Flora MacDonald,

beautiful savior of Bonnie Prince Charlie and pride
of the clans, hoped the voyage to North Carolina
would be the happy beginning of a new and peaceful life. She did not anticipate treachery, thievery,
storms at sea and the attacks of pirates. Nor did
she expect that tormented love could rival the impact of war to cause catastrophe.

THE SCOTSWOMAN
by
Inglis Fletcher

ABOUT THE AUTHOR

INGLIS FLETCHER's greatest fame rests on her books about early North Carolina, although her first two novels, White Leopard and Red Jasmine, were about Africa. Travel was long one of Mrs. Fletcher's chief enthusiasms. With her mining engineer husband, or often alone, she journeyed to remote mountain camps in Alaska and into the interior of Africa, where she went to study witchcraft and native customs.

Once back in the United States, she began, haphazardly at first, to hunt through records in California's Huntington Library for information about her early North Carolina ancestors. As she searched through the colonial documents, her interest grew until the names became live, vivid men and women and eventually the characters in such stories as Raleigh's Eden, Men of Albemarle, Lusty Wind for Carolina, Toil of the Brave, Roanoke Hundred, Bennett's Welcome, Queen's Gift and The Scotswoman. The Fletchers lived in an old plantation house called Bandon, right on the scene of the historic events that come alive in Mrs. Fletcher's writing.

The Scotswoman

INGLIS FLETCHER

BANTAM BOOKS · TORONTO · NEW YORK · LONDON

THE SCOTSWOMAN

*A Bantam Book / published by arrangement with
The Bobbs-Merrill Company, Inc.*

PRINTING HISTORY

*Bobbs-Merrill edition published April 1954
2nd printing .... March 1955
Bantam edition published November 1974*

Bantam Books are published by Bantam Books, Inc. Its trade-
mark, consisting of the words "Bantam Books" and the por-
trayal of a bantam, is registered in the United States Patent
Office and in other countries. Marca Registrada. Bantam
Books, Inc., 666 Fifth Avenue, New York, New York 10019.

PRINTED IN THE UNITED STATES OF AMERICA

Foreword

THIS book is primarily a work of fiction, though fact plays a strong part in its background. All of my Carolina novels have introduced historical figures, but this story is the first in which a historical figure has the major rôle.

When I first thought of writing a book about the Highlanders in North Carolina it seemed a simple thing; but the deeper I went into the subject the more I became aware of the numerous controversies that have grown up about the life of Flora MacDonald, perhaps particularly about her career in North Carolina. Also, the more I read, the more bewildered I became because of the ramifications of the clan system.

I think if I had not gone to Scotland and met that delightful and knowledgeable gentleman, the Reverend Mr. Donald Mackinnon, in Edinburgh, I would still be lost in the mazes of the intermarriages of the MacDonalds, the MacLeods, the MacKinnons and the MacQueens. These are all folk of the Isle of Skye, delightful but confusing and sometimes annoying with their use of the same surnames and even the same given names.

The Reverend Mr. Donald Mackinnon, who hails from Skye and who is the best living authority on Flora MacDonald, set me straight on the names and personalities, and also on the history of Flora and her people. He has given years of study to Flora MacDonald. He was the editor of *The Truth about Flora MacDonald* and is well advanced with the definitive biography of the delightful and heroic Scotswoman.

He was not only interested in my endeavor but most generous with his time and patience. He had

none of the contempt that many a historian exhibits
for a writer of historical fiction. Instead, he had a fine
understanding of the problems that beset me.

There have been numerous books written about
Flora MacDonald, the savior of Prince Charles Ed-
ward Stuart. After reading them I came to think that
each one was written to refute the findings of earlier
authors. In truth, some of the earlier books need correction, so inaccurate are they in terms of modern
scholarship.

Important points in Flora MacDonald's career still
remain mysterious and remote. Why did she come to
America? Why did she embrace loyalty to a Hanoverian king? Why did she take her place with the leaders of the Highland Uprising in North Carolina?
These questions still remain unanswered by contem-
porary history. In seeking my own answers I have
found much of the drama and poignancy her story
holds for me.

Some other questions about the MacDonalds remain unanswered or imperfectly answered. Did
Flora's daughter Anne and her husband, Alexander
MacLeod, travel to America with her or did they precede her by two years? For purposes of this story
they travel with her on the *Baliol*, though authorities
differ as to the actual fact.

Several interesting occurrences while I was writing
the book are worth mention. One concerns the twins,
Dougald and David. I had written almost half of *The
Scotswoman* when the Chief Dame Flora MacLeod of
MacLeod came to North Carolina, to the homecom-
ing at Old Bethesda Church near Aberdeen. With her
she brought her two grandsons. It happened that they
were twins of the same age as the twins in my book
and very similar in character.

I invented a family of fictitious MacQueens,
worthy though impoverished representatives of that
ancient and noble family, whose daughter emigrates
with Flora MacDonald in my story. Later I discovered that a real family of MacQueens came to North
Carolina at much the same time; these people I made
the girl's guardians in America.

My English major I call James Blair. Janet Schaw reported in her journal meeting a Captain James Blair in Antigua in December 1774 and described him as "a very agreeable genteel young man." He may have been an officer in the Royal American battalion. I have borrowed his name.

It is an almost impossible task to separate the Highland Whigs from the Highland Tories of North Carolina at the time of my story. I am still sometimes confused by the problem. My best test has been the lists of the prisoners taken after the Battle of Widow Moore's Creek Bridge. I am sure anyone named on these lists was a Tory.

A further problem has been the proper language to employ. The Scots who came to North Carolina were Gaelic-speaking. Some had no other tongue. In my own family I have three lines of Scots ancestry—the Morays, the Spruills and the Clarks. By marriage I am connected with the Fletchers, Hays, Roses, Chisholms, Fraziers, MacGregors and MacAlpins. In spite of this Scots background I hesitated to make my characters speak in Scots dialect. At last I decided to write mostly in straight English, rather than make mistakes in the altogether delightful dialect of the eighteenth-century Scots.

As I said earlier, it was only after I went to the Isle of Skye, visited Flora's homes there and met the Reverend Mr. Donald Mackinnon that these difficulties fell away and I was able to write.

The Scotswoman was written in Skye, in Edinburgh, in London and at Bandon Plantation.

I wish to thank Mr. E.T. McKeithen, of Orchard Hill Farm, Aberdeen, North Carolina; Mr. E.E. Wicker, of Pinehurst, North Carolina; and Col. Jeffrey Standback, of Widow's Purchase, Mount Gilead, North Carolina, for their great interest and research in the Flora MacDonald legend, both factual and traditional, and for the knowledge which they so willingly shared. My thanks also to Mr. and Mrs. Ernest Ives, of Paint Hill Farm, Southern Pines, North Carolina, for their interest and assistance; to Sir Angus Fletcher, of Fireplace Landing, Long Island, for many kindnesses; and to Dr. Hugh Lefler, of the History Department of the University of North Carolina, from whose classes I learned much about the Scottish settlement on the Cape Fear River.

Here, too, I want to express gratitude to Mr. Henry Hoyt, of New York, for books on the Scottish Clearances; to Register House, Edinburgh, Scotland, for documentary material; and to the Hayes Collection, of Edenton, North Carolina, for a letter from Johnston to Hewes dealing with Allan MacDonald as a prisoner of war. Mr. John A. Oates' history, *The Story of Fayetteville and the Upper Cape Fear*, was my constant book of reference; and Samuel A. Ashe's *History of North Carolina* was often useful for historical detail in a wider area. *The Highland Call* by Mr. Paul Green and the modern edition of the *Journal of a Lady of Quality* prepared by Evangeline Walker Andrews and Charles McLean Andrews gave me hints which helped me to recapture the colour of the times.

INGLIS FLETCHER

Bandon Plantation
Edenton, North Carolina
April 27, 1954

Author's Note

AFTER *The Scotswoman* was in pages, I received a letter from a direct descendant of Allan and Flora MacDonald concerning the spelling of the name. It has long been a controversial point whether the correct version is *MacDonald*, *Macdonald* or even *McDonald*.

I chose *MacDonald*, used throughout *The Scotswoman*, from several old books, for I wanted to use the spelling of the period. Consultation with authorities in Scotland and examination of Allan's own signature in the American Loyalist Claims, English Public Records Office, supported my decision.

Now I find that *Macdonald* has been matriculated in the Court of the Lord Lyon of Scotland.

The controversy over the spelling of the name is just one of the many concerning Allan and Flora MacDonald that have sprung up through the years. It seems unnecessary to attempt to alter the version used in *The Scotswoman*. How many spellings are there of Shakespeare's and Raleigh's names? I have forgotten.

INGLIS FLETCHER

Bandon Plantation
Edenton, North Carolina
September 20, 1954

Contents

Book One
Skye

Book Two
The Sea

BOOK THREE

The Valley of the Highlanders

BOOK ONE
Skye

1

Last Visit to Prince Charlie's Cave

DAVID MACDONALD stretched forth an arm to help his twin, Dougald, from the boat. In his eagerness David had leaped ashore just as the boat struck bottom. Dougald too had jumped up, but now he tottered to maintain his balance under the jolt from his brother's leap and Old Neil's efforts to shove the craft to a firm berth.

"Hold on, Dougald," David cried, "or you'll get the pipe wet, and we'll have no music tonight."

Dougald simply took firm hold of David's hand and leaped, deftly despite the cumbersome bagpipe strapped across his chest, to the damp, gravelly sand.

For a moment both lads paused to gaze back across Little Minch. Dougald's eyes went first toward Dunvegan Head and he thought of the school he had just left, this time for good. Then he, like David, looked farther north, in the direction of Trotternish Point, where was Monkstadt, their home these last seven years.

After only a moment's quietness David recalled Old Neil, who was still working to make the boat fast. "Here, Neil, I'll do that. Dougald, you take off the knapsacks. Let's be going, for we've no time to waste this year."

Aye, and that's true, Dougald thought as he swung the knapsacks from the craft to a large rock. Our last visit to South Uist and Prince Charlie's Cave, and it must be cut short.

David adjusted his load and picked up his walking-stick before he looked at his brother. Then he saw that Dougald had paused again, this time to look up and down the coast of the island, cut by crags deep moss-brown at their shadowed bases and gold, green and lavender at their sunlit tops. When Dougald turned David saw the sadness of his countenance and felt in his own heart a strong clutch of regret.

"Aye, Dougald, it's hard to leave ... but we've no choice." A moment later his usual buoyancy returned, and he added, "The voyage and the new land will bring adventure. I, for one, am somewhat glad we're being sent."

Dougald smiled, for he knew his brother's adventuresome spirit and he knew, too, that once they were started he himself would be excited by the voyage, the ship, new people and a new home. But he could not yet say this. The news had come too quickly, too unexpectedly, and he had not yet got beyond the single thought: I must leave misty Skye, dear Lady Margaret, and my schooling; David and I shall not again climb the slopes of Mount Hecla.

Finally he turned to Old Neil, who had guarded them when as lads of twelve they had made their first excursion to this island and who had brought them and returned for them every year since. With a slight laugh he said, "This is not like that first trip, is it, Neil? This time you'll not have to chase us through the bracken and the furze and splash through the quagmires to make sure we find our way and don't break a leg in the process." Then his voice changed and he said, almost to himself, "Aye, this is vastly different from that first time."

Old Neil said nothing as he hoisted his sack.

David laughed and said, "That doesn't make Neil any happier about the trip. He's glad this is the last outing. I heard him grumbling at home when he found he'd have to come along this time. He——"

Old Neil broke in to protest, "Nay, lad, I do no' mind being along wi' ye."

"Then what was it I heard you growling in the kitchen?" David asked. He then scowled, lowered his voice and quoted, " 'To my mind, the laddies be getting too old to be takin' a holiday and playin' their childish games.' "

"True enough, David. I do think it's time for manhood's business. Yet I'm glad you've got this one last time to say farewell to the island. You'll be missing it sorely, and this memory will be good." Neil bent to grasp his walking-stick and then waved up the rocky slopes. "And now I think it's time we be startin' up."

David, the sturdier and always the more athletic of the twins, led the way up a devious path that had over the years become their fixed route. They always stopped at the same estates, or tacks, visited the same cottages, wound through the hills to see the sky's reflection in their favourite lakes.

Dougald, walking a little more slowly than his brother and Neil, mentally forecast each scene of the tramp. We know it so well, he thought. In a way it's foolish of us to come year after year. Yet it's just the knowing it so well that makes it so very hard to leave.

Soon they would be at the small cottage where they usually spent the first night. It had long been unused, though its walls were firm and its thatched roof was partly intact. From the knoll on which it stood they would look out over the four gleaming lakes, like stained-glass fragments leaded together by strips of brown peat. Across these lakes they would see the long, serrated ridge of Ben More and they would see, below, a brook quietly wending through a glen to Lake Kildonan. Near by would be the ruined church—as intimate a part of the landscape as the rocks around it, with its old graves nestled into the grey earth. This cottage in the shieling at Alisary was a destination of special meaning—there Flora, their cousin, had first met her Prince Charlie and pledged to save him—nearly thirty years ago, it was.

Flora ... They were to stand beside Allan and Flora and wave farewell when they sailed next week. It's too soon! he inwardly cried. It interrupts all. To get him home in time Neil and David had come to take him from MacCrimmons' school early. He would not finish his lessons on the pipe, his learning of the Ceól Mór, the Great Music of the bagpipes, which he loved.

"I suppose," he said aloud, "Lady Margaret thought about it long before she could decide. Then, all at once, the time was close and now we've got to hurry off with hardly a farewell."

"Yes," David answered, "she was quiet for a week or so. I couldn't understand what the trouble was, but finally she told me—crying, she was—that she wanted us to go to America. It's best for us, she said."

Old Neil, who listened to all and who knew Dougald was finding it hard to face the unexpected change, added, "Once she'd made up her mind you must go, there was no question but it'd be with Flora and——"

David laughed and called back, "She wants to be very sure we don't forget the Highlands. She's afraid we'll become real colonists, with no care for the home country."

As if that could ever be, Dougald mused. Yet he was glad they would always be with Flora—he would yearn for Scotland, and Flora, wherever she was, would be the Highland spirit's incarnation.

Now there was but the slight rise of the heathered knoll between them and the cottage. David ran the little distance and dropped onto the step before the door. "Though we can't stop the night here this trip, we can rest awhile. I need to breathe a bit."

Dougald eased his knapsack from his shoulders and stood looking down the vale to the roof of the large house and the fences of Aridith McCullin—the Farm of the Mill—the first home of Flora. Then he pivoted, scanned the familiar walls of the small house and said abruptly, "I've always such an odd feeling about this place. It's not merely that Flora and Prince Charlie met here. It's ... it's that Father's life and Flora's link somehow at this spot, though he was never here. I feel that when he, and the brave soldiers like him, could fight no more for their rightful King, she took up the work." He turned back to his brother. "Do you feel that, David?"

"Aye, and often I've dreamed of doing my own part. But I fear fighting for the Stuart is over. . . . Yet, how I'd love to swing the claymore for him! That's the MacDonald blood, I guess."

Old Neil, resting on a flat boulder, observed the

two boys, now sitting side by side. They were as alike as two leaves branching from the same stem, nearly identical in stature, features and colouring. Both were brave, tall lads, close on to six feet in height, and they had forward-thrusting jaws, long straight noses and wavy chestnut hair. Their eyes were the colour of the restless sea, at times grey, at times blue. Their bodies were strong, stalwart with heavy bone and solid muscle. Only those close to them saw that Dougald had a slight tautness, a subtle, finer-drawn quality in his features, while David showed the smallest touch of being rough-hewn. It was as if a sculptor had quickly modelled a first head, then carefully, consciously reproduced the lines and texture in a second.

Inwardly there were greater differences between the twins. Dougald was quiet; he spoke seldom and then meditatively. David was more restless, outgiving. But they shared a genial sense of humour that prompted them now and again to assume each other's rôle, and momentarily deceive all, even their foster-mother. When Dougald the silent talked and jested and David the gay became taciturn, there was nearly complete transformation. Such tricks never lasted long, however, for David soon had to burst into his customary broad smile, and Dougald to relapse into his more familiar pensiveness.

The differences between David and Dougald were really but different expressions of the same inheritance. In David the strong Scots love of caber-throwing, of warfare and of good farming asserted itself; he loved action and the present. In Dougald the Scots reticence was combined with the love of skirling pipe-music, the commemoration of Clan MacDonald's past deeds, the vision of Clan MacDonald's future glories. The boys shared in equal measure the passionate honour, loyalty and courage of good clansmen and good warriors. Deep inside both was the pride that their greatness went far back—that it made their people fight valiantly in 1715 and 1745 for the Stuart, that it kept their father beside his Prince until his wounds dropped him, that their cousin had saved the Prince's life.

"Lads," Neil said abruptly, "mayhap it's time for forgettin', no matter how hard that is." When they looked at him with a kind of shock in their eyes, the old retainer went on: "I don't mean you should let the memory of your father and Culloden and Flora and the Prince die. Nay, that's part of you, and a good part. But a new land means a new life, and you must live it as it comes to you. Some think—Flora does, and Lady Margaret—that the clans can grow strong again in North Carolina. Over there, they say, you can have your rightful jurisdiction, such as was taken away in '48. There a man can wear the kilts without having some skulking soldier dragging him before the magistrate. Perhaps so, but perhaps the old customs and the old thoughts won't fit in that new country."

"Neil," Dougald cried, "that's a dreadful thing to say! What would we be, if not a clan, living and working together?"

"Dougald lad, I no more than you want the MacDonalds to change. But I'm an old man who's lived through many changes, and I know a man sometimes has to give a little." He used his stick as a prop as he rose stiffly. "You've both been brought up on Culloden—your father taught you that, as rightly such a soldier should to his sons. Now Flora and Margaret have long talked to you of Charlie and the MacDonalds' part in saving him." After a pause he said, almost to himself, "When memories help a man live on they're good. But if they hold him back, they're bad."

"Then you really do disapprove," David said, "of our coming here now, just before we go."

"I have told you I'm glad. But I said what I said because this ought to be an end of childhood.... And I fear it may be an end of something more. Yes, lads, I sometimes fear."

"Be quiet, Neil!" David commanded in a harsh voice as he jumped up. "You're spoiling our last visit. I don't even want to stay here now. It's true the new day is coming; I looked forward to it. But if we must deny this for it, the voyage and America are spoiled too."

"Neil doesn't mean to deny anything, nor to spoil it, Davie," Dougald said, rising to put his hand on his brother's shoulder. "He speaks like this only because he loves the clan, and us."

Then Dougald handed David's knapsack to him and strapped on his own. "Let's move on. The more I think of leaving, the more I want to visit the cave. And, Neil," he added with an affectionate smile, "you may be right that it's childish, but tomorrow I'm going to play the pipes louder and with more spirit than ever and I'm going to say the words clearer than ever!"

This time it was Dougald who strode ahead. It was a long, hard climb up the crags of volcanic Hecla, but the Hebrides' long summer's evening gave them plenty of time. By nine o'clock they were at the cave. With delight the boys and their old guardian absorbed the vista of mountains and moor, sea and lake which stretched northward to the Butt of Lewis, lying deep beyond the sun-reflecting haze, and southward to Barra Head. Across the Minch they could see Skye, shading from the purple, brown and dull green of the north where they had lived most of these last years to the shadowed cliffs of the Red and Black Cuillins, the mountains of the young men. Beyond those craggy mountains lay the fine, new Armadale Castle, where the young Laird of Sleat, Lady Margaret's son, was already residing and where they themselves had lived during the past winter. They gazed beyond Skye, then, and could imagine the blue mainland of Scotland. Near its heart was Loch Garry, where as children they had lived with their father.

Dougald lowered his knapsack and walked to the entrance of the cave, but David called him back. "Let's eat first. I'm fair faint with hunger. Look! We've got a feast—scones, meat, milk, cheese. Neil, if you start the fire we'll soon have the tea, too."

"And that sounds good! I'll help Neil," Dougald said, as he scooped up an armload of brush and carried it to the centre of the barren clearing. Neil had already stuck two forked sticks into the ground and on them balanced a third for the kettle. It took only a moment to build a crackling fire of the dried shrubs.

While the others laid out the food and waited for the water to boil, Dougald wandered to the edge of a ravine. Though it was still a clear twilight—nearly the whole night would pass in a silvery brightness—he could see small pin-points of light below. He could picture the children hurrying homeward for supper, some carrying pails of foaming milk; others herding sheep, pigs and cattle to shelter.

The contrast, he thought, of these islands—running children and humble cottages on stony heads beaten and buffeted by a sea forever churning to crush or envelop the reaching spine of islands that defies its domination.

Dougald stood there so long that David called out, "Tea is brewed. Come to eat!" A touch of impatience in his tone betrayed his ravenous hunger.

For a moment longer Dougald could not turn away. He felt he must memorize each detail of the spare yet graceful land. Softly, so David, who had little patience with "poetry-talking," would not hear, he chanted,

> "Farewell, lovely Skye, lake, mountain and corrie,
> Brown isle of the valiant, the brave and the free."

"Come on, lad! No more of your dreaming. We lose the best part of the evening."

David's briskness finally drew him to the fire. Dougald carefully arranged the pleats of his kilt so they would protect him from both the dampness and the hardness of the rocky soil. He promptly began to munch bread and cheese and to drink the freshly brewed tea from a pewter mug.

"You know, lads," Old Neil said between swallows, "I sometimes wonder that Flora has not come to Corrsdale to say farewell to her old home and the cave. 'Tis really more likely she'd be commemorating these spots than you young tads, not yet born when it all happened."

"She's not come often of late years at all," David

said, taking up the thought. "I always assumed it was because she needed no prompting to recall every moment of that terrifying, glorious night." In his enthusiasm he jumped up and strode about the clearing pointing in the directions of his thoughts. "Just think! She and Prince Charlie meeting at the cottage below, then again over at Roshinish. Look! Even in this light you can almost make out the spot, there on Benbecula. And after that, darting across to Skye in a poor, frail boat and in the terror of a fearful storm; then trying to land, only to be turned back by the English boats and militia."

Coming back to the fire, he concluded, "The MacDonalds have much to be proud of, and Flora most of all. Sure, if I'd done all that, I'd not need reminding."

"No doubt, you're right, lad: she needs no reminding. And it's true she has got some little mementoes about her that she never puts by.... Yet she's a spirited woman, not one to go so calm and cool away from home and fame."

While Neil ruminated, David leaned forward on his crossed knees and gently swished his tea around in his mug. Finally, with a slight frown he said, "Such talk makes me a bit uncomfortable. You wouldn't know much about this, Dougald, being away the last month, but I heard Flora say a strange thing to Lady Margaret. It sticks in my mind because I can't quite understand it." He took a determined gulp of tea. "I wish it would fade away!"

"Why, David," Dougald asked with some surprise, "what could it be to worry you? You told me yourself Allan and Flora have to go because of losses on the tack. That's sure no uncommon plight these days, as a farmer like yourself well knows." Then Dougald turned to Neil for confirmation and said, "Surely you'll agree Flora's spirit would make her do what is best for Allan, whether or not it made her happy."

While Old Neil nodded that Flora MacDonald did indeed have this kind of courage, David continued to furrow his brow. "That's true enough. Yet ..." He suddenly shook his head and smiled. "It's nonsense for me to pay so much attention to a chance remark. Flora said she wasn't going to talk of the Prince any more—that was all. I guess it just sounded odd to me—to think of not hearing her tell the tale in her vivid way."

"That is too bad, though," Dougald cried. "I was hoping she'd repeat it at the banquet. Her story is the proper climax to our 'ceremony.'" Seeing Neil wrinkle his nose in tolerant mockery at the word, he laughed good-humouredly. "Scowl if you will tonight, Neil. Tomorrow morning you'll find your blood stirred when we wake you to the 'Highland Muster-Roll.'"

With that Dougald reached for his pipe, rose and played a strain of the rousing march. David quickly packed away the food and utensils and in a moment had stones and brush swept away from a makeshift dancing area.

"Let's have a fling," he cried, drawing himself erectly into stance and placing his hands on his hips. "Neil, will you join, or shall I go it alone?"

But Neil was too weary from the day's climb to enter the strenuous dance. "Skip it yourself, laddie. One or two, it makes no difference when you can't make the foursome. That's the way I like best to see it."

At once Dougald had the shrill notes of the traditional fling whistling from his pipe, and David performed the steps with all precision, his kilt swinging in rhythm to his agile legs. The notes filled the air, slid down the mountain, and returned in a vague, cacophonous echo.

David flung himself from the last gyration to the ground and laughed breathlessly. "That was good!"

Neil, who relished every shrill whistle or booming bass note from a pipe played well, complimented Dougald supremely: "You're ready to pipe for the clan, lad. A little young you are, but you can soon prove yourself to all."

"If only you are right, Neil, I'll be very proud. But I've not even finished my training, so there's little hope I'll be made the piper."

"A man's gift," Neil replied, "can make up for a year or two of study. You must play as often and as well as you can, for if the pipes are to live, it must be in the new land—where the laws don't tell a man what he can and canna play."

Dougald pensively burnished the drones of his beloved pipe, his *piob-mhòr*, with his hand. He sympathized with the bitterness of Neil's tone. One reason he'd so much wanted to finish at MacCrimmons' was that the Highland pipers were slowly being silenced by harsh Hanoverian prohibition. Even to teach and to learn was law-breaking, though the MacCrimmons kept their school going, despite the danger. That stern injunction, Dougald thought contemptuously, proved only how passionate a call the pipe has—a call he would try to keep alive.

Suddenly he swung the pipe back into place and played an ancient lullaby he had heard throughout his childhood. The peculiar shifts in rhythm and the whining, wailing notes were as haunting as the still phosphorescence of the night.

" 'Tis a proper tune to end the day with, lad," Neil said, unwinding his kilt and wrapping himself in his warm plaid.

Soon the boys too were in only their woollen trews and long knee-socks. David, cocoonlike in his plaid, considered the best place to sleep. "I read that the Arabs wrap up their feet and put their heads to the fire," he said. "Perhaps I should try that."

"And singe those fine brown curls?" Dougald laughed. "There will be never a lassie in Skye will look at you if you wear a bald pate."

"Och—" David pretended horror—"and the party coming soon. Make room, laddie, and I'll sleep the good Scots way, my toes toasting all night."

The boys lay easily on the hard ground. When they were wee lads their old gillie had oftimes repeated, "A Scot, even a laddie, will grow a strong and robust frame from the out-of-doors," and "The earth, covered with bracken, is the best bed for a strong man."

David, reminiscing, stretched and said quietly, "Old Robbie was right. The ground is a good bed; it feels soft to my back."

Dougald, already near sound asleep, mumbled, "Aye, Davie. Good night."

The sun, which had only dimmed during the brief night, gathered a daylight brightness to it. Gradually the brown and grey islands were washed with tints of mauve, crimson and yellow.

Dougald roused with the first shining and, so near consciousness had been his waiting for this hour, knew immediately he must be both silent and quick. "David," he whispered, "get up! Don't wake Neil."

Both rolled from their plaids, stripped and ran to a near-by stream to bathe. As they slapped their legs with the icy water, they regretted they had no whisky to rub on them, as every man who wears a kilt and sleeps outdoors should, to prevent a cold.

In only a few moments they had dressed and were standing at the edge of rock overlooking the vale. Dougald lifted the mouthpiece of his pipe to his lips, paused and looked at David. When David nodded slightly, he set the melody in keen, bold notes. In a true voice David sang:

"Little wat ye wha's comin',
  Little wat ye wha's comin'.
  Duncan's comin', Donald's comin',
  Colin's comin', Laughlan's comin',
  Dugald's comin', Laughlan's comin',
  Alister and a's comin'!

"The Laird o' MacIntosh is comin',
  Macrabie and MacDonald's comin',
  The MacKenzies and MacPhersons comin',
  A' the wild MacCraws comin'!

"Little wat ye wha's comin' " ...

As children the boys had studied and recited this march as if it were a catechism. In its earlier version it listed the clans who in '15 united under Mar to restore the Elder Chevalier, unfortunate James who throughout his life saw a German on his throne. In its

later version it enumerated the clans who had pledged
allegiance to the Chevalier's son, Bonnie Prince Charlie, when, in '45, he sailed from France to rally the
clansmen for an invasion of England. The Young
Chevalier swept with headstrong resolve across the
Highlands from the Hebrides to Inverness, then down
to Edinburgh, with triumph all the way. Then he
dipped into England and retreated to Scotland with
growing trouble all the way, until, finally, he had his
Culloden.

Early David and Dougald had made up a little
drama of the events of Charlie's campaign. They had
often performed it for their veteran father and since
his death and their coming to Monkstadt they had repeated their traditional dialogue yearly, here, alone,
on South Uist, which had played as vital a part in
Charlie's story as had their native Loch Garry region.

Now Dougald lowered his pipe and spoke the first
words:

"When Charlie came to Scotland, he came first to
the MacDonalds, for they were famous for loyalty.
To the shame of the clan, the MacDonalds he first
visited denied him. . . ."

David then spoke in a commanding tone:

"I am your own Prince Charlie, come to claim my
rightful throne and to establish Scots' liberty under
their God-appointed King.

"MacDonald of Boisdale, are you with me?"

"Nay," Dougald answered, in a low voice.

"Alexander MacDonald of Sleat, are you with
me?"

"Nay."

Dougald resumed the narrative:

"But few were the MacDonalds who would not
fight for their Prince. At Moidart and Arisaig
MacDonald of Glenalladale and young MacDonald of
Clanranald took up arms for him. And there, at Bor-
rodale, our own MacDonald of Glengarry pledged to
raise his clan.

"When Charlie got to Corriearrick the Glengarry
sept welcomed him with cheers, and proudly the men

stepped up one by one to swear for him. Our own father stood before his Prince."

David again spoke the Prince's part:

"Angus MacDonald of Glengarry, I have sworn
rather to die here in the Highland hills than live longer in exile from my people. Are you, Angus MacDonald, with me—to fight if need be till death, that
Scotland may be ruled by the Stuart?"

"Aye, I am with you, if need be till death, that all
Scotland and I and my sons and my grandsons may
be ruled by the Stuart."

Dougald had given his father's answer in ringing
tones. Now he lifted his pipe to play a marching beat
which swiftly gathered a climax of martial thunder.

The instant the music ended, David picked up the
story with quickened pace:

"Our father marched his Prince to Edinburgh and
loudly proclaimed him King. Our father followed his
King to England, never thinking to turn back when
others faltered. He'd ne'er ha' turned back, but they
told him he was going to fight Cumberland and then
they led him back across the Esk. On the hungry, tir-
ing journey home he sang deserters back to the ranks.
At Falkirk he put old Hawley to flight; at Inverness
he took Fort Augustus. And then he marched to Culloden. . . ."

Dougald's voice cut in sharply:

"On April 16 at Culloden Angus MacDonald of
Glengarry stood at the side of his King, at the left
side, where never a MacDonald should be. There was
sleet in his face and pain in his belly.

"But he fought nonetheless for the Stuart cause . . .
till the cause was killed at Culloden, and he fell
wounded on the plain.

"And the Butcher Cumberland trampled him and
the Butcher's men rode over him, until he was left for
dead.

"But he rose and limped to his Loch Garry home.
When the red-coated soldiers came he stood on a
twisted leg to take their bloody oath:

"'I, Angus MacDonald of Glengarry, do swear
never   to   take   arms   against   the   King   of

Britain. . . . And I do swear never to pipe the pipe, the instrument of war. . . . And I do further swear never to wear tartan, plaid or any part of the Highland garb. . . . If I break my oath in any particular, may I be cursed in my undertakings, family, property; may I never see my wife and children, father, mother or relations; may I be killed in battle as a coward and lie without Christian burial in a strange land, far from the graves of my forefathers and kindred.'"

After a long moment Dougald completed the tale:

"Years after, he commanded his sons: 'You are unsworn. Play the pipe, wear the kilt and never forsake your King.'"

The boys bent their heads in pride and sorrow, and their eyes had tears in them. Yearly repetition of the words with which they honoured their father had only heightened their realization of his bravery and suffering. Nor had the years eased much their own loss when he died, twenty-one years after the battle, still lame.

At last they drew out their dirks, and David said, "Now we will swear ourselves to an oath fitting a Highlander."

Together they repeated words famous among Scotsmen who assert the ancient right to serve voluntarily a rightful lord. "It is not riches, neither is it honour, but it is liberty alone that we fight and contend for, which no honest man will lose but with his life."

Each scratched the inside of his wrist with the blade's point and then touched the bloody tip to the wound of the other.

"A blood oath is unbreakable," David said.

"A blood oath is unbreakable, save only by death," Dougald echoed.

Old Neil had awakened with the first pipe notes. For a while he purposely ignored the boys and matter-of-factly started the tea. Later he had silently watched the ceremony, almost against his will. Now, seeing the entire sincerity of the boys' emotion, he felt no urge to scoff. What if they had whittled down history to a personal achievement of their father? What if they were grown men clinging to a childhood and a past that could not come again? He was proud of them and wondered whether he was not wrong, whether their firm rooting in the past would not be their best preparation for the future.

Because he could not tell them aloud of his pride, Neil called merely, "If you be finished, lads, come sip your hot tea. We've a long journey to make today."

Dougald, always sensitive to undertones, said happily, "Ah, Neil, I'm glad you heard us." Then to ease their mood into an everyday one, he laughed, with only a trace of embarrassment, and added, "It's no doubt the islanders are glad it's the last time—what with my blowing that gets stronger every year."

"That I'll vouch for; you fairly blasted me out o' my plaidie this morning," Neil answered. "Now eat, lads, and let's be off."

Quickly they packed up and swung their plaids over their shoulders. As they moved slowly down the hill the sun glinted from their silver breastpins with centres of cairngorm. A breeze from the Minch shook the sprigs of heather, their clan emblem, in their bonnets.

Half-way down they paused with one accord and looked back to the hills. Dougald began the Clanranald March, softly at first, then louder until the music rang down the valley. David put his hands to his mouth and shouted the ancient battle cry of the MacDonalds: "*Dh'aindeoin co theiradh el*, Gainsay who dare!"

2

Kingsburgh

On the day after the boys' journey the sun and blue
sky gave way to chill, foggy rain and bleak greyness.
Loch Snizort tossed angrily, and even Snizort Beag,
that little arm of water penetrating to the center
of Skye, ruffled factiously. At Kingsburgh House,
lying on the edge of the Beag, Flora MacDonald
looked up from her packing to watch the drops
stream down the window-pane. 'Twill make Allan's
work that much the harder, she thought. With a sigh
she realized that never before had she needed to
worry because her Allan, stronger and handsomer
than most of the young lads of the island, was working late in the fields and in the rain. But this morning
she had seen his shoulders slump with the fatigue of
overseeing the heavy packing as well as the final farm
business. Too long he'd borne the enmity of rocky
ground and demands for higher and higher rent from
his laird. Now, she knew, were it not for his faith in
better success on the lush lands of North Carolina, he
would begin to despair. Nay, she corrected her own
thoughts, he has already despaired; that is why we
must leave.

She bent again to fold small garments, her youngest
child's dresses. It was hard for her not to cry when
she placed them in a trunk that would not go with her
on the long voyage to America. This chest would go
instead to Edinburgh, where eight-year-old Fanny
was already in the care of friends. "Some think it
best," she mused aloud, "to send even the wee ones
over the seas, but I cannot do it. Who knows what we
will find, or how long it will take us to settle?" She
shook her head sadly as she remembered her hope

that all her children would grow up on Skye, where the MacDonalds belonged, where they were known. Now the three boys were away in service or at school, Fanny was in Edinburgh, and Anne, Sandy and Jamie were to sail to America. "But I've no right to complain," she scolded herself. "Poor Anne's children will even be born abroad and will likely never see the home country."

A frantic pounding on the door interrupted her. She straightened, stood fixed for a moment, wondering who would have come at this evening hour and in drear rain. Then she picked up a lamp and threw open the door.

There, crouched in the shadow of the frame, was a cowering figure. A plaid hooded the face, so she could not distinguish who it was. In a hoarse whisper the trembling man pleaded, "Let me in, Flora MacDonald. Let me in. It's Peter MacQueen and it's hunted I am."

Immediately Flora stepped aside and, when the fugitive had ducked by, latched the heavy door behind him. "Go by the fire, MacQueen, and catch your breath. Then tell me what it is."

Still crouching and gasping, MacQueen explained. "The steward's come, Flora. He's come to turn me out." The old man whirled about defiantly and raised a shaking fist. "But I turned him out. Chased him from my house."

Flora nodded and waited to hear the rest.

"Thank the Lord I sent Molly and the lass to the hut on the hill. That black-hearted de'il came back with soldiers, he did. He's sworn to throw me and mine in prison for 'defying the King.'" MacQueen's drawn lips spat the words in scorn. "But he ne'er saw any of us a second time. I saw him coming and fled over here." With a sudden return of panic he jumped to the window. "The de'il may have followed me here. I must hide."

Flora quickly drew the draperies and led him back to the fire. "Then don't be standing where you can be seen. Sit down. Rest a moment."

"While Molly and the lass are cold on the hill? Oh,

Flora MacDonald, where'll I take them? Where'll we go now?"

"I don't know yet, Peter, but we'll care for you all somehow." Inwardly she wondered, though, how, with less than a week left and with the soldiers hunting such refugees without mercy, they could protect the MacQueens. "Now I'm going to fetch Allan, and you must wait. Do not dare put your face to the window again. If they come inquiring, hide and pretend the house is empty."

Flora threw her plaid about her head and shoulders. She drew all the draperies and latched all the doors but that in the kitchen. Once she passed MacQueen and he caught her hand, clung to it and cried, "God bless you, Flora MacDonald! I knew you'd help. I knew you were the one to come to."

"Of course we'll help, Peter. Could we, do you think, forget our years of friendship? Your past hardships wrought no change in our feeling for you. Now, while I'm gone, try not to worry."

Outside Flora strained to see through the thick rain and blackness. Twice she called for her husband, but the wind swallowed the words, so she gave over fruitless calling and bent her head against the rain. The wind fought her as she struggled across the open ground behind the house; in the darkness she stumbled over the rocks that no island farmer could ever clear wholly from his land. Once behind the byre she was protected and she threw back her plaid to listen for any sounds that would tell her where her husband was. Hearing nothing but the pound of the irate sea, she forged on to a thatched shed some thirty yards beyond. The farther side of the shed was open, and within, by the light of several lanthorns, she could discern milling sheep and dim forms of gillies working among them. Three sheep dogs ran back and forth before the opening and barked frequently to keep the sheep from bolting away.

"Allan! Allan, are you in there?"

A stooped old man gestured with long-handled shears. "Oot thar he be."

Then she saw a knot of men by the outer fence and

started toward it. The sound of her husband's voice froze her. He was saying, "Nay, I've not seen MacQueen. Why do you want him?" She held her breath until the other men, soldiers, as she now saw, answered insolently, "That's our affair. See you don't harbour him," and marched away.

At her low call Allan strode toward her. "You ought not to be out in such weather," he said anxiously. "What brings you?"

"MacQueen's evicted and come to us."

"So that's it. Go stay with him. Once these stragglers are under shelter, I'll be in."

She held him back to tell him to send Sandy to Monkstadt for David and Dougald. "Molly and the girl are hiding in that hut on MacQueen's place. Have the lads search them out."

Allan nodded. "Aye. Now get you in out of the rain."

Flora hurried past the shed and back to the house. The soldiers are gone now, she thought, but what if they return? And my young Jamie, sleeping upstairs. I must get him away.

Inside again she latched the door behind her and breathlessly told MacQueen what had been done. Then she ran swiftly up the stairs to look in on her thirteen-year-old son. He still slept, and she decided to let him sleep on. After all, no one would dare force his way into her home.

When she returned to MacQueen she noticed that the old man was wracked by shuddering chills, and she unfolded a blanket from an open trunk and gently tucked it about him. Much good it will do, though, she thought angrily. 'Tis more than damp shakes this man.

While she hung more blankets to warm before the fire Flora felt a welling bitterness. What need was there to stalk down these poor, industrious creatures as if they were animals? And sure, the new landlords were stalking down human prey just as much as if they had guns instead of laws in their hands.

From a pot the maid Katie had put on the fire when MacQueen came she dipped a bowl of steaming broth. The old man accepted it absently, but instead of eating he merely cupped his hands around its warmth.

"Sip it, Peter," she urged gently.

He answered only, "Where'll we go, Flora?"

How often, Flora thought, has Peter had to ask himself that question in the last few years! Peter, a man of breeding and responsibility and social prestige. Six years ago he had been tacksman of an estate as large as Kingsburgh; he had managed it well and had always deserved the love and respect of the islanders. Then an oppressive laird stepped in, bringing troubled and lean years for the MacQueens. Oh, Peter had held his head high during the first hard years! He had refused, independent and proud as he was, to give in and go to his clansmen on Harris and Lewis, though they would have welcomed him. His wife and daughter had rallied to him; Moira had come home recently from school at Edinburgh to help if she could and to reduce expenses.

Aye, the courage of the MacQueens had won the admiration of all—all but the harsh laird. What did he care for noble blood and a stout heart? He cared only for the hard cash that turning the tack into a sheep run would bring him. So finally MacQueen had had to relinquish his tack. Even then, he'd chosen to fight his own battle, make do with less. But the soldiers respected no man who did not manage a great estate. They had been harrying MacQueen, threatening him, and now they had forcibly cleared him from his home. The eviction had done something frightening to Peter; it had shown him what a losing battle he fought. Oh, dear God, Flora cried deep inside herself, protect the MacQueens! And protect us, that Allan and I may never have to see our children suffer want, as MacQueen's lass does.

Flora strode angrily across the room, her hands clenched before her. She wondered how long Allan would be; once she cautiously lifted a drapery to peer out. She could see nothing and let the material fall. Once again she anxiously paced the floor.

That MacQueen's plight was by no means unique

gave sharp edge to Flora's distress. Nearly every week she heard of some poor Highlander's being shoved off the land he'd been born to. Lowlanders, absentee English lords and even a new breed of Highland laird, all conspired, under the benediction of English law, to turn the proud and independent tacksmen into servile chattels or hunted outlaws. She knew well how they worked, these usurpers. First there was that strange new demand, a rent. Even she and Allan were suffering from that. Rent for land held in common by clansmen from time immemorial, for land meant, once bestowed by the chief, to be hereditary ever! Then after the rent, for the poor crofters there was forced labour that took a man away from home nearly three months of the year so that he could never earn the payment. Ere long they came for the tithe in kind—the rich man's rich wife's portion of hens and oats and barley that should be feeding a poor man's own starving wife and children. Finally the white-breeched steward came, the stranger who had no feeling for how it killed a Highlander to get down on his knees to an outsider and beg for bread to eat and time to pay.

"Oh, I'm glad, Peter, you stood up to that thieving steward!" she cried involuntarily. "They may take our land, but they'll not break our spirit."

But Peter said, " 'Twill only make them harder on us."

True, she had to acknowledge within herself. Every year they had grown harder. And why? Because the Highlanders had been loyal and true. Oh, they said it was because the farmers had no deeds, those paltry sheepskins, to prove their land was their own. As if their labour didn't make it a hundred times more rightfully theirs than some silk-waistcoated earl's who would never even visit it. But really this long bleeding of the clansmen was for Culloden, that bloody moor where the Prince's soldiers had promptly paid in full for following him. Aye, for Culloden it was, where this very MacQueen had nearly died ... and for her own part in the Bonnie Prince's escape.

"They never forget ... but neither shall we," she said aloud in her anger.

MacQueen roused himself at these words, looked up wearily and, pursuing his own train of thought, said, "It's the frail little Moira we must care for. You're leaving soon. Take her with you, Flora! Take her out of this cruel land."

"I'm thinking you'd better all come with us. There's no place here for you now."

Just as MacQueen was shaking his head in defeat, Allan called at the door. Flora let in a pinched, cold woman who sank immediately at her husband's side. "Take comfort, take comfort with us," crooned Flora softly, wrapping blankets about the sobbing woman. The young daughter followed her mother into the room, but she hung back. She was a slender, pale girl, and had she not been cold and tired she would have been a beautiful Scots lass, with her thick auburn hair, fair complexion and green eyes. Her features were regular and strong, and even now, in her fright, they were composed. Slowly she examined each of her rescuers in turn, as if trying to decide which would be kinder to her. Flora, seeing her hesitation, took her hand and smiled. "Come, Moira MacQueen. Warm yourself so you may help me soon. You must join us in our work and voyage. And it's happy I am to have you. You'll comfort me when I think of the children I must leave behind."

Allan was pacing the room in concentration. He stopped once before his son, waiting quietly as was his wont, and took hold of his arm in a quick, confiding gesture, as if to say, "I know I can count on you." Then he asked David and Dougald, who lingered inconspicuously beside Sandy, whether they could stay the night. "I'll need you tomorrow." Both David and Dougald had been waiting anxiously apart from the others. They had been told little of the MacQueens' story and now wanted more than anything else permission to stay and learn the rest. Without hesitation both nodded yes.

"There's nothing for it," Allan said so all could

hear, "but we'll have to smuggle them away with us. 'Twill be some risk, but many have done it."

MacQueen had said nothing since his wife and daughter entered. Now, at Allan's words, he violently pushed up in his chair. "I'll not go! You'll not take me across the sea from my own home!" he cried in a wild tone.

Allan pushed him back with a gentle but firm hand. "Easy, MacQueen! You must do what you must do. Your kin in North Carolina are getting along well. They'll be glad to have you and help you."

But Molly, too, whispered that she and her husband were too old for such a voyage. "It's just the lassie we fear for. Take her and that will content us."

"And where will you and Peter go?" Allan demanded. "Do you think you can make do on a scrubby tail-end of land on Harris, such as they give the evicted ones? You'd starve in less than a year."

Flora supported her husband. "Think, Molly. Think what such a life would mean."

" 'Twill be a better life for me than one in a foreign land." The old woman sobbed.

Moira saw that her parents really intended to send her away alone. She ran to them to kneel and plead. "Then let me stay too. I can help you. I'll not go away and leave you to starve as he says."

But the old father and mother were as determined that their daughter should go as that they should stay. "Hush, daughter, we know best. You'll go with Flora MacDonald."

Allan, already so hard beset by trouble on his own land, was all at once exasperated by the weeping of the women and the old man's stubbornness. "Good God, man, you'll stay here, where the very earth hates us farmers, when in America there are green pastures for the sheep and the crops come healthy almost without being sown? You'll stay here where there's constant danger, when there a man can live a quiet life, providing well for his own?" His voice grew louder and his pacing quickened. "I tell you, I no more than you want to leave my home. I'm no young fool of a lad thinking of the excitement and adventure. I'm a man thinking as you ought to be thinking—of where I can find the security to do a man's job."

"Hush, Allan," Flora said, putting her hand on his arm. "That does no good, as you can see. Mayhap if I were Molly MacQueen, just that little bit older, I'd not be able to do it either. We'd best think what's to be done with them here." She crossed to take Moira's hand and to lead her to the boys. "These three lads are sailing with us, lass. You know them all—at least you did before you went away to school. Let them tell you something of the new land."

While Flora drew Allan aside to speak with him in undertones, Dougald stepped close to the girl. He was happy to be told to talk with her, for his heart went out to all troubled creatures, and it had been instantly touched by the grave eyes in that sensitive face. But he could think of no words at all, and in embarrassment he blushed. David, though, was not abashed. He laughed and told Moira sincerely that he was immensely pleased she would be along. "We'll make you gay," he promised. "Just wait till you hear our Dougald pipe and see me dance. Aye, soon we'll have you dancing too. You'll see that—"

He was shocked into sudden silence. All whirled toward the door. There it was again—a knock, efficient, peremptory. Flora's face paled, but without hesitation she motioned the MacQueens to another room, and then snatched up the blankets and ran to the trunks. David dropped into an easy position in a chair and began to relate some recent happening at home to Sandy, who leaned against the mantel. Dougald stood perplexed for a second by the soupbowls he had scooped up from the floor; in desperation he tucked them under the folds of a blanket.

From his station by the door Allan waited for his wife's calm nod. Then he opened it. "Ah," he cried in the heartiness of relief, "the courier!"

A short, leather-clad man pushed his way through the door. "What ails ye, Allan MacDonald, that ye do not invite a poor drenched soul in out o' the rain?"

With total disregard for the comfort of the others, he shook as vigorously as any spaniel just out of the water. "Must be ye've seen the soldiers too. With guns they be, and creepin' about like bloodhounds." He grinned with mischief. "Would na say a word about their business. But I'll soon find out. What else is a courier for, I always say, but to find out the news."

"What is your news, Jemmy?" asked Allan, trying to get the talkative messenger back to his own business. "It must be important if it brings you out on a night like this."

"'Tis important to you, I dare say. The *Baliol* sails Wednesday, out of Campbeltown in Kintyre. All you islanders who want to be on her mun make haste."

"Wednesday!" Flora echoed. "It cannot ... so soon."

Jemmy grinned again and resettled his plaid. "'Twill be a joy to all if you canna go so soon, Flora MacDonald. We're not wanting to lose you."

Flora was wholly absorbed in the pain of the moment. Nothing, not even the original decision to leave Skye, had been so searing. For the first time departure—actual leaving, actual being gone—was more real than all the past, holding her back. She heard Allan answer in strained tones for both of them, "We'll be on her." Oh, Allan, she cried mutely, more pressure on you—still fewer days left for all there is to do!

"Weel," Jemmy said in good-humoured complaint, "I see I mun get my bowl of soup at the next house tonight." As he turned he shrugged philosophically and added, "'Tis wise I move on. Every hut and hovel will want this news. Many's the family that will sneak aboard that vessel, I wager."

He started out the door, but when all were ready to sigh in relief, he stuck his head back in to say slyly, "By the way, MacQueen's place is all dark and empty. Ye wouldn't know anything about that, would ye?" When they shook their heads he pursed his lips and said, "Weel, that's more news for me to ferret out." Finally he left.

Allan spoke decidedly. "We'll argue no longer. That old gossip suspects us, and I never have trusted his tongue. Come, MacQueen. We'll fetch your things over here for the time being. You can show my men what's to be moved. Lads, you stay here in case of trouble." In less than a moment the two men were gone.

Flora could not at once overcome her alarm at Jemmy's insinuations. She could not believe the militia would actually dare to invade her home; yet she had a sense of suffocation. Unreasonable elements seemed to surround the house, and the familiar sounds of the wind and rain outdoors repeatedly made her start. I'm foolish, she told herself; we of Kingsburgh are always safe from search. Yet I'd feel better if Jamie were away. There's no telling what a group of furious soldiers will do when they're after poor hunted folk. She quickly made a decision and felt more at ease. There was no fright in her voice when she said, "Sandy, 'tis a stormy night, but I'm going to send you out in it. You'll have to go to Dunvegan to tell Anne of the *Baliol*. A gillie could go, but I'd rather you went. I want you to take Jamie." She turned to Molly. "It might be best for you and Moira to go with Sandy. No one will be looking for you over there."

Molly shook her head firmly. "Nay. I'll wait for Peter. He needs me now." She rose and crossed to Moira. "But you, lass, mayhap you ought to go where it's safer."

"Don't make me go, Mother," Moira said beseechingly. "I want to be with you and Father, help you if I can. 'Twill be hard enough for me to bear going away to North Carolina. Don't make me leave you any sooner than necessary."

Flora listened and thought to herself that Molly and Moira really ought to go to Dunvegan. Then she decided not to argue. She knew that she would want to be with Allan were he in such need. She said simply, "Very well. I understand, and I am most willing to conceal you here as best I can." She motioned to Sandy. "Please bring Jamie."

With no more comment than "Aye," Sandy went up to awaken his brother. When he returned, steadying the sleepy boy in front of him, Flora had coats and blankets ready. She bundled the child in warm wraps and soothed him: "Don't be frightened, Jamie. Mother's sending you to sister Anne's for the night. We have to close the house before we thought." She saw that he was not awake enough to comprehend, but she went on in a crooning tone which comforted him until Sandy guided him into the night.

As if the slam of the door released his pent-up excitement, David jumped up. A sense of danger and of responsibility made his eyes sparkle. "Just think," he whispered excitedly to Dougald, "we're playing our part in saving someone! And with Flora MacDonald, too!" Leaning toward Moira, he said, "You must know the story of our Flora—how she carried Bonnie Prince Charlie over the water to safety. Now she's doing that for you too. Clear across the Atlantic she'll take you. You're a fortunate lass. They'll tell your story along with the other."

"Be quiet, David," Flora commanded with unaccustomed severity. "Is that what you've learned from your father's story and mine—that danger is zestful and misery gay adventure? Shame on you!"

David reddened. He never blushed from bashfulness, but he was sensitive to reprimand. It hurt him deeply that the Flora he worshipped should scold him for being proud of her.

"This is a time for thinking what to do for the MacQueens, not for glorying in their suffering." Flora frowned slightly in displeasure.

Dougald did not want to interrupt but felt he had to defend his brother. "Please, Flora, David meant no harm. He's as concerned about the MacQueens' trouble as the rest of us. But all his life he's waited for a chance to save someone and prove he's got true MacDonald blood."

"The MacDonalds want to see right is done, to relieve suffering—not glory in it because it offers a chance to be brave." She rose to speak with authority to the tall lads. "I know how each year you retell the stories of the '45. I know that you bravely shout till the mountains ring, 'Gainsay who dare!' But don't you know that means 'I must do this because it is right, and if others deny me, let them beware'? 'Tis no call to glory, but a call to honour. And honour may be a very quiet thing."

She had walked away a few steps. Now she turned back and saw in their faces a puzzled, even a betrayed, look. When Dougald asked, "Would you want us not to be proud of your story?" she regretted her brusqueness.

Something very deep in her said that if others forgot her story, if the MacDonalds ceased to include it in the epic of the clan's glory, she would lose something not only dear but essential to her. She knew that one deed of her youth had directed her growth as a woman. One decision of signal difficulty had transformed her from a callow girl to whom compassion, honour and courage were abstractions, as to these lads, into a woman who knew that compassion, honour and courage are soul-piercing emotions which grow only from generous love of others. But with what words could she explain such private perceptions to the children? At last she felt she must answer something. "Nay, but I, and your father too, would want you to be aware of the meanings."

After another pause she went on, as if groping for the right words. "'Tis just this I'm trying to say: A human act, like fighting for your Prince or saving someone in danger, is not the easy thing it looks years after. It's trying to see the right, then conquering your fear to do it. The real act is the inward thing. And later it's looking back, when you see people like the MacQueens suffering partly for what you did, and knowing that though you did right, you've caused hurt to others."

"Flora, do you mean you wish you hadn't saved the Prince?" David asked.

Her answer was sharp. "Of course not. It was right. I'm only saying I'm sorry much unjust suffering has come from it. 'Tis the same with Peter MacQueen. He's got much evil to bear now, and he knows that if he and others hadn't fought at Culloden, he'd not be suffering. But that doesn't make him wish he'd not fought."

"But fear—you said you had to conquer fear. Were you afraid?" David persisted.

"Of course I was afraid, just as I was a moment ago when the knock sounded on the door. Your father was afraid, too, when Cumberland's fresh troops attacked the poor, worn Highlanders." She hesitated a moment as if asking herself whether she should say more. Finally she added, "You never knew, did you, that at first I said I would not help the Prince?"

The boys were silent in their disbelief, but Moira bent forward and looked earnestly up at Flora as if to reassure her. "That makes the final act more noble," she said.

"I don't know about that," Flora replied with a smile. "I just know I'm glad I finally decided as I did." She paused in recollection. "This is the way it was. As you already know, I went at my stepfather's bidding to Alisary, not knowing why I'd been summoned. Alone I waited. It was near midnight, but the light was still on the hilltop. When the stranger came, I could see him well, and I was surprised to find a man so fair and noble hiding in that isolated spot. I thought to myself, This is no rough outlaw, but who...? Then realization came. That golden lad was my Prince, my lost King. Every night the past two months, ever since Culloden, I'd been praying to the good Lord for his well-being. Then I sank to my knees and thanked God I'd seen him safe with my own eyes."

Flora's voice had grown soft as she relived the reverence of that moment. Then she recalled herself. "The Prince raised me and explained my stepfather's plan. I was to row Charles, disguised as my maid, over the Minch to Monkstadt. Thence I was to convey him, somehow, down to Portree. At first all I could think was that one weak creature like me could never protect a man all the soldiers were hunting for.... That was when I first said no.

"Again he told me how much he needed my aid. And again I said no. I told him that my kin at Monkstadt and Armadale would suffer for it. I swore I'd never tell I'd seen him, but I would not bring misery on others who had no part in the escape.

"I believe that if he had asked me once more, I'd never have changed my decision. But Charles Stuart bowed his head and said he understood. He said his greatest sorrow was that the Scots had paid so dear for him. Without another plea for himself he turned away.

"I watched his weary walk, his bent head. Then it was that for the first time I really saw a man in need. Charles was hungry and tired, and within him he bore a heavy burden. If he were caught, he would be killed by one of Ferguson's two thousand men. Searching for him night and day, they were. Just the way he straightened his weary shoulders made me see that this man was more than a Prince. He was a human being, a hunted one, and I was thinking of sending him back to death and danger.

"Then it was that I agreed to go."

Flora looked straight into the eyes of first one boy and then the other. "I too had to learn what it is to be a true MacDonald.... It's to know that any human being, whether he's the Prince or Peter Mac-Queen, must be helped when he's in danger."

Molly MacQueen roused herself. "I hope, Flora MacDonald, that you would do it again, despite what's come of it. My Peter would."

Flora did not answer; she seemed in her silence to be dispelling her memories. Then she touched David's hair lightly and said, "Forgive my anger, laddie. Now see whether you can help us think what to do."

"I have been thinking, Flora. How would this be? Young Alex will be at Armadale most of the winter, so he won't know if we harbour the MacQueens on his land. The soldiers will think Kingsburgh House closed after Saturday. If Mr. MacQueen would never put his face out of the door, he could stay here awhile. Before long the soldiers'll be off chasing someone else. Then Mr. MacQueen could find a new place. Lady Margaret would help him."

"I'd feel better to see them permanently settled, but mayhap this is best in the circumstances. . . . Still, when young Alex does visit Monkstadt he's sure to look in on Kingsburgh. Then Margaret will have no more say in the matter. Alex listens little to his mother, I fear. What then?"

Dougald spoke up. "Lady Margaret will never let Mr. and Mrs. MacQueen go hungry, that I know. She has great respect for them. And besides, it wouldn't be the first time she's smuggled food through the back door." Dougald paused. "But that would be an awful way for you to live, Mrs. MacQueen. You're sure you won't come with us?"

"I would rather hide the rest of my life here on Skye, or even go over to Harris, as Allan said, than go far from my home. You don't realize, Dougald, that for Peter and myself there's not time to begin all over."

Flora had listened to the conversation. Now she spoke slowly. "It may not be so bad as you think, Dougald, for the MacQueens to stay here. In fact, it may be the safest place." She paused to debate within herself, then walked to the passage that led to the room across the hall. "Come," she said to the others. "I will show you something."

When the others joined her Flora was standing meditatively beside the fireplace. The twins and Molly and Moira waited, unable to guess what she intended to do. Then slowly Flora stretched forth her hand. She searched with her fingers along the panelled wall. At last her hand paused in its groping, turned, and there was the slight click of a hidden spring. A section of the wall swung back and a narrow, dusty stairway was revealed.

Moira gasped in surprise, and David cried out, "A hidden room . . . above . . . a hidden room! Flora, that's where old Kingsburgh hid the Prince! I've always wondered."

In a hushed tone Flora answered, "Very few people know. The chamber is sacred." Her voice trailed off. She felt that she had been hurled back in time. Just here she had stood to watch Allan's father lead the young prince to his sleeping room. Just here she had been when the Prince, holding his candle high, so that it cast strange shadows over his fair, laughing face, turned to look at her over his shoulder. He had been in a merry mood—and why not? Together he and she had outwitted Ferguson, the English officer. They had outwitted that lieutenant who lay in wait at Monkstadt. They had safely come, with old Kingsburgh for a guide, to this house, where they could relax and breathe freely. Here, the servants having been sent away, Flora and Mrs. Kingsburgh had served the Prince with their own hands. After dinner, when the women had retired, the Prince and old Kingsburgh had enjoyed long, deep draughts of punch. Flora had heard the Prince's voice below; he was singing, with somewhat pathetic bravado, "The King shall enjoy his own again." She had feared some outsider would see the light, come close to the windows to hear the voices. So she had slipped downstairs to see that all was well, and she had got there just in time to see the men disappear into the hidden stairway. She had stood there, smiled back at Charles, and imagined the room above, which she had never seen.

Flora wrenched her mind back to the present. I know well now, she thought, what that room contains. How often have I lingered there, reliving that night! She turned with a sigh to speak to Molly. "You will be safe up there, you and Peter." Then she swiftly crossed the room and from the hall called Katie. "Hurry," she ordered when the serving-girl appeared. "Go up the secret stair and make up Prince Charlie's bed. We have guests in need of it."

Katie's eyes opened wide. "What? The Prince's bed? Never have you let a soul sleep in it—only that fat London man who wrote the books, him and his friend."

Flora frowned. "You know, Katie, that Dr. Johnson and Mr. Boswell asked to sleep there. I'd never have suggested it myself." She started to turn back into the room, then looked again at Katie. "Forget all that now; just make up the bed as fast as you can."

"Well, just as you say, mistress," Katie said with a shrug. "But surely you don't mean for me to use the blessed sheets the Prince slept on. They at least have never been used since."

"Nay, not the sheets. Those I'm taking with me, and they're packed already. Now do make haste. And say nothing to the other servants."

Flora went back into the room where the others waited, still with perplexed looks on their faces. Before she could speak, Mrs. MacQueen protested. "Flora MacDonald, you don't mean for Peter and me to sleep where our Prince slept. We can't live in a room that's a shrine to you."

Flora walked to Molly and put her fingers to her lips. "I've made my decision. What is more fitting than that the room which harboured Charlie should harbour also you and Peter? Peter fought bravely at Culloden, and both of you have suffered in the Prince's name. The chamber was first a refuge; then it became a shrine, as you say. Now it shall be a refuge again."

Flora stood aside to let Katie, sheets in one hand and a candle in the other, lead the way to the hidden chamber. She gestured to the boys before she started up the stairs. "You come too. I know you want to see."

When they had all climbed the stairs, they found Katie opening a small window to air the room which, long unused, was heavy with dust. David and Dougald hurried about to look at every piece of furniture and into every nook. Molly simply looked about her and gradually tears came to her eyes. Moira went to her side and placed a hand on her shoulder. "Please, Mother, don't weep. 'Tis joyous you should be to be granted safety in this famous room."

Flora could pay no attention to the others. For her

the room was filled with memories, not people. By that window was cut the tress of hair now worn in the locket under her bosom. Involuntarily her hand went to it, and equally involuntarily she asked herself why never a word had come from her Prince: no little note, no message.

Sternly she told herself that he did not write because he feared to endanger her. Any message from him would have been damning, would have betrayed her at once to the English. But after all, she thought, I suffered imprisonment long ago. And Kingsburgh did too. There's been much time since then and no danger.

Katie's voice interrupted her sorrowful memories. "There it is, mistress, as fresh as I can make it in a moment and with everyone in the way. 'Twould be better if you'd all go down, and let me finish the job right."

Flora went at once to the stairs. She was thankful that Katie had recalled her to the present. Allan hated this room; he would have to know she'd been here, but he need not find her in it. "Hurry," she said to the others. "Peter and Allan will soon return. We must be ready to make plans with them for tomorrow."

A short while later Allan and Peter returned. Allan asked for Sandy and then nodded approval on learning that he and Jamie were on their way to Dunvegan. When he heard that the MacQueens, still refusing to emigrate to America, would be concealed in the secret chamber, he scowled for an instant. "I suppose you've been up," he said to Flora. Quietly she admitted she had, and he turned away before he said anything more. At last he looked at Flora. "It's your affair, if you want to open the room. I, for one, think it's a good idea."

Allan then began to make arrangements for the morrow. "David, you'll go home to talk to Margaret. Flora, you'd best go along, and take Molly with you. Dougald, if you don't mind, I'd like you to go with the gillies to Portree. Someone ought to be along to see that everything is stowed aboard properly. Peter, if you'll stay here, I'll show you something of the tack, and point out the gillies you should go to when you need anything. I'll set out a couple of scouts. There'll be little danger—not so long as I'm here." Allan placed his hands on his hips and stood with his feet planted wide apart. "Do these plans suit everyone? I'm sorry to give everyone a chore, when I know you'd all like to use the last days for a final hunt or pleasure visit. But there's much to be done. God grant we finish in time!"

Flora found she wanted to speak to Allan alone. She briefly touched his arm so he would know to wait, and then she hustled the MacQueens and the boys from the room, saying that they must all have rest for the many things to be done tomorrow. When the house was at last still, she said to her husband, "Sit with me a moment, Allan. We've not been able to speak at all together." But for a time she merely sat, with her hand over his, and said nothing. He too sat absorbed in thought and weariness.

Finally Flora turned to say, "Since Jemmy's been here and since we're so rushed and scattered, I've wondered whether we ought not to wait. There'll be another ship, and now there's not enough time.... I confess, I wish we could delay awhile."

Allan's voice was as determined as before. "The same reasons that make us go at all make us go now. I've not been able to tell you—the sheep-counting's done. We brought in twenty lambs less than last year. That's a poor total to report to young Alex," he added bitterly. "I've twice his years and experience; yet I've got to write again and say, 'I can't make your farm pay.'" He stood up and furiously smashed a fist into his other palm. "Oh, God, yes, I could make it pay, all right! But how? By Alex's own methods—by turning into a tacksman that squeezes his poor farmers as MacQueen's does." He turned beseechingly to her. "Flora, it's got to be now for me. I can no longer earn our living by begging it from above, and I won't steal it from below."

"Oh, Allan, I am so sorry! I see your hardships and to myself I sometimes wish the past undone. My heart aches to see the MacQueens. And it aches to see you, who never raised a hand against the Hanovers, defeated. How can they take such brutal revenge?"

"Don't speak so. 'Tis not revenge we're suffering. The Hanovers won at Culloden. They knew Charles would never come back." He sighed heavily, as if weighed down by immeasurable forces. "Nay, 'tis just this vise we're caught in, all of us, of the old pressing against the new. The old chiefs dying off, and the new ones bringing English ideas from the universities. The land wearing out and forcing us into trade. There's just no room for us Old Scots here any more."

"But how can we Old Scots, with our hearts tied so strong to our hills, make homes far away among strangers, Allan?"

"We can because there's a place there for us." He strode about in rising enthusiasm. "Don't you see the trouble here is we're bred to the land? Aye, and we're used to living in traditions of our own, while our world has got so old and small we have to live close with others and accept new strange ways. There with all the good land and peace and trade with England, a man can live his own life, without having to take sides in hatreds and competitions that have grown up over the years."

"But Hugh, my own stepfather, writes that not all the Americans like Hanoverian rule, any more than all Scots do."

"True, there are hard-headed ones there. I've listened well to all that. But the colonists are the King's subjects, and always will be. And there's an ocean between. What family squabble will make men want to fight after they've crossed a vast ocean, especially when it's the trade with the home country that brings money into the colonies?" He stopped behind her and placed his hands on her shoulders. "Nay, Flora, I know, I feel it deep inside me: 'Tis in America now that a man of strength can prove himself."

Flora sat quietly while she thought of all he had said. She knew she would not again remonstrate with him.

Certainly Allan was a man of strength, and above all else he needed a chance to prove himself. Slowly she rose, smiled tenderly and said, "I know you are right, Allan. We'll have success over there." But at the same time she prayed mutely, Dear God, let America be all he expects!

3

The First Remove

Morning brought no time for further discussions or plans. Even sorrow and worry, which underlay all Flora did, were choked down by the urgency of preparation. In the lochs of the Hebrides the winds and waters are unpredictable. There could be no telling, as Allan had said, how long the journey from Portree to Campbeltown would take. Four days were the briefest time their coastal ship dared allow, especially since it would put in at Armadale to allow them a last good-bye. Today, being Friday, was therefore the last day to make ready.

Breakfast preceded dawn, and work came with the sun. Allan was thankful they had been beforehand in their packing. Much was yet to do, and the day would be a harried one, but an early start and a will to finish would make it possible for them to attend the farewell gathering that night. He downed his porridge hurriedly and shoved back his chair. "I must see that the gillies get to work," he said, and then promised Flora he'd come back to the house as often as he could to superintend the loading.

She urged him not to tire himself. "I've got two strong lads and some of the men to help me. And all I must do is see they get everything that's to go."

Allan was eager to be outdoors but, seeing that MacQueen, who was to be shown the stock and storage, was yet spooning his gruel, he stood behind Flora for a moment. Fondly he pressed her shoulder. "I'd rather work the night through than have you exhausted," he said. "Go up to Monkstadt as soon as you can and rest. I'll make sure all's ready here."

Then he motioned to MacQueen and disappeared

out the door. MacQueen put down his spoon and rose promptly. Rest and the knowledge that he and his wife had a shelter had restored his spirit. He was ready for battle again and declared he personally would run any sneaking soldier off the land. Flora, seeing the flash of familiar courage in her old friend's eyes, asked whether he would not now reconsider and sail with them. "Nay," said MacQueen resolutely. "At my age a man has but one thing to look forward to—being buried on Highland soil, near his forebears. No one's going to take that from me." He swiftly went out the door and a moment later could be seen swinging up onto a fine bay. Then he and Allan clattered off.

Dougald walked to the window and studied the sky. "Beautiful day," he commented. "Maybe I can get in a little hunting on my way back from Portree. An extra grouse or two could probably be used tonight." He turned and spoke to Flora. "But I'll be hard put to get back before dinner unless we get started with the loading."

Flora was an efficient woman, and already she had Katie and another maid busy clearing the kitchen. "We'll stay tonight at Monkstadt," she said, "so you can pack the last of the china and the plate. Be sure it's tight in its flannel."

Katie grumbled that no one needed to tell her how to pack a dish or two, but Flora was too engrossed with the many details to care or to mind. "Come, Dougald, I've a special task to do." She led him outside where a pile of wood and a box of tools lay ready for the building of packing boxes and the boarding of windows. "Make a box, just so long—" she measured with her hands—"and so wide. It must be as watertight as can be. But don't nail it shut. Here's a lock. I might want to look in that box during the voyage. Now be quick about it, for David will need your help with the carrying."

She left Dougald to wonder what special object was to be placed in the flat, long container he was making, and stationed herself in the large front room where David and his helping gillies were beginning to move the trunks. When David reached for a chest near him she cried, "Not that one! 'Tis fragile crystal and must go last." She surveyed the trunks, which to David looked all alike, and designated two. "There, to the left. That's bedding, and beyond's the winter clothing. Take those now."

No object left the room until Flora had tested the locks and ropes and re-examined each label. "'Tis little enough we can take. I want nothing lost en route," she murmured. In the intervals when the men were below she ran from the room to tell Molly little things about the house or search for the third or fourth time in a long-empty drawer.

After a little, at a time when David was back for another load, Dougald brought in the strangely shaped box. "Here it is, Flora, but 'tis baffled I am to know what will fit in a shallow pan like this."

She gestured for both boys to follow, and as she led the way to her chamber above, she said, "I will show you. Yours will be the special charge of my most cherished possession." From a corner of the room she lifted an old mirror. The lads looked at it curiously, for it seemed ordinary enough to them. 'Twas no more than an old gilt frame, about two feet long and a foot wide, and the glass was dark and speckled.

She placed it against the wall where the morning light fell in a yellow rectangle, and bent to touch a hidden spring. The glass swung back to disclose a finely drawn and tinted portrait of Prince Charles. The light made the lines and colours vivid, so that the clear eyes under arched brows, the long nose and the curved, almost sensual lips, all framed in bright flowing ringlets, had the vitality of life. The lads each drew a quick breath. For a moment they felt they were looking directly on their hero. They felt that he, with his dignity and touch of arrogance, with his little humour but strong power and purpose, was gazing back.

"'Twas thus, lads, he looked when I first saw him. Then after, when he sorrowed, sweetness came into those eyes. And still after, when we parted, kind thanks and blessing were there." She slowly closed the mirror and fastened the invisible catch. "You must never let it come to harm, lads."

Under her watchful gaze the lads nailed the mirror into its secure case. She followed them downstairs and saw Dougald carry the box reverently. Both lads lifted it into a cart. As Flora turned back from the door she noticed David wedging it between two heavy sacks of meal. The house was wholly still. Through each door leading off the front hall she could see only barren floors and walls—walls smudged in squares where portraits of MacDonalds had hung for generations. There was suddenly nothing for her to do in her own home.

She stood tensely, one hand at the small of her back, the other slowly rubbing her forehead, and refused to give in to the sudden tears that welled up. On an impulse she wheeled and ran to the garden, where she dropped to her knees and began to dig with her fingers for bulbs. All the while she whispered to herself, "Allan said nay, but I must have them.... Soon as we have a house I'll plant them ... with the Scots earth still hanging about them.... 'Twill give me courage to see a living thing grow in that strange soil."

"Flora, Flora, where are you? 'Tis finished we are." It was Dougald, coming around the corner in search of her.

Her face, when she turned it up to him, was tear-streaked and she was biting her lip. That was a sad scene, with Dougald sinking to his knees beside her and awkwardly placing his arm about her shoulders. "I'm so sorry, so sorry, Flora," he said.

First swallowing, she reassured him. "Nay. 'Tis I who am sorry. I've seen the loss in your own eyes. But you and the others bear up, as I ought to do." She pressed his hand lightly. To herself she said, I must not do this again.

Dougald waited a moment, then said quietly, "Flora, I'm ready to make the first trip. Let me call David and see you off to Monkstadt. I'll do all the moving and meet you there."

"But there's the girl. She's staying to show Katie what to pack for her and to prepare for the voyage." She was still distracted and asked him helplessly, "With Allan busy here till late, how will she get up to Monkstadt?"

Only then did Dougald rise. He turned slightly away before he spoke. All morning he'd been trying to find a way to talk to Moira and now, although an opportunity was offered naturally, his eagerness made him shy. Finally he said hesitantly, "If you think it would be all right, I could come down for her." Flora did not answer immediately and he began to stammer slightly. "I mean ... she n-needs to rest. ... The coach will be at Monkstadt. So she won't have to ride, I could ... could take her up by boat. ... I ..."

Flora stood up and turned him to face her. "That's enough explaining, Dougald," she said gently. " 'Tis right you should care for the lass. Go now, and be careful."

The lad ran off toward the house, and Flora followed as soon as she had gathered up the plants and wrapped them in her apron. When she reached the garden door she stood quietly to let Dougald finish telling Moira that he would return for her. He spoke in abrupt sentences and then waited for her to reply. Moira only nodded, murmured, "I'll wait," and kept her eyes on her work. There was a frown of disappointment on his forehead as he glanced at Flora. Then he left the house without looking back.

When Dougald's footsteps had died away, Moira dropped the gown she held and looked out the window after him. But when she heard Flora come in, she sat down again, and said nothing.

"He's a fine young man, Moira," Flora said, careful to speak casually.

Moira looked up, replied, "Yes," and then asked, "Are you ready to go now? Shall I fetch the others?"

Flora looked into the beautiful, quiet face and seemed to forget momentarily that she must make haste. "Tonight, you know, our kin will gather. I hope you will feel one of us and join in the gaiety.

Your parents will be there, too, and they will want to see you happy, as in the old days."

Moira found it hard to speak, but at last she raised her hand in a gesture of confusion and said, "You are very good to me. It's just that I don't know how to thank you."

Flora answered, glad that at last Moira had revealed her feelings, "If that's really all that makes you so still, you must not worry. We want no thanks but seeing you happy. So smile now, and think of the reels you'll dance tonight with ... with our boys." Flora wanted to name Dougald, for she feared his shyness would make the girl think him dull. But she could not guess what Moira was thinking and decided it was best not to single him out. "They are very fond of you already" was all she added. "Now hurry. Call David and your mother. We must be off."

After Moira had left Flora waited until Molly had gone out to the stable. She stood alone for only a moment. Then she spoke a very quiet, inward good-bye and sighingly closed the door.

When the great doors at Monkstadt swung back to let Molly, Flora and David pass, the three arrivals stared in momentary surprise at a stranger who was talking with Lady Margaret. In turn Margaret and her guest broke off their conversation at the unannounced intrusion. The sight of haggard Molly told Margaret that it was the MacQueens' trouble which had brought Flora and David back to Monkstadt before they were expected. She rose and came forward.

"Margaret, we must speak with you," Flora said in an undertone.

Lady Margaret nodded and said so the guest could hear, "Of course, but first let me present you to Admiral Weston's niece. She's come to sail to America with you." She led the others across the room and made the introductions. "Miss Weston's mother is one of the Argyll Campbells. Miss Weston has been at Rosshire, visiting her aunt, and now she visits me, to my great joy." Then to the English girl she said, "You will excuse us a moment. There is some business ..."

Her voice trailed off as she led Flora and the others to chairs slightly apart.

Miss Cecily Weston, from Devonshire, thought it best to study the iridescent greens of the Minch through the window, but she found it difficult to keep her eyes away from the others, who spoke in low tones that she could vaguely hear. She could not guess what the trouble was, though it must have to do with that tired-looking Mrs. MacQueen, over whom Lady Margaret hovered. It seemed somewhat odd to her that the worn woman should be in an aristocratic house like Monkstadt. But that tall, strong young man made himself very much at home. Of course, Miss Weston remembered, he lives here, with a twin brother. She saw that though the young man attended carefully to all that was said by the older women, his eyes strayed frequently over Molly's shoulder toward her, and she turned back to the window.

Before long her gaze returned to the group. She could scarcely believe that the small, graceful figure was the famous Flora MacDonald. So often had she been told of Flora's great, if misguided, patriotism and daring that she had created in her mind the picture of a larger, more domineering woman. For a time Cecily observed the expressions on Flora's face. Yes, she finally decided, that woman could have rescued her prince from under his pursuers' noses. She's very gentle, but those eyes, with their quiescent vitality, could readily flare into passionate resolve.

I don't like her politics, but I do like her spirit, thought Miss Weston, who was herself a woman of resolve. Her beauty was of the fair, blonde, English kind. Nothing in her colouring promised flashing high spirits, but she had a magnificent, willowy erectness, which was somewhat deceptive: she did not bend easily. Habitually she carried her shoulders square and her head high. Her features were delicate, but strong. Her expression was usually sweet and serene—even when, as now, she was confused and when she suspected all her prior notions of the Scots were to suffer rapid change.

As she settled into a more comfortable position she

said to herself, They have certainly welcomed me
kindly. I've received as much hospitality as I would
be shown in any English manor—or more. She
looked at Lady Margaret and she thought, No one
could be more gracious than she; she's everything Uncle said she would be. Look at her now, smiling so
gently at those people, assuring them not to worry
about whatever it is, and all the while including me in
her generous gaze to keep me from feeling neglected.

Cecily felt it was she who ought to apologize for
imposition. How embarrassing it had been to arrive
late in the night and find that her uncle's letter had
preceded her by only a few hours! Lady Margaret,
welcoming her at the door, had betrayed no sign that
the unexpected visitor had flurried the household. All
was prepared. Lady Margaret had laughed consolingly and said, "Now don't worry about your letter
coming late. I'm afraid our postal service depends on
the whim of the courier. Only when he deems enough
letters have accumulated does he make his rounds.
'Twas only the news of the Baliol that lured him out
at last." Then Margaret had told her how happy she
was that Cecily had come to her. "Your uncle and my
dear Alexander, gone so long now, were very close,
you know," she had said.

At a quickening in the voices across the room Miss
Weston bent forward a little. The boy rose, said
something about a Kingsburgh House and came
toward her.

He bowed deeply and said, "Please forgive us. 'Tis
rude to whisper about and then run off just when
we've met you. We wouldn't, please understand, but
there's so much to do."

Inwardly Miss Weston was amused at his concern,
but she lifted a silencing hand and assured him she
felt no slight. "By all means, don't let my coming
delay you. I know what a rush you are in. I myself
feel breathless to think we must start so soon. But
since we sail together—you are going too, I think?"
When he nodded yes, she went on, "Yes, well, we'll
have much opportunity to talk later."

"Oh," David answered, "we'll have that tonight.

All the near clansmen will come to see us off. We'll have a proper farewell party, and you'll be able to see our Highland dances."

"I shall look forward to that. Will you dance?"

"Aye," he said, and then found courage to add, "with you, if you will allow it."

Miss Weston tilted back her head to laugh in pleasure. "I should be honoured. But you'll need patience to teach me the unfamiliar steps. Promise to dance a few times first with a Highland lass, so I may see you perform without the cumbrance of an awkward partner."

David almost replied, "You'll never be awkward," but he bethought himself of his manners and his duties and only thanked her before he hurried away.

The boy left and Cecily could hear his diminishing song, "Wha wud na be in love wi' bonnie Maggie Lauder? . . ." While the three women continued to consult for a moment, she marvelled that she had been reluctant to come to these kind people. When her uncle had suggested she visit Lady Margaret MacDonald and thus meet and sail with Flora and her party, she had refused. "After all," she had protested, "I can't really think, Uncle, that people I've been taught are barbarous will make good protectors."

The admiral had been annoyed. He said testily, "It's time you get over foolish prejudices. It's true the clansmen have caused us no end of trouble. They're a fierce and independent lot. But take 'em one by one, and they're as honest and generous as any people in Great Britain. Why, there wasn't a better man, nor one more loyal, than Alexander of Sleat." He'd then gone on to insist she visit Monkstadt, saying he wouldn't feel easy unless she travelled with friends.

"Margaret is a fine woman," he had told her. "She was one of Eglington's beautiful daughters. And the famed Flora MacDonald, well, she's got strong character." He had chuckled in recollection. "I met her, y' know. Was standing by when Prince Frederick interviewed her. He twitted her about saving the Pretender because she was in love with Charles's pretty face.

But she was queenly, I'll say. She looked right back at him and said, 'I'd have done the same for you, sir, had you needed me.' And y' know, the Prince was pleased, even if he wouldn't show it."

Such talk had soon whetted Cecily's curiosity and she decided to cut short her sojourn at Balmagowan, her Aunt Amantha's estate in Rosshire. Nonetheless she had teased, "But, Uncle, do you want me to sail with an old enemy of the King?"

His answer, as also the suddenly solemn tones of his voice, was surprising. "I want you to sail with the MacDonalds, Cecily. And I want you to know Allan MacDonald. He's a reliable man."

Once more Cecily studied Flora, this time to wonder what sort of man her husband was. It would take a strong man, she decided, to win the love of such a woman, and a still stronger one to live in the shadow of her fame. "I'm eager to meet him," she said under her breath, "with or without instructions to do so."

She bit her lip in chagrin at her tactlessness, for Flora looked up as if she had heard. But no, she only smiled and said, "Can you indulge our family business a moment longer? I'm sorry we must neglect you so."

Cecily smiled again to show she was in no way affronted, and relapsed into her thoughts. Would her other uncle, the one she was to visit in North Carolina, be like these people? she wondered. She liked their colourful tartans, the soft burr of their accent and the reticence of their manner. But she doubted Farquard Campbell would retain strong Scots traits. He's been thirty years in America, she thought a trifle contemptuously, and now has got so rich he'll never come home. He'd rather live among that isolated lot of adventurers and thieves than take his place in the society to which our family belongs. And then it crossed her mind that the disgrace would be hard to bear at home if her uncle, her mother's own brother, had really become too much of an American, as rumour had it. Well she remembered that the Earl of Dartmouth, with the business of all the colonies on his mind, had troubled to come see her when he learned she was making a trip to North Carolina. "Talk to Farquard," he had demanded. "Find out whether it's true he meets with the malcontents. Make him see that if it's true, he is, he's being beguiled by hotheads with no respect for the Crown and no realization that their own welfare depends on England." Well, surely, she thought, Farquard can't be so foolish as all that.

Her meditation was dispelled by a new sound. Mrs. MacQueen, she saw, was shaking with deep, slow sobs. Cecily involuntarily rose to go to her, but Flora MacDonald stopped her by rising and coming across the room.

"'Tis best to let her weep it away. 'Twill relieve her."

"But what has happened to the poor soul? Has there been illness, or . . . ?"

"Or death? Neither, but to her something harder to bear." Flora told the sad story of the MacQueens' long persecution and final eviction.

As she listened, the English woman sank slowly back into her chair. Her eyes widened in mixed astonishment and disbelief. She gazed at Flora as if she wished to be sure she could trust her, and finally she said, "You mean these people are wrenched from their homes, and without cause?"

"Nay, I glossed the tale. There is cause—the English will to starve our people to powerlessness." Flora's voice hardened as she described the oppression. She concluded, "Most of these pathetic creatures are forced, regardless of age or health, to roam the heaths. Forgive me, but 'tis the English who do this."

"But I'm sure . . . it's some misunderstanding. . . . The English would not . . ." Cecily tried to formulate her instinctive denial. She saw a victim of misfortune with her own eyes; she could not doubt Flora's truthfulness. But to conceive that the King would wilfully abuse any subjects, as Flora asserted, was impossible. She envisioned suddenly the kind of clansmen she'd had drawn for her by her governess: lazy men who preferred scavenging in the hills and robbing coaches to clean, hard, honest labour. Finally she found words for her thoughts. "I think the trouble must be

that we English do not know about this. We are
taught stupid things about the Scots. I grasp that now.
You see, there is still the bitterness of your insurrec-
tion. But most of us simply do not know."

Flora wished to refrain from argument with a guest
of Margaret's home. She looked down into her lap for
a moment, then, raising her eyes, said, "I see you and
my husband agree. He will not have the English at
fault, but the times." Her hand moved in a vague motion. "I am no historian. When he speaks of pressures
of trade, and age-old misunderstandings that gather
force as we Scots and English come closer together, I
have to be persuaded." Her voice took on tension
again. "But I fear I forget such arguments at the sight
of Molly there and at the memory that my own husband was denounced on the church door as one who
could not pay his bills. I remember only that 'twas an
English steward who put MacQueen off his land and
'twas an English school that taught our own laird to
oppress his people."

With quick insight Cecily saw that Flora's politics
and heroism were rooted in her sense of injustice to
individual persons. And it at once became clear that
Flora likewise did not wish to blame all English cruel-
ties on an individual, innocent woman. Flora un-
clenched her hands and reached forward tentatively.
"Do not think ill of me for this passion. I am happy
you will be with us. And even happier," she added after
a momentary pause, "that when we reach the New
World you will see Scots happier, because safer."

"Let us hope so," Cecily murmured, but inwardly
she thought, If you Scots let your hatred turn you
against the King in this present unrest in America,
there will be neither safety nor happiness for you.

The sight of misery like the MacQueens' was as
hard for Cecily to bear as for Flora, but Cecily could
not easily find her countrymen at fault. She had been
bred not only in a fashionable young ladies' lesson-
room, but also in an admiral's home. There, men of
state were frequent dinner guests and affairs of state
were constant dinner talk. She understood that a people who denied the King wilfully forfeited the benefits

of English rule. She understood also that among nations there was inevitably and always a fierce struggle for supremacy in trade and armies. It is clearly the husband who has the broader view, she decided.

Aloud she said, "I am extremely distressed. In my eyes my countrymen can never be the villains you describe. Perhaps the trouble is partly that your Scots landlords take advantage of unjust law. I have heard of many instances of that. Never mind—" she nodded toward Molly—"that pulls at my heart as much as it does at yours. Is there any way I can help?"

Flora stood up. "For the parents there's little can be done. They refuse to leave Skye. Fortunately we can trust Margaret to care for them. The girl, though—" She broke off when she saw Miss Weston's surprise. "Yes, there's a daughter. We will take her to her relatives in America. There she will have a better chance."

"For her there will surely be something I can do."

"Perhaps. When you meet her you can see. She needs protection, goodness knows! But she is both proud and reticent, and may refuse English aid."

You too, Flora MacDonald, are proud and reticent, Cecily thought. But you are brave and generous too. Then her thoughts went back to the unknown girl. She resolved to do all she could for the homeless child. Perhaps thus, she thought, I can rectify some of the wrong impressions of my people.

Cecily leaned back to look up at Margaret, who had come to stand beside her. The older woman was saying, " 'Tis a sad sight we greet you with, my dear. I hope this evening we can make you forget some of this unpleasantness and see a happier side of Highland life."

Cecily rose and spoke sincerely. "This sad sight has moved me much, Lady Margaret."

"Then," said the older woman, "you will understand why I must leave you to go make arrangements for the MacQueens. Flora, I saw Katie come in with your gown. You must dress. Soon folk will be arriving, and we must be ready for them."

Lady Margaret waited until Cecily had assured her

a few hours' rest would be welcome. Then she left the room and Flora and Cecily followed her. At the door Cecily touched Flora's elbow to hold her back for a moment. "Where is the girl now?" she asked.

"With Dougald, one of the twins. She will arrive late this afternoon. God grant the weather holds, for they come by boat!"

By mid-afternoon Dougald was still some little way from Kingsburgh. On the return trip, after the carts and waggons had been emptied of their crates at Portree, he had left all responsibility to the gillies. In due time the waggons would creak into the yard at Kingsburgh; he didn't have to worry about them any longer. He had cantered ahead with John, a young gillie who often served Dougald on excursions out of Kingsburgh. Together they had turned away from the path to flush out the fowl hiding in the furze and bracken on the hillsides, and they bagged three ptarmigan.

The excitement of the hunt had caught Dougald up; two hours had slipped by while he and John had stalked their prey, and, though they had ridden generally in the direction of Kingsburgh, they had some fast galloping to do, if there was to be time for the boat trip with Moira.

Dougald's "Halloo!" made John wheel and fall in beside his young master. The gillie was not a talkative companion, but that mattered little to Dougald, who always preferred his own thoughts to idle chatter. For a while Dougald studied the land they rode over. He wanted to hold it back, not let its reality slip by into memory, which, he feared, would grow dim amid the scenes of the New World. At times his attention wandered. In Portree he had found no bundles from the MacLeods of Dunvegan Castle. Did that mean something had happened to Flora's daughter Anne, that she would not be able to get to Portree for the sailing? Then Dougald remembered that the MacLeods had decided later than Flora and Allan that they would emigrate. Probably their belongings were not quite ready to be moved. No doubt, he said to himself, Anne's got all packed by now and is on her way to Monkstadt with Sandy and the others.

Dougald drew rein when he saw Kingsburgh House lying before him. The thought that somewhere down there Moira was expecting him made him exclaim happily, "Ride! Ride! Quickly! My lassie waits." At once he was glad John had cantered ahead. What kind of a fool was he to be taken with a girl so quickly? This new, grown-up Moira was like a stranger; he'd no business having dreams about her. Yet he could not deny he did dream; he felt sure that, could he but find the words to begin, he could say much, and her perceptive eyes would look on him with understanding. Then he laughed at his own hopes.

Nonetheless, when he reached the house, he leaped from the saddle and ran in calling, "Moira! I'm back!" Keen disappointment went through him when he heard in answer nothing but the echo of his own words. Quickly he ran through the house, upstairs and down, and only then was he persuaded it was empty. Slowly, kicking at the stones as he went, he walked out the front door. When he lifted his head, his heart jumped. A girl, her skirts blowing with the wind, was down at the landing-place. He ran a few steps forward and looked closer. It was Moira! Dougald relaxed to sigh aloud, "She does wait for me."

First shouting for John, Dougald raced down Prince Charlie's Steps and stopped breathlessly beside Moira. He was so relieved to find her, and so stimulated by the wind and salt spray that cooled his face, that he spoke merrily. With a sweep of his arm he indicated the sailing-boat. "Your gondola awaits, milady."

Moira looked up at him and for a moment responded to his gaiety. A lovely smile came to her lips. "You're kind, Dougald," she said simply.

Dougald shook his head. "Not kind. Just pleased you're going up to Monkstadt with me." Some of his customary embarrassment returned and he added, to conceal his feeling for her, "I'm tired of this day's lonely travel."

Moira did not reply, and Dougald turned away. He first watched John climb into the boat with the day's catch and then he watched the clouds hanging over the Long Island. "What think you, John?" he asked. "Is there danger of a squall? If so, I don't want to take Mistress Moira out."

John lifted his face and sniffed the wind. He observed the clouds judiciously. "Nay, Master Dougald, I think it be safe. There'll likely be a blow, but not for three or four hours or more."

Dougald felt a slight tug at his arm. Moira was trying to get his attention. "Please, Dougald, let's take the boat. I don't want to go back to the house. That's why I waited here—to get away from Kingsburgh. The rooms that used to be so festive and gracious are barren now. I seemed to see my dear father and mother there alone and frightened. . . ."

"Come, then," Dougald cried as he jumped into the boat. "Your sad thoughts are good reason for us to be going." He paused. "Moira, I didn't stop at the byre to see Allan and your father. There's no reason I should go up. . . ?"

When his questioning tone was answered by a negative shake of her head, he firmly grasped a post with one hand, ordered John to hold the boat steady and handed Moira down. Briefly he held her hand in his. "Turn your face to the north, Moira, where your mother and your friends look for you. See how quickly we take you to them."

With a great shove of the oar he sent them free of the scaffolding and rocks. John ran up the sail and pointed them toward the mouth of the Beag.

For a couple of miles the little boat sailed briskly, spanking through the short, sharp waves noisily and heeling with the gusty wind from the west. Moira loved the rushing salt air and hung over the bow covering to let it play over her face. Dougald, succumbing to lassitude after his long day's ride, leaned on his elbow and watched her. For the first time since he had met her he saw high colour in her cheeks, and that made him glad he'd arranged to give her this sail. As her exhilaration rose she glanced back over her shoulder frequently to laugh at nothing but the freedom she felt.

For a little while Dougald left the management of the boat entirely to the gillie, who crouched over the tiller. Before long John began to look anxiously at the low bank of clouds scudding in on them from the west and south. Finally he eased the tiller a trifle to bring them a little close to the craggy shore that lay ahead. "Wind'll swing south and blow," he muttered.

At once Dougald noticed the slight shift in direction. He too studied the bank of cloud. It was going to blow, no question. Now he began to wish he hadn't carried Moira out on the sea. "Bring her up a bit," he told the gillie. "If the squall hits from the west at all, we'll need some room. We don't want to pile up on the crags."

Moira, too, was sensitive to the sharpening of the air. She turned about, sat quietly and kept her eyes on Dougald, as if awaiting instructions.

Rapidly the storm came down on them. The light of the summer afternoon was all at once simply gone. Out of the south the wind struck them, carrying sheets of almost horizontal rain.

The little boat staggered and heeled as the full force of the wind and spray hit it, shrieking and tearing at it. The coast line was blotted out. They were alone in the blackness of the storm.

John, fighting the kicking tiller, managed the boat well, bringing it up into the wind before it could capsize, and Dougald jumped to double-reef the sail. They survived the first fury of the storm.

After the great gusts, the wind steadied to a gale that whistled through the ropes and made the flapping sail crack like a pistol. With the sail reefed down scarcely larger than a handkerchief, they let it fill cautiously and started off, running before the wind. The first crisis was over, but they could see nothing and could judge their course only by the direction of the wind.

Soon, off to the right, they could hear the waves roaring against the rocks of the shore. Dougald knew they were thundering in at a long slant and throwing spray high on the rocks. It was lucky he had made the gillie head farther out into the loch or at that moment they might be grinding on the boulders at the base of the cliffs.

Moira was now crouched by the gunwale, drenched but alert. Dougald could see she wanted to help, and he thought something to do would help her keep steady. He reached for a bucket and put it in her hands. "We'd best keep her free of water," he shouted in her ear. "Bail her some."

The waves were coming at the stern but at an angle, lifting it crazily, sliding under with a sucking noise and a sickening, slewing drop. The sail bellied and strained and the little boat flew. It was nervous work, but once they were caught in the storm, running before the wind was their safest manoeuvre and they couldn't stop until the wind dropped or they came into more protected waters. Uig Bay lay somewhere ahead to the right, if he knew how to find it, but in that sea if they tried to come about the waves might swamp the boat in the moment she was broadside to them.

He seized another bucket and set himself to help Moira with the bailing, for a little water came in with every wave.

For perhaps twenty minutes—it seemed an eternity—they flew blindly up the loch. Dougald and Moira, the bailing finished for the moment, peered about, trying to guess where they were and how far they had come. It seemed to him the wind was abating, though it was still tearing at them.

Then suddenly the clouds astern of them seemed to open and a gleam of pearly light spread around them. The light revealed that they were much too close in shore. A rocky, jagged coast lay near at the right and curved out to a point full in their path. Instinctively John shoved hard on the tiller. At the same time, Moira, seeing in the open sky a promise that the squall was blowing out, jumped to her feet to point at the break in the clouds.

Dougald saw it all. The gillie's sudden swerve to avoid the rocks let the wind get at the sail in front. It began to gibe. The heavy boom, driven by the full force of the wind, swung in across the boat. In another instant it would have struck Moira and almost sliced off her head or knocked her into the seething sea. Dougald leaped, his arm out to catch her about the shoulders and bear her down out of the path of the boom's vicious swing. He could feel her sink under his weight and knew thankfully that it would miss her. But on the arm, just below the shoulder, he caught a hard blow that dropped him sprawling across the gunwale, half in, half out of the boat.

A minute or so later it was all over. White-faced, holding his left arm with his right, he scrambled to his knees and peered about. Moira had gone down in a heap in the bottom of the boat. She was breathless but unhurt, and she pulled up to her knees and clutched at his shirt. "Oh, thank you! Thank you," she whispered. Together they looked ahead.

The boat had swung around Kilbride Point and John was making for the quieter water in its lee. In the growing light they could make out Monkstadt, not a quarter of a mile away, and they clung to the sight of it.

Dougald's left arm felt numb until he tried to move it; then a fierce pain stabbed his shoulder. He gritted his teeth, cautiously fingering his sleeve, and held his body carefully still as the boat glided into shore.

As they touched sand John spoke for the first time. "The lad's bad hurt, lass. You'd best run up to the house and get help. I'll see to getting him ashore."

4

Gathering at Monkstadt

THE steep slopes up to Monkstadt House were strange to Moira. She fixed her eyes on the lights glimmering through the rain and scrambled from rock to rock. Though she often tripped and once fell she felt no pain, so great was her will to bring prompt aid to Dougald. But at the crest of the hill she stopped short in panic. With the MacDonald clansmen had come dozens of retainers, who now camped in the yard and hovered for warmth and dryness over sputtering flames. Directly before Moira a huge man was plucking a new-caught pheasant by the fire. His swarthy features were distorted by the flickering flames and about him rose the acrid odour of burning feathers. She stifled her cry of alarm, threw her hand over her mouth and darted around him toward the house beyond.

"Ho! Who goes there?" his harsh voice cried. In a trice he took one long step and jerked her back by her arm.

When he saw that it was but a slender, frightened girl—surely no threat to his masters within—he relaxed his grip. "Now say: Wha' want ye?"

She nearly fell when he released her, but managed to pull herself straight and gasp, " 'Tis Dougald. Below, in the boat. He's hurt."

"Good lass, for bringin' word." He whirled to an older man close by. "Take her to the house. You, over there—" he beckoned to another—"down the cliff with me."

The older man stepped forward to support Moira. "Steady, lass. We mean no harm to you." He took a step toward the house.

"But Dougald," she cried as she tried to pull back. "Let me go help." Even as she said it she slipped into black release, and was caught, insensible, by the man.

Within the great house there were the laughter and bustle of a clan reunion. Everywhere there were the squared blues, greens, yellows and reds of the MacDonald tartan, mingled with the colours and designs of the particular septs. The staccato of many greetings and reminiscences was set against the unending rustle of the ladies' fine taffetas and silks. The MacNeils from Barra, accompanied by the Morrises and the MacCauleys, and the MacLeods from Lewis and Harris had already changed from their riding clothes into their dress kilts and plaids and were in the great hall. The MacKinnons were brave in their red, green and white dress tartan. Lesser folk had changed into their best attire from the rough woollens they'd worn for their journey in carts and by foot. Secure in their trust of the vigilant retainers without, the men carelessly swirled their kilts and the ladies fluttered plaid ribbands. The presence of the graceful and English-accented stranger only heightened their determination to exult in their Scots traditions this night, and prove the hardiness as well as the beauty of their heritage.

One of the Lewis MacLeods, standing by the hearth with Miss Weston, surveyed the room as she said, "It surely won't be long before Flora's daughter and her Alex—my cousin, you know—arrive. They sail with you." The speaker looked back at the guest. "As soon as they come in, I'll present them. 'Tis a shame you can't visit them at their ancient home." The woman laughed. "Even the stringent Dr. Johnson was impressed by the spare turrets of Dunvegan Castle."

"And with your heroine, Flora MacDonald, I hear," Cecily answered.

As so often in the past hour, the conversation broke off as they turned to watch new arrivals enter. With each opening of the door, the clusters of visitors regrouped and new conversations sprang up. Now it was the Talisker branch of MacLeods that entered and was welcomed.

Cecily found Flora beside her. "I'm dreadfully confused," she said in an apologetic tone. "Your many Alexanders are all mixed up in my mind. Is your daughter's husband the same Alexander Lady Margaret speaks of as being away?"

"Oh, no," Flora said as if it were impossible to think the two might be confused. Then she smiled. "I guess it must be difficult for a stranger. We like to carry on our family names. You see, Anne's Alexander is a MacLeod of Dunvegan. You will meet him, for he is to go to America with us. My Alexander—Sandy—is my seventeen-year-old boy. He too will sail with us, though now he is with Anne. And Young Alex is Lady Margaret's and Sir Alexander's son, though not much like his parents. He is our strict and English-bred laird."

Cecily was silent as she tried to absorb the information and make sure she would not again confuse the names. She heard the door open again, and then heard Flora's sharp intake of breath. When she looked up she saw not a party of happy relatives but a rugged-looking man with a limp girl in his arms. At Flora's surprised "'Tis the MacQueen girl," she pressed forward and with Flora bent anxiously over Moira.

The retainer outlined the little he knew of the accident and assured them the child in his arms was only frightened. He confessed he knew not how seriously Dougald was injured and concluded, "They're bringing him up. You'd best be ready."

Margaret had listened from the stairs. "My boy," she said faintly, her fingers tensing momentarily at her cheek. "Run! Run, someone, for Doctor John, Doctor John Ban MacLean." She took a step or two down the stairs, then turned to hurry back to turn down Dougald's bed. But first she appealed to Flora: "Care for the girl. Don't let her mother see her like that."

When Flora stepped back to ask the man to carry the girl upstairs, she discovered that Cecily was already leading him toward the stairway. "To my room. I and my maid will care for her," Flora heard her say as she disappeared.

A moment later Dougald himself stumbled in. His lips were drawn tight and with each movement he grimaced in pain, but he was on his own two feet between the gillies who had rushed down to help him. When he saw Flora's anxious look and the concern on the faces of the relatives circled about him, he drew a tortured breath to say, " 'Tis nothing. . . . Just a blow on the shoulder."

"Nothing, lad?" Flora exclaimed. "Your shirt sticks to you with blood. Hurry, men. Margaret waits above." She led the way.

As they half lifted him up the steps he grasped the banister for support and caught Flora's skirt to make her stop. "Moira—how is she?" he asked in a low tone those below could not hear.

Only when he was convinced that the girl was unhurt and well cared for did he allow Flora to lead him on. But once in his room and gently received by Margaret, he sank gratefully face down onto the bed. Twice he had enough respite from pain to tell her not to worry; the rest of the time he lay with clenched hands and teeth to keep from crying with the fierce throbs which pummelled his shoulder.

Time passed meaninglessly for him while Margaret pressed damp cloths on the stiffened shirt. At last a sting of air told him the linen had been removed. Then he knew no more until old Doctor MacLean warned him, "Brace yourself. I'm going to feel for a fracture." Dry old hands massaged the pulsing flesh and flexed the arm.

He heard the familiar voice again. " 'Tis nothing serious, Lady Margaret. He'll be mighty sore for a few days, but there's no break. Thing to do is keep this wound clean." Then there was the unbearable fire of whisky in the gash and Dougald reared.

"Hold on! You make it bleed again, and we'll have it all to do over," John Ban cried as he pushed Dougald down. After he had bound up the wound with strips of fresh linen, the doctor rose stiffly and

drew Flora out the door with him. Dougald heard
him say, "Before I go, I'll tell you how to care for
that wound."

Lady Margaret stepped up and laid a hand on his
forehead. She was still white-faced and solemn. "Oh,
my dear Dougald! I thought I'd lost you. I am so
thankful."

The burning of the whisky eased and Dougald
could think clearly and talk coherently. He managed
a wan smile as he said, " 'Tis glad I am to hear that,
Lady Margaret.... I feared you wanted to be rid of
David and me, sending us off to America the way you
are." That was not what he had meant to say, but
somehow the accident, and having her hover over him
as she had done when he was a much younger lad,
made him lose his restraint. "I don't want to leave
Skye, Lady Margaret. Must I?"

She sank to the bed, and took his hand in both
hers. "Don't, don't, Dougald. You are my own true
son, and David, too, with the good MacDonald blood
coursing through your veins. What will I do without
you?"

"But why then? Why do you send us? There's
much good I could do here."

"A man must have opportunity to do good. There's
really no opportunity here. You've no land of your
own and soon, with all the emigration, there'll be no
clan of your own." She raised her head to look about
the room. Making sure that Flora had gone, she
spoke in hushed but determined tones, "I want neither you nor David to suffer Allan's misery—losing
and losing and losing till he's not sure whether he
really has it in him to succeed. You'll love a fine
woman some day, as Allan does Flora. Will you want
to see her suffer as Flora now suffers?"

So that's it, Dougald thought, that's why Allan,
despite his manly handsomeness and his strength, always seems a little unsure of himself. He remained
quiet and his thoughts turned to Moira. He did not
want her to suffer.

At his silence, Lady Margaret rose. "I've tired you.
Now rest. Doctor John said you might come down for

supper if the pain is not too severe. So sleep now, and you'll feel stronger."

He turned his head to watch her leave. "I'm better already," he told her, "and I shall come later."

Almost at once he slept, but his aching and throbbing shoulder made his sleep restless. When, a short hour later, the glow of a small candle appeared at his door, he was at once awake. At first he could not tell who the woman was; in the arc of light he could see creamy shoulders and a slender neck rising from lustrous green silk and he could tell from the silhouette that heavy hair was piled high on an oval head. The woman took a step toward him, raised the candle slightly and in a young, hesitant voice said, "Dougald?"

He fell back in amazement as he heard the familiar voice come from the strange, mature young woman. "Moira! Is it you?"

She laughed softly and came a step nearer. "Aye, 'tis me, but I hardly know myself. The kind English lady has dressed me in a gown of her own. 'Tis too large for me." Then, characteristically, she forgot herself, even in her unaccustomed finery, and her voice deepened as she asked, "Oh, Dougald, are you really all right? 'Twas such a brave thing you did!"

"Don't say that. I didn't do anything, Moira."

"Of course you did. You saved me, and saved us all perhaps. And now you are in pain." She timidly touched his shoulder.

He laughed in sudden happiness. "There! Your touch has cured it. I'm feeling better, and I'm coming down to supper."

Her smile came then. "Oh, Dougald, I'm so glad. I couldn't bear to think of you lying here in pain." She straightened primly and fumbled to manage the long and slithery silken skirt. "Now I must go. Thank you again."

"Don't go. Sit here until the dressing-bell rings."

"I must. 'Tis not proper for me to stay long. And I must either get back into my own dress or have this pinned up. I shall stumble over my 'train.' "

"Wear that one, Moira. The green becomes you, with your auburn hair. You are very grown-up."

In the light of the candle he saw a deep flush spread over her neck and cheeks. "Please, Moira," he pleaded. "Just sit there, in that chair, till the bell."

As if his words had been a signal the gong sounded. Moira waited only till its echo died; then she brushed a shy kiss on his forehead and fled.

During all the excitement of Moira's and Dougald's arrival, David had been "helping" in the great kitchen. There busy preparations for the banquet had gone on all day. Now, just before the serving, stewards shouted orders about wines: Canary, Hippocras, Rhenish and the finest claret, red and white, were all to be served. The cooks bent over stoves and fire-places to turn beef, mutton and lamb on long spits. In a side kitchen a special set of cooks were dressing and cooking the venison, grice, ptarmigan, plover and duck that the retainers had brought in. The savoury mixture of odours had lured ever-hungry David back again and again.

Old goodwife Aggie sat on a high stool where her eye could search out every corner of the room. She was nearly eighty, but she still ruled the kitchen as sternly as she had when the present laird, young Alex, was born and when she had warmed his first wee drap of milk, as his mother was too ill to nurse him. At the moment she watched the turning of the fish, for it would come first at dinner. One by one the delicate salmon, the trout and perch from the cold streams in the hills were turned in the skillets. This was to be a feast her folk would remember in the new, wild land. "A silly business, this traipsin' over the world!" she muttered.

A reckless potboy who plunged his finger into a fine sauce warming on the back of the stove caught her attention. With her cane she whacked his legs and made him jump. In his fright and guilt the boy touched his hand to the stove, then screamed and thrust his fingers to his lips.

"Rub it in butter!" she called to him, as his tearful

eyes looked accusingly at her. "And let it be a lesson." She eased herself from the stool and hobbled past a table piled high with sweets to the cabinet of special concern. There lay the rows of haggis, the special Scots delicacy for ceremonious occasions.

David, seeing her concentrated stare at the plump puddings, thought it safe to tear away a juicy bite from a brown, steaming roast. She slapped him as vigorously as she had the potboy. With a good-natured laugh he popped the morsel into his mouth and, after exaggerating his pleasure in it to tease her, said, "I'll make a wager, Aggie. The haggis is a failure this day, and everyone will be filled with woe."

She shook her cane at him. "You're wrong, lad. In all my cookin' life I've never failed on a haggis. Look at that table there, and say whether or no you see fine haggis." She forgot her annoyance with him and bent to examine the puddings again. "I canna see anything amiss, but I do have my fears. 'Tis not St. Andrew's Day, and what good will come of a haggis any day but St. Andrew's? But Lady Margaret, she would have it."

David's exploratory finger came into her range of vision. She pushed his hand back and scolded, "Now, no touching! I want only perfect rounds when the MacCrimmon and the MacCarter pipe the haggis about the high table."

"'Tis our own Dougald who'll pipe them round tonight. Oh," he said in answer to her sceptical look, "he can woo new beautiful sounds from the pipe, such as you've not heard before. Old Neil can tell you." He gestured at the old man who had just entered in search of one of his boys.

"And it's I who'll tell you Dougald will pipe nothing tonight," Old Neil announced. "Up, lad, to visit poor disappointed Dougald." He shoved David ahead of him and told the tale of the mishap as he followed.

David, sorry that he had been jesting and playing while his brother needed his help, threaded his way through the ladies and gentlemen standing about the hall. From snatches of conversation he could tell everyone was discussing the accident and speculating about the young girl who had been whisked upstairs so rapidly. "Everyone told but his own brother," he muttered rather angrily as he took the stairs two at a time. Then he burst into the room they shared. "Doug! Doug! I just heard."

He stopped short when he saw Dougald propped comfortably between full feather pillows and writing in his journal. "Well, you're certainly not the sad sight I expected to see!" he exclaimed in some chagrin.

"Davie! I've been wondering where you were," Dougald cried as he laid down his quill pen and note-book. "As for me, I'm all right. The ladies just fuss too much." He lifted his left arm experimentally, but found it stiff and painful. With a wince he added, "Och, but I am sore!"

"Poor fellow! Neil told me about the pipes. I was just standing over the haggis and thinking how fine you'd be when you played them in, when Neil found me. 'Tis a sad thing.... And I'd boasted so, too—about you and your playing—to that beautiful Miss Weston. I wanted her to hear you."

"That's the second time I've heard of some mysterious woman. Who is she?"

David described the lovely features and noble carriage of the visitor and explained her reason for coming to Monkstadt. When he finished with a breathless "I'm going to dance with her," Dougald began to laugh.

"So she's charming enough to have you agog. How old is she?"

David had risen to strip off his clothes. He cast a disparaging look at Dougald as if to say, "What can that matter?" and whistled as he stepped into a tin bath-tub that old Neil had placed near the wash-hand stand. He poured water from the ewer over his lithe body. The water splashed over the boards of the floor as David, anticipating the merriment ahead, executed a little skip. Without warning he suddenly sang at the fullest of his power, "Wha wud na be in love? . . ."

" 'Tis good that Lady Margaret gave us a room

away from the others. You'd wake the seven sleepers."

"Why shouldn't I sing when my heart is as gay as a lark's song? Tomorrow the journey begins—away to a New World and new adventures!" he answered through the rough towel with which he was rubbing his hair dry.

"And a glamorous woman on deck," Dougald teased. "Oh, I begin to see what kind of fellow you are."

"Aye, a fellow as sensitive to beauty as you, my lad, if beauty of a different kind. Now up, 'tis your turn. I'll pour the water so you needn't raise your arm."

David's raucous energy filled the room, and Dougald suddenly wanted to be quiet. He thought of still Moira and her feminine tenderness. "You go on, David. I want to rest a bit yet. I've got some more writing to do."

"That journal! What is it now you're putting in—the boat trip?"

"Nay, not the boat trip, or at least not the accident. What's that to waste words on?" He meditatively flicked the tip of the feather of his pen across his lips a time or two. "As a matter of fact, I was writing about your gay New World and adventure. Only to me this whole voyage is a sorrowful business."

"I don't understand you, Dougald. You'll sure not be home-sick, with all the Scots in North Carolina. And think of all we'll see and all we'll have to do there. They say the hunting is unbelievable. The prey abounds and the mountains to stalk in are high and green and beautiful."

"Aye, no doubt it will be beautiful. But there'll be no gorse or heather. And won't it be sad to see tall trees everywhere that'll remind us there were no trees at home?" He turned on his side and propped himself so he could look seriously up at David. "I guess, Davie, it's beautiful or sad depending on whether you look at what we're going to or at what we're leaving. I'm the kind that looks back." He leaned forward. "Eight hundred years we are leaving. Eight hundred

years the MacDonalds of Clanranald have been on
Skye and on the Long Island. Though all is hardship
here now, and though we dare gather only when
ringed about by our fierce retainers, yet I'd rather
stay here, where, out beyond the armed men who
prove I'm not free, I can hear the sad and mighty
sea."

David had finished his dressing as he listened and
now he paused just before leaving the room. "There's
that word again—sad. Sometimes I think it's not that
things are really sad, but you, and you impart your
sadness to them. But still, if you really feel so
strongly, why don't you speak to Lady Margaret? It's
likely in her heart she'd be glad for one of us to
stay."

"I did," Dougald answered to David's astonishment. "I told her I'd rather stay."

"Well, what happened? I'm sure she didn't order
you to go."

"Nay, of course not. But she wants it. 'Tis hard
enough for her to send us, believing as she does it's
best. My staying, when she believes it's wrong and
when she wants it nonetheless, would make it
harder."

"So, then." David's voice was more cheerful now.
"I for one am glad you're coming. And if it's all decided, mope no longer." He opened the door and
sniffed. "Smell that good food? It's waiting for you, and
so are we." As he descended the stairs he was thankful that something in Dougald's reasoning—he wasn't
sure quite what—would make him sail tomorrow.
"'Tis a grand adventure we'll have. He'll soon love
it."

Dougald, left alone, could not rid himself of his
mournful mood. He gingerly eased himself from the
bed and walked to the window. Below, the shadows
of the gillies darted about the fires. How many of
them, he wondered, had heavy hearts this night, how
many sad for the folk who were leaving? For those
who were left behind there would be none of the excitement of new things. They would have only the
tedious, familiar tasks, and their dear ones would be

gone. One at least felt the loss; only a lonely man could play the mournful song which rose to Dougald's window.

The door opened and closed behind him. "Come, lad. Hot food and company will do you good." It was Neil, bringing more hot water. The old man had an anxious look on his face. As long as he had cared for Dougald, he had never learned to feel easy about his periods of unusual pensiveness. The lad had always been a regular healthy young MacDonald at some times, and then could be teased, coaxed or cajoled into good spirits and obedience just as David could. But there had always been other times, when the boy seemed detached, as if not all his spirit was at home in the busy farm life of the clan. Now, as usual, Neil decided it was the musician in Dougald that accounted for his moodiness. "No doubt ye're thinking o' the songs ye'd like to play tonight. 'Tis sorry I am for you."

"Well, I can bear the disappointment, I suppose. But I had hoped to make a fine showing tonight." Dougald crossed slowly to the centre of the room and got ready for his bath. "MacCarter can pipe for us, as he always has. He's as fine a piper as MacCrimmon, who'll be over with the MacLeods."

"Nay, lad, MacCrimmon'll not be here tonight. 'Tis more the sorrow that you canna play. 'Twould have been the best time for you to take your place, when one o' the traditional pipers could na come."

"Why, Neil," Dougald asked in surprise as he stepped into the tub, "where is MacCrimmon? 'Tis the first time he's let his MacLeods feast without him to pipe for their pleasure."

Old Neil answered as he tilted the heavy pitcher over Dougald's head and shoulders. "Flora's boy Sandy just arrived. The MacLeods could not be ready in time to come up. So tomorrow Anne and Alex will meet you at Portree."

Dougald, with water streaming down his face, said nothing. He now understood why he'd seen no carts from Dunvegan at Portree. He blindly groped for the towel he knew Neil would be holding out to him, and awkwardly dried himself as thoroughly as he could with his one good hand.

"Here, now, let me," Neil said, taking the towel back again. He laughed slightly. "The first night you came to Monkstadt I rubbed you down. And now, after these seven years, I do it again, on your last night."

With Neil's help Dougald drew on his trews, shirt and hose. The kilt was fixed in place and the sporran buckled so that it hung in the exact centre of the kilt. Automatically Dougald stretched both arms upward to set his bonnet on. The sharp wrench in his injured arm madé him blanch.

"We can risk no more of that," Neil said. He glanced about to find something for a sling. "This will do fine," he said as he held up a pale-yellow scarf from the floor beside the bed. "Don't know how it came to be there, but it's perfect." He knotted it and slipped it over Dougald's head.

Dougald realized that the scarf must have been dropped by Moira, probably when she bent to kiss him. With his right hand he smoothed its soft folds but for Neil's benefit he pretended great perplexity.

"Please, Neil," he said when every pleat and pin was in place, "fetch me a cup of tea. I guess I'm a little weak. The dressing has tired me." And he rested on the edge of the bed to let a slight dizziness pass.

Neil hurried out, saying there was a full teapot just down the hall, so the guests could warm themselves as they took off their wet things. In a moment he was back, chatting as he came in about the people he had seen. "There's that Mrs. MacQueen, beginning to look perky with all the company and gaiety. She was having herself a sip of tea. And Eileen, the Mac-Cauley girl, she be hoppin' up and down stairs like a rabbit. Just saw her nearly fall over Davie, sittin' as he is with that pretty Moira you came up with." Neil was so busy picking up shirts and straightening the bed he did not notice Dougald's attentive look. "Who'd have thought," he went on, more to himself than the boy, "the little lassie who went off to school a couple of years ago would have come home such a fetchin' young lady?"

Dougald all at once set his cup down decisively. "Thank you, Neil. I'm going down now." And he was gone.

5

Bad Tidings

THE dinner gong had called David and Moira and all others who lingered on the stairs or in the upstairs chambers to the floor below. In response to the chime every guest had leisurely drifted into the great dining-hall, where three long tables had been laid with glistening plate and china. Logs burned brightly in the huge stone fire-place, and on each table clusters of tapers in candelabra repeated the yellow flames in miniature. The polished shields and claymores on the walls were highlighted with myriad reflections.

Cecily, leaning back in her elaborately carved chair at the high table, listened but absently to David, who had deserted Moira to escort Cecily to her place. She was admiring the mediaeval pageantry of the hall, with the hanging weapons and tapestries which told of the MacDonald clan's illustrious history. Now and again, through the kitchen door, she caught sight of a phalanx of waiting-men, some already holding trays. Beyond them she could see cooks frantically darting about to place ladles in soup tureens and forks on platters.

"Have you met all these people?" she heard David ask.

Following the sweeping gesture of his arm, she surveyed the others at the table. Yes, she knew the Mac-Leod lairds from Lewis and Harris, and both their ladies. Clanranald, right down the table, she had spoken to for some time. As MacNeil of Barra, Mac-Cauley, MacKinnon and MacRee seated their wives and stood behind their own chairs, she softly recited the names to David. "Have I got them all straight?"

"Aye. 'Tis remarkable you can remember them all."

"I have to confess that though I remembered the lairds, I was till now terribly confused about their wives. 'Mrs. MacNeil, Mrs. MacKinnon, Lady Clanranald'—why, there must be a dozen of each here tonight, and I wasn't always told which branch they belonged to."

By now all but four of the chairs, two on either side of Cecily, were occupied. One place was no doubt for Margaret. That at the head of the table was probably for Allan. If so, Flora would sit directly across, at the first place on the right-hand side of the table. Cecily quietly asked David if her conjecture about the seating were correct.

"Aye."

"And the fourth chair?"

"For Reverend Mr. McKeogh, who sails with us. He's been the pastor of our kirk here and will be so in North Carolina." David had spoken as if his mind were elsewhere. In a different tone he commented, " 'Tis Flora who really represents the clan. She should preside."

"Oh, really? And do all of you feel so?"

He shrugged, and Cecily thought, That's an ambiguous gesture! It could mean "Who knows?", "Obviously," or "It's not polite to say." Aloud she said, "I, for one, am happy for the arrangement. I want very much to meet Allan."

"He'll come in soon. 'Twas but fifteen or so minutes ago that he arrived, with Mr. MacQueen." He looked about. "I suppose Flora waits for him." Then he looked down at her anxiously and spoke in a tone which showed that his new subject was much more important to him than Allan's late arrival: "You will dance with me, won't you? This morning you said you would."

Cecily was both amused and annoyed by David's persistent attention. It was flattering, certainly, and he was a sweet lad. But she'd left Devonshire partly to escape from unwanted attention from men she felt unsuitable for her. And though this lad was hand-

somer and nicer than most of the Devonshire dandies,
as she liked to call them, he was most certainly a
young, callow lad and not for her. Oh, she thought,
how I would like to have merely the friendship of a
mature, intelligent man, a man of my own age!

But of course she smiled and promised again to
dance. "Only on condition, though. First you must
take pretty Moira for your partner—and others of
your Skye lassies, too. I must have a demonstration."

David looked about the room. "I don't see—" he
began, then broke off his sentence. "There she is, with
Dougald in the doorway."

Cecily could have identified Dougald even had
Moira not been talking with him. "He looks exactly
like you!" she exclaimed. Then she laughed, for she
saw that Dougald's sling was the yellow scarf she had
draped about Moira's shoulders. Tonight anyway, she
thought, I'll be able to distinguish the twins. The gallant Dougald is wearing Moira's, or my, colours.
Then she looked more carefully.

"But he seems very morose," she commented to
David. "I can't imagine you ever looking that way."

"Dougald's the sad one of us. And tonight he's
more so than ever. Can't pipe; can't dance. And can't
bear the thought of leaving Skye."

"But you can? You want to leave this beautiful
house and your charming foster-mother?"

David scowled. "You ought not to put it so. 'Tis
not that I don't like Skye—I love it—but that I want
to see the world." With surprising seriousness he added, "And want to be something in the world. Skye's
no place for that."

Just as Cecily started to ask what David wanted to
be she saw, rather thankfully, Lady Margaret approaching the table. "Run on now, David. We'll have
to talk later, for Lady Margaret will want the chair
you're leaning on. Don't forget to entertain Moira."

She could tell from the sag of his shoulders as he
walked away that he was a trifle hurt. I shouldn't
treat him like a little boy, she thought. But, after all,
there's no point in letting him make both of us look

foolish. And I'm sure Lady Margaret would not appreciate my leading the lad on.

As Lady Margaret took her seat, settled her skirts about her and apologized for leaving Cecily alone for so long, Cecily moved her chair to make room and pleaded, "Don't, Lady Margaret, ever worry that your hospitality fails. Everyone has been gracious." She could say with wholehearted sincerity, "I marvel that with the rush and the unexpected trouble you can have us here and set such an elaborate, tasteful table. And I only wish I were a help, not an extra burden."

Margaret, her hand pressed against her chest as she gasped slightly for breath, said, "It's all taken care of now. I simply had to take Allan and Peter up to change. Then Reverend Mr. McKeogh was to come. I waited so I could bring him in to you." She looked up at the pastor, who stood solemnly behind his chair, and presented him to Cecily. "You will be glad he is emigrating too. Though you're not of our kirk, you will want a man of God. And John McKeogh is that. Turn to him if you have need."

Cecily could not help an inward shudder as she scanned the dour features of the minister. He was so unlike the genial priest of her own High Anglican church that she could not imagine herself turning to him for sympathetic understanding. Yet, she reproved herself, it is not for me to say whether or not he is a helpful, devout man; mayhap his very stringency suits the Scots temper and makes him better for them.

Lady Margaret was looking about and, as she checked the place settings, nodding in welcome to kinsmen. "This is the first time in all my years at Monkstadt that a dinner has got off to such a straggly start." She turned back to Cecily. "I did so want tonight to be perfect, for you, as well as for those of my own who are leaving. But there's no perfection, I guess, in a world of hurry and hard necessity."

Cecily felt sorry for Lady Margaret; she knew that so much of this housewifely fluster was a cover for painful feelings. I saw this morning, Cecily thought, how capable and calm she can be. And she told me how it's killing her to send her lads away.

There was intermittent scuffling of feet around the table. Cecily looked up and saw that the lairds and the minister were still standing, and growing tired of it. As she watched the impatient men she saw them suddenly straighten. A split second later she was surprised to see the women rise in a body. A touch on her hand and a whispered "'Tis Allan and Flora" from Margaret made her turn her head. When she did she automatically rose too.

At the far end of the room, framed in the dark oak of the doorframe, stood Allan MacDonald. He was a striking figure, in his finest kilt, snowy linen shirt, colourful tartan, bonnet and hose. The silver of his shoe buckles, breastpin and sword gleamed. The leanness of his strong features was accentuated by the uneven light.

Allan was not looking at the guests but at Flora, whose hand rested on his arm. She was clad in a gown of the MacDonald tartan, the ancient hunting tartan of fresh green and pure white. Across her shoulder she had draped her softest plaid. Beyond her clan colours and emblems she wore no ornament, and in these simple habiliments she was regal. Her brown hair had not a streak of grey; her eyes were as blue and as direct in gaze as they had been when, in younger years, she had outfaced soldiers to protect her Prince.

Flora took time to look, it seemed, at each person individually. Nothing in her mien betrayed worry or regret. Lady Margaret, yielding to the pride she felt, whispered to Cecily, "Someone said Flora MacDonald has captured serenity and dignity and wears them as armour, no matter what sorrow her heart holds. Is it not true?"

Even as Cecily agreed, one of the chiefs at the high table raised a bumper of wine and cried, "Ol elmi—I drink!" Every guest caught up his glass, filled early for this purpose, and echoed the cry.

Flora curtsied low and then began to walk as if in state between the two lower tables. She nodded to friends on both right and left and thus made her way to her place. Allan handed her to the platform and adjusted her chair. Only then did he bow.

Cecily, between Allan and Lady Margaret, looked at the faces of the guests, still all turned toward Flora. She saw there a warm devotion that she had rarely discovered on the faces of the English nobility when in attendance on King George III. Although she rejected the thought as somehow traitorous, she could not keep from saying to herself, He commands more polished forms of reverence, but she commands love.

She leaned forward to acknowledge Margaret's presentation of Allan. With entire sincerity she said, "I have been waiting to meet you."

His handsome and sensible countenance affected her favourably. Her first impression was that Allan MacDonald was indeed the strong man Flora's husband would have to be. Yet, when she assured him she had met his wife and that meeting her had enhanced her desire to know him, she saw that he scrutinized her rather nervously. It was as if it was very important to him to know just what she meant. Cecily had to stifle an impulse to say, "I mean because I knew you'd be as fine a man as she is a woman." But that wouldn't do; he'd know then she suspected that for some reason he was insecure, on the defensive. So she smiled warmly and said, "I am highly honoured to be able to sail with so famous a family."

Allan now appeared to recapture his ease. In a wholly pleasant tone he said, "Most of us gain what fame we have from our relation to Flora."

"I'm not sure of that," Cecily replied. "Certainly I heard of you when I was yet in England. But it is true, undeniably true, that your wife is widely known."

"I'm told this is your first visit to Scotland, and will be your first to America. What takes you there?" Allan asked.

Cecily had intended to tell him, almost as soon as she met him, of her mission to Farquard Campbell. Allan was, she knew, trusted politically, and furthermore she felt that Allan might know better than she how to approach Farquard. Despite some Scots blood in her veins, she was terribly un-Scots. She was not sure just what one said to bring a recusant Scotsman home to the King's fold.

Despite her intention, she found she could not bring herself to mention her political duties. That glimpse of some insecurity which she thought she had caught made her reluctant. So, as if she thought only of her own pleasure, she said, "Mostly adventure. I began to find Devonshire tedious."

With a gallantry natural to him, Allan replied, "Devonshire did not find you tedious, I'm sure."

Cecily laughed spontaneously; she was good-humoured and frank as well as sophisticated and proud. "Oh, sir, you are most kind, but I fear many of the Devonshire matrons shook their heads over my disgrace. I was the proud young lady who just wouldn't be married. So I'm off to see the world—an 'audacious' voyage, they call it—and give them time to become reconciled to my spinsterhood."

Margaret overheard and joined in. "I'm afraid I side with the matrons, Cecily. Marriage is the natural state for a woman, especially as beautiful and spirited a one as you."

Allan spoke rather wearily. "True, but how many men would please such a woman?"

Cecily saw Flora's arm move and was certain that she had quickly touched Allan. She's trying to tell him that he pleases her, Cecily thought.

Serving-men approached the tables and lifted their trays. Silence fell over the room and in that silence the black figure of the minister rose. John McKeogh stood erectly; his arms, instead of stretching over the guests and fare in blessing, hung close by his sides. He bowed his head and in a slightly rasping voice began to intone the prayer.

The very spareness of his words, so unlike the graceful petitions of the High Church tradition, was moving. Cecily heard him state the basic Calvinistic belief: "Almighty God, who seest that we have no power of ourselves to help ourselves, keep us both outwardly in our bodies and inwardly in our

souls. . . ." The impending journey was likened to a
dark night: the travellers would step into it blindly;
they must rely on God to guide their every step.
"May the angel of Thy presence be with these
voyagers wherever they may go; may all their steps be
ordered of Thee in wisdom and love. . . ."

At the Amen Cecily raised her head; she saw that
all others at the table were still sitting silently, their
eyes closed. Over them stood McKeogh, his thin lips
pressed closely together. One could feel the power of
his will; Cecily felt that though all were praying
silently and in their own words, they were in a deep
communication with one another through the medium
of this commanding parson. Only when, without a
word, he relaxed momentarily, as if to release himself
from his rapt concentration, did the other guests look
up. No one spoke until the minister had seated himself.

The serving-men lowered their trays so that the
guests could serve themselves. A succession of fishes,
fowl and meats, as well as puddings and vegetables,
were placed on the plates. The wine-glasses were re-
filled almost before they were emptied. There was an
atmosphere of total relaxation, a feeling that there
was time enough for graciousness and pleasure. The
Scots have made an art, Cecily thought, of putting to
the best use all peace and privacy granted them. A
stranger coming through the door would never suspect that this lavish banquet is occasioned by fear and
hardship.

"'Tis very unfortunate," Flora leaned forward to
say, "that you've no chance to see Dunvegan. The
castle is a rare sight, with its mighty turrets. My dear
Anne has been happy there." Flora sighed. "She went
there as a bride. I wanted to be with her when she
said her farewells, but with the MacQueens' trouble,
it was impossible. Poor Anne is, I know, having a
hard time pulling herself away. No doubt that's why
she is not here tonight."

"And is it really necessary," Cecily asked, "for
your daughter to emigrate? I mean, there can be no
danger to the clansmen who still retain their land and

great homes. If Anne's husband has such a fine estate. . . ?"

"Alex is a younger son," Allan cut in. With some bitterness he continued, "Even were he to inherit land, 'twould make little difference. He wants his sons to have prospects, and the Highlands offer none. 'Twould be a sorry sort of man who'd choose to have his children grow up here, things being as they are." He gestured to one of the lower tables. "There, the fourth on the right. That's my Sandy. A fine lad he is, with not a hope of a future in Skye. I won't have this one selling his service for the rest of his life to an English merchant, as the oldest has had to do."

Cecily looked at the boy and noted that he resembled his father, though he was paler and much more slender. He might be of frail health, she thought. Perhaps that's why Allan wants to keep him especially close. She turned back to Allan to say, "But the older boy—you speak angrily of his being in English service. From your wife I understood you are not the Anglophobe many of the Scots are."

"Don't misconstrue me!" he urged. " 'Tis not the English but the service I object to. And more than that it's the distance. Charles—that's the older lad's name—is in the East India Company's service. There's a chance he'll go half-way round the world one way while we go the other." He took a heavy breath. "I'd like to be able to see my sons. . . . Well, this one, and little Jamie too, I'll keep with me. And in America I'll be able to find a way to make them their own masters and later leave them something besides debts."

Flora revealed nothing of her own feelings; she spoke calmly in support of her husband: "We count much, Miss Weston, on the New World. Our kin who are already there describe unheard-of plenty. We look forward to good land and freedom from faction and oppression."

"Aye." Allan spoke up. "Rich farms with space enough between that there'll be no feuding. For that we're sending our best young men over. Margaret there, she's a good example. She's sending the twins so they may prosper in freedom and peace."

For a moment Cecily was silent; she wondered how realistic the Scots' understanding of North Carolina was. And she wondered, with all this talk of freedom, what their sentiments would be if there really were in America the division she'd heard of. At last she cautiously said, "I've heard some rumours of anti-English sentiment in the New World. You do not credit such talk?"

It was Margaret who answered. "We listen to it, but it sounds more like talk than anything else. Allan has thought that out and feels it's safe to go."

"Of course it is," Allan said emphatically. "Any man of sense knows rebellion is no good. Just disrupts the country. And if a rebel were successful before long he'd rue the day he sought his independence. He'd soon be begging for the prosperity and security of an ordered government."

So that, thought Cecily, is what Uncle meant by saying Allan is reliable: he will see the right side in this squabble, as he did in the uprising.

Flora sat down her glass and said, "You probably don't realize, Miss Weston, how eager we Scots are for peace—real peace, without armed men about always, and oaths to swear to an alien monarch and terms of service for our laddies."

"No," Cecily said, "I wasn't aware you feel so. I thought the Scotsman's greatest pride was that he fights his enemies without hesitation. I thought you taught your lads to fight almost before you taught them to walk."

"It's really a paradox, Cecily," Lady Margaret said. "We do believe a battle's better than submission to a wrong. And we hate for anyone to tamper with our independence. But just as much we hate the bloodshed and heart's sorrow of the battle-field." She raised her hand to her chin for a moment, as if pondering something. "Aye, it just now comes to me. This paradox is made very clear by the Scots women. We send our men, even our youngest sons, to battle with the cry, 'Return with your shield or upon it!' Yet many of our oldest songs are mothers' laments bewailing war and chiding men for making it."

They sat silently for a moment, as if talk of war, no matter how improbable, had cast a pall over them. Margaret finally looked up. "Now, let's forget this unhappy talk. See, the lads are going out now." She turned to Cecily. "You're going to see one of Scotland's finest sights now: an ancient custom, going back centuries."

Cecily's curiosity was aroused. Every young man in the room except Dougald had suddenly risen and without a bow or a word of explanation turned on his heel to stride through the nearest door. Then stewards came forward and removed the candelabra. The hall grew cavernous as deep shadows obscured the walls and corners. At last only the erratic fire-light illuminated the diners' faces.

Cecily could not help laughing. "I doubt, Lady Margaret, that I'll see anything in this light."

"Don't worry, you'll see, and I think you'll be impressed with our Scots 'candles.' 'Tis foolish in a way, I suppose, not to use the lovely English ones for the haggis, but I want to recall the past tonight. And from time immemorial the haggis has been enjoyed by the light of burning wood."

A dim figure entered and took a station at the foot of the high table. The fire was behind the man, and Cecily could see the silhouette of the bellows and drones of the bagpipe.

A clarion pipe note cut the air, and on each side of the hall the shadows were thrown back before brands burning in swirling flames. David on the right and Sandy on the left were leading in the young men, twenty-two in all. Each one carried before him, like a standard, a heavy pine splinter, almost a log. They circled the room, the orange flames billowing upward and back as they marched. Then they formed two long lines down each side of the dining tables. The arched torches made the room blaze with light and sent spirals of acrid, resinous incense to the beamed ceiling.

Cecily gasped in delight. Never before had she seen

such a display of handsome young-manhood giving itself wholly to creating beauty and light for others. "But how can they do it?" she cried. "Those torches—they are really young trees!"

Allan had been smiling up at his son, who stood behind Cecily's chair. He looked back at her to say, "Any lad who can throw the caber can manage a brand. And there's not a healthy Scots lad on Skye who can't trim the tree himself to make the caber, and then toss it end over end, just as he should to make it fall right."

While Allan was speaking, waiting-men filed in from the kitchens. In time to the music they marched forward with platters of steaming haggis. First Flora and Cecily were served, then all the others. As the last servant withdrew the piper followed him out, his melody diminishing into a thin, reedy wail. The lads remained immobile, their torches burning high over the tables.

Cecily wanted to say how impressive the ceremony was; she sought to find words which would convey her sincere admiration for the boys. "It makes me ashamed," she said finally, "of our delicate English gentlemen, who nowadays think vigour a mark of vulgarity. Oh, this is a refreshing sight!"

Like the others she began to eat her good meat pudding. But the contrast between the Devonshire men she had described to Lady Margaret and these "braw lads" stayed in her mind. They're young yet, she thought, and one can't say what kind of deeds they'll do. But I'll wager they'll not make a career of picking up ladies' lace handkerchiefs, as those others do.

She cut off a bite meditatively as she speculated on the prospects of these lads, prospects that occasioned so much concern in their elders. It did not seem to her, from all she had heard at home, that America, at the moment anyway, was the ideal place to which to ship off a nation's best manhood. Turning to Lady Margaret, she asked, "Are all these fine lads going to America?"

"I suppose most will go eventually. Of course hun-

dreds just like them are there already. But on your
ship only David, Dougald and Sandy will sail. And
young Jamie too."

"I do wonder that you can send them," Cecily said
involuntarily, "when there's so much uncertainty
about what's really happening over there." She saw
Lady Margaret's surprise and apprehension. "Forgive
me. I ought not to interfere in your affairs. Forget my
stupid remark."

"Nay! I begin to fear. This is the second time
you've spoken as if you think there's serious trouble
in North Carolina. What is it, Cecily, you're trying to
tell me?"

Cecily waited before speaking again. At last, when
everyone else was absorbed in conversation, she decidedly put down her fork and turned so she might
speak with Lady Margaret without being overheard.
"Perhaps I ought not to speak, but my heart says I
must. I know you Scots are leaving your homes because of severe hardships here."

Lady Margaret interrupted, "You don't mean
America is not really a rich land of opportunity?"

"No, no! Don't be alarmed about that. Everything
I have heard says it is a land of plenty." She picked
up her fork again and cut off a bite of haggis which,
however, she only pushed about her plate. "There is
rumour of political intrigue in America." She looked
directly into Lady Margaret's eyes. "I have no
doubt—in fact I've been told—there will be no serious trouble." She paused then and said, "But if it becomes necessary, England will send troops. Already
she requires an oath of allegiance of immigrants—
such an oath as Flora says you hate. I thought you
ought to know this if you are sending your foster-
sons. But speak of it to no one."

Lady Margaret's face blanched. Have I done right?
Cecily wondered. She consoled herself with the
thought that she had betrayed no secret and that she
ought in conscience to warn kind friends.

Margaret asked in a desperate, muffled voice, "Cecily, are you trying to tell me there is going to be

fighting in America?" Her cheerful manner had wholly disappeared.

"No, of course I'm not. I don't believe there will be. But there is unrest." Again she turned in her chair. "Lady Margaret, I'm sorry I have distressed you so. But seeing your fine lads and hearing your hopes for them made me speak. You have been gracious to me, and I would help you. From what you and Allan and Flora have said, I cannot but think you do not understand the country you emigrate to." She glanced about to make sure no one was listening. "I simply wonder whether at the moment your lads will find more safety there than here."

Cecily waited for some response from Lady Margaret; there was none. Thinking that, considering her own uncertainty about the state of affairs in America, she ought never to have spoken, she tried again to explain herself: "We have hopes that no outbreak will occur. And if it does, it depends largely on the emigrants themselves whether they will incur difficulty. As I told you, an oath of allegiance is demanded. You see, many of your Scots have carried bitterness over the sea with them; some of your people, it is rumoured, speak against the King. You can understand that England will not allow that."

Margaret looked across the table at Flora before she spoke. "Those of us who supported the Stuart can never, I believe, change our allegiance. . . . Cecily, it could be tragic if Flora and my boys go."

Cecily gently touched Lady Margaret's hand. "That has occurred to me too. But let us remember that I don't really know exactly how things are. I hear such talk at home, but, after all, it is the business of my uncle and his associates to exaggerate any potential danger to England, and so to be ready to forestall it."

For a moment Cecily watched the thoughtful look on the older woman's face. When she saw that Lady Margaret was going to say nothing, she straightened in her chair and resumed eating. After a moment she raised her head to look at Flora, and to marvel that, at this hour of farewell, there was a perfectly serene expression on her face.

At the proper moment Lady Margaret, somewhat more composed than a few moments before, rose to lead her guests from the dining-hall. First Flora and Allan followed, then Cecily, talking with the Clanranald and his lady. In a long procession all, including the boys, who put aside their torches and wiped the sticky resin from their hands, moved toward the long front parlour. The deep murmur of adult voices was pierced intermittently with a shrill laugh or exclamation from the young folk.

The halls resounded with full, rich notes of the great Highland pipes, so different from the sharp tones of the Lowland instrument or the flat notes of the Irish one. The call of these pipes aroused, in the old as well as young, eagerness for the dances which were to follow. Subtly the slow leisure of dinner was dispelled.

Lady Margaret alone could not be cheerful. It seemed to her that at every fifth or sixth step she heard someone wish Flora and Allan success in the New World and heard Flora reply, "We have strong faith in better fortune there." These happy phrases jarred her. She felt she and her clansmen had been the victims of some horrible hoax: blandishments from a rich but untried world had tempted her to send away that which she loved most. And her own loss would not have been the most crucial consequence: what if she had made the wrong decision for the lads?

They shall not go, she resolved. But immediately the thought of keeping them at home, which should have comforted her, brought images of young Scots lads in red-coated uniforms and images of strong men whose efforts could not make the land yield. She remembered enthusiastic letters from Flora's stepfather, Hugh, which described untold prosperity.

Suspended between her alternatives, she finally stopped just inside the parlour door, and let the others go ahead. Flora, still with her hand on Allan's arm, passed to go toward the draped alcove at the other end of the room. A few feet beyond Margaret she turned to invite Cecily to sit with her. "We'll have a vantage point," she said, "from which to see the dancers. But you must feel free to descend and dance yourself."

As Margaret absently smiled at Mrs. MacNeil, who whispered her compliments on the splendid feast, she saw that Old Neil was at his place by an enormous bowl. The sight pained her. Sir Alexander had, in his lifetime, always mixed the Atholl brew with care and pleasure. In those days a younger Neil had stood to one side to hand to his master the bottles of whisky and honey and the small scoop of oatmeal from which the drink was made. Alexander had tasted and tasted until he was sure the flavour was perfect, just as Neil was tasting now.

Oh, Alexander, Margaret cried to herself, I have always missed and needed you, but tonight more than ever I need you! If that were you, there by the punch-bowl, you'd soon come to my side. I could tell you what I've heard and you would know what to do.

Neil was gesturing to her. He wanted to know who, in the absence of young Alex, laird of the house, would preside over the toasts. Margaret looked about and saw Dougald—Dougald who wanted to stay on Skye, who had to stand apart from so much tonight. She beckoned him to her side. "Would you like to offer the toasts? You will know the proper way."

How pleased he is, she thought, to do the honours of our home! She heard him instruct a boy to fill the beakers and then watched him hand them round himself. First he presented the brimming cups to the honoured guests in the alcove, then to the chieftains and their ladies, and lastly to the young ones.

In the traditional manner Dougald stepped with his own full beaker onto the raised hearth. "It is the honour of the household of Monkstadt, of Lady Margaret MacDonald of Sleat and all the other members thereof to celebrate Flora MacDonald of Clanranald, the saviour of her Prince. *Ol elmi!*"

From every corner of the room the cry was repeated: "*Ol elmi!*"

Even as he lowered his beaker from the first toast, Dougald was beginning the second: "It is the honour of the household of Monkstadt, of Lady Margaret MacDonald of Sleat and all the other members thereof to celebrate Allan MacDonald of Kingsburgh. *Ol elmi!*"

And again the cry echoed.

Margaret waited until she was sure that Dougald would invite the chiefs to drink in the name of their own clans and septs. Yes, he remembered the right way; he was turning to the laird of Clanranald, stepping off the platform and offering his place. Now one by one the families would toast Flora and her husband.

Slowly she made her way up the length of the room, pausing at each ringing "*Ol elmi!*" to lift her own beaker to Flora and Allan. But her mind was elsewhere. She thought of the thousands of Scots who crowded on any boat sailing westward to get to a land they knew too little about. Our desperation has made us rash, she thought sadly.

When the final toast was called she was at the foot of the raised alcove. She drank, but to her silent hope for wisdom in the decision she must make. Then she stepped up and took her seat, slightly to the right of Flora's.

Cecily, she saw, was listening to something David was explaining with a great number of gestures. As David strode away, a second later, Cecily said to Flora, "They're going to do a strathspey. David says it's much like our reel."

"But slower, and more stately," Flora answered.

The measured music began and during the first bars the dancers grouped themselves into the facing rows required by the strathspey. David had gone to Moira, who till then had stood by Dougald's side, and now he led her to a position immediately before the alcove.

Margaret's eyes went back to Dougald. Poor lad, she said to herself, he ought to be in bed. She sum-

moned a servant and sent him to tell Dougald to go
upstairs if he was too weary to stay. After the waiting-
man had begun to thread his way through the guests
at the edge of the dancing area, she regretted her action. He doesn't need me to tell him such things any
more.

The dance had in the meantime begun. In honour
of Flora the song chosen to accompany the strathspey
was one celebrating Charles Stuart and Flora's role in
his story. The familiar melody had evoked a soft look
in Flora's face and she was singing, under her breath,
the words:

> You're welcome, Charlie Stuart,
> You're welcome, Charlie Stuart,
> You're welcome, Charlie Stuart,
> There's none so right as thou art.

Usually those verses moved Margaret also. She too
had abetted the Prince, though not so daringly and
courageously as Flora. Flora had got him past the soldiers; she had endured gunfire when she tried to land
him; she'd gone overland after him, to Kingsburgh
House, and then with him to Portree. Margaret herself had not even seen the Prince. She had known he
was concealed in the cave below Monkstadt and had
sent old Kingsburgh to his aid. But Flora, to allay the
suspicions of a young lieutenant—brash in the King's
service he was—played the spinet in this very room.

> Had'st thou Culloden Battle won,
> Poor Scotland had not been undone. . . .

Tonight these much loved words could not evoke
poignant regret. They only reminded Lady Margaret
that she and her husband had quarrelled, in all the
years of her marriage, only over her share in helping
the Stuart. 'Tis odd, she thought, that he was High-
land-born, but was against Charles, while I was Low-
land-born and English-educated and was for him. He
thought I disgraced him, and I thought he disgraced
the MacDonalds.

She could still hear Alexander's voice, proclaiming angrily that 'twas the MacDonalds who disgraced themselves and brought on all the woe. "They should never have leagued behind a Frenchified fop," he'd spat out. "And if they had to do it, they should have fought no matter where they were placed." He'd always insisted that the clansmen had obstinately laid down their arms because Charles had failed to give them their hereditary battle position. "Right side indeed! Why, in the days when MacDonalds acted like MacDonalds we fought and sat anywhere." Then he'd told her for the dozenth time about his famous ancestor who, when placed low at the table, announced, "Where the MacDonald sits, there is the head of the table!"

A booming voice startled her. She had not even realized the strathspey had ended, but MacLeod of Harris was already calling out compliments to the dancers. " 'Twas handsomely done. You do your elders proud." Then he laughed. "But you've not outdone us yet. We'll show you the old rincefada, which none o' you know. Come, Lewis, Clanranald, and all. We'll show the old style o' dancing!"

Nine of the older people moved onto the floor and stood in three ranks of three. The front row had a scarf, which fluttered against the dancers as they moved forward to slow, soft music. The music began to quicken, the dancers stepped forward more rapidly, each group passed under the scarf of the three in front. Then they wheeled in semicircles and performed a variety of complex conformations, which eventually brought them back to their original positions. The same pattern was executed again, this time to a faster beat. The young folk, who had rarely seen this ancient dance, clapped their hands to the accelerating rhythm until the room with filled with the echoes of slapping palms. All at once, after several repetitions, which got ever faster, the three rows, always straight, wheeled back to the original square formation and the music stopped with their last step. There was a burst of laughter and merriment when the performers had to fall into their chairs, the women fanning themselves and the men wiping their brows.

In an effort to shake off her preoccupation with fears and memories, Margaret rose and stood behind Cecily's chair. "Do you like our dances?"

Cecily looked up. "They are very beautiful. I wish I knew the steps."

"That one," Margaret said in a tired, even tone, "is a dance which pleased James II when he landed at Kinsdale. 'Tis said he himself danced with the lady of the household, and vowed he never had a pleasanter time."

Flora motioned to the centre of the room. "Here comes David, probably to claim the dance you promised him, Miss Weston."

"Oh, no!" Cecily exclaimed in mock dismay. "The steps I've seen are all mixed up in my mind. I hope he'll let me beg off."

But David pleaded: "We've decided to learn the rincefada. We'll all be as new at it as you. So do come."

Cecily was handed down. Her laugh rang back and also her words: "You did dance beautifully with Moira. She's all grace."

"David is having all the fun tonight, I fear," Flora said to Margaret. "Poor Dougald stands on one leg and then the other, wishing he could join in."

"He shouldn't do it. I've already told him he ought to be resting."

"He'll not rest as long as Moira's down here and looking so fetching. I meant to tell you. He's much attracted by her. That may make him happier about sailing."

Margaret shook her head in quick denial. "No. Just before dinner he spoke to me about staying. He may be taken with her—she's pretty and sweet and well-bred enough—but he's both too sensible and too young to let a slip of a girl he hardly knows change his deepest feelings."

But she turned to look for him and found herself unreasonably annoyed when she saw him leading Moira out the door to the garden. How wrong of me!

she chided herself. Moira MacQueen is a fine girl, even if her father has lost his land. Surely I've been long enough in the Highlands to have got over silly prejudices of class. It must be that I can't bear the idea of the lads growing up and loving and marrying.

She sank into Cecily's chair. For the first time she noticed that Allan was no longer in the alcove. "Where's Allan, Flora? I didn't notice his going."

"He left right after the strathspey," Flora answered, and Margaret noticed again a peculiar apathy in her voice. She's very indrawn tonight, for all her cordiality. 'Tis not like her to bottle up her feelings, whether they be gay or sad.

Margaret's thoughts went back to Allan. After the strathspey ... Allan did not like to hear the praises of the Stuart sung—no more than Alexander had.

"I was just thinking, a moment ago," she said, "of how Alexander and I quarrelled over the Prince—to my great regret. Has it been so with you and Allan?"

"Never. Neither he nor I would want that."

"Nor did Alexander and I," Margaret said a trifle reproachfully, "but it happened. Of course, it's been different for you. You married some years after, but I was a wife defying her husband."

"I'm sorry, Margaret. I didn't know. That's always a bad thing, of course."

Margaret knew that Flora's cool manner was the product of her need for control. This must be unbearably hard for her, and now I must tell her this dreadful news of Cecily's. But perhaps it will persuade her and Allan to stay. I want them to stay.

"Flora," she began indirectly, "I begin to be frightened of sending the lads.... I mean, I lose sight of any good reasons for emigrating. You see, what Cecily said is true: you and Allan and my boys are not really pressed—not like the MacQueens and others. You could make do here." She lowered her eyes. "And I begin to wonder whether things will really be so much better over there."

"And I have no doubt of it. What a change it will be, to see the little money hoarded up and held back all these years grow and provide for our needs instead of shrink into nothing!" Flora smiled suddenly. "And what a change it will be to be able to be as Scotch as we want. No spying, no interference. You should come too, Margaret. We'll turn those mountains into a clan holding. The green fields will be dotted with the gay colours of our tartans, and the green glens will echo with our songs."

"Are you really sure, Flora, it will be so?"

Flora stood up suddenly, and looked tenderly down at Margaret. "I understand your last-moment indecision. I myself have wept alone in my room and sworn I could not, would not go. But now I do honestly believe America is best for us Scots." She walked to the edge of the platform, then turned and looked at Margaret. "But I can't say whether America will be best for David and Dougald. No one can, and you must make your own decision." She bent her head and in a pleading tone added, "This talk is very difficult for me, Margaret. It awakens the pain I had numbed. And for what use? The will to emigrate has grown strong in me. I do not believe anything can make me hesitate now."

Margaret thought, I have to give you pain, for your own sake. She stood up. "You're right, Flora. I must make decisions by myself now. And I've made one." She surveyed the room. Neil was making more punch, new pipers were stepping in for the old, and waiters were already setting the buffet from which those guests who were departing yet that night would take food. Satisfied that her guests would want for nothing while she was gone, she turned back to Flora. "Come. I must tell you something, and this is not the place for it."

On her way to her chamber Margaret paused only to order a maid to fetch candles and holders enough for all the kinsmen staying over and to command, "Call me at once if anyone starts to leave or retire before I am back."

She then looked to ascertain that Flora was behind her, and went on up the stairs. She let Flora enter the room ahead of her and then locked the door.

"I do not mean to be mysterious," she said in a more relaxed manner, "but——"

"Please, Margaret. You owe me no explanations. We've known and trusted each other many years."

Margaret drew up a chair for Flora and then sat down on the edge of a settee. In a low, hurried voice she related the few facts Cecily had told her. "We heard dimly of faction," she concluded, "but troops—that's new and fearsome. And an oath besides. How tragic, Flora, if you and Allan and the boys left unrest here only to plunge into greater unrest there! This at least is home."

Flora sat quietly. Margaret saw that her shoulders sagged, as if in defeat. "I'm going to call Allan, Flora. A man should decide on this."

"No! No, don't call him," Flora cried, rousing herself quickly. "He must not know of it."

"What do you mean? Would you let Allan go unknowing what likely waits for him?"

Flora spoke with determination. "Allan knows as much as we know. Where there's trouble, as he himself told us there is in America, there are likely to be troops. And the Lord knows we've lived under oath nearly all our lives!" She sighed deeply. "Going is too important to him. I won't let him pass by his great opportunity out of fear for a trouble that may be nothing. He's thought this over; he believes it's safe to go. But my Allan's not a man to be reckless with his wife and children. If one more doubt were added, he might sacrifice himself and say nay."

Flora stood up and walked to the window. She clutched the drapery and leaned her head on her fists, as if struggling for control.

"Tell me the trouble, Flora," Margaret said calmly. " 'Twill help you."

"It can't well be told. You asked earlier about Allan and me. You were wrong. Between him and me there's been no jealousy, no anger, nothing but love and striving to make a good life. Others have said foolish things—about my harbouring in my heart a love of Charles, and about Allan's fearing my memories. They, too, were wrong." She let the draperies drop and walked slowly back to the settee. Margaret was surprised to see that she was not crying.

"I said only tonight to Dougald that Allan has lost until he's afraid he can never succeed. Is that what you fear, Flora?" Margaret asked.

"Partly . . . but not all. Allan is on the verge of losing his faith in himself. What man wouldn't with the trouble he's had? But think, Margaret, of what Allan's like. He's a huge, strong man, an intelligent man. He ought to be leading others, helping them. Instead he has to submit to being led, to asking help." She took a long breath before she went on. "It's not just the land, nor even the proclamation against him on the church door long ago. He's not a man to rise or fall by money or land alone. . . . I fear, I fear it's partly me."

"I don't understand, Flora. There's been no better wife than you."

"There's been no woman who wanted to be a better wife. But some things have hindered me. There's been myself. Years ago your own Alexander told me, 'Allan has to find his way. Don't you try to do it for him.' "

"And have you?"

"I've tried always, always not to. But one thing neither Sir Alexander nor I myself ever thought about. I became a legend; they called me the Queen of the Scots. I am proud of that, but it meant they came to me, not to Allan. It meant he had to live as Flora MacDonald's husband. Allan needs security above all else. If he has it, if he can see himself as a man in his own right, he'll succeed. He has everything for success . . . except the opportunity to use his abilities."

Margaret thought about Flora's words. It seemed wrong to her that Flora must forego her own happiness so Allan might have his.

Almost as if she heard the thought, Flora said, "Don't misunderstand me, Margaret. I go to find my own happiness as well as his. Mine depends on his."

"Aye . . . but is there no other way?"

"I hoped so, for a long time. But of late years he's

been more and more reluctant to act. 'Twas I, in the end, who had to write away to find places for the children. He hadn't the heart to write another petitioning letter. But if he had, I'm sure he'd have succeeded where I failed."

Margaret got up to open the window. "That I really don't understand. Only tonight he told us he wants to have Sandy and Jamie with him."

"Aye, he does, because he feels he's failed to provide anything good for them here. You can't expect him to say that."

When Margaret did not answer, Flora walked to the door. "I have said enough. Perhaps too much. But now you know that I will never again ask not to go to North Carolina. Already I have fought it out. I have discussed it frankly with John McKeogh. Now I know it is God's will that we shall leave Scotland." The cold severity left her voice; in a pleading manner she added, "I rely on you to keep my trust. In my heart I believe we will find in America all we are looking for. Pray that we do."

"Wait, Flora. Let me tell you that . . . that I honour you."

Flora made a denying gesture but Margaret went on. "And I'm grateful to you. Knowing that you go for a deep personal reason will help me decide about the lads. It is not so imperative for them."

Flora came back and rested a hand on Margaret's shoulder. "That is for you to decide. But it's odd. I find myself wanting to say to you what your Alexander said to me: 'A strong man ought not to be overprotected.' Both lads are strong. . . . I'll add something of my own too, something I've learned in these many years: all men need security and a chance to prosper. America may offer them. There's as much reason to hope it will as to fear it won't."

Flora waited but Margaret replied nothing. At last she said, "I'll speak to MacQueen. He may not want Moira to go now." She left, closing the door behind her.

Margaret was roused, some time after Flora had

gone downstairs, only by the maid, who announced, " 'Tis the MacCauleys. They'll be goin' now."

Slowly Margaret descended the stairs. On the first landing she met the MacCauleys, the widowed laird and his daughters, and bade them farewell. Then she made her way through the halls to the parlour. There the Grant lads were executing a fling to the loud pleasure of the onlookers. Nowhere could she see David or Dougald. And, strangely, she was glad. Her intention had been to call them to her and tell them they would both stay on Skye. But again doubt made her hesitate. First she would say good night to all and see them safely to their horses—or to their beds if they were staying. Then surely she would know what to do.

6

Final Decisions

DOUGALD, tangled in his covers, tossed until he woke himself up. He could not comprehend what evil dream had been tormenting him, making him writhe and moan. As he lay in the pearl-grey light of the dawn in his room, he sought to order the impressions of his sleep. Slowly his discomfort began to localize itself; he realized that his tormentor was not some ugly creature of his sleeping brain but his wounded shoulder, throbbing and pulsing with second-day intensity. "I'll really be lame today," he groaned under his breath. "Today, of all days!"

Gingerly he freed his legs from the twisted sheets and rolled over on his side, so that he might look across David, sleeping soundly, to the window. He gazed at the sky. Such a fresh blue, he thought, as if last night's storm had washed clean the ceiling and walls of the world. 'Twas a momentous storm, he said to himself as he recalled the many unexpected things it had caused: the near-capsize, the pain which made him hold back from the festivities, and later the numbness that enabled him to ignore his wound and talk with Moira. Oh, he thought at a particularly sharp pang, if only that numbness would return! "Patience," he muttered. "The second day is always the worst."

Very quietly he swung his feet to the floor. As he sat on the edge of the bed, with his arms lying limply across his knees and his head bent, he thought back on the night before. He remembered his misery at the party. It had been hard to stand back against the wall and watch David and Sandy and John MacNeil squire Moira about. She had smiled on them, and on other lads too, as she danced. Auburn tendrils about her oval face had been burnished by the light to form a halo for her smile. The sight had made him wish he had the power to follow Lady Margaret's advice and go to bed so he would not have to watch her with others. But he couldn't, for every now and again she had come to stand beside him and to talk courteously as she fanned herself.

With his uninjured arm Dougald now pushed himself up and, still in night-shirt and bare feet, walked to the window. He opened the casement and sniffed the sea-scented air. "And 'twas with me she went to the garden, no one else," he whispered.

By leaning out slightly he could see the whole expanse of the garden, stretching from the side of the house to the little knoll a hundred yards out. On the rise a garden-house overlooked the sea on one side and the hills on the other. There he and Moira had talked. There he had learned she was indeed sensitive and intense, as he had hoped. His pain was forgotten and his heart pounded as he relived the little time they had been out there together. . . .

At his invitation to stroll in the garden Moira nodded and placed her hand promptly on his arm. It pleased him that she was not coyly indecisive; changing from a worn tartan skirt to a silken gown had not made her assume coquettish airs. As soon as they were out of the house she stopped to take a deep breath. "It's so good, Dougald, to breathe the cool, damp scent of the earth and sea and to listen to the silence." She pressed his arm lightly. "Thank you for seeing I wanted to escape."

"But I didn't," he shamefacedly admitted as he led her to one of the gravel paths. Because she did not answer and he thought she might be disappointed in him, he tried to explain. "I'm sorry. But . . . well, you seemed to be having a very gay time. I couldn't dream you would really want to come out with me— away from all your admirers." Still she said nothing, and he tried again to make her speak. "Why did you want to escape, Moira?"

After a moment she pushed damp curls from her forehead. "It was all too sad to be pleasant. There was your Flora, taut with trying to be serene. And . Lady Margaret—did you not see how pale she was at times?" In a tone so low he almost could not hear it she added, "My parents, too, sitting back so tired."

"I thought they seemed relieved to see how well liked you are by those you'll sail with."

"Aye, 'tis true. 'Twas for them that I stayed and smiled so long."

They walked in silence until she sighed, "I shall miss them ... oh, so much!"

Dougald did not know what to say. He knew that no kindness from friends, no new sights nor new way of life ever wholly compensated for the loss of father and mother. His sympathy kept him from saying anything tritely consoling. Inwardly he vowed that he would do, and see that others did, as much as was possible to help her.

After a little while, however, he thought it right to point out that she really would be living in a better, more comfortable way. "You must remember this: you will hear from your parents and have the satisfaction of knowing they wanted you to go. America seems to hold out a promise. Your father and mother want you to reap it just as Lady Margaret wants David and me to." He tried to phrase his thought more clearly. "It's like gardening, I guess. Young seedlings have to be transplanted to the best soil. So must we be."

As he spoke Dougald began for the first time to perceive that one might want, passionately want, to start anew in a new land. He was surprised to hear himself say sincerely, "Look forward, Moira, not back."

" 'Tis all I can do," she said resignedly and then kicked a small stone from the walk. "Do you know, Dougald, I secretly think Mother and Father are somewhat glad they were evicted. As long as I can remember they've talked about sending me to the New World. But I was the only child. They never could bring themselves to it. First I was too young; then I'd no kin there; recently, ever since MacQueens have been in North Carolina, it's been that I had to finish school in Edinburgh first." She stopped walking and let her hands fall to her sides. "But they never paid attention to the best reason for not sending me: I don't want to go away from here."

"Moira," Dougald pleaded, "don't be so sad. I haven't wanted to either. But I know there are good reasons. Probably our elders know best."

She folded her arms tightly across her chest and swayed slightly from side to side in rhythm to her denial. "They don't! They don't! They don't!"

Just as Dougald started to ask how she could be so sure, she ran a few steps ahead, then whirled so she could look back on the outline of the house and the rough hills behind it. She threw her arms wide. "Look at it. Its roofs, jutting and thrusting every which way, make it look like a castle. And those hills—strong and sturdy and silent like the men bred in them. Our Scotland is beautiful. 'Tis in its beauty, poor though it be, that we belong."

She stood fixed, as if she would never cease reaching out for the crags of her homeland, and it pierced Dougald's heart to see the look of infinite sadness which came to her face. Only when there was a rustle behind the hedge and the sound of murmuring—probably lovers, Dougald thought—did she come to herself. She seized his hand and in a catching voice said, "Let's run, Dougald! There! To the garden-house!"

Both stumbled rather than ran. She had to hold her skirt above the puddles left from the storm. Dougald could not balance well with one arm in a sling. Besides, the jogging rhythm started a pounding in his shoulder. But at last they came to the steps. She let go his hand and ran up them ahead of him. When he reached her, he heard her draw shuddering breath. Involuntarily he touched her face. There were tears on it.

"Moira, Moira, what is it? Just the sadness, or something else? Tell me."

"Can I tell you? Will you understand and not

laugh nor be afraid of me? Others are, and I am of myself."

Gently he drew her to the steps. "Sit down and tell me. Of course I won't laugh. And how could I be afraid of anything about you?"

She did not answer at once, but finally she said, "Oh, Dougald, I see such awful visions! I seem to know before things happen how they'll turn out." Her voice was muffled and broken as she lamented, " 'Tis dreadful, 'tis awful to be so afflicted."

Dougald sat thoughtfully. He knew what Moira meant: she believed she had second sight, a capacity to see into the future. Many of the Highlanders he had talked with claimed to have it. Mostly it was the hill people, living on isolated patches of land where the imagination could feed on loneliness, who told of visions. But even old Aggie, living in the bustle of the kitchens of Monkstadt, was forever conversing with apparitions. He'd never known quite what to make of accounts of supernatural visitations. He patted Moira's shoulder awkwardly. "Hush. Don't cry. 'Tis nothing fearful to have the second sight. There's lots of folks who do."

"Aye! Old witch wives!" she cried bitterly. "But not young girls. And people scoff. They say I lie; they turn away—or they used to. I don't speak of it any more." She raised her head and looked at him. "But you—you will understand."

Dougald smiled reassuringly at her. In the dim light that filtered through the clouds, her face seemed worn. He did not pretend to know whether it really was given to men to see the future. But he did know that at least part of Moira's present agitation was the effect of strain and tiredness. He thought also of the old wives' tales reiterated before the fire to children of the moors and mountains. They'd breed unusual premonitions in anyone, he said to himself.

Impulsively he took her hands. He promised himself that he would protect her, teach her to be happy and confident again, as she could never be on Skye. Aloud he asked, "What vision was it this time, Moira, that frightened you?"

" 'Twas Flora," she answered in an awe-struck voice, "but Flora standing for us all. She was walking under tall trees. There was a look of unutterable woe on her face. She was murmuring, ' 'Twas not God's will that brought us to America.' "

Dougald held her hands more tightly. "But all things we do are foreordained by God. If tomorrow we depart for Campbeltown, and thence to the New World, 'twill be He who sent us." He sighed heavily. "It may be we'll know some sorrow there, as you think. But that too will be His will."

"But, Dougald—mayhap we mistake His will. Mayhap He lets us choose and we go against it, and that is where our sorrow comes from."

Dougald had to frown in perplexity. Many times he'd asked himself why, if all was foreordained, one had to make so many decisions and try so hard to improve oneself. But he had never found an answer.

At last he released her hands, stood up and walked a few steps into the little house. "I don't well know about that, Moira. I've wondered often, have even questioned John McKeogh about it. But he only says, 'God's ways are hard to scan.' "

She made no answer and he paced about, his mind jumping from his ever-plaguing questions about God's will to some new questions about the difference between second sight and just plain high-strung nerves. Finally he remembered that he wanted to cheer her, not let her premonitions flood him with despair and melancholy. "But come now," he cried, striding toward her to help her rise. "I don't know what's before us, but I begin to believe in the venture." He laughed. "For some inexplicable reason, your doubts feed my hopes. I begin to think our fears are born out of troubles in the past, not troubles in the future."

He stopped abruptly, astounded that he was speaking as he had dreamed of speaking to her—confidently, persuasively. The realization made his bashfulness return. But he saw that her face was tilted up to his, and he managed to say a little more. "Moira . . . perhaps if we both resolve not to be afraid, if we try to think of North Carolina as a place better, not worse, than the Highlands, we can make something glorious of our new life."

His words must have helped her. She placed her hands on his arms, very lightly so she would not make his shoulder throb. "I hope you are right, Dougald. Perhaps you are. Already it's easier for me, knowing that someone understands how I feel … and cares a little for it."

She started to descend the steps. Dougald caught her arm and turned her toward him. He kissed her tenderly. Almost imperceptibly her lips returned his kiss.

In silence they strolled slowly toward the house. Just at the edge of the terrace she said, "Please, Dougald, you go in. Tell Mother and Father I wish they'd come out here. I want to talk to them without all the others about."

Dougald lifted his head from his hand with a sigh. He'd not even had a glimpse of her after that, though he hung about in the parlour waiting for her. The pound of the Grant lads' feet, as they danced the fling, had given him a headache. Finally, tired but reluctant, he'd come to bed. On the stairs he'd seen Lady Margaret, dispensing candlesticks. Moira had been right: she was pale. But when he spoke to her she had only sighed and said good night.

The sound of the door opening and closing behind him made him jump up and then gasp in pain. "Lady Margaret," he said when he saw her standing beside his bed, "I did not hear you."

She put a finger to her lips and nodded at David. "Don't waken him—not yet." Then she sat down in the chair Dougald had just risen from. She rubbed her hand wearily across her forehead. Dougald saw deep lines beside her mouth and dark smudges under her eyes. Never before had he seen her like this; usually she was smiling and beautiful, despite her years and sorrows.

He assumed that it was the coming departure that had kept her watchful through the night and he sought to console her. Dropping to his knees and taking her hand, he whispered, "Dear Lady Margaret—

dear Mother—I wanted to tell you not to feel any longer that you are forcing me to do something I do not want to do." He saw a perplexed look in her eyes; she seemed to have no memory of their last evening's conversation. "I mean, except for missing you, I shall be happy in North Carolina. I've discovered I want to go. Truly I do."

She stood up abruptly without care for the way she pushed him back. Dougald thought for a moment it was hot anger which moved her, and he was confused. Then he saw that the look on her face was not an angry one, though he was not sure just what it was. Her hands were trembling, but he was fearful of clasping them again. He simply got up and stood before her.

"Dougald lad, must we ever be at odds?" she cried. "You shall not go. I have found out things. You shall not go. Nor shall David." She looked at the bed as she said David's name, and saw him staring at her with a surprised look. Her hand went to her mouth. "Oh, I did not want to tell you yet! I was going to speak first to Dougald ... because I knew—or rather I thought—he'd be happy where you'd be sad." She looked down as if she could not meet either boy's eyes.

David threw back the sheet and was on his feet in a second. "Not go? Why? I want to go. I want to sail tomorrow with the others."

Margaret simply bent her head still lower and said nothing. Dougald sensed that she felt they were betraying her. David's surprise had made him sound as though he cared not at all for her or for her reasons. And he himself, by changing his mind, seemed to be leagued with David against her.

"Lady Margaret," he said, gesturing to the chair behind her, "sit down again. Tell us what's made you change your mind." Somehow his words, meant to help them understand one another, seemed cruel. He could not remember any other time when he and David had thought their foster-mother owed them explanations. In an effort to soften his words, he added, "This is so unexpected we don't know quite what we are saying."

Margaret seemed to know that Dougald was trying to take the edge off David's refusal to obey and his own resistance to her will. She looked up with a sad, wan smile. "I keep forgetting you've got judgement of your own, that I've no right to order you about as though you were still the little boys who came here seven years ago." She could not keep a slightly injured note out of her voice as she said, "But I do hope you'll listen to what I have to say. You'll see that I am right."

David looked a trifle belligerent. Dougald recalled that only a day or two ago David had exclaimed, "Och, and I'll be glad to get to America! There I can find something besides farming to do. I hear they're pushing inland all the time over there. Going right into unexplored territory. That's what I'd like!" Now Dougald wondered whether any reason, no matter how valid, would make David accept delay patiently.

"Please, Lady Margaret, go on," he said aloud. "We want to know whatever it is."

Once again she related the reports of dissension in America.

"That we already know," David put in a little brusquely.

"Aye," she acknowledged. "But do you already know there's almost sure to be fighting? Do you know you'll have to swear an oath to support the King of England as soon as you get there?"

At the mention of fighting David's face had taken on an excited look. There's nothing he'd like better, Dougald thought. But the reference to an oath for the Hanover quenched the excitement.

David looked at Dougald. "We've already sworn otherwise, haven't we, Dougald? Over on South Uist. We've sworn to fight for Scots honour and liberty."

Dougald nodded, but his mind was on a phrase Lady Margaret had used: "almost sure to be fighting ...'" How did she know that? And was her certainty a product of her own fear? She had always been prone to persuade herself by using strong words.

"We ought to know it all exactly as 'twas told you,"

he said. "Can you remember just what you heard? And how did you hear it?"

Margaret was in better possession of herself now, and she repeated clearly all Cecily had said. This time, Dougald noticed, she did not make war seem so inevitable.

When David had heard Cecily's name he had exclaimed, "Miss Weston? 'Tis odd she didn't mention this to me." Now that Margaret had finished, he snatched up his clothes and stepped behind the arras. "I shall ask her about it."

"Don't be childish, David," Lady Margaret ordered. "I've told you all. And you needn't awaken her as if she were some informant to be roused any time you want to know something."

David was nettled, but he continued dressing. "I'm sorry I was rude. I don't know what's the matter with me." He emerged from behind the curtain and sat down on the edge of the bed to put on his shoes. "Did you speak of this to Flora?"

There was a pause before Margaret answered. Then: "Aye."

Dougald knew now what it all meant. The facts, if they were facts, were threatening, no denying that. And Lady Margaret wanted to protect her lads—she wasn't going to send them from the frying-pan into the fire. On the other hand, she was clutching at any excuse, now the time for leaving was come, to hold them back. How ironical, he thought, that only yesterday I should have been overjoyed!

"Flora is going despite this news, isn't she?" he said.

Margaret nodded. "But for personal reasons, Dougald. I can't tell them, but you don't have to go for the same reasons. Stay. Please stay."

That she asked instead of ordered moved Dougald. He saw that David, too, was thinking hard; he'd lost all his impulsiveness.

When neither lad spoke, she stood up. "I know you're trying to see it my way. I realize, too, that if you insist on going, it's I who've encouraged you." But she looked at Dougald as though she really did not understand his desire to go. "I try to be just about this."

She walked to the window and looked down to the sea below. Without looking at them she said, "Something has happened in these last few days, something I didn't know was happening. You're not my bairns any longer."

Dougald went to her side. "Don't say that as though there were now some terrible division between you and us. We haven't withdrawn, we don't deny you. How could we, loving you as we do?" He appealed to David for help in his explanation. "Am I not right, David?"

"Aye." Then David rose and went to her also. "Lady Margaret, I don't say things as well as Dougald does. . . . But I do think some, and I've thought this: We've come to the age where we want to make our own decisions and have our own adventures." He paused, then added, "I might as well tell you. I was happy to let you make the decision to send us, for it's what I've been wanting." When she bit her lip as if deeply hurt, he pleaded with her, "Please understand. I don't want to leave you. But I'd hate not to take up the challenge of America."

Margaret seemed to struggle within herself. Finally she took David's hand in both hers. "I don't think I can understand wholly, not all at once. But I do see part of it. Flora warned me. She told me you lads should not be over-protected. Have I smothered you by loving you so much? Oh, please, don't let it be that I'm driving you away!"

"Nay, of course you're not." Dougald spoke up immediately. "I know why David wants to go. He can use all that space and freedom in America to try things out, find out what he really wants, what he really is. How is he ever going to know here?"

Margaret nodded and pressed David's hand before she released it. "I see. I've known for a long time that you would eventually have to strike out on your own. I've just hidden the knowledge deep within me. Make your own decision, David. But do think well of the dangers."

When David finally spoke, he had tears in his eyes. "Thank you, Mother. I'm going to go now and think this all over. Do you mind if I speak to Flora?" Margaret shook her head, and David started to turn away. Then he came back. "I'll tell you after breakfast what I've thought out. I feel I'll go today with the others. But, Mother, if I go, the one thing I'll ever be sad about is leaving you." He kissed her and then slowly went out the door.

Dougald waited until he could no longer hear David's footsteps. Then, in as casual a manner as possible, he asked, "Did you tell the MacQueens of this? They ought to know. Mayhap they'll not want to send Moira."

Margaret answered absently, "Flora talked to them. She said they are almost irrational in their conviction that Moira must go."

Dougald said nothing, but he knew that he too would go. And he was glad the MacQueens had so decided. Yet it would be bad if Moira went to a place of new danger, and he hoped devoutly that things were not so serious in America as Lady Margaret believed. Last night he'd had a vision of what going to a fresh, new world could mean. There, perhaps, old wrongs and sorrows could be forgotten. The superstitions that haunted a people who'd lived in dark hills for eight hundred years might evaporate in the sunlight of a new beginning. I would go, he thought, for Moira alone. But it's bigger than that. All the will and drive that have been growing in me want a challenge. In an odd way he was rather elated that there were obstacles to success and happiness in America. With the strength of his body and the acuteness of his mind he could forge a life that would be right for himself and Moira and all the other Scots.

He could not tell these thoughts to Lady Margaret. Yet he wanted her to know something of his reasons for leaving her. Finally he said, "Last night, Mother, I got a glimpse of what you had meant about the new chance in America. It never meant much to me when you spoke of good land and flourishing trade. For such things alone I would never go. But I started to hope that when men live in a prosperous, growing country they can be happier. They can smile and sing more. They can have more faith in themselves." He paused. "That's why I'm going."

For a long moment Margaret said nothing. Then she walked to David's bed and picked up the nightshirt he had dropped there. As she folded it and smoothed it with her hands she said, "I hope you are right. Your reasons are good." She smiled as she put down the garment and stepped up to Dougald. She took his face between her hands and said, "But 'tis not reasons that reconcile me. I know now that what I feared was foolish. You and David are becoming men. We are closer than ever, now I've acknowledged your needs. You both called me Mother this morning. Remember, I'll be that to you, no matter where you are."

She walked toward the door but half-way there she stopped. "You'd best be getting ready. We leave for Portree directly after breakfast. I know you can't do very much with that arm. So tell me if I can help."

She was gone, and Dougald stood looking after her. At last he said aloud, "It must be right that we go. Otherwise this moment I've been fearing for so long, when David and I would have to oppose her and assert ourselves, would never have worked out so well."

7

Sail On!

ABOUT eight o'clock in the evening, when there was still light in the sky and Portree could be seen from the *Jessie's* decks, the last of Allan MacDonald's party boarded. They had not known at first whether they should row out to the ship. Anne, Alex and Jamie had not yet arrived from Dunvegan, and Flora had been reluctant to board before they came. It seemed strange to her that the MacLeod party should have missed the gathering at Monkstadt and now, on top of that, should be late to Portree. She wanted to delay until she saw them drive up safely in their coach. Yet it was she who had refused to go to the inn to spend the night. She could not endure the thought of walking again through the rooms in which she had last seen her Prince.

Now, aboard the *Jessie* at last, Flora thought that it had done little good to row out. She was irresistibly drawn to the portside. She gazed long at the entire town, from the fishing sheds at the dock to the last grey stone houses on the hill. Then her gaze rested on Portree Inn, outlined against the cliff. She wrenched her gaze away and turned to answer Cecily Weston's comments. "Yes, Portree is a very charming village." ... "Yes, you and Anne will provide companionship for each other."

The casual words came hard to Flora. The *Jessie* and the passengers, even Allan, on her decks were less real than memories. For twenty-eight years Flora had stifled recollections of her last sight of Bonnie Prince Charlie, and today especially, all the way from Monkstadt, she had girded herself against her thoughts. Now, with the inn before her, she could not keep them back. The years dropped away and the past was present. After old Kingsburgh had decided to send Charlie on to Portree, she had ridden hard, with only Neil MacEachen for an escort. Her mission, and her wish, was to precede the Prince and make arrangements for him. Finally she had dismounted before the inn, walked through the door and there found Donald Roy MacDonald. He was waiting to smuggle the Prince to Raasay.

Later—her fears for his safety had made it seem much later than it really was—the Prince had arrived. When he came into the chamber where she waited, he was wearing the MacDonald kilt which Donald Roy had brought for him. Brave and tall and handsome Charles had looked. But the life had gone out of his blue eyes, and lines about his mouth had brought age upon him.

The image of the defeated Prince was painful. Flora swiftly turned her back on the village, resolved to recall no more. But when she had turned and taken a few steps, she saw Raasay Isle stretched out before the harbour. That sight was even more painful than the other. Raasay Isle was the first and last Highland refuge of the lonely Prince. Charles had landed with high hope. He left with none. The throne of Scotland was lost on that day when Donald Roy conveyed the Prince to Raasay Isle. Never again would a Stuart rule in majesty.

There were tears in Flora's eyes, and she could see Bonnie Prince Charlie's image through them. She raised her hand in a last salute. No doubt Cecily, waiting quietly, thought the gesture a farewell to the land, to friends, to home. It was that. But Flora knew it was mostly a farewell to the Prince she had served faithfully.

The past had been relived to its last defeated moment. Flora sighed and looked about her. The decks were filled with emigrants who tried to make themselves comfortable by leaning against crates. Toward the middle of the ship Allan was showing a gillie where to stow trunks and where to spread pallets for beds. The scene was one of transience and confusion. Everyone was trying to make a place for himself and his belongings in this crowded craft. For a moment Flora closed her eyes against the sight. Then she opened them and scanned the water and the dock for some sign of Anne. Nothing. She slowly walked to Allan to see whether he needed her.

It was very dark, very late, but Flora paced the deck and waited for Anne. She stepped over an open package of food and a pot lying beside it. As she did so she recalled that few had been the voyagers who made use of the steady decks for cooking. No one felt much like eating, not when farewells still rang in their ears and when straining eyes could still make out the homeland. Milk and biscuits had been passed among the children. One hardy young gillie, who left no folk behind and who truly believed the streets of the New World were paved with gold, had fetched out some potatoes and begun to eat hungrily. But even he, when he looked into the sad eyes of the others, had lost his appetite. He had pushed the food back into his bundle and leaned against a trunk to whistle tunelessly.

For about an hour now, ever since Flora had been walking about, the gillie had been silent. No doubt he was asleep on the deck, as were some of the others. But there were a few, Flora could tell by different sounds, who still watched. Behind her there were whispers and smothered laughter from David and Sandy. They're too excited to sleep, she thought, and I'm too sad. Beyond the lads there was heavy breathing with many a sigh. Moira had cried herself dry of tears and now was half asleep, though she was restless and shudders racked her. Cecily's low-toned words of comfort made a monotonous background for Moira's sighs.

"Stow that fowl crate!" It was the captain, calling to the dim, busy figure of the mate near the foremast.

New murmurs told Flora that Moira had roused at the captain's call. Flora thought for a moment of going to her. Poor thing, she was hurt by the brusque way her parents had sent her off. She hadn't realized that Peter had growled angrily about Moira's "snivel-lin'" only because he'd been close to tears himself. No, Flora decided, I won't go over. I think I'd just cry and start her weeping again.

Flora looked up at the sky, and thought that the whole day, despite its clear sunshine, had been as dark as this night-time hour. Darker, she corrected herself as she looked at the white stars and the glow of the moonlight beyond the head of land to the star-board side. There was nothing to light the long day, nothing that can be remembered with joy. Perhaps to-morrow will be brighter. Anne and Jamie will be with me. We'll visit Armadale. After that there will be nothing to tempt me back.

She stepped carefully between the figures on the deck. What madness was it, she thought, that made us all deny our chance to turn back? Last night I could have let Margaret talk to Allan. He'd have stayed, for my sake and for our sons' sake. We'd not be tonight on a crowded little boat, heading for a bigger, more crowded one that will take us away from home for-ever. "Well," she said aloud, but so only she herself could hear, "I kept quiet last night just so I could look on what I'm looking on now—Allan resting easy at last, certain that the load of bad fortune was left behind in Skye. And that was not madness."

If blessings mean anything, she mused, we ought to be free of ill luck. Nearly every islander has come to wish us well. The next day was the time for the cere-mony, yet when they had come aboard many had al-ready arrived to pay homage. Crowds of people, all wearing MacDonald or MacLeod or Clanranald colours, had pressed down to the pier. The women had dropped to their knees to offer up prayers at Flora's feet. The men had shaken Allan's hand and shown faith in him. Many had pleaded, "Send me back passage money, Allan MacDonald. I'll serve ye seven years, if ye'll be having me, master." She'd been proud of him when he replied, "Sure, if I can I'll send it. And it's no slave to me you'll be if you come. I wish you all could be going with us to pros-perity."

The mate's voice sang out loudly, "Boat lights to the port side." Flora hurried to the edge of the deck, conscious that several others stirred behind her. She strained to see the figures that carried the moving lights in the small craft. Her breath caught, for she thought she had made out the figure of a woman. "Yes! Yes!" she cried aloud. "It is Anne. And that's—Jamie beside her." Although she could see that they were busy about something in the small boat and were not looking up at her, she stepped forward and waved eagerly.

"Flora! Keep back!" Allan cried, catching her arm. "You don't have to swim out to meet them."

When she realized how foolhardy she'd been in her eagerness, Flora trembled a little and clung to Allan's arm. "Thank goodness you look after me," she said with a shaky laugh. Then she freed herself and ran to Anne, coming over the side with the help of Alex below and the mate above. "Anne, I'm so glad to have you with me at last." Then she saw the paleness of Anne's face in the moonlight. "Has it been so hard for you? You look faint."

Anne answered nothing, but fell crying into Flora's arms. Alex pulled himself up and, after looking down to see that a gillie was helping Jamie, said, "You'd best make her lie down. She's . . . not well."

Flora saw that both Alex and Allan were bringing up boxes. She turned to Cecily and requested, "Please bring Jamie to me," and then walked Anne away.

"What is it," she asked when she had got Anne to a clear space where she could lie down. "Such wailing does no good. Tell me so I can help you."

Before Anne could draw breath to answer, Alex rushed up and dropped to his knees so he could cradle Anne in his arms. "Hush! Hush! There's no need to carry on so. There's many a woman has sailed the seas in your condition."

"Alex! What do you mean?" Flora asked, catching his arm.

He paid her no attention and went on consoling Anne. "Don't, don't. We'll have been there a long while . . . it will seem like home . . . when he's born."

Flora pushed him aside, and bent over Anne. "Oh,

my dear, I was thinking just the other day ... of you, having your children away from Skye. But I never dreamed——" She broke off to speak to Alex in some anger. "Why didn't you send a message? With Sandy coming over, you could have told me. I'd never have allowed her to come."

Alex stood helplessly with both arms dangling. "She's the one who wouldn't let a message be sent. I haven't known what to do with her. I'll do anything she wants."

Anne tossed on her pallet and sobbed out childishly, "Oh, Mother, I don't know why I came on! I don't want my baby born on the seas, nor in a far country." .

Flora held Anne's hand tightly and brushed the hair from her forehead. "I know, dear. I know." She looked up and told the men to go away. Cecily was standing off to one side with a bewildered Jamie. "Would you show him where he is to sleep, please?" Flora asked.

When the others were gone, Flora turned back to Anne, bent and took her in her arms. "Anne dear, this is a joyous thing. I am so happy to be having a grandchild. He'll be strong and handsome like his grandfather and father." She squeezed Anne a little to cheer her. "You must be happy too. Think of Alex. He wants to be proud about it. But you worry him too much."

Without saying anything Anne nodded and sniffed as if she were sorry she'd caused so much fuss and would try to be braver.

"Now listen to me, Anne," Flora went on. "You don't have to go to North Carolina. There's time, if you want to return." She paused and saw that Anne turned her face away. "Well, dear, what shall you do? You can go back. I'll stay with you. We can follow the men later, and they'll have everything ready for us ... a home for the child."

"Alex would stay too. He said so."

"Of course he would, if you want him to. So why do you cry? You're very, very fortunate. You're healthy, and will have an easy time of it. Soon you'll have a plump little bairn that I can dandle on my lap." Flora pulled at the blanket to make it smoother under Anne. Her voice rose in anticipation. "Shall we go back home, where you'll be more comfortable? We'll have him christened here, by our own pastor."

"Our pastor will be in America, Mother." Anne's voice was low.

"Aye . . . I forgot. Well . . ."

"No, Mother. I'm ashamed of my spasm. But it's over. I don't want to go. I'm afraid. But everything that is ours seems to be in America now." She tossed on the pallet and clutched at Flora's hand. "What is it? What force is it that pulls us on, when everything in us is dragging us back?"

Flora said nothing. She remembered that earlier she had refused to call the will to sail madness. But what was madness except acting when all reason said not to? Then suddenly she understood: That's just the point. It's not reason that holds us back. It's sentiment, and fear of the unknown. The reasons remain the same, as Allan said before. Hope grows in the soil of North Carolina. None grows here. She pressed Anne's hand. "I think," she said aloud, "that the same things pull you as pull me. Our husbands and children need to go. That's the same as our needing to go."

Anne whispered, "Yes, that's what I've felt in me these last two days since I've known. Even this little unborn baby needs it. But it's very hard."

"Aye, dear. But this kind of difficulty is no cause to fail. Now, rest. I'll stay with you till you sleep."

Anne was exhausted from emotional strain and soon she slept heavily.

Flora stiffly rose after Anne had grown quiet. She found Allan waiting. "How is she?" he asked anxiously.

She patted his hand in reassurance. "Tomorrow she'll be very happy she's with us. You'll see. She'll start talking about the grand new home they'll build for their son." She laughed a little, very tenderly. "Before long she'll say God foreordained that her son, born in the new land, should embody the new life."

Flora took Allan's arm and held it close. "Mayhap she will be right."

Allan sighed in relief. "I was worried. And poor Alex, condemning himself for uprooting his family— I'll try to encourage him."

They walked back and forth for a while, letting the sea air cool them. Finally, when once again the captain called an order, Allan spoke. "Well, tomorrow farewell. After that, Armadale. Then direct route and new things."

Flora awoke at dawn, when the first faint light on the eastern sky fell upon her pallet. She sat up at once, with a weight of heaviness and apprehension on her. For a moment she could not think why she should be disturbed. By looking about she could see her family—all safe, all sleeping still. Anne, her eyes slightly swollen from her tears, was on the next pallet. On the other side was Allan, half screened by bales and boxes. The feet of the four lads protruded from behind a stack of crates. Cecily, she knew, had kept Moira near her on the opposite deck. There was no sound from that direction.

Somewhat relieved to see that all rested quietly, Flora rose. She looked for a moment into the grey mists that hung over the islands of the sound. Then, before she moved to the edge of the deck, she bent to cover Anne's shoulders. Tenderness flooded her as she thought that Anne was to experience both the joy and fear of childbearing more sharply than most women, because of the perilous voyage and the new home before her.

After looking fondly at Anne and then at Allan, Flora softly walked away. She looked across the sixty feet or so of water between the *Jessie* and the dock of Portree. Groups of men and women were gathering. To Flora it seemed early for so much activity; she wondered momentarily at the cause. Then Allan's words of last night returned: "Tomorrow farewell." Today was the day of the blessing of the ship. Somewhere in Portree the young Laird of Clanranald was rising. He was no doubt already preparing to come to the pier to pronounce the traditional, formal words that signified long, perhaps permanent separation. Flora was torn within herself. She did not want to suffer the sound of those words, nor the pain of seeing Margaret, the laird, his lady, the MacQueens and many other friends waving good-bye from the dock. Already the blue water divided her irrevocably from her dear ones; she could not embrace them again. Yet she did not want to disappoint Clanranald, who had ridden here so that he might preside over the ceremony and thus show his devotion to his kinswoman. And, indeed, she would not want to sail away without the blessing that from time immemorial had protected Clanranald seafarers. Though this little *Jessie* was not the ship that would carry them over the heaving billows of the Atlantic, the benediction said over her deck and sails would extend to any ship that carried the MacDonalds on this journey. "Aye," Flora said softly, "I shall weep at the ceremony, but I shall later take comfort in it. I must strengthen myself, and take part with whole heart."

She saw that the dock was filling with people. It would not be long before the ceremony would begin, for the *Jessie* must sail with the best early-morning winds. Flora hurried to the sleeping area and shook Allan, Anne and the others by the shoulder. "Make haste! The crowd ashore grows thick."

Swiftly Flora straightened her gown and combed her hair. Before she was quite finished, Katie, whose loyalty had made her resolve to follow her mistress to the ends of the earth if necessary, bustled up. A gentleman, she said, wanted to speak with Flora. Wondering who it could be, Flora put the last pin in her dark hair. She made her way to the deck. There she saw John MacKenzie, law agent for the Barony of MacDonald. She ran to him with joy. She knew he had come on no legal business, but instead to give her a final word of her children; who now lived in the MacKenzie home at Edinburgh. "So good!" she cried. "So very good of you to come, John!"

Mackenzie clasped her hands in both of his. "I've but a moment, Flora. I just wanted you to know that you need never fear for your son and daughter. My wife and I already think of John as our own. Soon it will be the same with Fanny. She arrived safely."

Flora pressed his hands tightly. "All my life I will be thanking you—for riding the long way from Edinburgh as well as for caring for them. Tell Fanny—tell both John and Fanny—that I love them. I shall pray for them every night. We will send for them ere long."

With a reverent bow MacKenzie kissed Flora's hand. "I will deliver the message. And, Flora, I shall pray for you and Allan. God grant you success at last!"

He stepped into the small boat and the craft was pushed away from the Jessie. Flora thought her heart would break. "There departs my last link with the children," she whispered to herself. "For how long shall I have only the echo of John MacKenzie's message to sustain me?"

There was a pressure on Flora's arm. Allan had come up to stand with her. In a slightly sharp tone he said, "Think not of John and Fanny now. They are well and safe—thanks to you. Look to the shore. Hundreds are there to see you off."

Obediently Flora scanned the water-front. There were solemn faces, disillusioned eyes, both symbolic of the inner loss every Highlander had endured as the clans broke up. These islanders yearned to live again in days when every clansman rose at the call of his chief, fought beside his chief until the battle was won. They wanted, as their petitions to Allan had shown, to journey to the new land where the chiefs would rise to power again, where the clansmen could openly express their loyalty. It was too much to bear—having to leave them behind. But Flora said nothing of her thoughts aloud. Allan was persuaded that all these folk had come only to see her; he was tense and uneasy and eager to be away. She would not speak of the islands or the islanders.

Now the ceremony was beginning. A tall Skyeman pulled off his bonnet so that his hair shone blue-black in the sun. He stepped forward to stand directly opposite Flora. With a wave of his bonnet he shouted, "The song! Let's have the song!" At least a hundred voices joined in singing the words Flora herself had written long ago, when her heart still played with romantic recollections of the Prince.

> "Oh, hie to the Highlands, my laddie!
> Be welcomed by hearts warm and true,
> For there's where ye'll see, my ain laddie,
> The tartans and bonnets of blue.

> "And list, when they tell ye, my laddie,
> Their valiant deeds of renown,
> Of battles they fought for Prince Charlie,
> The true-born heir of the Crown, Oh!"

With innate musicianship the islanders began to vary the simple melody. The final verse and last refrain were sung in at least a dozen parts, each carried by strong, resonant voices:

> "Ye'll hear of the chieftains of old,
> Those sons of valour and worth,
> But Charles's own favourite clan was
> MacDonald, the pride of the North.

> "Oh, hie to the Highlands, my laddie!
> Be welcomed by hearts warm and true,
> For there's where ye'll see, my ain laddie,
> The tartans and bonnets of blue."

The simple words made more poignant the memories that had, throughout this time of departure, been crowding upon Flora. They also accentuated her sense of Allan's discomfort. He did not sing with the others. Flora was glad when the song ended and Clanranald and the old dominie of the kirk of Portree stepped to the front of the crowd.

The two men made a striking picture: the dominie in straight dark coat and the great laird in brilliant Highland dress. At the sound of a hunting horn the dominie lifted his feeble hands. In response the hundreds of men doffed their bonnets and the women bowed their heads reverently. The dominie's voice rang out:

"Ship bearing the folk of Clanranald, I fervently invoke God's blessing upon you, on your captain and your mate, both unmatched in bravery and courage.

"O God, render Thou the breath of the sky propitious, that it may urge this ship over the water to safe haven. Almighty Father, who has called forth the oceans and the winds, bless this bark. Take our stout heroes under Thy protecting power. Do Thou, O Son, bless the anchor, the sails, the shrouds of our helm. Bless the tackle, yard blocks and masts, and be their pilot over the waves. Our stays and halyards keep sound. Preserve them from danger. Let the Holy Ghost be around them, Who knows every harbour under the sun."

In chorus the passengers answered, "We submit ourselves to Thy Protection."

The dominie went on with the ancient prayer. It evoked images of gold-helmeted warriors of time gone by. "May God bless our swords, our keen blades which flash aloft, our heavy coats of mail, our heavy shields. O God, bless all our armour, offensive and defensive."

The men on shore and the men on the Jessie waved their arms over their heads as if brandishing weapons. The pastor continued: "Bless the bows of bright and polished yew that we bravely bend in strife; our birchen arrows that will not splinter; and the badger's rough spoil that contains them; and whatever warlike stores that are now on board a MacDonald bark."

The dominie dropped his hands and stepped back. The Laird of Clanranald spoke in a voice loud and clear. "Let us bless yon ship."

The captain echoed, "Let us bless our ship."

The mate and the passengers lifted their faces to the heavens and cried, "God our Father, bless her. Jesus Christ, bless her."

Clanranald asked sternly, "What do you fear, if God the Father be with you?"

From the deck the reply came swiftly: "We do not fear anything."

"Do not be deterred," Clanranald cried, "by womanish softness from acting like the hardy and bold. As long as the side of your ship be unrent, as long as four boards of her keep together, as long as she can swim under your feet, be not appalled by the angry ocean."

Clanranald's oldest gillies pressed forward. "The pride of the sea we submit to the brave. The fury of the waves will yield to the fearless. Send your ship swift as an eagle over the deep vales and mountains of the sea. Strike quickly; deeply wound the heaving billows. Make the surges fly like sparkling showers of living flame."

The laird spoke the instructions to the captain and mate. "Lo, the prow will cut the roaring waves. Her strong sides begin to creak. Let the steersman, he of the main sheet and the jib sheet, go to his task. Let the pilot sail past the BHREACAIN, the whirlpool, in safety."

The sail was spread to catch the wind; the windlass creaked as the anchor was hauled up. Every passenger stepped close to the deck's edge, as if to close the slowly widening distance between himself and the beloved faces ashore.

A final admonition came from the faithful Clanranald retainers. "If thy foe on land find thy courage increases with danger, he will the more readily yield."

Flora's hand went to her breast. She had hoped those words would be omitted; there must be no foes in the new land. She saw that the laird had stepped forward and cupped his hands to make his voice carry. She listened and did not hear the traditional words. Clanranald, his voice unsteady with emotion, was calling out his personal wish: "Flora and Allan MacDonald, and you other of our kin and friends, may you find no foes! May God, in His divine goodness, direct you to a rich New World where you will find full lives and happy in a land where there is peace for every man."

Silently Flora's lips formed the words "Thank you.

Thank you, my beloved laird." She could not see Clanranald any longer, nor the others pressed around him on the dock. Tears blurred her vision. She felt weak and had to cling to Allan's arm for support. To herself she vowed, I will put my trust in Clanranald's blessing, his devout wish for us. And I will endure no more farewells.

Allan bent to look with fond concern into Flora's face. It was as if he realized at last that departure meant vastly different things to himself and to her. His exhilaration was betrayed by his smile; feeling the boat under way made zest for the new life surge in him. But his concern was expressed by his words: "Dearest Flora, be brave. Remember their love and hope for us. And think of Armadale, which still lies before you. Your home is not yet behind."

Flora lifted her handkerchief to her lips. She straightened slightly, but stayed close to Allan so that she could feel his strong arm beside her. She searched carefully for words. Allan must not know that her heart would break if she touched Skye's earth again, saw another familiar face. Finally she said, "Nay, Allan. This is farewell to lovely Skye and to all I've known here. I do not want to clutch at the past any longer. We pass Armadale in the night. Let it slip by. I understand wholly what Anne said last night: 'Now everything that is ours lies in the New World.'"

"But, Flora ... my darling ... you wanted so very much to stop. Your mother's grave is at Armadale. You said you could not sail without praying there."

Flora raised her head and looked directly into Allan's eyes. "God will hear my prayers wherever I am." She smiled and took his hand to draw him forward. "Come. I want to look to the west—to the wide Atlantic, and home."

BOOK TWO
The Sea

8

Campbeltown in Kintyre

WHAT with one day of bad winds and several stops to take aboard emigrating crofters from Eigg, Coll and Tiree, the *Jessie* did not round the headland of Kintyre until the morning of the fourth day. The call of the mate brought relief to all on board. Allan and Alex, huddled together to discuss how to get the "smugglers" to the *Baliol*, looked up eagerly. They would have time, such necessary time, before they put out to sea.

Although there was yet a fifteen-mile sail to Campbeltown itself, every passenger fell to gathering belongings and sorting boxes. Flora, her parcels gathered together at last, sought out Jamie and made the restless lad stand beside her on the deck. "Look close, lad," she commanded. "You'll have to have sharp memories to recall your Scots home." To Cecily, standing beside her with a small satchel, as if she would step ashore at any moment, she said with a rueful smile, "I've enough memories. I wish this were the end instead of the beginning of the long voyage. And wouldn't it be a wonderful miracle if the North Carolina shore could look, when we get there, as familiar as this?"

"You contradict yourself." Cecily laughed. "You want it different, and yet the same."

Allan, left alone when Alex went after Anne, came up to lean eagerly on the bulwark and gaze ahead. "We'll see her now—the ship that takes us away. It won't be long."

No one could find much more to say. Jamie wriggled out from under his mother's hands and joined the boys nearer the prow. The fleeing crofters, uneasy about their fate in the port, crouched still on the far side of the deck. They, like the others, could only wait.

But when, more than an hour later, the *Jessie* swung into the Campbeltown harbour and the mate sang out, "*Baliol* ahead!" everyone was caught up by excitement and lined the bulwarks to gaze on the vessel. They followed the direction pointed by the captain, standing at Allan's elbow. Perhaps a quarter of a mile off shore a three-master stood at anchor. They could see tiny figures bustling about her deck. There were boats plying between her and the cluster of buildings that made the town.

The captain studied her for a moment through his glass. Then he turned slightly so he could look toward the dock. "She's taking aboard her water casks, poultry, and fresh provisions now. Ought to be ready, all right, to sail on tomorrow's ebb, sir."

Allan strained to see. Finally, still peering across the water, he said, "They'll be expecting Flora ashore. And I've a bit of business there, myself." He looked directly at the captain. "We'll go ashore in one of the boats. And you, if you'll be so good, can lay your vessel alongside the *Baliol*." He made his explanation in a casual tone. "Be easier if our gear—and such— go aboard directly. There's no need of any pother about it in the town and we won't run the risk of . . . of it's getting lost or left on shore."

The captain nodded blandly. "I conceive you, sir."

Less than an hour later, the *Jessie* was tied snugly alongside the *Baliol*, which, even heavily laden as it was, stood a good yard above the bulwarks of the smaller vessel. Allan MacDonald went across immediately to seek out the captain.

In a few minutes he was back, looking worried because the captain was ashore. In his hand Allan carried a letter addressed to Flora. It had been sent out to the ship earlier in the day and left with the mate for delivery.

Flora opened it and glanced through it quickly. "Our relatives here in Campbeltown have invited us to supper, all of us." She turned to Alexander MacLeod.

"That means you, too, of course. And any guests. How about you, Miss Weston?" As she turned to ask the question she saw Allan's scowl. "Do we have time, Allan, before we sail?"

"There's time enough, but I've got business in the town. Alex does too. And somebody will have to see that all our gear is transferred." He glanced at the boys, one after the other. "Dougald, you know our things from taking them to Portree. Would you do it? Soon as you can come ashore in one of the boats and join us. You, David, must help me with some errands in town."

Allan did not wait for any disagreement. There was too much to be done, and quickly. He hurried off to arrange with a boatman for passage ashore. In a surprisingly short time he was shepherding the others into a waiting boat. Before he himself climbed down, he took Dougald aside. "If there's trouble—there won't be, I think—send for me ashore. Whatever happens, get the folk aboard and out of sight. But the *Baliol's* mate is used to this. He'll take charge."

Dougald stood but a moment to watch them pull away. When he turned back men were already at work passing up boxes and trunks and furniture to the *Baliol's* decks. He quickly crossed over to the other ship and was dismayed at the careless tossing about of the gear. No sooner had he checked an item off a list Allan had given him than some sailor sent it sliding down the deck to rest where it would or to crash into some other object. It worried him to see crates, some of which he knew held precious and fragile things such as Flora's mirror, shoved about and then left lying for anyone to step on. He went with a protest to the mate, but was brushed aside.

"We'll get under way first," the mate said. "Then we'll stow everything ship-shape. We've a smart ship, as you'll see when we get to sea." Dougald could get nothing more out of him.

In a short time the last trunk and box, the last sack of oatmeal, the final crate of cackling hens had been transferred. Dougald drew an anxious breath. Now it was the human cargo's turn.

The *Baliol's* mate jumped down among the waiting emigrants. He rattled off instructions in a businesslike tone that showed he'd done this often before. "Before ye go aboard I want to make some things plain. A few of you have arranged to travel in the cabin. This won't concern you and you may stand aside. You others will bunk down in the steerage. It's no castle, but it'll start clean. I understand Allan MacDonald and Alexander MacLeod are your paymasters. We'll count you aboard and our tally should check with the list they give the captain.

"You'll supply your own food on the voyage or go hungry. We may be at sea longer than two months. Have you got enough to feed you and will it keep?" He scanned their faces. No one had voice to answer. "If ye've any doubt you had better send for some before we sail. A shore-boat will have biscuit and likely oatmeal. The prices will make your eyes bug, but it's better to be robbed than starved. You can cook forward in the galley when the weather's good. If we run into a gale there'll be no fires aboard. Ye'd best cook ahead if a storm threatens.

"The ship supplies fresh water for drinking—not for washing. You'll use sea-water if you have to wash. It'll salt your porridge free, too."

Dougald thought the mate's humour very bitter. Some of the emigrants seemed to shrink down as they listened; it was not a pleasant prospect they had before them—hunger and thirst, perhaps, on top of the fear they already had within them. Ah, the mate was referring to that now.

"There's militia in town and eyes watching. There'll be some of you who'd as soon not see the soldiers. You'll do well to keep out of sight below till we're well out to sea. Meantime we'll keep the hatches closed. You'll have a stuffy night but I'll wager you prefer that to a jail ashore."

The mate drew a breath and straightened. He planted his hands on his hips and surveyed the entire group. "Now, if all's clear and nobody wants to change his mind about sailing with us, we'll take you aboard. One at a time. Two of you men stand here and lend a hand to the women and bairns. The bosun will show you the way below when you get on the ship."

By families, the poor gillies and crofters began to line up. One by one, loaded with bundles, they came to the bulwark, and with a quick heave the two sailors stationed there hoisted them to the *Baliol's* deck. It seemed to Dougald, watching, that the anxious sailors above stuffed the frightened souls down the opening to the steerage as roughly as they had the crates.

Moira MacQueen was hanging back. Now, in the worst hours of the ordeal—when she must hide in the steerage of the ship and pray that no officer on the shore a short mile away suspected her existence—she had to be alone. Dougald jumped back to the *Jessie*, ready to say, "I'm staying, Moira! I'm staying with you." Then he caught himself. All the MacDonald party must appear ashore, so no one would think there was anything amiss. And should officers come, Moira could better escape notice if no MacDonald seemed particularly concerned about her.

There was no use, he felt, telling her he wanted to stay but couldn't. Instead he picked up her bundle, handed it to her and in a low voice said, "You must, Moira, on account of the soldiers. I know it's hard for a girl alone. I wish you could be with us. Later maybe Flora can fix it so you will be." He saw that she was listening and looking less lonely. "Keep below tonight. Keep quiet."

She gave him a slow, serious look, and then, as if in his words she had found the support she needed, she took the bundle from him. With square shoulders she walked to the bulwark. Just before she took her place in the line, she turned her head and called back, "Be merry on shore, Dougald. Do not be worrying about me." She managed a smile. "I'll be waiting for you and the others. There's no chance for me to run away or get lost."

Dougald lifted a hand, not in farewell, but in salute. A zest for the voyage rose in him. They'd be off in the morning. In the meantime, he would hurry into town and complete his farewells. Not through any misstep of his would a red-coated militiaman say, "Could be there's something going on on the *Baliol*. Let's have a look and see."

From the Campbeltown pier a crowd of MacDonalds hailed Flora and her family. They stretched forth hands to help the party ashore, and at once led the way to waiting coaches. Only when Allan explained he had errands to do did they pause for a moment. As soon as Allan had promised, for himself, his sons and Alex, to join the company later, they closed the carriage doors and galloped away.

Allan took no time to watch them ride off. He inquired for the captain of the *Baliol* and found him making his headquarters in the parlour of an inn. Alex stepped up first and paid passage for himself and his wife and one servant in the cabin and for several men travelling in the steerage. Allan reported a bigger score: Flora, his own sons and the twins, as well as himself, along with a maid and old Neil, for the cabin; Moira and a couple of farm wenches and no less than eight men in the steerage. His fingers were uncertain as they counted out the gold pieces. They left a great hole in his meagre supply.

"Ye'll be a bit crowded in the cabin," the captain pointed out as he contentedly pocketed the money. "Your two families make a considerable number. There's Miss Weston, with your party." He gestured vaguely above his head. "Here at the inn there are half a dozen more gentry with their servants waiting to sail with me. One's a woman, French by her name. One's only a lad, some kind of foreigner though he speaks English pretty well. You'll have chance enough to get acquainted before we see America," he added dryly.

"When should we be aboard?" Allan asked.

"I plan to run out with the first of the ebb if the wind's at all possible. That's not long after dawn. Ye'd be well advised to sleep on the ship."

Alex MacLeod, clearly thinking of Anne, spoke up. "Can we hope for an easy voyage?"

The captain thought they could. August, as he explained, was a good month for the North Atlantic, and unless they had the bad luck to encounter a hurricane beyond the Azores, September was the finest time for the western ocean.

"You'll be going to good Scots country up the Cape Fear," he went on. "In the early days, except for fear of Indians, a man could live there at his ease. Folks were too busy coping with the wilderness to worry much about politics except in their own neighbourhoods." He shook his head disapprovingly. "But on my last two trips I've found the American colonies much torn by foolish factions. North Carolina is uneasy, and no mistake. But I expect you have had reports."

Allan could bear to listen to only a bit more talk before insisting that they leave to find a chandler's shop. He could not hear more, he was afraid, without betraying that he felt a chill at the pit of his stomach. He had indeed heard reports, and he had not fully credited them. But this captain looked to be a steady fellow, a man of experience. It was impossible to shrug off what the man had seen for himself. Could it be, he asked himself, that from poverty-stricken Skye we are travelling to a restless, uneasy North Carolina? He all at once doubted that he would ever find himself in a quiet, stable land where a man's work brought him its worth. He felt destined to see his abilities caught and carried down in a whirlpool of others' making. Well, he decided with a pound of his fist that the others did not understand, I'm committed to this hazard. I must play it to the last florin.

With an effort he pushed away his dark mood and returned to the practical needs of the moment. "They say fresh food is a wonderful restorer along with all the salt meat and mouldy biscuit on a voyage. I put off getting some things to the last so they'd keep that much the longer. Let's find a barrel of hard apples and a sack or so of potatoes. We brought poultry enough with us from Skye."

A day in Campbeltown as the guest of Flora MacDonald was an illuminating experience, Cecily Weston had discovered. First there was the very old town itself, not very large to cosmopolitan eyes and no longer very important. A thousand years earlier, Duncan MacDonald told her, it had been the royal seat of an ancient western kingdom. A sculptured stone cross was almost six hundred years old. For centuries the place had been a MacDonald stronghold. On the rock of Dunaverty she could make out the tumbled stones of the ruined castle of MacDonald of the Isles. All around her were the symbols of a long, proud history created by these Scots whom she had thought of as little more than savages.

But the antiquity's the least of it, Cecily said to herself. If Flora MacDonald was ever here before it must have been for a brief visit more than twenty-five years ago. She couldn't know these people, nor they her. To them she was of course a famous person, the Prince's preserver after the '45, but beyond this she was a stranger. Yet in a few minutes they were all talking like old friends, and Flora was sorting out the indescribably complex clan lines of each one, finding in this person a remote kinsman, in that a definite cousin.

On Skye Cecily had learned to expect deference to Flora. Now, observing equal homage in Campbeltown, she realized that Flora's fame and influence were greater than she had thought. Flora herself was natural and unpretentious amid the acclaim. But the acclaim was there, and it proved that Flora MacDonald did, as David had said, represent the clan.

That makes it hard for Allan, just as I suspected, Cecily thought as she watched him talk with some of the menfolk in the room. He'd come in late with the boys and MacLeod. It had seemed to her that more than ever he had that air about him of not quite filling the space he ought to. He should have dominated the room, yet it was always Flora who captured attention. And he made an effort to be cordial; she did nothing. If I were in his place, Cecily resolved, if I had to live two dozen years in my wife's shadow, I'd not stand for it. But then she thought that Allan's way was better. She really liked his sweetness, his effort to be worthy of Flora. Yet she wondered whether she would like that quality in her own man.

When Cecily saw a serving-man start to refill her wine-glass, she waved him away. She was already getting sentimental, and needed no more stimulant. But it wasn't just the wine that made her sigh frequently. It was feeling again, as she had on Skye, that the Scots were people she loved to be with. These more cosmopolitan folk of Campbeltown were, in their own way, as Scots as the folk of Skye. Of course, they wore no tartans—not with the militia always a stone's throw away. But they loved their heritage and exulted in it. Cecily did not want the evening to come to an end.

But the farewell was coming inevitably. The mood had already changed to quiet melancholy. Someone was beginning a song. Cecily had no idea what the Gaelic meant but surely the song was a lament or song of parting. She could see the sadness of the words on the faces of the singers and feel it in herself.

Then Duncan MacDonald, host and spokesman for the group, was making a little speech of farewell.

"During these hard years, Flora MacDonald, knowing you were at Kingsburgh has been a comfort to us all. What you did, now many years ago, has stood as a symbol and an encouragement. It must be an old thing to you to hear about your loyalty to your rightful King and your courage and steadfastness, you being but a girl in that time. And remarkable it was. No doubt you were proud to serve your King, but a thought I have had many times, tonight you have confirmed for me: you'd have done the same thing for any man were his need as great. Part of the thing that moved you then was compassion and love for any creature in need, a crofter as quick as a King."

Duncan bowed slightly to Flora, then turned to continue his speech. "So, Allan MacDonald, you are taking from us part of our independence, part of our resistance to cruelty and tyranny, part of our loyalty, part of our love and compassion, far across the western ocean. We shall be the poorer for the loss of them here at home, but we pray God these fine Scotch plants, nurtured by you and yours, take firm root in the land across the sea. Our blessing goes with you."

To speak such words was passive rebellion, Cecily supposed; they were more than a little treasonous. But Duncan MacDonald's clear sincerity moved her. Individually she liked these Highlanders so much she found herself responding to their sense of injury and wanting to champion and protect them. It was strange and unsettling to get one's sympathies twisted about.

The speech marked the end of the visit. Allan MacDonald and Alex MacLeod, a little way across the room, were urging the others to start for the *Baliol*; the host was providing two men with lanthorns to escort the party down to the harbour. Cecily rose reluctantly and accepted her shawl from David.

The night was warm, and the stroll to the pier a short one. Everyone lagged a little, hating to place his last footstep on Scotland's soil. The few words spoken were low and quiet; even the lads were subdued.

When they were near the dock one of the guides, and Allan too, hurried ahead to hire a boat. The rest straggled out more unevenly than ever. Flora slowly dropped to the rear of the little procession, and finally she stopped, when the others were some ten feet ahead.

Cecily, watching quietly, saw Flora's face assume an expression of deep grief. She turned slowly to the hills; her arms reached out in a gesture like an embrace. It was as if she would take Scotland to her bosom in this last hour. A long moment passed. Then, without tears or words, Flora dropped her arms to her sides and turned back to the waterside.

When Allan called that the boat was ready, Flora was in complete command of herself. No one who had seen her a moment before would have guessed she felt regret. She calmly told Cecily that she was trying to think of an arrangement more suitable for Moira. "From the beginning, now, I want her to be one of us."

9

The Departure

A LANTHORN hung amidships on the *Baliol* guided
the MacDonald party back to the ship, looming in
the dark. As they came close, they could see a little
knot of servants lounging within the circle of the lanthorn's dim light and could see the captain move forward to meet them.

Sandy and David clambered aboard and stationed
themselves to give a hand to the others. As Flora and
Anne set foot on the deck, Flora's maid Katie came
forward to take charge of them. The mate had been
moved by chivalry, and a fee from Allan, to give up
his cabin in the stern to the two ladies. Katie had
made up the berths and now wanted to lead her mis-
tresses to them. Before Flora would go, she asked to
see Moira and for that night received a flat refusal.
"Foolish risk," the captain asserted bluntly.

A smaller cabin, regularly used for passengers, had
been assigned to Cecily Weston and the other female
passenger, the lady with the French name mentioned
by the captain. Cecily's fat, middle-aged maid Martha
lighted her way to it, protesting that it was hardly big
enough for a hat-box and that it was an outrage to put
two ladies in it with their maids. She almost filled it
herself, she said, and she thought that foreigner, who
hadn't bothered to appear yet, might just as well stay
away. When Cecily saw the cabin and compared its size
with Martha's bulk she decided Martha's idea might
be wise, if not feasible.

The great cabin—in point of fact, far from ample
in spite of its name—was to serve as a general gathering place by day but was to become a dormitory for
the men by night. Narrow berths lined the side walls,

and a row of hammocks was to be lashed up at night.
Old Neil had put bedding in a hammock for David.
For Dougald, in deference to the still painful shoulder, he had made up a berth. Sandy and young Jamie
MacDonald had hammocks. Their father and Alex
MacLeod and the pastor had been given berths.

Tired by the long day and well filled with Duncan
MacDonald's food and drink, all went at once to bed.
Sleep in these unfamiliar quarters, however, was not
easy. The other passengers arrived in ones and twos
throughout the night, each time with noise and talk.
They groped about noisily in the dark or struck a
light, and roused the sleepers. Soon after midnight a
rooster crowed loudly and set all the chickens in the
long-boat atop the deck-house cackling.

By far the most annoying disturbance was occasioned by the arrival of the woman who was to share
Cecily's cabin. She reached the ship with an enormous number of bags, mantua-maker's boxes and
other impedimenta, all of which had to be carried
hither and thither at her direction. At last she got to
her cabin, and the startled sleepers were about to settle back in relief when suddenly the noise was redoubled.

Poor Martha was the unwitting culprit. When her
mistress was in bed she had made up a pallet for herself in the narrow space between the two berths. As
the lady entered she tripped over Martha's feet and
fell on top of her. Thus rudely awakened, Martha began to howl and struggle. The lady, equally jarred,
struggled and screamed with almost as much vigour.
The uproar they made between them roused the
whole ship, and brought half a dozen people ready to
give aid. When a light was struck and the cause of the
confusion was revealed, the rescuers were hard put to
it to conceal their amusement. The lady, it was clear,
was in no mood for laughter. She dismissed the spectators haughtily.

So the night wore on, with sleep in broken
snatches. Again the rooster crowed, but this time the
sky was bright to the east. Dawn was breaking.

From the high poop the captain ordered the anchor

up, and the sailors on the forecastle, breaking into a lusty chantey, began to take in the cable.

The song soon had the passengers astir. First four boys tumbled out on deck, eager not to miss a step of the departure. Next came the older men, looking sleepy and dishevelled, and then the women. Almost a score of them altogether, they made quite a crowd. Although here and there one of them withdrew by himself, most of them, infected by the boys' excitement, were soon commenting on the scene before them. Then, after a few exchanges, they all fell silent for a moment as they realized they were mostly strangers to one another.

A hail came from forward: "Anchor's aweigh, sir."

Sailors were swarming aloft in anticipation of the next order. The captain stepped forward and bellowed, "Break out the topsails!"

The sun was just rising over the hills back of the town as the sails filled and the *Baliol* came up on its course and gathered steerage way. The voyage had begun.

Allan MacDonald was hungry now that the first excitement was over. He had sent young Jamie to find one of his men or Katie and get a pot of tea and some biscuit. He stood at the bulwark on the starboard side, watching the long curve of land to the south of them gradually slide behind, and nursed his appetite with what patience he could muster.

Another passenger came and stood beside him, studying the retreating shore. Allan had already noticed him several times and was not sure he liked his looks. He was tallish, though slender, and carried himself erectly. When everyone had hurried out to watch the ship get under way, this man alone had emerged carefully dressed. Now, he still wore a white wig tied in a club, and fine yellow nankeen breeches and a blue coat of expensive cut, all very neat and elegant.

He appeared in his early thirties. Allan thought he could detect traces of the military man in him and more than a little of the fop. Without any real reason, Allan decided one or the other aspect must be assumed, but he had no hint which was genuine. Well, in six or eight weeks at sea he had plenty of time to find out. Meanwhile he'd introduce himself and offer the stranger a cup of tea if Jamie ever secured a pot for him.

When the other man spoke his voice announced that he was English, not Scots. "I am honoured to make your acquaintance, sir. My name is James Blair. My family lives in Kent, but I've been in London of late years when not travelling. Though this is my first trip to North Carolina, I've been to America once before. I was in Boston not long ago."

Allan bowed to acknowledge the introduction. "Indeed, Mr. Blair, you travel more freely than I. I'm moving my whole family to North Carolina. 'Tis a great step for us. We wouldn't undertake such a voyage lightly. It must have been an important consideration that moved you to cross the Atlantic twice."

Blair answered in a silky voice, and Allan thought he made a rather involved explanation. "My older brother gets the lands in Kent. There is nothing for me there. I went to Massachusetts with the idea of laying out in lands some money that I inherited from my mother. One winter convinced me Massachusetts was not for me." He ruffled his cuff fastidiously. "First, the winter itself was a painful experience of frost and snow. No less dissuading were the people of Massachusetts, a turbulent people with no respect for tradition or birth or even law. Indeed, they're stubborn and stiff-necked and think even their treason is godly. I grew so discouraged with them I came straight home instead of investigating the other colonies. In London, however, I had such good reports of the climate and land in North Carolina I resolved to try again. So here I am."

At this moment Jamie appeared, leading Katie with a tray. Counting on something for himself, he had had her bring several cups. The two men paused while Katie poured and distributed the tea and passed the hard biscuit.

In the interval Allan had got his questions ready. "For climate there's a clear difference, I agree. But—

except there are more Scots in North Carolina—
what's the difference in the spirit of the two colonies?
Can you tell me something of that? I don't rightly understand why the people of Massachusetts are so
mightily discontented. Is it a serious thing?"

A tea-cup seemed to Allan to bring out all the foppishness in Blair. He took a judicious sip, holding his
cup affectedly. "Excellent tea," he declared, after he
had savoured it, raised his eyebrows and nodded. "To
answer your Massachusetts question first, the government has seen fit to make the colony pay some part of
the cost of the late war against the French. It has
therefore established certain taxes. These they claim
are unjust in principle. Since they have no representative in Parliament to vote taxes, they are pleased to
say they're taxed without representation, which they
call tyranny. With forests stretching down to the harbours in several ports, they're prodigious shipbuilders
and sailors. They'd trade with the world, at the expense
of merchants at home in England who expect to enrich
themselves through the produce of the colonies. At
the least curb these Boston merchants and ship-own-
ers are up in arms. Even His Majesty's troops in the
town don't prevent the free expression of their resentment against the smallest check. There have been
serious disorders already, and there may be real trouble within a year or two."

"Is there none loyal to the King, then?" asked Allan.

"Oh, many," Blair replied. "But the loyal men are
cowed and outnumbered. In Carolina the balance
swings the other way, at least according to a letter
from Governor Martin which was published recently
in London. Though some merchants and shipping
men, and some planters, incline the way of Boston,
the majority are loyal to the Crown and feel no great
injustice in a fair tax, most of which is spent for the
welfare of the colony. No doubt we'll encounter some
hotheads, but in the main, I'm told, we loyal men
shall do very well in Carolina. That's why I plan to
settle there and buy land."

"I'm glad to hear you say so, sir," Allan replied. "I

like a country steady. Where things are troubled, as the Highlands have been, with intriguing and night-riding and God knows what, a man's efforts go for nought. Only yesterday yon captain was hinting to me Carolina would be little better than Boston as you just now described it. It disturbed me. It's a relief you expect better things there than in the north."

Blair took his time about replying, and when he did he seemed to be choosing his words with care. "There are malcontents and hotheads in Carolina, too, but not so many. Governor Martin, according to report, is a fair man but a firm man. He'll stand little nonsense. There may be trouble there, but it will be short and the men of sense and loyalty will prevail."

Blair talked like a solid young man with a head on his shoulders, Allan decided. But could his words be trusted? Allan felt the man had not been open with him, though he could not say just why. Perhaps it was the queer mixture of fop and soldier. Till he learned better, he decided, he would keep any more talk to matters of no importance like food and drink and weather.

While Allan MacDonald was sharing his morning tea with James Blair, Dougald, Sandy and David were interesting themselves in making new and unusual acquaintances. Among the passengers was another boy, a little younger than they—sixteen or seventeen, they estimated—fair and blue-eyed but in some indefinable way recognizably foreign. He had come on deck as quickly as they, and he had shown the same eager interest in every step the sailors took in getting the ship under sail.

Dougald had even talked to him a little in the intervals when they were waiting for some new move on the part of the crew and happened to be standing together. He hadn't known quite what to say, and had finally been direct: "My name is Dougald MacDonald. What's yours?"

"It's Hungarian—easy to say but hard to spell. You say it John Auld-yo; you spell it A-u-l-d-j-o. The *j* is sounded like a y."

"Do you know," Dougald exclaimed, "my twin said you were foreign! I don't see how he knew. You are very fair and you speak fine English."

A slight change came over the lad's face at Dougald's words. "My mother is German. That accounts for my complexion. As for my speech, I've been four years at school in England and my tutor now is Scots." A puzzled smile curved his lips. "I can't understand the language most of your party speaks."

"Oh, they; well, they speak Gaelic, the ancient language of our people."

"But you?"

"Oh, I speak it, too, and English as well. Most of us speak both. But you must speak several languages."

"Yes. Magyar, of course, the language of the Hungarians, and German, and English, as you see, and also French fairly well, and a little Italian and Spanish. I can read Latin and I'm making some headway in Greek. But I like English. It is difficult at first, but when one begins to master it, it says so much."

Dougald had introduced him to the other boys at this point. Auldjo noted they were all MacDonalds. "You are brothers, yes?" he inquired.

"No, two pairs of brothers. David and I are twins. Sandy and Jamie are brothers, too, but our cousins. We are all MacDonalds, and bound together."

John Auldjo looked puzzled, then smiled. "Ah, I understand. It is the clan, which I have heard of. It is very interesting. You have a chief, and all the others are under him."

"Yes, but our chief is not with us. The father of Sandy and Jamie here, Allan MacDonald, will be the head of the MacDonalds on shipboard. He and his wife Flora."

"Ah, yes, yes. Of her I have heard many times. She is the lady who rescued Prince Charles many years ago, is she not? A heroine indeed!"

Dougald was inwardly delighted that even a foreigner knew about her, and could imagine how proud Flora's own sons were.

Auldjo went on, with a touch of shy formality: "I hope I may soon have the pleasure of meeting her. My tutor, Mr. Dee, has spoken to me often of her. I studied about the Jacobite risings of 1715 and 1745. It will make history come alive to speak with her."

"You're travelling with your tutor?"

"Yes, I am to see the world. We go now to America. But as I travel I must keep up my lessons. Mr. Dee is most particular about keeping up the lessons."

At this moment Mr. Dee appeared, a cold, buttoned-up man with no expression on his face. He was near-sighted and wore spectacles on his thin nose. He seemed quite unaware of the bustle and excitement of the sailing. "Time for lessons, Master John," he announced firmly.

To the active, vigorous MacDonald boys the morning of sailing was no time for lessons, and a man like Robin Dee was incomprehensible. Lessons! Tutor! Who'd want to bother with such things? Yet John Auldjo gave them a polite word of parting and followed Dee to the cabin without a single protest. With sailors moving about on the yards, high above the deck, astounding!

Alex MacLeod had his man rearranging his things compactly so he could lay his hand on what he wanted in the course of the journey. Since he was sharing the great cabin with at least ten men and their servants, some of whom might be rascals for all he knew, he was entrusting his money and valuables to his wife. She could tuck them away safely in the private cabin she shared with Flora. But he didn't want even his clothes lying about where they might be lost or walked on by anyone.

At the far side of the cabin another passenger seemed to be doing much the same thing. A shortish, middle-aged man he was, dressed in quiet colours but wearing a clubbed wig—the kind of fellow you'd never notice twice. In every way he was ordinary and undistinguished; it seemed to Alex there was nothing about him to attract interest or attention.

But since they were engaged in the same task, Alex

considered it mere politeness to toss an occasional remark across the room—about the difficulty of stowing
things without shelves to put them on, about the easy
motion of the ship, about the lack of privacy they
would have to put up with. Alex was still uninterest-
ed, but found himself giving his name and discovering that the other man's was Henry Holseman. It
wasn't a conversation exactly—just a remark tossed
across the cabin and a minute or two later another
remark tossed back.

They were this much acquainted when Dee came
in with the boy, John Auldjo, and retired to a quiet
corner with a book. When Alex threw a sentence
across to Holseman, he noticed Dee glanced up as if
in protest at the disturbance. The first time Alex was
not sure, but the next time he called out there was no
mistaking Dee's look of injury. Evidently talk irritated
him. To amuse himself Alex decided he would give
Dee some reason to feel injured.

"If you've no objection to telling about yourself,
Mr. Holseman, I'm wondering why you are going to
North Carolina. You don't look like a man who'd be-
come a planter."

Holseman had been on his knees, fitting boxes
neatly under his berth. Now he stood up, gathering
his thoughts. "You're right that I've no ambition to
be a planter. I'm a merchant. I believe there's much
money to be made in the southern colonies and in the
West Indies by a smart man. I've several schemes in
mind. These I naturally prefer to keep to myself, for
reasons you can well imagine.

"You see my affairs are very simple," he said easily. "Now I find it much more difficult to fathom why
gentlemen such as you and—is it your wife's father?—
Mr. MacDonald should be going. Didn't you mention
a few minutes ago that you have come from Dunvegan
Castle? A famous place, known all over Europe. Now
why should men like you be going to take up a planter's
life in a raw colony?"

Alex answered frankly. "I'm a practical man, Mr.
Holseman. True, I have been living at Dunvegan Castle, and it is a fine place. But it isn't mine and won't

be; I'm not the heir. True, also, I wouldn't starve if I stayed on there. But the land is poor. There's no money about, and little opportunity for a practical man. There's precious little for me, and there will be less for my children." Alex thought of Anne and the child she was bearing. He went on hopefully, "I want to pass on a good living to my sons. The lands in Carolina, I hear, are rich and yield well even with lazy farming—as much of it is, I've been told. With our Scots industry and careful management I look to become a rich man."

Holseman considered the answer for a moment, then asked, "But the other, he's an older man. Should already be settled."

"Allan MacDonald is a man of more feeling. It pains him to be between the landlord and the small tenants. One of his cousins has evicted some six hundred tenants. Their potato crops have been failures. They're near starvation. It wrings Allan's heart. He won't play the landlord's game, and, since he won't, nearly every year lately he's shown a loss." Alex paused for a moment and shook his head. "We're just dwindling away in the western isles. We must break it off and find a new world we can turn to our purpose."

As he finished, Alex glanced over to the corner where Mr. Dee sat with the boy, and remembered why he had begun the discussion. With a feeling of scoring on an opponent, he noticed that they had given up the effort to continue with a lesson and each had his nose buried in a great book.

The two men relapsed into silence and went on with their tasks. MacLeod was nearly finished when Allan and James Blair entered the cabin, and almost at the same time Cecily Weston and her cabin-mate issued from their private cubicle.

Cecily politely presented the gentlemen to Madame Rachel la Fabrère. Alex could not help studying her. She was beautiful and no mistake. Her hair was so blond it shone like silver and her skin was as fair as a baby's, with a faint pink blush just under the surface. Skin and hair set off her sparkling eyes and made them seem even brighter blue, made the red of her lips more vivid. Every movement of her tall, lithe body showed an almost exaggerated grace.

She'll make a rare stir among the bachelors, Alex told himself wryly. A man could find a good friend in Cecily, but this Madame la Fabrère was no such creature. She'd want all the men strutting for her. Even young Sandy MacDonald might feel his pulses pounding in her presence. And she'd not be above amusing herself with the lad in an odd moment if no bigger game was at hand.

As the group shifted about, Alex found himself between Holseman and Blair. Holseman leaned across him and whispered to Blair, "A French countess, I'll wager four to one."

"Taken for ten guineas," Blair drawled. "No, Holseman, I won't take advantage of you. I've known the lady."

"Who is she?"

"She's English as Devon cream, though she has picked up a bit of an accent from living on the continent. She married a Frenchman—I suppose she married him; at least she took his name. He was alive the last time I heard, though of course she may be a widow now."

"Why on earth should she be going to the colonies, and travelling alone?" Alex asked. "It's strange."

"Only two possibilities cross my mind," Blair said. "One is of course a man. She is a woman of ... comprehensive affections. Then her husband is a man of many interests and many intrigues. He has strange acquaintances, highly placed and infinitely disreputable. He may be spinning some plot that calls for an agent in the colonies. If she is acting as his agent she'll soon seek Philadelphia or New York, the money centres."

"In the meantime Madame la Fabrère should enliven our voyage," Holseman murmured. "She's pretty enough."

Outside, Alex could hear orders shouted, men moving about, cordage creaking. The motion of the ship, which had been small, for the sea was quiet, changed from a slight pitch to a roll. The *Baliol* had evidently

altered course and come about. They must have rounded the southern point of Kintyre and set a course
westward just clearing the topmost points of Ireland.

As the ship settled on its new way Cecily Weston
seemed to come to a decision. She went over to Allan
and asked him where Flora was. "I must talk to her at
once," she said.

Flora was nervously pacing the deck in the open
space just forward of the poop. As Cecily fell into
step with her, Flora seized her arm and confided,
"I'm fair beside myself thinking what to do about
Moira. I promised Molly MacQueen I'd care for the
girl. How can I do that when she is shut away down
in the steerage? I don't like her being there. What can
I do? The captain refused again this morning to let her
out."

"That's what I came out to talk about, Flora. I
want to help her. Besides, I have a practical reason
for wanting Moira with me. You know my maid
Martha. She's a good soul and something of a
chaperon for me, travelling without family as I am.
But on a ship, even in calm weather like this, she isn't
going to be a particle of use. Quite the contrary. After
her *embrouillement* with La Fabrère last night I decided I can't bear to have her with us in our tiny
cabin. Furthermore, she'd love to be down with the
gillies' wives. She's made friends with some and will
be forever running down to gossip. I might as well
put her there at once."

Flora looked as if she couldn't imagine what all this
had to do with Moira. Cecily came to the point.
"Couldn't I take Moira in with me? So far as the rest
of the passengers are concerned she would seem to be
my new maid, but between ourselves I'd treat her as a
friend, a very young friend. There need be no hurt to
her pride. If there is anything to arrange with the captain, I'll take the responsibility for it. What do you
think?"

Flora halted and turned toward Cecily; her face
had brightened and her shoulders straightened as if
she had thrown off a physical weight. "The very

thing!" she cried. "As for her pride—you're referring to what I said at Monkstadt. Now I well know Moira's a sensible girl, and will be happy for the arrangement. But keep her as much as you can away from that La Fabrère woman, for I'm sure she's no good influence. Let's be about it. Certainly the captain can take off his precious hatches by this time and let those poor people out to breathe a bit of air."

Resolutely they climbed to the poop. As they gained the level deck they paused momentarily to look around. Quite close on the right—Cecily was no good at estimating distances—the shore of Kintyre stood sharp and clear in the sunlight. Scotland was still with them, but ahead stretched a great, empty expanse of sea.

Lounging with their elbows on the rail stood the captain and James Blair, talking quietly—almost intimately, it seemed to Cecily. As the ladies appeared the two men paused in surprise and stood erect. Blair sketched a slight bow.

Flora stepped forward and addressed the captain. "Last night and again this morning I asked to see Moira MacQueen, who is travelling under my protection. Each time you told me you could not open the hatches to the steerage for fear of meddling by the soldiers." Her voice rose in indignation. "Look about you. There are no soldiers here. Take off your hatches. Let my poor people out to have comfort in this good sun and fresh breeze."

Cecily was surprised by Flora's assumption of authority, by the power of her personality. And most of all she was surprised by the captain's deference and acquiescence; he was agreeing that it was time to open the hatches, offering to go and attend to it personally.

At the risk of spoiling his mood, she drew him aside. "One moment, Captain, before we go down." She explained about Martha, her bulk and her uselessness at sea, about her desire to have Moira with her as a maid on the voyage. "I came to know the girl at Lady Margaret MacDonald's home. She'll suit me admirably. Now if this makes some small difference in her passage money, I'll render myself responsible for it. If you'll just step aside with me I'll be happy to adjust it now."

With alacrity he led her to a more sheltered spot and money changed hands. Between us—Flora's personality and my money, Cecily reflected ironically—we two ladies have subjugated him.

When they rejoined the others, Blair drew out his snuff-box. "I shall accompany you, if you have no objection, and be a spectator of the little ceremony of removing your hatches. The young lady I shall doubtless see in attendance on Miss Weston, but it may be edifying to observe these others you have penned below, Captain. Yes, an edifying though perhaps malodorous experience." He took a delicate pinch of snuff.

Cecily's disgust rose until she could almost taste it in her mouth. She could not avoid rich fops like Blair, creation of their tailors and dancing masters, even on an English vessel. "As you like," she answered him. "However, if your senses are so squeamish you'll do well to fortify yourself with perfume as well as snuff. It would be an act of double benevolence. Your sweet-smelling person would regale the women and show the men to what heights of delicacy the English gentleman has risen."

Blair flushed and bit his lip, but made no answer. In silence the four descended to the main deck. The captain summoned a sailor and ordered him to remove the hatch cover. When it was laid aside, they all stepped up to the coaming and peered into the steerage below.

A wave of warm, stale air came up at them and, undeniably, smells—a *mélange*, in fact, of all the smells people and their possessions give off in a confined space. Cecily felt her own nostrils involuntarily draw in. She stole a quick glance at Blair. His impassive face gave no sign of distaste. Daylight from the open hatch extended only part way into the dim space below. Two smoky lanthorns did little more than give the gloom a yellowish cast. Soon Cecily's eyes adjusted and she could make out the scene below. Some of the figures, having noticed that the hatch was open, were groping toward the ladder that led up to the deck. A few were busy at some task, caring for a baby or tidying themselves. But most were apathetic, sitting on the floor with their backs against a wall or lying on a pallet. In the deceptive dimness they seemed very closely packed and crowded.

The captain climbed half-way down the ladder and in stentorian tones called out his permission for them to come on deck and take the air. He warned not to crowd at the ladder.

As he regained the deck Flora turned on him with her eyes flashing with indignation. "It's a sin, Captain, to put people in such a dark, stinking, airless hole—worse still, charge them silver for the privilege of being packed in like sheep. You should be ashamed!"

This time the captain knew his ground and replied with spirit. "You're wrong, mistress. I command a smart ship. That steerage was clean and fresh when your people went in. What they do to it is on their own heads. I warrant there'll be a reek when we run into some weather and three out of four of them are sick. But that's unavoidable. As for crowding—well, I've just above a hundred here; many a master would take on above a hundred and fifty. I insist I'm a humane man; any discomfort they suffer is due to nature, madam, and can't be laid at my door."

The emigrants were coming up in a stream, some of the men carrying babies or helping their women negotiate the ladder. They spread into every available open place about the decks. Many of them rushed to starboard to feast their eyes on the receding shores of Scotland. On their faces Cecily could see the first, and worst, shock of the voyage. They had been uprooted from all they knew and loved, gone through the tearing business of saying farewell, started off into the unknown, been pushed below and shut up in a dark, airless hole. If their condition kept on getting worse at this rate they had nothing to face but despair. Some of them were crying as they looked back at Scotland. Some just looked numb and stunned.

Telling Cecily to watch for Moira, Flora moved off

among them, speaking an encouraging word to each one, giving comfort where she could.

Blair at Cecily's elbow was taking snuff again. "An instructive spectacle," he said lightly. "Scotland's loss is not mortal. I question Carolina's gain. Mrs. MacDonald's allusion to penning them like sheep seems most apt, though perhaps 'like hogs' would be the truer simile."

"Mr. Blair," Cecily said in cold, furious tones, "I've travelled to the north and know these people. Uneducated, yes; ignorant and easily imposed on, yes; but they are men with manly courage. You see them here half beaten down, bewildered. They do not touch your heart. That speaks ill of your heart. It pleases you to liken them to animals—like animals driven to the slaughter perhaps. In every other way they are human beings, better human beings than many people of fashion in London."

"I mentioned, I believe, that I had been much in London of late years," said Blair with a thin smile.

Cecily said pointedly, "I recall you did."

He smiled charmingly. "I must take it as a compliment that you remember my history. By the by, I believe I know your kin in London quite well. The family of the Duke of Bedford, is it not?"

"That part of my family, sir, I have left behind. I am travelling alone to visit my Scots kin in America." Her voice was cool. She had about her an aspect of remote dignity that could not be gainsaid.

Blair bowed mockingly. "I shall remember, Miss Weston. You are an adventurous lady on your solitary travels."

Cecily did not bother to answer. She had spied Moira at the foot of the ladder. "Get your bundles, child. You're coming to live with me in more suitable quarters."

Moira hurried away and was back instantly with her arms full. Blair had the grace to go down and relieve her of her burden and help her up the ladder. Half frightened by her night's experience, half delighted by the prospect ahead, she scarcely knew whether to laugh or cry. Cecily hurried her away.

10

Stormy Seas

IT WAS almost noon on the third day out. On the high poop the captain paced back and forth, unconsciously adapting his steps to the easy roll of the ship as she met the slow, steady swell. A thin sunshine came directly down on the *Baliol* sailing at the exact centre of an empty circle of ocean. The captain was only taking the air, for it was the second mate's watch and all was going smoothly. A capable man, the captain thought. Hands in pockets, the mate was studying the taut topsails, and the captain expected him any minute to order hands aloft to trim them for the seventh time, with a view to improving perfection. He'd not shake any more speed out of the *Baliol*, but the captain liked his mates to be brisk seamen.

The captain stepped forward and looked down on the main deck. Every available open space was filled with his emigrants taking advantage of the sun. They were settling in, it seemed to him. Some of them looked almost cheerful, with the good weather and the easy sea. They had been a despondent lot on the first afternoon, with Scotland sinking below the horizon astern and Ireland low down to port. He remembered one woman in particular; tears streaming down her face, she'd called out to her husband, "Och, I never knew it would be like this! Duncan, take me back. I canna stand to go so far from home." Experienced seafarer that he was, the captain had little patience with her wailing.

One woman had been sick—not seasick, some kind of cough. A sailor had tried to hearten her by telling her the open sea would cure her. "Ocean winds are wonderful healing for coughs, ma'am," he kept insist-

ing. He told her fine tales about men half dead of
consumption who had gone ashore at the end of a
voyage strong and healthy. The captain hadn't noticed that she benefited much from the man's encouragement. He had examined her himself to see she had
nothing catching. To his mind it was only an asthma
aggravated by the close air all night in the steerage.

Some of the men were as mournful as the women.
They had rocked and groaned as if in torment. Partly
they were sad at leaving their friends and homes, and
partly they were frightened by the great change, the
unfamiliar ship, the confined quarters in the steerage,
the orders from strangers such as himself. They had
had no experience of the ocean beyond a small boat
on the Minch and he supposed this voyage was a
fearsome thing to them. Yes, they'd been a sad lot
that day.

And Sunday had been as bad. They had wanted
kirk as usual, and the minister, McKeogh, had prayed
and preached to them. He was a dour man and no
mistake. For Christian comfort he had given them
hell-fire and damnation and souls in peril on the
deep. The captain's lips curved in a sardonic smile.
McKeogh's congregation had already had their imagi-
nations well freighted with the terrors of the sea, but
the old doctor had not scrupled to load on more. After an hour's exhortation they were carrying such a
weight of apprehension they could scarce stand.

McKeogh had particularly dwelt on the uncertainty
of life. The captain chuckled to remember how the
old minister had referred to the sturdy *Baliol* as a
cockle-shell, a frail peascod that alone stood between
them and the drowning in cold water. Below the chill
sea-water, through which they might well pass, he'd
said, there awaited an eternity of fire and brimstone.
'Twas enough to make a man look to his ship's caulk-
ing, the captain reflected.

The gillies had broken out in a cold sweat, and the
captain didn't much blame them. The dominie had
gone on to paint a grizzly picture of the new land
awaiting them: no man could know what dangers hovered there for them; all men had best commit them-

selves to God's mercy. One woman was so terrified by the prospects of America that she tried to jump overboard. Less than twenty minutes after the sermon ended, she had given a great cry and, with her baby in her arms, had scuttled for the bulwarks. None of the sailors had been close by. Fortunately her loud wail had brought young David and Sandy MacDonald at a run. When she was half over the bulwark they had seized her around the middle and pulled her back. The captain thought sure she'd let the bairn slip, but the boys had saved all.

Dragged back to the deck, she had sat blubbering and clutching the baby while young David patted her shoulder and tried to soothe her and Sandy went to fetch her husband.

The ship had sailed sweetly on Sunday, but there had been storms on the deck. People, the captain reflected, were as unpredictable as squalls, and if a man carried passengers he could look for unexpected gales to blow up out of calm sunshine.

By now, though, they were shaking down for the voyage. The mates had the ship trim and orderly. The passengers were getting their sea legs. Groups of them were learning to prepare their food in the galley. They had their gear stowed as well as they could, and the steerage aired out and clean. Each one knew where his place was below. Of course they were still landsmen, he reminded himself, and if the ship ran into a gale they would go to pieces again. Maybe his cabin passengers wouldn't be much better in a pinch. Some of them might be. Miss Weston was the niece of an admiral and there was a self-possession about her that made him think she'd keep her head. But that Madame la Fabrère would be a caution. Unconsciously he smacked his lips. His mind drifted off in imaginative contemplation of smooth, softly pink skin covering smooth, curving female flesh. Caution or not, she was a beauty to set a man dreaming.

Shouted orders brought him back to the ship. He grinned. The mate had the hands going aloft to trim topsails again.

The next morning dawned sullen red. A thin haze, very high, veiled the eastern sky. James Blair stepped out on deck and sniffed the air doubtfully. He climbed to the poop where he found the captain talking to the mate. They moved so as to make a place for him but did not interrupt their earnest conversation, which, as he had anticipated, concerned the signs of weather ahead, and not far ahead.

The captain pointed off the starboard bow to the west, where a solid army of black cloud, still low on the horizon, was implacably advancing, led by dark, swirling streamers of cloud. Less distant but still far off, an occasional swift flash as a whitecap caught the sullen light coming through the haze above showed that flaws of wind were scouting out in front of the cloud. As Blair took in the whole prospect he shivered. "How's the glass?" he asked.

"Dropping fast," the mate answered.

The captain shrugged impatiently. "We'll get wind, no question of it. Let's be making our preparations for it. There's no more than enough time." He turned to the mate. "Get your hands aloft and shorten sail. Batten down the hatches. Put up dead-lights on the cabin windows. Double-lash the boats on the deck-house. And first off, warn the emigrants in the steerage to cook porridge ahead. We'll have no fire in the galley after the wind strikes. Be about it, man. I want those topsails furled as quick as you can take them in. Take in your jib and bend on a storm jib. While you're at it, put a double reef in the mainsail, but leave that till the last." The mate hurried off, shouting orders as he went.

Blair watched the mate go into action, and his expression was unhappy. "From those orders, Captain, I presume you are expecting a real gale?"

"The glass promises a severe one, Mr. Blair. From the looks of that cloud bank it should strike us in about two hours' time."

"Damme!" Blair exclaimed. "It never fails that as soon as I go a-voyaging we have a storm and I am most ingloriously sea-sick."

"Come, come, Mr. Blair, a military man like you

discommoded by a bit of rough sea? It's not fitting, sir."

"Now, Captain, as I've several times explained, I'm on my way to Carolina to look out a plantation for myself. What's martial in this?"

"Don't try to deceive me, Mr. Blair. Behind the somewhat ill-acted foppishness you have put on as a mask I can see the uniform in everything you do. You may have resigned your commission, but I dare swear you have been an officer in your time."

Blair laughed easily. "So you have found me out? I'll confess you are right about my past. I was with Gentleman Johnny Burgoyne in '62 at the capture of Valentia d'Alcantara. I've been well into the American wilderness and in some apprehension of meeting a large party of hostile Indians. Yes, I've encountered most of the hardships a military man comes to expect. In the ordinary way of things I'd make bold to say I've met them with reasonable equanimity and occasionally even with enjoyment—on land.

"You'll note, Captain, that what valour I have operates on land," Blair continued ruefully. "My stomach, there is no gainsaying, is no sailor at all. It resents being taken to sea and mutinies most infamously. I must have made upward of a dozen voyages, and on each one, resolve as I will to control it, at the first sign of wind my stomach rebels and turns upside down if not inside out. I'll wager that in two hours it will make me heartily wish I were dead. But in my then state I'll lack the manhood even to finish myself off. By nightfall you'll find me a shell of a man, a very empty shell. Where there's no help a man must endure. And so I will, but in my bunk."

The captain laughed. "A lugubrious prospect you face. I thought I'd guessed right about your military bearing, but until just now I had no confirmation. So you were in Portugal in '62? Do you still hold the King's commission?"

"Yes, Captain," Blair said less affectedly. "I'm a major with an errand or two in Carolina. I don't mind your knowing, though I'd as soon some of your passengers did not guess it. I've acted the dandy only to put them off. You were acute to see through my little ruse. I hope my acting was more successful with the others. From the sharp words Miss Weston gave me I dare swear I have deceived her at least—and fallen in her estimation as a consequence, I regret to say. But enough of this. You must see to your ship, and I—I really will be sick."

Cecily Weston was a little surprised to find herself stimulated rather than frightened by the impending storm. She had confidence in the ship and its master, and she knew her uncle had come through scores of storms as threatening. The wall of cloud, she noticed as she peered out the cabin window, was close now, seeming almost over the ship. The queer greenish-yellow light seemed both dark and glaring at the same time. Every little while a fierce flaw of wind would catch the edge of a sail, shake it and make it crack like a pistol. The noise came into the cabin undiminished.

The regular swells had given way to confused hummocks of water colliding glancingly and throwing plumes of spray. Under Cecily's feet the ship plunged and bucked like a nervous horse. Though the uneasy motion did not affect her, Cecily could see that Moira was not so good a sailor. Unless the girl lay down at once she would soon be deathly sick. She made Moira take her own berth and did what she could to render her comfortable, then left her to rest.

She found most of the cabin passengers gathered in the great cabin and looking as if they were waiting for something unpleasant. Dougald MacDonald wore an anxious frown and came up to her at once to ask about Moira. As soon as he heard about her sea-sickness, he wanted to rush to the cabin. Cecily restrained him—she really couldn't permit him to visit the girl in her room—by assuring him Moira would be more comfortable alone. And that's probably true, Cecily thought, remembering the private and ugly nature of sea-sickness.

Dougald, she was glad to see, soon joined the other MacDonald lads. They were exhilarated by the crash

of the waves and the howl of the wind, and Dougald
caught their excitement. Together the four of them—
Sandy, David, Dougald and bright-eyed Jamie—slipped
out on deck. Soon they rushed back to report on
the sailors' precautions. One man, they said, was even
tying down the poultry crates in the longboat on top
of the deck-house. Could the seas reach so high?
Rachel la Fabrère moved a little closer to Holseman.
Her complexion was no longer rosy-pink but milk-white.
Blair, although Cecily did not think he looked frightened, was certainly beginning to be sea-sick. Anne
and Alex MacLeod, sitting together with clasped
hands, also seemed to be fighting sea-sickness.

Just then a sailor came in and hung a lighted lanthorn from a hook fixed in the low cabin roof. Other
sailors began to cover the cabin windows with strong
wooden shutters—dead-lights they called them. The
cabin was soon walled in solidly against the storm,
with no light except the feeble lanthorn. Robin Dee
had been ignoring what was going on about him. He
was sitting impassively in a corner, his glasses gleaming blankly astride his thin nose, no expression on his
face, a heavy book with a Latin title on his knee.
Only when the dead-lights left him almost in darkness
did he close his book and look about him in annoyance.

The boys entered again, and shut the door carefully behind them. The storm was close on their heels.
In less than a minute Cecily heard a roar of wind, a
rush of water, a groaning of timbers. The ship staggered and rolled down almost on her side, lay on her
beam-ends for agonizing seconds. A box, not wedged
securely under a berth on the windward side, came
sliding down the inclined cabin floor, hit an obstruc-
tion, tipped over, came open and spewed its contents almost at Cecily's feet. The lanthorn swung,
throwing crazy shadows. Then, staggering and shuddering, the ship rallied and rolled back. The cabin
floor levelled, the swinging lanthorn hung almost
straight down, still swaying. It would be so much
easier, thought Cecily, if we could only see out!

The *Baliol* pitched and rolled like a mad thing. It

was almost impossible to stand. She saw Blair, sitting on the edge of his berth, grab a can and be miserably sick. At last he subsided full length on the berth, spent and helpless. Outside she could hear great waves come crashing on the deck, then, as the ship shook them off, the seething sound as the water poured out through the scuppers. Blair fell out of his berth as the ship rolled. David and Sandy, picking their time, helped him back. Anne and Alex Mac-Leod were both sick. A sour-sweet odour permeated the cabin.

The ship shuddered as a great wave engulfed the decks. There was no noise of spray, for the solid green water came aboard with tremendous impact. Almost at the same instant the cabin door burst open. Cecily caught a brief glimpse of tumbling seas in a drab gray light. A knee-high wall of water was pouring in over the high door-sill and spreading inches deep over the cabin floor. All the passengers were as if frozen. Cecily found herself doing something that even then amused her. For all she knew, the cabin would fill full in an instant and drown her like a rat in a trap. In that moment on the edge of eternity she swung her feet up into the berth she had been sitting on, so as to keep her shoes dry!

A sudden roll of the ship flung the door back around and the weight of the water slammed it shut. Several of the men leaped up and barred the door securely, for the latch was broken. Water swished back and forth across the drenched cabin floor. Outside the storm pounded on.

Old Neil was puttering around with some boxes he had prepared before the storm struck. Finally he produced a bottle of wine, some cheese and biscuit. Only Cecily and the boys and young John Auldjo had the courage to sample his fare.

Flora MacDonald lay in her berth, with Allan at her side, holding her hand. The violent motion as the storm struck had made her sea-sick, but after a single paroxysm she had felt relieved. She felt limp and empty and the pitching and rolling of the ship made it hard for her to stay in the narrow berth, but the extreme wretchedness that reduces the victim of seasickness to despair had passed. Allan's strong arm steadying her when a sudden toss of the ship threatened to throw her off her berth gave her a sense of being cared for and protected, a luxurious feeling she had seldom had time for in her busy Kingsburgh existence. No duty called her. She could lie like this as long as she liked, savouring the feeling of security, of unhurried leisure.

She squeezed Allan's hand and smiled at him. "It's a foolish thing, but I'm taking pleasure in this great storm." She spoke reflectively, tenderly. "Though the ship may be close to danger, I feel your arm warding off all harm, your strength cradling me, Allan, and I feel light as a girl and lie easy. At home someone always had need of me. Night and day I was called to be doing for somebody who was in want of help. I was like a bow always strung tight, and many a day I had no time to be a weak woman and find relief in leaning on your arm. Sometimes—and I don't think it was pride to blame but only the habit of doing myself what I saw to do—maybe I almost forgot your arm was there for me to lean on. And my comfort this minute reminds me the loss was mine."

"Flora, my love, it's always been my first desire to shield you and keep you." Allan leaned down and she felt his lips tender on her cheek. His voice as he went on was half embarrassed by his sincerity, half rueful. "But I'm awkward and always behindhand. A thousand times it's been in my mind to take burdens off you—as you said, to give you my arm to lean on. And while the thought took shape, you—you were like quicksilver. Before I could so much as stretch out my hand, you were off doing for yourself and others what I would have been proud and glad to do for you." He sighed deeply. "Ah, your speed was my admiration and my despair. A thousand times I've lagged behind my desire."

"I'm taking strength from your arm now, Allan. I'll not run before you in this narrow cabin."

"Nay. And it's a joy to have you here with me playing the weak woman."

"Not playing, Allan. At heart I always was. It was only pity or duty that kept me always stirring. I had no desire to do it." Flora sat up, still leaning on his shoulder. "I tell you true I am glad to be on this ship, even in this storm, crossing the sea to a new land. For I'll learn new ways. I'll not run off ahead. I've loved no one but you, and you've loved me, but too much I've missed some part of the good of it through my ... quicksilver ways. I'll wait for the feel of your arm at my waist."

Allan pressed her hand tightly. "Now that I am free from all my ill luck back there, perhaps I——"

"Och, Allan, in the American forests, you'll be my oak tree and I'll shelter under your branches." She laughed. "Here we are past fifty and planning and talking like a lad and a lass." She sobered and gave him a long, clear look straight in the eyes. "You're a good man and a strong man, Allan MacDonald, and you have my love."

She leaned toward him and their lips met in a long kiss of love and understanding.

It seemed only a minute later that she was asleep, cradled against his arm. They had forgotten the angry sea.

James Blair lay in his berth. The curtains were drawn so that he could see out into the cabin only through a narrow slit. With the dead-lights shutting off the windows and only the yellow light of the lanthorn, he didn't know whether it was night or day. He must have been asleep, but he had no idea for how long. Probably for some time. The noise of the storm had lessened and the ship's action had eased. He felt better, too, though very weak and empty. The storm must be almost over, he thought.

Suddenly curious, he reached out a hand and twitched aside the curtain. Near by were Dougald MacDonald and John Auldjo. "What time is it?" he asked.

"Between four and five in the afternoon, sir," Auldjo told him.

Something still eluded him. He shook his head impatiently. "What day of the week?"

Polite as always, Auldjo was plainly puzzled by the question. "Thursday, sir. Are you all right? Is there anything we can do for you?"

"Quite all right, thank you." Blair rolled on his back, staring at the ceiling, and tried to link himself with the present. He must have been sick most of Tuesday, all of Wednesday and the best part of today. He remembered falling out of his berth. People had come to help him. Once, when the rolling had been particularly bad, old Neil, the twins' servant, had tied him in his berth to save him another fall. When he had been helplessly retching, sometimes one of them had held his head. He remembered Neil bending over him and, less clearly, several others—Robin Dee, Holseman, David, even Cecily Weston, who didn't like him. He rather thought Rachel had been there too.

Well, he'd never recapture it all; he had been too ill. He relaxed and eavesdropped on the boys.

Dougald was explaining that with the farming and peat-cutting and learning the use of weapons and hunting he'd had but little time for reading. And that little time, coming toward evening, when he was sleepy after a day in the open, he had often devoted to a nap instead.

"But, Dougald, you were part of a knight's household. Why were you so interested in sports and weapons and developing your muscles?" Auldjo asked. He sounded genuinely puzzled.

"We Scots—" Blair heard an oratorical note in Dougald's voice—"take pride in our strength and endurance. It's by exercise we acquire them."

"My father has often impressed it on me," said Auldjo, "that a man with a supple and well-taught brain can always get a thousand or ten thousand men with strong backs to do the fighting and the working for him. That's why he makes me study not only books but the world and mankind.

"Mr. Dee, my tutor, likes the early Christian fathers and Plato for philosophy, Euclid and others for mathematics, Montaigne, Racine and Shakespeare for human nature, and perhaps Descartes for system. Some of them write beautifully. My father says they are well enough but they are not practical. He says 'Go to Suetonius' *Lives of the Caesars* for human nature and Machiavelli for practical training.'"

"What is this Mach ... Machiavelli?"

"He was an Italian who wrote a treatise on how to rule, a book called *The Prince*. Its only aim is power; it has no ideal. The idea is for a cold man to take advantages of all the hot men's feelings, their loyalty and patriotism and their greed and lusts equally. He will be generous or cruel, lie or tell the truth as his interest directs. In the end, the book says, he will be the master of all the hot men who let their feelings guide them." Auldjo laughed. "My father wants me to learn to rule on Machiavelli's model. My father is in most ways a cold man but I think his ambition for me is a feeling and as such his principle would not approve it. It may be a chink in his armour."

Blair was lazily amused by young Auldjo's application of the doctrine to his own father. The whole theory will be a dash of cold water in innocent Dougald's face, he thought.

The trouble in Dougald's voice as he answered told Blair he was right. "Have there been such rulers? Do they not think of God?"

"In my study of history I have come on scores of them," Auldjo told him. "They care for themselves, not for other men or for God. But—how shall I say?—they spin a difficult web and many catch themselves in its toils in the end. Not all—and this hope of escaping draws men always to the philosophy." Auldjo paused, then returned to the original topic. "It is surely true a man of mind is served by many men of muscle. Oh, study teaches many things!"

The lads' talk started Blair on his own reflections. His mind turned to the plot and counterplot coming to a head on the American continent. There were enough hot men of feeling there, and cool men spinning webs, too. He had his own part in webs. It suddenly occurred to him that he had given no thought to his part for three days. Well, no matter. With the storm occupying all thoughts, there had been no risk. . . . Or had there?

He got cautiously to his feet. Though he swayed with weakness, he drew out his keys and then reached under his berth. Among the damp boxes and chests there he located a small chest. After fumbling with his keys he unlocked it and raised the lid. Manoeuvring so that the still-drawn curtains of his berth partially screened him, he drew out a small metal dispatch case and slipped it under the blanket in his berth. He closed the chest, without locking it, and slid it out of the way beneath the berth.

With some ostentation he yawned and stretched and climbed back into his berth. With the curtains adjusted to admit only a narrow band of light, he was ready. From a small pocket in his waistcoat he took a tiny, delicately made key and fitted it carefully into the lock of the dispatch box. As he turned the key, he realized with a sick feeling that anyone who had helped him in his sickness might have filched his keys, used them and put them back. Well, he'd know only by opening the box. Holding his breath, he lifted the lid; he sighed when he found a well-stuffed packet of oiled silk.

He spread the contents on the blanket, four or five notes covering money he had won at cards, half a dozen old letters and bills, a letter of introduction to Governor Martin, sealed, a letter of credit addressed to a Wilmington banker, likewise sealed, two more sealed letters. All these he gathered hastily and put back in the oiled-silk covering. There remained several packets each of a number of folded sheets, looking much alike.

He opened the first and held it to the light. It was headed "An Ingenious Method for the Curing of Tobacco." He tossed it aside. He opened the next and read, "The Plants and Crops Suitable to the Carolinas." He tossed it aside. As he opened the next his fingers trembled slightly. "The Economy of the Plantation." The fourth was about indigo and rice. He had picked up these notes from natural historians in London, partly out of curiosity.

Now he came to the last packet. He held his breath as he lifted an open sheet to the light. It was blank! Quickly he turned it over, shuffled through the other sheets. They were all blank. Here was a kettle of fish! Someone had stolen his packet and courteously left blank paper in payment for it.

Who? How? Blair could feel beads of sweat break out on his forehead. He lay flat and began to think with cold, furious concentration. The packet was addressed to Governor Martin in North Carolina. The information it contained was for loyalist use there. It had no value anywhere else and in perhaps six months it might be out of date and of little value even there. The colonial Whigs would give the shirts off their back to get it and destroy it. The Governor and the Tories would pay well to get it back.

The thief, then, fitted one of two categories. He might be a colonial secret agent, a Whig assigned to counter the activities of Major James Blair and at the moment very much the victor. Or he might be an opportunist adventurer, working alone and not in the pay of any faction, who had got wind of the packet and stolen it as a speculation. He would have to take it to Carolina in order to find a buyer. Once there, he would offer it to the highest bidder. Unless the packet had already been destroyed, it would stay on the ship and travel in someone's custody all the way to Wilmington. Blair had the rest of the voyage, he concluded, to track it down and recover it.

God help him if he failed! The packet was of the highest importance to Governor Martin in keeping the colony loyal. As for Blair, the Earl of Dartmouth himself had put it in his hands and ordered him to use all diligence in delivering it to Governor Martin. If it were lost, he might as well resign his commission and give up his career.

Whoever had stolen the packet must have had an informant in Dartmouth's office. He must have known Blair carried it. Everything about the operation indicated an opponent of some stature. Instinctively Blair rejected all the servants and lackeys. The emigrants were automatically ruled out; they had had no opportunity. The thief had to be an agent or adventurer . . . or adventuress.

The captain? He was a sharp fellow, and had easily detected Blair's military background, but could hardly be a colonial agent. Madame la Fabrère? That coquette with French veneer was certainly an adventuress. She'd not be above turning a dishonest dollar in international intrigue. Blair rather inclined to suspect her. Cecily Weston? She wasn't an adventuress but she might be an agent. He recalled she was a niece of Farquard Campbell, who had a checkered record at Cross Creek if he remembered his packet aright. He must keep an eye on her. Holseman? He frankly couldn't say. Off-hand, that sort of nondescript personality was not up to an exploit as touchy as this, but perhaps drabness was a disguise. Robin Dee? Who could tell what was going on behind that wooden face? Dee, too, would bear watching.

Blair was in a fever to be doing something to repair his loss. Anger against the thief, whoever he was, burned in him. A strong impulse urged him to confront the persons he suspected one by one and shake the truth out of them. Without thinking further he pushed himself to his feet. Sweat broke out on his forehead and his knees shook. The blasted sea-sickness had left him weak. Well, perhaps it was best so. Discretion had returned. He must wait, watch, lay some traps. Perhaps at the Azores, perhaps in the western Atlantic he would get an inkling of his enemy's identity. In the meantime he must lock up his box and give no sign that he knew the packet was gone. He must seem unperturbed. Let the thief think him a fool and a fop. By the ease with which I've been duped, Blair said bitterly to himself, I cannot judge myself anything else.

11

Fayal

DOUGALD MACDONALD and John Auldjo sprawled on
the poop deck. A light, steady breeze ruffled their
hair and tempered the sun. The slashing wind and
rain of the great storm now seemed unreal to the lads,
though the crew was busy about the decks and aloft
repairing the damage they had left in their wake.

The *Baliol* had a good Scots ruggedness, Dougald
thought. A day and a half before, when the weather
had first moderated enough for the passengers to venture on deck again, Dougald, in his inexperience, had
decided she was little better than a wreck. One of the
boats on the deck-house had been stove in, and three
crates of chickens smashed. At the height of the storm
the jib had split with a noise like a shot. In an instant
the heavy canvas had torn to ribbons, and the bulk of
it had gone flying off to leeward, the mate had told
him. A few shreds were still visible. It was just after
that, Dougald supposed, that the captain had tried a
fore-topsail to steady the ship. A great gust had splin-
tered the fore-topmast and brought it crashing down in
a confusion of rigging. The mate said they had had a
lively time chopping away the rigging with axes so as
to let it drop overboard. One swing of the broken
mast might have crushed a man like an egg. From the
broken latch on the cabin door to the jagged stump of
the foremast the ship had looked broken and hurt.

One gang of sailors was bending on a new white jib
with fresh cordage. A larger gang was rigging a stubby
jury spar to replace for the time being the broken
fore-topmast. Dougald was beginning to realize the
sturdy *Baliol* was at heart as strong as ever. All the
damage was on the surface.

The captain came over to the boys and was patient with their eager questions. "No, we'll not replace the fore-topmast now," he said. "We'll attach the jury mast to the stump of the old one until we make port in the Azores. See the two men at the cross-trees?" He pointed toward two sailors working at the top of the foremast. "They're preparing a socket. We'll raise the new spar bottom end up till the butt reaches the lower lip of that slanted socket. Then we'll rig a tackle from the main-topmast and pull the tip of the spar up till the butt slips into the socket, and finally make the spar fast to the old stump. It's a tricky task, turning the spar end for end if the ship's rolling at all. Watch it while we're turning it. You'll see the mate's a good man with a tackle."

The critical moment of the operation was at hand. The emigrants were moved out of harm's way. Sailors jumped to their stations on deck and aloft. Under the mate's direction the new spar was hoisted up, butt first. At the cross-trees four men busied themselves attaching the shrouds, with ample slack, and rigging a cradle of rope to keep the butt of the spar from slipping off the lip of the socket.

Dougald and Auldjo got to their feet and shaded their eyes against the sun's glare. Two groups of sailors each seized a rope attached to the tip of the spar and moved out to the bulwarks to keep the spar from swaying sidewise. Eight or ten men began to take in on the tackle rigged from the main-topmast. Slowly the tip of the spar came up as the sailors walked away with the rope.

The spar was level. The tip came higher. Suddenly the spar jerked and threatened to roll. "Steady!" roared the mate. The motion halted while he climbed the foremast and inspected the cradle. "Haul away slow," he ordered. Higher and higher came the tip, a little past forty-five degrees.

Dougald was puzzled. It seemed that if they lifted the spar any higher they would only drag it off the lip of the socket, for the pull from the main-topmast was on a slant. But he held back his questions. The mate was everywhere, superintending each move. Finally he was satisfied. "Pay out handsomely," he roared. "With a rush now!"

The tackle slackened. The spar teetered. Then with a sudden jerk its own weight and balance slipped it full into the socket, erect and quivering. The men at the cross-trees, who had prudently kept out of the way, jumped in to wedge the socket tight and make fast the bight of rope they had passed around the spar and the old stump.

The men on the deck gave a great shout as the new mast settled into place.

"Wonderful!" Dougald exclaimed. "I didn't see how they could finish it."

Auldjo rubbed his hands. "I thought that would be the way of it. This was an illustration of part of what I told you in the cabin, Dougald. Your strongest caber-thrower couldn't have lifted that spar an inch. A man who understands the laws of motion, using only a few pulleys and some rope, can easily place it where he wants it high overhead."

Dougald nodded soberly. "There's much in knowledge, mechanical or philosophical," he agreed.

According to the captain, the *Baliol* would sight the Azores in the morning. The evening air was soft and balmy and Blair, more dapper and ingratiating than ever since his inglorious bout with sea-sickness, had insisted you could smell the land. "I vow you can smell the flowers and the Fayal wine," he had told Cecily. "Come forward with me so as to be free from the reek of the ship, and I'll prove it to you."

Cecily had suspected that he invented the claim as an excuse to lead her forward to the bow of the ship, away from the others. Nonetheless, and though her distaste for his suave and fastidious manner had not lessened, she had accepted his proffered arm. As they strolled forward, she deliberately smiled more cordially than usual. She was eager to see something of the islands, and intended to obtain a satisfactory chaperon. Martha offered only dull companionship, and Moira was too young and pretty to be any protection at all. Cecily had covertly appraised Blair and decided he was the most presentable. And, she thought, it shouldn't be too difficult to make this ladies' man very willing.

When they reached the bow she left her hand on his sleeve while she raised her head to the light breeze and sniffed inquiringly, then again even more delicately. A light laugh escaped her. "I did you an injustice, Mr. Blair. I do positively smell the land."

"An injustice? Ah, I see: you thought my claim only a ruse to secure charming company for a stroll. I might have been guilty ... consider the temptation ... but, as you see, the breeze was really freighted with scent."

Cecily nodded and moved slowly to the rail. A silence fell between them. There was only the slow chunk and swish of the bow as the *Baliol* lazily shouldered through the light seas.

At last Blair came to lean nonchalantly beside Cecily. He looked at her admiringly, but when he spoke there was surprisingly little of the gallant in his voice and words. He asked about her uncle, Farquard Campbell, and about his business and political connections in Carolina. His questions revealed an unexpected knowledge of Carolina politics. Although Cecily could easily deal with the queries, she was puzzled and reluctant. As long as she had thought Blair no more than a macaroni it had been easy to ignore him or toy with him, as she pleased. Now an undercurrent of seriousness, an insistence in his remarks, made her wonder whether he was trying to test her knowledge of the colony, whether he had somehow got wind of the mission the Earl of Dartmouth had given her. And how annoying if he'd led her away from the others solely for this purpose! This Blair was a disquieting man. And rather handsome, she thought irrelevantly.

After a few noncommittal replies Cecily decided she had told enough of Wilmington and Campbelltown and Uncle Farquard. "I am most eager to see the Azores," she said. "It will be a pleasure to go ashore tomorrow."

"Why, pray? Except, of course, as a change from

these cramped decks. What is there to see? Only more islands, with bumboats crying out their fruit and vegetables for sale, and naked boys offering to dive for pennies, and ashore Portuguese merchants dogging your footsteps and urging you in villainous English or worse French to buy their wares. Italy or Spain is very well. But islands in actuality are always a disappointment. They are at their best as we have them now, a faint scent of flowers in the night, a promise they will assuredly not keep."

"You are a jaded traveller, sir. But I wasn't thinking about the Azores that way. These seas were Sir Richard Grenville's once. It was somewhere about here that he met the huge Spanish fleet with his little *Revenge* in the greatest sea fight an Englishman ever fought. Grenville is my great hero and I associate these islands with his story."

"Ah, yes," Blair said with a laugh. "Grenville was a Devon man, like your father and uncle, wasn't he? Perhaps a relative? He seemed to have a vast number of cousins. When he took a mere selection of them to Roanoke Island in America it was feared he might depeople Devonshire."

"It pleases you to make merry with a great venture, but you seem to know your history."

"Some smatterings merely. It caught my interest for a time at the university."

Cecily turned away so Blair might not read her thoughts in her face. She wondered how an obviously intelligent man could have become so casual. For she had decided that it was Blair's unconcern about all things that most irritated her. He had a way of treating every sight and every topic as something faintly tiresome. Who is he, she thought with a quick spurt of annoyance, to belittle great men? How dare he mock Grenville and call comic the ill-fated venture into the New World? She turned back to insist, "Grenville was both a Devon man and the greatest of Elizabeth's captains."

"The greatest? What about Drake? And though he won no glory here, and sought none, what of Howard?

Does their ultimate success against the Armada spoil their memories for you?"

"Drake?" Her voice was full of scorn. "An opportunist, as Raleigh was. And Howard thought first of money. Besides, I can't forgive him sailing away and leaving Grenville to fight alone here."

"Granted, Howard was a calculating man, but he calculated well. Grenville made a grand gesture in encountering the entire Spanish fleet with his single ship and died like a hero of chivalry. Howard won the war."

"I don't care for merchants of victory, Mr. Blair," Cecily said, looking at him directly for a moment, "Give me Grenville, Elizabeth's great captain. He towered above your Drakes and Howards."

Blair gave her a look of kindling admiration and stepped closer. "How loyal you are! If I were ever in trouble I'd want you on my side."

"You'll never meet trouble, Mr. Blair. Like Howard, you will sail away before it touches you."

Blair bowed ironically. "I take that as a fine compliment. You mean I am so prudent that though I capture no glory I shall win all my wars, whether they be of Mars or Venus."

Already Cecily regretted her last remark. Blair's neat parry of her thrust made her feel clumsy and ill-natured. Besides, as she tardily remembered, she was here with him because she had a use for him next day. If he was to volunteer to be her escort she had best make herself a pleasant and witty companion. She marshalled her social arts and graces and looked up with a smile. Soon she had him laughing with her.

When she judged the time right, she returned to the *Baliol's* arrival the next day. She was determined, she said, to see as much of the islands as she could, despite his discouragements. She would take Martha ashore as chaperon. For the day Martha would do very well. She regretted only that she could not count on Martha for protection in a rude seaport town at night, for the captain had spoken of the cantinas, the fine food and wine and the music. "But I shall have to return to the ship at dusk. . . ." She let her voice trail off with delicate regret.

Promptly and warmly Blair invited her to sample with him the entertainment offered by the cantinas. She expected no less, but, of course, she displayed proper surprise and pleasure. At last she accepted demurely, thinking to herself that she was little better than Madame la Fabrère.

They stood a little longer, lulled by the lazy swish of the sea at the *Baliol's* bow and breathing the sweet air. At last, by tacit consent they turned away and Cecily let Blair guide her through the darkness of the narrow decks.

Near the poop they came on Rachel and Holseman, leaning on the bulwarks and staring out into the obscurity of the night, apparently in desultory conversation. Holseman had a long-stemmed clay pipe in his hand. As they approached him, he turned and said, "What was the result of your experiment, Miss Weston? Are we near land?"

Cecily nodded. "After test, I had to grant Mr. Blair had the right of it. I distinctly caught a sweet scent of fruit and flowers wafted by the breeze."

With a faint note of victory in his tone, Blair said, "The fragrance tempted us both. Tomorrow night we go to one of the cantinas and find out whether the taste of the island's produce lives up to its scent. Miss Weston has engaged to be my guest."

At once, Rachel la Fabrère turned to Holseman and urged him to take her for dinner ashore the next night. When Holseman proved a little reluctant, she hung on his arm and pleaded prettily. Her lovely face, flower-pale in the darkness, almost touched his lips. He was soon overcome.

Still clinging to Holseman's arm, Rachel spoke to Blair. "And wouldn't it be pleasant if we joined forces?" Cecily was inwardly annoyed at Blair when he readily agreed. Evidently he did not care so much as he'd indicated about a tête-à-tête evening with her. It piqued her that he had succumbed to Rachel's obvious wiles as readily as to her own finer arts. One would almost think, she said to herself as she watched Blair smile at the others, that he is deliberately cultivating us all. The sudden suspicion made her annoyance sharper.

Rachel wanted to shop a little in the town, perhaps for a peasant costume, perhaps for some silver filigree work. Holseman, wholly entranced by now, agreed to accompany her. Coolly assuming that he and Cecily would go ashore together, Blair promised they would be in the town square about seven.

In his assumption Cecily saw an opportunity to give vent to her irritation. "As I told you, Mr. Blair, my mind is made up to see something of Sir Richard Grenville's islands. Not just the little shops but the country-side. To you one island is like another and every island a bore. To look about as I intend to would fill you with ennui. So I am resolved to take my woman Martha ashore with me, hire a carriage and drive up into the hills. Then I may enjoy the landskip without fear of your masculine censure. I'll join you in the town square about seven, if you please, sir."

Even as she spoke Cecily remembered that her object had been to escape Martha's unstimulating companionship. Now her annoyance with Blair had trapped her. So be it! He was clearly discomfited and that gave some satisfaction. If she would lesson a man, she must pay the cost of it.

The morning light brought the peaks of the Azores hovering in the sky, with a stream of mist below cutting off their bases and giving them the effect of dream mountains floating on the mist.

Though the islands were close around them, the breeze was very light, and it was afternoon before the *Baliol* entered the harbour at Horta, on Fayal.

The captain had chosen Horta, he explained to Flora and Allan, because there was a British consul there, a Scot named Malcolm MacLeod. "I want to have him endorse my Mediterranean pass," he said. "I'll be going to the consulate in an hour's time. He would be eager to talk to you, I know, and will probably want to invite you to dinner. Why don't you take your whole family and go ashore with me?"

"As for meeting the consul," Allan answered, "we'd be glad to. About the pass I don't understand. We go nowhere near the Mediterranean. What is this pass?"

"It's a safe-conduct to protect us from trouble with the Barbary pirates. The British admiralty issues it, and it has to be endorsed by the consul in every port of call. On this run I don't worry about most of the Barbary ships. They sail mainly in the Mediterranean or close to shore in the Atlantic. But ships from Salé range these waters, and they're commanded by the worst sort of corsairs, adventurers of all nations. Captives go to slave markets, which break a man's courage. So I'll just see Mr. MacLeod and have him endorse my pass."

He was as good as his word. In just an hour his boat was ready to set out for the shore. Flora had assembled her full household, including Moira and the twins, a party of nine.

At the consulate Malcolm MacLeod turned out to be a man from Harris, a sober, solid man, a little pompous. Though his wife was away on a visit to England, he invited the whole party to dinner, for he was excited by the chance to talk to Flora MacDonald. Except for the captain, who pleaded business, they all stayed as a matter of course, though the lads might have preferred something livelier for their first afternoon in a foreign port. David was disgruntled, too, that he was not included at all in Cecily Weston's plans. But when he noticed that Moira, who was to sit between him and Dougald, was looking particularly beautiful he began to feel reconciled. It was not long until he thought of a way to make the visit more exciting. Whispering in Moira's ear, he proposed that they escape right after dinner. "Tell Dougald," he explained in an undertone, "that we'll go along the dock and look at the boats. There'll be native fishermen there, and probably women at market stalls. I'll buy you a trinket for a memento."

His gay attentiveness did not betray his plan to buy something for Cecily too, something that would make her notice him.

Moira was delighted with the idea. Her eyes sparkled as she bent her head close to his to say, "If they won't give us permission, let's go anyway." Then she shifted in her chair and held her napkin over her lips while she murmured to Dougald, "David and I are going to the docks after dinner. You——"

"Just the two of you?" he interrupted, surprised and hurt.

"The three of us—you too. If you want to, that is." She looked at him quizzically.

He hesitated a second. Then: "Well, I suppose I'll go. But I'd hoped you and I might ride through the hills. The landskip ought to be beautiful. And I heard about a convent I thought you'd like to see." Dougald's voice revealed his disappointment.

The corners of Moira's mouth quirked up as she smiled in anticipation of the afternoon. "That was sweet of you, but the dock will be much more adventurous. Anyway David ... well, he wants to do something too, and the convent wouldn't interest him. You come with us."

"All right. But hush! Allan's glowering at us. Grace is to be said." Dougald bent his head and Moira demurely looked down at her plate.

After grace Allan leaned forward with a questioning look and started to ask something. Malcolm MacLeod, expansive and loquacious in the presence of his illustrious guest, didn't notice. He had long been away from the Highlands and had to be told both news and gossip. The second course was well under way before Allan could ask his question. "And what do you hear, please, from the colonies?"

MacLeod liked an audience and again he took charge. Every ship passing in either direction, he said, gave him a budget of news. He was singularly well placed, he believed, to arrive at a large view of what was transpiring in America. He prided himself on being an expert on the situation, perhaps a better one than any the Earl of Dartmouth had at his disposal. He paused, sipped his wine rather pompously, then turned to Allan.

"You're fortunate not to be going to Massachusetts—barbarous name, isn't it? I predict real trouble there before long. People are inflamed over constitutional questions, especially taxation. No doubt news of the Boston Tea Party last December penetrated even to Skye."

In response to Allan's nod the consul went on. "Well, following the disorders last winter the Crown sent over a new governor, General Gage. He took office in early April. I don't like it much. Gage has been long in America and has an American wife. His appointment might look like a concession to the Bostonians."

Alex MacLeod leaned forward. "But surely, even if Gage himself sympathizes with the Americans, his order must be to be stiff with them."

"So you know about Gage?" The consul asked.

"I know he's a trusted man, with much military experience."

Malcolm nodded agreement, then added, "But had you heard that Gage thinks England's repressive policy will lead to conflict? Recently he sent an urgent request to London for more troops. Since the Crown is determined to break resistance in Massachusetts, his request must in prudence be granted. I dare say transports carrying fresh regiments will pass through here in November."

Malcolm stopped when he saw the distressed look on Flora's face. But, having said so much, he could scarcely chop about and unsay it. Besides, it was all true and he might have said more. With a shrug he turned to listen to Allan's question: "But Martin, the Governor of North Carolina, is he as much exercised about conditions there as Governor Gage is in Massachusetts?"

"No, he is not. Of course, he admits that there are malcontents and hotheads in North Carolina, but he believes the loyal men overweigh them. His dispatches are confident that he can control things." Malcolm used his napkin with a flourish. "Martin is an American, by the by. He was born on his father's great plantation in Antigua."

Flora paid no heed to the last remark. She asked

anxiously, "Just how far is it from Massachusetts to Carolina?"

"I forget the precise distance," Malcolm MacLeod replied, "but from Boston to Wilmington must be six or seven hundred miles or even more. Yes, a good long way."

Flora looked heartened. "That's about the same as from Skye to London. And much that goes on in London we at home never hear of at all. If Boston is to have trouble may not the distance keep it from Carolina?"

"That's hard to say, Mrs. MacDonald. There are differences of opinion about how much the colonies will unite. They've got good sea communication, and now they have committees of correspondence, as they call them. They write back and forth about grievances—seditious fellows most of them. But still, in a pinch, each colony will consult its own interest. That's always been the way, and no doubt it will be so now." Malcolm pushed back his chair. "To say more about the colonies would make a to-do greater than they deserve. Let's not allow the American rabble and its misdeeds to monopolize the day. I'll show you something of the islands."

Everyone arose and leisurely started out the room. A few moments later they reconvened at the ornate official coach in the drive. Flora stepped aside at David's beckoning and listened to his plea. "I don't see why not," she said after a moment's consideration.

She watched David run over to Moira and gallantly hook her arm through his. With a little skip that joggled the sun-shade hanging from her wrist, Moira started off with him. Dougald fell in step slightly behind, but soon was at Moira's other side and laughing at something she looked up to say. Flora felt no worry about letting them go. Moira would be safe with those two sensible and hardy lads, both devoted to her.

Cecily Weston went ashore about five in the afternoon, when the heat of the day began to moderate. She was accompanied only by Martha, who was in a complaining mood and gloomily certain that they would both be murdered by a bloodthirsty and lecherous banditti they were sure to meet. Cecily was determined to take a more cheerful attitude but she was not finding it easy.

At the boat landing she found several small mule-drawn carriages waiting for passengers. She was attracted to one because it was drawn by a plump white mule which seemed the apple of its driver's eye. Cecily had a little Spanish, and although the driver's Portuguese had an outlandish sound she could follow the drift of it. She gathered he was calling his mule his little fair one and sympathizing with it as he estimated Martha's weight. She supposed the driver was an appealing native type—he had a smiling mouth, great dark eyes, curly hair and a flower worn with unconcern over one ear. His English was oddly accented, but voluble and moderately comprehensible. To the island girls, Cecily thought, he is no doubt a Lothario. But I'll wager he has garlic on his breath. She stifled her distaste and asked him his name.

"Jesus, señorita. A good name, is it not?" He sounded the *J* as an *H*, in the Spanish manner.

"A very great name indeed," she agreed with him absently. "Well, Jesus, drive us to the top of a high hill so that we may look all around."

They jogged through the town and followed a rising track. As the little carriage climbed the view began to open. The island was a scene of tropical beauty, soft and lovely. All around were vineyards, most of them loaded with fruit, but here and there was one already picked, fragrant with grapes in press. Little whitewashed houses with red-tiled roofs were scattered about the hillsides, covered with flowering vines. Occasionally a larger, more pretentious house proclaimed the greater wealth and position of its owner. Very attractive, Cecily noted mechanically.

As they mounted higher, the soft blue sea stretched away farther and wider, with other islands touched by the low sun showing far off across the water. Somewhere out there the *Revenge* had met the great Spanish fleet. One stretch of water looked very much like another.

When the little mule paused to rest and draw breath, Jesus jumped out to block a wheel with a rock. As he stood beside his little fair one he struck a rather dashing attitude and sang a small folk song, perhaps to cheer the mule but with one eye on his passengers. Cecily felt an impulse to get away. She climbed out of the little carriage and called back over her shoulder, "Come, Martha, let's walk and give the mule a proper rest." She started along a rough path leading out to a point that commanded a wide prospect.

Jesus followed them, the guide in action. "We say Fayal is an island of nobility, very fair and tropic. Would the lady care to see where the great English captain fought many years ago, Ricardo Campo Verde?"

Campo Verde? Cecily realized finally that he was oddly translating Sir Richard Grenville's name. "Where?" she demanded. "Where?"

His arms came up and gestured vaguely across a broad expanse of sea. "Out there, that way." His eyes lighted with interest. "Do you know he was a very devil? He comes back to the island every time we have a great storm."

"Nonsense!" said Cecily sharply.

"I swear it. Everyone on the island knows it, even the little children. Myself I have never seen him, but I have heard his voice bellowing out in the storm, giving orders to those he commands, whether men or devils I know not."

She saw it was quite useless to argue with him.

She noticed with relief that the sun was sinking close to the sea. By the time they returned to the town it would be the hour fixed to meet Mr. Blair. Her excursion into the past had proved a tasteless adventure. Martha and Jesus were not the right companions for it. It's odd, she thought with a wry smile, how the presence of a man, even a man for whom one feels distaste, lends spice to an afternoon's drive—or to an evening's entertainment. The prospect of a more exhilarating evening made her hurry the protesting Martha back to the carriage.

On the way down Martha objected to going back to the ship and leaving her mistress alone. "It isn't safe for you to be in this heathen place without me. They'll steal your purse and cut your throat," she insisted.

Cecily laughed. She was feeling better, almost gay. "I'll be with Mr. Blair. He should be almost as good a protector as you, Martha. If you like, when we reach the landing-place I'll give you the few gold pieces I have with me and you can carry them back to the ship. With my bag gaping open and clearly containing nothing of importance surely no sensible brigand would try to rob me."

In the square Rachel and the two men were waiting, idly watching the courtship of the Latin evening promenade. Blair came forward as Cecily was paying Jesus. In her present mood she was repenting of her brusqueness toward the driver and gave him a generous tip to make up for it, an amount that made his eyes shine.

With Blair she went down to the boat landing to arrange to have Martha ferried back to the ship. By good luck one of the *Baliol's* own boats was at the landing. Remembering the joking promise she had given Martha, Cecily opened her purse, took out four or five gold pieces, rolled them in a handkerchief and put the little bundle in Martha's hand. "Now," she said gaily, "I'm safe from robbers."

When she and Blair returned to the square she noticed Jesus was still hanging about. He had paid little attention to Holseman, but he at once approached Blair as if able to sniff out the leader of the party. Now we shall see, Cecily reflected, whether his persuasions which failed with me will work with these men.

Jesus swept a bow, aiming it at Blair but somehow including the others. "The gentleman seeks a cantina of the finest, where the food and wine are of the best, where the music and dancing are a delight. I, Jesus, know just such a place. Let me guide you there."

Blair shrugged impatiently. "We need no guide. We can see from here at least half a dozen restaurants and cantinas."

"These?" Jesus assumed an expression of theatrical contempt. "Sailors' places, good enough for men tired of the sea and ready to take anything ashore. Full of pigs and peasants. If the gentleman wants no more than country wine and strong cheese he will do very well. Take any one of them. Pah!

"The place I speak of is for the few. The wine is old and fine, the food to dream of. The dancers are—how you say?—ravishing. They get into the blood. And the music——" He kissed his fingers. "There you see the rich travellers, the great captains. It is of an antiquity. Once the bravest corsairs met there. Even now adventures take place there."

Blair looked at Holseman, eyebrows raised, undecided. Cecily was filled with inward amusement as she watched. In the end, as she might have expected, it was Rachel whom Jesus impressed. She was all eagerness as she came up and took Holseman's arm. "Of course we must go to such a place as this man describes. Now we know about it we would never be satisfied with one of these sailors' places. Lead us to it quickly."

The driver bowed to her, rolling his eyes, then looked quickly to the two men for confirmation.

They exchanged another doubtful glance, and Blair looked questioningly at Cecily. At her indifferent nod he nodded to Jesus. "Very well, take us there."

"One moment," he said, and hurried off. He was quickly back with a second carriage like his own and another coarsely picturesque driver. "Let the ladies and gentlemen step into the carriages. You shall be at the spot before dusk."

They drove for a mile or so along the shore. The old inn was set on a low promontory of rock, a deep cove at one side. It was a long building, nestled at the foot of a higher hill behind, its red-tile roof half smothered in vines full of purple flowers. Overlooking the sea was a terrace of flagstone, as long as the building and almost as wide, edged with a stone balustrade. At one end was a Moorish arcade. Cecily could form no idea of its age but decided it might have been here for centuries,

Jesus led them to the terrace. With something of a flourish he waved an arm and said, "The Inn of the New Moon." He beckoned to the host, who was already on his way to the party. "Manuel," he said importantly, "these English wish a good table where they may watch the sunset. Give them the best from your kitchens and cellars. See to it you satisfy them."

Manuel welcomed the party with a deep bow, led them past the sparsely occupied tables on the terrace to a heavy dark-oak table in the arcade. As they settled into their seats, Rachel noticed a table occupied by six men. They were tall men, with arrogant, handsome features and dark eyes of flashing brilliance. They were richly dressed, and by the easy manner in which they sipped their wine and talked they seemed at home in any society. She beckoned Manuel to her. Nodding toward the six men, she asked, "Are these men frequent guests here? They stand out among the islanders. Are they perhaps important travellers off a ship in the harbour? I am curious about them."

"I do not know them, madame. If you like, I'll ask their waiter what he has overheard. Now let me summon your waiter. Have you special desires as to your dinner?"

Cecily turned to Blair. "None of us has been here before. We do not know the local dishes. There will be other dishes on which Manuel's head cook prides himself. Why not put ourselves in his hands? Let him choose for us, both food and wine, asking only that he make the dinner memorable."

The men agreed, with some relief. Manuel bowed to her. "Your trust honours me."

After a brief colloquy with their waiter he moved off. Cecily saw him stop another waiter and talk to him for a moment. Soon he threaded his way back to their table. To Rachel he reported, "The waiter does not know the gentlemen. They speak in Portuguese and Spanish and another language he does not recognize. He thinks they came from the large ship anchored not far off the cove. They have chosen their dishes in a way I can commend and they order our finest wines and brandies. In every way they appear gentlemen of taste and means. I go now to see your waiter makes no mistakes in what I told him for you."

A wine waiter brought them tawny sherry and poured it into delicate glasses. Holseman sat turning his wine-glass with nervous fingers on the stem. He was abstracted, paying no attention to the conversation.

Cecily tapped him on the sleeve. "Is anything the matter?" she asked softly.

With a little start he turned to her and smiled weakly. "I believe I've seen one of those men over there before, the one with a scar on his left cheek. It disturbs me that I don't remember where."

Cecily looked as he directed. The man with the scar was the tallest of the lot. He made a striking appearance in a coat of dark-blue velvet laced with gold. He had a long, disdainful face with a great hawk nose. His mouth, with its sensual lips, looked cruel. As she watched him covertly, he looked in their direction and his eyes met hers briefly, then moved on to Holseman. It seemed to her that as his glance fell on Holseman there was recognition in it.

At this moment the musicians, who had been playing softly, suddenly struck into a lively gypsy air. Two dancers, a man and a woman, whirled into an open space on the terrace, boots stamping, castanets clicking. They were young and fresh, lithe as two panthers, yet trained. In the stylized movements of the Flamenco, so often empty, they were magnificent. It was astounding to see such performers off in this corner of the world. At least as to the entertainment at the Inn of the New Moon, Jesus had told the sober truth. If the food—and the adventure—he had promised were as good, this would prove a memorable evening.

As the dance ended, Cecily noticed that again Holseman had not been paying attention. He was watching the man with the scar. Suddenly he paled. His fingers left his glass, which he had been twisting with the same restlessness. He ducked his head as if to avoid observation but kept watching the stranger from under his brows.

He knows who the man is, Cecily thought. He is afraid.

12

At the Inn of the New Moon

As THE sunset faded, Manuel had lamps brought out
and hung on brackets. They shed a soft glow over the
terrace and under the arcade. Serving-men moved
about quietly, pouring wine and distributing great
platters of chicken prepared with yellow rice, fruits,
salads, and exotic dishes for which Cecily knew no
name. Everything was delicious, and the wine was
superb.

In the clear space on the terrace a woman had replaced the dancers. She sang in Spanish, with a haunting contralto voice, a malagueña telling of the pain of
love. All conversation at the tables ceased. The faces
of the diners wore expressions of sadness as the singer
wove her spell. When she finished, a storm of applause and cries of olé burst out from her audience.

To Cecily's surprise, Holseman, who shortly before
had shrunk into himself, was particularly enthusiastic.
He clapped vigorously, called out praise and almost
rose to his feet. His arm brushed Cecily's bag and
knocked it to the floor. Although the accident was mi-
nor, it seemed to disconcert him. He bent at once to
retrieve the bag, fumbled, finally dropped to his knees
and almost crawled under the table in pursuit of it. He
was very awkward, Cecily thought, but at last he
scrambled up and, with an unconscious tug at the
strings, handed her the bag. His muttered apologies
were profuse. Remembering she had removed all but
a handkerchief and a copper or two from the bag, Cecily assured him no harm was done. Absently she
tucked the purse away beside her.

Again the musicians broke into the pulsing rhythms
of the dance and the young male dancer sprang out to

leap and stamp and whirl. He had the lithe grace and power of a tiger. In his close-fitting costume every movement suggested an immense virility. Probably every woman there found him exciting. Some more than others, Cecily noted with sardonic interest. Rachel la Fabrère's cheeks were flushed, her eyes sparkled and her breath was coming quickly as she watched with complete absorption.

After a few moments Rachel wrenched her gaze away and scanned the room. She summoned Manuel with a gesture of her hand. "When he has finished, tell your dancer, pray, that I wish to speak to him."

While the audience still clapped, Manuel brought the young man to their table. Rachel praised his dancing warmly. "It appeals to me, and makes me, too, wish to dance. Manuel will have no objection, I am sure, if I dance with you. Though I have never danced for money I am no beginner."

The young man hesitated.

There was a faint chink of metal as she put something in his hand. "Come, come," she said, "I'm not accustomed to waiting. A *pas de deux* should offer no difficulty, a close dance of whatever sort you prefer. Tell your musicians what to play."

Either her coins or Manuel's meaning look persuaded him. In rapid dialect he called to the leader of the musicians and then led her out on the terrace floor. Rachel's blond beauty contrasting with his black hair, her softness against his lithe strength made them a striking couple. It was evident from the first sway of her body that Rachel had not been boasting when she said she was no beginner. Without a second's rehearsal she adapted her movement perfectly to his. As soon as the young man recognized her skill he began to employ quicker, more difficult steps. He danced in a large circle, his body held stiffly erect, his heels tapping smartly. Rachel danced within the circle, her heels keeping perfect time with the castanets. The dancer closed in gradually until they danced back to back, then, with a smooth gyration, face to face.

"*Olé! Olé! Olé!*" cried the diners.

Rachel's head was thrown back, her lips parted. The dancer bent over her, his eyes lazy and languorous. They swayed together as the music died. It had been a sensuous dance, in spite of its briskness and heel-tapping. Rachel lifted her face. Her slow smile was inviting and her eyes compelling. Thus she and her partner moved in slow unison, oblivious of the audience which continued to shout, "*Olé! Olé! Olé!*"

Caught up in Rachel's unexpected exhibition, they had forgotten the six strangers who had excited their curiosity earlier. The leader, the hawk-nosed man in the blue velvet coat, must have left his place while Rachel was dancing, Cecily decided later, for Rachel was scarcely seated when he appeared beside their table.

He was very cool. He took time for a leisurely, appraising look at each of the two women. It was an ambiguous look, impersonal, yet distinctly complimentary. Then he turned to Holseman.

There was no question now whether Holseman knew the man. His face was as white as cheese and damp with cold sweat. He was waiting uneasily for the other man to speak. He had not long to wait.

"Hello, Van Arnim. Well met, in my territory this time," the stranger greeted him, cold menace in the last phrase.

Holseman wiped his face with a napkin, gathered himself, but his voice sounded false when he spoke. "There must be some mistake. My name is Holseman, not Van Arnim."

With easy contempt the stranger pushed away Holseman's disclaimer. "Holseman, Van Arnim— what does it matter? You may use any name, but you are still the same treacherous, double-dealing fellow I resolved ten years ago to kill on sight. This is the night I balance our account." The stranger's hand went to his sword hilt.

Abruptly Blair pushed back his chair and rose to his feet. "One moment, sir. I don't know you. But you are armed, and you threaten my guest here, who is unarmed. Please to explain yourself, sir."

"I am Ricardo de Vega, ship captain and gentleman. You may know my name, sir."

"Your name is well known, sir, though whether as pirate or Robin Hood there is some difference of opinion. But, touching the killing of my guest here, I do not perceive that your name is a matter of moment. What explanation can you give for your threat?"

De Vega drew himself up. "I owe you no explanation of any sort. However, this man is a double and triple secret agent, betraying even himself. To say truly, he's no agent at all, for he seeks always his own profit and never that of the government whose money he accepts. Though he looks meek and unimaginative, he has a certain genius in betrayal.

"Ten years ago he made earnest effort to betray me to a most unpleasant death. It is no thanks to him that I am still alive. I did not die, but because of him I now find it expedient to command a ship putting out from Salé rather than from my own Spain. Though he failed in his main scheme, thus much he injured me. Both for his success and for his failure, my projected death, I vowed revenge. Are you satisfied, sir?"

Blair, unheated by De Vega's vehemence, replied very coolly, "Not completely satisfied, if you will pardon me, Señor de Vega. All this is on your unsupported statement. Besides, I don't know that Van Arnim's —Holseman's—act deserves cold-blooded murder."

Again Blair, without intention, had piqued De Vega. "Murder, sir? I have no intention of it. I wear here a rapier. Several of my friends are wearing blades as long and as sharp. One of them, at my request, will be most glad to lend his blade to Holseman-Van Arnim-Van Snake. A mercenary rascal of his stripe has no right to the privileges of a gentleman, but I'm ready to give him his chance in a duel."

Blair bowed. "In that case, sir, I withdraw any objection, providing the ladies are protected from unpleasantness."

At De Vega's word that he was not to be summarily cut down, Holseman, Cecily noticed, plucked up heart. She wondered why. Was he so naïve as to believe that, even were he so fortunate as to kill or wound De Vega, the five formidable-looking friends would accept the issue without further action? For the first time Cecily felt some sympathy and admiration for the nondescript little fellow who was regaining his composure to a remarkable degree.

Cecily had been so taken up with De Vega, Blair and Holseman that she had not looked about her. Now she noticed that De Vega's five cohorts had come up and were closely grouped about the table, along with a distracted Manuel. Manuel was protesting that he had many guests and the gathering violence would drive them away. For a moment, with real hope, Cecily believed that his suave argument would ease off the ugly situation.

But Manuel was quicker than she to perceive the futility of his attempt. He saw that De Vega was determined to force the issue, there or elsewhere, and he took the lesser of two evils. "Gentlemen, if you are not to be dissuaded from fighting, at least let me urge you to do it in a suitably private spot. Behind this arcade there is a yard with good footing. Let me have lamps hung there as they are here, to provide light. It will be more convenient in every way."

This much they conceded to him. De Vega and his five companions, Holseman—looking smaller than ever and more nondescript—and Blair followed him toward the hidden yard, leaving Cecily and Rachel alone at the table.

The New Moon's other guests wanted no involvement with De Vega—or with his enemy. They were getting out, some incontinently without waiting for their bills, others with dignity, as if they had finished and were ready to go in any case. Aside from a few waiters and musicians, the two women were soon left alone.

Rachel was half crazy with nervousness. She gnawed at her knuckles, then jumped to her feet and walked back and forth. "Who would have thought that mild little man would have a history?" she kept saying to herself. "I thought he was completely harmless."

She was listening. Suddenly she darted toward an open window set high in the wall. She was not tall enough to see out of it. "Help me!" she cried. "Let's move a bench under the window. I must see what they're doing."

Cecily tugged at one end of a heavy bench. As soon as it was under the window Rachel jumped up and her head almost filled the small opening. For a moment she watched spell-bound. Then her hand went to her mouth. "Mother of God!" she breathed.

With quick resolution Cecily mounted the bench beside her and used her elbow firmly to make space for herself at the window. Outside she saw seven or eight men, including Blair, forming a rough semicircle at the edge of a lighted spot close to the wall. Within the enclosed space De Vega and Holseman were fencing. Evidently they had commenced only as Rachel had spoken, for they were warily feeling each other out. De Vega was turned toward her, and she shivered at the expression on his cruel hawk's face: he was enjoying himself.

But little Holseman was by no means finished, though he was still nervous. He showed courage when the rapier was in his hand; and he was a surprisingly skilled swordsman. De Vega began to press the attack, his sword moving like lightning—feint and thrust, thrust again—but each time the smaller man parried neatly. He was not, like De Vega, debonair, but he was full of desperate energy. Sometimes his own point licked out in attack. Though he was much less powerful, he was, as long as he was fresh, a worthy antagonist.

All the spectators were intent and utterly silent. There was no sound but the rasp and whisper of the engaging blades, the faint padding noise of the fencers' feet as they lunged and recovered. The tension grew almost unbearable.

After a quick, indecisive exchange, De Vega suddenly thrust. His blade glided past Holseman's guard toward his heart. A tiny strip of white cloth fluttered away. Breathlessly Cecily waited to see if the torn edges would turn red with blood. Seconds passed. The cloth remained white. The whisper and clash of the darting blades went on.

A sudden cry in the night made Cecily gasp involuntarily and look out into the darkness. A darker shadow was coming on the run. A voice called, "Captain, a British ship of war's entering the harbour. She's coming in."

De Vega moved with incredible speed. His sword engaged Holseman's, seemed almost to take hold of it. Then with a sudden powerful twist of his wrist he sent Holseman's rapier flying out of his hand. The little man's eyes bulged with terror as he faced De Vega helplessly, empty-handed.

With a harsh laugh De Vega stepped back and dropped the point of his sword to the ground. "We'll postpone this. I have no desire for a brush with a ship of war tonight. We'll put to sea at once. Take him—" he gestured at Holseman—"along. I'll finish killing him on the deck of my own ship."

Blair stepped forward to protest: "You promised him a fair fight. You can't carry him off to murder him at your leisure."

"He shall have his duel on my ship just as he has been having it here. I give you my word."

"I should accept the word of a pirate?" Blair demanded hotly.

De Vega ignored the insult. "Yes, and for the best of reasons. We are a party of seven, well armed. You are two, with only a single dress sword between you." His finger moved in a small gesture, pointing at three men in turn. Their swords came out, and one was an inch from Blair's throat. De Vega went on smoothly. "Do you care to dispute longer the value of my word?"

Blair flushed indignantly, but he yielded to the inexorable logic of the threatening swords. The three men held him in place while the others hustled Holseman away. Then they, too, disappeared into the darkness, heading evidently toward a path down the rocks to the cove.

He was alone under the light. For a moment he stood there rather abjectly. Then he walked toward the arcade, and Cecily and Rachel.

Manuel found them a carriage. Rachel, still stimulated by the evening's events, began to chatter as they drove away from the inn, but neither Cecily nor Blair was in a mood to respond. Gradually Rachel subsided, and they rode silently through the night.

At the landing Blair hired a boat to carry the two ladies out to the *Baliol*. "I shall be along later," he said. "If the British ship of war those rascals mentioned is the vessel I think it is, the captain is a friend of mine. He should hear what went on tonight and some other matters I have to discuss. If you'll excuse me, I'll be about it."

13

An Adventurer's Legacy

On the boat out to the ship Cecily and Rachel began
to recover from their shock and fright. They talked a
little, speculating quietly about the main actors in
the drama at the New Moon. De Vega, so far as they
could guess, was just what he appeared—an adventurous
corsair, very skilful with a sword and no doubt just as
masterful in managing a ship. From what he had let
drop, they supposed some intrigue had gone wrong, and
as a result he could no longer live safely in Spain. He
had said his vessel now sailed out of the notorious little
pirate kingdom of Salé. What his channels of information were they had no idea, but they supposed he was
acquainted with adventurers of all nations.

Drab little Holseman was harder to relate to the
background that De Vega had suddenly revealed.
"Do you suppose," Cecily conjectured, "that he deliberately cultivated nonentity as a sort of disguise? He
was almost unnoticeable."

"It is hard to believe that any government would
hire him as an agent," said Rachel. "He looked
wholly ineffectual. Who would expect him to do anything useful?"

"Perhaps he wasn't an agent. Maybe he was traf-
ficking in secrets on his own and expecting to sell
them to the highest bidder. It seems more likely
somehow."

"Do you suppose De Vega will kill him?" Rachel
asked. Neither woman felt like facing the question. A
silence fell. Rachel studied the thick pattern of stars
overhead. Then with a quick change of mood she said
something frank that made Cecily like her for the first
time. "That dancer was a magnificent creature." She

laughed. "I had more than a mind to get off in a private corner with him. What happened afterward drove him clear out of my mind."

Once on the ship, Cecily felt a great wash of fatigue. She wanted only to get to bed. Rachel, still keyed up, wandered off to find someone to whom she could relate the night's adventures. Relieved to find herself alone in her cabin, Cecily at once began to strip off her clothes. As she reached for her nightgown, laid out on her berth, she noticed her handkerchief tucked under the edge of her pillow. Martha had put it there without unrolling it. Idly Cecily took the handkerchief and poured the gold pieces into her hand. She must put them away.

She picked up her bag and loosened the strings. She frowned when her hand came on a tightly folded packet of papers. Certainly she'd carried no packet when she began the evening. Her mind went back to the moment when Holseman had retrieved her purse. Yes, he had knocked it on the floor at the inn and fumbled for it an unaccountably long time. And he had pulled the strings tight just before he gave it back to her.

It seemed Holseman was not so inept as he had pretended; he had devised and executed a clever plan in a moment's time. An important packet was on him. De Vega was on the scene; his very presence promised trouble. At all costs the packet must not fall into the pirate's hands. The solution was to make someone from the *Baliol* its unwitting carrier. And then, if Holseman were searched, there would be nothing to find. No doubt, if he had come through his duel successfully, he would have found a way to recover the packet, and Cecily would never have known she had possessed it. Poor Holseman—his luck had run out, but his plan had been ingenious.

Cecily had to see what he had taken such pains to keep from De Vega. She moved close to the dim lanthorn. With instinctive caution she turned her back to the cabin door so as to hide the packet with her body if Rachel unexpectedly returned. Only then did she draw it out of her bag. It was thick, perhaps ten sheets folded and sealed. Whoever had sealed it had let the seal slip while the wax was still soft, blurring the impression. She could make out nothing. On the face of the packet someone had written: "To Governor Martin in North Carolina. With all haste."

Questions flooded her mind. Could Holseman have been a British agent? Martin was surely loyal to the Crown, strongly so. Yet Holseman was not English. Plenty of officers were continually travelling to the colonies. Wouldn't one of them be a safer messenger? Had Holseman perhaps stolen the packet from a British agent and planned to sell it in America to whoever offered most, Tory or Whig? She had no answers.

The realization that she had become involved in some dangerous plot weighed on Cecily. She tried to think what she should do, but her weariness would not let her. Carefully she put the packet away. With a sigh she lay down on her berth. She would decide what to do in the morning.

Blair's boat was drawing close to the British vessel. "What ship is that?" he hailed.

"His Majesty's ship-of-war *Somerset*."

"Give your commander, Captain Borset, my compliments and inform him that Major James Blair requests permission to come aboard."

After a short delay Blair was summoned aboard and a marine led him below to the captain's cabin. The two men greeted each other warmly. Within seconds they had the door closed and were closeted together.

Borset poured brandy into glasses. "This meeting is as happy as it is unexpected, James."

"It's not so happy for me, Phil. The fact is, I'm in a devil of a fix." Borset looked puzzled and Blair explained: "The Earl of Dartmouth entrusted a packet of papers to me to carry to the governor of North Carolina. Like a fool I let them be stolen from me. I thought I had a scheme to get them back before we reached America, but tonight's events have probably checkmated it. My whole career in the army is in jeopardy."

Quickly he related how he had been helplessly ill during the storm, how he had found the packet gone when he regained control of himself. "Confidentially, the packet contained two lists—one of the regiments which can be sent to the colonies, and one of persons suspected of sedition whom Governor Martin should watch and curb, and giving him his orders on how far to go with them. The list is based on reports from our agents in Philadelphia and Boston and other places, as well as from local sources in Carolina. I suspect a number of names on it will come as a surprise to Martin. I'm told flattery works on him; his vanity leads him to underestimate his opponents. In short, as a judge of men he has but an indifferent talent.

"The list may prove important in our handling of the province, but I can't imagine it having any value except in the colonies. The thief might have been an American agent seeking to protect his fellow rebels. Or it might have been some adventurer hoping to offer the packet confidentially for sale to the highest bidder in America.

"There were a dozen passengers on the *Baliol* who might have robbed me. My scheme was to study them, fix on the person who had it and get it back. But tonight we had an adventure ashore that may have spoiled my plan."

He went on to tell about Holseman's interrupted duel with De Vega and its aftermath. "God knows where the packet may be now! If Holseman was the thief, no doubt De Vega has it now."

Borset sucked reflectively at the tip of his mustache. "Was Holseman your prime suspect, James?"

"I'm not sure, Phil. That's the maddening part of it. There's a Scot named Dee I can't make out. On the surface he's tutor to a Hungarian lad but he might be anything. Then there's Rachel la Fabrère. She's a beautiful woman, light as they come and no good. She was married to that rascal in Portugal who gave us so much trouble with his intrigues a dozen years ago, though she may have run off from him. You remember La Fabrère? Utterly unprincipled, and clever. She's the kind of opportunist who would steal the packet if she happened on it. Then there's Cecily Weston. She's a niece of the old admiral. When I found that out I thought she was above suspicion. On the other hand, she's also a niece of the Carolina merchant Farquard Campbell, who's been more than friendly with the dissident Whigs there. I can't leave her out as a possibility.

"I rule out Flora and Allan MacDonald. Flora, of course, frankly admits aiding Charles Stuart a generation ago. But both of them are forthright, honest people, and I can't associate them with this sort of backstairs intrigue. They don't fit.

"So, to come back to your original question, yes, I suppose Henry Holseman is my prime suspect. And much good it does me now that De Vega has spirited him off."

Borset poured more brandy. The two men sat silently pondering for a moment. Philip Borset stared at his glass as he swirled the brandy round and round in it. Finally he spoke. "You're in a fix, but all is not necessarily lost. Holseman may have hidden the packet in his berth or in one of his boxes. Wouldn't it be a trifle bulky in a man's pocket?"

After Blair had indicated the size and appearance of the packet, Borset continued, "In the morning I'll send over a couple of officers in a boat; come myself perhaps. The chances of our uncovering the packet aren't too good, but I can at least insist on searching the ship and interrogating the passengers. We just might turn it up."

"The search isn't a bad idea, Phil," Blair said. "But leave me out of it, if you can. You may turn up the packet, and again you may not. In either case, it's best if I can go on playing my innocuous rôle. Secrecy is my best defense against a second theft ... or my best insurance of recovering the thing if you don't."

Borset rose and absently put the stopper in the brandy decanter. "Just as you say. It's a bad spot you're in. I hope I can help you out of it."

There was a twisted smile on Blair's face as he

looked up. "Thank you, Phil. You're one of the best men I know to have around in a pinch. But it was damned foolish of me to let the thing get stolen in the first place. If I don't get that packet back, I guess I'll deserve whatever punishment they mete out to me."

"Well, James," Borset said consolingly, "there's still a pretty good chance. If De Vega's got the papers, he'll probably try to sell them to a Crown officer. I'll give him a chance to get to me. Of course, I'd nab him and hand the papers over to you. If De Vega hasn't got them, then neither has Holseman. They're on the *Baliol*, headed for North Carolina, and you right along with them. I think it'll work out."

Blair pushed back his chair and stood up. "Let's hope you're right. And thanks again, Phil." He shook hands with Borset. "See you tomorrow."

Cecily's first sleep was sound, but before dawn she woke to toss and worry. The little packet weighed on her more heavily than it had last night. She could no longer delay making up her mind about the course she should follow.

In a way Holseman had entrusted it to her. And if, as was probable, he had come by it illegally, it made little difference. The envelope was addressed to Governor Martin. It really belonged to him and should go to him. Cecily felt that it was now her personal responsibility to deliver the packet. Good, she decided; I shall hide it and say nothing; when I get to North Carolina I shall hand it over. Only so shall I know it does not fall into the wrong hands.

Having so decided, Cecily smoothed her pillow and lay back upon it. Only momentarily, however, did she feel at ease. It occurred to her, although she tried not to think of herself, that she might be in a dangerous position. Should some agent try to recover the packet, she would not be able to guard it well or to protect herself. She twisted nervously on the thin mattress and pulled up the sheet.

She longed to ask for advice. But whose? Instinctively she felt that this was a man's business. There was Blair, but she could not trust him, and he'd insist she turn it over to him. She might send a message to the captain of the warship. No, the outcome would be the same. The captain was a friend of Blair. He was on his way back to England. He'd merely take the papers and give them to Blair with instructions to deliver them to Martin. Allan seemed a possibility, or even Alex MacLeod. But, on second thought, Cecily decided against telling either of them. Allan was loyal, but not very firm or independent. And Alex, well, she simply had no idea what he was like politically.

With a resigned sigh Cecily decided to stick by her original plan: she would keep the packet and speak of it to no one.

Then she sat up in bed. Flora MacDonald was the answer. She could be trusted; she had had experience with secrets. Yes, Flora would know what to do.

Cecily glanced at her clock and saw it was too early to visit the other cabin. But she was satisfied. She would sleep an hour or two and then, after breakfast, have her talk with Flora.

After breakfast she asked Flora if she could speak to her privately. Flora took her at once to her cabin, where they could be undisturbed. There Cecily told her everything that had happened the evening before. "The thing that troubles me most is what to do with the packet." She mentioned her suspicion of Blair. "It's nothing I can put my finger on, just a feeling."

"Allan felt it, too," Flora said. "He had the impression the man might be an army officer under his macaroni manner."

"It may be best just to say nothing and deliver the papers to Governor Martin myself," Cecily said rather woefully. "But it's a grave responsibility."

"True, my dear, but keeping the packet yourself is the only way to fulfil your responsibility. And after all, it may contain most important and secret political information. The fewer who know about it the better." Flora sat looking at Cecily without seeing her, as if she were looking at something far away. "Yes, I'm sure we're right."

Cecily, finding that she must in the end keep silent, was glad that at least Flora shared the secret. Absently her hand reached into her bag and pulled the packet half out. "But where shall I hide it? It would never do for Madame la Fabrère to see it. I trust her even less than Blair. In our little cabin neither of us has any privacy."

For a moment Flora continued to stare off into the distance. Then she seemed to come to a decision. "You trust me, Cecily?" She reached tentatively for the packet. "I could keep it here."

Cecily spoke quickly. "Of course I trust you, Flora. If you'll keep it here I shall be immensely relieved."

"Very well. I will take care of it for the rest of the voyage. When we reach Wilmington, I'll turn it back to you to give to the governor."

Cecily stood up. "You're kind, Flora. I knew you'd see the right thing for me to do." She turned to gaze out the cabin window. "You know this is the first journey I ever took alone. Sometimes I'm a little frightened when I think of the unknown country ahead and the uncle who is almost a stranger, except by letter." She hesitated, then laughed at herself. "I wanted adventure. Now that I begin to have some, I discover my faint heart. And how silly of me! My little pleasure trip is nothing to the change of home and friends you face. Yet I run to you with my very first problem."

Flora took Cecily's hand in hers; her clasp was warm and firm. "I should be miserable, Cecily, if people did not feel they could come to me. And as for adding an extra weight to my burden—why, you don't. I bear no burden. I have always thought change is to be welcomed, not refused."

Cecily marveled at Flora's serenity; she looked into her eyes and thought, They're wonderful! They're deep enough to see into the beyond.

After his breakfast Blair went out on deck, where he sat restlessly or paced up and down. Six or seven hundred yards off lay the Somerset quietly at anchor. Though he watched it impatiently, for some time there were no signs of activity. Finally, in the middle of the morning a boat was manned and put off for the *Baliol*.

When it came close he could make out his friend Philip Borset and two other officers, all in full uniform, and eight or ten sailors. Phil is making the visit impressive, Blair reflected. A moment or two later the three officers and all the sailors, except two left as boat tenders, filed aboard. Borset went straight to the *Baliol*'s captain and spent some time in conversation with him.

All of the regular passengers and their servants were requested to gather in the great cabin. Blair had no inkling of how Borset intended to proceed or how he had explained this rather official visit to the merchant ship. Though he hid his feelings, he was aflame with curiosity. He was among the first to appear.

When they were all assembled the captain spoke to them. "This gentleman, Captain Borset, is the commander of the warship anchored near by. He has come on board on a matter of importance and also of some delicacy."

In spite of his anxiety Blair was amused to note how the usually bluff and salty captain was furbishing his manners and his language in the presence of the naval officers. He seemed almost a different man.

The captain continued. "As you all know, several of the passengers of this ship were involved in violence ashore last evening, and one, Henry Holseman, was carried off by a man described as a corsair from Salé.

"Captain Borset has reason to believe that this Holseman was not, as he tried to appear, a simple merchant, but an agent. Though Captain Borset is not certain, he believes that Holseman was carrying certain documents rightfully belonging to His Majesty's government.

"It is Captain Borset's duty to recover these papers if possible. It is not known whether this pirate gained possession of them when he carried off the man Holseman. If Holseman had them on his person the captain will know where to search. On the other hand, they may be here on the ship, hidden by Holseman or perhaps passed on to someone else. Captain Borset's visit this morning is to inquire into Holseman's movements before his disappearance. As loyal subjects you will answer his questions and give him any assistance you can.

"He will want to question you severally, especially those who were with Holseman last night. I must ask you now to step out on deck. You will be called back one by one to answer Captain Borset's questions. Thank you."

Borset had told almost the true story, Blair thought as he moved out on deck with the others. He left out only my part in it.

On deck Rachel drew Cecily aside. "This business worries me," she said miserably. Cecily noticed that she was pale and not far from tears. "I may as well tell you. My husband is the kind of man who deals in stolen secrets. These officers may be looking for something he has somehow got hold of. I don't know. The fact is I'm running away from him. He's an impossible man to live with, scheming, cold, thinking only of money. He's bitterly jealous, too. Oh, I suppose I gave him cause! I like a little gaiety, dancing—even love."

"Why are you telling me all this?" Cecily asked. The life Rachel was revealing took her aback.

"Don't you see?" said Rachel, desperation in her voice. "If these men are looking for papers he took they'll suspect me of complicity. I'll tell the truth and say I know nothing about them. They'll demand proof and I'll have to say I've run away from him. Will they believe it? Not a word of it. The only thing I'd hate worse than going back to my husband is being shut up in an English prison. What can I do?"

Cecily was shaken, half disgusted and half fascinated by Rachel's disclosures. Rachel's fears sounded fantastic, but she supposed some connection between Holseman and La Fabrère was possible. Plotters and secret agents no doubt knew one another and dealt with one another. Fantastic or not, Rachel's distress was so clearly genuine Cecily could not resist feeling some compassion. But she could give her no comfort.

Blair moved about among the passengers on deck, watching for any signs of fear or guilt. He noted Rachel's agitated conversation with Cecily but could not guess its nature.

A sailor was ushering in the passengers one by one. Borset began with the MacDonald family and their servants. Each of the four boys he kept scarcely more than a minute. He was as quick with Flora, and with Moira MacQueen. Allan he kept a bit longer but Allan came out smiling and looking well pleased with himself. Evidently Phil had remembered what Blair had said the night before in behalf of the MacDonalds and had kept his questions perfunctory.

Then Blair's own turn came. He was ushered into the cabin. Borset sat at a table. Flanking him on one side was the *Baliol's* captain, and on the other side an officer was taking notes. The second officer, assisted by a squad of sailors, was busily searching the berths, boxes and trunks in the great cabin.

Blair approached Borset eagerly. "By now, Phil, I suppose you've finished going through Holseman's effects. . . . Nothing? Nothing? . . . It was too much to hope that we could go straight to it."

"Not the packet, James. We came on a couple of things that show him to have been an accomplished rascal, if that needed proof. Nothing to show any connection with the other passengers, though."

"Have you searched the cabin of Miss Weston and Madame la Fabrère yet? I have some hope we may turn up something there. You know, Phil, I'm half mad with impatience, waiting about on deck while you do everything. Isn't there some ruse by which I might stay here without raising questions?"

Borset leaned back in his chair, brought his spread finger tips delicately together as he reflected. "I suppose I could hold you as the suspected thief. The trouble with that scheme is that I should be regretfully forced to put you in irons, and down in the hold you'd hear nothing. No, I have it. Why don't you climb into one of those curtained bunks?" He smiled whimsically. "You can play Polonius behind the arras, only don't get stuck by some Hamlet."

"The very thing!" Blair hid himself and began adjusting the curtains so he could peer out.

"Are you out of sight? We're ready to go on." He turned to the captain. "Shall we take the tutor next? What's his name? Ah, yes, Robin Dee."

The search and the questioning went on with Blair absorbing every word and now and again risking a look at the suspect. When an interrogation was completed and the young officer at the table was finishing his notes, Blair poked out his head and discussed with Borset what had been brought out. They were puzzled about Dee. He would say little of himself. They could not determine whether he was a simple scholar or a very cool rogue. He was readier to talk about his employer, young Auldjo's father. The boy, too, talked about his father in an oddly impersonal way.

After the boy had been ushered out, Borset remarked, "Auldjo senior must be a complete villain, different from Holseman only in that he is richer and his dishonest schemes are on a greater scale. Without stirring from Europe he's as great a pirate as De Vega. No doubt he has used De Vega more than once. They're probably friends. But all this doesn't help us."

Blair kept urging that they get quickly to Miss Weston and Madame la Fabrère since they were the most likely to have something 'to reveal. They had been in the inn the night before. Because the questioning had thus far done no good, he favoured moving directly to them.

"No, James," Borset said easily, "let them stew a little longer. The more apprehensive they grow, the more likely one of them is to betray herself. I'm for leaving them to the last."

Blair settled himself in the berth. "Very well, Phil," he said. "I regret I'm so urgent, but this affair has me devilish worried. Besides, this is a musty corner and I'm cramped. So hurry as much as you can."

Finally Rachel la Fabrère was ushered in and

seated at the table. Borset had turned aside to look at his lieutenant's notes. As her beauty struck him his quick look of appraisal turned into an admiring stare that paid full tribute to her creamy complexion, the blue of her eyes and the swell of her bosom. "Reports concerning you, madame, most sadly failed to do you justice." He gave her a slight bow. His eyes followed with interest the faint flush that spread over her face and neck in acknowledgement of his remark.

With a sigh he turned back to the business before them and led her through an account of her experiences the evening before. Blair had to confess to himself that her story squared with the facts as he knew them. She utterly denied having known Holseman before she boarded the *Baliol*. Though they had been casual acquaintances on board, she insisted he had never in the slightest degree confided in her. "In point of fact," she asserted with a pretty wave of her hand, "he was for me only something to mitigate the boredom." Borset kept going back and going back, putting his questions in a dozen different ways, but she stuck to her answers.

Though Rachel was frank enough about the events of the voyage, she was both reticent and vague about anything earlier. Borset could not draw her out. As to the future she was even more unsatisfactory. Asked why she was going to America she would say only, "But for pleasure, of course!" She said she had no friends there, had no plans for settling in the colonies. She had wanted a complete change; she was curious about the New World. Why not a voyage?

Blair suspected she had wanted to get away from her husband. Perhaps they had quarrelled. Perhaps he was involved in some scheme so dangerous that she was afraid to be near him if it went wrong. Blair couldn't really credit that idea; he had difficulty imagining a scheme riskier than some of those in which she had taken part. In spite of her denial of any friends in the colonies he suspected a new lover in America. But Borset was doing everything short of torture to get the truth out of her and he was getting nowhere. At the end of an hour they let her go.

When Cecily Weston entered the cabin she was clearly irritated by her long wait on deck. She was formal and short with Borset, and it was easy to detect a note of sarcasm in her voice. In spite of himself, Blair felt admiration for her poise, the kind that comes, he reflected, only from generations of breeding and family standing. It was hard to think of her as a secret agent, no matter how dedicated, and impossible to think of her as an adventurer of the Holseman stamp.

Phil Borset's first remark was to put her at her ease. To Blair, however, she appeared already perfectly mistress of herself and he supposed Borset was in fact overcoming in himself the slight feeling of inferiority she inspired when she was on her dignity. He referred pleasantly to her uncle Admiral Weston and said he had once had the honour of serving under him.

He began his questioning by leading her through the events of the previous afternoon and evening, going into great detail. He was particularly insistent about the afternoon when she had driven into the hills alone with Martha. Had she talked to anyone? Had she seen anyone she knew? Had she mentioned her plans for the evening? Blair supposed Borset was trying to establish some sort of connection between her and De Vega. She seemed frank and open in her answers, and nothing helpful emerged.

When the questioning reached the period when the four of them had been together at the inn Blair could check her answers against his own recollections. So far as he could tell, she met every question without hesitation, fully and accurately. Although he could not see how a transfer of the packet could have been managed after the men retired to the duelling ground, Borset questioned her closely about the time when she had been alone with Rachel. Her answers shed no light on the present location of the packet.

Borset took a new tack. "What can you tell me about Henry Holseman? How long have you known him?"

"I never saw or heard of him before I met him on

this voyage. Frankly, he was an insignificant little man and I paid him scant attention on the ship. He did not confide in me. It was only because he was squiring Madame la Fabrère that he happened to be with me last night. Indeed, I had no desire for the company of either. It was Mr. Blair who encouraged them to join us. He will bear me out, I believe, if you consult him."

Borset moved on. "What of De Vega?"

Cecily gathered her thoughts. "I suppose the household of every naval officer who has served off the coasts of Spain and Portugal has heard of De Vega. My uncle has spoken of him a number of times. Certainly I never expected to set eye on him. Now I hope I never see him again. He has a cruel face, sensual, utterly ruthless."

"Have you been on close terms with your uncle, Miss Weston?"

"I have made my home with him."

"He is a man of the highest and most unquestionable loyalty to the Crown. I mention this because I understand from the captain here that you're going to America to visit another uncle, Farquard Campbell, a North Carolina merchant. Is that correct?"

"It is, sir."

"Though Farquard Campbell is a wealthy man and a representative in the Provincial Assembly, it is widely known that he is friendly with rebellious, not to say seditious, groups. It is hard to make out his politics, for he seems to try to stay in with every faction. Do you share his political views in the present contest between the colonies and the Crown?"

Cecily Weston drew herself up. "This seems a leading question." Blair leaned forward with eager attention. Cecily continued: "My uncle has been long in America. Most of the letters we have exchanged have dealt with family matters, not with politics. We have not written often. What political convictions he would admit to I do not know. Some of the beliefs he is supposed to profess I happened to learn recently when I mentioned my projected voyage in London. The Earl of Dartmouth was good enough to sketch them for me. If the Earl is right, I deplore my Uncle Farquard's politics and shall endeavour to remedy them on my arrival. Does this answer you, Captain?"

"Quite," said Borset faintly. He exchanged a look of defeat with an aide. "I must tell you, Miss Weston, what you would have discovered in any case—that your cabin has been searched, as has the whole ship. I need scarcely add that nothing untoward was brought to light. Thank you very much for your patience."

When the door closed after her Blair clambered stiffly from his hiding-place. "Dartmouth!" he exclaimed. "I didn't suspect she knew Dartmouth. I suppose I may as well go on to Wilmington or New Bern before resigning my commission. Wouldn't you say so, Phil?" He took a restless turn about the room, then managed a faintly cheerful tone. "I'll use the rest of the voyage as best I can. Perhaps my proverbial good fortune will save me yet."

14

Sea Encounter

THE *Baliol* had cleared the harbour of Horta about dawn and started the second leg of its voyage, to Antigua in the West Indies. Repairs had been completed. The last basket of fruit and the last crate of poultry had been loaded.

All day they had cruised among islands shining like emeralds set in a sapphire sea. Though the wind had been light, they had gradually left Fayal dim and distant astern and they had passed other islands.

Now it was late afternoon. The twins, Moira and Sandy sprawled on the poop watching an island, perhaps a mile away, slip behind. It was a long island. Here and there a church or a rambling convent gleamed white against the green of rich pastures and vineyards that climbed to the very hill-tops. The tile roofs of little houses marked out dots of red against the green hill-sides. In the clear light, the distance made farms, houses and buildings look as small as toys.

The ship was sailing almost due west. As the sun sank into the sea with a blaze of splendour, a golden light rose slowly from the horizon, flooding the bowl of the sky higher and higher until all the west to the zenith was as bright as a field of daffodils. The sea took the color of the sky and even the ship's sails were tinged with it—a golden ship moving through golden water.

From the poop they could see the emigrants crowd the bulwarks to watch the strange sight. Some of them were afraid. One of them called loudly, "God is in that sky. He will smite us for our wickedness." Others cried him down. "It's a glory. His blessing on us. Now all will go well."

While they were babbling on the deck below, there was a hail from the crow's nest. "A ship. Crossing our bows."

Dougald and Moira moved to windward so they could see past the sails, and looked ahead. Some distance off, black against the golden sky, a full-rigged ship, which had apparently come out of a cove hidden in the shore, was crossing their course and heading farther out into the channel.

Moira stood trembling, her green eyes wide and round. There was fear in them, and her hand on the rail shook. "It is evil," she whispered.

"It's only the strange light," Dougald reassured her. "It gives an ordinary ship a spectral look."

"No, that ship carries evil men."

A shout from the captain interrupted them. "You aloft there, can you make her out? What flag does she carry?"

"Can't make out, sir. Against this light everything's black. She's shifting her course, close-hauled now."

The black silhouette, though farther off-shore than the *Baliol*, was coming rapidly closer. Moira, wide-eyed, staring, repeated, "A ship of evil." Involuntarily, Dougald shivered.

Near them the captain was muttering to himself, "Wish I could get a clear look at her. If she's a privateer she's got us in a devilish position. We're pinned between her and the shore." He raised his glass and studied the strange ship again. Then he came to a decision.

"Pipe to quarters!" he bellowed.

The crew had been waiting for the order. Sponge tubs, rammers and primers came out with a rush. The sailors manned the pumps, wet down the decks with leather hoses and spread sand. They bent to the tackles and raised the gun-ports. Powder bags and shot were rammed home in each gun. Each port-fire had his slow match alight in his tub ready even before his gun was run out through the open port.

Another party of sailors were bringing up pistols and cutlasses and distributing them.

Blair, in his shirt sleeves and wearing his sword, dashed up to the poop. "Is she a privateer?"

"Can't make out so long as she's in that glare. If she is, I'll be as ready for her as I can be. We don't carry much metal—only a few six-pounders and one pair of nine-pounders, all of them rusty from salt. If I could get clear, I'd rather run than fight. In two hours, maybe an hour and a half, it would be dark enough to give her the slip."

"If you have to fight, I want to remind you all the men passengers and many of the emigrants will fight for you. Can you arm them?"

"Cutlasses . . . a few pistols."

Blair turned on Dougald. "Get Moira below." He nodded at the other vessel. "We'll be in range of her guns in another couple of minutes."

As Dougald hurried Moira off the poop, he heard the captain talking to Blair. "You're an officer. You and Allan MacDonald muster the Scots and lead them. They'll not work the guns. They'll fight only if we're boarded, so you've maybe half an hour."

Dougald resolved to join Blair as soon as he had Moira in a safe place. He'd take her to Anne, with whom Alex was staying.

In the cabin he found Allan MacDonald, Sandy, Jamie and David, tying back their hair, stripping off their coats and preparing for action. Old Neil was getting out their pistols and swords. They greeted him with grim gaiety. "Come on, Dougald! Shirt and breeks. Pistols in your sash. Here, let's wind a handkerchief around your head. It will keep the hair out of your eyes. If they board us, we'll have plenty of action." Neil tied the kerchief and knotted it tight.

When they hurried out on deck to join Blair, the other ship was in plain view ahead and to the south of them. At that moment it came about smartly and set a course, sailing on the quarter, to intercept the *Baliol*. As it swung about they could make out a long row of guns. "Armed like a frigate," Blair muttered.

"She's no merchantman. The question is: is she hostile?"

As if in answer, the stranger's bow-chaser barked and a ball kicked up spray twenty yards in front of the *Baliol*. She was closing the gap between them rapidly, evidently the faster ship and in a position to take full advantage of the wind.

The captain shouted down to Blair on the deck below, "You and Mr. MacDonald keep your men out of sight behind the bulwarks. We'll save you as a little surprise if they try to board us."

The mate was moving from gun crew to gun crew on the starboard side. "Don't get too eager," he told each one. "These light guns won't do any damage at long range. Keep your gun trained but don't fire until I give the word. Watch for my signal."

Dougald, crouching behind the bulwark between Blair and Sandy, had two surprises. First, John Auldjo, a pistol in his belt and an awkwardly held sword in his hand, slipped between him and Sandy. As always, he was cool and rather formal. "I am not sure we are right to fight; the stranger is much stronger. But, since it is decided, I shall take part. May I stand beside you, Dougald?"

Dougald had scarcely got into a new position when he heard Sandy call, "Mother, get back in the cabin."

He turned his head and saw Flora walking quietly toward Allan. She had braided her hair and wrapped it close about her head. She wore a simple, close-fitting dress and heavy brogues. "Don't try to give me orders, Sandy. I'll stay by you and Jamie and Allan until I'm needed elsewhere."

Just then the look-out shouted, "She's a Barbary ship, from Salé."

"De Vega's!" Blair exclaimed. Dougald, next to him at the bulwark, could hear him talking to himself. "Wonder what he wants with us. He knows we carry a Mediterranean pass. Probably something Holseman stirred up. Will he want to fight or just to parley?"

Cecily Weston and Rachel, banished to their cabin

by the captain, were finding suspense intolerable. The cabin window was on the port side It revealed nothing but an expanse of sea and the island beyond.

At last Cecily could stand it no longer. "I'm going out. I'll take a cautious look, and if I must, I'll come back immediately."

Cecily closed the cabin door behind her and stood for a moment looking around. Before her was the whole expanse of the deck, with the gun crews ready and the Scots, some with claymores and dirks, others with pistols and cutlasses, crouched ready to surprise the enemy. As her eyes swept the deck she felt proud. She saw the MacDonalds, Blair and many of the emigrants, strong and handsome. Her eyes went back to Sandy and the twins, and then to Jamie. He was so young. Too young to be a warrior. Yet in her heart she knew that the whole warlike breed had been reared on tales of danger and heroism, and young as they were, they were grown almost to manhood. Already they deemed it their privilege, as well as their duty, to fight.

The look-out's cry, "Barbary ship—pirate ship!" drove the lads from her mind. She knew it was De Vega's. She feared he might be seeking the packet. If he searched the ship ... He must not find the papers in Flora's cabin, she resolved quickly.

She made her way along the deck to where Flora was waiting with Allan. "Flora," she said, "I must speak to you alone."

Together they went back to the great cabin. There Cecily hurriedly explained her fear. "You must give the papers back to me. I brought them onto the ship. I don't want you in danger because of me."

Flora considered briefly, her face grave. "No, my child, no. De Vega certainly saw you sitting next to Holseman at the inn. He will suspect you among the first. He doesn't know that I so much as went ashore. Let things stand as they are."

"Perhaps we should destroy the packet." Cecily spoke tentatively.

"Never," said Flora firmly. "It is addressed to Governor Martin and to him it shall go. It may be immensely important. Since so many people are after it, it must be. Wait here a moment. I'll go to my cabin and hide it more securely."

She hurried off. In a few moments she was back. "Worry no more about the packet, Cecily. Search as they may, they'll never find it. Let's go back on deck. The weariest work is waiting helplessly. Maybe we can find a way to help." She took Cecily's arm and began to lead her toward the door.

After a moment's hesitation, they stepped out. It was a shock to see how close De Vega's ship had come. It was scarcely a hundred and fifty yards away, sailing parallel to the *Baliol*. After the first warning gun from the bow-chaser De Vega had held his fire, for what reason Cecily could not guess. The *Baliol's* captain, she recognized, was prudent in postponing an engagement as long as he could. He was hopelessly outgunned and she supposed as badly outmanned, in spite of his fighting Scots.

A voice from De Vega's poop deck bawled, "Heave to! We're going to board you."

"On what conditions?" the captain demanded.

"We'll name them when we're aboard," came the arrogant reply.

The captain roared down to the mate, "Fire! Try for her masts and rigging. We can't sink her. We might stop her." The five starboard cannon roared in a ragged broadside.

Instantly De Vega's heavier broadside replied, deck height, not crippling the ship but knocking out three of her starboard guns and scattering the gun crews. At the same time pirates swarmed into the rigging and began raking the *Baliol's* decks with small-arms fire.

Cecily cried out, "Bring the wounded into the cabin. We'll do what we can for them." Pausing only long enough to see that the men had heard, she and Flora went in to enlist the aid of Moira, Rachel and Martha. They would be in charge of the sick bay.

The privateer never shifted her course an inch. She was unhurt by the *Baliol's* puny broadside, almost unaware of it. She sheered in closer and closer. Dougald, crouched behind the bulwark, was angry and ashamed when he thought of the futility of their gunnery. Only one round, only half a minute, and they were silenced. It would be different, he resolved, when De Vega's men tried to board. Then the Scots would be in it. He would be in it.

The two vessels were ten feet apart, forging through the water. Then five feet apart. De Vega's men threw grappling irons, which took hold of shrouds and rigging. In seconds they had the two ships lashed together. A swarm of pirates began to jump to the *Baliol's* decks.

"Now!" Blair and Allan MacDonald yelled with one voice. The hidden Scots leaped out and joined the crew with a rush. They met the boarders with pistols fired point-blank and fell on them with cutlasses and claymores.

Dougald, at Blair's elbow, felt no fear. He fired his first pistol full into the face of a raider. His second brought down a man who was raising his cutlass to swing it down on Blair. Then he was hacking away with his claymore. The surprise of the Scots' onslaught made it prevail. A few of the pirates scrambled back onto their ship. The others went down. Except for the dead and the dying, not one corsair was left on the *Baliol's* deck.

High on the poop De Vega rallied his men with volleys of curses. He was a brilliant figure in his rich clothes. His broad hat with a drooping plume was a reminder of the old tradition. His men responded to his magnetism.

He jumped lightly down to the main deck, and drew his sword. "This time I'll lead you. What are you? Cowards? Dastards? Women?" He poured a rich contempt on them. "You ninnies, will you let these merchants shame you? Pistols primed? Got a cutlass? Come on then! Follow me. I'll skewer the man that falters."

Lashed by De Vega's tongue and led by his sword, the second wave of boarders was irresistible. The sailors soon gave up. The Scots, resisting stubbornly, were driven backwards, outnumbered and at last over-powered. Dougald bowed his head; defeat rankled. The Scots had been brave enough. Many lay groaning on the deck. They had fought hard. But they had been beaten, easily beaten, by a motley crew of foreigners.

Pirates with pistols cocked and cutlasses ready held the Scots helpless, while four or five men collected their arms. De Vega stood away from them, with an empty stretch of deck before him.

Blair knew the *Baliol* was now defenseless. His mind was racing in search of an idea, any expedient which would help the ship's company—and, equally important, keep alive his chance of regaining the packet. The only possible way, he thought, is to play on De Vega's vanity.

With his rapier sheathed, he stepped around the man guarding him and slowly approached De Vega. He addressed him coolly. "When I saw you at the inn on Fayal the other night you had an appetite for duels." De Vega's eyes lighted with whimsical interest, and Blair went on. "Your men are well armed and are three to our one. I have nothing to bargain with. But do me the favor of calling off your rascals and accepting my challenge. Let us fight this out between us."

De Vega laughed lightly. "Of a certainty, you have nothing to wager. Never mind, I accept your challenge. If you win, we leave the ship at once."

"Good," said Blair shortly.

"One moment," De Vega interposed. "I have a couple of matters of business to dispose of first. I didn't come to capture your ship. I respect your Mediterranean pass. I came to search.

"Before I hanged your friend Mr. Holseman up there—" involuntarily every face looked up, and then blanched at the sight of the black-clad body dangling from the yard-arm—"he mentioned, under some discomfort, that he had left a valuable packet on the *Baliol*. He would have bargained with it. He offered to share with me the fortune that could be made from it. I suspect it contains jewels. I want this packet.

"Second, he told me you carried a boy named John Auldjo. He is the son of a man with whom I have had dealings. Not a friend, a ... former associate. I'll take the boy, too, and see to his manly education. Oh, I shall give him every consideration, for I expect his father to reward me most liberally for perfecting the boy."

By some clairvoyance he picked young Auldjo out of the crowd of prisoners. "You, boy, step forward. What's your name?"

With perfect self-possession, almost with indifference, the boy answered, "John Auldjo."

De Vega turned to a villainous-looking fellow with a squint, evidently one of his mates. "Convey the boy aboard our ship. Take his tutor, too, for company. Then choose a dozen men and search the ship. Find the packet."

Young Auldjo turned to Dougald as the pirates approached him. "Have no concern for me. These men know that I am worth a larger ransom alive and in health. They will take pains to keep me so. Good-bye, Dougald."

Blair felt a great urge to interpose in the boy's behalf, but it would have spoiled his plan. His only chance was the duel. If he could win, there was a good chance De Vega might keep his word.

As the boy was escorted to the other vessel, De Vega turned once more to Blair. "Your pardon, sir, for keeping you waiting. My time is short. There is no point in waiting for the outcome to give instructions, for I shall infallibly win our duel."

Blair bowed. "No apology needed, sir. Make the boy's freedom, too, ride on my blade."

De Vega stripped off his coat and tossed it and his plumed hat to one of his men. "Agreed. Now, sir, if you are ready ..."

They faced each other. At the outset both men were cautious. Then the pace began to quicken. Blair was cool and serious. He had to be. In the first few passes he had felt the strength of De Vega's wrist. The man's sword moved like lightning. And De Vega was at ease, smiling and laughing and talking with insolent unconcern. Blair resolved to make a quick bid for victory. He manoeuvred for his most deceptive thrust. De Vega soon allowed him to reach the position he wanted. With a grunt of satisfaction he lunged. By a scarcely perceptible movement of his wrist, De Vega caught the thrust and turned it aside. "Not bad, not bad at all!" he exclaimed with a smile. "Of course it doesn't work with De Vega. But what does?"

As the duel went on Blair was forced to realize that his opponent was toying with him. Well, there was no help for it. He went on doggedly but without hope. At last De Vega's enjoyment of the exercise began to wear thin. "Enough of this fooling!" he cried. Blair felt his blade engaged. Then De Vega gave a sudden jerk with his powerful wrist. Blair felt a shock that made his arm tingle to the shoulder. His sword clanged on the deck a dozen feet off.

Disarmed! He stood stoically. De Vega calmly sheathed his sword. "You're a brave man, sir, but as a swordsman you aren't fit to face me." He added, "If it's any comfort to you, almost nobody is."

He turned to one of his lieutenants. "Drive these prisoners into the forecastle and lock them up while we search the ship."

After the brief cannonade some of the wounded had been carried into the great cabin. The women were busy bandaging and nursing them. Cecily was surprised to see Rachel working seriously with the others. She was even more surprised by Rachel's skill and coolness. She was evidently experienced and knew just what to do. Once, as she finished dressing a jagged splinter wound in a man's shoulder, Rachel looked up and caught Cecily watching her. "There may be more to me than you think," she said with a tight little smile. "I haven't spent all my time dancing. One learns what to do."

She demanded more lint and bandage. They had almost run out. Flora offered to bring some linen from her cabin. She hurried off. Minutes passed, and she did not come back. Cecily stopped work and went to look for her.

In the MacDonald cabin she found Flora sitting on the floor, very pale and holding her left arm. An open cupboard high up and an overturned chair told the story. Flora must have climbed onto the chair to reach for something in the cabinet and fallen.

Between set teeth Flora said, "My arm's broken, I think. Whisky on the shelf." She slumped back, her head on the edge of the low berth.

Cecily poured liquor into a cup and forced a little through Flora's lips. She had no idea how to help her. Perhaps Rachel would know. She ran back to the great cabin. Rachel came with her at once. Together they lifted Flora carefully into the berth.

Rachel found the break, midway up the forearm. "I'll do the best I can. There's nobody else." She looked about. The roll of linen Flora had been seeking when she fell was on the floor beside the overturned chair. It would provide plenty of bandage. She needed something for a splint. After a brief search she found a dagger in a very stiff sheath. The sheath would do.

With the dagger she slit Flora's sleeve and turned it back out of the way. She poured more whisky and offered it to Flora. "This will hurt. Better take a stiff gulp to dull the pain."

She grasped Flora's left hand and pulled with gentle, steady strength. With her other hand, feeling delicately, she made sure the broken bones were in position. "Now, Cecily, the splint. Put it there." She gestured with her head. "A little farther up. That's it.

"Now comes the hard part. We must bandage it without letting the bones slip out of place. Take her arm gently in both hands, elbow and wrist. Gently now. That's right. Now steady."

She began to wind the bandage, to hold the splint firmly in place. As long as she could she felt the break to make sure the bones stayed in place. She had made eight or ten turns when the search party led by the man with the squint appeared at the door.

"What's going on here?" he demanded.

Without moving her head, Rachel answered sharply, "I'm setting a broken arm. What do you want here?"

"I'm to search the cabin."

"Well, you can't do it now. This bandaging is not to be interrupted. Mrs. MacDonald is in pain and I won't have her bothered. Go search elsewhere."

"My orders were to search," he insisted.

"Search then, but do it somewhere else."

The man hesitated.

Cecily was deeply concerned for Flora. "If it's something connected with Holseman you're looking for, leave her alone. She scarcely knew him. I was in the party at the inn the night your captain took him. If you must search, try my cabin. It's over there."

One of the men behind the leader interposed. "Do what she says. Don't bother the lady with the hurt arm. De Vega can talk to her when he gets tired of fencing. Come on."

They trooped off to search Cecily's cabin. It would look as if it had been struck by a tempest, she supposed. Rachel was finishing the bandaging. At least they had not hurt Flora.

Rachel went back to look after the wounded in the great cabin. Cecily stayed with Flora.

A few minutes later De Vega appeared at the door. He was again wearing his elegant coat and his plumed hat, the very picture of a corsair. "My men tell me they postponed searching here because of an injured lady. What is the matter?"

"She fell and broke her arm a few minutes ago. She is scarcely conscious."

De Vega glanced over at Flora lying in the berth. "Who is she?"

"Her name is Flora MacDonald. She is—"

He held up his hand. "I know her well by reputation—the saviour of the last of the Stuarts."

"Pray do not disturb her. She did not know Holseman. She was not at the inn that night, nor was any of her family."

He hesitated, then shrugged. "Well, let her be. I'll question you instead. You are from Devon. Your name is Weston. You sat next to Holseman at the inn the other night. I remember your face."

Cecily opened her eyes wide. "How did you know my name?"

"I have ways of finding out things. What can you tell me about Holseman?"

"Nothing, really. I never saw him before we all boarded this ship."

"Had you heard of him?"

"No."

"Before he died, he ... confided in me that he had come into a valuable packet. He didn't say, but I gather it contains jewels. He said something—he was not very clear-headed toward the last—about entrusting it to one of you ladies."

Cecily's mouth opened in honest surprise. "Jewels? I never heard of any jewels aboard the ship."

Her mind was working furiously. Had Holseman, seeking desperately for something to barter for his life, invented jewels to go in the packet he had carried? The true packet he had probably thought not attractive enough to De Vega, but diamonds were another matter.

Her surprise evidently impressed De Vega. "Ah, well, perhaps it was one of the other ladies he had in mind. I noticed as I came in that my men had already searched your cabin. They didn't leave it neat; I'm afraid their housekeeping leaves something to be desired. They found nothing."

De Vega stopped on his way to the door. Half turning, he said, "Speaking of other ladies, was Holseman telling me the truth when he said the second woman in your party at the inn was Rachel la Fabrère?"

"Yes, of course."

"I didn't recognize her. In the past I've known both her and her husband, not always in a friendly way."

"If your ill will is chiefly directed against her husband, you should know that she has left him. She is running away from him." Cecily volunteered this information in the faint hope that it would help Rachel.

"Take me to her. I'd relish a word with her."

They found Rachel in the great cabin. De Vega greeted her with an exaggerated bow and sweep of his plumed hat. "I did not recognize you the other night, madame. A thousand pardons! I hear that you, like me, are at odds with your husband."

Rachel said nothing. She was very pale.

De Vega's voice turned deadly cold. "Where is the little packet Holseman entrusted to you?"

She burst into denials. She had no packet, nothing from Holseman at all.

He reached out and seized her by the arm, gripping it brutally. He turned his head to Cecily and spoke in silky tones. "I believe I'll take her with me. She may have the packet hidden somewhere about her and I can search it out at my leisure. If I have a mind for her, she might serve to amuse me for a month or so at sea." At Cecily's expression, he laughed. "Oh, feel no concern for her. She's quite used to strange beds. She looks at me now and knows I am a man. In two days' time she will be begging me to take her to my couch. And in the end I might sell her back to her husband. Perhaps not. He would kill her and take satisfaction in it, and I would rather cause him discomfort than her."

A bellow came from the deck. "De Vega, De Vega, A British man-of-war closing in on us. Hurry! We've got the boy."

"The devil!" he exclaimed. "No time to lose." With a quick shove he sent Rachel sprawling to the floor. "Keep the wench."

He was gone. On deck they could hear him shouting orders. "Get back on board. Cut us loose. Aloft there, set topgallant sails."

In a few moments his ship was slipping off into the gathering twilight. She was too fast for the British vessel to pursue. It was the *Boyne*, coming in from Massachusetts. Someone released the prisoners in the forecastle. Except for the dead and wounded, everything was as before.

Cecily went to Flora's cabin to see if she was comfortable. "All is well, Cecily," Flora whispered. "I hid the packet in the back of my mirror."

15

The Western Ocean

DAVID MACDONALD, wrapped in a light blanket, lay
on his back and watched the stars wheel slowly
back and forth as the *Baliol* rolled gently. He and
Dougald had seen some of the sailors and emigrants
sleeping on deck after the weather had turned warm.
A night or so later the twins had carried their own
bedding up to the poop deck and spread it near the
stern. Since that night, unless it looked like rain, they
had slept on deck regularly.

Though it was close to dawn, David noticed
Dougald was still sleeping deeply, sometimes snoring
a little. He would just lie quiet so as not to disturb
Dougald. He stretched cautiously and relaxed again.
His mind ran back over the voyage. As far as the
Azores, and beyond to the point where De Vega had
lain in wait, the company aboard the *Baliol* had had a
hard time. A few of them were gone—Holseman,
John Auldjo, Robin Dee. Some had been killed in the
fight with De Vega. Others still lay in their bunks
suffering from wounds. Even those who had come
through without a scratch had been shaken. Queer
how different reality was from the adventures you
dreamed about in advance.

Since that evening of golden sky and ocean everything had gone well. The winds had blown fair and
gentle. The seas had smiled. No more storms, no
more trouble.

The ship's carpenter had repaired the bulwarks and
gun-ports broken by De Vega's cannon. All day long
sailors had sat patching old sails or sewing new ones.
Their neat stitching had fascinated some of the emi-
grant women, who had been eager to try their hands

with the heavy, three-sided sail-needle. When they had tried to push the needle through the thick cloth with a sailor's palm instead of a thimble they had found it wasn't so easy as it looked. The strap intended to hold the palm in place was too big for their hands and let it slip. When they had proved clumsy—and most of them had—the sailors laughed gleefully.

Every day or so David had seen new creatures in the sea. He remembered his mixed pleasure and amusement when he had seen his first school of porpoises playing around the ship, tumbling, bobbing and chasing one another in sheer high spirits. Now, farther south, it was not unusual to see flying fish rise out of water and skitter above the waves in flight from pursuing dolphins. Sometimes one had landed on the decks. As soon as it had dried out, its colors had faded. Twice he had seen a fifteen-foot grampus wallowing and blowing in the trough of the sea quite close to the ship.

The weather had grown steadily warmer, and for the past few days it had been burning-hot at noon. The captain had had an awning stretched over part of the poop so that the cabin passengers might sit in the shade. Flora was often there, her arm in a sling. She never complained, and Rachel said she thought the break was knitting well. The younger women had blossomed out in bright muslins and cool calicoes, and all but Moira wore saucy little straw hats. People talked often about Rachel's beauty, but David thought both Cecily and Moira were prettier.

His sentiments toward Cecily were changing. In the beginning he had wanted her to be his special friend. She had paid him attention and been very kind to him. But in the great storm and afterwards, and again on the Azores, she had turned to the older men—to Allan, the captain and especially Blair. Oh, she was cordial to him, but even so, she sometimes made him feel he was merely an amusing child. An unwanted memory pricked him. After all the thought he'd put into selecting a keepsake for her at Horta, she said, when he gave her the intricately carved fan, "How quaint of you! What a nice lad you are—to spend your few hours on that exotic island purchasing souvenirs." Her words and her faintly mocking tone had hurt.

David rolled suddenly to one side. Then, with a determined sigh, he told himself a hard truth. Cecily was a lot older than he, and a difference of age did count with women, he supposed, just as Dougald had once suggested. Now David accepted the fact, and experienced a kind of relief. He gazed up at the quiet stars again.

A few minutes later David had to smile to and at himself. He realized that recently he'd been having a lot more fun with Moira than with Cecily. She seldom concealed her heavy auburn hair under a hat, and the sun had turned her face and arms a smooth brown. The fear and the suddenness of leaving Skye had worn off. In the holiday air that pervaded the ship Moira was full of gaiety and low laughter. Yesterday, when she had worn that pale-yellow dress, his eyes had turned to her every few minutes. She was the prettiest thing on the ship.

Dougald never talked about her, but he kept watching her, too. David wondered how Dougald felt toward her. He and Dougald had never been rivals; they could both have her as a companion. As he thought of Moira a pleasant drowsiness stole over him. He drifted back into sleep, the smile still on his lips.

Two afternoons later Dougald sat under the awning on the poop and tried to read a book John Auldjo had left behind, Montaigne's Essays, put in English by John Florio. He had just read how Montaigne's father had musicians play sweet music to awaken the boy pleasantly in the morning. Montaigne had been raised to live easily in a soft world. A Scots parent would have thought more of hardening his sons for a difficult life. It was as much a question of geography as of right and wrong. How should a boy be raised who was destined to voyage to America? he wondered.

He turned over twenty or thirty pages without looking at them and began to read again at random. The words failed to hold him. His eyes involuntarily strayed to the stern where David and Moira were fishing. A basketful of fish beside them proved their industry, but, nonetheless, it seemed to Dougald that they were mostly laughing and joking. Dougald was despondent. When he was with Moira, he always seemed to be serious, almost solemn. With all his heart he wished he had David's power to amuse her. But he hadn't, and it was no wonder she preferred David. There she was now, laughing aloud. If she liked David better, David she should have. He wouldn't stand in the way. There was nothing he wanted more than to have both of them happy. Well, almost nothing.

He mused miserably. Unnoticed on his knees, the copy of Montaigne fell shut. The dream of making a new life in America with Moira at his side, which had made him board the ship buoyantly, now seemed far beyond his reach.

The pair at the stern rail were pulling in their lines. David had a good bite and the line was jerking tautly in his hands. Just then Moira uttered a little cry. Dougald was not sure what she had done until she cried out that the barbed hook was stuck in her finger. With a bound he was at her side, while David was still encumbered with the fish he was unwilling to lose. Holding her finger, Dougald studied the way the hook had lodged. If he just pulled it out, it would leave a jagged tear, not to mention the pain of it.

With his free hand he pulled out his dirk, which was razor-sharp. If he made a tiny cut just there and turned the hook, it would come out, he thought, without hurting Moira badly or enlarging the wound. Though his whole attention was centred on his task, he realized David had landed his fish and was watching intently. Without looking up, he said, "I can manage this, David. Go to Madame la Fabrère and get some clean bandage. Hurry." David did as he was told without question.

"I'm going to make a tiny cut to let the barb out,

Moira. I'll try not to hurt you. Hold your hand as still as you can, and don't watch." She nodded soberly.

Steadily, gently, he cut just deep enough with the sharp dirk. A drop or two of blood welled up, not much. Moira had scarcely winced. He let his dirk drop and took the hook in the fingers of his right hand. He rolled it just a trifle, worked the barb into the slit he had made. It was easier than he had expected. With no resistance it came free in his hand. After a quick spurt of blood, only a slow ooze followed.

At the sight of the blood he had drawn, Dougald felt an immense pity for Moira. He saw her eyes swimming with tears she had held back. He must have hurt her cruelly. "Poor Moira," he whispered. With a great upsurge of boldness and concern he kissed her quickly on the cheek.

To his utter amazement she uttered a delighted little laugh. Suddenly, forgetting her hurt, she reached out with both hands and seized him by the ears. She pulled his head forward and gave him a firm kiss on the lips. Just as suddenly she released him. "Oh, Dougald, you solemn goose," she cried, "I do like you so much. It's always been you." She blushed. "Oh dear, I've given myself away!"

He was speechless. Before he could gather his wits, David was coming back with the bandage. While Dougald's fingers prosaically and neatly wrapped the clean white cloth about Moira's wounded finger, great organ tones of joy swelled and rolled through his heart. "It's always been you," she had said. Later, examining himself in a bit of a mirror, curiously as if he were a stranger, he found a drop of her blood on his ear.

The ship slipped along easily. One day was like another, but each evening found them nearer the Leeward Islands. The captain began to predict that they would reach St. John's, the chief town on Antigua, about the end of the week. One morning, after he had calculated the latitude, he told the passengers the ship would reach the line and pass into the Torrid Zone late the next morning or early in the afternoon.

At noon the ship crossed the Tropic of Cancer. Since it was not to cross the Equator and have the time-honoured celebration of that, the captain allowed the old hands to hold an initiation ceremony for those first entering tropic waters. It seemed wise to encourage anything that would relieve the tedium of the voyage. The ceremony was a rude mummery with a sailor in an oakum wig playing Neptune, come aboard to welcome the ship into his tropic kingdom. Neptune sat as a judge on each candidate for initiation. Some he ordered shaved. They were lathered with a mixture of kitchen grease and pot black and scraped with a notched stick for a razor. Others, blindfolded, he ordered pitched into the sea. They were tipped backward into a tub of water. Though it was only horseplay, some of the more superstitious Highlanders believed the big sailor was in truth Neptune and his judgements frightened them badly.

There were many new-comers to the tropics and Neptune was still at his work judging them in the late afternoon when the lookout reported a sail on the horizon, to the south. As the stranger came closer it revealed itself as a light schooner. Both vessels changed course to pass close by.

By late supper-time they were meeting. The *Baliol* backed her yards. The schooner came up into the wind. Both vessels lay drifting. The master of the schooner shouted across the water, "Where are you bound?"

"Antigua."

"Don't go there. There's a virulent fever stirring. Five hundred dead already and many more going down every day. Every ship has fled."

"Any fever aboard you?"

"No. We got away clean. I wouldn't go back for a thousand pounds."

"Thanks for the warning."

The schooner put her helm over and resumed her course. The *Baliol* continued to drift while the captain considered the news. Darkness began to fall. Most of the cabin passengers gathered on the poop as the last light died in the west.

A few minutes later the captain began to bark orders. Sailors ran aloft and the sails were trimmed. The *Baliol* settled on a course a little north of the faint glow to the west.

When everything was adjusted to his satisfaction, the captain came over to the knot of passengers sitting under the awning on the poop. "Some of you wanted to go to Antigua," he said. "I have freight for the islands. But there are too many souls aboard to risk yellow fever. I've decided to set a course directly for the Cape Fear. If any of you are disappointed, there's no help for it.

"If the wind holds fair as it is now we'll see the cape in four days. Mind, I don't promise. A man is a fool to vouch for the wind. But my judgement is about four more days."

At the announcement Cecily felt an unusual ill humour settle on her. She supposed the captain was right and there was no help for it. But the voyage was growing very monotonous, and she had set her heart on going ashore at Antigua. She had heard much of the island's beauty, of the almost regal luxury of life there. She might even have had another adventure, though nothing, she hoped, so serious as had befallen them in the Azores. Certainly she didn't want another mysterious packet to hide.

With an impatient gesture she strolled away. She'd just have to fix her mind on Carolina and be content that the end of the journey wasn't too far away. But there was no denying she felt robbed now she knew she would not see the flowering island. Perhaps she was being childish. When she thought coolly, she had no desire to risk a virulent fever. Still, she was annoyed.

In the lanthorn's light she noticed Blair, standing to one side and gazing at her. A few minutes later he made his way to her side. "You looked uncommonly put out just now when the captain made his announcement," he said in a low voice, "and most uncommonly attractive. Were you so eager to visit Antigua?"

"Not so much eager to see Antigua as most anxious

to gain a brief respite from the tiresome features of this voyage."

"At the risk of discovering I am one of the tiresome features, may I make a suggestion? The night before we reached the Azores we smelled those small islands at a considerable distance. The scent of a continent should reach much farther out. Let's go up to the bow of the ship and make the experiment there."

Cecily hesitated, then shook her head. "We're much too far away."

There was a challenge in his manner. "America is a very large continent. Who knows what odours it can generate? Let us at least try."

She recognized the challenge. For a moment she looked him steadily in the eye. At last she shrugged. "Oh, very well."

They descended from the poop, picked their way along the dark main deck and climbed at last to the forecastle. A cool wind had driven the sailors below. They were alone.

No sooner had they reached the bow of the ship than Cecily carefully sniffed the air, as if to justify her presence there alone with Blair. There was nothing but pure ocean breeze, unmixed with the smells of land.

"Off the Azores I accused you of a trick to get me to come for a stroll with you. Remember? That night you were right. But tonight you have really used the ruse I suspected then."

Blair laughed. "I confess it tonight. But the end justifies the means. You're here with me."

His complacency revived some of her old antagonism for him. She sought a new point of attack and found it in the afternoon's initiation. "You men!" she cried. "Always tricking someone—and for nothing more than vanity and childish amusement! Look at your foolery this afternoon."

"It was pleasing enough to those who took part," said Blair stiffly. "What was amiss?"

"Look at it sensibly," Cecily answered with the air of a weary schoolmaster with a dull pupil. "A big sailor with a wig of oakum played Neptune and scared a succession of poor gullible Highlanders half silly. You men blindfolded them one by one, daubed pot black on their faces, scraped them raw with a stick. In the end you threatened to throw them into the sea and tipped them into a tub of water with their clothes still on. Admirable, wasn't it?"

Blair's forced smile was a little sheepish. "I dare swear," he said, "that each man, after he got his blindfold off, heartily enjoyed the initiation of his fellows."

"My point exactly," Cecily pursued him. "If one of you suffers, he can't wait until the rest have suffered as much. Would women do such a silly thing? Of course not."

She saw she had made him sulky and her irritation drained away. After all, he'd no doubt invited her to join him because he saw her boredom; and his attention, if not wholly desirable, was flattering. She felt an impulse to coax him back into good humour, but she couldn't think of a way.

Still a little disgruntled, he spoke boyishly. "You make us out sorry creatures. Yet many a woman can put up with us and is glad to."

To atone for her sharpness she answered in a fond, teasing way. "I know. It's dull without a man." Her hand touched his shoulder soothingly. "I can't think why. What good is a man?"

He had been half angry with her. At her touch he knew how to answer her. His arms went around, imprisoning her. In the dim light, as he bent forward he could just make out the smile on her lips. "A man is good for this," he said quickly as his mouth came down on hers, covering the smile.

She pushed her hands against his chest, pushed and tried to shove him away. She moved her head to free her lips from his kiss. His arms about her were too strong. In a moment she felt her hands moving traitorously, slipping around his neck. Do what she could, her lips were opening, yielding. Something warm like brandy was moving in her veins. Her body grew soft in his arms.

His lips left her mouth. Rapidly they brushed her

closed eyes, one after the other, touched her cheeks, her chin, and found a warm hollow on her throat. Now he was holding her yielding body surely with one arm. His other hand strayed, touching her hair, pressing her to him. Wherever it went, it made her warmer still. This was madness; she shouldn't yield to him.

He stopped kissing her. They stood silent, leaning against each other and breathing deeply. Her dress had a laced bodice. His hands went to the cords tied in a bow. "Let me," he whispered.

She leaned toward him slightly, involuntarily. Then suddenly she was afraid. Her hands clutched to her bodice, she broke from him and ran to the ladder. He did not pursue her. . . .

In her bed, turning and tossing restlessly, she wondered if she was sorry. She was not sure that she liked James Blair, but he had the power to waken her blood. He was a man who was good for this, and she wanted such a man. For hours she could not sleep.

Across the cabin Rachel lay fast asleep. Rachel and her dancer. Rachel and De Vega. Cecily and James Blair. Sisters of the blood. And who was to judge her sister?

In the morning Cecily dreaded meeting Blair. She didn't want to be alone with him. In a group it would be little better. She was sure she would blush at the constant memory of their experience the night before and everyone would know.

The passengers gathered under the awning on the poop deck, as they did every morning now. She spoke to them idly and watched covertly for Blair. He soon appeared, greeted Anne and Flora and then turned toward her. She looked about desperately for some means of evading him. There was Allan MacDonald approaching, a roll of paper in his hand. He would do, she thought gratefully.

"Oh, Mr. MacDonald," she called, "what's that you have there?"

He came briskly over to her. "It's a map. When I found we were so close to North Carolina, I borrowed a map of the colony from the captain." How fortunate! He was itching to explain it to someone.

He unrolled it and she took it on her lap, holding it flat. His finger pointed. "See," he said, "here is the coast. Cape Fear is just there, pointing almost straight south. The river runs parallel behind it, to the west. We should be skirting the cape and coming up the river on Tuesday if the captain's prediction holds."

Now they were very close to Carolina, the map took on reality for Cecily. It represented earth and water she would be touching in a few days. Her mind took it in and memorized it.

Allan was going on. "It's a fair river, I'm told. We enter it with the cape on our right and a rather large island to the left. Very soon after we are in the river we shall pass Fort Johnston on the west shore—that is, to the left. Fifteen or twenty miles above the fort we shall come to Brunswick. Here it is—" he put his finger on a dot on the map—"but we shan't stop there. Then another fifteen miles or so will bring us to Wilmington. Of course there are plantations scattered along the shore, and perhaps villages, for all I know. At Wilmington we leave the ship."

"Is Wilmington a fine town?" Cecily asked with real interest.

"I'm told it is well built," Allan explained, "but it stands on low ground and the air is damp at all times. In summer the heat is oppressive, and mosquitoes are a torment. I'd never care to live in the lowlands. You won't be staying there either. I understand Farquard Campbell's main seat is far inland at Campbelltown."

Cecily nodded. "Yes, 'tis named for him. But will it be close to where you go? I'll want to see Flora often."

"Aye, but a mile or so from Cross Creek, where we shall stop while I seek out lands to my liking."

"How will we go inland—by boat or road?" Cecily asked.

"Either way. Part of the way the road is but a track through the wilderness, I believe, but it is passable for a carriage and travellers can stop the night at some plantation. The journey takes several days by road or boat."

"I'm strangely impatient to taste it all," said Cecily eagerly. "Perhaps I shall go to New Bern before visiting Campbelltown. Is it on your map? Where?"

Allan scrutinized the chart for a moment. "Here it is. See, to the north, on another river."

"It is Governor Martin's capital, is it not?"

"I believe so. He has a kind of palace there, built by an earlier governor."

"I shall want to see it soon."

"Well, no doubt we'll get our first glimpse of Carolina on Sunday or Monday. We can contain ourselves that long, I hope," said Allan with a sigh, "though I confess I'm as eager as you are."

16

Stephen Moray

STEPHEN MORAY, silversmith, spoke to his horse. The mare at once responded by breaking into a brisk trot, her best gait for covering at steady pace the straight, hard-packed path that led from Cross Creek to New Bern. For a good part of the journey Stephen jogged slowly beside the coaches of several travelling companions; now that they had turned off on the road to Wilmington he wanted to make good time. A truly regal commission for his craft awaited him and he was eager to receive it.

As he posted along in rhythm to his mount's gait, Stephen's thoughts dwelt on the riders who had bidden him farewell. A goodly party that had been—all important folk led by Farquard Campbell, the rich merchant of Campbelltown. Campbell had chatted about his errand; he was going to meet his niece, who had arrived on the ship *Baliol* from Scotland. He had never seen her, he said, but report had it that she was a fair lass with a good head on her shoulders. "And a fortunate thing that is," Campbell had said. " 'Tis foolishness to send a maid here now. But it won't be so bad if she's got the sense to mind her own affairs. If everyone would do that, we'd not have all this trouble." Stephen smiled to himself recalling Campbell's words; he wondered how the lanky merchant reconciled the "mind your own business" policy for others with his own active interest in local politics.

Well, that was Campbell's affair. Stephen lost interest in it and thought of the other travellers. They were all going to the ball for Flora MacDonald, who with her husband and other members of her clan had come in on the *Baliol*. Such a to-do they'd set up about her! Every rider had chimed in some memory or anecdote about Scotland's most famous woman. A couple of them could speak from firsthand knowledge, for they'd fought in the '45. Others, even the old man who had emigrated in the early thirties, long before Flora MacDonald became famous, knew the whole story. Stephen doubted that there was a Scot in all Cumberland, Anson and Montgomery counties who couldn't recite the tale by heart. He himself, born here in the province, had learned along with his nursery rhymes the tragic history of Charlie's defeat at Culloden and of his refuge in the islands. Even after he was orphaned and left to pick up knowledge where and when he could, he'd never lacked for teachers of Scots history. Whenever he was with a few Cape Fear Highlanders, he'd heard how the clans stood shoulder to shoulder to go down in glorious defeat.

Stephen shrugged carelessly as he remembered that often he had been with Cape Fear Englishmen who had another version to tell: the clans hadn't stood so bravely together—some had fled to the hills—and no defeat was glorious. Be that as may, Stephen thought, the outcome was the same. Whether taken on the field or in the hills, the poor Scots had been made to swear the great oath. It still tasted bitter in their mouths and rankled in their blood. Though free of the oath, Stephen hated it and his sympathy went out to all who lived under that sword of Damocles. "An oath," he'd often said, "ought to say what a man believes in his innermost heart and what a man wants to give his full strength to. 'Tis an iniquitous way of undermining manhood to make a man swear to what he cannot believe. What shall he do with his heart and strength if they're tied round with loathed commitments?"

With a sad shake of his head Stephen reflected that many of the Scots he knew were now asking themselves that very question: What to do now, when there's a call for men to stand up to the Hanoverian and tell him he can't override a subject's rights? Some of the veterans of the '45 half whispered, "After all, we came here partly to get some rights. And shall we let them be taken away, and our farms and prosperity with them?"

Others weren't too clear about the meaning of the talk of human rights and the English constitution. They'd come too recently to understand the issues that evoked such talk. But they were clear about the losses they'd sustain if trade didn't improve. " 'Tis not for us," they said, "to talk about loyalty. We're sworn. Let's just pray the quarrel's soon settled and we can go about our affairs in peace."

And when the talk came to such a point someone would try to cheer the others by saying, "Well, 'tis just the hotheads who stir things up. Like as not most people won't have anything to do with them and their rashness." Here the old and cautious ones would sigh and hopefully nod their heads. But nowadays someone was likely to answer, "Maybe the hotheads are right. Lots of people are taking their side."

Then there'd be a little flurry of panic, but most of them would end by hoping to God there'd be no trouble, at least no trouble they'd have to take sides in. An old man would raise a knobby, calloused hand and say, "Hush! Hush! We have no part in this controversy. We have our farms to cultivate, our timber to cut, our new fields to plow. Wait. It will die down—or be checked. Let's hold our peace till then."

So most of the Scots turned the rich, ripe earth and set their turpentine buckets and moved farther west into virgin land. But more and more frequently they had to look up from their toil with a worried frown because someone among them would muse aloud, "What shall we do if it comes to blows between England and the colonies?"

As he rode through the pine barrens that verge on the coastal plain in the Cape Fear area, Stephen remembered the tension he sometimes felt around him. But, he thought as his mind reverted to Farquard Campbell, there's never the smell of fear about him. For all that he probably knows more of what's going on and what's likely to happen than any of the others. His fine mounts, his gold piled up, his influence seem to divide him from the rest, insulate him from danger, though he sometimes reaches out to put his hand close to the fire. Be interesting, Stephen thought with a smile, to see what Farquard will do with his niece here. If she's really an admiral's niece, as he said, she's probably a staunch loyalist. She's not going to like some of Farquard's friends.

Suddenly Stephen laughed aloud, leaned forward to pat Black Bess's shoulder and shouted, "Heigh-ho, and the wind blows free!" He felt young, adventurous and awfully glad that he was just starting what he knew would be a fine career. His trade was nothing less than the trade of Benvenuto Cellini, great silversmith of Rome and Florence. God willing, he would win fame, too. Yesterday's message was a good omen: "Governor Martin requests your presence at the Governor's Mansion at New Bern, to confer about the silver for the household." Stephen was prepared; his spare time was always taken up with the sketching of exquisite designs for the aristocratic patrons he was ever confident of winning. Now he was carrying for the governor's approval the most beautiful design he had ever sketched.

'Twas wise of me, he thought, to leave Boston when I did. This commission could never have come had I stayed in the shop of Paul Revere and forgotten my craft in enthusiasm for politics. 'Twas right I came away when I'd learned all about silver that he had to teach me. I'm an artist, not a politician.

Stephen thought back on his strange apprenticeship in Boston, the city of sedition, as lots of people called it. While he was working in the shop and absorbing every secret of the great smith's skill, he learned also some of the secrets of the great smith's thinking. He learned that Revere was as much an apprentice in a political way as Stephen in an artistic. A shabby man called Sam Adams was Revere's master, and would have been Stephen's too, if Stephen had let him. Many a time Adams had appeared beside the bench to inform Revere of a gathering to be held in someone's room. Each time he had expressly invited Stephen to come along. Not infrequently Stephen had gone, to sit obscurely in a corner and listen. Soon he

followed easily the disputations on England's latest
manoeuvre. He could see exactly why Sam Adams
and the others agreed that Governor Hutchinson
ought to be removed. A royal governor's job was to
administer for the welfare of his colony. What right,
then, had Hutchinson underhandedly to urge England
to use stern repressive measures in Boston?

There had come a time when Stephen had got so
angry at one of these meetings that he'd forgotten to
sit inconspicuously in the corner. The talk had been
about Lord North and his sneaking attempt to beguile
Boston by sending cheap tea. North thought the colonials too thirsty and too stupid to see that the tea still
carried a hated Townshend tax. With Adams, Revere,
Hancock and the others Stephen had vowed, "Nay!
I'll ne'er taste a drop from that poisoned leaf!"

His indignation had made him feel at one with
Adams and his pupils. And that feeling had, in turn,
made him decide never again to stroll through the
snowy streets to meet with the others. Stephen felt
strongly about injustice, but he did not at that moment want to fight its cause. He wanted to launch
forth in his trade, prove the skill he felt in his fingers
and mind. Choosing a craft that demanded years of
study and practice and making his own way had
delayed him. He was past thirty. He'd no business
espousing Boston's cause; it was time for him to go
home to North Carolina and put up his shingle: STE-
PHEN MORAY, SILVERSMITH. So he'd retreated into
silence again. He mildly applauded the Tea Party, but
when Revere asked him why he did not huzza loudly
he said, " 'Twas a brave action for you Bostonians.
But 'tis nothing for me to take part in. I'm a North
Carolinian, and I'm going home now." He had
thanked Revere, for his debt to the artist was immense; he had also wished him well in his fight for
his city's freedom.

Swiftly Stephen and Black Bess had galloped down
the coast to Cross Creek. Each mile had taken them
farther from Boston's cries of "Tyranny!" till the matter began to slip from his mind. Then, as he neared
home, he heard the cries of Virginia and of his own

colony. There was word that Wilmington had sent the tax collector flying and that no one was of a mind to drink taxed tea. A little later news of England's intolerable acts of punishment came to North Carolina from a harassed Boston. Stephen, like his friends, was indignant; yet so far he had kept his vow of silence. He had set up shop in an old house with a shack that would do for a stable. At first he'd stayed close at home, but later there had been a few commissions to ride out for, and satisfied purchasers to deliver wares to. Now he felt established. This journey to accept the Governor's order was the proof of his success. And if he sensed at times that he, along with his fellow Scots, would soon have to make a decision, he pushed the thought away, sang again, "Heigh-ho and the wind blows free!" and promised himself he'd worry about that when the time came.

Black Bess responded to the spur. She flew along the road as fast as his enthusiasm could wish. All at once and without a command from Stephen, she slowed to a trot, then to a walk. Stephen immediately put a hand to his pistols. There were all manner of men on the highways and paths these days, and he did not mean to ignore Bess's warning. There might be something around the bend that one would not want to gallop into headlong.

Once around the curve in the road, Stephen saw that there was no danger. MacKiethen and MacNeil from Cross Creek were ambling along on slow-gaited horses, probably making a return trip from New Bern. Stephen came to a halt before them and asked for news.

"Going to New Bern, are you?" MacKiethen asked. "Well, you'll find a lot of loose talk going around. The Council's meeting and some folk are fair worrit. Wild words fly about—"

MacNeil broke in. "Pay no need to the pother, lad. Martin seems a well-meaning man, and he's got his Council in bounds. Look at the way he manages the Assembly. Just dismisses it, if the talk gets too free."

"I'm not so sure it's a good thing to have the Assembly dismissed," Stephen said. " 'Tis the only voice we've got, and we'd be hard put to make any laws or get our wishes over to England without it."

MacNeil nodded as if agreeing in part with Stephen. "Aye. True, lad. But I'm not for letting a bunch of hotheads get together and talk us all into trouble."

With a laugh MacKiethen put an end to the conversation. "Let's be on our way, MacNeil. We can't solve anything by letting the day slip by while we stand chatting in a dusty road. Good luck, Moray, on your business, whatever it is. And safe journey home."

The two travellers rode on to the west. Stephen nudged Black Bess toward New Bern. "Trot along, Bess, and we'll get to town before nightfall."

Well before dusk Stephen was close to the outskirts of the town. He caught glimpses of open clearings among the trees and gracious houses with little lawns and gardens behind them. Eagerly he rode toward the next turning, beyond which the River Neuse lay. It was a broad river, not narrow like the Upper Cape Fear at Cross Creek and Campbelltown. The Neuse, even as high up as New Bern, was wide enough for great ships to sail from the ocean. As he followed the river down to the town, Stephen might see a large vessel, such as could never put in at Cross Creek. But when the expanse of the river lay before him, no lights sparkled on it. No matter, it would be enough on this trip to see the red-brick houses of the wealthy and especially to see the palace built by Governor Tryon. Any edifice, he thought, that nearly caused a revolution among the back-country folk who had to pay for it ought to be truly luxurious—to make up for all the trouble it had caused. Twice the Council had been forced or cajoled into appropriating funds, and the people had groaned with the knowledge that so much of the scarce money in the province would be sealed up in the brick walls of the mansion.

Stephen pounded through the lanes of the town; many of the houses were made of brick and clapboard, and precious glass, imported from abroad, glittered in many of the windows. But even the increase in richness and beauty did not prepare Stephen for the grandeur he discovered as he rounded a corner and saw full before him the noble palace of the Royal Governor. The design was chaste, the effect sumptuous. The tall central building and the two smaller buildings which flanked it were of pink brick. The three houses were connected by curving white colonnades, etched coolly against the dark, lush greens of the garden shrubs. Stephen, standing in the gateway of the high brick wall which surrounded the garden, breathed, "Verily, it's the grandest building in the colonies, just as they say!"

For a moment the citizen and the artist in Stephen were at war. That the Governor paid for his unprecedented luxury by depriving the people was distasteful to him. Yet beauty, at any price, was to be cherished. The artist in him said that Tryon had been wise to fetch an architect all the way from England to draw the plans—a Moor he was. Stephen thought of the pictures he had seen of noble, exotic Moorish palaces and mosques, and he found it remarkable that a man of that bizarre, geometric tradition of architecture should be able to draw plans for buildings that harmonized with the broad rivers and vast forests of the New World.

Briefly Stephen lost all sympathy with the Regulators, those reformers of the back country who made a fuss over expenditures for beautiful buildings. They are mere yeomen, he thought, who care only for the rainfall and the fertility of the soil. They do not recognize pure loveliness when they see it.

While Stephen gazed on the façade of the palace and thought that his silver was the perfect ornament for the general magnificence of the house, a bugle blew. Wheeling his horse, he looked down on the parade ground and across it to the river. A company of redcoats marched smartly along the road from the river, took position and began to drill. Two officers faced the flag-pole and presented swords. A sergeant pulled at the ropes that held the flag aloft. Slowly he lowered it, while two corporals of the colour guard stood by to fold it for the night. As they caught the flag's edge, the sunset gun sounded. Then the bugle called retreat and the company marched away to the beat of drums.

Stephen watched the soldiers move away. They were soon a splash of red colour amid the green tones of the shrubbery. The sinking sun coated the river with gold. Stephen wished for his paints and a bit of canvas; he wanted to capture this fleeting, brilliant scene. It seemed prophetic: the most graceful emblem of American culture, created of English desire, hemmed round, cut off by English soldiers.

A small coloured boy ambled up the path. Before him he herded half a dozen black-faced sheep by lazily stretching forth a shepherd's crook. A dog ran hither and yon, snapping at the hoofs of the sheep, keeping them closely grouped.

Stephen guided Black Bess to the side of the road. He looked down at the boy and asked the way to Miller's boarding-house. The child only stared at him with wide eyes. Stephen gave up hope of an answer and rode on into the town.

A crowd was clustered outside the printing office, still reading and discussing the news in that day's New Bern *Gazette*. They readily made a place for Stephen, who dismounted and, holding Bess's reins loosely, joined them. He wanted to ask his way, but found himself curious to know what unusual article in the paper held them so late into the afternoon. An old man was saying, "They'll be here tomorrow morning, noontime at the latest. I can scarce contain myself, so much am I wanting to show the laddies the heroine of Scotland."

"They say she's a wonderful-looking woman for her age," a woman said. "How old do you suppose she is?"

"Fifty-two or three. Somewhere about there," an old man with a wig said. "She's a young woman yet, for all she's had seven children. But I do wonder how she's changed. I saw her in London—handsome she was—when even the English rallied to her, admiring her stout heart. They would not let her be put in the Tower."

Stephen laughed to find anticipation here equal to that of his travelling companions. "I dare say," he commented to a man standing near, "it won't matter what she looks like. She'll receive a royal welcome. A whole passel of folk from Cross Creek have gone down to meet her in Wilmington."

"Aye," the man replied, "but she'll get no gayer a reception there than here. Old Martin himself will entertain her at the palace. He's bound to profit by her popularity, make no doubt of that. He thinks government's a matter of bowing at balls and paying compliments."

Stephen laughed as he reached down and picked up a neglected paper lying in the dust. "Martin's a bit outmoded, I think. There's been little compliment-paying for the last ten years, leastwise between England and us." He slapped at the paper until most of the dust had blown away in little yellow gusts. Bold print proclaimed, FLORA MACDONALD VISITS NEW BERN FRIDAY. "By the way," Stephen said as he turned to leave the crowd, "which way is it to Miller's boarding-house?"

After listening to the man's directions, Stephen tugged on Bess's reins and led her slowly down the street. There was barely light to read the paper, but Stephen made out that the "idolized saviour of the last Stuart claimant to the throne" would be fêted at a public reception at the Governor's Mansion on Friday night.

He let the paper drop and whistled idly as he strolled along. By criminy, he mused, I'm going to make my business last through Friday! I don't want to miss seeing Flora MacDonald. Like my own kin she seems. He put himself to thinking of practical matters. Yes, he surely had enough money to tarry a few days. While there he planned to buy silver for the ornate tea-set which Farquard Campbell had ordered a few days ago and for which he had generously counted out his Spanish Jos. If the Governor just wasn't in too much haste to have his flat-ware, there'd be nothing to hurry him back to Cross Creek before the week's end. And why should Martin demand unusual promptness? The most illustrious guest Martin would probably ever have would have come and gone in a few days.

When Stephen turned into the lane that had been described to him, he saw the boarding-house at the end of it. It sat on a point of land stretching a little into the river. Against the water, which was black now, Widow Miller's place looked neat, comfortable and self-contained. Stephen tied Bess to the fence and swung open the gate to walk up to the house. Two loungers at the steps were quarrelling, and Stephen was amused, but not surprised, to discover that the subject of their altercation was the Scots heritage. One of them raised a menacing fist at the other and cried, "Ye're wrong—dead wrong! The clans of Scotland will always be the clans of Scotland, wherever the people be. And they'll always have loyalty to their chief above all other men. Why, just look ye at the excitement about the MacDonald who's coming!"

In an accent that betrayed he had no Scots blood the other answered, "Let be with all that. It's the famous lady that calls forth all the hubbub. MacDonald's no chief."

"That shows how little you know. Allan MacDonald will be a chief now—chief of the clansmen in America. You'll see the charred cross carried all over North Carolina to announce the gathering of Clan MacDonald. Everyone of their connections and friends—the MacKinnons, the MacQueens, the MacNichols and MacLeods—will come rushing, just as in the old days they came out of their glens in wartime."

"You talk like a MacDonald yourself." The other laughed.

"Nay, but I give respect where respect is due. I'm an Argyll man, Campbell by name. My mother was a Fletcher of Glen Orchy."

Stephen, interested despite his desire to get into the house and wash the dust from his face, broke in. "I thought the Fletchers and the Campbells were enemies. 'Tis what they say up in Campbelltown, near where I come from."

"So they were in the old days, after Glencoe. The Campbells massacred the MacGregors. A horrid deed that was—I say that though I'm a Campbell. But later 'twas somewhat forgiven." The old man laughed and showed he had a trace of humour. "At least, 'twas forgiven enough for my father to marry my mother. The Fletchers, you know, are a sept of the MacGregor Clan."

Feeling that he'd best wedge his way between the men at once if he was to escape a lesson in clan history, Stephen nodded and pushed by. Before he could knock, a round-faced, bright-eyed woman of middle age opened the door. "I heard your voice, a different voice from those two wrangling ones that are always outside my door. Come in. Come in and tell me your name."

Stephen pulled his hat off and stepped within. All the while he was asking for a room for three days Mrs. Miller was fanning herself with her starched white apron. She was the kind of bustling housewife who would be hot and breathless from scrubbing and serving even on the coldest winter days. After listening to Stephen she shook her head in consternation. "Now, now, isn't it a shame? If you'd come but an hour ago I'd have had a room. But a message came from Wilmington that three or four persons of importance will arrive tomorrow. Tonight I can put you up in a nice room, but after that there'll be only the attic."

For a second or two Stephen considered whether his desire to see Flora MacDonald was strong enough to make him endure the discomforts of Mrs. Miller's garret. Finally, after turning his hat about twice, he said, "For tonight I'll surely stay. Could I tell you about the other days tomorrow? I'm not actually sure how long my business will take."

Widow Miller beckoned him to follow. "That will be fine. I surely do hate to discommode you, Mr. Moray, but these visitors coming tomorrow are very important." She paused and turned on the stairs so he would get the full significance of her announcement. "They sailed over on the same ship Flora MacDonald came on. Two fine ladies they be. One has a companion and a servant. And there'll be a gentleman with a valet. I just couldn't refuse such people. Where would they go?"

Stephen laughed inwardly at Widow Miller's assumption that hers was the reputable boarding-house in town. But he nodded gravely to show he fully appreciated the situation and did not mind the inconvenience. "I quite understand, Mrs. Miller. Now if you'll just show me my room for this night, and have some warm water sent up, I'll be obliged."

The October darkness descended early on the town, but there still remained two or three hours for the day's business. Stephen washed carefully; he shaved and braided his hair into a club. Then, when he had changed into clean, frilled shirt, nankeen breeches and a blue broadcloth coat, he caught up his cloak and the scroll of his designs and clattered down the stairs.

While he was fastening his heavy blue cape about his shoulders, Mrs. Miller bustled up to inquire whether he would eat at her table that night. When he shook his head no and said he'd do some business and then go to a meeting, she tried to find out what affairs he could have that were so urgent. Stephen brushed off her inquiries. There was nothing she shouldn't know about his visit to the Governor nor about the chat he hoped to have with some friends who ought to be in New Bern, but he didn't like gossipy ladies. Even with brusqueness he couldn't wholly escape Mrs. Miller's solicitude. She called after him as he went through the door: "Better take a lanthorn. There's plenty of roughs about the town. The molasses ships from the Indies are in and ships from Salem too. You can't tell what seamen will do when they're ashore, roistering around the taverns and inns."

Stephen had no fears about sailors. He loped down the steps without the lanthorn and once in the street he lost no time.

In five minutes he was hitching Bess to a post before the Governor's Mansion. With long, sure strides that somewhat covered up his nervousness he went up the steps and into the antechamber. There, to his surprise, he found four other men waiting. As he shrugged off his cape and draped it over the back of his chair so it would not wrinkle, he decided to say nothing to the others. There was no telling what sort of business, official or otherwise, they might have, and Stephen thought it just as well to steer clear of anyone who might be prejudiced in Martin's eyes. The commission meant too much—in money as well as in prestige. He sat down and studied the floor, but now and again he scrutinized the faces of the others.

He felt certain that he had seen the one sitting in the far corner before. The man was old, nearly in his dotage; his head was sunk on his chest, and his features were buried in a thick, white beard. His eyes, despite the heavy brows drawn low over them, were alert. Stephen could see that they frequently turned toward him. The gaze made Stephen uncomfortable; to get away from it he looked at the others, all middle-aged and, he thought, rather undistinguished men. Just as he was turning his eyes back to the floor, he saw that the old man had raised his hand. Yes, he was beckoning to Stephen.

A person of so many years deserved respect. Stephen arose, still plaguing his memory for the name of the man and the time and place where he had met him. But his efforts were of no use, and when Stephen stood before the ancient he was at a loss for something to say.

The other, however, began at once. "So," he wheezed, "young Stephen Moray, fresh from apprenticeship in Boston, has come to claim the prize."

"The prize, sir?" Stephen asked haltingly. "I don't understand. . . . I don't know what you're talking about."

"No? And you don't remember who I am either, do you? But I remember you. You came as a younger man—seven, maybe eight years ago—to my shop. Yes—" the old man nodded as a look of recognition came into Stephen's eyes—"I'm St. Ledger, the smith you first came to when you decided to take up the trade. You wanted to know who was the best master. I told you Revere."

Stephen felt his face grow red in shame. How could he have forgotten this man who had given him the best advice he'd ever been given? But it was surely understandable. St. Ledger had changed mightily. He'd grown pitiably old. His hands did not look as though they could hold a hammer or squeeze the bellows. It was almost impossible to imagine that this man had once turned out very handsome pieces of silverware.

"Sir, I'm sorry to have been rude . . . but you . . . you've changed much. And you perplexed me with your talk of a prize. I know of no prize."

St. Ledger pushed himself up in his chair and motioned Stephen to an empty seat beside him. "What are you trying to tell me, Moray? What would bring you here, tonight of all nights, if not the Governor's silver contest?"

"Contest?" Stephen's heart sank. The letter had said nothing about a competition. What a cruel hoax it was, to bring him here whistling with glee, and then let him discover he might well not get the commission!

"Yes." St. Ledger leaned so that he could speak confidentially in Stephen's ear. "You're in it, and I'm in it, and so are all these others. That first one is Isaac Marquand of Edenton, and the others are Griffen of Staunton, Virginia, and William Ferris of Annapolis, now of Edenton. All are good craftsmen."

"And who will judge of our designs?" Stephen asked in a disappointed voice.

"Wallis, Wallis of Edenton, and the palace architect Hawkes."

Stephen began to feel a little better. Wallis he knew well; in fact, he was going to see him at the tavern tonight. He knew that Wallis, an excellent goldsmith, would allow no favouritism to influence his decision, and he felt no qualm that his visit with him just before the contest might seem a bid for favour. The goldsmith was a judge Stephen had faith in; he liked youth and young ideas. Often Stephen had heard him say, "We over here are different from the people back home. Our houses are different, our lives are different. Even our character is changing. So let's have styles that fit us, not the folk in England." Stephen looked at the other contestants and saw conservatism written on their faces. Their patterns would be derived from French and English models. But his own were based on the simple, clean line that Paul Revere had taught him to value. There was hope, great hope. Stephen was suddenly eager to unroll his designs on the Governor's desk; he was confident they would win applause.

Even as he was thinking this, the door to the office within was thrown open. A rather small, slender man stood in the doorway. That could not be Martin, famed for his rotundity. St. Ledger elbowed Stephen and whispered, "Archibald Nielson, Tryon's old secretary."

Nielson spoke politely but without ceremony. "Gentlemen, His Excellency has asked me to say that it is impossible for him to see you today, as he is engaged in preparation for guests. He has asked me also to invite you to leave your designs on the table. They will be examined, and the award will be announced at the ball to be given Friday night. You are all invited to attend."

Without waiting for protest or explanation or other remark the competitors might wish to make, Nielson turned on his heel and firmly closed the door.

"Well!" exclaimed Griffen. "There's a cavalier manner for you. I've a notion to ride home and be done with this."

St. Ledger chuckled as he put his design on the table. "But you won't, Griffen. You'll stay, for you want to win as much as the rest of us. And you want to go to the ball too."

With a shrug Griffen put his scroll beside St. Ledger's. Marquand stepped up next, and then Ferris. Stephen was last to lay down his design. But he placed the scroll beside the others with a fairly light heart. The pattern is good, he said to himself with confidence, but without pride. If it deserves to win it will.

Outside he bade farewell to St. Ledger and cordially wished him success. Then he leaped to Bess's back and clattered off toward the tavern. His plans were settled. He'd take the attic room and patiently await the outcome. He had to admit that he was not very sorry things had turned out as they had. He wanted to go to the ball. He was eager to see the MacDonalds, who would soon be making a home in his country.

17

Decision Approaches

THE tavern was crowded with men of all stations.
There were a few of the sailors Widow Miller had
fretted about, but they were easily outnumbered by a
more respectable type of diner who engaged in quiet,
usually serious conversation with friends. As Stephen
pressed through the main room he surveyed the faces
clustered about the many tables laden with bottles,
glasses, cups, plates and cutlery. Over to the left the
other silver-contest candidates were dining. For a moment Stephen felt uncomfortable; they might draw
ugly and erroneous conclusions about his meeting with
Wallis. Then he raised his shoulders in his habitual
nonchalant shrug and thought, Let them; I'm not going
to forego Wallis' company for their suspicious minds.
But despite his independence, he was glad to find his
friend in a small alcove off the common room. They
could talk freely without being overheard or seeming
conspicuous.

As always Wallis looked commanding. He was an
elderly man who had so thriven in banking that he
had finally given up his trade. His brocaded coat
and fancy dull-yellow waistcoat were elegant and
fashionable. Affluence had not, however, refined all
the homespun quality from his appearance and character. He wore a white wig, which, with his austere
features and lined skin, made him look both old-fash-
ioned and honest. When Stephen walked into the alcove, Wallis was busy with a venison steak and a
mound of flaky rice, drenched in gravy. The New
Bern *Gazette* was propped in front of him and he was
so engrossed in its news that he did not look up until
Stephen spoke. When he saw who it was, Wallis

folded the paper and gestured with it to an empty chair. "Stephen, it's good to see you. Sit down. You'll forgive my having a bite before you came? I was half famished."

Stephen dropped into the chair and motioned toward the gazette. "Reading about our illustrious guest? I'm hoping very much to see her."

"Yes, reading about Flora MacDonald. I, too, am eager to see her, but yet am not wholly pleased about the moment of her arrival."

Stephen laughed. "You mean Josiah Martin ought to have his mind on matters more important than speeches of welcome or contests among silversmiths? There is nothing he likes better than composing a speech or proclamation."

"That's true enough. Remember last August when he convened his Council only to read them a proclamation enjoining anyone from attending illegal meetings? I read it and it was a fine, ringing document. But even his Council members took part in the convention that Mr. Harvey directed a couple of weeks later. As a literary man Martin may be said to lack force."

Wallis wiped his mouth with his immense white napkin, then went on. "But that wasn't what I meant. It bothers me to see these Scots landing in greater numbers all the time. They understand little of the conflicts so unfortunately existing between us loyal Americans and the English Parliament and Ministry. They are open to any specious argument and may be seduced into opposing our just demands."

As Wallis scraped up the last of his rice, Stephen poured himself a glass of wine. "Well, surely they have cause enough to come. With the lairds changing their lands to deer runs, forcing them out with impossible rents, they must emigrate or starve. What would you have them do?"

Wallis pushed his plate back and leaned on the table. "Stephen, you misunderstand me. I'm a Scot myself, and so are you. My family came over in 1739. I was already a man grown, married a year. Your family came at much the same time. You're a young man. I don't know whether you were born here or brought as a babe. In any event you know how we make our livings here in the colonies. You know how, these late years, the Ministry has hemmed our trade about with restrictions—to our great loss of profit. It's also .threatened our freedom of religion and sought to invade our rightful liberties as British subjects.

"I've nothing against these Highlanders who have been coming in such numbers these last months. They are fine fellows, I suppose, but many of them are raw, ignorant gillies and crofters who know nothing of our ways. Though they come here to escape oppression and poverty, they have no acquaintance with any-thing else. They are at the mercy of the first man who will speak them fair. And you can be sure nobody will speak them fairer—and mean less—than our Governor Martin. Of course, Allan and Flora MacDonald will not be so gullible; I have in mind the generality of the emigrants."

The arrival of a waiter with Moray's dinner inter-rupted the discussion. Stephen ate a few bites in silence, then replied, "Your concern over these new Highlanders surprises me. As you know, I came back to North Carolina only last winter after some years in Massachusetts. There the contest was clearly drawn. But I wasn't aware that in these parts there was need for a man to declare himself one way or the other."

Wallis sipped his wine while he chose his thoughts. When he spoke he was very serious. "Stephen, your stay in Massachusetts has blinded you to what is afoot here. You speak of taking sides as only a possi-bility. We have already done it.

"Evidently the events you saw there impressed you as local issues. They are not local issues. A principle is at stake, a principle that affects every American in every colony.

"We have begun to develop a new life here, like nothing in the old world. The land, the forests, the harbours give every man great opportunities. And we have been pressing toward governments that give a man freedom to work and prosper—I could see no end to the hope of the New World. It looked like something new under the sun. With the constitution and with our charters we believed that our rights and liberties were inalienable!"

Stephen had put down his fork to listen. Now he smiled. "You tell me nothing new, Wallis. This is your favourite theme."

" 'Tis no romantic theme, lad. Now the Ministry, abetted by Parliament, every day makes clearer its view that we hold our precious rights and liberties only at its pleasure. You know how the Ministry has sought to bring us to our knees. There's no need for me to run through all its measures. But take a few." Wallis' voice had grown sterner. He counted the grievances on his fingers to emphasize his point. "First, it put through the Quebec Act and with the stroke of a pen handed over our western lands to Quebec. I say nothing of its making the Roman Catholic the established church there, though in principle it imperils our religious freedom. But our lands—by the same process any colony can be cut up and parcelled out at retail. It's intolerable.

"Next there's the billeting of troops. You saw them quartered in Boston homes. You saw them use their Writs of Assistance for arbitrary search wherever they pleased. And tell me, lad, if there, why not here in New Bern or Wilmington or anywhere?"

Stephen swished his wine in his glass and stared at it. "Aye. . . . There's nothing to prevent its coming here."

"We've always voted our own taxes through our own assemblies," Wallis went on without listening to Stephen. "Now Parliament is trying in a dozen ways to tax us. We've always refused to admit any validity to its tax measures. Last winter the Ministry tried to seduce us into accepting a tax by shipping over tea at cheap prices."

"In Boston I watched it thrown into the harbour," Stephen interrupted.

"Right. The only way they could strike at the principle was to destroy the tea. I suppose it was good tea and even with the tax it was cheap. But you know what the issue was. If we accepted the taxed tea we accepted Parliament's right to levy taxes on us. Pay the little tax and we are soon forced to pay a great one—at the pleasure of a body in which we have no voice, over which we have no slightest control. Stephen, that tea went not only to Boston but to Charleston, Edenton, Wilmington, and so on. This is not Boston's controversy but all the colonies'."

Wallis threw up his hands. "I could go on all evening. These are only a few of the ways in which the Ministry seeks to undermine our liberties, ruin our trade to the enrichment of merchants in England, tyrannize over us. When we seek to protect our just rights, the Ministry proceeds to punish us with harsher measures. Now the port of Boston is closed and the people in great distress as a result.

"Time after time we have appealed to the King. Our allegiance is to the Crown. But the Ministers get to him first, and he does not listen to us. We are only trying to maintain our ancient freedoms, but they give him false stories of our rebellious spirit. As a result he gives us no redress.

"We'll counter the Ministry's moves with our non-importation and nonexportation agreements now being discussed by the Continental Congress. They should have a ruinous effect on many English merchants and make them exert some pressure on Parliament. But many of our leaders here in Carolina—Harvey, Hewes, Sam Johnston, Caswell and others—fear we shall have to fight to convince the Ministry we will not submit tamely to its tyranny."

Stephen asked anxiously, "Do you believe that?"

Wallis sighed deeply. "God knows I hope we can get off at a cheaper rate, though I'm as much against submission as any man. But I can't go along with . . . well, with Hooper and others of his mind. They say that the colonies, pulling together, are grown too big for the mother country. They look to a time not far distant when we shall sever the tie with England; they foresee an American nation standing independent. I don't say they advocate separation. They see it as something coming willy-nilly. I can't agree.

"Most of us put our trust in the King. We have al-

ways been subjects of the Crown and expect to continue so. But not at the cost of knuckling under to the
King's Ministers. That we dare not do."

Wallis broke off and laughed apologetically. "Forgive me, Stephen, for subjecting you to a speech. I
don't like strong talk; I'm a moderate. But so many
people miss the import of today's events. Boston's
cause is the cause of America. The sides are drawn
and the contest far advanced, here as everywhere in
the colonies."

"Don't apologize, Wallis," Stephen said. "Your
speech is falling on good ground. Maybe I needed it.
In Boston my sympathy lay with Sam Adams and
Hancock, Paul Revere of course, Dr. Warren, John
Adams and all the others. But I had my way to make
in my trade. I wasn't a Bostonian. Even when my
spirit cried out against Boston's wrongs, I kept telling
myself it wasn't my fight.

"When I came back to Carolina, I set up shop in
Cross Creek. Up there almost everybody is a Highlander. Most of the people don't know what is going
on in the country below, and they have no knowledge
of the American past to set against the troubled times.

"The leaders know, of course. I rode down with
Farquard Campbell. He sympathizes with the Whigs
and lends himself to their counsels. But he is for acting very slowly. He wants the Ministry to mend its
ways, but he counts on the good will of the Crown.
He would act by petition and peaceful pressures. He
is for avoiding a direct test of strength by arms."

"As a banker, I've known him for years," said
Wallis. "He's mighty well off. There are those who
say he fears war because his wide holdings would
make him sure to incur losses. What do you think?"

"No," said Stephen. "His stand on this is not mercenary. I see him as a true moderate, hoping both
sides can be pacified and made to agree to compro-
mises. His thoughts are hard to guess, but I suspect he
has another consideration. In his neighbourhood he is
a leader of the Scots. Like you, he distrusts the igno-
rance of the raw Highlanders and—"

Wallis broke in. "Well he might. That's just what I

started out to say. The questions at issue in this conflict are so strange to the Scots it will be long before they understand them as we do. And there will be Martin setting himself up as a sort of laird. He'll have them believing they hold their land through him and if they don't give him their support he will dispossess them. Just see if it doesn't work that way."

Stephen held up a silencing hand. "What I was going to say is that I think Campbell believes the Scots can be made to hold aloof and take neither side. It looks as if it might really work that way. We've had clan leaders come up from South Carolina with the same message, urging us to keep clear of the whole controversy. It's the burden of the talk at Cross Creek and Campbelltown.

"But my point, Wallis, is that I've listened to this kind of talk ever since I came back. And it fits with the idea I had when I left Boston. I'm a silversmith, and a good one. I like my trade and want to work at it. I've no desire to spend my life in other men's quarrels."

Stephen broke off with an embarrassed smile. "Now, confound it, I've been making a speech. Politics surely induces oratory. Now I've come to my point I shall be brief. I shall think long tonight. I don't go into a thing lightly, and I promise nothing. But what you have told me has blown up the coals of some old thoughts of mine. Maybe it's high time for me to get into this fight."

The older man gave him a steady look. "Good man," he said quietly. "If you decide to serve the cause, I'd suggest you start at home. There's much work to be done at Cross Creek. The local Committee of Safety . . ." He pushed back his chair and stood up. As he gained his feet he gave Moray a friendly pat on the shoulder. "Let's go out to the bar, sample a glass of punch and listen to the talk."

At the bar men were packed tight, talking in small groups. Wallis knew most of them, Stephen found, and introduced him to a bewildering number in the next few minutes.

Three local men asked them to have a drink. One

was John Hawkes, the architect. Stephen was interested in him because he was to be second judge, along with Wallis, in the silver contest. With him were James Coor, a builder, and James Davis, a printer. Evidently they were deep in a political discussion, for as soon as they had paid Stephen the courtesy of a few sentences of welcome they took up where they had left off—in the midst of an argument about the Port Act which had closed Boston to all shipping.

"Much as I pity the people of Boston," Davis said, "in the long run this act plays into our hands. It helps bring the colonies to united action. Here's an example." He fished in his pocket, drew out several papers and selected one. "South Carolina instructed its delegates to the Congress in Philadelphia as follows: 'to consider the acts lately passed, and bills pending in Parliament with regard to the port of Boston and Colony of Massachusetts-Bay, which acts and bills in the precedent and consequences affect the whole Continent of America—also the grievances under which America labours, by reason of the several acts of Parliament that impose taxes or duties for raising a revenue, and lay unnecessary burdens on Trade'; and so on for half a page, enumerating more grievances and empowering the delegates to do what seems best to obtain repeal of the offending acts and redress of the grievances. That's from South Carolina, very distant from Boston."

Coor had a long letter from Richard Caswell, one of North Carolina's delegates to the Congress, describing his trip to Philadelphia and the spirit he found there. The letter was going from hand to hand.

Stephen liked the looks of Hawkes. It seemed to him Hawkes's taste would chime with his and he would appreciate the clean lines Stephen had learned to use in his designs. With Wallis and Hawkes as judges, he knew he was in good hands.

As he studied Hawkes, his ear caught another discussion going on behind him. He glanced around and saw a group of four or five. They were speaking of Flora and Allan MacDonald. One man, a tall, strapping fellow, his face flushed with drink, had seen them at the ball held in their honour at Wilmington. He was much impressed by Allan. "He's a fine figure of a man. Now Flora looks distinguished, but she's only a slip of a woman. Young-looking but past fifty. Of course I know her story, but a man wonders how she could have done what she did to save the Prince from all the soldiers around. With Allan it's a different story. You have only to look at him—standing above six feet tall, straight as a tree, strong, a look of command on his face. They say he'll be chief of the MacDonalds on the Cape Fear. He might be chief of all the Highlanders in America, let me tell you."

One of his companions, a little man far gone in liquor, stared at him owlishly. "Big, is he? But whash he done? Flora saved Prince, twenny-fi', thirty years ago. All time since, whash Allan done?"

Allan's big champion clapped the little man on the back and made him stagger. "What he's done isn't the question. It's what he can do. The man's a born leader. You wait and see."

"Why wait?" the little man grumbled. "Flora's great lady now."

Stephen turned back to his own party, his lips involuntarily quirking into a smile. James Coor touched his elbow. "Step aside with me a moment. I've something to tell you."

Stephen nodded. With a word of excuse to the others, Coor led him to a corner beside the bar. Although there was a loud group almost at their elbows, so long as they kept their voices down they would talk without being overheard.

Coor leaned close to Stephen's ear. "I've been talking to Wallis about you. He says your heart's in the right place and maybe you could help us. I don't know whether you'll agree. Will you at least promise to hold confidential what I'm about to say?"

Stephen looked him squarely in the eye. "That much I promise willingly. As to the rest, let me hear it first."

Coor took a deep breath. He was a sincere man and at the moment very serious. "All right, here it is," he said. "Our agents in London have picked up word that the Earl of Dartmouth has sent Martin a list of persons suspected of sedition. According to their reports, it ought to reach his hands today.

"It's too late to intercept it, though we are not missing any chances of doing that. Some of our best patriots will be in danger, possibly grave danger. If we could get that list we could protect some of the men named. It would let us know how much the Ministry has found out about our secret leaders."

Moray moved impatiently. "All this I see. But why talk to me of it?"

Coor grinned without humour. "A good question. I'll be frank with you. Most of the committed Whigs are well known to Martin. He has better sense than to let one of them wander through the palace unobserved. Now you've been very reserved about your political views. You're in nobody's black books, though Wallis tells me you hold the right opinions.

"Tomorrow night you'll be at the Governor's ball. The designs in the silver contest will be on exhibition in the room adjoining his study, and ten to one the doors between the two rooms will be standing open. Surely a moment will come when you can slip in there without being noticed. Martin has a habit of just tossing private papers into the centre drawer of his desk. We'd expect the list to be there. It may be locked, of course, but the lock's flimsy. A good pry would break it. It's much to ask, but will you try to get the list for us?"

Stephen stood for a long moment thinking, his eyes on his toes. At last he raised his head, facing Coor squarely. "It's a hard choice you're asking me to make. I've a good chance of winning the competition. If I'm caught five minutes later with my fingers in the Governor's desk, I'll spoil my new-won reputation as a silversmith and be disgraced. They'd be sure to say I was after money."

Coor's face hardened and his eyes narrowed. "Come now, young fellow," he said; "you're risking a commission for a trumpery silver dish. Some of these men whose names are on this list are risking their lives. Wallis told me you'd been doing some soul-searching, which any man is entitled to, but you were ready to throw in with us. Don't do it with half a heart. Make your first venture a deep one. Come, man, tell me you'll undertake it."

A momentary anger against Wallis went through Stephen's mind. He had been pretty free with the confidences Stephen had given him at supper. When had Wallis talked to Coor? It must have been only a few terse words while Stephen's attention went to the strangers who were talking about the MacDonalds.

Coor must have divined what he was thinking. "Most of this Wallis guessed from your Boston experience. He told me this afternoon. Only a sentence tonight to add you were on the brink of decision." He grinned again. "I'm here to push you over the edge."

Stephen was still torn two ways. At last he said, "Let me sleep on it. Tell me where to send you word and I'll let you know in the morning. I wish there were someone else."

Coor laid a hand on his shoulder. "Even the best of us always wishes there were someone else. All right, take the night to think. I have faith you'll choose right and give me the word I want in the morning. Drop by the *Gazette* office about ten." He shook hands solemnly. "Let's get a fresh glass and join the others."

Back with the others, Coor held up his full glass. "We thought we'd go straight to the spring for another drink."

Hawkes was ready to leave. Stephen took it as a good omen that Hawkes's good wishes and handshake seemed hearty and sincere.

As the rest of Stephen's group talked quietly, voices near the door rose angrily. One outshouted the others. "I don't care whether John Harvey or the devil was moderator, that convention was damned seditious nonsense. If I'd been governor I'd have clapped all the leaders in jail." There was a brief scuffle and Stephen saw the tavern's host slipping purposefully through the crowd toward the centre of the disturbance.

Within a minute all was quiet. A visitor coming in

would have seen only a group of gentlemen enjoying their glass. But Stephen knew that just under the surface passion ran hot, men were staking their lives on their beliefs. Carolina's destiny was at stake and would not be settled by tavern talk.

It was near midnight when Stephen let himself into the Widow Miller's house. Before he started upstairs he slipped off his brogues so as not to disturb any of the guests. As he started through the hall, he glanced through the open door of the dining-room and saw the Widow Miller, her head bound in a kerchief, directing her maids who were polishing silver and crystal, while two men were rubbing wax on the already gleaming floor.

He smiled to himself. Surely this extraordinary activity was worthy of a visit of the King himself and his consort Charlotte. He stepped inside the room, beckoned to the Widow Miller and told her he'd be happy to take the attic room the next night.

In his room he went quickly to bed but not to sleep. He lay restless and could not close his eyes. He couldn't see ahead. What would war do to the future of a young silversmith? Should he even be thinking of his individual future? Coor had faced him with a decision, and the next night might decide his future. He got up and went to the narrow window. The moon, nearly full, rode high, casting a sheen on the rippling river. Suddenly he felt a fierce possessiveness of this fair country.

Finally he went back to bed and soon drifted into uneasy sleep. He dreamed he won the competition at the palace, over all the other silversmiths, but Governor Martin wanted not a silver table service but twenty-nine cannon of fine silver and gold. He was sure he could never find the materials for so great an order. He knew he had both won and lost. His despair awakened him. As he looked at the stars shining in the square of window, he knew also what he would tell Coor in the morning.

18

Exchanges at New Bern

"WELCOME! Welcome to New Bern!" The shouts went up from every side. Woodsmen's caps, Scots bonnets and felt tricorns waved; aprons and bonnet strings fluttered 'in the late-afternoon breeze. Allan waved happily to the crowd and forgot his tiredness. Only an hour ago he and Flora had wondered together whether they could hold up through another enthusiastic reception and ball. Wilmington had fêted them grandly before it let them journey inland, and on the ride both had realized their great need of sleep, rest and permanence. Yet now, when greeted by the warm admiration and genuine rejoicing of the New Bern folk, Allan felt a resurgence of energy. He wheeled his horse and fell in beside the carriage. Flora placed her hand over his, on the sill of the window. She leaned across to hear his words: "Did you see, Flora, the familiar faces?"

"Aye. Both those we've actually known on Skye, and those who look like their relatives, our dear friends at home."

Allan's voice was hearty. "It refreshes me almost as much as sleep and bathing would. I'm glad we came—if you are." Flora had smiled and nodded to show she felt the same way. Allan's thoughts went to Anne, who had gone directly up-river from Wilmington. "Too bad Anne and Alex and the laddies couldn't come along," he said. "They'd have enjoyed seeing New Bern."

"Nay," Flora answered. "Anne was too tired and too sick. I'm glad the MacLeod folk met her. A bumping land journey would be hard on her. As for

Sandy and Jamie, they had dancing enough at Wilmington."

For a few moments Allan rode in silence beside the carriage. He glanced over his shoulder to see that the others had followed safely. It was a good-sized retinue. Cecily and Moira followed immediately in Farquard Campbell's coach. That one promised fair to be a strange man, Allan thought. Farquard had seemed delighted to welcome his niece, yet not so delighted as to accompany her to New Bern. He'd said he might as well do a little business while he was in Wilmington. Some merchant called Harnett—Cornelius Harnett, that was it—could advise him on his imports. He'd been caught with a supply of tea, he said, and wanted to know what would be banned next. Even Cecily had thought her uncle's business a little ill-timed. She'd shot him a puzzled glance and then said, in a half-successful teasing tone, "Uncle Farquard, distances are great, I know, and you wouldn't like another trip down here. But still, must you pack me off? I'm tired of travelling without my family. Let me stay overnight also." Campbell had laughed in his easy way and patted Cecily's shoulder. "Nay, lass, go to the New Bern festivities with your friends. My business wouldn't interest a woman."

Cecily had pouted ever so slightly, though Allan couldn't guess why. Except, of course, that Cecily tended to be a pretty independent miss and just might take it into her head to meddle in affairs of men. Allan laughed then at a play of words that came to mind. Cecily might well meddle in affairs of men, but not in affairs with men. She'd certainly brushed Blair aside repeatedly, and been firm about choosing Moira as company for the land journey.

Allan could tell that the whole party was as stimulated as he. David cantered back and forth and around because his gaiety wouldn't let him ride as slowly as the coaches. Dougald had reined up to wait for Campbell's coach and Moira. Nowadays the lad often had a bashful blush to his cheek that showed he was smitten. And good time for Dougald to have a little experience with women, Allan thought, momentarily remembering a bonnie lass he'd known thirty years ago on Skye.

It was with confidence and aplomb that Allan leaped from the saddle before the Governor's Mansion. He'd brought his family safely across the water. He was delivering them to the Royal Governor's door. They had been invited to stay there during the New Bern visit.

David rode up and asked for instructions. Allan told him to accompany Cecily and Moira to the inn. "Take Dougald along. Later, when Flora and I will have met the Governor, we'll call you all over and introduce you."

When Allan turned back, a plump man came running down with short, jerky steps. He hurried to Allen with hand extended. "Alan MacDonad, it is welcome you are to Tryon Palace, the seat of our government here, and my home."

Allan had time only to return the handclasp firmly before Governor Martin stepped over to help Flora from the carriage. "Allow me," Martin said, motioning a footman aside. "It is my privilege and pleasure."

He ushered Allan and Flora up the steps and into the hall of the palace. The door was left open and the cries of the New Bern citizens could still be heard. Briefly Martin hesitated before one of the doors leading off the foyer; then he said, "But of course, Mrs. MacDonald will want to refresh herself. I shall have to suppress my eagerness to talk with her." He nodded toward a coloured girl. "Lizzy, take Mrs. MacDonald to her room."

"Thank you, Governor Martin," Flora said. "Let me just keep an eye on the gillie and Katie while they bring in my things. He has a habit of dropping them, and I have Dougald's precious pipes as well as an antique mirror I value." Flora seemed to be delaying, seeking some opportunity. When Allan, at the Governor's gesture, stepped into the next room, Flora touched Martin's sleeve. "Excuse me. Can you arrange to have a talk with me—a private one, and soon?"

Martin was clearly surprised. "Well, but . . . of course. . . . Yes, Mrs. MacDonald. Whatever you say.

Will after supper be too late? When you are more settled, and I more free?"

At once Flora nodded and turned to follow Lizzy.

The Governor looked after her, cocked his head in perplexity, then settled a genial smile on his face as he went in to Allan. "As I said, sir," Martin remarked as he closed the door, "it is an honour to North Carolina to have you and your famous wife. It is in addition a benefit. You Scots are frugal farmers and loyal men. We need both. Yes, Allan MacDonald, you will have much opportunity to benefit your country and your King here in the colonies."

The tight knot of fear that had hidden in the pit of Allan's stomach ever since the ship captain predicted trouble in the colonies began to loosen. He drew himself erect and unconsciously showed his military bearing. "Thank you, Governor Martin. My aim has been always to provide well, and serve well. If North Carolina offers the opportunity to do those things, I am thankful."

Supper was over and, after some pleasant conversation, Flora had retired to her room. The Governor had not yet called for her, but she felt confident he would before very long. She appreciated that many demands were made on his time; and she felt a certain pity for him. The rigours of public life were no doubt great. Even as she had left the room, at a time when folk ought to be thinking of going to bed, he had sighingly mentioned a conference he had yet to attend. After that conference, she surmised, he would see her.

For a while Flora tried to sit quietly. She did not want to take the packet from its hiding-place until it was needed. Already it had had a devious enough career, and she would take no chances on its being lost or stolen again at the last moment. Finally, however, she could not wait. It occurred to her that damp might have spoiled its pages, blurred the ink. Then too, she wanted to see how seriously she had torn the papers when she ripped the seal and shoved them into the narrow crevice behind the mirror. She rose and pulled the bell; when Katie appeared she asked her to open the crate.

"Now, mistress," Katie remonstrated, "this is no time for looking on the Prince's picture. Oh, I know you're eager, after this long month of travelling, but it'll just have to be locked up again."

Flora was firm. "I must see it," she insisted. "And I can't lift it from the box with my lame arm. Be about it, Katie." In a few minutes the box was open and the servant was dismissed. Carefully Flora dusted off the mirror. Her fingers deftly, though nervously, felt under the ornate, gold edge. The front swung back, and the Prince looked out at her. His half smile seemed to say, "I've kept your secret well, Flora Mac-Donald, as you did mine."

Quickly Flora reached for the papers. Her fingers trembled slightly, and the papers slipped from them, some falling within the frame of the picture, some falling on the floor. How clumsy of me! Flora thought as she stooped to collect them. She rose and automatically began to sort the leaves. Several pages obviously contained a continued list of names. Yes, they were alphabetical, and it would be a simple matter to put them in order. At the top of one was the name, Coor, James. Flora riffled through the sheets to find some more names beginning with C. Here it was: Cameron, Ian; Campbell, Farquard.

Farquard Campbell! The name made her pause and remember the man she had met but two days ago. Now what would his name be doing on a secret dispatch to the Governor? Flora resolved not to examine the papers further, but as she shuffled them together she could not help but look at the heading to the list: "Persons suspected of seditious conduct; to be interrogated."

Flora thought of Cecily. She ought to know that her uncle's loyalty to the King was under suspicion. Twice Flora paced across the room, her eyes continually glancing toward the mysterious docket. It was an ironical thing that Cecily herself had protected it. It would be bitter to tell her. But it must be done.

With firm steps Flora went to the door. She would

find a messenger to summon Cecily. Flora had hardly started down the hallway when a young man emerged from another room. He spoke politely and asked whether he could be of help. When he understood that Flora wanted a trustworthy messenger, he offered his own services. "I'm Archibald Nielson, Mrs. MacDonald, a kind of volunteer aide to Governor Martin. I shall be happy to do your errand."

Cecily was leaning against the door-frame of Rachel's room. An amused smile came frequently to her lips, for Rachel was leaving Cecily's life as explosively as she had come into it. Hat-boxes, trunks, cartons and jewel cases were strewn haphazardly about the room. The bewildered maid was running from one to the other in response to Rachel's contradictory orders. Cecily wondered how Rachel had got her possessions in such total disarray in the few hours she'd been at Miller's boarding-house.

As if in answer to Cecily's thought, Rachel exclaimed with hands thrown wide, "And who should have guessed my friend would get sick and send for me so quickly? I was looking forward to the ball, to dances with the dapper Mr. Blair and the rustic local gentlemen. But this is the way of generals—they order and will be obeyed."

Cecily wondered what the general's letter had said. Rachel had completely refused at first to listen to the messenger who came to carry her to Philadelphia. At first her voice had been petulant, then angry. Once, before the messenger could finish a sentence, she had stamped her foot. But then the persuasive letter had been given her; there had been a silence as she read. Rachel had next spoken in silken tones. "Of course ... he needs me." And to Cecily she had explained carefully, "He is so very ill."

Between them, the messenger and the serving-girl bundled the litter together and toted the trunks to the coach. Rachel, still trailing unattached scarves and furs, emerged from the dressing-closet. "I am so sorry to rush off without good-byes," she said to Cecily. "Will you explain to Mrs. MacDonald and to Allan?

And tell them I shall miss them?" With startling sincerity she added, "I am fond of Mrs. MacDonald, and of you. God bless you both!"

Then she was her quick, superficial self again. Her heels clattered as she ran down the stairs. Cecily watched her go, and surprised herself by thinking, I'll miss her gaiety, and even her silliness.

While Cecily was yet on the landing, a knock sounded on the door below, and in a moment she was summoned. A slender man awaited in the hall. He introduced himself as Mr. Nielson. As soon as she heard his message she fetched her cloak. The summons was not a surprise; Flora had said she would try to make an appointment with Martin at once. Without telling anyone where she was going, Cecily went out the door and waited for Nielson to guide her to the carriage. Widow Miller's boarding-house was still strange to her. Once she stumbled against the paling fence, but Nielson caught her.

"Careful," he said, keeping hold of her elbow. "Mind the round stones. They can throw you if you do not have care."

Mr. Nielson seemed a courteous man, but his advice was a trifle foolish. "How can I mind the stones when I can't see them," Cecily asked with a touch of asperity.

He laughed. "My mistake. Of course you cannot see in the dark."

"But I can. I have cat's eyes, but I can't see stones under my feet in time to save myself."

Once again Nielson laughed, as if he found casual teasing pleasant. "So you have cat's eyes? I'm sure you don't display the cat's ability to scratch, or any other feline attributes."

"I can scratch if necessary, sir," Cecily replied. The conversation, pointless as it was, was amusing. There was a good firm quality to Mr. Nielson's voice that made Cecily want to hear him speak more.

"A feline woman is a danger to a man. He can't resist seeing how far he may tease her and still dodge the sweep of her claws. In the end of course he has scars for a souvenir, though he's as much to blame as the cat. Upon my soul, though, if you hadn't warned me, I'd never have thought of you as cattish. Now your companion, Mistress la Fabrère, of whom we all know ..." His voice trailed off, but the inference was clear.

"There are tom cats as well as tabbies, Mr. Nielson," Cecily said.

This time Nielson threw back his head. There was genuine mirth in his laugh. "*Touché!*"

Nielson swung open the door of the waiting carriage. He handed Cecily up the small step and, when she was seated, drew a rug over her knees. After a word of direction to the coloured coachman, he got in beside her.

"Mrs. MacDonald seemed somewhat agitated when she asked me to come for you. Knowing you'd be tired —and she too—I thought of suggesting she wait till morning. But I decided against it. I'm glad I did. It pleasures me to escort you."

"Thank you, sir. It pleasures me too," Cecily said. For the life of her, she could not keep the pertness out of her voice. The carriage lights shone on Nielson's handsome face. She saw he was smiling. She laughed then and asked, "What is it about you that makes me want to say impertinent things?"

"Are you saying impertinent things? I think you're quite delightful. Most young women here are quite dull—so seriously engaged in looking over each bachelor with the idea of marriage in their minds."

"And you're a bachelor, one of their possible victims? Fie, sir, you shouldn't be so hard on the young ladies. 'Tis the business of a proper young lady to find a husband."

Nielson looked at Cecily with mock sternness. "Now don't align yourself against me. I'm a bachelor and intend to remain one. And I must say, I thought for a moment your spirit was as independent as mine."

"You've seen through me! Yes, I'm dedicated to spinsterhood. So we can have great fun together."

He took her small hand and shook it solemnly. "My new friend, pleasure is ahead of us."

"Not enough, I fear," Cecily said with real regret. "My uncle will come in a day or two to carry me away to Campbelltown."

"Then we must make the best of our time. May I have the first minuet tomorrow night at the ball? And the supper dance, and the last contre-dance? And perhaps one in between?"

"So many!" Cecily cried in flattered surprise. "Is that the custom here?"

"No, indeed; it's my personal custom. We shall have everyone talking. Do you mind?"

Cecily could not help considering for a moment. She did not care what the local dowagers thought, but Blair . . . ? She tried to dismiss the thought of him but found she could not. Therefore, she compromised with Nielson. "Let them talk, but not too much. Only two dances will I promise now."

Nielson sighed in exaggerated disappointment. "So be it! I'm grateful for the little you give me. Ah, the palace, already! I must hurry you in and deliver you to Flora MacDonald at once."

As soon as Cecily entered, Flora rose. She was dressed in a black silk gown, trimmed with her clan colours, and her feet were shod in small fur slippers. "Dear Cecily," she said as she walked forward, "so good of you to come!"

Nielson lounged against the door, as if reluctant to leave. "My first mission for you was most agreeable. If there's anything more I can do—here in this consultation—I should be happy . . ."

With a wave of her hand Flora cut him off and dismissed him. "You have been most helpful, Mr. Nielson. I'll not impose longer on your time and goodwill. Miss Weston and I have some private matters of importance to discuss."

When Nielson had bowed courteously and left the room, Flora asked Cecily to sit down. Now the moment of revelation had come, Flora was confused how she should begin. Was there any tactful, kind way of telling a girl a member of her family might be a traitor?

"Cecily," she began hesitantly, "the time has come to hand over the packet. I've told Governor Martin I want to see him, and have already taken the packet from its hiding-place."

"Good!" Cecily exclaimed as she restlessly got up. "I shall be glad to have that responsibility off my mind. You know, Flora, it was really a good thing that you hid it. I've tried not to think about it, tried to pretend it didn't exist, but I've been mightily curious. And I've wondered often whether we did the right thing—concealing it, I mean. Now at last I can quit worrying about it."

Flora could not share Cecily's relief, and she wondered whether Cecily's worries were not just beginning. Slowly she said, "I told you that when I hid it I had to rip the seal." She walked to the mirror and opened the secret compartment. Rather irrelevantly, as if glad for a change of topic, she said, "Come. See the picture of the Prince. 'Twas with him I hid the packet."

While Flora picked up and nervously fingered the papers Cecily gazed on the portrait. "He was handsome," she commented. "I can understand why you wanted to aid him."

Vigorously Flora shook her head. "'Twas not his bonnie face that moved me. . . . But let that be. Here are the papers. I think you should know. Accidentally I saw them."

Cecily turned excitedly. "You did? Can you tell me what they say?"

"Well . . . I hardly know how."

While Flora was groping for words there was a knock at the door. Hurriedly Flora folded up the packet again, and slipped it into the pocket of her dress. "Yes?" she called.

It was Nielson's voice that answered. "Governor Martin will see you now, Mrs. MacDonald."

Flora opened the door to tell Nielson she and Cecily would be along directly. Then she rapidly patted her hair into place and slipped into her shoes. "I'll have to tell you later," she whispered to Cecily.

"I'm disappointed," Cecily murmured as she followed. "But, after all, perhaps it's best I don't know."

Nielson showed them into the Governor's office and departed. The room was spacious and warm; it was brilliantly lighted by twelve candles and a fire which blazed in the fire-place. Martin rose from his desk when the women entered, and greeted them with a suavity that showed no trace of weariness. Nonetheless Flora regretted that she had been forced to request an interview that had to be held late at night. "I'm sorry, Governor Martin, to keep you at your duties so late."

"I'm happy to receive lovely ladies at any hour, even when they come on business." As he placed chairs for them he asked, "Is this the Miss Weston you told me of at dinner, Mrs. MacDonald?"

Flora hastily presented Cecily and apologized for her remissness. "'Tis a little flustered I am, Your Excellency. Cecily and I have an unusual duty to perform. My thoughts are taken up with that."

Martin leaned on his desk. "And what is this mysterious business?"

"I think she can best explain it. It is really her story," Flora said, looking at Cecily. "Go on, dear, tell Governor Martin just how you found the packet."

There was a silence while Cecily sorted out all the details of Holseman's peculiar character, his abduction and her finding of the packet. Finally she began to speak. She told the entire story lucidly and calmly.

The Governor listened without comment. Once, at the first mention of Holseman, he looked up in sharp surprise. He tapped the table with his fingers, but refrained from interruption until De Vega was mentioned. Then he said abruptly, "In the pay of France."

Cecily waited but Martin motioned for her to go on. Quickly she told of De Vega's boarding the ship, and of Flora's offer to hide the packet. "I was immensely glad she did hide it," Cecily concluded. "De Vega searched the ship rather thoroughly. My cabin was a mess."

"And still he did not discover the packet?" Martin asked in some confusion.

"Fortunately, he did not search my cabin," Flora explained. She indicated her arm and told how she had broken it in the midst of the battle. "We may be thankful that De Vega turned out to be something of a gentleman. He forebore to discommode me with a search."

Flora reached into her pocket and drew out the packet. "Here, Your Excellency." She hesitated before she handed it into Martin's waiting hand. "I'm afraid the seal is broken. To insert the papers in the hiding-place quickly I had to unfold them." Flora felt that honesty demanded she tell Martin how much she had seen. But she could not, not in front of Cecily.

"Of course," Martin said, "I understand." He rapidly separated the leaves and scanned them. "Ah . . . the regiments . . . good . . . So, it's to be only interrogation," he muttered. Then he folded the sheets compactly and walked around the desk to lock them in a drawer. As he pocketed the key he smiled at Flora and Cecily. "The packet is important, and it is fortunate that you protected it. But I regret that your safety was jeopardized. His Majesty will be deeply indebted to you both for your courage and discretion."

As the Governor came back around the desk Flora stood up; she was eager to be able to talk to Cecily alone and finally tell her about her uncle. But Martin would not let her leave at once. "I'm sorry that I must ask yet another question. The documents are self-explanatory except on one point. They do not name the courier who was to bring them. And that man, though obviously he suffered ill luck, is described as a trustworthy intelligence officer whom I must use in other affairs. Have you any clues to the identity of the courier? Did anyone approach you, make you suspicious?"

Flora shook her head, and Cecily said in surprise, "Why . . . I just assumed it was Holseman! Captain Borset all but said so!" She paused and thought for a moment. "No, I guess I could have misunderstood him. But if it wasn't Holseman, then … then I simply don't know who it was."

The news did not seem to dismay Martin. "Never mind," he said, "the officer will have to report to me, and soon. Now I want to thank you again for your wisdom, courage and loyalty. Mrs. MacDonald, you've not always been on our side. I had thought I'd have to exact the pledge to the Hanover from you. But I see it's not necessary. Your action is a stronger pledge than an oath. It's a pleasure to welcome you. I wish all our North Carolinians were as trustworthy as you two. I fear we have many disaffected folk."

Disaffection again! thought Flora, disturbed. Ever since she and Allan had planned the voyage to Carolina, they had been warned repeatedly. But they had not discussed the warnings, had not heeded them. She had tried to shield him from news of ominous conditions here. He, perhaps, was trying to shield her. Now they must consider the reports together. He and I need peace, security, not fear and danger, she reasoned. 'Twas I, partly, that led him to believe we'd find them here. I must tell him the Governor confirms the previous news of faction.

Flora followed Cecily into the hall. Mr. Nielson was waiting, and said the carriage was already at the door. There would be no opportunity to speak to Cecily tonight. Tomorrow would have to do. Somehow Cecily and her uncle did not seem so important now. Flora had suddenly realized that to the royal government she herself was a long-standing enemy of the King. Martin had already betrayed curiosity about her politics. Well, it was convenient that by chance she had helped deliver the packet and thus had allayed suspicion. But she and Allan were not on the Hanover's side. They were not on any side. Thus they must remain.

"I hope your consultations did not disturb you, Miss Weston," Archibald Nielson said with concern. "You're not so gay as when we rode together earlier this evening."

Cecily looked up and smiled. "It will require but a

little of your conversation to restore my spirits, Mr. Nielson. Actually I'm more light-hearted than before. I'm rid of a responsibility that sat heavily upon me. But at the last moment Governor Martin spoke of disaffected folk. The mere mention of disloyalty distresses me. I do not understand how men can think treasonous thoughts. Oh—" she raised her hand to keep him from answering at once—"I know that sometimes men have true grievances. The Scots in the Highlands did; since my visit there I do believe that. But grievances can and must be handled another way. Treason! Traitor! Such acts, such men are horrible— and contemptible."

Nielson was quiet, evidently surprised. Only after a moment did he reply. "You did not need to silence me. I certainly was not going to defend traitors. Though, I must confess, I think certain conditions might drive a man to strong, and rightful, resistance." He looked at her with surprising sternness. "Would you repudiate any traitor, even if he were your friend . . . or relation? What about your personal belief in such a man?"

The question shocked Cecily; it could refer only to Farquard Campbell. Nielson's pointed question told her more surely than anything she'd heard previously that Farquard was on the wrong side. First the Earl of Dartmouth in London and now Nielson here. She liked Nielson so much she was tempted to discuss Farquard with him fully and frankly. Then she decided he was too new a friend. It would be safer to misunderstand the purpose of his question and steer the conversation into a more casual vein. Assuming a light tone, she said, "I can't imagine myself in such a position. Of course, I'm inordinately fond of Flora and the other Scots who opposed the Crown. But that happened long ago." Cecily managed to chuckle. "You're not suggesting, are you, that I give up her friendship for a deed over twenty years past?"

Nielson responded in the same bantering tone. "Of course not. But you know, I'm hoping to see more of you. I'm resolved to pay my addresses only to beautiful Tory ladies. Now that you've passed the test, I can invite you to an excursion. Will you ride out with me Saturday? What a tragedy for me if you had exhibited Whig sympathies!"

Just then the carriage stopped before the inn. Nielson jumped out to help Cecily. She paused on the coach step and looked into his eyes. "A ride would be pleasant and, I suppose, perfectly safe. You've assured me your heart is invulnerable to maidens' charms." She stepped to the cobblestones.

Nielson took her arm. "Not to charms, to wiles. And I don't believe you would be guilty of coquetry. Now please say, what about the excursion? I'll show you the local wonders—the creeks, the swamps, the forests. Yes, we'll go to the turpentine woods. Have you ever seen turpentine in the making?"

"You make it very attractive. Yes, I should like—" Cecily broke off. "Oh, no, I can't. We leave Saturday for Campbelltown."

"Why not tomorrow then?"

"Well . . . but there's the ball," Cecily said, her disappointment showing in her voice.

Nielson laughed. "Unless you're the kind of damsel who spends all day preparing, we can do both. It's not very far to the pine barrens. I promise to have you back for supper."

At the door Cecily turned to bid her escort good night. In the shadows she saw a movement as a man stepped forward. No features could be distinguished in the dim light, but she knew, from his height and the set of his shoulders, that it was Blair. She flushed. He was sure to think her light; first there was her response to his kiss, now her being out with a man she had just met. If he'd heard her accept Nielson's invitation, his opinion would be worse. She suddenly wanted Blair to know that between her and Nielson there was nothing but comradeship. It was impossible to say so, and anyway her pride would not let her. She tensed herself to greet him with the coolness she had shown since the amorous moment on the *Baliol*.

To her chagrin he barely nodded to her. His attention was all for Nielson. "Don't you recognize me, Archie? It's Blair. You didn't expect to see me here,

did you? Well—" they were shaking hands heartily—"I didn't expect to see you either. And most
certainly not with my friend, Miss Weston."

"James Blair, by gad! You're the last person I expected to meet in America! It's been since . . . let's
see ... Portugal, wasn't it? You were a pretty raw
lieutenant then, and I was a very new-hatched subal-
tern. It's been a long time."

Again the men shook hands. Finally Blair recalled
Cecily's presence and apologized for their neglect.
"But really, Cecily—Miss Weston—running across
Nielson is a stroke of good fortune. We were great
friends in Portugal. The fortunes of war—or of mili-
tary careers—carried us apart."

With a dazed nod Cecily acknowledged his remarks. Blair had been a soldier, an officer? Was he
still one? Yes, even now he was telling Nielson he'd
been promoted to a majority. This didn't fit at all
with everything else she knew of him. And come to
think of it, his manner now was forceful and direct; it
had nothing of the supercilious macaroni in it.

"Forgive me for interrupting, Mr.—or should I say
Major?—Blair," Cecily found voice to say. "I don't
want to stand in the way of your reminiscences. Let
me bid you both good evening."

Blair was quick to answer. "No, Miss Weston,
don't go up yet. Archie and I will postpone our recollections a few moments. I must speak with you." He
opened the door and let both Cecily and Nielson pass
in front of him. Then he gestured to the empty parlour. "Step in here just a moment."

In a disarming tone he explained quickly: "I just
want to ask a personal favour. Don't either of you tell
anyone that I'm an officer, please. I've had ten odd
years of uninterrupted service, and determined on a
vacation from it. I've not worn my uniform all this
trip and I've acted like the gentleman of leisure I've
long wished I was. So don't give me away."

With a laugh Nielson said he could sympathize
with a desire to play civilian. "I left the service myself. And right now I, too, am on a kind of vacation—just serving Martin until my personal affairs are

wound up here. Then it's back to England and the life of a country squire!"

Cecily tried to smile, and did manage to look less confused than she felt. "By all means, Mr. Blair, your rôle is no concern of mine. Your secret is safe. And now, good night to you both."

She quietly left the room and ascended the stairs. The enigma of Mr. or Major James Blair plagued her. This latest revelation made him much more attractive than he had appeared on shipboard.

In Blair's sitting-room the two friends were just getting settled for an hour or two of conversation. As Nielson accepted a glass of brandy, he said with a smile, "Come now, Blair. What's all this about a vacation? I followed your lead, but I didn't believe you for a second. And I doubt that the intelligent Miss Weston did."

Pulling a chair close to the table, Blair shrugged. "It doesn't make too much difference now. If it had, I'd have let you pass without speaking. I knew the military business would come out. But as I say, it doesn't matter much now. My guess is, though, that at the moment Cecily is a bit confused. When the time comes, I'll explain the whole thing to her."

"How about explaining it all to me right now? I'm curious as the devil."

It was with a sigh that Blair answered. "I'm afraid it's a story of failure, Archie. The long and short of it is that I was acting as special courier, carrying a packet to Martin. The thing got stolen from me, and on the chance I could ferret out the thief I kept playing the rôle of delicate gentleman I'd started with. It didn't do any good. I've got no idea where the blasted thing is."

Nielson whistled softly in surprise. "You're in a bad spot. But, good God, Jemmy, it doesn't sound like you—letting an important document be lifted off you! How'd it happen?"

Blair went through the story and could tell that Nielson sympathized. "You've got to admit," he concluded dejectedly, "that I look pretty much the fool. I can offer mitigating circumstances, but neither sea-sickness nor De Vega is a satisfactory excuse if I draw a court-martial. I might get one. I'm almost sure to if the dispatch doesn't end up in the right hands. And if it does, and I don't get in trouble, I may still have some trouble with my major assignment. I'm here to do intelligence. What officer will want to trust me when he hears how I was duped?"

For a while Nielson stared at the ceiling, and Blair kept quiet, for he remembered that Nielson did this only when he was thinking something out. Finally Nielson looked at him and brought his fist down im-patiently. "I can't figure it out. We had no word of a packet from Dartmouth, and no one, so far as I know, has made any shady overtures to Martin. Of course, it may be too early for that; you Baliol people just got here today. So far only Flora MacDonald and Miss Weston have seen the Governor. And Allan."

Nielson looked at Blair questioningly and was told that those three were the last to be suspected. With a wry look Nielson went on. "Well, then, we can only wait. This much I can promise you, James. I'll keep on the watch, and if there's any way I can save you, I will. I'm close to Martin and might be able to put in just the right word for you. By the way," he added, pouring himself another glass of brandy, "when do you intend to report?"

"When I can't delay any longer, or when I hear something about the packet. I suppose I ought to ap-pear tomorrow sometime."

"No. Wait till Saturday. Trust to my knowledge of Martin. He's so busy planning for the ball and enter-taining the MacDonalds that he probably won't notice your delay. And if he does, tell him you were tracing out some leads before the Baliol party dispersed and you couldn't afford to be seen going to a conference with him. Really, Blair, he's easily handled if he be-lieves you're on his side. And there's no doubt of that."

With a scrape of his chair Nielson got up. He stretched and strolled about the room. "Hate to sit down for very long," he murmured in explanation.

"Now tell me: What about this intelligence assignment?"

"Actually, there's little to tell as yet," Blair answered. He lighted his pipe, and, after blowing out the match, added, "I report to Gage as soon as I can. Of course, my departure depends much on Martin, but I hope to get away early next week. In the meanwhile I try to pick up what I can about the situation here. Everything I've heard since landing has indicated that over in England we don't have a very clear picture."

"I'll vouch for that, James. There are times when I think if Parliament had been wise and had looked ahead or had listened to anyone who understood America, none of this would have happened." Nielson scowled as he talked; dissatisfaction showed clearly in his face as well as his words.

"Just what do you mean?"

"It'd take me from now till next week to tell you all I mean. But I'll say this—" he dropped into a chair and tapped the table with his finger as he talked—"the home government has done a heap of muddling, as usual. Only this time it's serious business. Not long back the Americans were unhappy, but loyal men. Now, thanks to the Ministry, they're perilously close to being desperate, disloyal men. At home they thought they could foist any sort of law on them—the Stamp Act, for instance. But the Americans question the laws put on them, and, questioning, they marshal facts that show our inconsistency and double-dealing. They've lost their respect for Parliament and the Ministry. And only so long as they believe the King stands apart from his advisers will they stick with England."

Blair thought for a while before he answered. Then he said, "I don't know half so much about the sentiment here as you do, but are you sure you're not exaggerating? I've talked rather closely to several colonists since I've been here. Everyone was against war."

"Who'd you talk to?"

"Farquard Campbell, for one. At home he's thought dangerous—perhaps. But he seems to look on himself as a moderator. Now, mind, I don't approve what he's reportedly doing, but if he really believes he's working toward peace, he's not so dangerous."

Nielson merely harumphed as if unimpressed. Blair, his finger tips pressed lightly together and his elbows on the table, was trying to think of the name of a young man he'd met in the dining-room. Tall, broad-shouldered fellow, with clean, square features and an open look about him. Likeable. But what the deuce was his name? Morton? Murray? "Moray!" he said aloud. "Yes, Archie, I met another Scot here at the inn. Stephen Moray. Far as I could tell, he's got no interest in politics at all."

"That might well be true. He's an artisan, really an artist, and all bound up in it. But he was apprenticed in Boston, so you don't know what may be germinating inside him." Nielson suddenly jumped up again. "Listen, Blair. I may be wrong, but I'd advise you to pay more attention to signs of war than signs of peace. One thing is sure: Once rebellion gets started here, it'll be hard to stop. You've had a chance to talk only to a couple of Scots. They're not representative, though they're important. Wait till you know some of the colonials who've been here longer than most of the Scots. You'll see they're a new breed of Englishmen. And believe me, if England doesn't realize what kind of men they are, and deal with them accordingly, she's going to have a war on her hands. Just write that home when you make one of your reports."

Blair was cleaning out his pipe. He spoke without looking up. "How do you suggest we deal with them, Nielson?"

There was a pause before Nielson took a deep breath and answered, "This is between you and me, but I'd give them representation. I've been here long enough—nearly five years now—to have a lot of respect for many of these men. I don't see any reason for their being kept out of Parliament. Or rather, I don't see any good reason. Pitt—Chatham I guess it is now—put his finger on the real cause of our refusal, and our trouble. Remember when he charged the Grenville party with 'preposterous and infatuated errors' in its American policy? We're stuck with those errors. And we're going to pay for them, I'm afraid."

"Be careful, Archie," Blair warned with concern. "I understand what you're saying, but you could be misunderstood."

"I know. One reason I'm talking so much is that I usually keep quiet. But recently things have been frightening me. For a while I thought Chatham would have a strong influence on the Ministry. Still hope he has. Then too, I took hope from Dartmouth's appointment. He inherited a bad situation, but he seems to want to be fair. But I can't now see that he's achieving much, and I can see how touchy the patriots here are getting."

Nielson fell silent and paced about the room. To Blair there seemed nothing to say. He was thankful he'd run into Nielson and learned so much from him. But even Nielson's comments were little more than opinions. Blair found himself eager to be in Boston, at work on his assignment. He wanted to find out for himself just what was going on. At last he roused, when he saw Nielson reaching for his hat. "Another glass, Archie? To warm you up for the drive?"

Nielson refused the drink and slung his cloak over his shoulders. Blair detained him a moment. Rising, he said in a half-jesting tone, "Tomorrow, if you don't mind, don't be too charming. I wasn't getting on badly with Miss Weston. It's true she's a little piqued now, but that's usually a good, rather than a bad, sign." He saw Nielson grinning mischievously and added, "You wouldn't like to show me around the turpentine woods, too, would you?"

Nielson slapped him on the shoulder. "I'd be happy to, Blair. But don't forget—you've got to be running down suspects. Martin would never swallow your story if he found out you'd been gadding about with Miss Weston and me. But don't worry: I'll talk to her about you."

With a good-humoured grin Blair acquiesced. "All right, but mind you just show her the landskip. I know you better than to believe you'll tattle on me, so I won't warn you about that." Then he spoke seriously. "Archie, I meant it. I'm fond of her. And I have to go to Boston for a long time. Don't spoil my chances."

19

The Governor Entertains

THE night of Governor Martin's ball was fair and, for October, very warm. As the carriages began to drive up and deposit the guests at his door, the full moon was already shedding a genial light. Even the weather was joining in the welcome to the distinguished visitors from Skye.

As the rooms of the palace began to fill, Archibald Nielson's prediction that only Tories would accept the Governor's invitation was proved wrong. Whigs and Tories, moderates and extremes, people of all political persuasions, were turning out in force to meet Flora and Allan MacDonald. Before Martin and his dinner guests were ready to rise from the table, the palace was thronged.

The musicians, stationed near the grand staircase, played softly. Servants in Governor Martin's livery moved about passing trays of punch in delicate crystal glasses, and a hum of lively conversation filled the air.

Suddenly the orchestra broke off in the middle of a dance tune and began a dignified march. The doors of the drawing-room were thrown open. Thus warned, the guests crowded toward the walls, leaving a wide avenue the full length of the great reception room.

Stephen Moray, crowded close to the wall in the hall, craned his neck to see the Governor's party make its grand entrance. The Governor and his guests of honour led the procession. Josiah Martin, in his most elegant dress, walked at the left, with Flora, radiant, on his arm in the centre. Flanking her on the right, Allan stood a head taller than the Governor. All eyes went to the MacDonalds. Behind them fol-

lowed the members of the Governor's Council and
their wives.

The tall, straight figure of Allan MacDonald
brought out a low murmur of approval from the female guests. He wore Highland dress, which not only
became him mightily but set him off from all the
other men in the room, who were dressed in woollen
coats, brocaded waistcoats and, most of them, white
satin small-clothes. He wore his own hair, and his
well-brushed dark-brown curls gave his face a youth-
ful look which none of the gentlemen wearing white
wigs or powdered hair could match.

A girl next to Stephen gave Allan a long look and
sighed. Scarcely realizing she was addressing a man,
she turned a little toward him and said, "I fairly lan-
guish at the sight of kilts. A man looks so handsome
in them, and I love to see them swish as he walks.
They make a man immensely fetching, don't they?"

Stephen looked ruefully at his nankeen breeches,
the best he had brought but something less than the
height of fashion, and blushed. In his heart he agreed
with her that kilts did give a man an air—that is, if
his legs were straight and his knees not too knobby.
He would have given a month's earnings to be wearing a kilt at that moment as he watched the girl's eyes
follow Allan in helpless attraction.

Though Allan won the women, Flora drew the admiration of both sexes. The warmth of New Bern's
reception had restored her full vitality, and her carriage was both regal and buoyant. Her high-held head
was noble. Her mouth, always warm and generous,
was smiling. Her large oval eyes were sparkling. Her
gown, cut low and square at the neck, was of satin
woven in bands of velvet in dark colours suggesting a
plaid. Its sleeves were full and slashed, with a lining
of white satin. At her bosom she had three cockades
fashioned of broad white ribband, the white cockades
of the Stuarts, which she always wore with formal
dress to show her allegiance.

One of the two women standing at Stephen's left
told her companion, "That's the same dress she wore
in the portrait Wilson painted of her. You've seen it,

haven't you? Women in Scotland wore dresses of that material after tartans were proscribed."

"It looks like a tartan, but I suppose it would evade the law," the other woman replied. "I'm glad we never had that law over here. The Cross Creek people wear their plaids as they please, and kilts as well, and I'm sure it makes them happy."

The procession advanced with dignity the length of the polished floor. At the far end of the room Governor Martin and the MacDonalds mounted the dais and turned to face the assembled company, Flora still in the centre and Allan at her left. With a lifted finger, Martin signalled the leader of the orchestra.

At his sign the musicians struck up "God Save the King." The whole assemblage stood quietly, many of them with their eyes fixed on the full-length portraits of George the Third and Queen Charlotte which hung on the wall behind the dais. They were by Allan Ramsay, the fashionable and talented Scots artist, Stephen had discovered. He wondered whether Flora knew they were Ramsay's work. For Ramsay had been impressed not only by her achievement but also by her expression, and he had persuaded her to sit for a portrait.

When the anthem was over, the Governor bowed Flora into an elbow-chair and took his place beside her in another. Allan stood behind Flora, and the Governor's secretary came to stand behind his superior and introduce the guests, who were lining up, the length of the room, for a formal presentation.

Stephen was too nervous even to watch the crawling progress of the line. For him the crucial moments of the ball lay ahead, and his anxiety to have them over and settled, no matter how they came out, was almost beyond bearing. He moved away.

At one of the tall windows in the reception room James Blair stood with Archibald Nielson, chatting negligently. His eyes roved approvingly, taking in the beautiful proportions of the room, blazing with the light of many candles in crystal chandeliers and side-wall sconces, the fine silks and satins of the ladies' gowns, the well-cut coats of the gentlemen. "Not bad at all," he murmured to Nielson. "You might think yourself at a reception in London for people of very good quality. At first glance, the generality here are more concerned with society and politeness than in Boston."

"The MacDonalds put people on their mettle. Look at Flora; she is like a queen. Allan makes a fine appearance, too." The two men watched as a couple were presented. The gentleman bowed and kissed her hand. The lady made a deep curtsey. Flora smiled winningly and had evidently a pleasant word for them. She sat very straight, her billowing skirt hiding her small satin-clad feet.

"She's a great lady. I grew to admire her very deeply on the ship coming over," said Blair, his air proprietary. Suddenly his manner changed. "If I'm to work as an agent here, I should learn about the political leaders. You know them, Archie, and you can help me. When each man goes up to be presented, tell me his name and a little about him, if there is anything important to know. Then I'll have both his name and his face imprinted on my memory. Agreed?"

"A pleasure, James. You get the best of the lot as the first. There goes James Hasell, the only fully trustworthy man on the Governor's Council. He's been a judge. He has served as deputy governor when Martin has been away. A solid, conservative man, loyal to the core, though you might find his spirit a little heavy in conversation. Martin has complete confidence in him."

"Good. That's enough of a portrait. Who comes next?"

"His name is Samuel Cornell. Except that he is one of Martin's Council, I know nothing about him. Probably moderate. Now I think of it, I do know one thing about him: he has a pretty daughter named Sukie."

"Ah!" Blair exclaimed with a mock leer. "Perhaps I should investigate him—and his family. I gather the latter will bear watching."

"Next comes Judge Maurice Moore. He has served with distinction on the bench. He sympathizes too much for my comfort with the Whig cause, but he's an honest man."

"Who's this fellow who looks as if he had been shaken with fever and dried out by the sun?"

Nielson's face wore an expression of distaste. "An arrant rebel and a rising man, though not yet one of the top leaders—Abner Nash. The next two in line are of the same stripe, Richard Cogdell and Alexander Gaston. I'll wager all three were on your precious list. Don't trust them."

"I shan't—at least not on land. At sea, as I told you, I'm a weakling and a natural gull whom anybody can trick. These two fellows coming up now look rather respectably Tory. Am I right?"

"Both members of the Council and on good terms with the Governor—John Sampson and William Dry. I'm not personally much acquainted with them. I give you only Martin's impression."

For half an hour the long line filed slowly up to the dais to pay tribute to the fame and charm of the MacDonalds. Nielson went on naming the men and limning their characters in a sentence or two, and Blair ticketed them in his memory—those to use and those to distrust.

As the line before them shortened, Blair sorted out his impressions of what Nielson had told him. "Almost as many Whigs here as Tories, Archie. It surprises me a little that they mingle so amicably, considering the warmth of the conflict."

"One must be on the spot for some time to understand it, James. In England it would be incomprehensible."

"One other point impresses me. Among the Whigs here are many understrappers, a number rising to leadership but almost none of the top men. Why is that?"

"The main reason is that there is little liking between them and Martin and this is recognized on both sides. Of course there are individual considerations besides. Mr. Harvey, for instance, is frail and in bad health. Harnett and Hooper both live in Wilmington, and Hewes's home is in the Albemarle country. They would not journey so far for a ball. Caswell, Hewes and Hooper went to Philadelphia for the meeting there, and so on. By the way, Hooper grew up in Boston and studied law there with an eloquent rebel you may remember, James Otis. Does this fact explain his extreme temper?"

"It would go far to. But enough of politics. Here comes Cecily Weston."

They made their compliments to her beauty and were soon in animated conversation, with much laughter and good humour.

When the final couple had been presented, Governor Martin rose and stepped forward to the edge of the dais. A brief roll on a drum gained him the attention of everybody in the room.

"Ladies and gentlemen," Martin began affably, "let me ask you to join with me in a very pleasant ceremony." He made a short, rather graceful speech about the silversmiths' competition, stressing the design for a large centre-piece for the dining-table. The judges—Mr. Hawkes, the architect, and Mr. Wallis, the Edenton goldsmith and banker—had made a careful study of the designs, he said, and come to their decision. Mr. Wallis would speak for the judges and tell the company something about the award.

He waited while Wallis came forward, introduced him to the audience and returned to his chair. Mr. Wallis' speech was short and to the point. "This award," he said, "is the first to be given officially in our province for artistic endeavour. In the early stage of settlement men's minds are rightly taken up with agricultural pursuits, with trade and manufacture. So it was here. Now we have attained to a more settled and secure footing in the land, and a degree of leisure, it is good that we recognize the Arts. Since our province has a numerous group of able silversmiths, we have thought it good to lend the encouragement of the government to the design of fine silver, something I am sure the ladies here tonight will approve."

A clapping of feminine hands endorsed his opinion. With a smile Wallis continued: "Mr. Hawkes and I have studied with the utmost care every design submitted. We agreed to base our judgement on beauty, good form and originality. A number of the designs are very fine, but I am glad to say Mr. Hawkes and I agreed at once on one as the best.

"We are delighted to name a man of undoubted talent, a young Cellini, I might say. He has designed some very fine pieces which I am sure you will all find beautiful. Governor Martin has caused to be prepared a certificate naming him as the victor in the competition. Mistress Flora MacDonald has kindly agreed to present it. May I say, before I name the winner, that you may see the drawings a little later, when they will be on exhibit in the anteroom to Governor Martin's study?

"Now comes the important moment. Will Mr. Stephen Moray step forward to receive his award." Wallis pronounced the name distinctly and with great emphasis.

At the far end of the room Stephen had been listening to Wallis with almost painful attention. He believed in his creative ability, and as Wallis had spoken he had been astonished by the intensity of his desire to have his gifts acknowledged. When he heard his own name and the burst of applause that followed it, he was at first powerless to move. He saw people looking about, trying to pick him out of the crowd. He saw Flora MacDonald rise and go forward.

At last he gathered himself and moved toward the front of the room, head erect and shoulders squared. The expanse of polished floor seemed interminable as everyone stared at him. He kept his eyes on Flora's face.

As he came close, something about her brought up from his heritage a surge of the old clan spirit. He did not know why he did what he did, but he could not have done otherwise. Without servility he dropped to one knee and kissed the hem of her skirt. Thus had Scots, since the days of chivalry, attested loyalty and fealty.

Flora's eyes filled with tears. She understood his

action and her heart rejoiced. She motioned him to his feet and handed him the scroll. Her voice was low but carrying. "Laddie," she said, "I am happy that a Scot so young and bonnie should receive this high award. May God go with you always!"

Again the applause rang out. Stephen shook hands with Wallis and, still a little dazed, took the hand Governor Martin extended.

The little ceremony had evidently pleased the Governor, for he was expansive. Still holding Stephen's hand, he said, "Young man, you are a fine artist and the province rejoices to claim you. This night should be memorable for you. What can we do to add to your pleasure? Make a request."

At any ordinary time the Governor's suggestion would have left Stephen speechless. Tonight, moved by his communion with Flora, he answered without hesitation. "I'd like best to hear the pipes. Next to that an old Scots song would give me pleasure."

The Governor smiled approval. "Very appropriate," he said. He turned to Flora. "Is there a piper among you?"

"Our ward Dougald MacDonald is reckoned well worthy of the MacCrimmons who trained him."

The Governor turned back to Stephen. "Then you shall have both your piping and your song." Once more he turned to the assembled guests and raised his voice. "In honor of Mr. Moray and of our Scots visitors, with your good permission we shall have an interval of Highland music."

As Dougald appeared, carrying his pipes, Stephen moved to the side of the room, taking his place beside the Governor's friend, Mr. Nielson, and a couple from the Miller house, Miss Weston and Mr. Blair. Both men congratulated him warmly. Miss Weston was very cool and said only, "Very commendable." Was he hypersensitive in thinking her attitude that of a lady condescending to a tradesman? He flushed slightly. As Dougald was ready to begin, he made no reply.

Dougald started off with "Flora MacDonald's Lament," a choice that combined a tribute to Flora with an expression of the sadness that filled the hearts of Scotsmen far from their misty isles. He followed it with an ancient war song. Before beginning a third tune he summoned David and Moira. "Dance a fling," he commanded, "I'll play a gay one." Moira was shy at first, but David threw himself into the dance with such gay abandon that she was soon matching him step for step in the same spirit. Dougald had every toe in the room tapping, and when the three finished the dance, panting, the applause was general.

The performers bowed and smiled shyly. Dougald called Moira and David to him and whispered to them for a moment. Then he faced the company and said, "Mr. Moray has had his piping, and I hope it did him good. He asked also for a Scots song. We will sing one chosen specially in his honour." He stepped back and took his place beside Moira.

He played the tune through softly on the pipes. After a phrase or two, Stephen Moray's eyes lighted up. Involuntarily he exclaimed aloud, "The Bonnie Earl of Murray."

Moira and David began to sing, their clear, pleasant voices blending sweetly.

> "Ye highlands, and ye lawlands,
>   Oh! quhair hae ye been?
> They hae slaine the Earl of Murray,
>   And laid him on the green."

The old tale of lawless violence, of loss and grief, stirred Stephen as it always did. The singers were going on:

> "He was a braw gallant,
>   And he rid at the ring;
> And the bonnie Earl of Murray,
>   Oh! he might hae been a king.
>
> "Oh! lang will his lady
>   Luke owre the castle downe,

Ere she see the Earl of Murray
. Cum sounding throw the towne."

As the song ended, Cecily Weston turned to Ste-
phen curiously. "What did Dougald mean when he
said he had chosen this song in particular to honour
you?"
. "That song, Miss Weston, is 'The Bonnie Earl of
Murray.' People have spelled his name Murray or
Moray, as I spell mine, but it is one name."
"Then—this is a song of your family?" she asked.
"My people like to believe so," he said proudly. He
smiled. "Some of them still hate Huntley as fiercely as
anyone could. After almost two hundred years."
"Let me see," said Cecily Weston. "My history is
shaky. Was the Earl of Moray the brother of Mary
Stuart?"
"No, that one was a generation earlier and the
Bonnie Earl's father-in-law. Actually he was Queen
Maria Stuart's half-brother, a bastard son of the King,
but the greatest lord in Scotland for all that."
Miss Weston looked at him for a long moment,
puzzlement on her face. At last, in cool tones, she asked
a question. "And you, Mr. Moray, you are a silversmith?"
The condescension in her voice made him wince
inwardly. He was as well born as she. What was
wrong with a silversmith? He liked being one. She
would learn that in America a man did not rest on
the achievements of his ancestors. Even if he had
money, as Stephen did not, he would prefer to work,
to do something for himself. It was a characteristic of
the life here. He would make her see.
As he opened his mouth to tell her all this, she and
Blair moved off. Nielson, following a step behind,
tossed over his shoulder a word of excuse or farewell—
Stephen couldn't tell which, for the orchestra, just beginning to play, drowned it out.
Governor Martin handed Flora down from the dais
and led her onto the floor for a minuet. Stephen
watched other couples detach themselves from the
groups lining the walls and take their positions.

The Governor and Flora led the dance, he with stiff precision, she with poise and grace. Allan was solemn as he moved with Mrs. Hasell through the dignified pattern of the dance. Moira and Dougald went through the steps preoccupiedly; each was absorbed in the other. Cecily, bowing to Nielson, was the most charming of the dancers. Her willowy body gave itself to every movement with effortless perfection.

The first dance over, a quadrille was begun. Contre-dances and more minuets would follow. The young folk had been impatiently awaiting this part of the evening. They were quick to seek the floor. The whole room seemed to respond to the grace and beauty of the women, to the manly tread of the bold, handsome men bred to strength and individuality. It was as though the polished beams and prismatic chandeliers absorbed and reflected the ardour and promise of the young people, the more stately brilliance of their elders. For a golden hour the ballroom in Tryon's Palace was full of something very like joy.

Stephen was tempted to yield to the evening's pleasures. A contre-dance would banish the sting of Cecily Weston's dismissal. Many of the women here would be delighted to dance with the prize-winning artist. Then, disconsolately, he pushed himself away from the wall. There was no time for him to enjoy his victory in the silver contest. Now he had to thank the Governor by stealing from him. His stomach contracted miserably, but nonetheless he started to manoeuvre casually toward the hall. No haste showed in his manner; he courteously chatted with the guests who waylaid him to offer congratulations.

Cecily lifted her lace handkerchief to her lip, and wiped away the fine beads of perspiration there. She breathed deeply to cool herself with the fresh autumn air and to regain her serenity. It really had been rude of her to flee to the garden, but she'd not been able to restrain herself. There had come a moment when the ball had ceased to be exhilarating and had grown depressing. Blair had not asked for a dance, and the succession of other partners had become wearisome. When at last he had sought her out she'd given him a curt refusal and run away. It had really been silly. A man so fickle in his attentions was not worth anger.

Slowly she began to walk down the path around the house and told herself that her dissatisfied mood would soon pass. Already the dejection that had seized her began to relax its hold.

She was passing close to a lighted window. Glancing idly in, she saw that it was Governor Martin's study, the room where she and Flora had given him the packet the night before. At the height of the ball she expected it to be empty. It wasn't. A single figure, taller and thinner than Martin, stood behind the desk, alone in the room.

She stepped off the path and moved close to the window to get a better view. It was as if she were in the darkness of a theatre and watching a lighted stage. Two branched candlesticks stood on shoulder-high bookcases, a third on the desk filling the room with soft light. Her eyes sought the man at the desk. He was . . . Stephen Moray.

Furtively his hands went to the centre drawer. Was the man a thief? At his cautious touch the drawer began to open. The Governor must have forgotten to lock it this afternoon. Moray seemed startled when he encountered no resistance. What could he be after? Suddenly she knew. The packet! She wished she could be surer, but she must do something without delay. He was sorting through a handful of papers.

She stepped blindly backward toward the path. Her heel sank into a hole in the soft ground and she almost fell. Without volition, her right hand flew out seeking the window ledge. The ring on her third finger grazed the window pane, making a sharp little click that sounded to her as loud as a pistol shot.

Moray started guiltily. His head turned toward the window. The papers in his hand dropped back into the open drawer. Then with elaborate unconcern he began to look at the hunting prints hung on the wall, moving toward the window. Now Cecily was sure he had no honest business at the Governor's desk. He was coming close to the window; she must get away.

She gathered her skirts in her hand and ran lightly to one of the French windows into the ballroom. At the door she quickly composed herself and entered. As quickly as she could without attracting attention, she skirted the ballroom to the anteroom of the Governor's study.

Here half a dozen guests were studying Moray's design, which had won the silver competition. She passed them calmly and they did not look around. At the open door of the study she paused and peered in.

In that second of pause her mind was racing. The room was a long rectangle with windows on two sides. Moray stood at the far end with his back to her, looking out the window, one hand at the side of his face to cut off the light from behind him. The desk was much closer. Holding her breath, she tiptoed into the room and headed for the desk. She reached the front corner and began to glide around it to reach the drawer. Moray had not sensed her presence.

The drawer stood open, as Moray had left it. Half a dozen documents lay scattered, one of them familiar ever since that night in the Azores when she had found it in her bag. The papers made a faint rustle as she pulled it out. Moray turned as if he had been stung. Slightly crouched, he stared at her in wild dismay.

Neither knew how long they stood staring at each other as if rooted to the ground. At length Cecily divined that Moray had recovered from the first shock and would make his counter-move. Could she reach the door before he cut off her escape? The packet, still in her right hand, seemed unprotected. In a scuffle he could snatch it from her and her strength would be of no avail.

While he was gathering himself, she thrust the packet into the bosom of her dress. The stiff paper was large and clumsy to hide within her low-cut gown. She worked at it with both hands as she began to run toward the door. Her movement seemed to release Moray. He sprang across the room with incredible speed. They reached the doorway almost together. His hands went out to seize her.

Feeling the packet was safely out of sight, she found a sudden self-command, a mastery over him. Before he could touch her, she spoke almost in a whisper, with cold distinctness. "Don't be a fool. There are at least eight people within five yards of us, admiring your designs. I have only to scream. It would go hard with you if they found you with your hand thrust rudely in my bosom."

Involuntarily he drew back a little. She knew she had defeated him. She drew herself up and, with a little smile on her face, walked easily into the anteroom.

Within seconds he was at her elbow, whispering furiously into her ear. She did not pause, but he kept pace with her. "If anyone's a fool, Miss Weston, it's you. That list you are guarding so stubbornly can do incalculable harm to innocent men—get them put in prison, their houses burned. All of them are loyal subjects of the King, as loyal as you are. Maybe all they've done is talk in a tavern against the unjust taxes Parliament tried to impose on us, or at worst sent a schooner to Martinique for a cargo of rum. Why should you work to destroy them?"

"I don't believe you," Cecily answered haughtily without looking at him. "You were rifling the Governor's desk. He's the King's representative. When you rob him you rob the King. You're a thief and a traitor."

"Can't you understand?" pleaded Stephen desperately. "I suppose you'd agree your uncle is a good man. I'd wager my life his name's on the list."

Abruptly Cecily stopped and faced him. "My uncle?" she cried. "You're lying." Just beyond the doorway where they were standing couples moved with deliberate grace in the stately pattern of the minuet, but it was as if Cecily and Moray stood alone on an island of bitter passion.

"Yes," Stephen whispered tensely, "Farquard Campbell. You must know he's a Whig. Why isn't he here with you now? He stopped in Wilmington to talk to Harnett about the nonimportation agreement."

Chill fingers of fear touched her heart, but she summoned her coldest expression and looked Moray in the eye. "I'll pay no heed to the words of a thief," she said haughtily. "And if you annoy me further, I'll report you as a thief."

Moray's mouth twisted in bitterness, as if there were alum on his tongue. He strode away. Cecily followed him to the doorway. She watched him snatch his cloak from a rack, and shoulder through the door with the wrap yet on his arm. Then, trembling from the strain of the intense moments just past, she made her way up the staircase.

Upstairs she found a secluded corner and sat down to wait for her heart to stop pounding. When she pressed her hand to her bosom she heard the crackle of the papers. They must be put back; only good fortune had let her get this far with them, without someone's noticing the unsightly, knobby bulge in her bodice. She felt sick and confused, as she drew them out and unfolded them. She intended to read the list, be certain about Farquard Campbell. Then, without reading, she wrapped her handkerchief about the papers. She realized that the presence of her uncle's name could make no difference. She had the power to destroy the message, but she would not do that. Martin had already seen the list. More important, Cecily could not force herself between the King and his purposes. She was too loyal.

With a sigh she rose and resolved to blot out thoughts of Farquard. The thing to do now was to conceive of a safe plan for replacing the packet. Instinctively she rejected a direct approach to Martin or Nielson. Moray might be a traitor who deserved to be reported. But she was no informer. No, she preferred to return the papers without calling attention to Moray. His needs would trip him up without assistance from her.

For a moment Cecily stood still. A frown appeared on her forehead and she bit her lip while she considered ways of getting the packet back to its drawer.

When she had decided, the frown disappeared. She looked perfectly serene when she went down the stairs a moment later.

Reflecting that her bag had once before served well to conceal the packet, she had fetched it. To be perfectly sure that no one would detect it she had also picked up her cloak and draped it over her arm. At the foot of the stairs she paused. No one was attending to her; it was as easy for her to enter the study undetected as it had been for Moray.

It was the work of a moment to slip the papers under other loose sheets. Carefully she left the drawer slightly ajar. Then she hurried from the room and was back in it almost immediately with Nielson, whom she drew forward by the sleeve. "You really ought to see whether anything is missing," she said anxiously. "Surely the drawer isn't supposed to be open."

Nielson shuffled through the papers. "They don't seem unusually disorganized. But, of course, I'm not sure of exactly what ought to be here." He frowned as he looked at some papers, Cecily couldn't tell which. "I'll speak to the Governor about it. He shouldn't be so careless."

Cecily watched Nielson lock up the packet bearing, presumably, her uncle's name. She nodded when Nielson excused himself and left by the room's side door to search out the Governor. Her head ached unmercifully now that it was all over and she dreaded the gay company she would find in the ballroom. Her thoughts went to Flora, as they had when she'd first been troubled by the packet. Of course, she couldn't tell Flora about Moray. But Flora was quiet and dignified, and Cecily could spend with her the time she must in decorum remain at the ball.

In the great-room Flora was strolling about, examining the members of each cluster of dancers or conversationalists. When Cecily approached her she cried softly, "I've been seeking you. I can't put off telling you any longer. Remember last night, when I started to tell you something about the packet? Well, I——"

Cecily froze. "I don't want to hear it. Not now!"

"You must. I dislike telling you, but your uncle Farquard——"

"I know. Excuse me."

Cecily stood for but an instant, her hand pressing against her cheek. Then she fled. She forgot propriety and hurried past the Governor and his guests without a farewell. She wanted only to find an escort to take her to the inn.

In the hall she met Blair, indolently chatting with some of the local gentlemen. Forgetting her desire to avoid him, she touched his arm. "Please," she said with almost pathetic simplicity, "I am not well. Will you see me home?"

He did not hesitate. He wrapped her cloak about her and guided her out of the house without bothering to find his own wrap. As soon as they were in the dark he slipped his arm about her waist and she allowed herself to lean on him gratefully. In the carriage he tucked the lap robe about her and asked solicitously, "Cecily, what is it? Are you seriously ill?"

She shook her head and smiled wanly. "No, don't be concerned. There have been too many festivities for me, I suppose."

She could see the outline of his face and was reminded of another night when Blair had hovered over her. But how different this was! Tonight there was no mockery on his face. Instead there was genuine concern, worry . . . and affection. He looked at her searchingly and shook his head slightly. "An overdose of gaiety doesn't sound right," he said finally. "No one has more high spirits than you. Tell me the truth, Cecily. Has something happened to frighten you? Has someone annoyed you?"

Tears welled into Cecily's eyes. She felt engulfed in issues and undercurrents that were too big for her. For a brief second she was tempted to put her head on Blair's shoulder and weep, just for the relief of it. But self-pity and womanish fragility were things Cecily never indulged in. The muscles in her throat tightened as she struggled for control. When she spoke it was in the light tone she always used with Blair. "Your question brings me to my senses. What a foolish miss I am—to turn, when in need of a reliable escort, to the one man who has made me indecorous advances." There was a tremor in her voice as she went on before he could speak. "I trust you understand it was my weariness that made me invite you to a carriage ride, not any . . . any wanton impulse."

With a pretense at laughter she put up her hand to push him a little farther from her. He caught her hand and pressed it against his lips as he murmured, "Dear Cecily, you're not wanton. Has that been worrying you?" He tipped her face up to his with his other hand. "A thing begun in jest, dear, can end very seriously—as has my feeling for you."

She felt a blush burn in her face and pushed his hand away so that she could look down into her lap, out the window, anywhere but at him. "But . . . well . . . you must think me——"

"Look at me, Cecily, and I'll tell you what I think." He waited until she turned slightly toward him, finally glanced up, then dropped her eyes again. "You would make me miserable forever if you didn't respond to me. I love you."

Surprise made her forget her timidity. This Blair was like none of the other Blairs she had known—the vain, insipid one of the early voyage; the reckless, amorous and ineffectual one of the final days at sea; the casual, distant one of the last two days. This was a Blair she had sensed in small, infrequent phrases and gestures. But she had not been able to believe he really existed. How had he come to her so quickly, rendering her soft and weak with surprise and joy? She looked into his eyes and cried almost plaintively, "I do not understand you! You do, you say, you are nothing that I expect. And now—love? We are strangers to each other. How can there be love between strangers?"

"Like this, Cecily," he said, drawing her against him and pressing his mouth compellingly on hers. She held herself rigid; this chaster kiss was more passionate than the earlier one. She feared to yield at all;

even a soft response would surrender her more completely than staying with him that other night would have done.

He drew away, and she felt bereft. "Close your eyes, Cecily," he commanded gently, and she obeyed. He kissed her again, and she clung to him.

When they at last drew apart, she held his face between her hands. "James ... James." She spoke his name with quivering lips that wanted to break into a smile, even a clear laugh of happiness. "Oh, James, my stranger gentleman-soldier, who and what are you that you can take me from myself?"

He took her hands to hold them. "I'll tell you, but later." He nodded toward the carriage window. "There's the inn."

They stood at the foot of the walk to watch the coach clatter off. The cool wind whipped her cape and skirts about him and he gently wrapped the cloak about her, and held her in the circle of his arms. "Let's just stand a moment, dear. How long will it be, do you suppose, before we have another moment such as this? A quiet, private one, beneath a quiet moon and sky?"

At his words she felt a chill that was not from the October wind. She asked, "What do you mean, James? I go only to Campbelltown. Will you not come there to see me?"

Without looking at her he said, "I go to Boston. For how long I cannot say."

She wrenched away from him. "You will leave me? Now?" Her face was pale in the moonlight and the hurt showed in her eyes.

His hands went out as if to touch her, but he withdrew them and thrust them into his pockets. Turning slightly from her, so that he did not see her face, he said, "I should not have spoken. I knew I had no right. But, Cecily—" he turned imploringly—"how could I not?"

She gathered her skirts about her in a gesture of withdrawal. She waited for him to explain himself.

He perceived her bewilderment and said contritely,

"I'm sorry, Cecily. I'm not explaining things so you can understand. The trouble is, I don't think I can." He ran his hand through his hair while he groped for words. Finally he said shortly and directly, "You know I'm an Army officer. But I'm not on vacation. Instead I'm on a very important mission. That's what I meant by saying I'm not free. The worst part of it is that I don't know when I will be."

Cecily stepped close to him and asked, "What kind of mission is it, James?"

After a pause he shook his head and said, "I can't tell you."

"You don't trust me." She said it in a flat tone.

"It's not that. What I'm asking is that you trust me." He caught her arms and turned her to face him. "It's much for me to ask. It would be much for you to give. There'd be long waiting, often without news. But will you do it?"

Cecily almost said "Yes" at once, but she held the word back. If he told her nothing of his mission, he remained as much a stranger as he had been. More of one really. She had at least been familiar and easy with the fop he'd pretended to be. She knew nothing of the officer he really was. Could she wait endless months during troublesome times for a man whose face and words and habits might become dimmer, vaguer in her memory?

During her silent moment of perplexity Cecily recalled the other problems and questions that faced her. Her aching tiredness returned and she felt incapable of finding any answers. Involuntarily she rubbed her neck to relieve the tension she felt. "James," she said pleadingly, "I do not know what to answer. I'm afraid to answer, for fear you will misunderstand me. Can you believe that at this moment I honestly cannot know my own mind and heart? It is impossible that I should all at once. Believe that I want to understand my feelings—and yours. But give me time."

He gazed at her earnestly. "I would willingly give you time, Cecily. But circumstances give us only tonight or an uncertain day many months hence."

"Tomorrow. There is tomorrow," she whispered.

He took her in his arms and kissed her. "Yes," he said against her hair, "we have tomorrow——half of it anyway. Will you give me your answer then?"

"I'll try to. But first I must think." She slipped away from him and ran up the steps. "Good night, James."

20

The Bitternesses of the Morning

A DRIZZLY mist blurred the outlines of the trees in front of the Governor's Mansion and obliterated the line between the river and the sky. Flora, standing by the drawing-room window, watched the spray on the pane, saw pin-points of water creep together to form heavy silver drops that coursed down the glass. With nervous fingers she traced one path after another. Frequently she walked toward the hall to look anxiously at the closed door of Governor Martin's study.

Mr. Farquard Campbell had arrived in New Bern in mid-morning. Now he was closeted with Martin and Allan, and Flora was left to wonder what the three men discussed. She could not imagine what sort of conversation could be carried on for long among them. They had little in common. One was a states-man, one a merchant, one a landowner—it could hardly be business which was evoking the murmurs she could dimly hear. Politics were on nearly every tongue, but she doubted that they engrossed the three men. Their conflicting views wouldn't permit open or sympathetic discussion. Martin's loyalty would oppose Campbell's—well, disloyalty was the word, Flora sup-posed. And Allan would probably refrain from saying much; he wanted to remain aloof from North Caro-lina's quarrel with the mother country.

Flora walked quickly back and forth across the room and tried not to wish that Allan would talk to her more frankly about the political unrest they'd learned of. He is right, she told herself, in keeping his own counsel, in not burdening me with his men's af-fairs. Yet she wished that Allan had made some com-ment to her when she'd told him about Farquard

Campbell, not just shrugged. And when she'd related the Governor's promise to exempt them from the oath of allegiance, he said merely, "It makes little difference about the oath. Sworn or unsworn, we're no threat to either the King or the so-called patriots. I'm not concerned in this business, and I hope you'll not involve yourself in it." The words had stung, but she had consoled herself by remembering that, for Allan, escaping the oath of loyalty to the Hanoverian was not the blessing it was to her.

With a little shake of her shoulders Flora determined to forget all she had heard about faction in North Carolina. Already her knowledge had led her to interfere in Allan's domain, in the decisions he, as husband and as head of the family, had to make. What good would her coming with him to America do if she forgot all that she had learned about him, and about herself, during the earlier years of their marriage?

She returned to the window and forced herself to sit calmly in the chair before it. She was thinking that she and her Allan were more fortunate than many married folk. They had been given a time for exploration of each other; every past joy and fear, every success and failure had intensified their insights. Now, in their ripest years, they were given a new beginning. The children were mostly grown, and she and Allan would again lean on each other, give wholly to each other. They would find a richer, more harmonious intimacy than they had ever known before. The cherished moment of the voyage, in which they had renewed their vows, returned to her. It was as if they had married again.

Often in these days Flora had compared the trip to the New World with a much shorter trip she and Allan had taken together. It was the journey across Skye to Flodigarry, Allan's first tack and the first home they'd all to themselves. Now, sitting by the Governor's window, she recalled the long, low main room of Flodigarry, where she used to sit, waiting for Allan to come in from his rounds of the fields.

All had been strange to her then, as now, and she

had soon come to love it. The room was simple, with its stone floor, great fireplace and deep-set windows. From the casement she had looked on the majestic ridge of hills that cut the island and on the flatlands, covered with heather of warm, dusty rust colour.

She would never forget her first sight of the house, her first entering of it. Allan had laughed aloud when he swung her from the coach that had brought them. He'd caught her in his arms and carried her across the threshold. "My Flora," he'd cried exultantly, "my bonnie Flora! This is our home. I am the tacksman of Flodigarry at last. And you are its mistress." The words still rang clear and happy in her memory.

Soon, Flora thought as she rose, I will hear words like that again from Allan. And this time the untroubled joy of beginning will not give way to misunderstanding. Here I can be exactly what I have always wanted to be: Allan MacDonald's wife, and nothing more.

On her way to the stairs Flora passed the study door. She did not pause. Resolved to banish weariness and worry, she lightly climbed the steps and went in to dress for the journey.

In the study the men were, despite their different sentiments, discussing politics. Allan, his chin propped on his hands, sat at a side table and refused to let himself be drawn into any sort of comment. He wondered just why he'd been forced to sit in on the interview, and, frankly, he wished the debate between Campbell and Martin would end. It was interesting—he had to admit that—but he'd much rather be on his way over to Cross Creek, and would be, as soon as the talk was wound up.

Allan had asked to be excused from the discussion entirely. While Campbell had been taking off his wet cloak and giving a boy some orders about a message to Cecily, Martin had drawn Allan into the study for some preliminary remarks. "I want you to hear what Farquard has to say. He always brings a good bit of news. Unfortunately he's been here in the colonies a long time, has imbibed a little too much of the colonial view. But he's basically loyal, and he's a good source of information. Carries weight, too, with many of the local men."

Allan had made it very clear that he didn't believe Farquard's news would interest him. "I've got no stake in this homeland-colony dispute. And the only stake I want is one on some land, fertile land." He'd laughed as he said this, and inwardly hoped Martin would offer to insure his getting a good plantation.

The Governor, however, took up the first statement. "You've a big stake in the controversy, and I in you. The Scots will turn to you, and you'd best have an idea of what's going on. In fact, I'd like you, if you could, to balance Farquard's influence a bit. I trust him, mind you, but I fear that many of your people, who really understand little of the issues disputed between England and North Carolina, will misinterpret his views. They might think he wants them to join the disaffected."

The words had momentarily made Allan want to stay. The prospect of power among the Scots, power like that held in the old days only by the great clan chiefs, lured him. Then he'd determinedly strengthened his resolve to confine himself to farming. That, surely, was his most immediate and most important task.

Saying that he had no wish to become involved in politics and that he must at once hire a carriage for the trip to Cross Creek, he'd moved toward the door. Just as his hand touched the knob, Farquard had swung back the door and cut off chance of escape. Heartily the merchant had shaken Allan's hand. "Glad to meet you again, Mr. MacDonald. And glad to catch you before you start your journey. I'm hoping you and Mrs. MacDonald will accept the offer of my carriage. I go direct to Cross Creek, and would be honoured to convey you."

Martin had swiftly accepted for Allan, pointing out that the hire of carriages was no easy matter. "Furthermore," the Governor had said, "this way you'll be able to stay for our discussion. Come now. Sit down."

"Aye," Campbell had seconded. "You've no idea

how much your presence is going to mean among the Scots. I can tell you that I'll be glad to have you work along with me for an amicable settlement of the controversy. The quicker you learn all about the grievances, the better."

With some ill grace Allan had sat down and resigned himself to listening. At first little of consequence had been said; Martin had a few questions about the colony's trade, and Farquard had answered them in dry, businesslike terms.

A few moments ago, however, a new, tense note had come into the discussion. Farquard, leaning forward in his chair and shaking a bony finger, had said in his cool, deliberate manner, "Martin, I've been warning you, and I'm going to again. You're forcing desperate means on the colonies. Oh, I don't mean you personally, but all you English statesmen. Harnett swears the trade restrictions the Philadelphia Congress recommended are going through—and not just locally. You mark my words. Every port up and down the coast is going to be closed before long, just as in '69. It'll work a hardship on both sides of the Atlantic, increase the bitterness and drive Englishmen farther apart than ever."

"The fools!" Martin had cried explosively. "The colossal colonial fools! Money's short now, but they'll stop trade. They're cutting off their nose to spite their face. Permit the trade, and they'd make enough money to pay the tax without feeling it. You're a shrewd merchant, Farquard. Can't you make them see that?"

Martin's flare-up of temper did not in the least perturb Campbell, who was stretching his long legs in front of him and crossing them at the ankles. He folded his hands across his chest comfortably and only then answered: "The other merchants are as shrewd as I am. You'll do well to disabuse yourself of any notion that they are bumbling around with no clear idea of their aim. You can believe me, Martin, when merchants forego a chance to make profit, even a little one, they've got something weighty on their minds. And these have. They've got a determination to make the profit their skill, not English law, permits them. The same is true of the shipbuilders and the manufacturers. They're not after a bigger allowance from England. They're after the freedom that any English merchant is supposed to have. What they want to know is why Parliament can curtail their production and profit and not do the same to the home merchant. And doesn't it seem reasonable," Campbell concluded, turning to Allan, "that they should ask that question?"

Allan confined his response to a noncommittal shrug. He had seen Martin's face grow red while Farquard was talking, and now was waiting for the Governor's counter-argument. Martin had entirely lost his casual, composed manner in Campbell's presence, and there was a catchy, agitated rasp in his voice as he said, "You're not telling Mr. MacDonald the whole story, Farquard, and you know it. That question, the one you say the merchants are asking, can be opposed by another: Why should Americans be allowed exceptions from colonial policy that no one else is allowed? Since when haven't colonials supported England's trade? Since when haven't they lived according to the laws Parliament makes for the good of the commonwealth?"

"Never!" Farquard retorted, and took a quick breath as if he was going to argue. Martin didn't give him an opportunity. He turned to Allan and said, "What Mr. Campbell neglects to say is that many hotheaded colonials—and not just merchants—really want independence from England. They want to live without law and allegiance." When he saw Campbell shaking his head in denial, Martin cried, "No? What more evidence do you want than the court situation here? All last year I tried to find what the agitators wanted. I offered to meet their demands, so far as English law and royal prerogative would let me. But would they compromise? No. They held out till they got what they really wanted all the time—anarchy in which there's hardly a court functioning. Any kind of lawlessness can go on—little they care!"

Allan looked from Martin to Campbell in concern,

and allowed himself to say, "You mean they think they can get on without enforcing the law? That's both foolish and dangerous."

Farquard got up as if impatient with the conversation. "What the colonials—especially the Regulators, whom Martin is talking about—think is that Crown-appointed judges and clerks were not enforcing the laws justly. No justice is little worse than injustice. So they're holding out for the right to elect the men who sit in the local courts. Furthermore, on their own initiative they'd established interim courts."

While he was speaking Campbell had crossed the room with long strides. Now he picked up his cloak and faced Martin. "I didn't come to harangue about last year's affairs. I came to give you good warning that you ought to heed. From the talking and listening and asking I've been doing—and it's quite a lot—I've decided this is the crucial time. England can still save the day or she can lose it. Right now she's in a fair way to lose it. Caswell, Hooper and Hewes—all the men up at the Philadelphia convention—are still trying to work through legal means to get redress. But they've got beyond the point of being satisfied with a little gain here or there. The tax, the restrictions on trade and manufacture, the bribed courts, the quartering of soldiers, the search—all the particular things they fought—now seem only examples of something bigger. It looks to them as if England's denying them subjects' rights in any way she can. They want those rights. They want representation and local authority. You're not going to appease them by a little concession here or there."

Martin's anger had increased as Campbell spoke and he retorted in a loud voice, "Farquard, you're beginning to sound like the traitors who call themselves patriots—" he spat out the word—"and it's going to get you into trouble. England's not going to tolerate insolence any longer. Nor am I. I've gone along with you, felt you were striving, in your own way, for the same thing I am—prevention of civil war and support of English authority. But now——"

Campbell cut him off. "Now I'm still striving for

the same things. My God, Martin, you know what I stand to lose! But I insist on showing you the best way to handle the problem. And don't you be threatening me. I'll make up my own mind, take my own risks. I'm going to finish what I came to say. If England pushes the colonials too far, if she continues to ignore their petitions, she's going to force them into illegal means. Mark my words, the growing repressive policy is the surest way to bring on open war. The colonies are loyal, now, say what you will. Most are bound closer to England than to the other colonies. But that can change over-night. You know what was said right here in New Bern last August; you know what's being said in Philadelphia now: 'Boston's cause is our cause. If England can oppress one colony she can oppress them all. Our power lies in uniting.' That's the thing you have to prevent. That, and driving them to do more than petition to get redress."

Having delivered his ultimatum, Campbell let all trace of anger fade from his face and voice. He stuck out his hand. "Come now, Martin. You and I will do no good if we don't listen to each other and co-operate. My warning was meant to help, not hinder. You pay some heed."

Allan surmised that the Governor and Campbell must have frequent disputes, for Martin seemed to take this one as no terribly serious matter. After but momentary hesitation he shook Campbell's hand and said almost jovially, "Right you are. But, blast you, Farquard, you get harder to listen to. And I meant it when I warned you. I know your purposes, but England doesn't. She's telling me already to observe your actions. I'll be able to do little for you if you get yourself in serious trouble."

Farquard didn't bother to answer; the thought of trouble seemed almost to amuse him. He stepped up to Allan and made arrangements for the drive. "After some little business in town," he promised, "I'll be by to collect you. Mayhap we can talk further on the journey. There's much more to be said. But for now, enough. The rain makes an early start desirable. So eleven thirty at the latest."

Allan agreed to the hour of departure and then watched the tall, spare merchant go through the hall and out the front door. He was not sure he liked the idea of travelling with Farquard. The man was earnest about politics. It would be hard to silence him.

The Governor interrupted Allan's thought. "You have a bemused look on your face, Mr. MacDonald. Are you perplexed by Farquard and his views? No need to be. As I told you, his facts are realistic, even if his position as a loyal patriot is not. Before long he'll give that position up, and see that I know how to handle this situation. Let him negotiate and arbitrate. In the crisis, it's not his words but my troops that will mean victory. Troops, yes, and the many loyal people here in the colony."

"Then you really believe some people are loyal?" Allan asked. "Campbell's remarks made me wonder whether everyone was a . . . a hothead."

With a short, belittling laugh, Martin said, "Everyone? By no means. I estimate that ninety per cent of the North Carolinians will rally if I raise the standard. That's counting the Scots, of course," he added meaningfully.

Allan began to see why both Campbell and Martin wanted to instruct him on colonial issues. They looked for him to enlist his countrymen for their respective causes. The thought that they represented alternatives between which he might have to choose gave him a despairing feeling. He pushed the fear away and renewed his vow to stay out of this fight if he could. Then he extended his hand and thanked the Governor for his hospitality. "You've been most gracious to my wife and myself. We appreciate it. But now we'll go west and devote our energy and time to carving out a good life for ourselves and our children."

"Of course. I mustn't hold you," Martin agreed, as he took Allan's hand in a completely friendly manner. "And don't hesitate to appeal to me if I can aid you in any way. Some benefits are at my disposal. . . ."

Martin let his vague promise hang between them; Allan chose not to acknowledge it. Benefits brought obligations; he was not ready to fulfill more obligations than those to Flora and himself.

Suavely Martin brought the conversation to a close. "You must forgive me if I now bury myself in the day's business. Convey my farewells to Mrs. MacDonald and tell her I was sincere in saying that she must visit me again—when Mrs. Martin is here. Now I must begin my conferences." As he escorted Allan to the door he idly commented, "The first interview is with one of your shipmates—Mr. Blair."

At Widow Miller's Cecily was humming a blithe song as she waited for Blair. Early this morning she had awakened to rehearse their conversation time and again. Each time she heard the echo of his "I love you" and "I'm asking you to trust me" she felt more certain that she would wait for him. "Yes," she had cried aloud, as she threw back the coverlet and stretched vigorously. "I shall not mind the long months, knowing that he's to return at the end of them. And I shall be busy planning and embroidering and buying." Her laugh rang out happily as she thought of ordering silver—but not from that thieving tradesman Moray.

The morning had been so busy that she had not noticed the hour. Farquard Campbell had come in on her while she was at breakfast and had urged her to hurry with her packing. In her happiness she had forgotten about the packet and the suspicion of her uncle. He was gone before she recalled it, but it made no difference. This morning was no time for a family argument. She'd pushed all political thought from her mind and rushed through the packing without even calling Martha. Martha was too clumsy; she'd be about folding dresses all day, and need supervision the whole time. Now, as Cecily straightened the last gown, she left off humming and murmured, "I'm ready for James." She looked at the clock. Eleven! The morning nearly gone! And James had not even sent a message.

She knew that if she waited in a room that had a timepiece she would soon be frantic. Uncle Farquard wanted to be on the way to Campbelltown in just half an hour. Already, she saw, three precious minutes had flown by. Impulsively she decided to walk in the little garden behind the inn. It was barren of all flowers but a few golden chrysanthemums, which would have lost their brilliance in the grey misty rain. The drabness did not matter. The damp, cool air would be refreshing, and the waiting would be easier without the ominous tick of the clock. She snatched her cloak and ran from the room, intent only on getting outside quickly.

She was half-way downstairs before she saw Moray, lounging by the banister post. He straightened purposefully, and she could tell he was waiting for her. Furiously angry, she did not give him a chance to speak.

"Mr. Moray, last night you spoiled my walk by your infamous thieving," she said peremptorily. "I know not what despicable act you contemplate now. But I don't wish to see it, or you. Let me pass."

Moray's temper was as quick as hers, but more controlled. "I intended to apologize, Miss Weston. Insulting women is not a habit of mine, and I was sorry for what I said. But you do not deserve apology."

Cecily's voice was scathing. "You fall back on the hauteur of your noble ancestors. But don't! No traitor is worthy of your lineage. Especially a traitor of the back-stairs sneak variety!" She gathered her skirts to her fastidiously, as if she did not want them to brush against his unsavoury person, and started to pass.

His restraint vanished. He caught her arm in a viselike grasp. "You listen to me! I'll teach you something about real villainy, the kind your high-born Ministers are fond of perpetrating. I tried to tell you last night—" he shook her rudely—"that list you so nobly saved endangers the lives and reputations of men devoted to England and her constitution. Men who are British subjects and who demand only to be treated as such." He drove her against the wall.

She faced him squarely and did not try to squirm away. She could never have loosened his grip. Though she raged inwardly, she spoke with cool contempt. "Their demands I care not for. Their—your—desert is to be treated as the rebels they are."

"Rebels! What right have you to call us that? Every man on that list—and many more—have openly asked that the constitution be upheld. What has happened to you home Englishmen that you no longer care for English liberties?" Stephen was almost hissing through his clenched teeth. His eyes were narrowed and he was pale. "You've learned that justice has not the profit of injustice. Laws used to be the same for all Englishmen—we struggled centuries for that. Now you've discovered you can fatten yourselves by making different laws for colonial citizens and for home citizens. Your merchants get more profit than the colonial merchant! Your homes are safe from illegal search; ours are not! Your taxes are set by men whom votes can recall; we have to swallow the taxes you impose on us or choke on them!"

Cecily felt weak. These were not the sort of things she expected Moray to say. He was forcing her to condemn—if she condemned him—honour and liberty. To escape the trap she said, "You rationalize your treachery, cloaking it with noble purposes. But what have your fine words to do with the point: your stealing a secret document? That, I must say, was a fine example of the English safety from search!"

He dropped her arm and turned away in disgust—both at himself and at her. His anger had subsided. "I am ashamed of that act—or, rather, of the way I had to do it. But I wish I'd got the list." He whirled back to look her straight in the eye. "Even you, who see so little, ought to be able to see that the existence of that list proves my point. We ask in a proper manner for proper redress of wrongs against us. You and your friends at home reply with a sealed list of 'dangerous men' to be acted against without warning. We act like free men, and honourable. You treat us like criminals. No one likes sneaking less than I. But when England sneaks, I must—to protect myself against her."

"So your name was on that list! How noble!" she jeered. "You fear for your own safety. You only pretend you steal to protect other men."

Moray took a step up the stairs. He glowered down at her. "There's no good in talking to you. You lose the point and distort the issue. But this I want you to know: My name was not on that list. I've wanted no part of a quarrel with my King and brother Englishmen. Brother Englishmen, indeed! They'll brother us as Cain did Abel if we let them! I see that now."

He leaped up the stairs and left her standing, shaken, at the foot. Cecily held to the banister for support and stared after him. She felt she hated Stephen Moray; he had made her feel cheap and prejudiced. Then she turned and ran through the house to the garden.

The October air, blowing sharply against her cheek, was chilling rather than refreshing. The golden chrysanthemums looked tarnished. Cecily took one look at the garden and ran on to the long, high arbour beyond. She dropped to a bench. For a moment she huddled there, wrapped in her fur-lined cape, and rocked back and forth. She wasn't thinking anything, just feeling hurt and deceived. When, however, her vision blurred with tears, she sprang to her feet and walked briskly up and down the length of the arbour, so as not to give in to crying. "I won't, I simply won't let that Moray spoil my morning! James will come soon, and I mustn't be in a gloomy mood."

After a few turns she had regained control. But, even though she was calmer, she could not recapture the light-heartedness of the early morning. When she tried to conjure up Blair's features, she saw Stephen's black eyes and square—yes, honest chin. When she whispered over and over again Blair's "I love you," she heard only Stephen's "you see so little." Finally she cried aloud, "The wretch! The wretch of a silversmith! A disgrace he is to his country and family!"

Her abuse of Moray was no relief. It only reminded her that her own uncle, too, was in a fair way to be a disgrace to his country and family. How could Farquard have got himself into such a position, consorted with that kind of person? Surely he'd not been wooed by elegant speeches like Moray's.

The image of Farquard rose before her. She recalled

the commanding assurance with which he spoke, the reticence he maintained about his affairs. Even two days spent with him had showed him to be, in these respects at least, a true member of her family. Was there anything, she wondered despairingly, that could move him—other than his own decision and determination?

Her shoulders sagged and she was on the verge of admitting defeat before she'd had one shot at the enemy. Immediately she pulled herself erect and spoke aloud in contempt of her own weakness. "Cecily Weston, you inherited as much Campbell blood as Farquard did. And right is on your side, not his. You'll talk to him, plead with him, beguile him if you have to. But you'll not let him be a traitor. Not if there's anything in the world you can do to stop him."

Once having made her decision, she sighed and absently pushed a blown strand of hair from her forehead. Already her thoughts had gone back to Blair. Where was he? What had taken him from the inn, from her?

At the sound of footsteps on the gravel walk without she whirled. Smiling, she waited. Then the smile faded and she was crushed with disappointment. Moira, her cheeks rosy from the wind and her eyes sparkling with excitement, ducked into the arbour and hid at the other end behind a thick post, made larger by the gnarled trunk of an ancient vine. A moment later Dougald came pounding up the path, stopped for a moment to look and listen, then went directly to Moira's inadequate hiding-place. He caught her hands and pulled her so she had to face him. They laughed together for sheer youth and happiness and did not see Cecily.

"You can't escape me, Moira," Dougald whispered breathlessly. "And don't forget that last night you promised you never would try to. You've broken your word. A kiss is the penalty."

Moira blushed and pushed lightly at Dougald's chest when he tried to draw her to him. "No, wait," she teased him. "You're not the old, solemn Dougald

I fell in love with. I can't kiss someone as strange to me as you're becoming."

But of course she kissed him, and the sight, as well as the innocent words, similar to those which had passed between Blair and herself, pained Cecily. She silently scolded herself for feeling that Dougald and Moira, by bringing their happiness here, were imposing on her. If anyone was out of harmony with the garden, the gloomy, romantic, blustery day, it was she.

Lightly Cecily scraped her foot on the gravel so that they would know she watched. Dougald's buoyant assurance dissolved into awkward shyness, and Moira's blush turned to one of embarrassment.

"Oh!" Moira cried after an instant's surprised silence. "Oh, Cecily! Dougald and I were looking for you ... supposed to be looking for you. Everyone wants you—your uncle, and Flora and Allan, everybody. They're all ready to go. Mr. Blair, too. He's not going, but he's all but searching all Widow Miller's rooms for you."

Cecily gave them a swift "thank you" and raced down the path, her skirts caught up in her hands. At the back door she paused to assume some dignity. Quietly she entered the hallway. Farquard was in the process of pulling his watch from his pocket. The weary air with which he did it told Cecily the timepiece had already been consulted several times.

"Uncle Farquard, I'm sorry. Can you delay a moment more? I want to speak to Major Blair for a moment."

Picking up his tricorn from the table, Farquard answered affably, "We'll wait in the carriage. I dislike rushing you, but the horses will not make good time on a rainy day like this." Then he could not refrain from reproving her; almost dutifully, as if he felt that as her guardian he must be stern, he added, " 'Tis a wasteful thing, lass, to be late for an appointment. The time of all of us has been squandered."

Cecily didn't bother to answer. She thought it foolish of him to make any fuss about a mere ten or fifteen minutes. Besides, she had seen Blair standing at the turn of the stairs, and she had no words or thoughts for anyone else. Quickly she started up, then stopped and stood still, looking at Blair in consternation.

He stood as purposefully as had Moray. His shoulders were as square, his face as stern and determined. "Come up here, Cecily," he ordered.

Slowly she climbed the steps. Her head was tipped to one side and she frowned slightly as she looked up at him and wondered at his cold manner. "James," she asked when she reached the landing and stood before him, "what is the matter?"

"I doubt I need to tell you," he said frigidly. "From what I hear you veritably manage my affairs. I must thank you for relieving me of responsibility—and for making a fool of me!"

Her hand flew to her mouth. "I ... I don't know what you're talking about! Made a fool of you? Never!"

"No? It's your word against the Governor's." His lips curled as he quoted Martin. " 'So, Blair, you, a trained intelligence officer, let a pretty slip of a girl put one over on you. I must recommend Miss Weston for a commission. She is more efficient than our experienced men.' " He laughed falsely in imitation of the Governor's bantering chuckle.

Cecily paled as she began to perceive his meaning. The packet—it must have something to do with that nuisance of a packet. Tears started to rise, but she choked them back so she could say levelly, "Tell me straight out what you mean."

"You stole the packet! Yes, while you were bending solicitously over my sick-bed." He paced back and forth on the tiny landing as he recounted his version of the theft. Cecily felt that he was crowding her down, that his anger and misconception engrossed him so that there was no room left for her in his heart and mind. But she would not be driven away until she had tried to tell him the truth. She listened as he raged on: "And weren't you clever in evading the issue when Borset interrogated you? Best of all, you took it to Martin—and left me to dodge around, unable to report. Right under my nose, the whole thing!" He held himself rigidly now, but his voice was vibrant with anger.

She reached out to touch his arm, to plead with him. "James, I . . . honestly I didn't know you had anything to do with it. And I didn't steal it. I swear I didn't. It was Holseman."

He shook off her hand. "Holseman, eh? Do you blame it on him, now he's dead? Or did he really steal it, and give it to his lovely, innocent-seeming accomplice?"

At this charge her anger matched his. White-faced, she drew back. "For shame!" she cried with a voice that trembled under its burden of contempt. "So this is the quality of your love! It converts to suspicion and base accusation at the first misunderstanding. I was trying to do what I thought best. What would you do if an official document just turned up in your purse? I didn't know whom to trust. Certainly not you, playing the fool the whole trip. And Borset was thick as thieves with you. Besides, he was sailing for England, and I knew I'd get to Martin before he ever would. Call what I did wrong if you want. I did the best I knew. If you say different, you're just venting your spleen on me. I couldn't help it if you were hoodwinked. Don't blame me!"

Cecily couldn't stop the angry words, but even as she said them she wanted to snatch them back. She knew what it was: Blair was getting rid of the anxiety that had been building in him since Holseman took the packet; she was getting rid of tension that had been building since her clash with Moray last night. This angry farewell did not need to be. After she had finished crying out at him, she waited, hoping he would beg her pardon, and let her beg his.

He looked at her as though he were wavering. An expression of grief crossed his face, then passed. Quietly but coolly he said, "Perhaps you are right. I should not blame you. But perhaps you were right also in saying the love between us is fragile. What would an officer do with a meddling wife? What would either of us do during the months of separation if we trust each other so little that this happens at the first trouble?"

If he had not used that word "meddling" Cecily would have run to him. But the adjective rankled, pricked up her pride. To hide her trembling hands she put them behind her back; to conceal her tears she blinked quickly. Then, in a strained but clear voice, she said, "I believe you are right, Major Blair. Farewell."

She walked steadily downstairs and without turning went out to the carriage. Flora sat within, already wrapped in lap-robes. She made room for Cecily and spoke cheerfully of the trip ahead of them. "I'm so glad to be riding with you, dear. A winter's separation faces us. We must have a good talk that will last us a long time."

Cecily smiled wanly and nodded. After a brief look at Flora she stared fixedly out the window toward the door of the inn. If it opened, she promised herself, she would jump down and run back. But it remained closed, and, after farewell shouts from the men and a crack of the whip, the carriage rolled away from Widow Miller's.

Inside the door James Blair stood with his hand on the latch. Stubbornness kept him from lifting it. He'd not run after a woman who'd nearly wrecked his career and didn't care enough to say "I'm sorry." But when he heard the carriage roll away, he thought only of holding Cecily again, of kissing her and feeling her turn in his arms. A day for that would come, he promised himself.

21

A Triumphal Procession

THE valley of the Upper Cape Fear River lay brown and gold in the sun. It had a lassitude like that of a woman who has just given birth to a child. Indeed, the land had given birth, throughout the hot blazing summer, to the crops sown in the spring. The long growing season had come, with pale-green shoots lengthening, thickening into dark-green stalks and leaves. The rains had come, at the right time for the young corn, tobacco and cotton. A few weeks past the rich crops had been harvested, and now the fields were empty or wore brown stubble that testified to their summer's endeavour. At the edges of the fields bright-yellow pumpkins and creamy squash were piled high.

The muted browns of the fields were framed by the vivid autumn colours along the riverbanks. The leaves of the sourwood blazed crimson to deep maroon; the sweet gum glowed yellow and red. The swamp maple and sycamore sent their dry leaves drifting down to carpet the earth with tawny gold. Hazel and hickory nuts and black walnuts hung heavy, ready for garnering.

Only the long-leaf pines remained green. They stretched upward, like slender ribs of a huge, shadowy Gothic cathedral. In the interstices of their trunks there was sanctuary for deer, fox, opossum and other small forest animals. Birds, too, had refuge there; the wild turkey, quail and partridge rustled the dry leaves in their foraging. Over the surface of the river the blue heron and white crane skimmed lazily.

It was noon of the third, the last day of the journey before Flora MacDonald and her party could see this loveliness of the land. The rain had blotted out vision until an hour or so before, when the clouds had vanished and let through the warming sunlight. The carriage lumbered to a halt at a clearing atop a knoll, so that the travellers might rest and might survey their new home. Farquard Campbell leaped from his mount to help Cecily down, while Allan went round to Flora. Dougald dismounted and wound his horse's reins about a tree trunk so that he would be free to hand out Moira and, if there was time, stroll about for her. David, whistling tunelessly as he had been throughout the long morning's ride, disdained to jump down. Instead he guided his horse to the highest point of the hillock so he could see as far as possible up the Scots valley and beyond it, in the direction of the mountain ranges he hoped someday to cross.

With a sweep of his arm Farquard Campbell indicated the expanse of land before them. "There it is—different from the Highlands, but just as beautiful."

"Aye," Allan murmured, "and kinder to a man." He drew Flora's hand through his arm and held her close to him.

She sighed and then said, "'Tis a fair sight, and I thank God 'tis a glen."

Farquard tried to interest Cecily in walking to the rim of the knoll and looking down on the river. An avenue barren of trees allowed them to see dark patches beside the water. They were the houses of Campbelltown. The village, at this distance, merged with its sister town of Cross Creek. For the new land, it was a healthy community.

Cecily observed all Farquard pointed out to her and commented politely but listlessly. At the moment Campbelltown seemed to her a place of exile, where no friends would comfort her. Flora would go beyond, to the north probably, as soon as Allan could buy a plantation. Moira would not be far, but she'd be with relatives and, anyway, she was too young and simple yet to be a very satisfying companion. Nielson, whose friendship would have helped her sustain much loneliness, was left behind. And James—James was away, perhaps never to return to her.

"You'll like your new home, Cecily," Farquard

promised. " 'Tis one of the best appointed in the settlement."

With a smile Cecily said, "I'd like to get to it as soon as possible. Could we go on now?"

She herself called Dougald and Moira from their short excursion into the woods. Moira scowled and on the way to the coach spoke up pertly. "The rest of us, Miss Weston, are not so eager to see the journey end. 'Tis not kind of you to cut short the little time left."

In contrition Cecily stopped. "Forgive me. I am being selfish. I've not the good reason you two have for wanting the trip prolonged." She smiled gently and motioned toward the wood. "Go enjoy your walk. I'll wait with Flora in the carriage."

The moment had been spoiled, though, and Dougald and Moira chose instead to run up to fetch David, who still gazed in awe at the reaches of the land he had come to. Allan called after them, hastening them on. He was as eager as Cecily to be done travelling. For him it would be a beginning, not an ending.

For the most part of the remaining journey into Campbelltown Flora, Cecily and Moira spoke of the past six weeks. Quickly the friendship among them had grown; now more quickly, in a day's time, it was to be broken off. "No," cried Flora once, after she had spoken of their separation, "not broken off. Like all things that ripen, it must rest in the winter. But come spring, we'll see one another again, and be better friends than ever. Think of all we'll have to tell!" She leaned forward to touch Cecily and Moira pleadingly. "You will both come to visit me in my new home? I love fixing up a house, and 'twill be more of a joy than usual if I can look forward to entertaining you two in it."

Moira's eyes had sparkled at the prospect. Softly she promised, "Aye, I surely will come."

With a tender smile Flora said, "You dare not fail. Dougald would perish." She paused in thought for a moment and then said, "About April, I should think. Yes, that's the time. The roads will be passable and you can come to see Anne's baby. In March, you know, it's to be born."

Thoughts of Anne, who was never wholly out of Flora's mind these days, engrossed her. She fell silent, as did the others, who had cares and hopes of their own to ponder on. She hoped fervently that in Campbelltown she'd have word that Anne had made her river journey safely and was now comfortable at Glendale, her new home. Only when a faint note cut the air did Flora rouse herself. "Hist! A pipe note, I'm sure." Colour flooded to her cheeks, and her eyes, tired shortly before, took on lustre. She reached for Moira's hand and together they leaned out the window. "Doesn't it sound beautiful, lass?" she cried in a low voice.

Cecily was hanging out the other window, but she was calling Farquard instead of listening to the *piobrach*. "Hush, lass!" Flora said. "We don't want to miss a note. Ah, but I forgot. You haven't the skirl of the bagpipes in your blood. You don't know how they make the heart beat faster and the blood run swifter."

"You hush, Mrs. MacDonald," Moira cried, but in a way that was not impertinent. "You'll miss the marching song of the Clanranald. And 'tis Dougald himself playing it."

"Nay! How could it be?"

Proudly Moira explained: "He rode on ahead. We planned it all when we stopped back at the knoll."

"The lass is right," Farquard said. He had ridden back in response to Cecily's call and now spoke to Flora through the window. "Allan's gone ahead too. Couldn't wait. And, of course, David wasn't to be left behind. They all wanted to be part of the crowd that welcomes you to your new home, bonnie Flora."

There was no time to say more. A throng of people, carrying banners, were marching up the road in time to Dougald's pipe. Allan was striding along before them, his progress impeded by the many Scots who pushed to the front to speak to him, to shake his hand or just to walk next to him for a second.

For Flora the greatest joy was seeing, toward the

edge of the crowd, Hugh MacDonald, her stepfather. He was as hale as ever, though his black hair had turned white. Despite his age he walked as briskly as the others. When the coach stopped, he was the first to run to the door. Clasping Flora in his arms, he swung her down and time and again repeated, "Wee Flora, my bonnie Flora! Here at last!"

Flora kissed him; tears were streaming down her face. "Oh, Hugh! The sight of your dear face makes up for all that's left behind," she cried happily. "Have you talked with Allan? Have you met the twins? Alex, Jamie—did they arrive safely? I can't see them." The questions tumbled over one another.

"I can't answer all that at once, lass," Hugh answered. "Give me time. Now the lads—they're here in the press of people somewhere. Fine lads they are. You can be proud. As for Allan, no, I haven't had a chance to speak to him. Twins? I don't——"

Flora laughed and cried at the same time. "Hugh, you're the same as ever. One thing at a time. How good it is to hear you going through items so methodically! I have missed you sorely." She kissed him again, then drew away. "But come, I want you to see Allan. So strong and happy he is now. The nervousness I wrote you about just disappeared after we decided to emigrate. Come, let me take you over."

Just then Campbell, having turned his horse over to the groom and helped Cecily and Moira down from the carriage, stepped over. Raising one hand high above his head, he took command. The babble of voices stopped abruptly, and Dougald ended the march with a grand flourish. The people pressed around, some smiling, some crying, in the joy of having Allan and Flora MacDonald among them.

In a loud voice Campbell called over the heads of the people to his groom: "Tether that horse, and come round to hold the reins." Then he reached over to pull Allan by the sleeve. "Help your wife to the box, where all the people can see her. Get up and stand beside her." He looked about. "The lads—get the lads, folks, and send them up here."

The menfolk boosted Allan to the step. He reached

down and drew Flora up beside him. Alex and Jamie were pushed forward and made to stand at either side. Moira did not join them; she had gone to embrace her aunt and uncle and then stand between them. They had come to receive her into their family. Cecily, too, hung back; this celebration was for only those of MacDonald name. Farquard, who was to present Flora and Allan to their new friends, refrained from climbing up on a rock so that he could be seen. He did not need to put himself in a place of special prominence; his voice alone drew everyone's attention.

As soon as the MacDonald party had assembled in front of the coach Farquard cried in a ringing voice:

"Good folk of Cumberland and neighbouring counties, you have come from the hills and the glens, as you might have done in our own Scotland. You have come to pay your respects to our valiant countrywoman and her brave husband. Some of you are MacDonalds, close to the welcome new-comers in clanship. Many are not clansmen, but you are close too—in friendship. I see MacNeils and MacKeithans, MacLeods and Morrisons, Bethunes and MacGregors, all here in the vanguard. What other clans are represented I cannot tell. You'll let us know in a moment when the clan battle cries go up.

"'Tis proud I am to present Allan and Flora MacDonald to you, and proud I am that by gathering here today you have demonstrated the clan spirit that lives on, thrives in the glens of the New World. Now, out with your claymores and up with your voices!"

As the shout went up, Campbell stepped back beside Cecily. Allan and Flora were left alone to receive the homage of the North Carolina Scots. Flora closed her eyes against the sight of the devoted faces, a sight too moving to bear without tears. Allan lifted his head proudly, looked full on the people and then at the land around them. When the cheer died, he spoke. "For Flora and myself and our children, I thank you. Already you have made us see that we have not lost our home and our people. We have found them."

A second shout rose to the highest tips of the tall pines. Flora opened her eyes and stretched forth her arms in greeting.

Farquard Campbell whispered to Allan during the cheering. Allan took Flora's arm, turned her, and helped her into the coach. Cecily was ushered up and handed in. Mounts were brought for Allan, Farquard and each of the lads but Dougald, who moved to the side of the carriage. He would march and pipe. The people churned about, to clear the road and to fall in behind and beside the carriage.

Moira ducked around the folk in front of her and ran up to the carriage. Clinging for a moment to the window ledge, she called, "Thank you, Flora MacDonald. Thank you for caring for me. God bless you." Then she let go and walked a few paces beside Dougald. A moment later she lifted her hand in farewell to him and dropped back into the crowd to find her aunt, and to stay with her.

Slowly the procession moved forward to the rhythm of Dougald's pipes, punctuated by rousing shouts from each clan. Allan and Farquard led, the coach and piper came second, the lads third. In such order they would go through the streets of Campbelltown, where Cecily would part from them. Then they would pass through Cross Creek and come at last to a plantation up-river, where Allan and Flora would stay until they had a home of their own.

BOOK THREE
The Valley of the Highlanders

22

The Silversmith

STEPHEN MORAY, bending over the high drawing-table in his work-room, reached for his already damp handkerchief without taking his eyes from the paper before him. He blotted the perspiration on his forehead and mopped his neck. There was a frown on his face at the pattern his pencil had brought out on the sketching-paper. That bunch of grapes along with a sheaf of grain was too much. He must get the effect of elegance without profusion.

His hand felt for his knife, but couldn't find it. Stephen finally looked up, casting his eyes here and there for it. Ah, on the bench. With two long strides he was across the narrow room and had his knife in his hand. As he turned he glanced out the window. Cross Creek was quiet, no doubt because of the hot late-May sun. Anyone who could remained indoors, and even there, in the quiet dark of the closed houses, the air grew oppressive. Stephen smiled to see a young stable-boy who had pressed himself flatly against the tavern to take a nap. The shadow which protected him had shrunk as the sun steadily rose toward its zenith until the narrow margin of an inch protected him. It wouldn't be long before that young lad hopped up from his stolen sleep.

Stephen jarred himself out of his dreaming and went back to the table. Immediately he began to scrape the cluster of grapes from his design. It didn't help much; the pattern had a basic clumsiness he didn't like. He pulled out another sheet of paper and started over with a freshly sharpened pencil. He began to whistle tunelessly in satisfaction as a delicate lyre design with a smoothly widening handle and a squared end emerged. It was elegant and chaste; he stood a good chance of getting a commission for a set of flatware in this pattern. And an order would come in handy at the moment.

Again his handkerchief was wiped across his forehead. It was really difficult to work on a steaming day like this, but for Stephen there was no choice. These days there was little time for attending to one's livelihood, not with Committee of Safety work and drilling in the afternoon. Today was the first uninterrupted four hours he'd had to give to his craft in a week. The worst thing was that few of the people who walked in on him came to commission silver; people weren't thinking much about knives and forks and spoons these days. He shrugged the thought away. He wasn't the only man whose career and personal life had been chopped up by the growing antagonism between the patriots and the loyalists. Some had suffered much more than he.

Suddenly he held his pencil poised and listened. He'd caught the easy rhythm of a horse cantering down the narrow road out of town. It stopped at the shop. Stephen threw down his pencil and hurried to the main room. A big man was already striding through the door. Stephen had no trouble recognizing him. It was James Coor, the New Bern builder who had persuaded him to go through the Governor's desk back in the fall.

Coor was damp with sweat, and he was mopping his red face with a big handkerchief as he entered. As soon as he had shaken hands he stripped off his coat. "Hot on the road," he grunted.

"Better have a wash and something to wet your whistle before we talk," Stephen said. He brought out a basin and a bucket of water, found a piece of soap and a towel. Coor filled the basin at once and began washing his face and neck. His shirt, Stephen noticed, was dark with sweat down the back.

"Want rum?" Stephen asked. "Or buttermilk? I've got some cold in the springhouse. Maybe you'd rather have that?"

Coor spluttered as he washed soap off his face. He

straightened up and began to towel himself vigorously. "Make it buttermilk. Too hot for rum."

When Stephen came back with the crock he found Coor, already at ease, sprawled on a bench with his back against the wall. As Stephen poured a generous glass, Coor said, "Cross Creek gave me a surprise this morning. It's grown. I haven't been here for three or four years and in that time it's become almost a city. There must be a hundred houses."

"At least a hundred," Stephen agreed. "We've outstripped Cambelltown by a good margin. The waggons coming in from the west come to Cross Creek and our merchants get their trade. Then the last four or five years brought hundreds of Highlanders. Most of them couldn't find suitable places at Campbelltown and settled around Cross Creek."

"I never realized the town had grown so," Coor repeated. "You get word of these changes but they don't mean anything until you see them. You're on the Committee of Safety here. Must be quite a job, isn't it?"

Stephen grinned half-heartedly. "Just before you came I was congratulating myself I was getting a whole morning with no politics. First time in weeks."

Coor's broad smile answered him. "And I spoiled your morning? I had to come up this way on business. I thought I'd like to see how things are here for myself while I was in the neighbourhood. Wanted to see you, too. Felt we asked a lot of you last fall, especially as you weren't really one of us then. You could have pulled it off if it hadn't been for that high and mighty niece of Campbell's. She's over at Campbelltown now, isn't she?" Seeing Stephen's curt nod, Coor asked, "Is she still giving you trouble?"

Stephen was suddenly annoyed at Coor's conviviality. His relations with Cecily Weston were his own affair, and he'd thank Coor not to pry into them. He was tempted to say just that, but he pressed his lips together and merely frowned.

Oblivious of Stephen's impatience, Coor dropped his feet to the ground and sat forward. "Tell me," he said, "how the news of Lexington and Concord was received here."

"Like all the other news lately, in several different ways, depending on the people," Stephen replied vaguely. Then, feeling that he was letting personal worry warp his attitude to Coor, he went into detail. "Most of the merchants are patriots. There are maybe thirty-five or forty of us of this persuasion. To us the farmers up there in Massachusetts were striking a blow for our rights and freedom, and a shrewd blow, too."

"Shrewd, aye. But that's a weak word for it. The first time we colonials have taken on British regulars, we bested them. By God, it was a glorious blow!" Coor shook his fist vehemently.

Stephen nodded in agreement. "The correction stands. But let me go on. With the Highlanders here in town it was different. Many were shocked. I think some of them are expecting a great doom to fall on Massachusetts as a result. Campbell is the leader of a great part of them. He wants no war and was sorry to see it come to fighting up there. He is dinning it into the old Highlanders' ears that this whole matter isn't their fight and the best they can do is sit quiet." Stephen scratched his head meditatively. "I suppose, since we can't count on their help, he does us a service when he tells them to take no part."

Coor took out a pipe and put it in his mouth empty. He clamped his teeth down on it and thought for a minute. Finally, removing the pipe from his mouth and fishing for his tobacco, he said, "Mayhap you're right. They'd make good fighters, there's no denying that. It's better to have them out of the quarrel than on the wrong side. If you have to, promote Campbell's view among them yourself."

"If need be, I will. But don't forget to consider Martin," Stephen went on. "We have no proof, but we suspect he's corresponding with other Scot leaders—to induce them to raise troops in the loyalist cause. Most of them are eager for peace. Martin knows that, and will argue that the best way to maintain peace is to overawe the patriots with a show of force."

Coor rose to his feet. "I suppose you are making every effort to intercept letters from the Governor." He nodded his head in satisfaction at Stephen's "Of course" and then, impatiently pacing back and forth, talked on excitedly. "You're right about Martin's argument. Fact is, he'll argue anything, anything at all that might win him supporters. He's a frightened man. Back in February he thought it would make him popular to have North Carolina exempted from Parliament's bill forbidding trade with the colonies. Through Tryon, in London then, he achieved it. I'll tell you, he won no popularity. People took it as a trick to divide us from the other colonies.

"Then he called the Assembly to meet in early April and the Convention summoned by Colonel Harvey met a day earlier, paying no attention to his proclamation forbidding it. Same as last year it was, only worse. The Assembly flouted Martin by joining in with it. Ever since, the Convention and the Committees of Safety have been doing just about all the governing that's being done."

Stephen resigned himself to a lecture. He slumped down comfortably in his chair and made no effort to cut off Coor's report. Telling this ardent patriot that these things were already known in Cross Creek, that Stephen himself had brought back word of some of them, would do no good. The man just had to rehearse everything he knew. Now he was off on the militia companies that had been formed, as if Cross Creek and Campbelltown and nearly every other town in the province didn't have its regular drill.

"Abner Nash has several hundred men drilling down on the parade-ground. The sight makes Martin uneasy, you can be sure."

With a disgruntled shift of his shoulders, Stephen tried to work a crick out of his neck. The sight makes me uneasy too, he thought. I don't like seeing any men drilling—on our side or the other. He envisioned the morbid mock drama he often took part in: patriots and loyalists presenting arms and practicing loading and dropping down to sight at each other across the village green. No man could see that without a chill. There'd come a day when it wouldn't be a pageant any longer. It hadn't ever been up at Lexington.

Coor wasn't saying anything, and Stephen hopefully looked up. His relief faded when he saw that Coor was merely guzzling another glass of buttermilk, no doubt to grease up his throat for more talk.

The glass banged on the stand and Coor resumed his pacing and his speech.

"I keep telling people we have to face up to the facts," he said. "The Congress in Philadelphia is still petitioning the King. So are most of the colonies individually. We all hope to get concessions. Dartmouth in the Ministry would like to see compromise; so would some of the other big men in England. So would a lot of our leaders. But we're at cross purposes with the Ministry on a couple of fundamental principles. And there's pride. Parliament, having talked so high, doesn't like to stomach talking any lower. But we can force them to. Our nonimportation agreements may do much to starve English merchants and manufacturers. They should put some pressure on Parliament. But not enough, I dare say."

Of course it won't be enough, Stephen thought. We haven't the means to fight a war indirectly—with trade and diplomatic pressures. England has the means, though. And if we delay too long, she'll have us in a strangle-hold. May have us there already. It'll be the sheer strength of our arms and the stiffness of our necks that save us. God, it's a sickening realization! Yet we've got to face it. Why don't more of the men around here come to it? Have we got to deal with chicken-livered men who talk big and fight little?

Even before he finished the angry thought Stephen knew he was wrong. There was a difference between judgement and cowardice. Most of the men he knew were wary, their fingers tense on the trigger. But they were holding themselves back, knowing that once the finger tightened there could be but one issue. The time for thinking was drawing short; they were using it to the full. They were vacillating about the principles involved—weighing them, testing them, revising them. Once they got the issues down into words of their own, they'd stick by them, never cry off. No, the danger wasn't in fear, but it might be in failing to see when the subtle moment for switching from thought to action had come.

"In Massachusetts the patriots found they had to fight," Coor was saying. "Face up to it: down here we'll have to fight too—with all the men we can arm."

Stephen rose to his feet and hitched up his breeks. "I know. But first we have one thing to do: get more men committed. How long have we got?"

Coor pursed his lips. "Six months to a—— What's the matter?"

Stephen had grabbed his arm and was listening intently. In his concentration he ignored Coor. After a moment, with a slow nod as if he were satisfied about something, he said, "You stay here. A horse stopped up the lane. Somebody's coming to the shop."

"Who?"

Stephen looked out the window and answered, "Alex MacLeod. Wonder what he wants."

"Shall we speak to him? Might be a good idea."

Stephen considered for a moment. "It might. I'll feel him out."

It was hard to steer Alex away from silver patterns, and Stephen, needing the order, put off probing questions for a while. Alex was bound to order exactly what Anne wanted and, in an effort to explain her wishes, clumsily gestured with his big fingers and spoke self-consciously of shafts, bevels and patinas. Finally, unable to be more articulate, he dropped his hands to his sides and said, "Oh, you know what I mean!"

"No," Stephen answered with an amused grin, "I don't. Try starting over."

Alex scowled and shook his head decisively. "Never! Give me some sketches and I'll show them to Anne. That way she can say just what she wants." Suddenly Alex smiled broadly and added, "It's im-

portant, you know, that she should be pleased. The
flatware is my gift to her to celebrate the bairn's birth.
Did you know I had a fine son? Born end of February."

"God bless the babe and the mother!" Stephen offered hearty congratulations and extended his hand.
"Will you allow me to make a cup for the babe? I realize I don't know your wife, but she's Flora MacDonald's daughter and I'd be proud to do something for
her."

While he was speaking Stephen had gone to his
drawing-table. He lifted the flat top and rummaged in
the papers underneath. "I take it Mrs. MacLeod
would prefer something ornate for her service." He
laughed easily. "Of course, I couldn't be sure from
your description."

"Aye, she likes rich, heavy things."

With a sheaf of papers, on the top of which was
the lyre design worked out that morning, Stephen went
back to Alex. "I'd recommend this first one or else
this fiddlestick pattern—" he sorted the drawings hurriedly—"this one. They're massive enough to carry
additional ornamentation, but yet they're graceful.
Tell her to indicate whether she wants a floral, fruit
or whatever motif. I'm sorry I don't have many that
are already heavily embellished. I can do it for her
right enough, but it's not my natural style."

Grateful that the burden of selection had been removed from his shoulders, Alex said thanks. He carefully rolled the patterns into a scroll. "I'd like to tell
you," he added as he turned, "that your work's been
highly recommended to us. We knew, of course,
about the contest you won. Then too, Farquard
Campbell gets up now and again. He told us about the
tea-service you made for him. He's mightily pleased."

The compliment was gratifying, but Stephen paid it
little heed. He was busy thinking how to switch the
conversation, now that he had an opportunity. It
shouldn't be hard; there was never an unbridgeable
jump between Farquard's name and politics. Finally
he said casually, "I didn't know Farquard got up-
country much. Seems to me he's always rushing about

our two villages with orders—the merchant's kind or the politician's kind. The man's got a finger in every pie. You've got to admire his energy."

MacLeod laughed. "Admire, yes, but not be engulfed by it. I like Farquard much, but wouldn't give a pence for his advice—except on business. There you can be sure I follow it."

"What then . . . ?" Stephen asked.

"Oh, this tomfoolery of his about dancing along the convolutions of the middle line. Farquard's obsessed by this idea of moderation. He thinks that he alone, by holding the hands of the patriots and the loyalists, can keep the two factions in amicable contact. Bosh! He'll just get himself pulled apart in the end."

Stephen, encouraged by these words, considered asking Alex to have a seat in the other room and stay for a bite of lunch. It could very well be a good thing to let Coor, who could be very eloquent at times, talk to him. Then, realizing that MacLeod was still speaking, he cursed himself for losing the thread of the conversation.

" . . . maybe it's my old Marine training," MacLeod was saying, "but I believe in getting in the thick of the battle or staying out entirely. No point in half-way measures, less point in cajoling and hand-holding."

"You sound," Stephen interposed, "as though you're giving advice. But to which side?"

Alex clapped on his hat and looked him straight in the eye. "I'm not talking about sides. I'm talking about a man's way of settling his quarrels. You look as though you'd probably feel about as I do. But I've got one edge on you: my business was war. For years I defended England professionally. Now I'm retired. Any quarrel I get into will be one I've a personal stake in. Then I'll fight just the way I told you: with the most effective weapon I can find to get rid of my enemy."

"Mr. MacLeod," Stephen said, making a quick decision, "has it occurred to you that you've already got a stake in the quarrel here? Why don't you stay and——"

Alex spoke up quickly and firmly. "I'm not ignorant of your position, Mr. Moray. Don't try to make
me commit myself. It won't work. Many thanks for
the patterns. I'll return them, with the order, as soon
as I can."

He left Stephen lost in a mixture of confidence and
discouragement.

An hour later Coor and Stephen were sitting on
opposite sides of a small table in the kitchen, each
with a mug of rum at his elbow. Coor was packing
his pipe.

"Now," said Stephen, shoving his empty plate
aside, "leave my fellow-Scots for a moment. I've got
an idea on that, but first I want to say something else."

Coor leaned back and waited.

"Just before MacLeod came in," Stephen went on,
"you estimated we had about six months to make
ready. It's not long, and it's fortunate that drilling and
laying in gunpowder and arms have already started. I
think of something additional we ought to do right
away if we can."

Coor pushed back his chair and went to the fire-
place. While getting a pine splinter with which to light
his pipe, he said, "Good! Any idea is welcome. What
is it?"

"It's about the Regulators. Martin is counting on
their support," Stephen explained. "After their uprising they never received a full pardon. They hold their
lands only on good behaviour and fear he might ruin
them if they were to defy him. But from what I can
tell, they're not with him heartily, and right now they
wonder just how much he can realistically offer. If we
send men among them to encourage their doubt, they
might leave his party."

"It's a practical thought, Stephen. You're in their
country. Can you make a beginning at once?"

"Aye. The Committee of Safety meets tomorrow
evening. We'll devise a plan."

Coor wandered about the room with a worried
scowl on his face. "You told me to leave the Scots for
a moment. I can't get them off my mind. Winning

over the Regulators would deprive Martin of a major source of support. The only other group he counts heavily on, and with more than a little reason, is the Highland faction. We've got to hold the Scots away from him. But MacLeod discouraged me. If he's typical, Campbell won't do us the service we hoped for. It looks to me as though some recruiting to counter Martin's efforts is in order."

"I told you," Stephen said, setting down his rum glass, "that I had an idea about the Scots. As you know, I'm a Scot myself and have some notion of how they think. They're still clansmen, Coor. No matter how independent they seem to have grown—like MacLeod—they'll follow their leader. Oh, not all. You can't hope for that. But a large per cent will. The thing for us to do is talk to the clan chieftains. Martin and Campbell have been doing it for some time. It's time we caught up."

"I don't know, Stephen," Coor said slowly. "A lot of the Highlanders I've met are making up their own minds. Look at you! And at James Moore—a general in the Continental Army. In addition there's a lot of faction among the Scots."

Stephen nodded as if he were in accord. "There is faction. But two things you fail to see. The line that divides the Scots is really time. I mean the Scots who've been here awhile see things differently from the new ones. Those groups will probably have to be appealed to on different grounds. In fact it's already working out that way. Martin relies most fully on the new ones. Campbell talks mostly to the old ones. There's something deeper, however, than their feeling about North Carolina, their sense of belonging here. The clan feeling's deeper." He rose to lean across the table and said earnestly, "I know. I've felt it in myself. Listen, Coor: when I first saw Flora MacDonald I all but swore fealty to her. There's many another that feels the same way. When Allan and Flora MacDonald came here the Highlanders instinctively gave them the devotion and service that Scots give to their chiefs. Those two together can close the gap that divides Scot from Scot. Together they might decide which way a significant number of the North Carolina Highlanders will go."

Coor stared at Stephen a moment as if he were seeing him in a new way. Finally he said, "I can't dispute your sincerity nor ignore your insight into your own people. I do tend to think your hopes of carrying all by carrying the MacDonalds are sanguine. Yet, your suggestion is excellent. It's the leaders we must work on. Tell me more about them."

Stephen shrugged. "I've told you much of it already. Allan MacDonald is the biggest man among the new Scots here, and next to him would be MacLeod, I suppose. Both of them are former officers, and it's likely they've a habitual loyalty to England. I've no proof, but I'd wager Martin is in contact with them. I also don't know, if he is, what threats or promises he's making. . . . Of course, I could be entirely wrong. He just might have others in mind above them, feeling that they, though very useful, couldn't assume full military charge."

"What's the best way to find these things out?"

Stephen considered his answer. While he was thinking he fetched the jug and poured fresh drinks. "Well," he said, sitting down again, "the first thing to do is to get out some keen agents. Let them concentrate on the Scots, find out if messengers are going back and forth and things like that. We'll know what to do next when we have that information."

Coor nodded and waited to hear more.

"The second thing to do is to send someone up to the big clan gathering at Mount Helicon. It's scheduled for the last week-end of the month. We could learn a lot there. The people will themselves show us the men they consider their leaders. Beyond that, they'll speak freely, ask questions."

"By God, Stephen," Coor cried, banging his fist on the table, "you'll go yourself! Why, you haven't mentioned the best thing about that gathering. A Scot among them could say some meaningful things, do much to show them our side. You're the man for it."

Stephen shook his head. "There are other men with much more experience than I—and less well known

as patriots. Those people aren't going to welcome anyone who comes purposefully to involve them in civil
war."

Coor waved his hand impatiently. "You told me
yourself you've a strong attachment to your heritage.
They'll know that. Besides, you know Farquard
Campbell well. He's accepted among them. Ride up
with him. Make yourself one of his party. . . . Oh, I
forgot. That niece of his, tutored by Admiral Weston—she could cause you trouble."

"No," Stephen said slowly. "No ... I don't think
she would."

With a pleased and teasing laugh Coor asked,
"You mean you've brought her around to our opinion? By Gad, you're the man for this job! If you
could win over that stubborn missy, you can win over
anyone."

Stephen got up with a violent scrape of his chair.
"I've not brought Cecily Weston round to anything.
But I have got to know her, and respect her."

"Fine, lad!" Coor said, slapping Stephen on the
shoulder. "And if she returns your respect, you'll be
able to keep her from interfering."

Stephen's jaw was firmly set and his voice was
cold. "I'll not trade on any friendship, not even one
with someone I have to consider in some ways my enemy. I don't think I'm the man for the job."

It was evident even to Coor that Stephen was
deadly serious. "Excuse the flippancy, Stephen," he
said at once. "But do take a little advice: Don't fool
yourself into thinking too close a friendship with a
woman of the other side wouldn't be a problem to
you—that woman especially. Three men were appre-
hended down in the country south of us a couple
months ago. Martin had them taken to New Bern to
wait around till he was pleased to see them. When
they finally got into his office he brandished a list in
front of them and warned them that England was on
to them. Made all kinds of threats. I'm willing to
wager it was the same list Miss Weston so assiduously
preserved."

Stephen scowled at the floor; he'd been dreading

such news. The memory of his failure still burned, and any reminder that Cecily Weston was one of the enemy burned more. Yet he had to ask the question: "Were reprisals made on these men? I hope to God no one suffered from it."

Coor shrugged. "All of them suffered loss of time and money. Their wives suffered weeks of terror. I dare say, if Martin weren't such a lax administrator we'd have had a lot worse results from that packet. He being the kind of man he is, we've been lucky. Thing I never could fathom was whether he knew you'd tried to take it."

Slowly Stephen said, "I doubt that he did. Miss Weston would never have told. She fights her battles directly."

After giving Stephen a speculative look, Coor said his farewells. "I'll be on my way. You'll go to Helicon, I know you will. Because you know we count on you."

After an early supper the next evening Stephen went to his barn and saddled Black Bess. It would have taken him only twenty minutes to walk to Farquard Campbell's place in Campbelltown, but he had decided to ride over. He had two or three reasons ready, in case he was asked, for he would never have confessed to the real one, which was that he would present a more gentlemanly appearance arriving on horseback.

In point of fact, Bess needed exercise. She had not been out on the road for almost a week and was full of spirit. She was skittish as he saddled her. When he mounted, she pranced and caracoled. Only a firm hand kept her from bolting in a wild run. Once on the road, he let her take a hard gallop for a half mile before he pulled her down to a decorous trot. The result was that she was somewhat lathered and warm when she arrived, and Stephen's nagging sense of responsibility made him give Farquard Campbell's horse-boy careful instructions for caring for her before he would let the lad lead her away to the stable. Stephen entered the house with the uneasy conviction that his manner lacked something of the negligent ease of the gentleman.

In the house he asked for Farquard Campbell and was ushered into the counting-room. Campbell was sitting at his desk, studying a ledger, with a mug of rum at his elbow.

Stephen accepted a mug of rum and inquired about the health of Campbell's family. Farquard reported that both his wife and his niece were in excellent spirits. "Miss Weston attracts much company to my house," he said. "Mostly young sparks not long from England," he added with a wry smile. "Courtly fellows and all friends of the Governor. Sometimes I think the minx is seeking to improve my manners—or my politics."

Stephen knew with despair what Farquard was talking about. Cecily filled Campbell's house with affected and elegantly dressed loyalists, and seemed at times to prize those befrilled swains as highly as she did her uncle or himself. Often enough he had raged home after leaving this house. There was no vanity in him, but he knew himself to be a stronger man than those others, and he knew Farquard to be a more gracious one. And, leaving himself out of it, he didn't see how a woman of Cecily's mettle could endure such company. But she seemed actually to court it.

He could not bring himself to speak openly any criticism of Cecily, so he found a weary defense for her, one he'd often consoled himself with. "Miss Weston formed her tastes in the home of Admiral Weston, where she grew up, and here she gathers about her gentlemen most like those she knew there. You and I, however," he said, recalling himself to his purpose, "might doubt that any of them would make you wiser in politics. I would expect the opposite effect."

Campbell laughed tolerantly and rose to stroll about the room with his hands tucked under his coat-tail, behind his back. "At any rate, Cecily is determined to make me over. She lessons me like a schoolboy when she finds out that I have talked to Harnett or Howe or heard from Caswell or Hooper or any of the other Whig leaders. She lets me know such associations will ruin me with the Governor and the King. She's right, of course, that Josiah Martin has a hearty dislike for some of the company I keep." Farquard paused beside Stephen and looked down at him. With a laugh he said, "You, for one. I might as well warn you." He moved on. "Of course, the thing is that both Martin and Cecily think any resistance to the Ministry pure folly. I must beg leave to disagree with them and choose my friends for myself, in spite of her."

Stephen lowered his head in his mug as he took a swallow of rum. When he looked up he got right to the purpose of his visit. "Are you taking your family to the clan gathering on Mount Helicon? That's what I came over to ask you about."

Farquard sat down in his chair, leaned back and crossed his legs. "I'll tell you, lad," he said. "My wife's health is not of the best just now. I've decided it would be unwise for her to go up in the hills and sleep in that cool air. She'll not go. But I'll go. Much of my year's profit comes from being the merchant for the Scots. I must keep close to them. I'd not miss a meeting of this size. It's like money in my pocket."

"I rather thought you'd be going," Stephen broke in.

"There's another reason, too," Farquard said. "For a long time I could speak for the Scots of Campbelltown and for most of those at Cross Creek. I'm not telling you any secret. You will know this is the reason I have political influence. But I've never felt I could sound out and speak for the Scots on the outlying farms. It never mattered much before, but now, with the fuse burning on the powder keg, it does matter. Those landowners are hardy men, easily enticed into swinging the claymore. Many are new to the country and don't know the issues. They could be led into battle easily. I'd like to prevent that, as you know. Now Allan MacDonald, who's among them, is a natural leader. If I can get him to see this thing my way, those Scots will stay neutral. The trouble is that I suspect Martin will try to make him his gull. MacDonald has had no chance to discover the lay of the land here. In fact, he's tried to steer clear of that.

Just wants to mind his own business. And that would be fine—except that no man can stay out of a thing like this for long. The trick is to find the way between the dangerous extremes."

Stephen digested Campbell's revelations in silence. He knew from experience that no argument would convince Farquard that open revolt might be the better way. Finally he said, "If you go up without your wife, I suppose you'll ride."

"No, my niece wants to see the Scots she came over with, especially Flora MacDonald, and she's determined to come with me. With a woman coming along, we'll need a mort of baggage. I'll take a carriage for her and the baggage. Whether I'll ride in it, too, or ride a horse, I've not decided."

"I've made up my mind to go myself," said Stephen. "I came over to ask if I might ride up with you. Would my company be acceptable?"

"You'll be as welcome as profit. A merchant couldn't say more."

"Then I'll go with you," Stephen said. "When do you plan to leave?"

"It's less than a day's journey. Can you be here about eight next Friday morning?"

"Aye, and thank you." Stephen rose and picked up his hat. "It's growing late and I won't detain you longer tonight. Don't get up. I can find my own way out." He came over to Farquard Campbell, shook hands with him and took his leave.

The counting-room had grown dim, but in the hall outside the western light was still flooding strongly through the window. As Stephen came out into it he could scarcely see. Blinking and squinting, he did not notice Cecily Weston, sitting with someone on the window-seat, until she spoke: "You'll pass without a greeting, Mr. Moray?"

In confusion he turned. He could see nothing clearly, only two dark forms moving toward him against the intense light from the window. Nonetheless, he extended his hand and said, "Forgive me, Miss Weston. The sun was blinding." He bowed to kiss her hand.

A mocking tone met his greeting. "Oh, Mr. Moray," said a higher voice than Cecily's, "you've got the wrong one entirely."

Stephen blushed as his vision cleared and he found himself holding the other girl's hand. She was that slender, auburn-haired girl living in town now. Her mischievous smile made him suspect she'd deliberately managed that it was her hand instead of Cecily's. Well, he'd not be discomposed by the jest. Greatly exaggerating his bow, he said gallantly, "Not the woman I expected, true. But by no means a wrong one. It's a pleasure to see you again, Miss ... Miss ..."

The effort to recall her name was utterly useless. All three burst into laughter. Cecily controlled herself sufficiently to come to his rescue. "It's Moira Mac-Queen, Mr. Moray. And she has changed, hasn't she? I was telling her this afternoon how different she looks from the exiled lass I met on Skye. She's really blossomed in America."

Moira took the compliments without any coy disavowals. "How could I help it? I'm happy here. I miss my parents, but I wouldn't want to go to them on Skye. I would want them to come here."

"America is a wonderful country, isn't it, Miss MacQueen?" Stephen said. He liked her directness and found himself relaxed, despite his faux pas.

"Yes, really wonderful," she echoed. "I rode out this other afternoon. Ah, the green hills—I find I love them! And once I thought nothing could take the place of the barren crags of Skye." She smiled confidingly. "You know, my Dougald promised me once that this is the way it would be. Only he said we'd find our happiness here together. We've been together only once the whole winter, he's so busy up-country."

"Now, Moira, don't go back to that," Cecily said gently, picking up a reference Stephen hadn't understood. "You'll see Dougald at Mount Helicon. Talk to him about your fears and hopes."

Cecily kissed Moira's cheek fondly and let her out the front door. As she turned back to Stephen she said, with a rueful shake of her head, "The child comes to me for advice. And who am I to give it?"

"The best person," he answered, taking her arm as they walked into the parlour. As usual he was forgetting his anxieties in Cecily's presence. Once she knew a person, she had a gift for conversation and for putting a guest at his ease. Of course, part of the relaxation he felt with her came from the ban they had tacitly placed on political talk. They'd found that the mention of faction and dissension ate up their friendship like acid, leaving nothing between them but distance and the memory of their early quarrels and continuing cross-purposes. After each such episode they had come to harmony again, but slowly, ever more tentatively. As his regard for her had grown he'd learned to dread these quarrels, for he was loathe to destroy amiability that meant much to him. Now, remembering the way their friendship had grown, he postponed something he had to say to her .

When they had settled themselves in the handsome Hepplewhite chairs before the fire-place he said, "You gave me good advice about those books. I enjoyed them, especially Doctor Johnson's *Rasselas*. I should have read that a long time ago. That new one—*Clinker* . . . *Humphry Clinker*—was pleasant, though nothing to compare with the story of the Abyssinian prince." He leaned forward. "Without you as mentor, I'd never catch up on the modern works."

"I'm glad to have you use my small store of books," Cecily replied. She pulled a small table toward her and lifted a cover. "Just as I thought. There are some tea-cakes left. Will you have one?" She passed the plate to Stephen and said as she did so, "I'm glad too that I have enough influence with you to keep you at your reading. Really, since you enjoy it so, you shouldn't have let the habit slip away from you."

He started to speak but she prevented him. "Now don't plead these years of apprenticeship and career-starting. I know all about them and have learned to apreciate your 'honest toil.' But I insist that a gentleman ought never let his interest in literature and such things wane. Why, Stephen, that sort of thing is the very mark of breeding! More than that, it's interesting, as you well know. That's one thing I like about Mr. MacLeod. He brought more than three hundred volumes with him, and finds time to read and discuss them."

Patiently Stephen suffered the lecture; he was satisfied that Cecily had imbibed enough of the free American air to classify him as a gentleman, despite his being in trade. Besides, she was right: it would be a sorry thing if in the hard work of settling this rich land men forgot about the richnesses of thought and art.

When he saw that Cecily had finished, he said, "Speaking of Mr. MacLeod, he was in the shop a day or so ago." He described Alex's groping through the technicalities of silversmithing and they laughed together. Man-fashion, he added the news of the baby's birth as an almost irrelevant detail.

"Stephen! Why didn't you tell me at once?" Cecily cried. "I'm so happy for Anne. I'll never forget how the poor thing looked on the voyage—pale and ill. Now she has a fine lad. Flora will be delighted." In her excitement Cecily got up to walk a step or two back and forth and then lean against the fire-place. "I can hardly wait to see her. No doubt she'll be at Helicon."

"Aye," Stephen said, rising, "I would imagine so. By the way," he added, trying to slip in casually an announcement he'd been reluctant to make, "I'll be riding up with you and your uncle. I just arranged it with Farquard."

At once Cecily's smile faded. "Are you going as a Scot or as a patriot?"

There was a pause before Stephen answered honestly, "I suppose you'd best say as both."

Nervously Cecily turned away and rubbed a finger along the smooth marble of the fire-place. "It's ironical! You yourself spoil for me the pleasure your company can give. Why don't you at least have the decency to go up there without an ulterior motive?"

"Please don't say that, Cecily. There's nothing ulterior about it. I simply can't divide myself and be less than I am."

He waited for her to make some comment, but she

said nothing. Finally he picked up his hat. "Well, I wanted you to know I was going along—not just appear and then suffer your obvious annoyance. Let's try to have a cordial trip."

He excused himself and left, hoping she would have got over her displeasure before the reunion.

23

Reunion

FLORA lifted the bairn, her first grandchild, and held him before her. She cocked her head to one side and crooned, "Bless you, laddie, little son of our new home. You're a joy to me. How'll I ever let you go back to Glendale, so many miles away?" She pressed him against her shoulder and swayed her body slightly to rock him. "Why, 'tis you, wee thing that you are, that makes all the travelling we've done, the starting over mean so much." She looked down at Anne, hemming a long dress for her child. "When I dandle the bairn, Anne, and think what a safe life you and Alex and Allan and I can make for him, here in North Carolina, I'm wholly reconciled to the loss of Skye. There he'd have had to grow up under a burden of trouble. But here he'll come into a good estate and freedom."

Anne snapped off the thread and twisted it about the needle as she answered with a gentle laugh, "I feel the same way, Mother, but it's no good talking so to Norman there. 'Little son of our new home!' He cares not for that—what he means, where he comes from, what he'll come to. He cares only for what he gets to eat."

"Nay, lass," Flora admonished, "don't talk so. A babe understands. Mayhap not the words, but the tone, the love. Look how he laughs." Flora spread her hand across the baby's chest and supported him so that Anne could see his smile. "He's a sturdy one, he is, for only three months," Flora went on. "I confess I worried when I heard you were coming here to Mount Pleasant before Helicon. Yet I wanted you too badly even to hint that it might be better if you didn't make the trip. I've yearned to see you, Anne. With Allan always in the fields, I'm lonely."

Anne stood up and gave her mother a quick hug, awkwardly, for she didn't want to disturb the child. "I know. We feel things much the same way. When Norman was born, I thought I'd never get on without you. You were always in my thoughts, as I know I was in yours. Can you guess what sustained me most? Remembering that night on the ship, that little cramped Jessie. You told me Alex wanted to be proud of his son, that you wanted to be proud of your grandson. I lay there sweating, and through clenched teeth I swore again and again I'd give you both your bairn."

The memory of pain and fear made Anne move away slightly with face averted. Then she looked up and said, "We feel the same about another thing, Mother—our husbands. I'm lonely without Alex. I'm going home with him Sunday, straight from Helicon."

Although Flora pressed the baby closer against her, as if she could never let him be taken from her, she nodded in agreement. "Aye, I do understand. I don't want you to go, but ... 'tis right you should." She sighed then. "'Tis a sad thing we're so far apart."

Anne had started for the kitchen to see whether Katie had clean diapers ready. Pausing, she said, "I'm afraid I'll never quite forgive Father for settling over here. Oh, it's a good farm, I know that. But Alex and I had to go west; his kin already had bought Glendale for us. Father could have bought land anywhere."

"Hush!" Flora cried, her finger to her lips. "I grieve, too, but I do not find fault or lay blame. You've seen your Alex—and him with more gillies than Allan——nearly kill himself to get the first year's crop in. You ought to know why we settled at the first good place we could find after the winter broke."

Knowing that further complaint would seriously displease her mother, Anne murmured, "I'm sorry for saying that," and went on out the door. Flora paid no attention, for she was feeling the bitterness that sometimes welled up in her when she thought of the distance between her and Anne and Hugh—distance that had kept her ignorant of her daughter's child-bearing, distance that had kept her, after her first brief reunion at Campbelltown, from once seeing her stepfather, a man she loved dearly.

Automatically Flora patted little Norman, whimpering now with sleepiness, and carefully eased herself into the rocking-chair beside the fire-place. She began to force away disappointment as she always did—by recalling how hard Allan had worked to make a home for her and their sons.

He had drawn severely on his great energy to accomplish a twofold task in this first spring. He'd found a home and got his crop in all at the same time. She'd been able to tell, from the way he protected and cherished her, that he too looked upon these months as a completely new beginning in their life together. In the firm, confident tones that reminded her of a younger Allan he'd said, "Now I'll find the house. I don't want you riding over these rough roads. I'll find a place worthy of you, Flora, and I'll furnish it worthy of you."

With the first thaws he'd saddled a horse and surveyed the country, and come back jubilant with news: he'd bought a rich farm up near Barbeque Creek, where their old friend John MacLeod had a kirk; a substantial house, nearly completed, stood there already, as well as several outbuildings—a kitchen, a byre and a barn.

Almost as soon as he'd announced his news he'd sent two of the men with waggons down to Wilmington. They would bring up the household goods that had been stored last fall. Then Allan and the lads and the rest of the gillies had galloped north, to fell trees and root out stumps, to put up fences and dig a well.

The day on which the furniture arrived he'd sent for her. When he lifted her from the coach his hands were rougher and blacker than she'd ever seen them before. "I wanted to wait," he'd said. "I wanted it all finished for you, dear. But we men aren't good at fixing a house. It's going to take you and the servants to make it livable, I'm afraid."

Allan never knew how inhospitable the unpainted

frame building had looked to her when she first examined it. He never knew how she'd blinked back
tears at the sight of a packed-mud floor and cracked
windows. It had made her almost sick to see her
lovely hand-carved furniture—the graceful desk, the
long fire-side bench of tufted Turkey carpet, the large
stretcher ·table—sitting awkwardly about in corners
harbouring dust and fine gravel. But she'd fixed her
eyes upon the mirror, and let it remind her of Allan's
good intention. He'd hung it in a prominent place in
the great-room, a place where she would see it and be
able to open it if she wished a dozen or two times a
day. Softly she'd said, "I'd feel terrible, Allan, if you
didn't need me to make your home. You did right to
send for me early. I'll have things set right before you
know it. Now show me about the whole farm."

The weeks that followed were confused in her
memory. Too much had been done in too little time.
The family came together only in short breathing-
spells between chores. Outside, Allan and the lads
worked alongside the gillies, splitting wood and guid-
ing the plough. One by one they'd ridden down to the
settlement for saws, pails, food and cloth and other
necessary supplies. Inside, she and Katie and the
bondswomen had scrubbed, polished, measured and
stitched. Everyone had responded to the inexorable
logic of time. Three months they had, to make their
impact on the new land. Success or failure in the New
World depended, for them, on setting the first year's
crop, on purchasing and pasturing the first year's
herds. Flora had understood and had willingly released her women, on occasion, to help outdoors.
Uncomplainingly she'd picked up the waxing or the
silver-polishing where the servants had left it off.

Yet it had been difficult, in the ever-present weariness of hard work, not to become quick-tempered
and harsh. Only once had they come close to quarrelling—and, of course, over a relatively small thing.
There had been a day on which Flora had unexpectedly wept. "We can't live like heathens," she'd cried,
surprised at herself, "without so much as a floor! Oh,
how I yearn for the cool, clean stones of Flodigarry!"

Allan, short of money as he was and needing every head of cattle and every bag of seed he could hoard the money for, had sat in silent discouragement. Thinking his silence meant denial, Flora had wailed, "Is it a home or a stable we're to have?" Still without answering he'd left the house, and nothing more was said. Flora was ashamed of her outburst. She knew it had resulted simply from strain that sometimes looked as though it would be endless.

A few days later a joiner had come. Only then had Allan referred to the floors. "I'm sorry about the delay, Flora, and even sorrier I didn't think of having this done before you came. This man from Cross Creek is good, they say. He'll have to do it, because I can't spare anyone from the fields."

It was strange, Flora thought now, looking about her, how those floors had been the turning-point for her. It seemed that the moment they were finished she'd been able to envision and then create this cheerful room, as gracious as those they'd lived in before. Simple hooked rugs were colourful against the soft, oiled surface of the hard pine. The heavy red damask curtains, given her so long ago by Lady Primrose in London, cast a ruddy, warming glow over the whole room. At night the mirror reflected her family, tired but harmonious again, as they sat together to rest from one day's labour and plan for another's.

Finally, the race between human effort and unremitting time had ended. One afternoon last week Allan had come in early, smiling and rubbing the sweat from his brow. He'd stopped once to turn and stare squint-eyed across the turned fields. Then he'd caught her hand, squeezed it and said boyishly, "We've done it! Every field is ready. And, God, I'm happy! I'm no longer a gentleman, but it doesn't matter. I'm a real farmer. I plough, I cut weeds, I handle a hoe. My back is weary by nightfall, my legs tired. See how my hands are calloused by scythe and plough handles." He extended his hand, and she gently ran her fingers over the hard, white places. He smiled and went on. "I like this life. My only concern is that you should be happy too."

"Aye," she'd answered with a smile. "I'm well content. I don't mind seeing you and the lads working with your hands. It's good to be weary at night from honest toil. But as for your not being a gentleman any longer, I can't agree. You were born one." She stood on tiptoe to kiss him fondly.

Together they had entered the house, spoken hopefully of the sunshine and rains that must now come if their labour was to reach fruition. "But that we can only pray for while we do the chores faithfully," Allan had said. "And in the meanwhile we can ease up, rest some." After a pause he'd grinned. "I can wait no longer to tell you the surprise I planned for you. When I saw we were going to finish in time for the clan gathering, I sent for Anne. She'll visit with you and go up to Helicon with us."

No words could have expressed Flora's deep joy. Quiet, unbidden tears had washed down her cheeks just as they did now, when she was rocking her grandchild and thinking back on that moment. The new life, though it was rigorous and demanding and isolated, was bringing the happiness of shared security and achievement that she and Allan had groped for all their life together.

She took her handkerchief from her pocket and wiped her eyes and then little Norman's neck, moist and faintly red. She was very gentle, for she did not want to awaken him.

On the next day, Friday, the sun was just showing over the tops of the pines when Allan spurred his horse and led the way down the lane. Behind him came the carriage, its seat overflowing with blankets and small wraps for the baby. The pace would be slow so that Flora, Anne and Norman might ride easily. All the lads—David, Dougald, Sandy and Jamie—had been sent ahead. No one expected them to restrain themselves to a sedate walk to Helicon. They'd been gone some fifteen minutes and were no doubt already past the mill and the third bend in the road.

In the coolness of that May morning hundreds of

other Scotsmen were leading their families along the roads to Mount Helicon. There was not a Highlander anywhere between the Cape Fear and the Pee Dee rivers—anywhere, in fact, in all North and South Carolina—who was willingly staying home from the reunion. Gaelic songs and Gaelic battle-cries filled the air. Most of the travellers forgot momentarily that they were representing Cross Creek or New Bern, the area up by the fork of the Deep and the Haw or the farmlands by the fork of the Uwharie and the Yadkin. They did not think of themselves as coming from Anson or Montgomery county or from any other place in their new homeland. When the clansmen convened no one pointed at an approaching rider and cried, "There's Angus MacNeil of Wilmington!" Instead they shouted so all could hear, "MacNeil of Barra!" "MacGregor of Argyle!" "Campbell of Rosshire!" "MacDonald of Skye!"

Every shire of the old homeland, every islet near it, would be represented—Jura, Eigg, Rum, the Shetlands, the Orkneys, the Hebrides. There would be old men leaning on knobby sticks and young men hardy enough to play the traditional games. There would be wrinkled women who had never mastered the accents of English; they gleefully anticipated two days of gossip in the rhythmic syllables of Gaelic. There'd be young matrons who called their bairns by Gaelic names, and young maids who'd spurned the American suitors of the winter and come in spring to blush and say "Aye" to Highlands lads.

Most of the rejoicing folk arrived road-weary toward nightfall. They called greetings to friend and stranger alike—there were, really, no strangers, just new friends—and made their way to their own people. Each clan camp was designated by a flag bearing the badge of the clan: myrtle for the Campbells, broom for the Morays, wortleberry for the MacQueens, heather for the MacDonalds.

Around these standards—a dozen or more there were—the clansmen gathered. On the first night the conversation was mostly the low, intimate greeting and reminiscence of family members. Here and there brothers and sisters and cousins celebrated reunion with a song. Much of the talk and the singing lasted late into the night, but never did it disturb those who, having travelled the greatest distances, chose to sleep.

The ground, covered with pine-needles, sent up a pungent fragrance about the sleepers. The pines soughed softly overhead, resulting in the light wind. Across the flames fell shadows of young men who kept the fires. Over all was the black dome of the sky, perforated by a million stars.

It was a quiet night. On the morrow, at the coming of dawn, the Highland folk would rise in gaiety and laughter. Tonight, under the towering, protective arches of the tall pines, they dreamed. Perhaps they dreamed of the Duke of Cumberland's edict—that one of every twenty Highlanders would be executed. Perhaps they thought of the other nineteen who were banished to America. Perhaps the roll of names of the first few who had asked for land grants passed through their dreams: the MacNeils, the Campbells, the MacAlisters, Mac-Dougalds, MacKays and MacGills. Perhaps they did not dream but slept oblivious of past and future.

Mount Helicon held them quietly throughout the night. Its sandy ridges, crowned with soft grasses, shielded them from the man-made tensions that agitated the settlements. Most of these Highlanders had pushed beyond the towns into remote valleys. They had dedicated their energies to winning the greatest battle man fights—that against time and nature. Now, having gained a measure of success, they had gathered to give thanks and rejoice.

When the first sunshine spread over Helicon's ridges they arose, splashed themselves with cold spring water and gazed clear-eyed and proudly down into the glens. They could see fields where forests late had grown. They could see, on the bank of Rockfish Creek, old Bethesda Kirk. In 1755 it had been founded by their ardent missionary pastor, the Reverend Hugh MacAde. Yes, their dogma and dicta were well established in the new land. Reverently the Scots paused before they gave themselves to games and gossip. The sight below, the symbols of their labour and their faith, awed them. It was a testimonial that the new land had welcomed them, their bodies and their souls.

For the young folk the awe-filled moment passed quickly. Here and there a quick flash of colour was seen as a lad flung his plaidie about his shoulders, as a lass reached for a kettle to fetch water.

"Wait!" the Reverend Mr. MacKeogh's voice rang out. "In the silence of this morn offer up a prayer, a prayer asking the Lord to show us how we may return thanks to this generous land that has taken us in."

Heads were bowed and each man and woman, according to his capacities and aspirations, prayed that he might serve his new home.

"Forget not," MacKeogh cried, "that this lush land, despite its sweet fruit, its vining flowers, its plentiful game, is like the Garden of Eden. There is evil lurking here. A serpent of discontent slithers among us. Steel your hearts to slay it!"

As if the sun had retreated behind a cloud, a chill came upon the people. Then softer tones dispelled it. John Bethune, the beloved present pastor at Bethesda, countered from his camp: "To live in peace with the land and its folk is the best way to return thanks. Every man here has a will to do that. Find the strength to follow your will, and you shall have served America well. Now, God bless you, and let you rejoice."

The frozen groups of folk began to yield to the bright sun and fresh May breeze. Youth called forth youth; age welcomed age. Women put their heads together to discuss the feast they would prepare. Children scrambled into the edge of the woods to gather wild flowers. Older men, whose stiff knees made them content to sit by the fires, watched beef roasting over the embers. A contingent of stalwart lads, led by David, disappeared in quest of a straight young pine tree suitable for a caber. Allan, his son Sandy in tow, made for the men who were clustering about Farquard Campbell's carriage, there to discuss the price of stock and seed. Allan swung along eagerly; for the first time in many years he would speak with the authority of a landowner who expected profit.

The caber contest was set for mid-afternoon, and at two-thirty the older men were hurrying to finish stripping and smoothing the pine tree that the lads had felled. The sun flashed blindingly on the sharp *skean dhus* with which the oldsters sliced off the bark and rounded the end of the log. Families had withdrawn to their own camps and were encouraging their contestants. Under every clan flag the caber-thrower was nervously warming up. Some ran to loosen their taut leg muscles; some swung their arms to take any stiffness out of the shoulders. Every once in a while one of the youths would crouch and heave as if he were hoisting the heavy pole to his shoulder; he'd rise and dart ahead, then catapult the imaginary caber into the air.

Under the heather flag David was jogging back and forth, bending, heaving, stretching all his muscles. After the fifth or sixth lap he threw himself panting onto the ground before Dougald and Moira. "Much good practicing now does! Either a man has the strength and the balance or he hasn't."

Leaning forward to touch him reassuringly on the wrist, Moira said softly, "Oh, David, don't fear. I know you're going to win for us."

Flora heard the last words and laughed. "'Us,' lass? Already?" She saw Moira blush at the teasing, and hastily added more seriously, "Now don't be sorry you said it. We want you in our family, dear. But I was surprised. Dougald's done nothing but worry about the time it will take him to settle independently. From his glum words of late—ever since his trip to Cross Creek I've heard them—I thought you two were going to have to wait till your old age to be saying 'we' and 'us.'"

For a moment Moira sat with her head down; she was waiting for Dougald to speak. When he said nothing she looked up obliquely and found that he had not even listened to Flora's query. With Allan he was watching some of the other throwers exercising, measuring their skill and strength. With some pique she said clearly, "Dougald would have so. But I've warned him—" her delicate lips grew firm in haughty independence—"that I don't intend to grow white hairs waiting for a man to wed me."

Flora patted her hand and said consolingly, "I'm sure, Moira dear, you won't have to. If our Dougald hesitates, there's good cause."

"I know, Mrs. MacDonald," Moira wailed, her pretence of indifference gone, "'tis dear of him to want everything secure for me. But I say that would be dull. Why can't we work our lives out together? If we don't, one of us may find some day that there's no room, no need for the other any more. Isn't that true? Cecily says it is—and I'm sure she should know."

"Why, lass," Flora exclaimed, "whatever do you mean? You talk as though Cecily were some unwanted spinster who waited in patience so long she was forgotten. I'm certain that can't be true."

David, getting up to run again at Allan's command, grunted, "Stephen Moray doesn't think of her as unwanted. Do you note how he tags after her? Humph!"

"Leave the match-making to the ladies, David," Allan ordered brusquely. "Your turn's coming soon, and you'll get only one toss. Swing your arms loosely. ... Aye, that's the rhythm."

Obediently keeping the beat, David said, "I'm not worried, sir. . . . The work I've done has been good conditioning. . . . I ought to be able to heave the caber ... a full pace or more above last year."

Allan punctured his over-confidence: "Are you forgetting that all the other lads have done the same hoisting and pulling and splitting you've done? Some have been doing it for several years. I tell you, it's the earlier emigrants you have to be careful of. Mind that advice, and take their measure."

Dougald shook his head and sided with his brother. "The other lads don't look as fit to me as David does. In fact, I'd have a try at the caber myself, if I didn't have to compete with him. But I know my place when David's on the field—it's along the side, cheering him on."

Moira had been listening and now could not be still any longer; she would not let Dougald take second place, not even to David. "Don't you be over-modest," she cried, getting up to stand beside him. "Having the best piper is as important to the family as having the best caber-thrower. And there's no doubt that you're the best piper."

Dougald took her hand and smiled. "Thanks, but it's more important to us to have the winning caber man. Allan's long been the best, acknowledged far and wide. Now David's got to keep the MacDonald leadership that Allan won for us."

"Dougald's right," Allan put in. "I hate to admit I can no longer hoist the pole as I used to. But I can stand back so long as a MacDonald takes the day. That's as it should be—one generation taking up where the other left off."

While he was speaking Allan had looked directly at David. Now he turned to Dougald. "I don't mean to belittle the importance of your task today. The MacDonald have never had the best piper of all the clans. Today we should have the best. 'Tis a glorious thing."

He called David to him and put a hand on each boy's shoulder. "I've been proud of the way you two have realized the task we've got here in the new land. Here everything's different so from Skye that we can't keep our name on the basis of the old days. We have to reassert it, prove we can conquer everything—from the land to the games—just as well as we could at home. That's a wonderful thing about America. A man is judged by what he achieves, now, today." His voice had grown raspy with emotion, and he concluded quickly. "Remember what I've told you: A MacDonald leads ... or he's not a true MacDonald." With a push he started David for the playing area.

For a moment Dougald stood looking after Allan quietly. Then he commented to Moira, "What a shame it is that Allan has to turn to David instead of to his own son! Sandy's a fine fellow, but he's no athlete. I think it's a constant sorrow to Allan."

Moira forebore to answer except with a warning press of her hand. Sandy was not far away, nor was Flora. Casually she looked at Sandy. He was wiry, handsome and clever. But his gift was for management and for balancing profit and loss. She looked back at Dougald's sensitive face, which revealed generosity and humour and vision. A little sigh escaped her as she realized that loving Dougald, a tenderer man, would take patience. He would deny himself what he wanted most if he thought that by waiting he could in the end give more. Already he'd described for her the land he wanted to buy, the home he wanted to build. He'd sworn to give them both to her as a wedding-token. How long would it be?

From the playing-field Allan waved to the family. "Come!" he shouted. "David is to throw!"

Catching Moira firmly by the wrist, Dougald raced across the meadow. Flora rose, slowly and with dignity, and took the baby from Anne. Together they walked on, interested but not consumed with interest, as they had been when their husbands used to compete.

When they arrived at the ring of spectators, Moira stepped back to make room. "Such a pity you didn't see. He was grand. But look! There! The farthest mark. That's David's."

A few moments later, after the last two contestants had heaved the tall pine log, a shout went up. "David MacDonald wins! Hurrah for David MacDonald and the whole MacDonald clan!"

Five of the men David had defeated hoisted him to their shoulders and carried him triumphantly toward Allan. All the contestants were gracious losers, though some of the heavier, older ones showed chagrin at being bested by a young lad like David.

David, feeling a little foolish about riding above the heads of the others, grinned with happiness. He reached down to take Allan's offered hand. "It was for you, Allan" was all he could say.

Moira hung on his arm, dancing along beside him excitedly. "Davie! Davie! 'Tis proud of you I am." With an exhilarated laugh she cried, "The next best man in the world you are! And in some things the best."

She fell back and leaned breathlessly on Dougald. " 'Tis you who are the best man in the world, my darling," she whispered, looking up at him, "as well as the best piper. When your turn comes, I'll be listening proudly."

A solemn mood fell over the people toward evening when the piping began. To many faces there came far-away looks which bespoke memories of notes echoing down Scotland's crags. Most of the folk sat with their kin or dearest friends and listened raptly or murmured in unobtrusive tones.

Flora sought out Cecily. Ever since Moira had spoken of her, Flora had realized that she knew little of Cecily's life down in the settlement. It was a pity that a little distance and a little time had proved to be high barriers between them, and a greater pity, Flora felt, that today, when she had had an opportunity to chat with Cecily, she had let herself be engrossed in her own family. In looking for a grassy seat from which to watch the pipers, she purposefully walked toward Farquard's carriage. She came slowly down behind the Campbell camp and made her way around the coach. Hearing Cecily's voice at the same moment that she heard the first pipe note, she caught up her skirt and stepped rapidly over the brush at the meadow's edge. When she got round to the other side, she halted in surprise. Cecily was tugging at Stephen Moray's sleeve.

"Don't go!" Cecily was urging. "I tell you, don't go to them. Politics are banned. This is a good Scots day of memories and songs. You'll convert it into something insidious. Then you'll report it and make trouble for these folk out of nothing." She pulled back her hand and rubbed her neck in the nervous gesture she always resorted to when tense. "For my sake, Stephen."

"You thwarted me once before, and men have suffered for it. Now——"

"No!" Cecily spoke in a harsh whisper. "Please don't say that. I have wondered so often whether I did right that night."

"Then don't interfere again."

"This time it's something different, Stephen."

Stephen was scowling, as if both angry and dismayed. He started to answer, but when he looked up at Cecily he saw Flora standing hesitantly by the coach door. Quickly he mastered his agitation and said courteously, "Good-day, Mrs. MacDonald. 'Tis a pleasure to see you again." Now he grinned disarmingly. "I've a special fond place in my heart for you. You're my national heroine and my personal benefactress as well. I've not forgotten the night you bestowed the award on me."

He had given Cecily time to recover herself. When she turned she was smiling graciously, warmly. "Flora, I didn't hear you approach. But I'm glad you did. We've hardly seen each other."

Flora perceived that a private matter had evoked Cecily's anxious words to Stephen. She did not want to force herself into the matter. "I only wanted to ask you to sit with me during the playing. Would you? Now don't hurry if you've some more talking to do. Why don't you and Mr. Moray come over to our camp when you're free?" She took a step to indicate she would leave them alone.

Stephen stopped her. "Wait, please. Miss Weston and I had no more to say. And I've got to speak to the men over there." He pointed to a hillock where Allan, Farquard, Alex and several others sprawled in the warm sand. "I'll go on over and leave her to you."

Without looking at Cecily he hurried away. She bit her lip and watched him go. Only after a moment did she recall Flora's presence and turn to walk with her.

"I do wonder," Flora said casually as she drew Cecily's arm through her own, "what business Mr. Moray can have with Allan. I hope he doesn't want a silver commission. My women can't keep polished what we already have."

Cecily drew back to look quizzically at Flora, as if she found the question odd. "I fear," she said, "Mr. Moray has many concerns beside silver, as you should know."

"That's an enigmatic remark, Cecily. My impression of the lad has been simply of a dedicated artist with gracious manners and disarming frankness. Of course, I've seen little of him. You——"

"I know better? Is that what you were going to say?" Cecily interrupted. "No. I find I cannot scan his character at all. He's most disconcerting. He really makes no pretense in sentiment, opinion or action. Yet he's a contradictory man of fine and fearful qualities. I am uneasy with him."

Flora thought some little time before she answered. They found shady seats among the trunks of some pine trees before she said, "I couldn't help hearing, back at the coach, the word 'politics.' The trouble is political?"

"Well," Cecily said rather shortly, though not rudely, "it's certainly true that I distrust his politics. That would be all right, but I trust him—as a person, I mean. He's at the house often. We've discovered much in common and tend to place confidence in each other. A plaguing situation. One must always be on guard."

Flora laughed. "Now, Cecily, aren't you exaggerating? Listening to your uncle's friends has made you overly sensitive to the friction that we hear of. I think much of it's local, for one thing. We're not troubled much, back in the country. But the big thing is that politics, even the gravest political antagonism, cannot stifle a real friendship." She leaned forward to touch Cecily's wrist. Her face and voice both took on a tentative expression that showed she was not meaning to pry. "Should I say love, Cecily? Is that what you fear with this handsome Stephen Moray?"

Flora waited for an answer, but none came. Finally she went on. "Politics can slightly change the character of love, my dear. But it cannot destroy it. The one is a man-made thing, the other God-made. Love is always the stronger."

Cecily had listened seriously as if she attached importance to Flora's advice, but her only comment was terse: "There are times when a man and his politics cannot be severed." Swiftly she changed the subject. "Let's talk of something else. I've news that will interest you. Our beauteous ship-mate, Madame la

Fabrère, has written me on most elegantly perfumed note-paper. New York, she says, affords brilliant society—the most brilliant, of course, in her salon. Our mutual acquaintance Mr. Blair graced her table one evening, she said. She hopes I'll travel north and do the same."

Flora was perplexed by Cecily's swift retreat in the conversation and also by the brittleness of her tone. Rather absently, to cover her confusion, she answered, "I hope you'll not go. A light woman——"

"Hardly!" Cecily exclaimed without letting her finish. "I confess, though, I don't know whether La Fabrère or Blair is the person I would most wish to shun."

"Oh, Cecily! You were always too hard on Mr. Blair. I thought him quite pleasant at the end."

"Yes, at the end . . ." Cecily's voice trailed off. Her head was propped on her hand. She was bent forward, so that her elbow rested on her knee. It was a position uncommon to Cecily, Flora thought. The awkwardness and weight of it betokened discouragement.

Flora tried to guess what bothered Cecily and sought for consoling words. Before she could speak, however, Cecily energetically pushed herself up and rose to her feet. She smiled in self-mockery. "Do forgive me. I'm very bad company." She swished her skirt about until it fell in straight, soft folds. "There will come a time, Flora, when I'll speak freely to you. Right now, we've met at a time when I don't know my own thoughts. I do know one thing, however, and I must tell you that: I've wished to see you, to draw on your wisdom."

Flora made a depreciating gesture, but Cecily insisted. "Oh, yes, wisdom—a kind of wisdom I never appreciated before. You've learned the proper woman's way. You possess yourself and yet are wholly Allan's." Unwanted tears choked Cecily's voice, and she turned away. But she managed to add, "You think I'm foolish, no doubt. But I'm learning too late that woman is not the opposite of man, but the complement. I've stood independent and opposed till it's too late."

Flora jumped up and put her arms about Cecily. "My dear, I won't ask what all this means. Tell me when you're ready. Don't tell me if you find you never want to. But take comfort in this: that lesson was not one I learned easily, nor so young as you. I had to be told it, several years after I was married."

Reluctantly she released Cecily; she wanted to help her, but knew that the decision to surrender to another must always be made alone.

Flora herself stood alone in thought some while after Cecily had run away. It was the poignant music of Dougald, playing the even-song, which lured her back to communion with the friends about her. She listened and shared in the response to the melody. For Dougald there were no rousing cheers as there had been for David the caber-thrower. There was instead the speaking silence with which men honour him who evokes racial memory and awakens courage for the future.

The traditional melodies had called the men on the hillock back to their families. By twos and threes they shook hands and ambled away, until Allan alone was left, a silhouette of a man in the fading light. Flora watched him stand poised in thought, then stoop, as if to pick up something. He straightened and she saw him absently pour sand from one hand to the other, while his head sank forward as it always did when he was disturbed. Suddenly he whirled; his arm shot forward to hurl the sand to the wind. He turned back swiftly and strode toward Flora. When he was close, solid and real again, she reached forth her hand and whispered, "I'm glad you're back."

24

Chief of the MacDonalds

THOUGH it was after the late dusk of a June evening, Allan spurred his horse onward. He knew he'd covered over thirty miles that day, as far as he liked to ride even his gamest bay, but he had to go on till he found safe shelter. Before long there was bound to be a plantation. He shifted the reins and fished in his pocket for his limp handkerchief. It was gritty with sand and smelly with sweat. Lord, how he wished he were home at Mount Pleasant!

A bend was coming and he slowed to round it with utmost caution. Once already he'd been ambuscaded, yanked to a halt, dragged from the saddle. He didn't want to go through that again; the memory of it was frightening enough.

A startling cry had announced the attack: "It's him! MacDonald! Get him!" The next instant he'd been wrestling desperately with a sinewy youth. Only his mature man's weight and power had taken care of that one. The second brigand, clawing at his back the whole time, had been easier to handle. Swinging about to grapple with him, Allan had crashed to the ground, not from his antagonist's blows but from the force of his own lunge. A mere stripling, scared to death, lay beneath him.

Allan had jerked him up by the shirt front, blazing mad and ready to twist the meaning of the assault out of the boy. Then he threw him back to the ground and leaped to the saddle. The other was groaning. There was no point in tangling with him again on the lonely, dark road.

That had been on the way down, ten or fifteen miles out of New Bern. The rest of the way that cry

clanged in Allan's mind: "It's MacDonald! Get him!"
Why get MacDonald? Who was it that lay in wait in
dark bushes for Allan MacDonald? Not just robbers,
taking any prey that passed. That was clear.

In New Bern he'd had another surprise. While
buying the items he'd made an excuse for the trip, he
learned about Governor Martin's flight from the city.
A week ago it was, even while he and Flora and the
rest had been having the reunion. A rebel called Abner Nash had run the Crown authority out of town,
and only because Martin was trying to keep six of the
Palace cannon out of the patriots' hands.

Tight-lipped, Allan had paid for his purchases.
Then he'd ridden by the Governor's Mansion. Last
fall he'd seen it sparkling with light and life; now it
was cavernously dark. Even the draperies had been
removed, leaving black holes of windows. Looking on
it, Allan had not thought primarily of Martin; he'd
thought that when the seat of government gapes
empty it bodes ill for the land.

Eager to blot out the sight, he'd spurred his horse
savagely and headed southeast, to Fort Johnston,
where Martin had taken refuge.

The Governor hadn't lost faith because of the
rout—that was clear from the first moment Allan had
spoken with him. But he was in a precarious position;
the fort was a sorry protection for him. More important, Martin—the whole authority of the Crown, in
fact—had been put on the defensive. Always a dangerous position.

Abruptly Allan's thought returned to the present.
A light flickered through the trees to the left of the
road. He found the lane leading back and turned the
bay into it. A hundred yards or so from the house he
dismounted and walked ahead of the horse. At the
edge of the clearing he stopped to look the place over.
It was a spacious house, built much like his own. He
thought of the feather-beds that must wait for guests
in the upstairs rooms. It was also a quiet house. Eagerly Allan walked toward it, tied the horse and
mounted the steps.

First a young coloured boy and then a soft-spoken

middle-aged man came to the door. "You're looking for shelter for the night? Come in."

"My horse . . . ?"

"My man will take care of him."

In the hallway the host introduced himself as Thomas Howe. At once Allan tensed; Howe was getting to be a famous name among the patriots. He saw that the man was watching him closely, perhaps baiting him. "I'm a brother to Colonel Robert Howe. Mayhap you've heard of him."

Non-committally Allan said, "Aye, a well-known man he is." Then, as observant as his host, he told his own name.

With a laugh Howe replied, "You hardly needed to tell me. There are your kilts . . . and your fame."

Allan didn't risk any questions. He'd found out it was probably patriots who'd attacked him before and been warned he might have trouble with any more he met.

Howe had paused with his hand on the latch of a door leading off the hall. "We'll be happy to have you remain with us tonight. I'm honoured to have such an illustrious man as my guest. Two of my friends are in the study. Won't you join us for a drink? It would probably help you sleep well."

Allan found that the very suavity of his host angered him. There was something afoot here just as there was everywhere a man turned these days. Well, if it had to do with him, he'd like to know straight out what it was. He would join them, and without so much as washing up. There was no sense in letting them confer while his back was turned.

Keeping his voice and expression entirely pleasant, he said, "I'll need nothing to make me sleep, Mr. Howe, but I could most certainly use a drink to quench my thirst. It's kind of you to offer." When he was in the room and facing the others he added, "I'm sure you and your guests will excuse my appearance. A man can't stay clean on the road."

Two other men had risen when Allan entered. One promptly reached to place another chair by the fireplace and the other said, "Welcome. We've been hearing much about you recently. Heard you were down our way."

Howe made introductions. The name of the man who'd spoken was vaguely familiar, but Allan couldn't place it. Harnett—he'd heard it somewhere. The identification didn't come, and he dismissed the problem to think about the other name. Coor. That one he'd never heard before, he was sure of that. But Howe had mentioned that the man was a friend of silversmith Moray's. He must be a patriot too.

Howe had gathered the glasses together and was replenishing them, adding a fourth. He held up the fresh tumbler with the amber whisky in it for Allan's scrutiny. "Enough?"

"Plenty, thank you." Allan spoke from his original position, half-way between the group of chairs and the door. He noticed the tableau-like atmosphere. Every man, himself included, was slow to speak or move. And the words had little to do with the thoughts they were thinking. He decided to put an end to it, just ask a few questions and see what sort of answers he'd get.

"Gentlemen, forgive me if I plunge into a matter that lies heavy on my mind," he said, taking a deep breath. "I'd just like to know why everyone seems to be waiting for me. I don't know who everyone is around this country, but everyone around this country knows who I am." He saw perplexity flicker over Coor's face and felt a good deal of satisfaction. Let the other fellow be confused for a change, he thought. Then he went on aloud: "I started ten days ago from my home, beyond Cross Creek, for New Bern. A simple trip for supplies. On the way I was ambuscaded. And it was me they wanted—not just any traveller. Now tonight, my arrival was no surprise to you, nor was my identity. I appreciate the reception committee . . . but I'd like to know why I was honoured with it."

Howe acted as if there was nothing strange in the question. He walked over to hand Allan his drink and gestured again to the chair. Without waiting for Allan to move, he took his own seat, leaned back and crossed one leg over his knee. With a smile he said, "Mr.

Harnett, Mr. Coor, why don't you sit down? I'm sure Mr. MacDonald will feel more at ease if you do. We have given him a rather . . . well, tense reception."

When Allan saw Harnett and Coor follow the cue given them, he too sat down. It felt good to sink into a comfortable chair after the day's hard ride and he was grateful to Howe for playing his game, whatever it was, coolly. This way he'd have a few minutes', if not a full night's, rest.

"Mr. MacDonald," Howe said, leaning forward, "you've asked for frankness. We shall give it to you. Our stilted reception of you comes from a simple thing: we were talking about you when you arrived. We were saying that you did not ride to New Bern simply for supplies. You went to see Martin, just as you then went on to Fort Johnston to see him."

"Aye," Coor said with a grim chuckle, "it's dangerous these days to see Martin. Some of the New Bern men probably wanted to prevent your sticking your head in a noose."

"This is the first time, gentlemen," Allan said, "that I've lived in a place where it was dangerous to visit the head of the lawfully established government."

Howe nodded as if he appreciated Allan's sentiment, but he went on quietly with his account. "You went to see Martin as a result of your conferences at Helicon. We know well enough why you went: Many of your fellow-Scots asked you to. That was to be expected. You are their natural leader. Of course, what we would like to know is: which way will you lead them?"

Allan found himself admiring Howe. He went to the point, and without melodrama or threats. All the while he'd been speaking a gentle smile had played about his lips, as if his rôle of interrogator was not customary for him and was amusing to him. Yet, no doubt about it, the man was in earnest.

In Allan's silence, Harnett leaned forward in waiting. Finally he said, "Which way, Mr. MacDonald?"

Allan stood up and placed his empty glass carefully on the small table beside his chair. "You and your fellows are irresponsible and premature. The assailants out of New Bern tried to kill me before I was well aware I was confronted with a question. They struck at me because it was possible I was a loyalist leader. Merely possible! Do you kill for a possibility? Now you three demand my answer to the question before I have it. I don't know whether I'll lead anyone anywhere."

"What did you tell Martin?" Coor put in, his voice louder and more insistent than the others.

"Just what I'm telling you," Allan said, looking him straight in the eye. "I went for information, because I saw I was in need of it. Even if all I do is tell my fellow-Scots I won't lead them, I have to have reason for my decision, understand this fight, find the right and honest answer."

"What did he offer you?" It was Coor again, driving bull-like toward his objective. "He made you terms, didn't he?"

Allan was suddenly tired of it. The interview had given him many things to consider while he made up his mind. He wanted to be done with these men, to rest and then work out his views.

"Mr. Coor," he said decisively, "what Governor Martin said to me was confidential. Even if it weren't, and even if I were of a mind to tell you, it wouldn't make any difference. I haven't made up my mind. If you're interested in me and in the way I go—and you certainly seem to be—I can tell you this: Everything that I see, everything that happens to me, will influence my evaluation of your side. Now, if you gentlemen will excuse me, I think I'll go to bed."

He watched their faces as he bowed formally and started to turn. Would they let him carry it off?

Coor lunged out of his chair, one arm outstretched.

"Mr. Coor!" Howe stopped him. "Did you have something more to say, something that Mr. MacDonald ought to hear? If not, I think we should let him retire. He's fatigued, and a long journey still lies before him."

Again Allan bowed. "You've been gracious, Mr. Howe, and helpful to me. Good night."

Outside the door Allan paused for a second, just

long enough to hear Howe reprimand Coor: "Don't be a fool! Molesting him is the surest way to lose him. He's telling the truth. We still have a chance."

The coloured boy appeared at the foot of the stairs and Allan followed him to his room. In less than ten minutes he was stretched across the bed. He wished he could ride on at once, but he needed rest and so did the bay. He forced his eyes shut; with an early start and better luck than he'd so far had he could reach Mount Pleasant in two days. He fixed his mind on home and finally slept.

Eight or ten miles away from Mount Pleasant Allan heard a hateful cry: "Allan MacDonald! Wait!" Out of habit he jerked up his rifle, cocked the trigger and sighted at the rider galloping down the hill. He saw it was David, and his arm shook as he let the barrel drop. This business had him aiming at his own kin.

When David reined up Allan reached across to clasp him gratefully by the shoulder. "A fortunate meeting. And forgive my aiming at you."

Struggling to control his horse's rearing, David panted. "Flora sent me. She was worried. I told her it was needless."

"Nay, it's very useful. But you say she's worried? Of course ... I've been long gone." Allan's voice was tired.

"Something's the matter, sir." David jumped off his horse and held the bay so Allan could dismount. "What is it?"

Slowly Allan walked to a muddy stream near by and fell to his knees to splash its water on his face. He mopped his neck with his wadded-up handkerchief and then fell back to rest against the trunk of a tree. "Come here, lad," he called. "I'll tell you."

". . . and that's the story," Allan concluded, having covered every stage of his journey down to the last lap. "That's the way things are in this country now." He pushed himself up and spoke more vigorously. "I've decided what I have to do: help stop this, if I

can, before it goes farther. I know what rebellion
would do to this land. It'd be worse than Skye. Our
ploughed soil would be trampled into a battle-ground.
Our turned furrows would be graves. What little we
could raise might be burned. What little wasn't burned
could not be sold." He ran his fingers through his hair
despairingly. "I don't understand it. The life here is
good; there's enough for every man. Why do these
fools want to spoil it? They don't, they can't know
how war devastates."

David had listened to the recital without comment.
Now he asked, "You'll take the commission Martin
offered you?"

"Aye," Allan said resignedly, "and go back to my
old profession of defending the country. I've got to
start gathering troops. It means you lads will have to
work the plantation."

David was on his feet in an instant. "Not me, sir!
I'm your first recruit."

Allan shook him a little by the arm. "You don't
know what it means. It's not just adventure, you
know."

David met his gaze. "Perhaps I do know what it
means. I've got the sense to value the land and the
opportunity we found here. Believe me, sir, Dougald
and I talk much of what we're going to do. He wants a
good plantation, and Moira for a wife, and children. I
want to go over those mountains." His arm reached out
to the west. "Only one thing can stop us—war, and the
kind of lawlessness you described to me." He suddenly
grinned a little and spoke more like the David who was
forever plotting excitement of some sort. "And there'll
be a little adventure, won't there?"

Allan smiled and nodded his head. "You're like me
as a lad. I wouldn't have wanted to stay home either.
Frankly, I hope Sandy and Dougald will feel the
same way. We'll need every man we can get. Now, you
want your first mission?"

David saluted smartly. "Yes, sir!"

"Don't take it as a jest. You know the dangers on
the roads. Ride carefully, by back trails if you can, to
Glendale. Tell Alex everything I've told you. Tell

him Martin offers him a commission as intelligence officer. He'll be appointed land agent to cover up his activities. If you have to speak about this to Anne, explain only about the land-agent appointment. War is a man's business. The women mustn't be worried with it—no sooner than they have to be anyway." Allan sighed and seemed troubled.

"I know what you're thinking, sir. It's about Flora. And I was wondering . . . if I ride on now, she's sure to become suspicious."

Allan looked up quickly. "Why should she? Nothing's been said, has it? About why I went?" He waited until David shook his head. "Well, then, there's no reason for her to be told. I'll say you asked to go hunting, since you'd have been away two or three days anyway if you'd had to track me down. She knows you well enough to believe that readily."

By the time Allan had finished speaking David had mounted. He was having trouble holding back his mare. Allan caught hold of the bridle. "Mind you, don't hunt either game or adventure. Get home as fast as you can. There'll be duty waiting. And, lad, take care." He slapped the mare's flank and sent her galloping down the road.

25

Fort Johnston

AT TEN in the morning on July 15 James Blair stood on the deck of a schooner carrying muskets, powder and ball to Governor Martin. As they entered the mouth of the Cape Fear River, Blair pursed his lips and gave a little nod of satisfaction. Together fate and his orders were taking him exactly where he wanted to be. And this time he wasn't coming on the scene as an ineffectual dunce but as an intelligence officer who knew his business: reporting on rebel military activity and raising loyalist troops. He was thinking also that from the little he'd seen of conditions here in North Carolina, an officer like himself would find plenty of work to do.

Swiftly he reviewed his plans: deliver the documents Gage had sent by him to Martin as quickly as possible and then head north to the back country. He hoped Martin would be at the fort, now that they'd made the detour around to it. But it would be just like him to have "retreated" again. Blair hadn't yet got over his amazement on learning Martin had fled New Bern and thus just handed the rebels the seat of government in a neatly wrapped package. The Governor's secretary had come down the Neuse River in a boat to hail the schooner and send them on to the Cape Fear River. Nothing had been said, in words, but Blair could see that even the new secretary, a man loyal to Martin, didn't like the retreat.

Things had changed significantly, Blair reflected, since he'd entered the Cape Fear about nine months ago. The sides hadn't really defined themselves then, and the Crown authority still had good chance to keep control. Despite his personal troubles at the

time, Blair had been fully confident of the success of
the cause for which he worked. Now it was harder to
be confident. He still believed that it was a cause
which deserved the best efforts of the best men, but
he couldn't deny that at least in North Carolina, from
reports he'd heard, the prospects were discouraging.
The Governor was holed up in an isolated fort and
the Whigs were in the ascendant. General Gage had
made it no secret that the Highlanders and Regulators
in the back country represented the only hope of holding the province until an expeditionary force of British regulars could restore obedience. So many Carolinians had now joined the rebellion that the list of
suspected which had caused so much trouble last fall
was all out of date. The fact was that Martin was an
optimistic bungler who never realized the strength of
the opposition until it was too late to meet it.

The schooner was coming in toward a little knot of
vessels anchored off the fort. The largest was a sloop
of war, emblazoned with the name *Cruizer*. She was
solid, though old and encrusted thickly with barna-
cles. Beside her there was a transport; he made out
the name *Peggy* on the stern. With them were a couple of smaller vessels, a schooner and a scow. They
all looked slack and somnolent.

Ten minutes later the schooner had dropped anchor. Blair returned shouted greetings to an officer on
the *Cruizer's* deck, then told his own captain to wait
for a message before beginning to discharge the arms
he carried. He started ashore in a boat.

As he approached the fort he was dismayed by its
appearance. The walls, made of blocks of some kind
of mortar, were crumbling; to Blair's practised eye,
they lacked the strength to stand any bombardment.

Greater dismay came when he was inside. An enthusiastic Martin greeted him with great satisfaction
over the shipment of arms, as if he thought they were
the answer to all his problems. He outlined a thousand plans for the future, but apparently had no realization of his present predicament.

Blair asked to see the fort's two officers, and was
introduced to Captain Collet in command, and Rich-

ard Wilson, his lieutenant. Collet, though a captain in the regular army, impressed Blair as impractical and inefficient. The suspicion was confirmed a few minutes later when Martin whispered confidentially, "Just between ourselves, I've little use for Captain Collet. Of course, I don't let on. But he's let the fort run down. He thinks of his own gain first, as well he might, for he's deeply in debt. He's high-handed with the neighbouring planters and contemptuous of them. They hate him to a man. They refuse to sell him supplies. They entice his men to desert. Three more ran off last week."

Blair was distressed that such a man should be in charge. He said nothing about it, but no longer wondered at the poor condition of the fort. "What force has Collet?" he asked in a low voice.

"He's supposed to have twenty-five, but at least half have slipped away. Aside from Wilson here, I don't believe half a dozen men could be depended on in a pinch."

Blair looked grave, and stepped forward a few paces as he thought about it. "Hmm, a very slim force." Then, turning, he asked another question. "Tell me, Governor, is it true that the Whigs in Brunswick and Wilmington have raised sizable companies of men? Aren't they likely to attack the fort?"

An expression of disdain came to the Governor's face. Waving his hand in a contemptuous, dismissing gesture, he said, "A rabble of them march up and down with old rifles and fowling-pieces, Major Blair. It was the same at New Bern. They make a ridiculous appearance. As to the fort, there have been rumours of an attack. Captain Collet says threats began as early as last March, but nothing has happened. I attach little importance to them."

Blair called Captain Collet back into the conference to ask about the threats. The commander's account of the situation squared with the Governor's and provided few additional details. His one real contribution was to disclose that though the fort's guns were good, they would be of little use. He had almost no powder and what he had was in bad condition.

"That is upsetting news, Captain, but important," Blair said. "It would be most unwise to bring up the arms we have aboard into so naked a place. If the Whigs were once to discover so rich a prize was here for the taking, they would be quick to attack. I'm surprised the fort's guns alone have not yet tempted them." He paced up and down, his hands behind his back, as he studied the situation. At last he directed a question at Collet. "What sort of intelligence do you receive from Brunswick and Wilmington?"

"My force is too small for me to send out scouts," Collet said defensively. "But loyal Tories have been going and coming, each one with news. The Wilmington Committee of Safety has patrols out to stop all messengers, but a good number get through."

"This is in general," said Blair, his voice tinged with impatience. "What of the movement of troops in the two towns? What is the news today?"

"As a matter of fact, there's been no news for two days," Collet admitted stiffly. "A couple of riders came in just as I was hurrying to greet you. I've not had time to speak to them yet."

"Let's have them in at once and hear what they have to tell us," Blair ordered, taking a seat. He hoped desperately that the couriers would bring some hard, realistic facts.

A moment later the orderly brought in two young men, both with a stubble of beard and the general dishevelment that testified to hard, secret riding. Blair half rose in his chair; he had no trouble recognizing them—David and Dougald MacDonald, and between them, for an anguishing instant, the image of Cecily Weston. When it was gone he sank back in his chair and looked the lads over in surprise. They'd filled out and matured over the winter. Men they were now, and if they were carrying dispatches down from the back country, they were doing men's work.

The lads had got over their start of surprise and were waiting to shake hands. Blair rose and greeted them warmly. "I'm glad we have able men like you working for us," he said sincerely and then added in answer to David, "Yes, I imagine it is a surprise to see me here, and in this capacity. I was not free before to disclose my profession. Now quickly, what news do you bring?"

"Letters and a message for Governor Martin and word of patriot activity up the river," Dougald said, going straight to the point. "Where is the Governor?"

"In the next room," Collet put in. "I'll take the letters and message to him."

Dougald and David both shook their heads, and Blair surmised that they had probably dealt with Collet before. "You go, David," Dougald said. "You've got the letters."

While David was extracting some papers from a leathern pouch hanging at his side, Blair asked Dougald, "Who sends you out?"

"Allan. The Governor made him recruiting officer a month ago. Or, rather, he asked him to be one. Allan thought it over and then went right to work. We bring his official acceptance and a report of what he's done."

By now David was gone. Blair asked Dougald to tell his news. "Is it something you picked up on your way down?"

"Yes, sir. We risked going into Wilmington and staying over night with the loyalist, Doctor Cobham. Word was all around town that Colonel John Ashe was mustering his troops there. He plans to bring them down-river by boat and attack the fort. Bob Howe is leading his troops from Brunswick to the same end. Ashe will embark tomorrow afternoon. Howe may already be starting. And Brunswick's only twelve miles away."

This, Blair thought with an inward groan, is what comes of Martin's contempt of his enemy and Collet's laxity. He wasted no time on his disgust and asked for more information: "Any idea how many men in the two contingents?"

"Cobham didn't have any certain figures, sir, but he estimated at least five hundred."

Collet stood up in agitation and advised, "Governor Martin must be consulted."

Blair nodded. "Ask him to come in."

Martin entered and took a seat at a round table. Collet and Blair pulled up chairs, and the twins lounged in the background. An informal council of war was begun. Dougald was called forward to repeat his information. Blair then took over.

"Let me set forth our alternatives as I see them, gentlemen. Here in the fort we have no effective force to meet five hundred attackers. We have to choose one of two courses. We can bring in the crews of the *Peggy* and the *Cruizer,* as well as some powder, and try to defend the fort. Or we can dismantle the fort—take the guns out to the ships, along with the supplies we can transport—and let the rebels have it." He paused briefly, then said, "Well, gentlemen, which is it to be?"

Martin, inclined to discount Dougald's report, was for doing very little. "Bring in a few marines and stick it out," he advised.

An indignant look passed over the faces of both boys at Martin's doubt of their account, but a slight signal from Blair made them remain quiet. Blair at once turned to Collet. "Your opinion, Captain?"

"I doubt we can hold the fort, though I wish I could share the Governor's confidence. But, as I said before, our guns, good though they are, will be useless without powder. The supply of that is very uncertain. A real attack pressed home would be too much for us. The danger might be extreme, don't you agree?"

"I certainly agree that the fort is a sorry affair. It's of little use to us. Without the cannon, it would be of little use to the rebels, too." Blair leaned forward to emphasize his point. "If we move the guns out to the ships we suffer no loss, and we preserve what strength we have. If we try to defend the fort and fail, we lose the cannon and, worse still, we give the rebels the colour of a victory, which will puff them up greatly. I'm for moving to the ships."

Blair had risen with his last words, but paused when Collet suddenly began to vacillate. "No, Major, on second thought, your plan is impractical. We don't have the men to move the guns."

Blair brushed aside Collet's worry and took his stance at the end of the table. "We'll need all the boats from the *Cruizer* and from the *Peggy,* too. Signal their commanders to come ashore. With their crews we can manhandle the cannon." He turned to Martin. "I hope you agree, sir."

Martin looked cast down. "I've little choice. Since General Gage has refused to restore my commission as colonel, I can't speak as a military man. If you gentlemen agree we should retire to the ships, I must acquiesce."

Collet had yet another reservation: "We had better ask the *Cruizer's* captain if he can defend the ship against Ashe's boats. I'd hate to abandon the fort and then have Colonel Ashe board and take the *Cruizer.*" He finished with a sullen mutter which betrayed the real cause of his about-face. "If we abandon the fort these cursed colonials will burn my house and all my furniture. They'll be happy to spite me."

Blair's fist clenched, but he calmly pressed his point home. "If Howe is marching, as our report has it, we have a very limited time. Let's get started moving out the guns and supplies."

Collet and Martin had to yield. The stripping of the fort was put in train.

Later, after Blair had satisfied himself that the sailors from the *Cruizer* were working with a will, he motioned David and Dougald aside for a private consultation. "I'd like one of you to stay with me four or five days," he said at once. "I expect we'll have more news for Cross Creek then, and someone must wait here to carry it. How about you, David?"

"Right, sir. I'll be glad to see what goes on here when the rebels come."

"Fine. Now, if you don't object, go help with the guns." Before David was out the door Blair was assigning Dougald's task. "Do you know any back road or trail that will get you around Howe's men? Colonel Ashe, you said, is coming by boat and will be no risk to a man on horseback."

"There's a path south of the road that I can get

to," Dougald answered after a moment's thought. "I don't believe the rebels will think to cover it."

Blair nodded in satisfaction. "If you can get through, you'll be far more useful going back to Cross Creek at once than staying cooped up here. I have a number of messages, including some that will ostensibly come from the Governor. Would you rather I wrote them out, or will you memorize them? It is much better, of course, not to have any papers on you if you should be stopped on the way."

"Just tell me," said Dougald steadily. "I'll remember."

For the next half hour they went over and over the messages Dougald was to carry home. Finally Dougald called a halt. "I've got them letter perfect." He stood up, eager to be on his way.

"Very good," Blair said, following Dougald to the cabin door. "But wait a moment. There's something else." Softly, so no one could overhear, he said, "I expect to follow you into the back country shortly, as soon as I can complete my duties here and make a few arrangements. I've been assigned to work as agent up your way. General Gage doesn't want the Whigs free to complain of provocation because he has sent officers openly to work against them, so we must pass as civilians. It's a good plan, but presents me with a problem. Most of the other agents are Scots who can be pretending to visit relatives. I'm English and I have no relatives in the Upper Cape Fear."

"Come to us," Dougald promptly said.

Blair smiled. "That would be pleasant, but no real solution. Allan MacDonald can take care of everything up your way. No, I need a place at Campbelltown. And, with your help, I think I can get one. At Farquard Campbell's."

Dougald shook his head and frowned. "He'd never allow it. Right now he's holding off both sides."

"I'm sure Miss Weston could win him over, if she would. The difficulty will be in getting her to agree. I left her on bad terms. You've got to plead my case well. She must allow me to come as her suitor. Even Farquard wouldn't have to know my real rôle, if she'd do that." He stopped when he saw Dougald's dubious expression. "What's the matter? Miss Weston's loyalty would surely make her wish to help."

"Oh, I've no doubt of that—of her loyalty. But . . ."

Blair looked at him sharply. "Are you implying she has a suitor in Campbelltown? That my presence would annoy her, even if we hadn't parted on bad terms?"

Dougald squirmed uncomfortably, for he'd caught the urgency of Blair's questions. "I'm not enough in Miss Weston's confidence . . . I mean, well, perhaps I'm wrong. I'll say this: I've an idea she may be glad to have a loyalist to talk to."

Blair took it all in and bit his tongue to keep from asking more questions. No matter how anxious he was, he wasn't going to force Dougald into betraying a confidence or gossiping. So he said merely, "But you don't object to giving her my message? No. Well then, relay it, and speak as earnestly as you can for me. Now, about your journey. Can you travel by daylight, or is your route safer by night? I want you to leave now, if you can."

"If Captain Collet can supply me with a fresh horse, I'll go now. The poor beast I rode down is pretty well exhausted. He's a good horse but worn out. I'd be caught at the first challenge if I had to depend on him. It's a fair enough trade, for when he's fresh he's a fine gelding."

"I'll see you get a good piece of horseflesh under you," Blair promised. "Meanwhile you'd better eat. And take along some provisions."

Half an hour later Dougald rode out, promising to use a path some distance off the main road. His first job was to feel his way around an army on the march. Blair didn't envy him and wondered uneasily whether he had the experience to manage it. But there was no alternative to sending out raw men, and also no time to worry about it. With a quick shrug of the shoulders, Blair turned back to the task in hand. Sailors from the ships were dismounting the guns. Even as he came up to them they were starting to lower one away. They had attached heavy ropes to it. Some forty men took hold of the ropes. Others shoved it out of the embrasure. Grunting and cursing, they lowered it slowly to the shore below the fort. After hurrying down to the beach, they seized the ropes again and sweated it aboard a small barge. A boat's crew towed it out to the *Cruizer*. On the ship they rigged a tackle and hoisted the heavy gun aboard. The lieutenant in charge of the crew evidently knew his business. The transfer, from start to finish, took just under two hours.

Blair glanced up at the afternoon sun. At this rate they would be at it most of the night, but it couldn't be helped. There was only one barge.

He found Collet talking to the *Cruizer's* commander, an elderly officer but, if Blair could trust his judgement, a pretty able man—perhaps lazy about routine, but good in a pinch. His crews, once given something to do, put their backs into it.

Collet introduced him, then reported, "The *Cruizer's* men are making good progress moving the guns. They should have them all aboard an hour before dawn. My men are getting up the small arms and supplies with a view to moving them."

"Let's hope we're not molested before dawn," Blair put in dryly. "If Ashe is embarking tomorrow, his men shouldn't be here for a couple of days. I'm much more concerned about Bob Howe's men from Brunswick. It's only twelve miles, and if he should decide to try to gain all the glory for himself he may get here tonight."

"With raw troops?" Collet demanded scornfully. "I'd be most surprised."

"You would be, indeed," Blair agreed with some scorn. "I hope you at least have scouts and pickets out to warn us of his advance."

"Sir," said Collet truculently, "I know my business."

"That's open to doubt, sir," said Blair. "May I remind you that you are a captain and I am a major? Now do you have scouts out?"

"No, sir. I did not regard it as necessary. Besides, if my men go out alone they may desert."

"Do you seriously mean you have none you can trust?"

"Perhaps three or four, sir."

"Then send out three or four, and be quick about it. I don't intend to be surprised here, with the ship's company scattered about unarmed and the fort lying defenceless."

Sullenly Captain Collet sent out a small patrol with instructions to report immediately the first sign of an advancing force.

While he was still seething with irritation Blair encountered Governor Martin. "What's the matter with this fellow Collet?" he demanded. "The man's an imbecile."

Martin defended his commander. "Oh no, sir, not an imbecile at all. He's a fine map maker and, I'm told, an accomplished engineer."

"He may be an expert with a pencil, but the man's a fool with troops. He's determined to do nothing in dismantling the fort. What's the matter with him?"

"I warned you," said the Governor, a touch of slyness in his tone, "that he's a very selfish man. His house and furniture are here in the fort. Now we are leaving the fort, the rebels are sure to burn them."

Blair silently wondered how a man could in conscience take the honoured name of loyalist and yet serve first his personal ends. Thank God, he breathed, not all our supporters are like that!

After darkness came on, the *Cruizer's* men worked by lanthorn light, weary now but dogged. At four in the morning the last cannon was at the water's edge, the barge in position to receive it. The men seized the ropes and heaved. The gun slid grudgingly part way aboard the barge. They paused for breath. As they began the final pull everything went wrong. One man's feet slipped. As he fell he struck two or three others and threw them off balance. At the same time the gun rolled. The barge tilted sharply up on its side. Off slid the gun and all the men into five feet of water. The barge smugly righted itself.

With the ropes attached, the cannon was not difficult to get out. But the men were wet and tired, their tempers frayed. It took almost an hour more to get the last gun aboard the Cruizer. By five-thirty, however, the fort was swept clean and the last boats were going out to the Peggy and the Cruizer. Howe's men were too late for the prize.

When Dougald rode out of the fort in the late afternoon, his first care was his horse. Captain Collet had given him a tall, raw-boned mare, not handsome but, Dougald soon decided, both strong and fast. She would do. He felt better.

As a matter of fact, he had not been quite frank with Blair. On his way down he had noticed several trails leading off the road to the south, and he guessed that they connected somehow, but he had only drawn on this surmise when he spoke of a back trail. He decided he'd run the risk of using the main road for two or three miles before turning off to grope his way through the woods. It ought to be a safe manoeuvre, for the Whigs wouldn't complete the march from Brunswick that afternoon and they would not camp where the sight of their fires might warn the fort of their coming.

He went forward cautiously, studying each open stretch before he ventured into it, and covered two and a half to three miles without seeing a soul. A curving, wooded stretch of the road lay ahead. He decided to chance it, keeping a sharp eye out for places where he could slip off the road into the trees and stopping often to listen. In this way he covered another mile. He was coming to the end of the woods. Ahead lay a long stretch of meadow, on both sides of the road.

He pulled over among the trees on the south side of the road, dismounted and led his horse to the very edge of the woods. Here he stopped and studied the road ahead. In the distance he heard the sound of a drum. At the same time, at the far end of the meadow, Howe's foot soldiers came into view. Passing them, a dozen horsemen swung around the bend; they were bearing down on Dougald at a canter. They had not seen him, he knew. They were coming only to reconnoitre the road he had just traversed. But if he mounted and rode crashing through the woods they might hear him and give chase.

There was only one thing to do. Quickly and quietly he led the mare behind a little hillock and into a thick copse. While the horsemen passed he stood at her head, ready to hold her jaws if she gave the least sign of nickering to the other horses.

After the horsemen had pounded by he felt less concern about his horse, Dougald stood caught up by troubling thoughts he hadn't expected. The sight of the alert scouts riding by had brought questions to his mind. The Whigs, he had to recognize, were just as sure they were right as the Tories, maybe surer. What if they were right? What if they were, as Moray was forever saying, trying to make something new and great here in America? The fussy Governor, the captain at the fort who wouldn't talk to him, what were they trying to do? Hold this country down under laws and orders from across the ocean, under a Hanoverian king. But, he assured himself, all the Tories weren't like the Governor and the captain. There was Blair, there was Allan MacDonald. He was with Allan. He was helping Blair at this moment. He had no right, and no reason, to doubt their wisdom.

The last of Howe's men passed by and disappeared around the first bend after the road entered the woods. Dougald waited patiently to be sure they were gone. Then he mounted and rode slowly through the woods to circle behind the meadow. People were likely to be riding between the troops and Brunswick all night. Even though the road might look empty, it was too dangerous from here on, at least until he got past Brunswick.

When darkness fell, he tethered the mare and lay down to sleep a few hours in a woods. He woke half an hour before dawn, munched some breakfast and prepared to be on his way. It was light in the east behind him as he started out, picking his way through broken woods.

An hour later, when it was full sunrise, a swamp forced him to come close to the road. He had the bad luck to round a bit of woodland almost on top of a patrol cooking breakfast at a tiny fire. Seven or eight men were lounging there. One of them jumped to his feet with his rifle cradled over his arm. "Hey, who're you?" he yelled in surprise.

Dougald raised one arm in friendly greeting. "I'm Sam Mac ..." he called, pronouncing a name unintelligibly, "carrying letters from Colonel Howe to Mr. Harnett. In a hurry, too." He spurred his horse and rode on, more than half expecting the thud of a bullet in his back.

At the names of Howe and Harnett all the man's suspicion evaporated. Dougald was far out of range before it occurred to him to wonder what a messenger in a hurry was doing coming out of the woods. It took a while, he reflected wryly, to learn to be suspicious, but next time he wouldn't be so easy.

On board the *Cruizer* there was nothing to do but keep on the alert and wait. Blair moved over from the schooner to the warship and made himself as comfortable as he could. Martin spent most of his time writing letters, long letters to Gage and Dartmouth, justifying his abandonment of the fort and painting rosy pictures of his plans for a rising in the back country. Collet slouched around the decks, alternating between sullen silence and angry diatribes against the cursed colonials. The captain of the *Cruizer*, on closer acquaintance, bore out Blair's first good opinion of him. He knew his trade of war. He and Blair watched developments on shore with lively interest.

As near as the two men could tell, the main body of Howe's force reached the fort about noon of the sixteenth, and invested it, though at some distance. His soldiers lurked in the woods and rarely showed themselves. There was no firing.

The next day nothing changed except that the colonials were a little less careful about concealing themselves. That night the two men on the *Cruizer* could see a ring of cooking-fires.

On the eighteenth they made out a flotilla of boats coming down the river, carrying Ashe's troops from Wilmington. The boats kept out of range of the

Cruizer's guns and landed above the fort. Blair estimated three hundred men. The whole force now gathering in the woods was above five hundred, as Dougald had reported.

The ships at anchor off the fort were put in readiness to beat off an attack by Ashe's boats in the unlikely event that the rebels should try to capture them. Blair took particular pains to put the schooner bearing the small arms in the safest position. The day passed in tense waiting.

After dark Ashe moved. His troops crept up to the walls of the fort. With a wild yell they charged the gate and poured in. They fought, Blair noted, like Indians. He could imagine how they had nerved themselves up to the assault and how let down they felt when they found not even a cat to oppose them. He smiled grimly to himself.

Now they were lighting torchs and beginning a systematic search. They wouldn't find much. The fort was stripped clean of anything useful to an army. As the torches moved about, Blair noticed Collet had come to the bulwarks to watch and was standing beside him.

The Whigs were setting fire to the barracks and to everything that would burn in the fort. Against the light of the fires, they were visible from the ship, busy at destruction. Now tongues of flames shot up at a little distance. Beside him, Collet was almost crying. "The rascals! The triple-damned rascals!" he moaned. "I knew they'd burn my house. There goes my furniture, everything I own."

In the morning, Fort Johnston was a smouldering, crumbling shell. Governor Martin stood on the deck of the *Cruizer* looking at it. "Here I am driven to a ship in the harbour. I'm determined to stay here and keep in touch with loyal men." His expression was wistful. "I wonder how long it will be before I set foot again on Carolina soil."

"It may be a very long time, Governor," Blair answered. "You know this is war. This is what happened in Boston. We may as well face it."

It was evening, just full dark, two nights after the fort had been burned. David MacDonald made his way stealthily to the stern of the Cruizer. Below him in the water a little dugout swung at the end of its painter. During two endless days of inaction David's restlessness, his longing for adventure, had been growing in him. That afternoon he had made up his mind to go ashore. He knew if he asked for permission it would be refused. In the afternoon he had noticed the dugout, looked again to make sure there was a paddle in it.

It was his passport to adventure. He had only to wait for dark. Now night had closed in. He pulled the dugout close in under the Cruizer's stern and retied the line. After a quick look around to make sure no one was watching, he went over the rail and slid down the rope to the waiting boat. It was easy.

With cautious strokes he paddled away, making for the shore a little above the ruined fort, where a patch of trees would offer hiding for his craft. The tide, he observed, was just about on the turn. When he came back in an hour or so he must remember it would be ebbing strongly. Ten minutes later he had pulled the light dugout up among the trees and was smoothing out the track he had left in the sand.

First he went to reconnoitre the woods where Howe's men had camped. They were gone. He found the ashes of their fires, nothing else. He didn't know whether they had gone back to Brunswick or only to Ashe's camp, a mile up the river. Anyhow, there was nobody around the fort.

He would go up and try to get a look at Ashe's camp, he decided. It was close to the shore. Should he go back and get the dugout, approach by water? He would get a better look from the woods. He ran a greater risk of discovery on land, but that only added spice to the adventure. Ashe would have some sentries in the woods, but he could easily elude them.

He began to work his way silently up-stream parallel to the bank of the river but well back from the shore. The going wasn't difficult and in twenty minutes or so he began to catch gleams of Ashe's camp-fires. He doubled his caution.

The encampment was in an open place running down to the shore. Dougald worked around to a small sand-hill behind the camp, crawling the last fifty yards on his hands and knees. He raised his head cautiously over the top of the hillock, and there before his eyes lay the camp.

Most of the men were already asleep, rolled in their blankets. Half a dozen men were on watch, sitting in the shadows with their rifles across their knees. Something was going on just back of the narrow beach. A big fire threw out a bright light. Near by, forty or fifty soldiers were hard at work, building something.

They had stacks of small logs cut into lengths of about a dozen feet. These a gang of men were arranging in rows and lashing together, with a few smaller poles placed crosswise to hold them firm. They looked like rafts. David wondered what Ashe wanted with rafts, since he had plenty of well-made boats.

Three or four of the rafts seemed to be done. A second gang was working on them. They were lashing on tall poles festooned with tow and half-barrels full of something sticky and gummy. One barrel had been broken and the stuff was oozing out. Finally David was able to recognize it: pine pitch.

Ashe's scheme was now clear. He was making fire-rafts. When the tide was ebbing, he would launch a score of them, hitched loosely together with light chain, set alight the pitch and tow and let them drift down flaming on the anchored ships. The chains would hold them against the helpless ships while the fire took hold. They would at least drive the *Cruizer* from her anchorage, and perhaps would destroy her altogether.

This was something the *Cruizer's* captain should know at once. David slid down out of sight behind the sand-hill and edged away into the woods. He went back a little more rapidly than he had come but cautiously, for all that. In fifteen or twenty minutes he was entering the upper edge of the patch of trees where he had left his boat. Well, he'd done it. He relaxed his watchfulness.

A voice spoke to him. "That you, Joe? This is the cross-grainedest night! Lost that bottle of rum we found in the fort. Would have sworn it was right in this hollow tree. Found an old dugout I don't want, hid in the bushes. Hey, Joe, why don't you say something?"

David had never hit an unsuspecting man before. He did now. The man was big and heavy but he had no warning. David smashed him on the jaw as if he were throwing the caber. The man collapsed and fell on his face. David's arm tingled clear to the shoulder and his hand hurt. He stood for a moment looking down at the inert patriot.

He had forgotten Joe. Joe's arm slid over his shoulder from behind and locked under his chin. Joe's other hand came over the other shoulder and began to add to the pressure on David's windpipe. It was quiet and efficient. David was fighting for air but he couldn't even gasp. Joe's arm was sinewy, and David's clawing hands could not budge it. His lungs were bursting. He could hear his heart beating; his eyes were bulging. Things were beginning to feel misty. He had to do something or he never could do anything.

Primitive instinct took over. He kicked back hard at Joe's shin. He could feel his heel hit and a momentary release of pressure on his throat. David lunged forward, holding hard to the arm under his chin, and putting all his strength into the heave. Joe came flying over his head in an involuntary somersault and lighted with a crash on his back. David snatched the breath he had been craving. But Joe was not through. He was turning toward David, coming up in a crouch. His left hand reached out and grabbed. Close together, half clinched, they traded heavy, grunting blows.

Behind him, David could hear the first man stirring, getting to his feet, muttering, "Didn't do nothing to you . . . and you hit me. Knife you for that." David knew he didn't have much time. He hit Joe hard in the pit of the stomach and doubled him up.

It gave David a start on the two patriots. He ran for his boat. He came to the place where he had left it. The marks were plain. But the boat wasn't there. His two antagonists were pounding through the trees in pursuit. David did not hesitate.

He ran down to the water's edge and plunged in. His clothes and shoes bothered him, but he had only a short swim. He could dimly make out the black shapes of the ships. The ebb was sweeping him down on them. He mustn't let it carry him past.

He remembered the line he had left dangling from the *Cruizer's* stern. He let the tide sweep him in against the stern, groped for the rudder post, braced against the suck of the tide and felt for the rope. At last his hand touched it. He got a firm hold and hailed the deck.

His third call brought feet pounding on the deck. Almost immediately he was hauled up, dripping, bruised and a little sheepish, but full of his discovery. Blair gave him a sharp scolding for sneaking ashore but admitted his report of the fire-rafts was worth having.

The mare was dead tired, but she had brought Dougald back. Campbelltown lay just ahead. It had been a gruelling trip for both of them. Whig patrols were growing bolder everywhere. Near Elizabethtown a party of horsemen had ordered him to stop, which he didn't choose to do, and pursued him for a mile or so, but, being ill mounted, they had dropped behind and given up. Dougald's hand dropped to the mare's shoulder as he blessed her for her speed. Once a bullet had come from cover and whined by his ear. He wondered how the hidden marksman could tell whether a target was Whig or Tory. Perhaps the man just shot at anyone riding by who didn't stop on call.

Dougald ran over the messages he had to deliver. Blair's word to Cecily Weston was by no means the most urgent, but she was here in Campbelltown. If he delivered it now it would save him a trip back. He decided to stop at Farquard Campbell's house and see her first. Maybe Farquard Campbell would lend him a fresh horse to carry him out to see Allan at Mount Pleasant and Alex MacLeod at Glendale.

It was cool and peaceful in the Campbell house as he waited for Cecily. When he sat down he realized that he was almost as tired as the mare. A great desire for sleep flowed through him and almost overwhelmed him.

Then Cecily Weston came into the room. "Dougald," she greeted him, "I'm so relieved you are back safe. Is David all right? I worried when Moira told me you had gone down the river."

"We were at Fort Johnston. James Blair came in on a schooner just as we arrived. David is staying with him a few days on the *Cruizer*." Dougald waited a second. He'd seen her hand clench involuntarily at the mention of Blair's name. What was the trouble between them? he wondered. Because Cecily said nothing, he went on as if he hadn't noticed. "The Whigs were marching against the fort. It couldn't be defended, so they decided to move everything out of it to the ships and let them take it. Mr. Blair gave me a message for you."

Gently and slowly he repeated Blair's words, almost exactly as he'd memorized them at the fort. "Of course," he concluded, "there's no way to give him an answer, so you don't need to tell me anything. He wanted you to know he was coming and he hoped you will give him your help."

Still Cecily said nothing and Dougald blushed. "I hinted," he said, trying to make things easier for her, "he might be one suitor too many for you in Campbelltown though your loyalty to the Crown would work in his favour."

It at least made Cecily rouse herself. "What did he say?"

Dougald grinned. "He wasn't very well pleased. But he didn't say anything, just asked me to plead his cause well. I hope I have. We need—" he couldn't stifle a great yawn—"officers like him around here. Excuse me. I didn't realize till now how tired I am."

"And I keep you standing over a message from James Blair! 'Tis you who must excuse me. Can I offer you a bed here?" She was brisk and gave no indication of her feelings.

Dougald thanked her but refused. He would stay in Cross Creek. He wanted to start early in the morning for Mount Pleasant and Glendale, and if he was to see Moira, as he wanted to, it would have to be before night.

At Cecily's order, Campbell's stable-boy saddled a fresh horse for him. He mounted wearily and rode on toward Cross Creek. In the town he decided to stop at the tavern, leave his saddle-bags and make sure they could give him a bed to himself for the night.

As he made his arrangements with the taverner, the man looked at him curiously. "You're one of the MacDonald twins, aren't you? Never know whether you're you or your brother." He laughed at his own wit. "Somebody else from your place is here. Allan MacDonald came in about half an hour ago. I think he's in the bar."

"Good!" said Dougald. "I'll find him." Now he wouldn't have to hurry out to Mount Pleasant to give Allan his messages. Tomorrow he could sleep as long as he liked. He'd see Allan right away and then go to Moira, with his mind easy.

He found Allan reading a gazette, his elbows on the bar and a tumbler of whisky close to his hand. He looked up with a quick smile of surprise and pleasure when Dougald spoke to him. "Well, lad," he exclaimed, "so you got back safe! How's David? Is he all right?"

Dougald explained quickly about David's staying behind with Major Blair and the Governor. "He'll be along in about a week. He'll have a hard ride. Whigs are out in a dozen places. I was lucky I had a fast horse."

"Well," said Allan easily, "we'll alter all that when we raise our Highland regiments up here. The Whigs won't dare to show their faces."

"I hope so," said Dougald. "Drink up your whisky and let's find a private place. I've many things to tell

you." Suddenly he felt more mature and more aware
of how things were really going in the province than
the man before him. He didn't remember ever feeling
this way before. Perhaps it was because he was so
weary. He didn't know that he liked this new matur-
ity.

Allan obligingly reached for the tumbler of whisky,
then paused with it in his hand. "You saw the Governor? You gave him my message?"

"That's part of what I have to tell you." Dougald
was patient. "Yes, I saw him, and a fine stew he was
in, too."

Now Allan's curiosity was aroused. He gulped
down his drink, grimaced and blew a couple of times.
"This native whisky seizes a man's throat," he said.
"Come along, Dougald lad. I want to hear everything.
Let's go to my room." He started briskly out of the
bar, with Dougald following more slowly.

Sitting on Allan's bed, Dougald began simply with
an account of what had happened up to the time he
had left the fort. "You see," he finished, "how weak
the Governor is, and how much stronger the Whigs
are near the coast."

Next he turned to the plans for the future and the
messages he carried to Allan. "The schooner that
brought Major Blair down from New York carried muskets for us up here. With the country so disturbed it
will be very difficult to convey them up the river.

"Governor Martin requested General Gage to
restore his own rank of colonel but Gage denied him.
He also asked for a colonel's commission for you and
a major's for Alex MacLeod. These also General
Gage refused to allow." He hurried on with his recita-
tion, knowing that Allan was struggling to conceal his
disappointment. "He is sending down from Boston
two of his own officers, Donald MacDonald and
Alexander MacLeod—not our Alex, of course. They
will be in command. He permitted Governor Martin
to commission you and Alex as captains but not as
higher officers. I was instructed to tell you all this."

Now he waited for Allan's comment, but Allan
simply told him to go on. He did so in a hesitant

voice. "Blair and the Governor realize it will be a disappointment to you to have the chief command given to another. They are helpless to change it, since General Gage is in full military command. They particularly asked me to make it plain it was not their doing."

Allan got to his feet and paced back and forth in the narrow space of the little room. Finally he admitted, "This is hard news, lad. Is anyone in our neighbourhood to be above me?"

"No, only General Gage's own officers, who will be here soon."

"Do they want me to go on rousing the Highlanders and recruiting them?"

"They are more eager than ever. Will you agree, now others are preferred above you?"

Allan stopped his pacing and turned to face Dougald fully. "Aye, lad, I'd go on with the work in any case. I want the land quiet and secure. How else can it be made so?"

Dougald remembered the faces of Bob Howe's men marching against the fort. He thought of Captain Collet's disdain of all colonials. He gave voice to a nagging thought. "I only wish the King's representatives would tell us what they are doing. It would be easier to serve the Crown with a whole heart if they trusted us more. Sometimes they make us pawns."

Allan dropped his hand on the boy's shoulder. "Nonsense, lad," he said heartily. "We're at the centre of their plans. I can say it though I've just been denied the command I expected. And we'll have our reward. No, lad, the Crown is the only cause. Think no more of it."

Dougald nodded unhappily. "I know. I shouldn't doubt."

Allan began pressing him for details of the affair at the fort. He told him as much as he could remember. Now he had delivered his messages, his fatigue began to wash over him again, threatening to overwhelm him. He yawned repeatedly, and found it hard to keep his eyes open.

At last Allan noticed how sleepy he was. "Aren't

you about ready to turn in and have a sleep?" he asked.

"I want to see Moira first," Dougald said. "She'll want to know I'm back safe." He grinned. "Besides, I'll relish a word with the lass."

It was deep dusk when Dougald reached the MacQueens' house. Moira's uncle opened the door, revealing a neat room cheerful in the lamplight. As he spoke Dougald's name there was a rush behind him and Moira thrust past to welcome Dougald home. Her hands went to his shoulders. "You're back safe. Oh, Dougald, I worried so."

At her touch he was whole again. It was worth all the fatigue to have her to come home to. The very sight of her auburn hair, of her sea-green eyes soft with feeling for him, did him good. For a long minute they stood looking at each other, her hands still on his shoulders.

They had private things to say to each other. He needed to be alone with her. How could he arrange ... ? Moira turned her head and spoke to her aunt. "Aunt Jessie, weren't you and Uncle Will going next door to the MacLeans? You said something about grey yarn Mrs. MacLean had for stockings."

Fussy, grey-haired Aunt Jessie came forward. "Why, no, child, I don't remember ... why, yes, now I recall. We were going to step over there. Come on, Will." She began putting a shawl around her shoulders and pushing her bewildered husband toward the door while she was still talking. "You're so particular about your winter stockings, Will. You should see if the yarn Mrs. MacLean has is heavy enough. These young people can get along without us for a few minutes."

Will MacQueen's eyes lighted with sudden comprehension at last. "Aye, aye, a sensible precaution," he said as he followed his wife to the door.

When the door closed, Moira sat down in a big chair. "Poor Dougald," she said, "you look exhausted. Come here." She motioned to the footstool in front of her.

Dougald dropped down on it, let his head sink into her lap. "Aye, I'm bone-tired."

Her cool fingers gently stroked his forehead.

"Moira, it's heaven to come home to you." He sighed deeply. "I've learned how much I need you, now, all the time. I wanted to have a house ready, lands to give you. You know how we've dreamed. Now, with these troubles, it might be years, forever. Moira darling, I can't wait so long. I'm too tired to hold out. Will you take me, though I can offer little?"

"Rest, sweet, rest." Her light fingers moved slowly over his closed eyes. "I'd take you with nothing and no place to lay our heads. Oh, Dougald, I don't care about things! We can get them together. It's you I want."

A great peace flooded over him, merging with his fatigue. He felt her stir, then her lips on his temple.

26

Flora's Quest

MOIRA stood at the window, looking out over the rolling fields of Mount Pleasant. Behind her she heard the satisfied rattle of Aunt Jessie's teacup and the familiar *tsk* which denoted relish. Then came Aunt Jessie's hearty voice: "My mouth was athirst, Mrs. Mac-Donald, for a good cup of tea. In Cross Creek a body can't find any. It's all that dreadful yapon mixture with its bitter taste."

Flora's low voice answered, "Oh? I didn't know that. It's awful the way I never get down to the settlement and learn what's going on. But, as I was going to say, please have another cup." There was a sound of poured liquid and then the tinkle of a spoon against a fragile bone-china saucer. Flora was still talking. "We never want for tea. Then too, only a week or so ago the Governor sent us six chests. . . . Poor man."

"Aye, a shame it is—his being exiled to the Cruizer. I don't hold with Martin, no more than with those upstarts who oppose him." That was Aunt Jessie again. Moira had heard these views many times. Yes, here was the inevitable next sentence: "I say we Scots should keep out of this. Months ago I told Mac-Queen I'd never speak to him again if he took sides." A significant pause followed. Then: "MacQueen and I are still speaking."

Moira knew that she was sulking like a child and that she ought to go sit down politely. She wiped her eyes and sniffed quietly. She most certainly did not feel like talking to them.

Only yesterday Moira had been singing about the house, laughing over nothing, making plans and changing them every five minutes. One fact was real to her, and she'd thought of nothing else: she and Dougald would be married soon. Her heart was set on an August wedding—or September at the latest. To-day she felt only despondence and resentment. On every hand someone was opposing the marriage.

First it had been Aunt Jessie. She'd had a dozen objections ranging from the incompleted trousseau to the disjointed nature of the times. That hadn't too much bothered Moira; there were others on whom she could count for support. She and Dougald had already made plans to ride up to Mount Pleasant together. They would tell Flora, and receive her blessing. Moira's throat had choked up just imagining the scene.

The plan had been spoiled inadvertently by Allan. News of the attack on Fort Johnston, of Martin's remove and of a secret meeting had to go to the outlying farms. Dougald was sent as courier directly from Cross Creek. He'd ridden off, although she'd clung to him, pleading, "This once, Dougald, you tell Allan no. We're more important than this evil message of war." She hadn't been able to hold him back, for he would not fail Allan. Watching him go, she'd felt her knees shake as the weight of premonition settled over her. Not one minute since had that image of Dougald galloping away faded from her imagination.

Yet she'd gone on with the original plan as best she could, calling on Aunt Jessie as companion for the journey to Mount Pleasant. Even that had been opposed. Aunt Jessie thought the projected visit scandalous. "I don't care if Dougald can't go home at once!" she'd exclaimed. "'Tis not for you to announce the engagement. The very idea of the bride-to-be rushing up to her betrothed's home to tell his family about it!"

Remembering Aunt Jessie's arguments and her own replies, Moira clenched her teeth. She had wanted to see Flora because Flora would aid her. Her strong will had prevailed.

The next morning they'd started, and for the whole eighteen miles Aunt Jessie had grumbled. Now, however, as Moira noted bitterly, Aunt Jessie was in the best of spirits. Flora had aligned herself with the opposition.

Again tears started and Moira pulled out a hand-kerchief. Behind her there was a lull in Aunt Jessie's conversation, and Flora softly called out, "Moira. Come sit with us. Please."

Slowly Moira turned, keeping her reddened eyes downcast. She felt torn. Never would she be able to hold herself away from Flora, who was so good. Yet, right now, she was close to hating her. Nothing in the world but Flora's no could stand long in the way of the marriage. It was a temptation to wring permission out of Flora, no matter how unfair the means. Moira, with her head still bent, sat down. She pressed her lips together to keep herself from speaking out her anger and hurt.

"Forgive me," Flora began as soon as she'd poured a cup of tea and placed it on the little table beside Moira's chair, "for going over the subject again. I know it's painful, but I feel I must make you understand. I—both your aunt and I—favour this marriage. But we want it to be a happy one. All we ask is a few months, dear, a few months that will perhaps insure your happiness...."

Flora's gentle voice trailed off. Moira knew some sign from her was expected. Stubbornly she kept her face averted. There was a rustle of taffeta and a light hand touched her shoulder. Stiffly Moira suffered it, but did not respond.

Quietly Flora went on. "You say you don't care that Dougald isn't settled; you say he now doesn't care. How long will a man like Dougald be able to endure being a husband who doesn't protect and provide? Not long, my dear. He's innately too responsible."

Again Flora paused and Moira refused to answer. What could she say without capitulating? Flora's words were almost the same she had often used about Dougald while she was waiting for him to reach a decision. But couldn't Flora, couldn't they all see that Dougald had changed? The urgency of the time had made him different.

"All I'm asking—and I'm asking it for your

sake—is that you at least have a home to go to. Stability is the very heart of marriage, and a home of your own is the basis of stability. There you can explore each other and put down your roots." Flora's skirt moved and Moira knew she'd turned away slightly. Almost to herself Flora was saying, "Allan and I have been wanderers from home to home. I've furnished so many rooms, thinking 'now we're settled; our lives will ripen in this good place.' Then before long we've picked up and gone on again."

The skirt swished again and the hand was put back on Moira's shoulder. "Mayhap I make too much of a home. But without ... what have you? You'll have your adventure. It's not enough. I know; I've had adventure."

"Exactly what I always say," Aunt Jessie broke in with vigour. "These children are excited by the very haphazard nature of their romance. They like the heart-breaking separation ended by sudden visits in the night. That's all well and good for courting. It's bad for marriage."

There was a silence. Flora finally brought herself to say, "Aye ... it might well destroy it. The purpose of marriage is for a man and woman to be together."

Suddenly Moira's resentment welled up. Was Flora daring to pretend that she and Allan were together? Was she daring to hold herself up as an example? She turned her face up at last and steadily watched Flora, who had returned to her chair.

"You know our Alex is a land agent now," Flora said. "He's looking for a new plantation for us, and Allan with him. That's why Allan's away——"

"Is it?" Moira interrupted, her voice high.

"Why ... of course." Flora flushed, but went on evenly. "I was going to say that Alex could just as well hunt for a plantation for you as well as for us. Or, if we move soon, you could have Mount Pleasant. It's a profitable farm. We're leaving it only because I want to be near my family."

Clutching the arms of her chair, Moira leaned forward. Her lips quivered in anger as she said, "Alex won't find anyone a plantation. He's not a land agent.

And like as not Allan's never so much as looked at land on his journeys. He's too——"

"Hush! Moira, we must be going." Aunt Jessie suddenly heaved to her feet and fussed with her shawl. "There's no call for rudeness."

Moira had not moved. She still leaned forward with her eyes intently fixed on Flora.

Flora met her gaze. "Please, Jessie, wait," she said. "Moira, explain yourself!"

Moira defiantly finished her interrupted statement: "He's too busy recruiting for the Hanoverian."

Flora sank back in her chair. ". . . recruiting for the Hanoverian?" she whispered. Her arm made a quick, nervous jerk and her tea-cup crashed to the floor. She didn't so much as look at it. It was as if she hadn't heard it. How could she not? Moira wondered irrelevantly; the brittle crash of it hangs on the air.

The moment was too tense. Again Moira lashed out, glad at last to be rid of a grievance that had, during the last month, grown like a cancre in her. "Yes, recruiting! That's what Allan's doing! You talk about stability and being together. Are you and Allan together? And what do you do for stability? Your husband's stirring up a war my Dougald will have to fight. He doesn't want to! When we were last together, when we decided to be married, do you know what he said to me? He said, 'I've no quarrel with this land. But now I have to fight—for Allan, and Flora and others I love and am indebted to. Help me do it, Moira!'" She stopped for breath, shuddered and went on in a lower voice. "I want to help Dougald. Together he and I will face this war you are all hiding your faces from. We'll have a real marriage—the kind you just described. We'll be together."

While Moira spoke Flora had sat as if frozen. Now she slowly slid to the edge of her chair, reached down and gathered up the jagged pieces of china one by one. Her fingers moved precisely; she put every splinter in the saucer, rose and placed the shattered cup on the fire-place top.

Moira suddenly burst into tears. "I'm sorry. Oh ... I'm sorry!"

The silence, ruptured only by Moira's sobs, was worse than the crash of the tea-cup. Aunt Jessie, plunging in to face the situation squarely, did not help much. "I must say," she said with forced briskness, "that I'm relieved to find you didn't know, Flora MacDonald. There are many of us folks who've said to each other, 'And what is it that's come over Flora MacDonald—supporting a King she should hate?' 'Tis a burden off my mind to know it's all Allan's doing. At least it's not you who's setting Scot against Scot. For there are some of us, you know, who'll have no part of this fight, no matter what you and Allan do."

"Does Allan tell them I am for the Hanoverian?" Flora's voice was low.

"I wouldn't know what he tells them. I don't attend those meetings he calls. But I hear things. Only last week my neighbour Mrs. MacLean said to me, 'I can't believe MacLean and I need to take sides in this patriot-loyalist battle. But if Flora MacDonald thinks it right we should fight, mayhap——' "

"You may tell Mrs. MacLean——" Flora cut off her impulsive reply. "Nay. Forgive me. I wish to be left alone." She reached for the ornate bell cord and pulled. "A gillie will bring round the coach."

Moira, who had stifled her crying and was trying to think of a way to make amends, was grateful for her aunt's next action. Mrs. MacQueen said nothing; she merely walked to Flora, squeezed her arm as women do when they feel for each other, and turned to leave. "Come, Moira," she called over her shoulder.

Before Mrs. MacQueen was out of the room Moira was kneeling before Flora. "Forgive me. Please forgive me. I should not have told you ... promised I wouldn't. Allan himself asked me not to. He loves you, and only wants to protect you."

It was several seconds before Flora answered. At last she touched Moira's hair and bade her get up. "You'd best go home, Moira. But . . . don't blame yourself. I would have learned about it soon anyway."

After they had gone, Flora sat alone. Katie came to clear away the tea things. Flora did not rouse. Katie came again to open a window to let in the cooling evening air. Still Flora sat abstracted. At last, entering for a third time with a sealed message addressed to Allan, Katie said, "Mistress Flora, what be the matter?"

Absently taking the letter and then running her finger around its edges, Flora answered, "Nothing, Katie—at least nothing you can help me with." She rose then and seemed to see the envelope for the first time. "Who brought this?"

"Two men, mistress. Rough-looking fellows smeared with sweat and dirt. They wanted the master, but finally believed he wasn't here and gave it to me. They looked like the ruffians one is forever seeing roaming around the countryside these days."

Flora nodded. "You may go, Katie."

"Shall I get supper as usual?"

"Aye, as usual. I imagine there'll be just Jamie and I for supper again tonight."

When the door had closed Flora sank back wearily into her chair. She felt defenceless, cold, exposed to raw winds. Moira had crashed through the protecting wall Flora had built around her home. The destructive forces gathering momentum as they swept across the land seemed to her to be converging on Mount Pleasant. Flora felt defeat, but no anger—not against Moira anyway. Why should the child be condemned for speaking the truth? A great gap had opened between Allan and herself. They were at cross purposes, deceiving each other.

Momentary fury at Allan's deception made Flora stand up, rip the sealed paper open in her rage. Why should she not violate his privacy? He'd left her but this one mode of knowing what he was doing. Unless, of course, she was to run about the countryside asking the neighbours. That she would never do, for his sake as well as her own.

Her hands trembled and, drawing the letter from
its folder, she tore it. She tried to hold the halves
steadily together but couldn't. With a breathless gasp
she ran to the escritoire and laid the torn pieces side
by side. By leaning heavily on her hands she could
press the papers flat and hold them in place. She discovered then, when she tried to read, that she was
crying.

The words, written in a small, slanting back-hand,
were blurred. The blurring did not soften the message
of the words that leaped out at her: "Allan MacDonald of Mount Pleasant ... intention to raise troops to
support ... ministry against Americans ... services
to Governor Martin ..." Flora glanced to the signature: THE WILMINGTON COMMITTEE OF SAFETY.
Her fist pounded down on the boldly scrawled title.
"Safety!" she cried aloud. "Danger!" Only then did
she know that at least half of her sickness was the
sickness of fear. Bigger than hurt, bigger than hatred
of the Hanoverian was fear for Allan. Her first prayer
in this crisis was "Dear God, protect him!"

She walked in agitation about the room, sometimes
pausing to re-read the cease-and-desist order. Mrs.
MacLean's words came back to her: ". . . if Flora
MacDonald thinks it right we should fight ..." Flora
began to realize the scope of Allan's influence. It was
not merely himself he was endangering, nor those
close to him—Dougald, Moira, Sandy, Jamie, herself.
It was the whole Scots people in the valley. How well
she knew them! In these sons of border feuders and
fierce old-world retainers there was a love of martial
airs and pipes. They'd lived in peace here in America,
but they'd not stilled their inborn lust for battle. All
that was needed was the rising of a chief they loved.
That, and a few notes from Dougald's pipe. They'd
snatch up their claymores and die in a war they had
no reason to be in. "Dear God," she prayed then, "let
the claymore remain sheathed! Let the clan war-cries
remain unshouted. Protect us from self-destruction."

She sat at the desk and leaned her head down on
her crossed arms. In that tired mood she tried to
think what she must do. There was, she knew, one

certain solution. She could speak out publicly, proclaim to all the Scots that she was not with Allan in his loyalty to England. She could ally herself with Farquard Campbell. She could ally herself with John Bethune, who preached neutrality from his pulpit. She dismissed this possibility as soon as it came to her. It would destroy Allan.

Yes, it would destroy Allan and also the happiness she and Allan had found. In this new home they'd come together in secure sympathy and sharing that they'd never had before. She'd been happier than ... yes, happier than on Skye. America had held a promise out to them and had already begun to fulfil it. In answering the challenge of the new land, she and Allan had found true harmony. Like the other New World Scots they had begun to prosper and to forget anxiety. Every time she'd seen the earth turned by the plough, or heard the ring of the farmer's ax striking down a tree, she'd felt another seal had been put on her happiness.

But now Flora perceived a truth about her happiness: it was based on isolation, retreat. When there were peace and plenty in the land she and Allan could not conflict. But, as Cecily had said, there are times when the man and his politics cannot be separated. With politics laying claim to human hearts, the one antagonism that had ever existed between herself and Allan was revived. Their natural political loyalties went in opposite directions.

Slowly Flora rose; she pressed her hands to her temples. She saw that the decision facing her now was much more complex than the one that had faced her in the '45. Then there had been just herself. She could serve where she would. Now there was herself and Allan. Therefore her choice was both more difficult and more meaningful.

As she lowered her hands and let them hang limply at her sides she realized she was nearing the lonely time of decision. Suddenly she wanted help with it. She wanted Lady Margaret; she wanted to draw on her wisdom. Margaret had opposed her husband in the '45. Margaret knew why Flora had followed Allan to

America. "Oh, God," Flora cried aloud, "I thought in fleeing to this country I'd left the past behind! It rises to torment me—in an oblique way I cannot fully comprehend."

The door burst open and Katie ran to her, taking her in her arms. "Mistress . . . Flora . . ."

Like a child Flora rested her head on Katie's shoulder and wept. "Good Katie, comfort me."

"There, there," Katie crooned. "Now tell me what it's about if you can."

Flora lifted her head and tried to smile. "Old friends we are, Katie. We've lived through much together. You're the only old friend I have here. No, there's still old Neil—worn, tired, but devoted. You two stand now for all the loved ones out of the past."

"I'm honoured, mistress, if you consider me a friend. I feel so."

Slowly Flora walked toward the window. "I was yearning for Lady Margaret just when you came in. I need my family now, and those who were with me in the '45. Katie," she cried with sudden resolve, "call Neil. Tell him to saddle horses. I'll go to Hugh. Yes, first to Anne, and then to Hugh."

"Oh, mistress, not alone! Wait till the master returns, or one of the lads."

"Do you know, Katie," Flora asked with a rueful smile, "when any of them will be back?"

Katie shook her head and said nothing.

"Well, then, I'll go with Neil. Help me get ready."

When, three days and two nights later, Flora turned into the road to her stepfather's house, she was sitting erectly in her saddle. The trimness of her blue velvet riding-habit, the jauntiness of the little white plume in her bonnet and the composure of her features belied any fear or uncertainty. Yet she and Neil had made a frightening journey from Mount Pleasant to Glendale and, now, on to Hugh's home. She now knew how foolhardy she'd been to set out with only an old man as protector. Anger against Allan and Flora MacDonald was hot in many hearts. One farmhouse had refused her a night's refuge. There an irate woman had denounced her as a turncoat. "Heroine of the '45! Now you see a chance to be heroine of the '75, do you? Go on with you! We want no war." The door had slammed loudly.

At another place she'd stopped to drink from a spring. As she leaned over the refreshing water she'd heard a scornful voice say, "I thought the Allan MacDonalds always drank tea! Governor's tea!" That time it was Flora who had turned her back. The taunter would not see her cry; no one would hear her disavow Allan.

The entire journey had been one of stabbing realizations. This land, she saw, was not one of peace and plenty, but one of clashing hatreds. North Carolina, probably all America, was on the verge of a death struggle between the old and the new. How ironic it was! Allan had fled Skye, saying, "Here we're caught in a vise between the old and the new." Well, now he was not caught in it; he was pressing his great weight down on the lever and forcing the vise closed. The image terrified Flora. She saw her people, her dear Scots—Allan among them—crushed. Unable to keep her thoughts wholly to herself, she'd described her vision to Neil. "Mistress Flora," he'd said sorrowfully, "there was a day on which I told the lads a man has to change with the times. There's some that could do it—the young folk mostly, like David and Dougald. There's some that never will be able to—older folk like me and the master."

Flora wondered whether Neil knew how much that statement had helped her. For the first time since she'd learned what Allan was doing she felt sympathy, understanding for him. He had faced a fearful challenge alone. But oh, she wailed within herself, he should have talked with me! I would not have let him choose the wrong way.

Without warning Flora's horse bolted. She was nearly thrown from the saddle, for she'd let the reins lie slack in her hands. A desperate grab and natural good horsemanship saved her. She clung to the horse's neck, speaking soothingly and wondering in fear if a marauder in the bushes had frightened the horse. A second horse pounded up to her and brown strong hands caught the reins. Flora was afraid to look up. Now she knew how often people were attacked on lonely roads. A steady familiar voice reassured her. "It's all right, Mrs. MacDonald—just a rabbit."

Gratefully Flora thanked Pete. To herself she thanked Anne, who'd insisted on sending another man with Flora for the rest of the journey. "I wish I could send more, but I can't leave our place undefended," Anne had cried in fright. Poor Anne, terrified and alone. She too was seeing her faith defeated; frantically she clutched little Norman to her and wept at the frustration of her hopes for him. "I dream at night that they've killed him. Our men bring in stories of rapes and murders on the road. In the daytime I can tell myself they exaggerate, but when I walk the floors at night I believe the stories of atrocity. I think of Alex, and wonder whether he lies stabbed in some pocosin. I run to awaken Norman just to hear him cry with life."

Flora had been glad she did not have to break to Anne the news of Alex's activities. When she mentioned the subject Anne had said listlessly, "I know all about it now. He didn't tell me. I found out just as you did—by accident. One night three men pounded open the door. They just wanted to leave a warning. If Alex continued as intelligence officer for Martin, he and his family would suffer." Then had come the plaintive, almost childish cry that sounded so much like Anne when she was little: "Mother, what will I do? How can I stop Alex? He mustn't endanger himself and us like this. And Father—how can you bear it?"

Flora had been able only to hold her gently and confess, "I don't know that I can bear it."

"You'll stop him, won't you? Yes, that's it! You can make Father give up this madness. And if Father does, Alex will. Please, Mother." Anne had sobbed brokenly and clung to Flora. "We all depend on you."

Ahead Flora saw Hugh's comfortable house. She spurred her horse to reach it quickly, for she felt how near she was to breaking down. Responsibility for Anne, Moira and so many others pressed down on her. She had thought she was at the age when she could sit still, let younger ones work out the tensions of life. But that was impossible, she saw. Strife was dismembering clans and families, and Allan was at the centre of the strife. For the love she bore him and also her people she must find a way to restore unity and peace among the Scots without destroying them forever in her own home. She had to find her course soon; already, in refusing to answer the angry farmwoman, the taunter at the well and Anne, she had tacitly approved Allan's actions.

Now behind Hugh's comfortable white house, Flora could see a dozen or so workers ambling in slowly from the fields, their day's strenuous labour done. In the air there was the jingle of harness chains as horses moved briskly toward the barn and a binful of corn. Flora reined and tried to distinguish a familiar figure among the men. They were all gillies or slaves. She started forward again, and in turning her horse looked toward the orchard on her, left. There stood Hugh, gazing at the fruit-laden cherry and apple trees. She was shocked to realize he'd not heard her approach, and shocked also to see him leaning on a cane. Age has overtaken him at last, she thought. He's no longer the keenest, strongest man ever known on Skye.

At her second loud call he turned, and a joyful smile came to his face. He hobbled toward her, his heavy shoulders, still broad, bent forward. He still wore the patch over his blind eye; his face was more hawklike than ever. Flora wondered whether this old Hugh looked, as they'd said the young one did, like the great Somerled MacDonald, from whom he was descended.

She smiled as he reached for her hands to help her dismount. He was, despite age, still the courteous Highland gentleman he'd always been. And no doubt within the stooped body the Highland temper and fierce courage still raged from time to time.

"Hugh ... Father," she said softly.

His voice shook, more with emotion than age, as

he welcomed her. "This is the best surprise I could have had. I've been thinking of you so often lately. You must have received my thought."

"I've thought of you too. I came because I need you."

He hurried her as fast as he could into the house. While she was washing the dust from her face and brushing off her clothes he called in gillies and ordered a banquet. He sent, too, for his grandson Ian. "Tell the young master to come right in. The work can wait, but Flora MacDonald can't."

Flora, coming down the stairs, heard the order. "I'm eager to see Ian. He must have grown tall by now."

"Aye, a sturdy lad and a good one," Hugh agreed as he led her into the great-room. From the doorway he had to kick back the rug, and a second later he pushed some grimy boots out of the way with his cane. "A bachelor's house, Flora. We need a woman to straighten us out. Your dear mother would be horrified if she saw this disorder." He took her hands again. "Now that you'll be with us for a while, you can take care of us."

"I wish I could, Hugh," Flora said sadly, "but I must return home at once. I told you I came in need. As soon as you have told me what to do, I shall go back."

"Not tonight?"

"No, but tomorrow." She paused, sighed, then added, "I'd thought we'd soon be moving near you. Now I doubt I shall ever be near my family."

Hugh seemed to wither at the words. "I've been waiting for you so long. I've thought maybe you could help me live out these years that I drag about with me." He silenced her dismayed protest by waving his veined, swollen-jointed hand. "I lost my zest for living when your mother died. I thought by coming here I'd regain it. Alexander said I wouldn't. Lady Margaret too. They said I'd carry my grief with me wherever I went. It's been true."

Flora rose and stood, her hands clasped before her. "They understood many things. I've been yearning

for Margaret all this past week. God bless her. I hope
she's well."

For some time Hugh sat with his head sunk forward on his chest, and Flora walked slowly about,
touching guns that hung on the wall, each with a
story she knew, or blowing dust from small objects that
betokened Skye and Armadale. The light had grown
dim in the room before Hugh finally raised his head
and said, "Tell me your trouble, Flora."

She sat down before him and in a strained voice
told about Allan. When she had finished she asked,
"What shall I do?"

Hugh leaned forward, his knotty hands on his
cane. "What do you want to do, Flora?"

She opened her hands in a helpless gesture. "Everything. Everything that contradicts." Nervously she
got up and walked about again. "I want to say to the
whole world, 'I hate the Hanoverian! We Scots owe
him nothing! Let him be defeated!' But that would be
siding with the rebels. Worse yet, it would be opposing Allan." She whirled and clutched Hugh's shoulder. "Why has he done this to me? This intolerable
position! He gambles with my love for him! Counts
on my remaining silent as he brings on war! And I
will. Only I can't. Not only he and I, but many Scots
here in North Carolina are in hazard. I have to think
of them too."

Hugh reached up and took her hand. He pulled
her around so she would face him. "What do you
want most, Flora?" He looked at her closely, his
uncovered eye glittering blackly, compellingly.

Slowly she answered, "Most? Most I want peace
and my husband with me in peace. These years
should have brought restful autumn. War is bleak and
endless winter."

"Have you told Allan this? You blame him for not
coming to you, telling you. Why should you not have
gone to him?"

Flora looked at Hugh a long time. Briefly she was
angry. She started to say, "I couldn't talk to him as
long as I didn't know." But she held back the words.
If she was honest, she had to admit she did know—

not that Allan was recruiting but that unrest was growing and he was troubled about it. She had refused to admit that a time for decision was at hand. She'd never spoken to Allan, had even forbidden talk of the general dissension. Recently she'd been careful not to ask where Allan and the lads were going when they rode away. She'd told herself she was leaning, as she'd promised to lean, on Allan. Never had she admitted to herself that she was trying to avoid contact with something she feared.

She had talked to others, but not to Allan. There was John Bethune, the pastor. He'd come to warn her that her lads spoke their minds too freely, that they would soon be standing in direct opposition to both neutrals and patriots. He'd warned her that many Scots looked to Allan and to that General MacDonald up in Boston as chieftains who could guide them. He'd pointed out that Allan and the general had always in the past defended the King. Yes, Bethune had tried to make her act. He'd said, "Neutrality must be active. Those of us who want to keep clear of this rebellion against the Crown must speak out against rebellion. I do, in my kirk. You must too, Flora MacDonald. The people trust you."

Bethune's words had made her think seriously. For a long time now she'd contemplated the devastation that taking part in this war would bring upon them. She'd prayed to God to keep them free of it. But overtly, so Allan and others could see, what had she done? Nothing.

While she was still thinking about his question, Hugh came over to her. He put his arm about her shoulders and held her close. "Florry—" he used the pet name he'd used when she was a child—"I remember how you were about helping Charlie. Do you? Do you remember why you did it?"

"Of course. He needed me."

"No," Hugh said. "It wasn't just that he needed you. It was also that he asked you."

The image of Prince Charles came to Flora. He was turning away in despair because she'd refused his plea for help. "What does this talk of Charlie mean, Father?" Flora asked.

"That Allan needs you, but is different from Charlie. Allan can't ask you. Not aloud. You must talk to him."

They were together a few minutes longer. Then the door burst open and a tall lad strode in. "Aunt Flora!" Ian MacDonald, a freckled lad of seventeen, gave her a great hug. "It's wonderful to see you."

Flora kissed him. He was dear to her, just between her own boys in age and, like them, he had the wholesome mark of the sun upon him. "What a comfort he must be to you, Hugh," she said, taking her stepfather's arm.

The three of them walked toward the dining-room, where supper was waiting. All the way Ian poured forth questions faster than Flora could answer them: "How's Sandy, the twins, Jamie? When are they coming to visit? Is the harvest good? How many sheep have you got? Have you dyed them yet so they'll not be taken up by the neighbours?"

Flora threw up her hands in mock distress. "Enough! Give me time. I'll tell you all as well as I can."

Hugh laughed. "You see I've got a real farmer, Flora. I'm well pleased with him." Then he indicated the seats and forbade more talk until grace was said.

27

Crossed Purposes

IN THE MILL below the plantation house at Mount Pleasant, Allan MacDonald paced back and forth before a body of tense men. His hands were in his pockets and his head was hunched forward. He spoke without pause, although his mind was on many things. Frequently he glanced to the sentry at the door. A series of men was posted from the road up to the mill. It was dark, and extra precaution was needed. On this early-August evening, as on every other evening nowadays, the woods were filled with patriot scouts. So far there had been no alert signal. Intermittently Allan's mind left the threat of danger and the meaning of his words. In those moments he was thinking of Flora, wondering when she would return from Hugh's.

Approximately two dozen men sat listening to Allan. None of them guessed that his attention was divided. They could tell that he was alert to the possibility of danger; they trusted his competence and gave themselves to absorbing his advice. In the past month Allan had visited farmhouses, talked over fences, debated in taverns. These listening men were a few of the many recruits he had won. They had pledged not only support for an eventual battle, but active, immediate service. With them Allan was establishing a network of contacts that would reach into every county where Scots resided.

Tonight some of these recruiters were discontented. They harboured resentment against Martin, who'd failed of his promise to Allan. They harboured resentment also against the General MacDonald, supposed to arrive tonight. He might be a great chief, but, to some of these hostile Carolina Highlanders, he was a

427

usurper of Allan MacDonald's leadership. These discontents stayed because Allan had asked them to. "Don't relax your efforts," he'd said. "'Tis not my commission we're fighting for, but our homes."

Now Allan was speaking tersely of their job. "We've a better chance for winning men to our side than before. Governor Martin has changed his plan. No longer will we alone, surrounded on all sides by patriots, try to put down the rebellion. Our local forces will henceforth be backed up by regulars. Chances of success, always good, have multiplied a hundredfold."

Allan swung on his heel and started across the width of the mill again. "You are not sent out to rally, but to recruit. Get pledges of support; that's all that's necessary now. Point out that the pledge doesn't interfere, for most men, with the work they have at home. Now they give loyalty. Later, when the time is ripe, they'll strike the single blow that will kill this conflict."

There was a pause while Allan watched the sentry, who was bent forward, listening. Had it been a real bird note or the signal? In unison the heads of the listening men swivelled. The sentry straightened. "All clear."

Allan resumed his pacing and his talking. "You've all read the pamphlets Martin sent up. There the standard recruiting procedures are set out. The Governor wants you to quote the present prices and point out that they'll get worse if the rebels gain ground. He wants you to ask farmers how much of their fall harvest they expect to be able to ship out and sell. He suggests that above all you remind the farmers they were given their land by King George. Martin believes that gratitude ought to overcome the traditional hatred of the Hanoverian, make Scots forget George is Cumberland's nephew and remember he's got Stuart blood."

"Captain MacDonald." It was a man in the second row speaking.

"Aye. Speak up."

"Shall we stress their oath not to oppose the Hanoverian?"

With a thoughtful frown on his face, Allan considered the question. "I'd think not. The ones who will bring it up are the ones the oath galls. They hate the Hanoverian for the aftermath of the '45. Why bring it up if you don't have to? Besides, according to the oath, they have only to remain neutral. They don't have to defend the King."

He resumed his restless strides. "If you meet one who sides with the patriots, remind him of his oath. Remind him a Scot never breaks his word. I wouldn't mention it to the others."

Again Allan stopped, this time to stand squarely before his men, his hands on his hips. "Use Martin's arguments if you want to. To my mind, as you know, there's but one good reason for fighting. But that reason is undeniable. It may be that only by fighting can we bring peace to the land. If the rebels aren't stopped, this country will blow wide open, and we and our wives and children will be blown up with it. Any man who wants to prevent that had better join up with the side that wishes to preserve order. The patriots, if unchecked, will first ravage the land and then leave us in anarchy. I don't want to see North Carolina torn up like Massachusetts. I don't think many of the rest of us Scots want that either.

"Let me stress one point—the crucial point—before you go. Neutrality is our worst enemy among the Highlanders. There are few enough who'll become patriots. Many—the majority—will stay aloof if they can. Your job is to show them the truth: things have gone so far that neutrality is useless, even dangerous."

He chewed his lip for a moment, nodded and went on. "I think that's all. You all know your assignments. Get started. I'll go out as soon as I've talked with General MacDonald. I should be back in a fortnight. Convene here in sixteen days. I'll have further instructions then."

There was a restless shifting about among the recruiters. Finally one man voiced the general sentiment. "You're going to take instructions from that MacDonald?"

"I'll take orders from my superior officer."

Allan's determination silenced further grumbling. The men rose, stretched their legs and set their bonnets firmly on their heads. A few moved toward the door.

"One by one," Allan ordered. "The patriots have dozens of spies out. Allow a slow count of five hundred between departures."

The door opened and the first man slipped through. For the next five minutes there was silence as they waited for the cry for help. None came. The next man went out. The tension was worse than present danger would have been. Allan paced restlessly, hoping to God that every man would get through his mission safely. His head ached. This was only the beginning of his night's ordeal. Unless Donald MacDonald was intercepted he'd arrive soon.

When about seven of the men had gone, one, who was waiting at the door, refused to leave without speaking first. "Sir," he began hesitantly, "as we've said before, the name of Flora MacDonald would help us. Could we——"

"It's your turn, Shaw," Allan answered levelly. "You've had your instructions. Hurry up."

Shaw reluctantly crept through the door. The remaining men exchanged disappointed glances, but none spoke again. In order they filed out, all but the sentry and Allan.

At about eleven o'clock the sentry called softly. Allan swung his feet from the bench he'd been resting on and jumped up. A few minutes later four men filed through the door. Kenneth Black and Colonel MacLean, local men who'd met often of late with Allan, led the way. They introduced the two newcomers: Major Alexander MacLeod and General Donald MacDonald, both British regulars from Gage's headquarters at Boston.

Allan extended his hand first to the general. He couldn't help being impressed with the distinguished-looking man of military bearing. "You're welcome as officer, chief and kin," he said.

While Allan was shaking hands with MacLeod,

Kenneth Black cut off the amenities. "Greetings can wait. We can't stay here. A patriot scout saw us about five miles back. We angled around, but he's sure to flush us out. He probably knew us and our destination though we aren't in uniform."

The general appealed to Allan. "What safer place can you recommend?" He smiled pleasantly, despite the need for haste. "I've had enough detainment and questioning."

When Allan didn't answer at once, Black spoke up. "It has to be your place."

Allan waited a long time, weighing his alternatives. He felt strongly that taking the officers there, even if Flora was away, would be a great injustice to her. "We can't go there," he said finally.

Black was already half-way to the door. "The time's come, Allan," he said. "You can't keep it away from your doorstep forever."

Again Allan shook his head. "Flora ..." He left the sentence incomplete. Black was right. Yet he'd always meant to talk with Flora before he drew her and the house into it. He stood there measuring his pristine duty to Flora against his immediate duty to these men. Essentially it was sentiment versus safety. "Very well," he said. "I wish there were another way, but ... my home is safest and nearest. Gentlemen, please accept my hospitality."

When Allan saw Flora standing in the hall he almost ran to her and cried out, "I'm sorry." His relief at seeing her safe and his sense of his betrayal made him for an instant think only of her. He had, though, to restrain himself, knowing that she no more than he would want outsiders to witness their conflict. Stiffly, without even kissing her, he turned to the men behind him. "I had not thought Mrs. MacDonald would be here to welcome you. I'm happy that she is."

Then he led the general forward and said, "This, Flora, is General MacDonald, chief of the MacDonald clan of America. General Gage has sent him here to direct the raising of a whole loyalist brigade in Carolina."

Allan had to admire Flora's control. She greeted the general with all the respect due her chief.

General MacDonald was courtly. He expressed his satisfaction at meeting her and being in her house. With a few pleasant words he recalled her old fame. "Your husband, ma'am, is one of my most trusted captains. I hope soon to secure his advancement to major."

Allan saw that Flora's smile and acknowledgement were strained. As much to save her as himself from embarrassment, he said quickly, "My dear, these gentlemen are here for a meeting. Some others are coming. We have things to discuss which are for men. You'll excuse us. . . ."

Flora held her head high. "Of course, gentlemen, I understand perfectly. I was just going to retire to my chamber in any case. I bid you all good night."

The men went at once to the great-room and settled themselves in comfortable chairs. Donald MacDonald recounted the difficulty he'd had since coming to Carolina in late June. He had been stopped by the patriots in New Bern and held there until he satisfied them of his harmless intentions. "I had to do some equivocating," he admitted ruefully. As a result, he said, he'd not been long in the back country, and along with Major Alexander MacLeod still had many questions about people and conditions here.

A knock on the front door interrupted the talk. Allan uneasily stepped to the doorway to see who had come. Alex was expected, but it just could be . . . no, that was Alex's voice. Allan turned back, ready to announce the new arrival. He was cut off by Alex, who made long strides across the hall to the great-room and spoke loudly, as if in warning. When he entered the room he was at the head of a number of men. The second behind him was Stephen Moray.

Even while Alex was still making a small cautionary gesture Stephen began to speak. He professed regret at coming uninvited and unannounced. "I stopped at Glendale on my way back from the west. When I found Alex was riding this way with a little company, I thought I might be safer coming with them this far, now that so many night-riders are out. From here I'll have only a short ride to get into Cross Creek in the morning." He had stepped into the great-room, and his eyes were busy going from face to face.

Allan mustered what grace he could to make Stephen welcome. As he introduced Moray, he took care to name him as one of the patriot leaders in Cross Creek, so as to warn the two British officers against him.

There was an awkward pause as Allan poured and distributed mugs of rum for the new-comers. Again Moray spoke up, this time to direct the conversation. "We hear a rumour that Governor Martin is thinking of leaving the *Cruizer* and making his way up here where so many of his friends are. Do you think it would be a wise move?"

Kenneth Black took it upon himself to reply, and Allan was grimly amused by his friend's equivocation. "It appears to me there are considerations pointing both ways. Since the lower country is so full of disaffection, Martin's leaving the *Cruizer* and his journey here would be attended with some danger, though he would be most welcome once he arrived. Then it is important that he keep in communication with General Gage and other leaders to the north, and that would be more difficult from a point in the interior such as this." Black pursed his lips as if he were seriously considering the problem, then said, "On the other hand, if he were here, many men now wavering would come strongly to his support. Some of them are afraid to declare their true sentiments. If there were a general movement to his leadership, they would put aside their fears. I am thinking particularly of the Regulators."

The others nodded approvingly. This was the kind of thing that might impress a patriot and would certainly tell him nothing he didn't already know.

Moray made his next question particular, though he couched it in the terms of mere politeness. He turned to Donald MacDonald. "A silversmith like me becomes well acquainted in his neighbourhood. You, sir, are a stranger. Are you from the north?"

"Yes, Mr. Moray. I'm on what you might call a family visit. I have the honour to be the chief of the MacDonalds in America. I'm down here to look up some of my cousins and become better acquainted with them."

"Then you are here for pleasure. Let me wish that you enjoy your stay." Stephen made a small bow. Allan MacDonald, watching him, was burning with impatience and irritation. He had not realized the fellow was so cool. Meantime, the carefully planned secret meeting couldn't go on. They must sit and bite their nails until Moray pleased to leave them. Now he was asking more questions. Why had Alex let him come?

Still addressing Donald MacDonald, Moray continued. "How do people in the north regard General Washington? I am curious, too, to find out more about the fight at Bunker Hill. You see, I served my apprenticeship in Boston and my interest in Massachusetts affairs continues."

Donald MacDonald paused reflectively. "I fear I can't satisfy you on either question. My journey has been a leisurely one. I left Massachusetts about the tenth of June. I believe General Washington had not yet arrived. And the fight at Bunker Hill did not take place until late in the month. I don't follow military affairs closely, and no doubt your knowledge on these points is superior to mine. I believe both sides at Bunker Hill now claim the victory."

Stephen drained the last of his rum. He turned at last to Allan. "I've ridden upwards of thirty miles today, and the evening is far advanced. No doubt you gentlemen have affairs to discuss. Mr. MacDonald, if you could conduct me to a place where I can sleep I'd be most grateful." He looked around the room. "You have a considerable company. If beds are scarce, I'll be quite satisfied with a truss of hay in the barn."

Allan did his best to conceal his eagerness. He led Stephen off.

In fifteen minutes he was back, rubbing his hands. "Well, gentlemen, we've had an unfortunate delay, but

I think we may safely continue our discussion if it is not too late."

General MacDonald looked grave. "We have our privacy once more, but I fear the damage is done. This Moray is an observant man. I've little doubt he saw this meeting for what it is—two British officers conferring with local loyalist leaders. It's unfortunate," he said, turning to Alex MacLeod, "that you couldn't shake him off."

Colonel MacLean had taken out a large handkerchief and was polishing a pistol. "Secrecy is important to our movement at this stage. We are practically at war and war has its unpleasant side. Should we perhaps silence him?"

Though his face was impassive, Allan gave an interior start. The man was suggesting plain murder.

Alex MacLeod spoke quickly. "Moray thought of that possibility. On the way over he spoke to everyone we met. We stopped once at a little tavern for a drink. He mentioned where we were going. At least a dozen people, patriots as well as loyalists, know he was with us and where we were bound. If we took Colonel MacLean's suggestion it would be laid at our door at once."

Donald MacDonald shook his head sententiously. "We didn't need that, MacLeod. After all, we are all gentlemen. We can't resort to cold-blooded murder."

"I could," said MacLean.

"No," General MacDonald continued, "Moray must ride away safe and unmolested in the morning. Let us hope he is less clever than I feared.

"Moray brought up a point we should consider. I have a letter from Governor Martin in which he asks my advice about coming up here. Some of you know him better than I do. What is your opinion?"

"Surely not what I told Moray," said Black with a laugh.

"Tell him to stay on the Cruizer," said MacLean tersely, still polishing his pistol. "The fact is, Martin's a bungler. If he could come with two or three regiments of regulars he would make a rallying point for volunteers. Alone, he would probably walk into a trap in Wilmington. If he should get here he would do us little good and perhaps commit some folly that might damage our cause. No, let him stay on the Cruizer and write letters."

It was a brutal appraisal of Josiah Martin, but Allan noted that a number of the men nodded in confirmation. The moment summed up the development the summer had brought. Martin's star was setting. No longer were the rebellion and counter-attack matters of negotiation and diplomacy. Effective measures would henceforth be military; strength, not tact nor perhaps justice, would spell victory. Allan knew he had done well to accept the leadership of Donald MacDonald and General Gage. Now only through such men could he serve the cause he had embraced.

The talk went on. The group brought up point after point and debated each freely. In the end, General MacDonald gave his judgement. Allan noticed some of the men were beginning to yawn. At last General MacDonald called a halt. "This has been a most fruitful meeting," he said. "I'm much better informed on account of it, and I'm sure Major MacLeod has profited as much. Before we retire for the night, let me sum up two points which must direct our policy in the months to come.

"First, though we must line up every soldier we can, let us keep our recruiting secret until the time comes to bring our army into the open. We do not now want to provoke a collision with the aroused Whigs.

"Martin wants us to employ the troops we are raising to stamp out rebellion here in this province. The plan has local advantages, but takes no account of the outbreak in other colonies. Also, it's not feasible unless there are supporting English troops. General Gage and I have another plan: I will lead the Carolina troops to Wilmington to rendezvous with a fleet of transports which will conduct them to a rallying-point, probably in Nova Scotia. From this point an army will march to subdue the colonies as a whole. Since this is our aim, we must avoid battle with the rebels in his province by all means of honour open

to us—especially as long as we have no support." Mac-
Donald paused and looked at Allan. "I know why you
fight. I give my word we will not be long away from
Carolina and the home you fight for."

Allan had felt his hopes drop and rise again. If the
loyalist forces were to be taken out of Carolina, where
was the peace and safety he was seeking? Yet he realized how much his own security depended on the stability of all America. And, after all, there was yet a
chance that the first battle would be fought here. He
would pray for those English troops. He recommitted
himself, knowing that he could never endure the coming months of war if he were not fighting for the peace
and order he believed in and needed.

All at once he realized that the meeting was over.
As host he must show all these men to their rooms.
After all this talk they were ready enough for bed.

In the barn where Allan had established him, Stephen did not allow himself to fall asleep, tired though
he was. He had played a risky game, thrusting himself on Alex MacLeod and forcing his way into a loyalist meeting. He had recognized most of the men and
made pretty certain that the two visitors were British
army officers sent down from the north to take charge
of loyalist troops raised in the province. His information ought to go at once to the Committee of Safety at
Cross Creek.

When he estimated that Allan was back in the house,
he let himself quietly out of the barn and cautiously
approached the house. He slipped up to a lighted
window and peered within. The men sat in a ring.
They were talking, and seemed likely to continue. He
could hear an occasional word but could not follow
the conversation.

Quietly he made his way to the barn. Fortunately,
when Allan had conducted him to the barn with a
light, he had stopped to look at Black Bess and knew
where to find her in the dark. He saddled and bridled
her and led her stealthily out of the barn. Without attracting attention they passed the house at a walk.

Once on the road, Bess started off at a steady trot for Cross Creek.

When Flora had gone upstairs to leave the men free, she had undressed at once and gone to bed, but she had not fallen asleep. Her eyes were wide open in the dark. After a time, rays from the rising moon came in through the window. The light made a ragged pattern on the floor. Outside an owl hooted; a dove sounded its mournful note; a horse in the stable neighed. A pine tree's branches scraped against the wall of the house, moving softly, swayed by a light breeze. Flora heard all the night noises while she waited for Allan.

She wondered what was going on downstairs and hoped the meeting would not last long. It was terribly unfortunate, she felt, that her return and the meeting had coincided. Now, coming directly from consultation, Allan would be more than ever full of loyalist plans. He would be more loath than ever to relinquish his part in them. Perhaps, she thought, I should wait until another day.

She clenched her fist in renewed regret that for so long she had closed her eyes to the unrest. Her withdrawal had done nothing to protect her home. The conference of leaders going on downstairs was dramatic evidence that Mount Pleasant was now a loyalist headquarters. Her withdrawal had only given Allan time to involve himself deeply. She prayed his commitment was not irrevocable. The fear that it might already be too late made her determine to speak yet this night. The time was inauspicious, but delay might be disastrous.

At first the time of waiting seemed long. Then she thought it was perhaps a good thing, for it gave her a chance to go over in her mind what she would say to him. Her words must define a way by which she and Allan could come together again, trust each other, share. She wished she could say simply, "I love you, as always. Let us forget all but our love." She could not say only that. It was the political struggle in the province that was dividing them; she must put her case in terms of political issues. It would not be easy for her.

She knew her plea must not include only Allan and herself but also the Scots people, whom she had promised to aid. Her mind reviewed a meeting she'd had en route home from Hugh's. A Colonel MacIntosh had sought her out, saying, "The Scots who want to be neutral sent me." Then the colonel had begun to argue the benefits of neutrality. Flora had been so glad to meet with one of her own conviction that she had said at once, "I need no persuasion. How can I help?" At first MacIntosh had asked her to issue a general statement that might be circulated among the Scots. She had been unable to grant that. Then he had asked for something she could do: talk to Allan. She had agreed. Now, tonight, she would fulfil that promise.

Patiently she rehearsed the arguments she wanted to use. When he came upstairs she would be ready to speak calmly. The depth of her feeling left no place for the irritation and bitterness she had felt at first. Everything petty had been inundated and washed away.

The night was far spent when Allan at last tiptoed into their room. It was good of him to try not to wake her, Flora thought. She smiled tenderly as she thought that in a minute, despite his care, he would forget and drop a boot. A good man he was, and she loved him even when he was wrong. After he had shut the door, she spoke. "I'm awake, Allan. No need to be quiet."

At once he bent over her and held her close. "I was so worried. Where were you? Was your trip safe?"

She pushed him away, afraid that she would lose her strength for argument. There seemed to her to be a very fine line between love and open antagonism between them. It made the love more precious, and made her want to cherish it at the cost of all else.

He took her withdrawal for displeasure. "About tonight . . . I'm sorry. I didn't intend——"

She interrupted him. "Never mind. I was a little taken aback to have those men in my home, but . . ."

"Then you knew?"

She sighed. "I learned while you were away."

"I'm glad. It's a great relief to me to have it in the open."

After a pause she said, "Allan, I want to talk to you about it. Will you light the candle?"

"Aye." He busied himself with his tinder-box. A flickering light showed the tiredness of his face. "I want to tell you all about it." He sat down on the edge of the bed and turned to her as if he was happy he could confide in her. "Now I see how foolish I was not to tell you before. But where shall I begin? With tonight I guess. Part of the meeting was fine. But for the rest—details! How many rifles among the Scots in Anson County? How many in Cumberland? How many muskets needed to supply arms to those with none?" He passed a hand wearily over his forehead. "I made up my mind I'd never haggle again."

Flora realized that Allan thought she had accepted the fact of his allegiance and would suffer it meekly. He might, from the way he was talking, even think she sympathized. Abruptly she reached forward and touched his arm. "Allan, you must give this recruiting up."

He threw aside her hand and stood over her. She looked up at him, saw his set jaw. "Wait, Allan," she went on hurriedly. "Let me finish. I ask this for your sake as well as mine. While you were away two men came from Cross Creek to bring an order from the Wilmington Committee of Safety." She pulled it out from under her pillow. "You are in danger. So is Alex. So are all related to you."

Allan took the folder, saw that it was open and that the sheet within was torn. "You read it?" After she had nodded, he held it to the candle, scanned it and then let the pieces burn. "This sort of threat is not the most fearful kind."

"Believe me, Allan," she answered, urgency in her voice: "You must stop. Even if you don't care for danger, there are reasons. I believe so firmly in those reasons that I have given a promise—a promise that you and I would stand apart from the conflict."

"To whom did you give this promise?"

"Colonel MacIntosh."

"How dared you!" Allan tossed his head angrily and turned away. "If you knew what I've been doing when you promised you must have known even then that I am not neutral, never can be."

"You can refuse to give any more active support. That's all I want. That's what the colonel wanted, and the people he spoke for." Flora caught her breath, then hurried on. "Let me tell you what he said."

Allan faced her. "I don't give a rush for his opinion. And I can guess for whom he spoke. What I care about now is you and your opinion. Why do you oppose me in this?"

Sitting up in bed, Flora leaned toward him earnestly. "We've seen too much civil war, and a bitter thing it is. We've seen Scotland ruined by it. We've seen too many brave Highlanders come out from their glens at the call of their chief only to fall stark and still on the battle-field. Behind everything else, that's why we emigrated here. I want to see no more fighting."

"But the fighting's bound to come," Allan interrupted.

She threw back the covers and knelt on the high bed so her face was almost on a level with his. Her large, unhappy eyes held his. "Wait, Allan, let me finish. When the Scots fight together they prevail. When the Scots are divided they often lose. When they fight each other, when some stand, when some are unsure of the right, all their courage goes for nought. They march out to defeat and death. Now if I believed you could get all the Scots together and enlist them all, and add the Regulators and the country Tories and raise such a force as to frighten the rebels into giving up, I'd not have a word to say.

"But the old Scots let it be known that this is not their quarrel. They don't mind if the Whigs and Tories fight to their hearts' content in the country below. Here in the back country they say neither Whig nor Tory has an enemy, and hence neither will come in arms. They'll plant and harvest as usual and take no part. You can't bring them to join in with you, argue as you may. They won't enlist, will they?"

He did not answer.

"You see?" she cried out. "You know they won't! It would be better if all we new Scots joined with them and stood aside. Then neither Whig nor Tory would have reason to send soldiers against us. But if you enlist part of the Highlanders—a thousand or two thousand—you'll not be a force strong enough to frighten the Whigs. They'll come against you, or you'll march against them. You'll be a forlorn hope surrounded by enemies. You'll bring Whig armies here, and they'll not let the old Scots stay neutral. Many of them are Americans at heart and hate the Hanoverians. Forced to take sides, they'll join the rebels, many of them. We'll have Scot against Scot and only sorrow will come of it.

"So I say let the Scots be one people, together. Give up this scheme of fighting. Let us all stand aside." She leaned toward him, her hands clasped in an almost prayerful attitude as she made her appeal. "Allan, don't help to divide us for another slaughter."

Impulsively Allan stepped forward and took her hands. "You say it well, Flora. This is the first time I have understood how you feel. Yet, though I understand, I can't agree." He sat down on the edge of the bed and tried to explain his view. "Put it as you say—if we all sit at home when the Whigs rise in arms, then they win. The first thing they would do is cut the tie with England. We would be a land without government, no stable courts, no order, no security, no certain title to our lands. We'd be at the mercy of any brigand, and I've experienced what that can mean on my travels lately. This is a fine country. It needs only rule and law. We cannot do without the Crown. I intend to support the Crown in every way I can. If this means fighting, I'll bring as many soldiers into battle as I can muster."

"You could be taking harmless men to death."

"It's a risk I face as much myself, and gladly."

"You—we—owe nothing to Governor Martin or to King George. We've a new, raw place here to make into an estate for our children. Surely your first obligation is to the boys, to us. Allan, please! We can still go back to our old plans. Find a home for us farther west. We'll isolate ourselves with our kin. We don't have to take strife into our lives. We can still escape."

Allan took two or three turns on the small bedside rug, then stopped. He caught hold of the post at the head of the bed and stood gazing down at her. "I'm sorry, Flora, but you're wrong. Things are such in this country that we can't escape. That's why I best perform my obligation to you and the children when I support the Crown. If we fall into the chaos of revolution, we'll have only a ravaged farm, whether here or farther west. When I go about enlisting soldiers to put down the rebels summarily, I'm doing it for the boys and you—for all of us."

Flora turned around and once more sat up in bed, her shoulders against the head-board. She refused to look at him. Bitterly she scorned him. "You've let yourself be beguiled—yes, beguiled by resounding phrases from Martin and by his promise of rank." Her voice broke and tears of disappointment were in her eyes, but she went on. "You should know by now how little Martin's statements mean. You should know, *Captain* MacDonald. 'Tis a low office for one who is sacrificing his home and his people."

Allan advanced a slow step toward the bed and drew himself up. "I tell you, Flora, I wasn't bribed by the promise of a commission, high or low. I'd be in this quarrel if I were but a common soldier. I'm in this because I must be in it. You too must be, though I hoped to be able to keep you out of it. You'd best listen, Flora. The day will come when you can't hide from it—not you, nor Colonel MacIntosh, nor Campbell, nor all the rest. I'm preparing for that day. If you step in and oppose me, you may well really divide the Scots, really leave us vulnerable."

Flora said nothing. There was the taste of defeat in her mouth and she wondered whether she had done well to follow Hugh's advice. Perhaps Hugh had not realized how far Allan had gone. No, she corrected herself, I had not realized how strong Allan has grown. She listened to his quiet movements. He was undressing, getting ready for bed. Throughout almost the whole discussion he'd remained calm and reasonable. Her anger began to fade, and she began to review what Allan had said. One thing she was grateful for: their goals were the same. It was not yet time to despair.

She looked at the window and noticed that it had become a square of grey with the first approach of dawn. She sighed and spoke gently, so he would know her anger was gone. "Ah, well, we'll not agree tonight. Blow out the candle and come to bed."

Stephen Moray reached Cross Creek by mid-morning after his night ride. Before he stabled Bess he made a circuit through the town, telling Robert Rowan and other patriots to be at his shop in a half hour. When they had assembled he described the meeting at Allan MacDonald's into which he had intruded the night before.

"It tells us," he said earnestly, "that the loyalists are intensifying their efforts to enlist companies of soldiers here. I'd stake my life that Donald MacDonald and that new Alexander MacLeod are professional officers in the British army. Gage must have sent them down from the north to direct the movement and lead it. MacDonald looks a formidable man."

Rowan had listened quietly to Moray's recital, nodding as Stephen made each point. At the end he asked only, "What steps would you advise to counter his work?"

Moray paused to marshal his thoughts. He answered succinctly. "Three. I'd suggest the provincial congress at Hillsboro appoint two committees—one to come into this country and meet with the leaders of the Regulators and Quakers or any others who have scruples about joining in with us to protect our constitutional rights, and one to meet with the new Scots and explain to them in simple language the nature of the present unhappy controversy and our just aims in it. The first committee must be empowered to offer the Regulators real protection if they will cast their lot with us. We can propose these measures at Hillsboro, but it will be the task of the congress to carry them out.

"The third step we can take ourselves. We must keep the Scots divided. Colonel MacIntosh and the other leaders from South Carolina, as you know, were up here not long ago preaching neutrality to the Scots. They helped and will help more. But we all must realize that the chief influence among the Scots on our side is Farquard Campbell. He is at it early and late urging them to hold aloof. All but a handful of the old Scots accept his view.

"He must be told of these British officers intriguing against him. He must be persuaded to work even harder to hold his old Scots in line and perhaps to win over some of the recently arrived Highlanders. We must offer him the best support we have. If we can keep the Scots in two camps we break their force in half."

Rowan sucked on his clay pipe reflectively. After a pause he spoke. "Three wise suggestions, Moray. They don't aim at the impossible; they could do good. I'll take care of approaching the congress at Hillsboro myself about the committees. I make no doubt the congress will think well of them. As for Campbell—you know him pretty well?"

Stephen nodded.

"Then ride over to Campbelltown and see him this afternoon. Do it yourself. You have a good, clear tongue in your head, and you'll know how to put the case to him."

Stephen's business with Farquard Campbell was quickly completed. Campbell listened without comment to Stephen's account of the night at Mount Pleasant. He wrote down the names of the men gathered at the meeting as Stephen gave them.

At the end, he laid down his pen and nodded. "So that's the lot for now. Allan MacDonald and that son-in-law of his, MacLeod, I knew were in it. MacLean, too. He's a spitfire, always ready for high words and action, but no judgement. Tell me more about these two officers, Donald MacDonald and Alexander MacLeod."

Moray gave him every detail about them that he could recall.

Campbell sighed. "I'm sorry Gage is in this. He's a smart man, and it looks as if he had sent down two capable fellows to work here. It will not be simple to hold the Scots quiet. I could wish Josiah Martin still in the Governor's Mansion at New Bern. He was no such antagonist as these three." He uttered another weary sigh and pulled himself deliberately to his feet, a tall, solid man. "We'd best have a drink of rum to fortify ourselves, since we have Gage and not Martin to contend with." He went to a side table and brought a decanter of rum back to his desk, where he carefully poured a drink for each of them.

Stephen had had no sleep the night before and little to eat that day. As the first swallow of the smooth Jamaica rum settled in his stomach he could feel it begin to spread warmly through his body.

Farquard Campbell sat down again and raised his glass to his lips with a slow consideration. When he had replaced it on the desk, he spoke. "Well, lad, I'll do what I can. Don't expect miracles. Some of the old Scots will stick by me—quite a number. They'll have temptations offered them, but many of them will stay quiet. I'm but one man. I'll do my best. You know yourself how far that will go. Tell them this at Cross Creek." After a pause he added, "You know who could do most for us—Flora MacDonald. MacIntosh has been sent up to her. I'll talk to him. Then, if it's necessary, I'll talk to her."

Farquard rose and put a hand on Stephen's shoulder. "As for you, man, take care of yourself. Your eyes look like holes burned in a blanket. If I were in your shoes I'd go home and sleep the clock around."

"I'm tired, right enough," Stephen admitted, "but before I go I'd like a word with your niece."

Campbell went with him to the door of the counting-room. In the hall he called loudly, "Cecily, here's Mr. Moray come to pay his respects."

Cecily came to the parlour door. She held a book

in one hand; her finger marked her place. She smiled
a tentative welcome and stepped back a little to allow
Stephen to enter if he wanted to.

Stephen saw that she was, as always now, unsure of
what his presence might mean. As he looked at her
the terrible, disarming tenderness she always evoked
rose in him. His intended casual greetings left his
mind entirely. He wanted very much to hold her in
his arms; he wanted to press his cheek against her
fine, soft hair and tell her about his trip. He wanted
her to share his ideals; he wanted her to comfort him
in his fatigue.

With a curious, one-sided smile, Cecily observed
him. "Well, Stephen, do you have something to say to
me?"

He heard himself answer, "Yes, Cecily. I've much
to say to you." As he followed her into the room he
knew he had made his decision. He knew Cecily well
enough not to expect her to compromise. She would
never share his patriotism. Very well, he would not
speak of that. He would speak of something equally
dear to him: his love for her. Surely patriotism and
love, if sincere enough, could exist side by side, each
taking the full share of the man. He closed his mind
against his earlier conviction that the sincerity of conflicting politics and love was what made them incom-
patible.

After she had seated herself in a high-backed chair
and motioned for him to take a place on the comfortable divan, Stephen slowly began. "You must forgive
my hesitation. I did not know when I called for you
that I would say what now I want to say." Feeling
that he was making a cumbersome beginning, Stephen
got up, took a turn about the room and started over.
"Cecily, I don't know how to say what I want to
say."

She had followed his every movement with concern
in her eyes. Now she said, "There is no need to
plunge in at once. Come. Sit down again. You seem
very tired."

"Yes, I am fatigued," he admitted, letting her push
him back onto the divan and place a hassock into

position for his feet. Her solicitude gave him courage. She would not concern herself if she felt nothing for him. When she returned to his side to tuck a little pillow behind his head, he looked up at her. "Thank you. But don't make me too comfortable, or I shall slip into a lassitude and never search out the words I want."

He saw her blush very slightly. As she turned to take her own seat she murmured, "Perhaps . . . perhaps that might be best." Hurriedly she picked up her book and said, "Let me read to you a bit. It's very humorous. Rest and we'll talk later."

The sense that she had divined his purpose and wanted to slip away from it made him act decisively. He leaned forward and closed the book in her lap. "No. I think too long we have postponed talking about some things."

She leaned back, as if composing herself to meet a challenge, and looked at him. "There are some things we seem unable to talk about amicably."

"It's not those things I want to bring up now—nor ever again, if that's the way it must be." He put his hand over hers and bent forward a little more. "Cecily, you must know I love you."

She rose quickly and looked away from him. "From the way you have opposed me, I could hardly think so."

He went to her and stood behind her. "From the way I have returned after every quarrel, from the way I've stifled all talk of things that would displease you of late, from many things, you must have known. But let's not argue about past indications. I'm telling you now, Cecily, straight out. I love you and cannot endure our casual relationship any longer."

"What other is possible to us?" Her voice was tight and high, as if the question cost her pain. "Our loyalties . . ."

Stephen put his hands on her shoulders. He knew she was torn; it was clear that she had thought of this, had even feared it. She cared for him, at least in some measure.

"Cecily, great happiness is possible to us, if you

return my feeling. The things which keep us apart will not endure forever. The war will pass. The rest of our lives we can live together, with nothing to separate us."

She bowed her head and seemed to think seriously about his words. His hands tightened on her shoulders and he began to turn her slowly to him. For a moment she rested her head against his chest, seemed to yield. Then in a muffled tone she said, "Give me time, Stephen. You don't know what you are asking."

"I'm asking you to marry me. Will you?"

She wrenched away from him and stood behind her chair. Her hands gripped the back of it so tightly that the knuckles showed white. "I cannot say! Not now. Please be patient."

He watched her tenderly and was almost happy. He was sure Cecily would refuse outright if she did not care deeply for him. Of course he would be patient; his last wish was to distress her. Aloud he said, "I'll be patient as long as you ask me, my dearest. Say but one thing: you care something for me. Just tell me that, to help me be patient."

She looked up at him with a pitiable confusion. "Stephen," she said softly, "you know I care for you. But I would not cause you unhappiness. Do not ask me to say more now."

Stephen felt that for the moment he could ask for nothing more. Her avowal of affection had stilled all his questions. He felt only a desire to reassure her, make her smile and thus erase the perplexity from her expression. He took her arm and led her around the chair. "Sit down, Cecily, my dear. Don't be distressed. May I stay a few minutes longer? We'll talk of other things."

She gave him a grateful look and pressed his hand. "I'm afraid I won't be good company."

"You always are, to me. Will you read to me now, as you wanted to a few minutes ago? Then we shan't have to cast about for conversation. I just want to be with you a little longer." He took his comfortable seat on the couch and was delighted when Cecily rose to put the pillow behind his head again. He watched her until she had sat down, opened the book and found her place. Then he closed his eyes and listened to the delicate precision of her voice as she read a familiar passage in Henry Fielding's *Joseph Andrews*.

Neither heard the knock on the door or the soft footsteps of a servant answering it. The firm tap of boot heels made Stephen rouse, but Cecily, engrossed, read on. It was Stephen who first saw the man in the doorway. The visitor was in dusty riding-clothes, but somehow he looked fresh and full of vitality, for all the marks of travel on him. Stephen knew him at once. It was James Blair, the man who had been with Cecily at the Governor's ball.

Cecily looked up, as if to ask why Stephen was paying no attention. Then she followed the direction of his gaze. When she saw Blair she paled. The book fell shut in her lap. Like figures in a tableau she and Blair stared at each other.

Suddenly, with a little cry, Cecily sprang to her feet. The book fell to the floor. Stephen bent to pick it up and as he did so Cecily looked at him as if she only then recalled his presence. Her expression was unreadable. She moved on to greet Blair. "James. James, my dear. I didn't expect you for at least a week."

Stephen clenched his teeth in anger as he saw Blair's hand slip lightly around Cecily's waist. He was somewhat appeased when she gracefully moved away. But she continued to gaze at Blair as if she could read some message, dear and secret to her, in his countenance.

Finally she turned and led Blair to Stephen. When she spoke her voice was strained. "You remember Mr. Blair, don't you? He and I are ... are very good friends. From the boat. We came out on the same ship."

For a moment Stephen thought she shot him an imploring look; then it was gone and she smiled brightly, as if nothing could have pleased her more than James Blair's arrival. "Do sit down, both of you. There's so much to ask about, to tell." She shrugged her shoulders and apologized to Stephen blithely.

"I'm sure you'll forgive our reminiscing. We haven't seen each other since New Bern last fall. I have to find out what's been happening to him. Oh, I know a few things. While you and I, Stephen, have been shut off in the rustic quiet of Cross Creek, Mr. Blair has been fluttering the hearts of fair ladies in New York. Yes, James, Madame la Fabrère wrote me all about you. Normally I should not have corresponded with such a woman. But what could I do? You did not condescend to send me a line."

A gay, artificial note had come into Cecily's voice that Stephen could not endure. It was obvious that she and Blair had a sophisticated rapport that he could not, and did not want to, share. Stephen felt so bitterly disappointed and deceived that he had to get away. Otherwise he would say something offensive to one of them. He rose even though Cecily was still chattering.

"Dougald delivered the message you sent," she was saying. "Unless he trimmed it down to make it easier to carry, it was a very plain message indeed. But I did not mind its plainness so much as its finality. You gave me no chance to ... tell you how I looked forward to your visit."

She spoke with an edge to her voice which could have been acerbity or hysteria. Stephen didn't wait to find out which. He curtly excused himself and went to the door. "I only intrude," he said pointedly, "on a personal affair. Cecily, when you have time to talk or read with me again, be so kind as to let me know. Until I hear, I shall not disturb you and your visitor."

He took hope when she rose hastily and moved a step toward him. She had an anxious look in her eyes and seemed about to speak. It must have been an illusion, Stephen thought as he saw her stop and return to Blair. She gave him only a formal good night, and let the servant show him to the door.

28

The Fall Interlude

DAVID waved until Dougald was out of sight and then trotted on through Cross Creek. It was not yet suppertime and he was in no mood to hurry to Cambelltown, especially since he knew Dougald was going to see Moira. Those two could make happy use of any delay. David had the whole evening to see Blair at Farquard Campbell's house and find out from him where the King's standard was being kept. There'd be no immediate need for it, and there was no immediate need for Dougald and him to get back to Mount Pleasant. They'd make a pleasant journey south and back. The October weather was exhilarating and the colours were beautiful. David looked forward eagerly to the entire trip. He remembered how impressed he'd been with the Highland valley last October when they first rode up into it; now if they went to New Bern he'd see the same hues and sights.

When he came to the short open stretch between Cross Creek and Campbelltown he spurred to a gallop. Stimulated by the crisp air, he took a great breath and shouted for the joy of it. All things—nearly all things—were going well. A distinct lull had come over the land, but David knew that it was only a time of waiting. Causes were ripening. Like the year, they were moving to their appointed ends.

He judiciously slowed his horse and let the reins hang loose as he thought over the peculiar character of the time. A crisis was coming, yet people were sending their roots deeper into the land. Well, that was understandable. Allan and others like him thought they'd stand the blow better if they, like trees, had a good grip on the soil. Also they wished so devoutly for the rebellion to be put down, and believed so firmly that it soon would be, that they really thought more in terms of peace than in terms of war. Among the Scots who recruited with Allan—except, of course, the professional soldiers like the general and his aide—one heard surprisingly little talk now of companies and arms. Mostly one heard about a utopian "later, when the peace comes."

Thinking about Allan, David shook his head in wonderment. The man had changed from the defeated Allan MacDonald of Skye. He had a faith and conviction that carried him through everything nowadays. It looked as though the old prophecy was failing. Allan wasn't Allan the unfortunate any more.

Perhaps, however, the prophecy about Flora was coming true. These days Flora sometimes gave him the feeling she was walking toward a dread doom. David felt affection and sympathy rise in him. Though she kept her face serene and spoke low and gently as always, Flora grieved inwardly. David shook his head in concern. He wished she would join Allan in the loyalist cause. Allan was right, and, besides, nothing Flora could do would stem the strong tide now. Lately she'd taken heart because Allan spoke of buying her a home near her kin and because there seemed to be less agitation in the land. If she took hope from these things, she was doomed—at least to disappointment. This was but a lull before the storm.

Again David's thoughts reverted to the coming conflict. The mission he and Dougald were on this October evening was a good sign of the time. They were making a leisurely journey. They took time to hunt and visit friends. But at the end of the journey was the rallying flag of the King's troops, a tangible symbol of war.

He had ridden into Campbelltown and down the street to Farquard Campbell's house. The light in the windows sparkled invitingly. David dismounted at once and loped up the walk.

The Negro house-boy let him into the parlour and promised to fetch his master right away. In a moment or two, Farquard strode in. "Welcome, lad. What brings you?"

Nonchalantly David replied, "Nothing of great moment, sir. I heard Mr. Blair was stopping with you, and thought I'd combine a ride with a visit. He and I knew each other on the *Baliol*, you know." David watched Farquard closely. He wasn't sure just what line he should take, for he didn't know how much Farquard knew of Blair's real capacity. The minimal truth seemed the safest way.

Farquard gave no sign of suspicion. He nodded and said courteously, "I'm sorry Blair isn't in now. He and Cecily went out for the afternoon. But sit down and wait. They'll soon return for supper." He gestured toward a chair for David and took one himself.

Campbell moved less agilely than usual, David thought, and had about him an indefinable air of preoccupation. David wondered just what was going through his mind these days. Surely, by now, he must be getting aware that his position was precarious. Probably no one would ever know exactly how much Farquard knew or which way his thoughts went. He was a deep man of complex motives; yet he was almost ingenuously sincere. It was a hard-to-fathom combination.

When Farquard had moved his chair so he faced David and made his long frame comfortable he started to speak. "I'm glad to speak to someone from Mount Pleasant. How are things there?"

David caught the phrasing of the question at once. Farquard at the moment wasn't interested in the people so much as in the problems. Deliberately he did not comprehend. "Things, sir? Well, the harvest was good—good enough for Allan to talk about buying a place over in Anson County. You probably know all about that."

Farquard pursed his lips and nodded. "I knew he was negotiating some with Caleb Touchstone. Flora's getting her wish, is she? That's good. I've heard her speak often of her great desire to live near her kin."

After David had agreed, Farquard went on.

"Seems a strange time, though, for Allan to move. He's swayed by Flora no doubt."

David knew what Farquard wanted to hear. It was common knowledge that he'd made a circuit of the Scots Valley a few weeks ago and stopped at Mount Pleasant to talk to Flora. No one had told David just what was said in that meeting, but it was pretty clear that Farquard had hoped to enlist Flora openly on the side of neutrality. She hadn't agreed—at least she hadn't acted. Farquard's questions now made David think she'd promised again to try to persuade Allan, and take her stand that way. Well, if Farquard wanted to know about Flora, there wasn't any reason he shouldn't be told. "About Flora's swaying Allan, sir, I don't quite know what you mean. They both want a house over in Anson, though I think she fears this is an unpropitious time to move. She'd rather they had the political strife settled before they move. This way Allan may not be able to work the land right away."

"Then she's going along with him on his recruiting?" Farquard's eyebrows shot up in surprise and dismay.

"It's no secret to you, sir, that Flora is neutral. But of course she knows Allan's view. She's not very happy." David crossed his knees and wondered when Blair would come.

Farquard got up and walked slowly to the window. "There's still time to hope. This fall's been quiet. A lot more words get written and spoken, but there's been less violence. The Continental Congress adjourned last month without closing the door on reconciliation. I pray our representatives are sincere in denying they want independence." He turned back to look at David in some discouragement. "But even I grow more fearful. The Congress also forged firmer measures of armament and drill. And that ultimatum Hooper presented in August was defeated by one vote. One vote alone kept us from making such demands that England could never have met them. There are a lot of our demands England ought to meet. But there are some we shouldn't make—the ones that are so strong they will forever cut off hope of compromise. I fear how the vote will go if another such ultimatum is considered later."

Farquard shook his head and looked back out the window. "There's Blair, coming in alone," he said in surprise. He watched a moment, then turned back to David. "Lad, you don't save the peace by breaking it. I wish men would learn that."

Further talk along that line was cut off. Blair entered with a greeting for David already on his lips. "I just missed you in Cross Creek. Saw Dougald there and he told me you'd come." They shook hands heartily. "It was very good of you to make the trip from Mount Pleasant just to pay respects." His words and tone were casual, as if between himself and David there was nothing but an old, fairly familiar acquaintanceship.

As soon as he had spoken to David, Blair turned to Farquard. "You must be wondering what I've done with Cecily. She's quite safe. We had stopped at the silversmith's, where she wanted to look at patterns. It was there I met Dougald."

Farquard frowned in some apprehension. "It's dark already, Blair. Cecily ought not to come from Cross Creek alone at this hour."

With a smile Blair reassured him. "I wouldn't think of letting her come alone. She wanted to look longer at Mr. Moray's patterns and also to talk with him awhile. I decided to come over to fetch David, who, according to Dougald, must return to Cross Creek tonight. Then I'll bring Cecily home. If supper's at eight as usual, we should make it. My watch—" he drew it out—"says six-thirty."

David, who had caught Blair's cue, was already on his feet. "Thank you kindly, sir, for entertaining me. I'll go back with Mr. Blair. Dougald expected me to be gone only a short while."

Farewells were said, and Blair and David were, within five minutes, cantering back to Cross Creek. Most of the way Blair did the talking.

"Yes, lad," he concluded, "I'm glad you and Dougald are going after the standard now; Martin's had it a good while. I've no doubt he guards it fervently, but I have great doubt we'd be able to get it from him quickly when the time comes to raise it. We might not even be able to find him. He's talking now of going to Charleston and talks still of travelling up to your country. Once you lads have got the standard from him, he can journey where he likes, for all I care."

It was wholly dark now, though the evening was clear. The full harvest moon hung red over the horizon. It was beautiful, but gave little light. Blair's voice came unembodied to David. It was clear and clipped. There could be no mistaking the directions. David gave a little sigh. He wasn't going to New Bern after all, but back toward Fort Johnston, for the flag was on the *Cruizer*.

They rode on in silence until they reached the edge of Cross Creek, where they would separate. About two hundred yards from the first house, David reined up and turned to Blair. "We'll get the flag all right, sir, and should have no trouble. But where'll we take it?"

"Can't Allan keep it?"

"He could, but he may be moving soon. Shouldn't it be kept nearer the centre of the district? The rallying-point won't be over in Anson County."

For a moment there was silence while Blair considered. "You're perfectly right. You'd best leave it here in Cross Creek or Campbelltown. I may still be here when you return, though I plan to go up to see Allan and others very soon. If I'm not here, don't leave the standard at Farquard's. He's getting pushed into a decision, but I can't be sure which way he'll go. Peter Hay is your man. You know where he lives?"

David said he did and turned his horse. "Goodbye, sir, and thank you. Mayhap we'll meet again soon, if you're up our way."

David rode around one side of the town, while Blair headed for Moray's shop.

Cecily, sitting on the bench in Moray's work-room, was leaning forward earnestly. Several sketching-papers lay in her lap. Carefully she kept one hand over them to keep them from falling to the floor. "Please, Stephen, we have but a few more minutes to talk. Let's discuss this thing, not spend the time in anger. I know—" her free hand reached toward him to signify agreement—"we've had no time together since James Blair returned. I know his return came at a most unfortunate moment. I know you've been confused ever since. What I'm trying to do is explain it to you—as best I can."

Stephen had a dark and angry look on his face. He strode up and down the room, sometimes looking at her but more often not. "Two full months have passed—more than two months really—and you've made no effort to see me. When at last you came, you came with him. Had it not been for Dougald's quite accidental visit we'd not have had this chance to speak." He turned suddenly and looked full at her. "Would you ever have spoken to me if chance had not brought us together tonight?"

Cecily heard a plaintive note amid the angry tones. She saw despair in his expression. He was not so much angry, she knew, as hurt. Quickly she rose; the sketches fell in disarray on the floor. She went to him and put her hand on his arm. Oh, she thought, if I could only tell him the whole truth! It would make it so much easier. Immediately she rejected the thought; she would not endanger James, whose purpose has not yet, thank God, been divined.

"Stephen," she said very softly, "that night, when James Blair walked in while we were reading, I told you I wouldn't give you an answer." She paused to make sure he was listening, then went on. "Think back, Stephen, to what I said to you. I said you didn't know what you were asking of me. Now you know what I meant. I'd had word he was coming. I didn't know what his return would mean to me. I intended to tell you. But I had no idea he'd arrive that night. I thought there would be time."

Stephen looked at her again. He ran his fingers through his hair. "I suppose that's true. I can't believe you'd not have acted openly with me."

She saw he'd got rid of his anger and started hur-

riedly to speak. They might have but five minutes
more to reach some understanding. "Stephen, I'll
have to say some difficult things very quickly. You
must try to understand, even when I can't explain
them well." In her concentration she began to pace
back and forth. With her fingers she crushed her
handkerchief and played with it. "I was speaking true
when I said I cared for you. I really didn't want to
care. We are too different, albeit very much alike.
Despite my will, I began to care."

He took a quick step forward and opened his arms
to her. "Then——"

"Wait!" Her arm warded him off. "I fought the affection, feeling happiness would never come of it—
not for you, not for me. You remember the antagonism of our first meetings. It has seemed to me that
some day that antagonism must burst out again. I've
feared we could stifle it only so long. I will be honest.
I tried to counter-balance my growing feeling for you
with my remembered feeling for James Blair." She
looked at him almost defiantly. "He and I are
alike—in every way." She turned away and walked
another few steps. "For a while I had no idea he
would return. When I found he was coming, I simply
didn't know what I felt. We had parted in anger. I
had intended to forget him. . . . I couldn't."

Stephen followed her and caught her arm. "You don't
need to tell me every detail. I want to know but one
thing, Cecily. Do you love him?" He tightened his
fingers as if he could by force compel her to deny
love for James Blair. "Say no."

She stood still and looked at the floor. Finally, very
quietly, she answered, "I still don't know."

Stephen dropped her arm and turned away sharply
in renewed anger. "Why do you tell me all this if not
to reassure me?"

"Oh, Stephen," she cried, "I am not being wilfully
cruel. I am torn, terribly torn, between the two of
you. I don't know what answer to give you now any
more than I did before."

Stephen leaned over his drawing-table. He gripped
the sides with his hands. "You act, Cecily, as if you

cared very much for him. You spend all your time with him. You let him speak endearingly to you before others. I dare not be so free. Is your feeling for us equal when your deportment with us is not?"

Cecily's retort came sharply. "Why I act as I do with James Blair is my own affair. I have tried to reason with you. Now I won't try any longer!" She spoke rapidly. "I am not a woman who likes to dangle men. I have hated hurting you. Throughout these two months I have relied on your patience and generosity—yes, and love. I hoped that when I could speak to you you'd understand, be patient a little longer. When I know my own heart there will be no ambiguity in my actions."

He ran to her and put his arms about her. "Cecily ... Cecily ... forget what I said. I've yearned to see you, to hear you speak as though you cared about what had happened." He held her more tightly. "I will be patient."

She detached herself from him. "Thank you, Stephen. I wish I were not so foolish. It is dreadful to know that I must in the end hurt one of you. I would not do it. You are both dear to me."

Cecily expected him to speak or to come to her. He stood with his hands hanging limply at his sides. He was very different from James, who would refuse to let her put him off. Dear Stephen. He was a good man; he would wait patiently. She moved quickly to him and took his hand. "I wonder whether anywhere there is another man as honourable as you."

Sadly Stephen gazed into her eyes. "Honourable? I wonder, is it for honour that women love?"

There was an assured knock on the door. Cecily was not forced to answer Stephen's question. She pressed his hand and then turned swiftly to pick up the scattered drawings. When Blair entered she was studying one with particular care. With a smile she beckoned to him. "Come see this. Isn't it lovely?"

As she looked up to see his reaction to Stephen's artistry, she noted again the leanness of his features. Her heart beat faster, and she wondered how honest she had been with Stephen.

Dougald looked up quickly when David entered the MacQueens' parlour. "Ah! Blair found you."

David grinned and nodded in answer but spoke first to Moira. "You look very happy, my sister-to-be, and that makes me happy. Just think! This is the first time I've seen you since the engagement."

Moira had run to him as soon as she saw him. He caught her hands, stepped back and looked at her fondly. "There was a time, lassie, when I thought I might be your bridegroom. I gave up that hope long ago. The best man always wins."

Dougald shot his brother a speculative glance. He felt no jealousy—there could be none between David and himself. And besides, there could be no doubt of Moira's love. His look signified only his great affection for David, his sincere hope that he suffered no sense of loss. Dougald could not quite persuade himself that David was whole of heart. Who could be, once he'd met Moira?

Blushing, Moira led David to the divan where Dougald still sat. She pulled up a hassock and sat before the brothers. Her elbows were on her knees and her chin was cupped in her hands. Against the fire her skin shone pale and her hair glowed red. A modest, tenuous smile came to her face.

"The thing I'm most happy about, David, is that the breach between Flora and me is healing." Her hand went out to Dougald and he held it while she spoke on to David. "I know how deeply Flora loves Dougald, how deeply he loves her. Not for a moment have I ceased regretting my outburst. The instant after I spoke I knew I'd do anything, even wait to be married, to show her how sorry I was." Her voice trailed off in recollection.

David leaned forward and spoke cheerfully. "Don't fret about it now. You know how good Flora is. She forgave you before you left that day."

"Is she all right?" Moira asked anxiously. "I've asked Dougald and he says she's troubled deeply. I thought so. My thoughts have gone to her constantly and I have seen her struggle under a weight of woe."

"She bears up, and none of us will know her sorrow. But we can all tell she thinks constantly of what she must do. We can only wait until she decides." David leaned back meditatively.

Dougald disliked this talk of Flora, for he understood well Flora's conflict. The same revulsion against fighting for the Crown that harassed her had harassed him. Perhaps, he thought, I feel it even more strongly. At least she doesn't think at times that she'd like to fight for the other side. He remembered his earlier chat with Moray. A sense that Stephen and he loved America in the same way had taken him there. It was perhaps fortunate that Cecily's presence had prevented intimate conversation. There was no use in even thinking about another course. He could not go against his own people.

Forcibly Dougald wrenched his thoughts to the happier subject of "later." He smiled and said, "Let's think of the future. Davie, I've been telling Moira about Allan's plan to move. We've talked very confidently of taking over Mount Pleasant. Of course, it would depend on Allan."

"Aye, David," Moira said, rousing herself from her musing, "and we've thanked you a score of times tonight for offering to help us work a place till we get started." She paused and then spoke wistfully. "Wouldn't it be wonderful if it did work out this way? Flora would be with her family; we'd have a home, as she wants us to. And we could be married around the new year—or early spring at the latest."

Fondly Dougald looked at her, sharing her dream. He shifted so he could see David too, who also shared their dream, though in a different way. "It's hard not to be over-confident. If Allan buys, he'll need to sell Mount Pleasant right away. I'd have to work the place off. It would take a couple of years at least. The sum Lady Margaret gave me to get started with won't cover the price and might not cover what Allan would need."

"Nay," David spoke up, "but our combined sums might. I'll lend you my share."

Dougald and Moira shook their heads simultaneously, and Dougald said what they were both thinking. "We aren't going to stand in your way. Once the rebellion's put down, you'll want to ride west. We know what an explorer you are at heart."

With a laugh David got up. He paced about the room to use up some of his energy and brushed aside the objection. "I'll get started on my own right enough. Don't you worry. All I'm going to need is the price of a new saddle and some supplies." He stopped between them and looked down. "Honestly, my lad and lassie, there's nothing I'd rather do than help you two along. You count on the money, and on me. Buy yourself Mount Pleasant or some other place. Remember, I'm an experienced tacksman. I'll serve you well."

Moira reached up and caught his hand. She pressed it to her cheek. "A dear brother I'm getting."

Embarrassed slightly, now he'd made his speech, David disengaged himself and picked up his bonnet. "Come, lad. This visiting is all very well, but we've a job to do."

"No!" Moira jumped to her feet in surprise and dismay. "I thought this once you just came to see me!"

"Unfortunately not, dear Moira," Dougald said with a sigh. "We have to come back to the present now and perform a mission."

"Not a dangerous one again?"

"Nay. This is very easy. We ride down for the King's standard. One day not too far hence we'll need it." Dougald reluctantly rose and threw his plaid over his shoulders.

Moira looked at him sadly. "It really is coming, isn't it? When we talk as we did tonight I almost forget." She pressed her clenched hand against her lips for a moment and her eyes were frightened. At last she whispered, "There are other times when I can't think of anything but the coming battle. I keep seeing disaster. . . . Oh, if I could only believe it would turn out well!"

Dougald took her in his arms. "Don't think about it. Think about the time after the battle . . . when we'll be wholly happy."

Moira nodded. She walked between them to the door with a hand on either lad's arm. Her eyes went from one to the other. "You must take care of each other."

Dougald kissed her good-bye. "Perhaps we can stop on our way home."

Again she nodded. "Try to. I'll be waiting. In case you can't, let me give you a message for Flora now. Tell her my thoughts are always with her—and my love. Tell her about our plans and assure her that I wait patiently, knowing she was right." She reached up and took the plaid he had carelessly tossed about his shoulders. Carefully she draped it across his chest and fastened it. "God would it were a magic cloak of invulnerability."

29

The MacDonalds Forever!

FLORA let the latch fall into place after the messenger had left. She did not open the letter at once, but tucked it into her pocket so she could draw her little plaid about her shoulders for warmth. The raw January winds cut through her this winter as they never had before. She stepped slightly to one side and, through the tall, narrow window beside the door, looked at the cleared land about the house. The messenger had already disappeared into the pine grove. The yard was empty and had the hard, hoary, crusty look of all farm land in winter. Just looking at it, Flora shivered. These had been severe weeks. Each morning the men had to go out to break the ice in the trough so the stock could drink. She felt very lonely, very isolated here in the new place.

As she walked back into the great-room Flora glanced about her. This was, as Allan had promised it would be, a much finer house than that at Mount Pleasant. There were three more bedrooms, and the great-room was very spacious. There were dark, rough-raftered ceilings which reminded her of her old home on Skye. Yes, if the house had been of stone, instead of clapboard, she would have been reminded of Flodigarry.

Allan had hoped she would be happy in this new home. He'd announced his purchase almost triumphantly: "You've been wanting it, Flora. Now I can give it to you."

She had almost retorted, "I don't want the new home westward if peace does not come with it." Because she had dreaded another argument, she answered instead, "But the money, Allan." And indeed, she could not believe that they could afford to buy a larger place so soon.

He'd brushed aside her protests. "The profit was good—thanks to our shrewd businessman Sandy. And yesterday I had a good offer for Mount Pleasant. I believe verily that fate meant us to have Caleb Touchstone's good plantation. And it is good! Over five hundred acres, and a mill and an orchard."

The purchase had been hurried through. It had pained Flora to see Mount Pleasant go to a stranger, when Dougald and Moira would have liked to buy it. But, to meet Touchstone's price, Allan had to sell outright. And, Flora thought now, perhaps it was just as well. Come spring Dougald and Moira would take a small place, one of a size they could manage without too much difficulty.

They had moved in November, a barren time of year. Though the pines, which surrounded the farm on all sides, were tall and stately and green, she wanted the summer-tender, the softer greens of hardwoods. The trees of the orchard stood grey and gnarled and lifeless. The fields were dun-coloured with drying stalks. Allan had been able to look upon this drab sight and envision summer's growth and autumn's harvest. Flora could not. She'd tried, but she could not envision the apple trees laden with bright-red apples. She could not imagine the stone springhouse filled with crocks of fresh milk and cream.

Once she had shaken her head and said, "I do not understand how you can speak so confidently. With your recruiting and the issue it will bring, you may not be able to farm this land."

"I will be able, Flora. I will. If not next spring, then the one after. When I'm done fighting there will be peace in the land, and this will be a rich and happy home for us."

Flora had not been able to share his faith. She could not believe in the coming of peace. She saw only Allan's preparation for war. Her fear had never abated; yet she had found some comfort and pleasure in the new home. It was nothing to the pleasure she had hoped to feel when they moved close to Anne and

Hugh, but she enjoyed it as long and as much as she was able. Before the coldest weather came, Anne had been able to visit and Flora to play with her grandchild. Hugh came once, though more often Flora went to him. Ian was often in the house, joining them at supper, chiming in with his natural-born-farmer's talk of "heavy land" and plough blades. Yes, there had been a semblance of cheer and unity.

The best part of the new home had been seeing John Bethune. Flora recognized that. He, with his devout faith in neutrality, his constant preaching of it, his never-ceasing endeavour to hold the old Scots to their convictions, gave her support in her own quieter campaign. He did not come expressly to help her in that way, nor had she invited him for that purpose. No, she'd engaged John Bethune as a tutor for the lads. He came once a week to read Latin to Ian and Jamie, and to Dougald, who joined in voluntarily when he was home. That laddie read books from Alex's fine library as though a thirst that had been drying him out for years was at last being quenched. The younger lads rebelled at the lessons, but Dougald often stopped by her chair to thank her for making them possible. That was usually after one of his trips to Glendale. There he studied the Roman and Greek philosophers the Auldjo lad had told him about.

Flora tried to hold these cheerful memories, but they slipped away. She sat down by the fire, and huddled a little for warmth. As she drew her plaid closer about her shoulders she noticed how thin her hand was. With a sigh she realized how old she felt, how very cold.

Resolutely she turned in her chair, intending to pick up one of the books that lay on the table beside her. A crackle of bent paper reminded her of the letter the messenger had brought. She drew it out and studied the envelope. It must, she thought as she began to tear the seal, be very important. Else no one would have ridden 'way over here in freezing winds to deliver it. She thought it odd, however, that an important letter would bear no emblem in the seal.

When she unfolded the crisp sheet, she understood

the lack of identification. This was a message from Governor Martin, sure to be confiscated if it fell into the hands of the rebels. She ran her eye over the elegant script. One sentence she read again and again: "We hope to have your help in raising the clans." A bitter sigh escaped her. Even now, when she saw almost no one, when she lived in lonely retreat, petitions reached her. And she had already endured so many. The words of them came flooding back to her.

First, General MacDonald's. He'd come in early December for a consultation with Allan. As always, she had fled upstairs to avoid contact with the "war cause," as she'd come to label Allan's side. But she had been a little too tardy. While she was yet on the stairs, the general's voice had arrested her: "Fionnghal!"

At the sound of her Gaelic name she had half turned. MacDonald stood on the lowest step. One hand rested on the banister; the other reached toward her. He looked at her from under his heavy brows. His gaze was determined. He spoke as her chieftain: "Fionnghal! A man's business is war. Let Allan take his man's part."

She had known why he spoke as he did. She stood firm for neutrality. Allan stood firm for the loyalist cause. The impasse was slowly nullifying both of them. Allan had gone on in his work of recruiting, forced forward by his strong conviction. But his energy, like hers, was sapped by their pull against each other. General MacDonald wanted Allan free of her hindrance.

She had faced him and made her retort: "Nothing, no one could keep Allan from acting a man's part. But . . . I believe he could do otherwise than he does, and still be a man."

MacDonald had answered, "Nay, Flora, he cannot. Once he could have perhaps. Not now. You wish him back in the past world you live in. You cling to a world in which we Scots had to live amicably only with our clansmen, those of our own name. Yours is the lost cause, the forlorn hope, not ours. We—Allan, Alex, the lads and I—live in a world with new and farther-reaching connections between us and the men around us. Allan has recognized the conditions of this New World."

"No!" she cried aloud, rising from her chair as if the general were present to hear her. "This is not a question of the old and the new. Those who have accepted the new are rebels. They are the breakers of tradition, the forgers of something never before dreamed of. That is not what Allan is. He upholds tradition!" Her voice sank. "But his tradition now is one the Scots should hate!"

Flora had come to see with clarity the essence of the struggle between Allan and herself. It was not the new versus the old. It was not even rivalry between the Stuart and the Hanoverian, though that could not be wholly ignored. Nay, it was really one way of having peace against another way of having peace. The identity of their goals had made the struggle the more heartbreaking. They wanted the same thing. They wanted it for each other's sake and for the sake of all their people. They respected each other, loved the more deeply for their unity of aspiration. But while she said, "If you want to enjoy peace, do not disrupt it," Allan said, "If you want peace, fight for it."

Flora bit her lip in concentration. She was trying to still her painful thoughts. Slowly she picked up the letter that had fallen to the floor. She sat down again and rubbed her fingers over the worn leather of her Bible. She had read the scriptures long into the night after General MacDonald had spoken to her. She had read the passages in Isaiah, Joel and Micah which say the swords shall be beaten into ploughshares. Now she did not turn to the pages. She knew each passage by heart. Joel said, "Let the weak say, 'I am a warrior.'"

Allan was a warrior now, but he was not weak. He erred, but, by virtue of the formidable force of his conviction, he was stronger than he had ever been before. She had begun some time ago to recognize that she would never sway Allan. Her hopes, in that dawn after their first discussion, had been in vain. They would never agree—not unless it was she who changed.

Many people had besought her to yield—not merely people like the general and the Governor but friends and kin on whom she'd counted for support.

Not long after the move to this house, the MacQueens had come. Mr. MacQueen had told her to give up her hopes of success. "You'll do no good opposing Allan. Things have gone too far. Allan has it in his heart to fight, and fight he will. You sit here by yourself, pondering right from wrong. Will you ever find the answer? What is right? I do not know. The seething passions in this land will devour us, whichever way we go."

She had asked him whether he had joined the loyalists.

"Nay. I would go the other way—to the patriots—if I went at all. But I'm under oath. I dare not take up arms against the Hanoverian, but I will not fight for him."

"Yet," she'd cried, "you seem not to think it wrong that my Allan should!"

"Nay, your Allan is not fighting for or against the Hanoverian. He's never cared either way about the Crown, except as symbol. He's fighting for his life—or livelihood. It's the same thing. I cannot blame him. More important, you cannot stop him."

Flora's hand clenched over the letter and crumpled its one edge. Nay, she thought, I have not stopped him. But I still have not come to believe we save our lives and the lives of those we love by sending them into a battle between the Americans and the English. Why we Scots should fight in that battle I cannot see."

Others saw. Anne, Anne who had begged her to make Allan desist, had spoken to her one day in mid-December.

Katie had started it, with the frank familiarity of an old servant. Yes, after she'd taken Norman from Anne and started up the stairs with him, she'd stopped and brought up something that had evidently bothered her long. "Anne, 'tis you who can talk to your mother. The tension in this house is saddening to everyone. Tell your mother to give in. Tell her when men have made up their minds to fight, the devil himself can't change them."

Flora remembered well how Anne had laughed slightly at Katie's bold concern. When they were alone and could not be overheard, Anne had said, "My reasons are not the same as Katie's, but they point the same way: Give in. I know I once felt otherwise. Now my Alex has convinced me that we must fight, and on the side of the King."

"What of your own convictions, Anne?" Flora had asked.

"My deepest conviction is that a wife must follow and support her husband, Mother."

The words had cut, but Flora had answered levelly. "What if the wife feels a twofold responsibility? What if she, like me, cares as much for her people as for her husband?"

Anne had lowered her eyes and admitted Flora's problem to be more difficult than her own. "Aye. I understand. Your voice speaks for many. Mine does not."

In the days that had followed Anne's visit Flora had come to wonder whether her voice did speak for many. All the people near who had sided with her deserted her. She was left alone, more alone than ever, to resist the cause of war. Neil had approached her in embarrassment one day. He had stood before her, and turned his cap in his hands nervously. But when he'd spoken his voice had been steady. "Mistress, there is a matter on which I would speak."

After she had signified that he should go on, he'd said, " 'Tis about this business of Allan's recruiting. Begging your pardon, but 'tis not like you to be lacking in courage or wisdom. All through the long years I've watched you, you've understood a man's problems. But now you seem not to know that Allan must go to war. I tried to tell you months ago, on the road to your stepfather's. 'Tis Allan's duty to fight this rebellion. 'Tis also his need. You cannot keep him from doing what his conscience says is right." He'd waited a moment, then asked, "Is it not the way of our women to buckle on the sword-belt of her man and put his shield into his hand? Is it not, Fionnghal?"

Neil's words had distressed her. Did the true valiance, then, of Scots women inhere only in sending their husbands and sons off to battle? Would she, if she opposed the warrior Allan, deny the man Allan?

When Hugh had come, but a day later, she'd confronted him with that question. He'd sat quietly, with his hands folded over his cane. "When you sought my advice before, Flora, I told you Allan needed you. I think the reason the Scots women have always stood uncomplainingly behind their men is that their men have needed them. I know that was true of me, with your mother."

Flora put her hand to her forehead. It was feverishly hot, as if a fire burned there as well as in the hearth. She wished she could forget all these words of recent admonition. They had enhanced her unhappiness a thousandfold. It is ironical, she thought, that I, the one who set out to do the persuading, am the one subject to the most arguments. There seem to be very few now who share my view. She felt caught in a mesh of reasons that she could not sort, and wearily rested her head on her hand.

The petitions of her family and friends had, she recognized, undeniably wrought some effect. Somehow the ends she had been striving for had been subtly transformed. The need for reunion with Allan had become more compelling than the need for changing him. The need for Scots unity was more compelling than the need for neutrality.

Once more she unfolded the letter and re-read Governor Martin's sentences: "We hope to have your help in raising the clans. No other person in all this Royal Province has the influence that you have. The people respect and love you.... If you will do your part, we will raise three thousand Highlanders."

She rose to carry the letter to her desk. For a moment she tapped it with her finger and wondered whether she should answer it at once. To sit down now, take the quill in hand and reply would resolve her anxiety. She knew that her answer would be final, whatever the consequences. There came always a moment when vacillation tore one apart. She was approaching that moment. Her old conviction rose strong in her. Swiftly she picked up the pen and dipped it in the ink. In her haste she bent to write without even sitting down. It would take but a line to refuse.

Before she had finished the salutation, she laid down the pen. Doubt again assailed her. She slipped the Governor's letter into the drawer.

On Thursday John Bethune came, not to teach the lads but to talk with Flora. His face was unusually grave when he greeted her. She knew he brought news. "What is it, John?" she asked as soon as he was seated.

From his pocket he extracted a letter. The envelope was blank except for the address. She started in surprise when she saw it, and Bethune looked at her penetratingly. "You received one, too?"

Flora went to the desk and drew her letter out. Holding it toward him, she said, "Would you like to read it?"

With a shake of his head Bethune answered, "Nay, I don't need to. The wording is no doubt different, but the question is the same." He leaned forward to warm his hands at the fire. The flames cast reddish tints on his face and accentuated dark lines of thought and worry. "Have you answered it, Flora?"

"Nay. I should have, but uncertainty stayed my hand. You, John?" She took her customary chair, across the hearth from him, and spread her plaid over her lap.

"I answered. I told Martin I would go as chaplain of the Highland regiment Allan is raising."

Flora sank back. "How can you? What about your preaching?"

While he rubbed his hands together and held them to the warmth he said, "The Reverend Mr. MacLeod will take over Bethesda. He's not too able, being in tender health, but he will manage." He straightened abruptly, put his hands on his knees and gazed at her in earnestness. "I see it as my duty, Flora. Most of my people will be in the regiment. How can I be of service to them if I stay here? I cannot let them go to battle without the comfort of the Saviour and the church."

Flora had closed her eyes while he spoke. She felt as if her last bulwark had been taken away. Yet she would not let John know how bereft she was. She looked at him and nodded understandingly. With her left hand she reached forward to touch his arm in reassurance. "Of course you must go. And you belie nothing of your principles. Although you'll be amid the killing of war, you'll be succouring, saving. It's the right way for you, John."

As if greatly relieved, Bethune rose. He hesitated, then asked, "How will you answer the letter, Flora?"

She shrugged. "I am not certain."

Bethune walked once to the window and back. When he was beside her again he said, "Your decision is most difficult. May God guide you in it! I won't presume to advise you, yet I will say this. A wife and mother may be to her family much what a minister is to his flock. You too have it in your power to succour and to save."

She pushed herself to her feet and gazed long into the fire. "I have wondered about that. I know that I will do whatever I must to insure the safety of our people. How best can I save them? Martin tells me that if I speak out three thousand will rally. Three thousand is a sizeable force. Three thousand would have a good chance. But ... Martin often exaggerates." She turned about to face him. "What do you think, John?"

With great sympathy he said, "I cannot guide you. Only God and your own heart can. Let's pray together for guidance."

They knelt on the bricks before the fire-place. John Bethune's petition was brief, but it sank deep into Flora's heart. The last words were "... and if we cannot escape death, let us not fear it. Death is a black camel that kneels at every man's door. But with Thy help, we conquer death."

After she had closed the door after John, she watched him ride away. His clergy's plaid flowed from his shoulder. When she could no longer catch a glimpse of it among the pine trunks, she walked back to the great-room. Perhaps it was time to answer the letter. She stopped short. Nay, there was one thing yet to do.

When Allan strode in from the mill that afternoon, he started, as so often of late, to go upstairs without coming in to see her. She called to him.

Her heart contracted when she saw that his eyes were slightly squinted in tenseness and caution. He, her husband, wondered and perhaps even feared what she might want of him.

"Allan," she said gently, "I want to say something to you."

He hunched his head forward a bit and looked at her quizzically. "Aye, Flora. I'm listening."

She walked half-way across the room, stopped and waited to choose her words. "You know, Allan, that I understand what you are striving for?"

"I know you've said you do. Sometimes it's difficult for me to believe it, when you unendingly oppose me."

She lifted her hand as if to tell him her first remark had been only a preliminary. "I have for a long time realized that you nor I, nor anyone but God, could prevent this war. My entire concern has been to keep the Scots—and you—from taking part in it, being swallowed up by it."

Allan observed her closely, but did not interrupt. She knew that he could not quite comprehend the meaning of her words. Nonetheless she persisted, needing to go through it all at least once more. "Don't you want that too, Allan?"

His head dipped forward. "Of course. And if isolation were possible, I'd be with you."

She took another step toward him and opened her hands supplicatingly. "If you were with me, we could unite the Scots and be safe."

He shook his head. Impatiently he rubbed his forehead with his sleeve. "I've told you many times, Flora: What you want is impossible. No one, Scot or otherwise, will escape danger if this storm breaks in its full fury. Besides, many Scots have the same convictions I do, and as deeply. They will not swerve."

He turned to leave. Quickly she spoke up, wanting to ask her last question before he'd gone. "Allan, if I joined you, how many Scots could we raise?"

Slowly he swung around. She thought for an instant that he was going to come to her and say, "Flora, will you? Please." He only waited, studied her face and then drew a long breath. "No man can predict exactly. In the end, everyone makes up his own mind, regardless of who calls. But, if you would join us, I think we could count on nearly three thousand altogether."

She knew he was waiting for her reply. She, though, was waiting for him to say more. After a moment in which both kept silent, he left the room. She heard his steps on the stairs above, and knew he was going in to wash and change for supper.

Flora stayed in the great-room a while longer. As Allan had said, each one must decide for himself. She thought over all that had been said that day and in days past. At last she went to the wall and opened her mirror.

She looked for a long time at Charlie's face. She did not see the handsome features of her beloved Stuart prince; she saw instead the discouraged man she had remembered while with Hugh. Once before she had refused to help, and then had seen she was wrong. Was this moment, when she was forcing Allan to go on alone, another in which she was wrong?

Before, by uniting herself in purpose with another, she had saved a lone man's life and helped her Scots. Perhaps now, by uniting herself with Allan, she could help save many Scots' lives.

Suddenly her loneliness fell away. She closed her mind to doubt. MacQueen had spoken the truth: she could sit alone pondering right and wrong forever. In the end she would not be sure of the right. Who could forecast the destruction of an impending storm? Not she. Not anyone. All she and other mortals could do would be to band together and face danger with the strength of unity.

That night at dinner Flora laid down her napkin carefully. She rose before the others and stood looking at them. For the first time in many weeks she smiled full on them and let her eyes answer the question that was always in theirs.

They all watched her. Dougald spoke their thought, their hope. "Flora is with us now."

"Aye." She nodded. "I am with you now."

Again there was silence, but only briefly. Suddenly David scraped back his chair and ran around the table to catch her in jubilation. The other lads rushed to her. David whirled her away in a mad dance of celebration. "The MacDonalds forever!" he shouted.

"Set me down!" she cried, laughing and crying from the joy of sharing with them again. "Look what you are doing to my hair. It's tumbling down."

David stopped at her request, but almost before she had regained her balance young Jamie whirled her on. Again she cried, "Set me down. My Allan has not moved."

As she went to him she pushed her loosened hair back from her face. Her cheeks were flushed and her smile happy. When she spoke her voice was breathless, from the dancing and from emotion. "Well, Allan, have you nothing to say?" she asked, laying her hand on his shoulder.

He reached up and covered her hand with his. Earnestly he looked at her. First he murmured, "You look like a young girl again, with the colour in your cheeks." Then, after a pause, he asked, "Are you sure, Flora?"

"Aye," she assured him in a firm voice.

"I thank God. I have needed you, and will need you more before this is over."

Jamie had run to tell Katie and Neil, who had always shared the family sorrows and joys. When Katie ran in she was flushed and panting with excitement. Neil, who'd had to come in from the barn, was ruddy with cold. When they were told, they went up to Flora.

" 'Tis the good Lord has caused you to see rightly, Fionnghal," Katie said.

Neil spoke next. "I knew you'd see your duty. You'll buckle on Allan's sword-belt and place the shield in his hand."

With a smile full of affection for these faithful friends, Flora answered, "Aye. That I will—just as you admonished me. And now, to symbolize this moment, when the MacDonalds join together to face whatever crisis is to come, I'll pin a clan emblem on each of you."

At Flora's direction Katie brought in a length of the clan ribband and scissors. One by one the men knelt before Flora and received the woman's blessing of the warrior. Over each bowed head Flora spoke the words "*Dh 'aindeoin co theiradh el*, Gainsay who dare!"

It was Jamie who knelt last. For a moment Flora hesitated and an expression of pain crossed her face. "You too? Must I send even my bairn?"

Allan stepped forward and put his hand on Jamie's shoulder. "We MacDonalds are together now—even unto this youngest."

Flora pinned the badge on Jamie and kissed his cheek. The exhilaration of the moment had passed, and serious thought of the import of her act returned to her. She did not waver, for now, when she was at one with her family, she felt a greater strength than she had known for many weeks.

That night she lay in Allan's arms and pledged to him all support she could give. The cares of the past months melted away. She put her lips to his dark head, so close to her shoulder. Her dear Allan was hers once more, and she belonged to him.

30

Await Tomorrow

In February 1776 loyalist hopes were buoyant. It was
true that the provincial Congress and the Committees of Safety had practically taken over all government; true also that Whig troops drilled and marched
as they pleased, especially in the piedmont counties.
More ominous, it was true that the greater part of
the Whig dominance had been won in the last ten
months. But, the Tories told one another, their day
was just dawning.

It was an epidemic hope, various and many-footed.
Governor Martin would always say at least sixty per
cent of the people were loyal at heart though in-
timidated by the rebels around them. In moments of
enthusiasm he sometimes said ninety per cent. No one
asked him how so many could be overawed by so
few. At such times he estimated there were thirty
thousand loyalists who would rise to the call.

In less sanguine moments he figured closer: three
thousand Highlanders, three thousand Regulators and
three thousand unclassified Tories—a sizeable body
still. Leaders such as Allan MacDonald thought three
thousand to thirty-five hundred might be raised at
Cross Creek, Highlanders and Regulators, perhaps
more. They had travelled through the hill country and
spoke from personal observation. When the call
came...

Even the least of these predictions was comforting.
But the real hope of the Tories did not lie within the
province. From the Governor down to the smallest,
they put their main reliance on British regulars,
several regiments of regulars. With solid redcoats for
their support, the Tories would rise confidently. The

redcoats would stamp out the spirit of rebellion and restore rightful authority.

It was not an empty hope. A year ago even a thousand regulars might have overawed the Whigs and pacified the whole colony. Now it would take considerably more than a thousand. But Governor Martin had long since written to request an expeditionary force and had received vague assurances. When the troops landed at last, everything would be different and, the Tories were sure, much, much better.

On February 4 a rider reached General Donald MacDonald in Cross Creek carrying a letter from Governor Martin now on the sloop *Scorpion*. Jubilantly Martin reported that he had received a letter from the Earl of Dartmouth, written on November 7, carrying the great news that an expeditionary force of seven regiments of regulars, bound for the Cape Fear, would follow close on the heels of his letter. Dartmouth was explicit: seven regiments and a fleet following immediately. He went on to say that the loyalist militia, especially the Scots, which had been organized and recruited secretly, should now embody openly, take up arms and prepare to join the regulars.

He was sending out word to leaders of the loyalists everywhere to embody at once and march to the coast. It was his hope they would reach Brunswick by February 15.

Donald MacDonald put Martin's letter down and rubbed his hands in satisfaction. The call had come. Now was the time for the Scots to rise and fight for their homes and lands, for the peace and security of the province.

With this positive and immediate promise of British aid, all the waverers would flock to the royal standard. His recruiting problems were at an end.

He opened his dispatch-case and took out a draft of a manifesto he had partially prepared against the day of the Scots rising. He read it through, sometimes uttering a sentence or phrase aloud: "I hereby command and charge all his Majesty's loyal people to repair to the royal Banner, agreeable to the Governor's

Royal Proclamation, of date the 10th of January last." He took up his quill and changed a word or two. "Employed in the glorious and righteous Cause of rescuing and delivering their Country from the Usurpation of Rebellion." It was brief and pithy. It had the right ring. "Given under my Hand and Seal—" he filled in the date—"this 5th Day of February 1776."

He would have copies made and publish them tomorrow. At the same time he would issue the call to assemble at Cross Creek. The Governor didn't seem to be aware of the distances that would have to be covered in summoning in the Highlanders. It was out of the question for the Scots to gather and march to Brunswick by the fifteenth. It would take that long to bring them all together here in Cross Creek. He thought, however, he could notify Martin that he would be at Wilmington by February 25.

He called in James Blair and sent him off to confer with Governor Martin, letting the Governor know when he believed he could reach Wilmington and finding out how the Highland troops should make their junction with the incoming British troops. "Come back as soon as you can," he told Blair. "We may be on the march. But choose the most open route back."

General MacDonald decided he would call up the volunteers himself from Cumberland County. Allan MacDonald had recently moved west out into Anson County. He would send Allan copies of all the important papers and put him in charge of raising the Scots there. He would send off a rider within an hour to acquaint Allan with the good news and instruct him to call out the men at the earliest moment.

Allan MacDonald burst into the house in high excitement, Donald MacDonald's letter in his hands, the messenger from Cross Creek at his heels. "Flora," he shouted, "the time's come! Seven regiments of British regulars on the sea, maybe already in Carolina—no need to go to Nova Scotia now. The general must see it. We'll put down the rebels here."

The news spread through the household like wild-

fire. Flora, the twins, Sandy, Jamie, the servants, all
came flocking in. Allan couldn't stand still. He
walked up and down, burst into triumphant laughter,
read them Donald MacDonald's letter and the copy of
Martin's letter, passed around General MacDonald's
ringing manifesto. All this was the news he had been
waiting for.

In two minutes the boys were as excited as he.
They were all talking at once. They are all boys,
Flora thought, even Allan. Their spirits were on fire
at the thought of going to war. But her mood was in-
dulgent. She had seized on one piece of Allan's blurt-
ed news: seven regiments of British regulars coming.
Pray God they be prompt! she told herself. If her
men could once be united with the regulars they
would probably be safe. She would need to worry
about them only for the short time they marched to
join the regulars.

Abruptly Allan returned to his immediate responsi-
bilities. "We'll rejoice later," he said. "Now we must
decide the best way to call up the Anson County
Scots."

It was Flora who thought of the fiery cross. "'Tis
war," she said. "Let's follow the ancient custom of
the Highlands. We'll find swift runners to take the
message to every mountain and glen. Our people will
hear the call and heed, as they did in the risings of
'15 and '45. They'll come 'out of the glens to follow
the MacDonalds.'"

They all caught up the idea with enthusiasm. David cried, "We'll burn a beacon fire, too, on the
highest hill."

Old Neil hurried from the room and in a few minutes returned with a squat bottle. "This is the very
last of Prince Charlie's liqueur from Skye," he said as
he poured the amber liquid into small glasses. "I've
been saving it for a wedding, but now is a better time
to drink it down."

They toasted the King and the royal family, the
Governor and General MacDonald, even the Mac-
Kinnons who had distilled the cordial, until at last the
bottle was empty.

In the morning all the family, including the servants and bondsmen and some of the neighbours, gathered at the stables.

Before anything was begun, old Neil stepped up to Flora and knelt on one knee. "Grant me one thing, Flora MacDonald. Let me give the bath of blood to the cross. Remember I carried the cross first in the '45. I ran from Monkstadt to Armadale, carrying the news and the cross. It was my cousin James who took it across the water and on."

"You shall be the first, old Neil, the faithful one."

Allan, as the chieftain of his family, slaughtered a fat goat with a swift thrust of his two-handed sword. "Lads," he said, "scorch the wood and bind it into crosses."

When the first cross was made and finished, David handed it to Flora. She took it in her hands and kissed it. Then she delivered it to Neil. "Bathe it in the blood."

When he once more stood erect with it in his hands, Flora stepped forward and kissed him on the forehead. "Go in God's care. Carry this emblem of war and carry it to those who fight with the MacDonalds."

It was the same for the other crosses. Before the four chosen to carry the crosses departed, they turned to Allan. Tall and bold he stood, his sword dripping with the blood of the goat. They lifted him on the heavy horsehide shield that had served a MacDonald for many generations. They carried him on their shoulders across the meadow, shouting an ancient cry in the Gaelic: "When danger arises, then is the hour for the chieftain to conquer in the field."

When they set him down, Allan drew his skean dhu from his garter and cut a thin line on each man's wrist. Every man pressed his wrist against his neighbour's, mingling the blood. No word was spoken. They were bound together by the tie of blood for the days to come.

Then Allan spoke. "We of Clan MacDonald will fight on the right hand of our Chief Donald MacDonald, as in the glorious day when Robert the Bruce granted the right to our ancestor Angus MacDonald, Lord of the Isles, as a reward for his fidelity.

"Now go forth, south and north, east and west. Display the cross to all. Speak only of the name of the meeting-place, Cross Creek, under the oak, and the time, before February 15."

Four horses stood waiting, saddled and bridled. The four messengers mounted, old Neil to go the short way, east, Jamie to go south, David to make the long journey to the west, as far as the Uwharie Mountains, and Sandy to go north.

Dougald had been chosen to light the signal fire on the highest hill. With him went Alex MacLeod of Glendale.

One of the bondsmen had his pipes. As the messengers rode off, he began a pibroch, an old tune with variations used when soldiers were rising and the burning spear was the sign.

So the MacDonalds dedicated themselves to war in the King's cause.

Companies were gathering everywhere in the valley of the Highlanders, meeting other companies and joining with them for the march to Cross Creek. Regiments were on the way from Chatham, Guilford and Bladen as well as from Anson. Colonel Thomas Rutherford, who had been working with the Whigs, now declared for the Crown and called for a loyalist muster on February 12. The next day, disappointed by the number which had come in, he issued a fiery manifesto. The roads were full of men converging on Cross Creek and Campbelltown.

On February 16 the troops began to pour into Cross Creek. On the same day Peter Hay proudly carried the royal standard from Campbelltown to Cross Creek. The MacDonald twins marched in the guard of honour that accompanied it. The town was full. Just how many had come in no one knew; people estimated all the way from thirty-five hundred to five thousand. And many of the Regulators were still to come.

On the face of it, the Scots army would be strong.

But General Donald MacDonald was suffering agonies of anxiety. People in each district responsible for calling out the loyalist troops had been told they could freely spread the news of the seven regiments of British regulars on the way, and they had. The story had been passed from person to person, and, as stories will, it had grown and picked up embroideries as it went. Hundreds of the volunteers stoutly maintained they had been told Governor Martin and a thousand British regulars would be at Cross Creek to meet them.

Now they went about slyly inquiring for the Governor and looking everywhere for the flash of red that would mean redcoats marching through the pines. No one had seen the Governor. No one had had so much as a glimpse of British regulars. In the taverns at night, people whispered about betrayal. The Regulators, who had little confidence in the Governor at best, were especially upset. They told one another, "If he deceives us in this, the chances are the whole story of the British army to help us is only a trick to draw us in. It will never appear. We will be left surrounded by our enemies."

Donald MacDonald and the other leaders worked frantically to reassure them. But do what they could, many of the Regulators turned back and went home. Sometimes whole companies, marching in ranks, turned away after a day in Cross Creek, and nothing could prevent them from going home in a body.

Even the Highlanders were slow to rally to the royal standard and commit themselves finally to the venture. Donald MacDonald had thought the work of recruiting was finished. He had rubbed his hands with satisfaction as the crowds had poured into the little town. Now once more everything hung in the balance.

Allan MacDonald had brought in many Highlanders from Anson. Perhaps he could help in this emergency. General MacDonald went to him and frankly asked his aid. "Though Major MacLeod and I are Highlanders like themselves and though I'm even chief of the MacDonalds in America, we're strangers to them here in

Carolina. They would have more trust in you, who live among them."

Allan knew the importance of the general's request. The whole rising was at stake. The Highlanders were hesitant and uneasy. Allan knew he might sway a good number of them, but he realized a greater number was needed. Only one person in Cross Creek could lift them to fighting pitch.

He raised his head and looked Donald MacDonald in the eye. "I'm not your man," he said. "I can bring in many of the Scots who are reluctant, but not enough. Furthermore, I cannot dissolve their half-heartedness. There's only one person in Cross Creek who can bring them heartily to the royal standard, and that's Flora. We must go to her."

General MacDonald rubbed the side of his jaw. "Will she do it?" he asked. "Last time I talked to her she seemed opposed to our plan."

Allan nodded. "She and I are together now."

Farquard Campbell had been impressed by the first rumour of the British expeditionary force. All his scheming had been to avert actual fighting and to work out some sort of compromise settlement. Now it seemed to him that he should throw his weight to the side of the Crown. If there was to be shooting, he'd take the side that would get it over with first. The rebels, it was becoming clear, would protract the conflict as long as their dissatisfaction lasted. The loyalists would end it sooner. But he believed in taking all precautions before making a final decision. He summoned in three of his bondsmen, three canny Campbells.

"I must know about this British fleet at the earliest moment," he said. "One of you will go to New Bern, one to Wilmington and one to Brunswick. The minute you have any definite word of the promised British fleet, send me an express by a sure rider. That doesn't mean its arrival only. I want news of any delay, or even any certain location of it—the Azores, Antigua, wherever it might be." He fixed a calculating eye on them. "Since conditions are likely to be disturbed, it may be wise to send several riders by different routes. At least one must get through with no delay. Understand?"

The boldest and cleverest of the three, the man destined for Wilmington, Peter Campbell, spoke up. "Farquard, will you cancel the bond of the first man to send you the information? I'd like to win my freedom."

Farquard Campbell eyed him steadily. "Yes," he said. "It would be a good bargain."

"Count on hearing from me," Peter Campbell said.

Fifteen minutes before two the next afternoon a great crowd was gathering around the mighty oak tree, such a crowd as Cross Creek had never seen before. Four pipers, led by Dougald, played martial music. The royal standard on its tall staff scarcely stirred in the light air.

At two precisely, Flora appeared, escorted by Allan and General MacDonald, Major MacLeod, Colonel Rutherford and other leaders. She wore a dress of the MacDonald tartan. For this occasion she had laid aside her favourite and customary ancient hunting plaid. To her it was a symbolic act: she hoped her men would encounter no prey on this journey. At the sight of her a great shout went up.

General MacDonald mounted the high platform with her and raised his arms high in a gesture of silence. "Friends," he roared, "Flora MacDonald, saviour of Prince Charlie in the '45, will speak to you. This is a great throng, and we want all to hear. Please let us have quiet." He paused, turned to Flora with a little bow, then faced the crowd. "I give you Flora MacDonald!"

A second time the Highlanders greeted her with a mighty shout, then stilled.

Flora's voice was ice and fire as she talked to them—ice as she poured her scorn on those who whispered of the Governor's absence as a betrayal, fire as she spoke of the mission of the Highlanders to maintain the security and order of the province, to protect their lands.

She read the Earl of Dartmouth's promise of the seven regiments of regulars as told in Governor Martin's letter. "This is the promise the Governor made you. He spoke no word of coming here himself. See, here is no betrayal, no deceit. Here are the faith and support of a great nation.

"What Highlander has hung back when his chief called? What mother or wife has grudged her sons or husband when strong arms and brave hearts were needed? Courage is our history and our heritage. Courage we have brought with us from our misty isles, from our glens and mountains. Let us show it here in our new home.

"But, as a woman with sons and husband and fellow clansmen in the ranks, I have a great hope that there will be no need for fighting." Her voice deepened, grew vibrant, reassuring. "It is my hope that the British regulars will arrive in time so that our Highland troops may join with them and overawe the rebels, without drawing a sword or firing a shot. This is my great hope as a mother and wife. And so I believe it will come to pass.

"Highlanders united never lose. It is only when our people are divided, when they are confused about who has the right, when many hang back, that they ever taste defeat. We here look to victory.

"If we rise as united clans, God will guide us. We will carry on our lives in peace and happiness.

"Let us now be one people, united in the task of preserving this province in order and prosperity. Let us all—every one of us—come now to the standard and engage together to carry this splendid enterprise to victory."

When Flora finished at last, her Highlanders again paid tribute to their heroine with a deep-throated roar. She had roused them.

Many of the Scots came in that day.

But not the Regulators. To them she was only a foreign woman. Though she spoke eloquently, they remained fearful and distrustful. That night more of them went home in a body. And the next day they slipped away in fours and fives.

And some of the Scots were as doubtful as the Regulators. The Whig committees had talked and talked, all during the fall, had put out papers explaining their grievances. Sometimes the seed had taken root, and not a few of the Scots had come to believe that the right lay with the Whigs. Flora had done her best, but the Scots were not all of one mind.

The next day General Donald MacDonald was forced to recognize that the volunteering at Cross Creek was virtually at an end. Indeed, desertions during the night had cost him some fifty men. To stay any longer would melt his troops gradually away, not increase them.

He called his captains together. "This afternoon we march a short distance out of the town. We are not so numerous as I had hoped, not above two thousand men, but those we have are good men, brave and able. There is nothing to be gained by lingering here. Pass the word that we shall muster and march at two this afternoon."

That afternoon a weak sun shone, but it was a chilly February day. By three o'clock the last preparations were made, and the men stood in ranks. A pipers' band, led by Dougald, struck up a march. The command was given and the columns moved forward.

Flora MacDonald sat stiffly erect on her white horse under the spreading crown of the great oak and watched the Highlanders stride by. Her heart swelled as they passed her, their faces quiet and determined, their kilts swaying to the rhythm of their step. Young faces and old blurred as her eyes filled with tears. With a great effort, she sat firmly erect as each line of men proudly saluted their beloved Flora.

She blinked her eyes to clear them. Once more each face stood out. She saw them all: Allan, bold and vigorous, a captain at the head of his company; Sandy, a lieutenant; Jamie, young though he was, looking every inch a soldier; the twins, their tartan kilts swirling to the skirl of the pipes—and so many more, all dear to her.

They took the road gaily. This was as it should be.

They should set out with high hopes, led by Donald. MacDonald, their chief and wise commander.

Just before the troops had marched he had spoken briefly to them. He had repeated that his plan was to lead them to Wilmington, there to take ship to Nova Scotia, where they would be made part of the main British army in America. If he could avoid an engagement, he promised there would be no fighting on the march to Wilmington. His words had given comfort to the women gathered to see their men off. They were travelling down the river only to take ship.

Though Flora took a degree of comfort from this assurance, she was sad to see her men go. There was David, very debonair. He was filled with exhilaration and joy. Camps were to be made, adventures to be had, battles to be fought. Life spread before his eager eyes as a series of splendid excitements.

Dougald had an expression in his eyes that troubled her. He had never needed to confide fully in her, for she had always known what was in his mind. He had none of David's joy in this campaign. Last night he had said farewell to Moira. They loved each other deeply and the parting was sad. But something more was at work in him. Could it be, she asked herself anxiously, that the promise he found in this new land he thought more likely to be realized by the Whigs, while his loyalty to Allan, to his people, to her, constrained him to march with the Tories? She knew his heart was torn.

Here was Allan, looking bold and competent at the head of his company. He would be a good soldier, for he was brave and ready. He would carry out the most dangerous assignments without fear or hesitation. Soon he would be a major; General MacDonald had promised it. Would he have the self-confidence and the decisiveness to make a good commander? For all their sakes, Flora hoped so. He attached such value to what he was doing. As he passed her, he saluted. A wave of love swept through her, perhaps partly maternal but a wife's much more.

The next company was Anne's husband's. He was much older than Anne, an experienced officer of Marines in the old days. He had an air more professional than that of most of the officers, but every glance displayed his pride in his present company of kilted Highlanders with their broad shoulders and sturdy demeanour.

Behind Alex's company came the Regulators who had joined in with the Highlanders—two hundred men out of the thousands Governor Martin had predicted. They wore buckskins and ugly caps very different from the jaunty bonnets of the Scots. They walked loosely, slouching along, the toes of their moccasins turned a little in as Indians walked. Their faces looked morose and uneasy.

As the last man disappeared into the forest road, Flora sought out Anne. "Take Neil to look after you, and you and Katie and the babe ride to Hugh MacDonald's. Wait for me there."

Anne made no objection, but old Neil raised immediate protest. "I don't want to go home or to Hugh's, Flora. I'm maybe a bit old to be a soldier, though I'm as tough as leather for all my years. 'Tis my wish to follow along with the troops and care for my lads. It's a reasonable request, Flora. Don't send me off with Anne MacLeod now."

Flora was tempted to humour the old man. She would even feel easier in her mind if Neil were with Allan and the lads to look after them. But there was no one else to escort Anne to Hugh's. "Neil," she said, "we can't have Anne and the babe riding the roads alone with Katie in these troubled times. She needs a man to keep her safe. No, you'll have to go with her."

His look of crushed disappointment melted her heart. She smiled at him as she might have at a bairn. "Neil, you must escort Anne to Hugh's, for I won't be with her. Bring her fairly to Hugh's door. It's only a day or so. Once there, you can turn straight around and come back. The troops won't have gone far in two or three days. You can follow along and catch up with them."

Old Neil, as pleased as a child, was at once in a hurry for Anne to start, so he might return the sooner.

"Why won't you be with us? Where are you going, Flora?" Anne asked, concern in her eyes.

"I'm riding to Haymount, where the men will camp, to be with Allan and the boys tonight. Young Malcolm MacKay will ride with me when I start home tomorrow. Allan has arranged it."

Reluctantly Anne turned away to gather her party and start off for Hugh MacDonald's home. Flora, accompanied only by the boy Malcolm MacKay, rode down the forest road in the wake of the little army.

That cold night at Haymount, Flora kept vigil. She sat on a pack on the ground, with Allan's head on her lap. Around her lay her sons and the twins and Hugh's grandson, Ian. She looked long on their sleeping faces, saying her silent farewell.

In the morning, while the men were eating breakfast and breaking camp, Flora spoke cheerfully to the boys. "I'm glad," she said, "to see more MacDonald tartans than those of any other clan."

David answered gaily, "Why, 'tis a MacDonald rising, Flora. That's what they say in Cross Creek."

Flora smiled. "That pleasures me well. Let them see how MacDonalds can fight."

It was time for her to leave. Allan put her on her horse. Each lad came to kiss her hand and Allan kissed her on the mouth.

She waited a little way down the road as the troops marched off, banners waving, pipes skirling—watched them go until the last man disappeared around a bend in the forest road.

Campbelltown and Cross Creek seemed very empty after General Donald MacDonald's little army marched away. The noise of crowds, the beat of drums and the skirl of pipes were gone. The ordinary tasks seemed trivial and useless. Farquard Campbell found trouble in keeping his mind on his ledgers, and Cecily walked about the house unable to settle down even to a book.

Rumours came fast. Moore and his Continentals were at Rockfish Creek. There would be a fight. This was the evening of the nineteenth. The next night the Scots passed close to Campbelltown, crossing the

river. There had been no fight. They planned now to
march down the north side of the river. Then Whig
troops moved into Cross Creek—men from Hillsboro
under Colonel Thackston and from Salisbury under
Colonel Martin. When Cecily asked her uncle what
this signified, Farquard said dryly, "Moore, I suppose, believes he and Caswell have the front door
blocked. He's sent Martin and Thackston to close the
back door behind Donald MacDonald. I wish I'd
hear from my men down below. If the British fleet's
late, MacDonald's position is uncomfortable."

The twenty-first and twenty-second of February
dragged by. No one came to the Campbell house.
There was no news. It was maddening, Cecily thought,
as she moved for the twentieth time from one room to
another. It was as if they had been transferred from good
air into some thicker element in which they hung suspended like a fish in water and time swam slowly.

Late in the evening of the twenty-second James
Blair reached Campbelltown and went directly to
Farquard Campbell's. He was dirty, unshaven and
red-eyed from lack of sleep. In the hall he slipped his
arm around Cecily and kissed her briefly.

Farquard led them into his counting-room and
made Blair as comfortable as he could. With a mug of
hot buttered rum in his hand, Blair gave a short account of his journey. It had been a hard, dangerous
trip. That morning he had encountered Moore marching toward Elizabethtown and had nearly blundered
into his arms. For two hours he had cowered in the
woods until Moore's Continentals had passed on down
the river.

He had made what arrangements he could with
Governor Martin. There had been no word of the
British fleet which Donald MacDonald was planning
to join. The tidewater was strongly Whig, and without
the fleet as a refuge he feared MacDonald would find
little security in Wilmington, assuming he could get
there. The Whigs were swarming everywhere to cut
him off with his Highlanders.

"Not a very cheerful estimate, I'm afraid," he ended with a wry smile. "What's the news up here? I've heard nothing."

They told him the little they knew. As they talked, in spite of himself he yawned and began to nod.

Cecily took charge of him. "You're worn out, my dear, and must get to bed. We'll have a little time together in the morning. Much as I want to see you, I want you to rest tonight." Her smile was a little tremulous, a little weary.

It was the morning of February 23. James Blair, shaved, bathed and fortified by a full night's sleep in a bed, was sitting down to breakfast, once more himself. Cecily surveyed him from head to foot, slowly and appreciatively. "A great improvement, James. If you go on like this, you will become a handsome man."

He grinned at her. "I feel like a new man. I hope you'll love this new me even more than the old one."

She poured him coffee and saw that the servants provided him with ham, a dish of eggs and good fresh bread.

"Do you know," he said between bites of ham, "there's nothing I'd like better to do than marry you this very morning? I suppose it wouldn't do." He smiled ruefully but tenderly in his effort to jest about their separation. "By noon I must start off to join General MacDonald and get on with finishing this war."

"Let me have your cup and I'll pour you more coffee." Cecily reached for it as if she were already a new wife. "I'm half tempted to marry you in haste as you say, just to make sure of you. But let us, by all means, be practical. Finish your war and come back for me."

There was a special fillip of pleasure in talking this intimate nonsense in a moment snatched from stress and danger. Blair knew he would never forget it. He would have it with him to rest him on long marches, to warm him on cold nights of a campaign. What a woman she was! His eyes were busy memorizing every line of her face. Impulsively he leaned forward and took her hands in his. His lips came toward hers.

Where they sat at table, through the wide doorway they could see part of the hall and the door of Campbell's counting-room. When the door of her uncle's office slammed loudly, Cecily looked up startled to see Stephen Moray standing there. Her heart jumped into her throat, and belatedly she withdrew her hand from Blair's. "Mr. Moray!" she gasped.

He had seen their intimate pose. It recalled sharply Cecily's promise: when she loved, her actions would make it known. His long, serious face was white with anger as he advanced to the doorway. Even now he could not berate Cecily. His fury concentrated on Blair, the British agent who had insolently assumed he could pull the wool over everyone's eyes. For weeks he had suffered Blair's presence, denied his cause and his compatriots for love of Cecily. Now he need deny them no longer.

He reached across the table, grabbed Blair by the shirt-front and hauled him up. His voice was a growl. "By God, I'll suffer your spying no longer!" His free hand moved toward his pistol. "You'll come with me, sir."

Blair moved with incredible swiftness. His right hand leaped out to knock Stephen's pistol away; his left thrust hard to Stephen's chest, sending him staggering back.

Cecily jumped out of her chair and stepped between the two men. She held her head high, a spot of colour burning on each cheek as she faced Moray indignantly.

He looked at her squarely. "I see you've chosen."

"Yes, I've chosen!" The pride in her voice stabbed and weakened him. She cried out again, "Get out! Get——"

Blair's voice broke in on her incisively. "Cecily, pray stand aside. I've never hidden behind a woman's skirts or taken asylum in a friend's house. I don't propose to begin now."

Taken aback by the commanding note in Blair's voice, Cecily stepped meekly out of the way.

Blair advanced toward Moray boldly. "Mr. Moray, I question that you have a shadow of right to detain me or question me. You have made yourself obnoxious in another man's house, upset his niece and gratuitously attacked me. If you feel you must do more to distinguish yourself, pray continue."

Moray found his anger drained. That Blair was an enemy was not important. Cecily had chosen him. . . . Raising his hand almost in a gesture of appeal, he took a step forward. Blair saw motion as threat. He stepped forward and swung his fist hard into Stephen's jaw. A quick flurry of blows followed. Stephen was no match for him with his fists. Another well-placed blow to the jaw sent Stephen spinning to the floor.

Blair turned to Cecily. "I'm sorry, my dear, but I couldn't let you fight my battles for me, as well as you were doing. I had better go before he comes to himself. I don't want to hit him again. It's quite a ride to MacDonald, and after my journey up I'm not inclined to make it by forced marches. It's as well for me to go now. I think we both know Moray will not harm you. Take care of him."

Cecily went with him as he fetched his saddle-bags and gave him a long kiss in the hall. "Good-bye, my love. Keep yourself safe."

He was gone.

When she returned to the dining-room, Stephen Moray had dragged himself into a chair. He was sitting hunched forward, his head down, and with one hand he was feeling his jaw with cautious fingers.

She knew that he was miserable and she felt pity for him. Pity was something she would not seek to appease him with. He would not want so poor a substitute for love. She stood beside him and touched him lightly on the shoulder. "I am sorry, Stephen, terribly sorry."

He did not answer, nor did he move. She continued to look at him, but already her mind was on James and her heart tight with fear for his safety. After a few moments she said, "Stephen, I don't think I want you with me now."

He pulled himself to his feet wearily. Whatever

dignity he had lost there in the dining-room he re-gained as he gave her a long sombre look.

"Then I will go." He bent to retrieve his pistol and then stood looking at it. Almost to himself he said, "General Moore marches today to engage MacDonald and the Highlanders. I'll go with him. Orders be hanged. When we're finished here I'll join Washington in Massachusetts."

Cecily, her whole being given to concern for Blair, hardly heard. "Massachusetts?" she echoed faintly.

Stephen was already at the door. "Aye. There are no memories to plague me there. Farewell. God grant you happiness."

A moment later she heard him ride away. Only then did the full import of his words bear down into her consciousness. She stepped forward, as if she would call him back from a battle she knew he did not need to enter. Then she stopped. She could call him back to nothing that he wanted. She had disappointed him enough—almost loving him, but, in the end, failing to surmount the barrier between them. Her prayers followed both men to battle; but her love went with James Blair.

Toward dark on February 24, Peter Campbell rode up to Farquard Campbell's house on a badly spent horse. He was taken at once to the counting-room, where Campbell sat at his table.

The younger man drew out a large handkerchief and mopped his muddy face. "Remember our bargain, sir?"

"I do indeed. Did you bring me the information I want?"

"Information, yes, but I don't believe you'll like it."

"Let me have it in any case, and briefly."

"A fast schooner came into Wilmington from Antigua. I scraped acquaintance with the captain and talked to him. He struck me as a reliable man.

"Now he had talked to the first mate of a dispatch-boat from Bristol. It had had an uncanny voyage, favourable winds the whole way. It hadn't left England until well after New Year's. This mate told him that the fleet the Earl of Dartmouth promised would sail in November was still lying at anchor in Ireland and showed no signs of an early sailing."

Farquard Campbell fixed him with a steady stare. "Are you sure of this man? He had no cause to mislead you?"

"As sure as I can be of anyone," Peter Campbell answered sturdily.

Farquard's closed fist struck the table. "Blast it! I feared Dartmouth was giving rein to his optimism. He's a man who can always make himself believe what he wants to."

Peter Campbell interrupted. "It will do you no good to speculate about Dartmouth. What are you going to do about Donald MacDonald and his High-landers? They're marching to nowhere."

"I know it, man. What do you think I'm putting my mind to?" Farquard asked in irritation. "How are you? I know your horse is spent. Can you stand another ride? General MacDonald's somewhere in the vicinity of Corbett's Ferry. I'd like to send a man of intelligence, like yourself, who knows the facts and can set them before the General. Will you go?"

Peter seemed to take stock of himself. "I'm strong yet, not too tired to ride. I want three things first. Cancel my bond now, so I'll know I'm free. Saddle a good strong horse for me, and give me a letter to General MacDonald so he'll know I'm to be listened to. That's all I need. I'll go and gladly."

"Good man!" Farquard said heartily. He went to a cabinet, searched briefly, and pulled out a paper. He picked up a quill and wrote rapidly: "For services rendered, paid in full as of this date, February 24, 1776." With a quick scratching of the quill he signed his name. "You've earned that already," he said, passing it over to Peter.

Peter read through what Farquard had written and pocketed the paper with obvious satisfaction. "One more thing," he said. "Do you recommend that General MacDonald should come back here?"

"That's not easy to answer," Farquard answered

thoughtfully. "If he goes on to Wilmington he's walking into a hornets' nest. If he comes back here he's certain to run into Thackston and Martin with their men and maybe Moore, too. Maybe they'll treat with him. He can try it. I'd not advise him to fight them. We'll need the Highlanders when the English troops finally arrive.

"Maybe his best course is to march part way back and disband in the forest. Let the men seek their homes in ones and twos. A few might be arrested, but hardly two thousand."

"Good!" said Peter. "I'll start as soon as I've had a bite to eat. If the going's clear, I'll see MacDonald on the twenty-sixth. If I have to dodge Whigs all the way, it may be the twenty-seventh."

31

Moore's Creek Bridge

GENERAL DONALD MACDONALD walked up and down the bank of Black River. In the water below him, icy in the cold February weather, fifty half-naked Highlanders, their teeth chattering, were struggling to raise an old flatboat. It would serve as the centre float in a short bridge across the narrow river. He needed it to get his little army across the Black and on the road to Wilmington again.

In one way he regretted that he had determined to avoid battle until the march was completed. A week before, on February 19, he and his men had been a few miles above Rockfish Creek on the south side of the Cape Fear. On the far side of the creek General James Moore was entrenched with just over a thousand Continentals. At that time his own Highlanders and Regulators had outnumbered the rebels by as much as seven hundred. Perhaps he should have attacked Moore then.

Moore had drawn him into an exchange of letters, several letters altogether. In strict fact, he reminded himself grudgingly, he had written the first letter himself. But that wasn't the point. Moore, he saw later, had been prolonging the correspondence to gain time. For instance, the letter of the nineteenth. How did it go? After saying that the terms of the Governor's proclamation didn't suit him, he had gone on: "However, should I not hear further from you before twelve o'clock tomorrow, by which time I shall have opportunity of consulting my officers here, and perhaps Colonel Martin, who is in the neighbourhood of Cross Creek, you may expect a more particular answer." And so on. And the next day Moore had written again, a stiff, hostile note, not to say insolent. It was insolent, positively insolent. Look at the way he twisted the truth in that rigmarole about an oath the rebels had made him and MacLeod swear: "I cannot conclude without reminding you, sir, of the oath which you and some of your officers took at New Bern, on your arrival to this country, which I imagine you will find difficult to reconcile to your present conduct." The only reason he and MacLeod had taken this foolish oath was that a pack of rebels had shut them up in jail and they had no other way to get out.

Moore had known what he was doing with his letter-writing. While the parleying was going on he had been reinforced directly by two contingents, and Colonel Thackston had joined Colonel Martin with more rebel forces within easy marching distance and almost in his own rear. Meanwhile two hundred Regulators had lost heart and gone home in spite of his persuasions to keep them with him. Others were deserting by ones and twos. So at the end of the letter-writing Moore was in command of a force just about the equal of his. Entrenched, he was far too strong to attack. MacDonald shook his head.

He had had to move before his little army melted away. He had marched back to Campbelltown, crossed the Cape Fear there and started down the north side. Roads on this side were more numerous and allowed more opportunity for manoeuvre, but there were tributary rivers to cross. At every bridge or ford a small rebel force could make a formidable resistance.

He had left Moore and his Continentals behind, on the wrong side of the river with no boats near at hand. Moore would be after him, but he had a good start. Somewhere ahead of him Colonel Caswell had about two regiments of rebel minutemen, perhaps eight hundred. Entrenched behind a river, such a force might cut him badly. But if he could once catch Caswell in the open he would know how to attend to him.

At dawn his scouts had reported that Caswell was entrenched at Corbett's Ferry, where the main road crossed the Black. That was no place to meet him.

Accordingly he had altered his route, veering off on a woods trail to reach the Black here, five miles up from the ferry.

He looked down at the shivering men in the water. "Captain MacLeod, how are you getting on?"

"We have the boat floating, sir. We're pumping it out. Be done in a minute." Alex had nothing on but a drenched shirt and didn't suppose he looked like much of an officer, but he had done his job. He'd be glad to get himself and his men out of this freezing water.

"Good man!" MacDonald shouted. He was already calling for the bridge crew to be ready with the split logs. He'd have his bridge up in twenty minutes, and with luck he'd have his little army across in another hour, waggons and all.

Five miles away, at Corbett's Ferry on the main road, Colonel Caswell was impatiently waiting for one of his scouts to come in with some definite word of the Highlanders' movements. He had been out of touch with MacDonald for several hours.

Almost at the same time two men appeared at the far side of the river and were ferried across together. He recognized one as a scout of his. The other said he was a messenger from James Moore.

Caswell questioned the scout first. "Where are the Highlanders? Are we still in front of them?"

"They've given us the slip, Colonel. They bridged the Black five miles up. By now I expect MacDonald has them all on this side."

Caswell banged his fist into the open palm of the other hand. "Blast it! He's a capable man."

He turned to the waiting messenger. "Let's see what Moore has to say." He held out his hand for the dispatch. "Anything to add yourself?"

"No, sir," the messenger replied. "It's all there."

Moore's letter was short. The Highlanders were ahead of him. He would follow by boat, bringing supplies. Meanwhile, he had ordered Lillington and Ashe to hurry down-river by boat to reinforce Caswell.

They would meet him at Moore's Creek, and Moore suggested Caswell retire to that point.

Caswell ran his hand slowly over his face, considering. There was no reason to hang on here. He ordered his men to fall in for the march. He took time to send off an express to Moore, giving MacDonald's position and announcing his intention of moving at once to Moore's Creek.

His men were fresh and should march faster than MacDonald's weary Highlanders. They had the good road and the Scots had to work their way through the woods. He ought to beat them to the creek by several hours. Just to be sure, he sent out scouts on his flank and front.

The head of Caswell's column reached Moore's Creek in the early evening without incident. They found Lillington already there, feeling rather proud of his rapid movement down the river. He had already dug entrenchments just behind the bridge.

Caswell looked them over. "These are just right for your small force, but now that we have more than a thousand men we ought to be farther back." He walked up on the little ridge overlooking the bridge and indicated a line about a hundred yards back from the water. "Let's put all the men to work digging in about here," he ordered.

By torchlight a detachment ripped the planking off the bridge. The round pine logs that made the stringers of the bridge they greased thoroughly with tallow and soft soap. By midnight the combined force of some eleven hundred men was out of sight behind its earthworks. The trap was set.

All night long the Highlanders struggled through the woods and swamps. When they came to a pocosin they had to slog through deep mud and stinking, stagnant water. At each step a man had to lift his foot squelching out of the sucking mud, move it ahead and feel for solid footing before he put his weight on it. It was exhausting even for a few yards. When a man fell his companions jerked him to his feet wet and covered with mud and slime.

General MacDonald soon realized that the Highlanders would not reach the bridge until an hour or
two before dawn. Though he had little fear of an am-
bush in the woods at night, he would need reliable information to determine his moves in the morning. He
asked Allan MacDonald to pick out a dozen strong
young fellows to serve as scouts.

Dougald and David volunteered. The general ordered them to take horses, ride ahead until they came
close to the creek, then to proceed on foot as near to
the bridge as they could safely approach. They were
to observe any enemy activity there and to report
back at once.

David was in high spirits as the two lads set out.
"The general's won my eternal gratitude for putting
me on a horse and getting me out of that mud," he
said gaily as he and Dougald rode off. "I'll pay him
back by going so close I could pull a rebel's beard,"
he boasted.

"Now, David," Dougald admonished, "this is serious business. The general is depending on us to bring
information back to him. If you get captured by some
foolishness, you'll fail him."

David was too pleased with himself even to be put
out. He contented himself with telling Dougald not to
be a grandmother.

The horses followed the dim trail without guidance,
which was lucky, Dougald decided, for the night was
so dark he could see next to nothing. When the two
lads decided they were less than a mile from the
bridge and close to the road, they dismounted and
tied their horses, marking the spot carefully in their
minds.

Silently on foot they made their way to the road.
With the road once located, they retired again to the
edge of the woods at the side and crept along toward
the creek and the bridge. They were cautious, but the
distance they had to cover was not great. In about
twenty minutes they came out on the bank of the
creek close to the bridge.

After the complete darkness of the woods, the open
space at the creek seemed light by contrast. They

could make out the shape of the bridge—clear across the creek. It hadn't been cut down. On the far side they could see the dying embers of half a dozen fires.

"The rebels had a troop here tonight," Dougald whispered. "No way of knowing whether it's still here."

"With only six fires I'd estimate less than a hundred men," David whispered back.

"Report six dying fires. Let the general figure out what they mean. He wants facts, not opinions," Dougald replied. "Keep quiet now and listen."

The two lads stood motionless for three minutes. The creek murmured. A vagrant wind rustled leaves all around them. Downstream a fox barked.

"Should we go look at the bridge close up?" Dougald asked.

"No use," David replied. "There's nobody here."

"We've collected an encouraging set of facts, but I don't like them," Dougald insisted. "This could be a trap."

"Give the general the facts," David mimicked. "Add that you think it may be a trap, but don't know why. We should be getting back."

They felt their way back to their horses.

About three in the morning, General MacDonald called together his principal officers without halting the marching column.

When the officers were grouped around him, he opened his mind to them. "I have been determined to reach Wilmington without fighting a pitched battle. Now it may be necessary.

"On this side of the river there are several tributaries to be crossed, as you know. We left Caswell at Corbett's Ferry while we crossed the Black in the woods. Ahead lies Moore's Creek. We have three courses of action open. We can retreat, giving up the idea of reaching Wilmington. We can cross at the bridge, storming it if it is defended strongly. Or we might make a long detour to the north."

Almost together, Colonel MacLean and Major Mac-

Leod spoke up. "Retreat's out of the question. Let's not consider it."

General MacDonald went on patiently. "To my mind, the long detour's impractical. Exhausted as they are, the men would be slow. We would only be giving the rebels time to gather their scattered forces against us. The approach to Wilmington from that direction is as easy to defend as this one."

MacLean was abrupt. "That leaves the bridge. No alternative to it, defended or not."

Major MacLeod disagreed. "If it's defended in force, we have no business attacking it. When we fight, we ought to choose our own ground. We don't have the numbers to spend men on charges against an entrenched enemy when we can avoid them."

Allan MacDonald backed up Major MacLeod. "We're here to rally," he said. "At this time a drawn battle, or even an expensive victory, would contribute little to our aims. I say fight only as a last resort. I pray God we take the right course for the King's cause."

Major MacLeod asked General MacDonald what the scouts had reported about the bridge.

"Dougald and David MacDonald were there an hour and a half ago. They didn't get right up to the bridge, but they could see it was standing. They saw half a dozen dying fires. Men had evidently been there. They saw no one. Dougald, however, smells a trap."

"What makes him think so?" MacLean demanded.

"Just the feel of the place. Too quiet, he thought," General MacDonald said.

"I'm for testing it out without committing ourselves," Major MacLeod said. "If the rebels are there in force, try another way."

MacLean was contemptuous of caution. "I say storm the bridge boldly. These rebels are rank amateurs. They'll run if we charge them seriously. A good brush will make soldiers out of our men."

Most of the captains muttered approval.

Major MacLeod, out-voted, said, "Well, if young

Dougald's right, we'll find out who the cowards are at dawn."

General MacDonald cut off the conference. "Return to your commands. The men will lose heart if they miss you. Keep them moving. They need at least an hour or two's rest if they are to attack."

The general needed rest, it was plain to see. His face was grey. At intervals he was seized with fits of uncontrollable shivering. An hour later, as the column reached the vicinity of the bridge, he pitched off his horse in a dead faint. When he came to, he was out of his head. Allan MacDonald and Major MacLeod, who helped pick him up, realized he was seriously ill with a bout of fever.

They ordered a stretcher prepared and had him carried back along the road to the house of a loyalist. Major MacLeod took command.

He allowed the Highlanders to rest for a little more than an hour. The eastern sky began to turn grey.

At Major MacLeod's order, the Highlanders were roused silently and told to fall in. No bugle shrilled, no pipe skirled. The weary men fell into ranks quietly, blowing on their cold hands and shivering a little in the sharp air that precedes a winter dawn. They were looking to their rifles.

Dougald and David took their places in Allan MacDonald's company. Allan stood firmly two paces ahead of them. They were scarcely in position when Major MacLeod came to speak to Allan.

"MacDonald, I'm making you a major as of this moment. You'll be in command of the main reserve. I know you'd like the honour of being in the front rank, but I must have someone solid in charge of the reserve.

"Captain Campbell will lead an advance party of volunteers. I'll go with him. I've been down to the edge of the woods and I don't like the looks of things. I have the same feeling Dougald did, though there's nothing I can put my finger on. I want to see for myself."

Dougald and David were among a dozen of Allan's

company who stepped forward. "We want to volunteer to go with Captain Campbell, sir," they said together.

MacLeod looked at Allan questioningly. Allan shrugged. "There'll be no stopping them," he said. "They're keen."

"Very well," said Major MacLeod. "Line up over there. I think Campbell ought to have about seventy good men. You lads can make a start."

Dougald and David took their places. Most of the volunteers who filled the ranks were young fellows like themselves, willing and eager. In ten minutes the number was complete.

Major MacLeod and Captain Campbell appeared and took charge of them. MacLeod gave them their instructions. "We have the honour to be first across the bridge. It may be deserted. There may be a thousand rebels behind it. Be ready for anything. We'll march now to the edge of the woods. When all's ready behind, you'll hear a gun fired. That'll be our signal. We'll advance across the bridge in good order, then charge. Understood?

"Very well, then. Forward march! Quietly now."

David was keyed up like a fiddle-string. A moment like this made a man feel himself a man. He stepped out proudly as the advance company marched to the edge of the trees. He stole a look at Dougald: he was as solemn as ever. A pity Dougald couldn't enjoy himself as he could.

At Captain Campbell's signal, the company halted. The dawn light was still grey and sullen but strong enough for sighting a rifle. David peered out into the open. On the far side of the bridge was a semicircle of clearing perhaps a hundred yards deep, rising toward a knoll behind it. No wind stirred. Not a needle rustled in the scrubby pines. The creek lay black and still. David fidgeted with his rifle and worked his jaws; his mouth felt dry. He wished they could get started.

To the rear a gun cracked. With the very echo of it Major MacLeod leaped forward, shouting, "King George and the broadswords!" Captain Campbell sprang into action; he cried, "Forward, my lads!" A bugle sounded. The *piobrach* skirled from the woods. Campbell's men stepped bravely toward the bridge with their kilts swinging.

Then they were on the bridge floundering and slipping on the greased logs. Some fell in the black waters of the creek; some were dying, some groping toward the land. Others kept their footing by thrusting their claymores into the pine stringers; balancing precariously, they got across. David saw Dougald, ahead of him, reach the far shore and turn to shout back. "Fetch sand," he yelled. "The bridge has been greased." With the pipes playing and all the confusion and splashing and yelling, there was no way to tell whether anyone else had heard Dougald's call.

Major MacLeod had fallen first. He scrambled to his feet and called for the men who had crossed to charge. At their head he reached earthworks thirty yards back from the bridge. The trenches were empty. "Nobody here," he shouted. "They've withdrawn. Come on, men!"

David followed with a will. He was more than half-way to the knoll. Major MacLeod was only a few steps ahead of him. He could see Captain Campbell over to his left.

Then suddenly he was deafened and half stunned by the roar and crackle of musketry straight ahead. Bullets whined by him. Most of them were high. Instinctively he bent low. He saw MacLeod jerk, stop and fall; struggle to rise from the black slimy earth; wave his sword, shout encouragement, and fall again. A dense cloud of smoke hung in the air above another line of entrenchments well back on the knoll. The ridge seemed to belch fire. David was right: the cursed rebels had set a trap and the Scots were charging into it.

Major MacLeod staggered to his feet again and waved his men forward. David, ready to do his best, kept low and moved forward almost on his hands and knees. He zigzagged to make a more difficult target. Again a rebel volley poured into the hesitating Scots advance. Major MacLeod shook as if in a high wind, then fell once more. He must have a score of bullets in him, David thought.

A cannon barked from the top of the knoll. The rebels were sweeping the bridge to keep the remainder of the Scots from crossing to back up the attack.

David looked behind him. More than a few of the Scots were down. Some were breaking for the shelter of the woods at the sides of the clearing. The others, with no officers to lead them, were milling around like sheep, simply waiting for whatever might happen to them. He was in a lonely place.

As he turned his head to look forward, he saw Dougald dart up to Major MacLeod and drop to his knees beside him. The major was still stirring. Dougald took him under the armpits and began to drag him back toward the bridge. Four or five shots rang out from the knoll.

Dougald faltered and fell back. A bullet had lodgement. He lay still beside the major.

David saw him fall. It turned him sick. He tried to crawl to Dougald while a volley whined over him, aimed at the little knot of Scots standing helplessly below. He had to flatten. He saw old Neil dart from nowhere to Dougald's side. God knew where he had come from. Thank God he was here!

Neil held the lad tenderly in his arms. The young face was stained with smoke and mud; the bright eyes were glazed. The chestnut hair fell across the smudged, contorted forehead.

"Neil, Neil, am I going?" Dougald whispered.

Neil's tears fell on the upturned face. "Laddie ... laddie ..."

In a gasping whisper Dougald moaned, "David ... tell him I died ... as a MacDonald should ... facing ... facing ..." His voice faltered. His breath came fast. "Moira . . . Moira . . . my dear love . . ." He sank back in Neil's arms.

Old Neil cradled him to his breast, then laid him down gently and covered him with his plaid. He took out his pistol and primed it carefully. All about was the noise of battle. From somewhere near the bridge

Allan's great voice rang through the uproar: "Follow me, Skye men! Follow me!"

Neil started toward his master. A rebel shot from a safe bulwark. Neil fell with a ball through his leg. He dragged himself back to where Dougald lay and stretched his old body beside the young one. If he was going to die, let it be there beside Dougald, so young, so very fair. He laced his long, bony, old man's fingers through Dougald's limp ones and listened to the pipes and their message:

> Yes, we cam' frae the Hielans, man,
> An' we cam' a' the wye,
> An' we saw MacDonald and his men,
> An' they cam in frae Skye . . .

Over and over the war pipes played the ancient song. Dougald had thought well of it, but it was not Dougald's pipe playing it now.

Allan found the two of them, the dead and the living, a few minutes later. Hand in hand they lay stretched out on the hard, dark earth, under a tartan of the MacDonald clan.

He called for aid. Any help would do. A surgeon came. A rebel he was, but kind. He loosened Neil's hand from Dougald's cold clasp and carried the wounded man away.

Allan knelt beside Dougald's body. The lad was so young to lie dead under the trees in a strange, foreign land. Gentle Dougald, whom they used to tease, saying he was no Skye man built for fighting. Flora would grieve, grieve deeply, for she loved the lad. But she would take comfort that he had died as a true Skye man should—facing the foe. Allan rose, ready to die himself if need be. His men needed him. He started the dangerous way back to them.

On the knoll, Colonel Caswell watched with eager interest as the accurate rifle fire of his minutemen stopped and broke the Scots' charge. He turned to Colonel Lillington, his eyes narrowed in speculation. "That does it," he said. "I'm astonished a general as accomplished as MacDonald put so few men across the bridge and attacked with so little spirit. They scarcely fired a shot, and there couldn't have been more than two small companies."

Lillington was studying the scene beyond the creek. "Something must have happened to make them lose confidence in their leaders. The main body is doing nothing at all. I can see it over there in the trees. May I make a suggestion, Colonel? We have boats. Why not put three hundred men across the creek up above in the woods and launch them against the Scots' rear? It's my belief they'll run."

"I was just entertaining the same thought," Caswell answered. "They are wavering. One more push should rout them. Will you set about it at once?"

"With alacrity, sir." Lillington hurried off.

Afterwards Allan wondered by what miracle he had been able to reach Dougald and get back to his men. He had watched the attacking party struggle to stay on the greased logs of the bridge. When he'd seen some of the Scots fall into the water, he'd sent his son Sandy, who was a lieutenant, with twenty men armed with poles to pull them out of the water.

Colonel MacLean had come and taken his place by Allan's side. Together they'd watched, seen Major MacLeod form his men in line and with Campbell lead the charge. Though the skies were grey, the light was good and the picture before them was clear.

When Major MacLeod had jumped across the empty line of entrenchments and turned to shout back at his men, Colonel MacLean, at Allan's elbow, had said, "I knew they didn't have the guts to stand up to us. They've pulled back out of harm's way. I'll take half the men and cross in support of MacLeod.

"You'll be in command on this side. Get some flooring on the bridge and bring the waggons over."

Allan had nodded, and MacLean had hurried off to move his companies out to cross the bridge. The men were standing in ranks and it was the work of seconds to start his companies in motion. His vanguard had issued from the trees as the first rebel volley worked its havoc. Seconds later the cannon on the knoll had barked, and the ball, sweeping the bridge, had sliced into the massed ranks of the Highlanders, killing or wounding eight or ten men.

MacLean had gasped, "My God! I was wrong. It was a trap set for us. I misdoubt I've killed poor MacLeod with my confidence."

He'd simply stood there, lost in his own thoughts. Without orders, his men drifted back among the trees where they would be hidden from the rebel gunners. They had lost their faith in his leadership and their stomach for any more fighting that day at one clap.

Allan had only a confused memory of what he himself had done. He'd had a searing sight of Dougald's fall and Neil's dart to his side. An old man like Neil out there—it was wrong. Allan, the lad's leader, should be there. He remembered scrambling forward into the black water. He remembered shouting to his men to follow, to give aid to the ambushed. He'd crossed somehow. When he'd looked back, the men were not there. They'd hung back. It was a rebel surgeon who aided. Even Caswell's men respected courage like Dougald's and Neil's.

Allan recalled the private rite, his moment of farewell with the lad. When he'd risen his mind had gone back to the larger need. He had known there was only one thing to do. He had to get back, save the rest of the men.

Now he went among them trying to restore discipline and morale. He slapped captains on the shoulder and spoke to them to put heart into them. "Come now," he urged each one. "Get your men in ranks. All is not lost. The lads over across had a harsh reception. But some half of them will get back somehow. We're sixteen hundred men. What's thirty-five or forty hurt? We're as good as ever, man. Where's your Highland courage?"

He was making some progress. Though the men kept looking anxiously toward the bridge and the hillside beyond, they were steadying down in the ranks. He'd weld them together again, make a fighting force of them.

One of the men interrupted him and pointed at a rider coming along the road from the west, evidently unaware of the trouble at the bridge.

Allan did not at first place the horseman, but his outline looked familiar. He shouted to the men, "Don't shoot! He's a friend." He stepped out into the road and signalled the rider to halt. As he did so, he recognized James Blair.

Before Blair could reach him, Allan noticed a second horseman, who had come in at almost the same time, being directed toward him by some of the soldiers as he picked his way through the ranks.

Blair jumped from his horse and came up. "Hello, MacDonald. I was delayed up above, but I've come as quickly as I could. What's been going on?"

Allan shook his head. "All sorts of bad luck. We've had the devil of a time. We were almost cut off at Corbett's Ferry but got around Caswell. Here we put our noses into a cul-de-sac. Then General MacDonald fell ill of a fever. Major MacLeod took command. We tried to fight our way across the bridge. MacLeod led the attacking party and ran into a rebel trap. He was killed and we lost about fifty men. MacLean and I are in command, but he's not feeling up to much. The check upset the troops and they're very uncertain. I'm trying to steady them down. You can help."

Blair gave him a steady look. "You've compressed much ill fortune into a few words. Of course I'll help. What's the program? Do we have another go at the bridge or try to find a way around?"

"Right now the men don't have the heart for a strong attack."

"Then it's find a way around."

The second man had been trying to attract Allan's attention. Now he broke into their conversation. "Did you say General MacDonald's sick and not here?"

Allan nodded.

"Then who's in command?" he demanded.

"I am, and Major Blair here, who came in just before you did."

"I'm Peter Campbell," the stranger said. "I come from Farquard Campbell and I have urgent news for you. Here, read this." He held out Farquard Campbell's note of introduction. "I have facts that will alter your planning. You won't want to go to Wilmington at all. You won't need to find a way around Caswell's Whigs.

"The fleet carrying the regiments of regulars you were promised never sailed. It's still in Ireland. There are no regulars on the Cape Fear and none likely to be in time to help you."

For an instant Allan was stunned. His head swam. Then he gathered himself to meet the emergency. Blair, too, had readjusted to the new circumstances they faced.

"My God," said Allan, "don't let this leak out to the men. If they hear of it, they'll bolt and scatter. We've got to hold them together as a fighting unit or the rebels will pick up hundreds of us as prisoners."

"Right," Blair agreed. "Tell me, what precautions have been taken to protect our flanks and rear?"

"MacLeod was relying on our keeping the rebels busy by attacking them. And the creek isn't easy to cross except by the bridge."

"We aren't keeping them busy now," said Blair with a wry smile. "It helps steady soldiers if you give them something practical to do. Let's order some pickets——"

Suddenly a commotion broke out in the woods to the rear and on the left. A great shout, a rush of feet and a scattering of shots announced an attack from an utterly unexpected angle.

Some of the Scots and most of the Regulators threw down their rifles and ran, screaming, "It's Moore and his Continentals! We're surrounded!" The panic was irresistible. Scot after Scot dropped his rifle and took to his heels. Allan himself was caught up in the rush and half carried along with it, as he pleaded and expostulated, urging the men to rally, to show their courage. He could do nothing with them.

In less than an hour what had been a force of fourteen hundred Highlanders and two hundred Regulators, a well-drilled little army, had disintegrated into a

crowd of helpless fugitives, scattering out for safety in
flight.

Soon after noon, General James Moore's army,
which had come down the river by boat and debarked
at Dollerson Landing the night before, arrived at
Moore's Creek Bridge after a march of ten miles.

Stephen Moray had travelled with it. He had expected Moore's troops to have the decisive engagement with the Highlanders, and in addition he had
thought the simplest way to reach a battlefield was to
travel with an army. Now he discovered he was too
late to take part in anything but the rounding up of
fugitives.

He was with Moore when the jubilant Lillington
reported, "It's as easy as hunting rabbits. The Highlanders were worn out when they came to battle.
They have had no rest since and little strength for
running. We gather them in."

At the farmhouse where General MacDonald had
been carried, he was taken prisoner. Although he was
still quite ill, he was no longer delirious. He denied
the Highland army had ever amounted to two thousand men. More had come in originally, expecting to
find Governor Martin and a thousand British regulars
at Cross Creek. When they found these rumours without foundation they had returned home. Others had
deserted later. The actual number he had led to
Moore's Creek was between fifteen and sixteen hundred.

Stephen Moray was given the task of running
through General MacDonald's papers. Among them
he found a letter from Farquard Campbell, detailing
Caswell's movements. This was a surprise! Everybody
knew Campbell was friendly with the Governor and
kept up relations with both sides, but the Whigs had
always supposed that his real sympathies lay with
them. Probably they were right. Stephen felt a kind of
sympathy for Campbell. The man had heartily supported the Whigs and gone far with them, to a point
just short of war. He was a man confident of himself,
sure he could play his own game. And his game was

to be a moderator between the two extremes. He'd always been frank about it. Now the conflict had come to plain fighting, there was no longer any room for a moderate. Campbell had been forced to choose a side. Stephen looked at the letter before him. "As one Scot to another, I feel I must tell you" was the opening.

The Earl of Dartmouth had distrusted him as too much a Whig. Now the Committee of Safety would have to arrest him as a Tory. Campbell's plight illustrated how little room a moderate had in a conflict like this.

The bag of prisoners was growing rapidly. Sometimes a Whig detachment would bring in as many as fifty at once. Many officers fell into the net: Colonel Rutherford, Allan MacDonald, his son Lieutenant Sandy MacDonald, Colonel John Pyle and others from the youngest lieutenant up to General MacDonald himself. John Bethune, who had come to Widow Moore's Creek only to console his people, was also made a prisoner.

In the late afternoon Stephen Moray felt a strong impulse to go out with one of the detachments hunting prisoners. He was restless after finishing with General MacDonald's papers and wanted a complete change. He spoke to Colonel Caswell about his desire, and, somewhat to his surprise, Caswell had him supplied with a horse and put him in command of a detail of ten men, all mounted.

They rode out along the trail the Highlanders had followed in coming to Moore's Creek. Even for February the air was damp and chilly on Stephen's face, and a few drops of rain fell from time to time. For a short distance the path wound through woods, fairly solid under foot. They rode silently in single file at a good pace. Then they came to a pocosin. The horses trudged through it at a slow walk, their feet sinking into the slime beyond the fetlocks at every step.

At one point Stephen halted and called the sergeant up beside him. He pointed down at regular marks in the mud. "What do you make of those, sergeant?" he asked.

The man studied the ground. "I'd say a horseman

not fifteen minutes ahead of us." The oozing mud had levelled out the footprints left by the Highlanders the night before. Now visible but already fading were the hoofprints of a single horse travelling in the same direction as Stephen's party.

"Must be an officer if he has a horse," the sergeant added.

"We can't move fast in this muck, but let's do our best. I'd like to overtake him before dark," Stephen directed.

They rode on, urging their horses. On solid ground beyond the pocosin they broke into a fast trot. An occasional fresh hoofprint told them their quarry was still ahead.

The trail ran through open woods, with little undergrowth. Through a long forest aisle they saw two men on foot. At the sound of the cavalcade behind, the two men turned aside, seeking a place to hide.

Stephen called over his shoulder to the sergeant, "Take five men and flush out those two fellows. The rest of us will go on after the horseman."

Stephen and the other four rode on. As they swept around a bend and looked ahead, they saw a saddled horse, standing by the side of the trail. The rider had dismounted and was sitting on the trunk of a fallen tree. When he heard them coming, he jumped to his feet and started to reach for his pistols. Then, realizing the hopelessness of contending with five armed men, he stood still.

As they came up and surrounded him, Stephen recognized him as James Blair. Triumph and misery flooded through him together as he realized Blair was his prisoner.

Two of the men dismounted and took Blair's sword and pistols from him. He stood quietly while they disarmed him. When they stepped back, he looked up at Moray very coolly. "Hello, Moray. I deserve this. I underestimated you Whigs. The mare there—" he gestured with his head—"badly needed a rest. I thought I might have a bite to eat while she was taking it. I didn't expect any of your patrols out this far. If I hadn't believed I was completely safe I would have hidden in the woods or made the mare go a little farther. I see I was wrong. You people seem to understand war better than we expected of amateurs."

Stephen was remembering the last time he had seen Blair, with Cecily, and all that had been said and done among them. What Blair had just said to him was very generous. He was taking on himself full responsibility for his capture, leaving Stephen free of obligation. It almost made him angry the way Blair always seemed to outdo him in grace and courtesy, and the worst of it was that the Englishman seemed to do it without effort or conscious thought. If they should play a game of magnanimity Blair would be sure to win. But he wasn't playing a game.

The thing was, Cecily Weston loved this man. He had tried to win her himself and failed. It was Blair she wanted, whether he liked it or not. Involuntarily he sighed. He knew what he was going to do, but Lord, how it went against the grain!

He turned to his four troopers. "Ride on back and see how the others are getting on. I'll bring this fellow along. We must hurry if we're to reach camp before dark."

The men mounted obediently. One asked, "Sure you can handle him all right alone?" When Stephen reassured him, they rode off.

From his saddle he stared morosely down at Blair. At last he spoke bitterly. "Blast it, I wish you weren't continually crossing my path."

Blair stared back, not a muscle in his face moving. Seconds ticked away.

At last Stephen stirred impatiently and gestured toward the mare with his pistol. "Well, get on your horse."

Still in silence, Blair mounted.

For a moment longer Stephen Moray appraised him with a long look. "When the times comes, she'll want you—alive and free. So I suppose it's your turn." He pointed his pistol straight up at the sky and fired it. "That's to explain your escape to the men. When you made a run for it, I missed you."

For a moment Blair hesitated. Then he raised his hand in salute and tribute.

Fire burned in Stephen's eyes. "Damn it, ride. Before I change my mind." He turned his horse and started back.

32

Aftermath

ALLAN MACDONALD was among the horde of fugitives swept up by the triumphant Whigs. Fate had left him, alive and unhurt, one of the many prisoners—above eight hundred. For a moment he raged, believing he'd rather be dead than a captive, and rather dead than a leader who had not brought his men through safely. The rage passed. He had done his best in fervent conviction.

As commander of the Highlanders, he went to see to the prisoners' welfare and to represent them in dealing with their Whig captors. Moore and Caswell had put Major Rutledge in charge of the prisoners. Rutledge, Allan saw, was a very decent fellow who would guarantee just treatment.

Only when he was easy about the men did Allan let himself return to personal worry. He knew now how his lads had fared. He ran over the list again. Sandy had been caught and was here with him, unhurt but fuming at being a captive. Jamie and his son-in-law, Alex MacLeod, were not among the prisoners. Neither one had been in the dawn attack, so the chances were they had not been wounded or killed. Men told him they had slipped along under the bank of the creek and won their way clear. About David he couldn't be sure. The lad had been in the forefront of the Scots' charge. Rutledge had allowed Allan to look for him among the killed and wounded, but he had found no trace of him. He could only hope that David had escaped unhurt.

Dougald, poor Dougald—at thought of him a lump formed in Allan's throat. Gentle Dougald had died a hero, hit as he tried to succour Major MacLeod.

Though the lad had rightly suspected a trap, he had
done his best to warn his fellows of the greased
bridge, charged with the boldest and gone as far as
any.

Allan thought of the loneliness of a soldier's un-
sung death on the field. He would perform one service still for the lad, and perhaps save old Neil at the
same time. He sought out Major Rutledge. "Major,"
said Allan, "I want to make one request for myself.

"My ward, Dougald MacDonald, was killed over
there." His hand pointed to the battle-field on the far
side of the creek. "You would be doing a great kindness to me, to my wife, Flora MacDonald, who has a
special feeling for the lad, and the lass he was to
marry if you would let me send his body home for
burial."

Major Rutledge measured him with an appraising
look. "How do you propose to accomplish it? You
know I can't release you or any of the other prisoners
for such a purpose."

"I realize you can't, sir. I believe I have a way out.
One of our old servants insisted on coming with us, to
look after me and the lads. He must be seventy-five.
Though he was wounded in the fight, it was by accident. He wasn't a soldier, so there's no need for you to
treat him as a prisoner of war. Let old Neil take the
lad's body back to Anson. Give him a pass and I'm sure
he can find some sort of cart or wagon for the journey.
The lad was his favourite; he'd die rather than fail."

Rutledge kicked a clod of earth. "Very well, bring
old Neil here in twenty minutes and he shall have his
pass."

"Thank you, Major. You are kind."

He hurried off to tell Neil of the arrangement he had
made. The faithful gillie rejoiced at the opportunity to
perform this last service for the lad he had loved.
Though he was weak from his wound, he swore to
Allan that he would carry out his task.

Neil assured him, "I'll manage all for the best. What
shall I tell them at home about you?"

"They say we'll be marched up to the Roanoke River

in the northeast part of the province and confined in Halifax jail. Major Rutledge thinks I can soon be freed on parole."

"I'll tell them. Flora will know you are safe."

It was time for Neil to go to Major Rutledge for his pass. Neither man had words for what stirred in his breast at this parting. They clasped hands in understanding.

On the third morning after the fight eight hundred and fifty Highlanders marched off for the jail at Halifax. Behind them they left the brave men who had borne the brunt of battle, buried in shallow graves beside their valiant commander, Alexander MacLeod, and young Captain Campbell.

The rebels had been more fortunate. A young man named Grady had been killed and one man wounded.

The Battle of Moore's Creek Bridge was over.

Evil news travels fast but not to the far places. The first Flora MacDonald knew of the disastrous battle at the bridge and the defeat of the Highlanders was when Neil drove the waggon bearing the body of young Dougald up to the house door.

Katie's loud and terrible wailing brought Flora out of the house, aware that some misfortune had overtaken them but not knowing what it was. She approached the waggon standing under the broad spread of the oak tree. She looked at Neil's face and knew that death had struck. With stiff lips she formed a name: "Allan?"

Neil shook his head. He spoke but one word: "Dougald."

Dougald! The others were children of her body, but Dougald was the true child of her heart. Always he had sensed her thoughts, as she had sensed his. Dougald, bonnie, bonnie Dougald! Her pity went out to Moira, the tender young lass.

The herd-boys came down from the hills, the maids and bondswomen from the kitchen and dairy, Anne, with her babe in her arms, Hugh MacDonald who was staying on the place in Allan's absence, the few ploughmen left at home in from the fields. They all gathered around the waggon. They looked at Dougald's face, white and very cold, wearing now the peace that death brings.

Soon after the farm people came, friends began to arrive from Cross Creek and Campbelltown. Cecily Weston came. The MacQueens came together, and many more.

Then it was that old Neil told them how the Scots had gone down in defeat at the bridge. He described how Dougald and David had fought and how bravely Dougald died. He told of the others, what had happened to them, how Allan and Sandy were taken prisoner, how David and Jamie and Alex MacLeod and Ian MacDonald had got clear away.

While he related his heavy news, the dogs set up a mournful howl. They had smelled the odour of death, not the blessed death that brings release to the old, but the swift, untimely death that comes to the young in the full flower of their days.

Katie began a chaunt in ancient Gaelic: "Hark, the whirlwind is in the wood, a low murmur in the vale. It is the mighty army of the dead, to bear him away through the air."

Flora spoke sharply. "Katie, be silent! We'll have no old Druid words spoken here."

Katie threw her apron over her head and, weeping, ran blindly to the house.

Cecily Weston, though controlled, was stricken with threefold grief this day. Deep sorrow, though perhaps the least, came from a message from Blair: "I can return only when this is settled." Then, like all the others, she had been deeply fond of Dougald and his death was a heavy grief to her. And the very morning of the day Neil had come by bearing the news of Dougald's death, the Whigs had arrested Farquard Campbell. She had worked long to make him a Tory, and now she felt responsible for his trouble. "They took him at his own dinner table—at which the guests were my Tory friends," she kept repeating.

They carried Dougald into the great-room and laid

him out there. Moira MacQueen had hung back from
the waggon. Now they led her in alone to look for the
last time upon the face of her love.

She was like a body frozen. She shed no tears. Her
face was stiff and blank, without expression. Her eyes
stared, without blinking.

"She's been like this ever since she heard the evil
news," Mrs. MacQueen whispered. "No words, no
tears."

"Don't worry," her husband reassured her softly.
"It's the shock. She'll break soon."

Flora took Moira to the room where Neil was resting so she could hear everything that had happened to
Dougald.

When the old man told her that his last words had
been "Moira, my dear love," she broke down at last
and cried her heart out on his shoulder. "Oh, Neil,
Neil, why couldn't I have been there to be near him
and hold his hand as he lay dying?"

Flora was against having a large funeral, but
friends and neighbours kept coming in. The cooks
were busy in the kitchen preparing food for those
who stayed to sit up through the night of lamentation.

At last most of the visitors left. Flora felt the need
to be alone and went to her room. She could not
sleep. She paced the floor, back and forth, back and
forth. In the night, Katie heard her walking and
brought her a cup of tea. "You must sleep,
Fionnghal," she said gently. Flora scarcely heard her.

What would they do to her Allan? Hang him as a
common traitor? Surely not that!

Jail? For Allan, who loved the freedom of the open
air and the wild sea, it would be like death. Allan the
unfortunate, here as in Skye before—the thought kept
rising in her mind. No matter how hard he tried, no
matter how well he did, his enterprises seemed destined to fail. She saw him moving steadily forward to
a doom waiting for them all.

She took some comfort that others were alive and
free, her Jamie and her son-in-law, Alex. Anne had
hope. She was young and resilient. But for Allan and
herself it was already too late. This venture, short-

lived as it had been, was their last great assay against fate, and fate had won.

They buried Dougald on the slope of the hill, under a great oak tree. Only their own family and the MacQueens, along with the servants, were there at this final moment. Flora wished that John Bethune could perform the rites. She sorrowfully put him from her mind. This hour belonged to Dougald.

It was a rare morning, the sky blue and cloudless. Spring was coming upon them. Tender buds were showing. The oak was pink with its falling tassels. The warmth of spring was in the air.

Birds were singing in the trees. Overhead, an eagle soared. A cardinal flashed to the oak tree and swung on a branch. Dougald would have liked that, Flora thought.

On the way home, as they came down the hill, Hugh MacDonald walked beside her, his hand under her arm. He spoke only once. "Flora, my daughter, I think God must have loved him as we did. Young Dougald will be at peace with Him."

His words and his touch gave her comfort.

That evening Flora walked up the hill where Dougald lay. She sat on a large stone to watch the sun go down behind the far peaks of the Uwharies. For a time she sat unmoving. The events of her life flowed through her mind as a drowning person's do. She saw her family, her dear family: Ranald, God knew where, with his Marines; Charles somewhere at sea; her Allan, and Sandy with him, captives on the road to Halifax jail; John and young Fanny safe, she hoped, in Scotland.

Her life was full of sadness. Here in America she waited on alone, without her husband or her children. All her hopes had been denied. Was the pattern of her life always to be misfortune, her family, which might have had a glorious happiness together, broken and scattered? Was it for this she had left her beloved home in the far isle?

The sun was setting in tender glory. Gentle colours

of evening filled the western sky. The night songs of birds came softly from the pines. Far down the hill she saw light columns of smoke rising from the chimneys of the bondsmen's cabins and her own kitchen. It was as though time itself were standing still. Everything was peaceful, tranquil ... except her own heart.

Then from within her a voice that might have been Allan's seemed to speak to her. "Don't grieve for me, beloved. I'll return to you when I can. Pray God for patience."

Suddenly her faith returned to her. She and Allan would be together again if she kept her confidence in the future. They would all be together again, all but Dougald, who lay at peace in the ground beside her.

With sureness now, she spoke to herself aloud. "You must be brave and have a stout heart in your adversity. You must keep hope alive in the breast of your daughter Anne, so that she will know all will go well with her and her husband and her babe. Most of all, you must watch over little Moira, grieving for her lost love. God give you strength to stand erect and fearless through this time of trouble."

The lovely glow of the sunset was fading. Darkness was not far off, and the air was soft with spring, the ever-renewing spring that brought grace and hope to the human heart.

Flora rose from the rock, wrapped her tartan over her shoulder and walked down toward the house, her head held proudly high.

EPILOGUE

The Prisoner and the Fugitive

FOR A TIME, life went on at the farm, though uneasily. Marauders, men of no party or of either party, rode unchecked, taking advantage of the lawlessness of war to burn and pillage. And there was Whig resentment against the leaders of the Highland rising.

Flora knew it would be politic to come out as a Whig. Many of the Scots had, after their defeat. She could not do it. She had found it hard enough to take her stand in the beginning. To abandon it now would be a disloyalty to Allan and to her own integrity.

The months ground slowly by. Sometimes she had a word of Allan. After a time in Halifax he was taken to Reading in Pennsylvania, and there he was paroled within the limits of the town. He was well enough but restless and unhappy, petitioning for exchange or any end to this half-life.

In the second fall the Whigs drove her from the farm and confiscated it. She was a fugitive, as Allan was a prisoner. She and Anne took refuge with Kenneth Black, but they were not allowed to stay there long. The Whigs harried them there as elsewhere.

The few treasures they had saved they put into a cart with a mule to pull it. They moved in the dark like fugitives. They stayed once in the deserted hut of a charcoal burner. That evening Flora touched Anne's shoulder. "I've been thinking, daughter. Why not go back to your place? The rebels have already pillaged it and burned the house. Maybe they won't come again."

Anne looked up with sudden animation. "Mother, I believe you're right. Do you remember the little cottage by the spring? I don't believe they thought to put the torch to it. We could go there."

They travelled by night in secret. It was early morning when they reached Glendale, the MacLeod plantation. The devastation was worse than they had thought from the reports. Anne's eyes filled with tears as she looked at the ashes that had been her home. "Oh, my pretty house!" she cried. The children clung to her skirts, their eyes big.

Presently, out of the woods came one of Anne's old servants and the children's nurse. They ran to her and sank down at her feet to kiss the hem of her skirt. Everyone was weeping.

At last Flora drew them back to the present. She was brisk, to stiffen them up. "Enough of these tears now. Where have you been living?"

"In the millhouse," the nurse answered. She caught up the children. "Come, little dears. Let me show you a young fawn that comes to visit us."

"It's a miracle the rebels didn't burn the mill, too," the man Robin added. "They ripped up the master's books and ransacked the house for gold before they burned it. They missed the mill somehow. We hid in the woods while they were here."

As they came up to the door of the mill, Robin suddenly brought his open palm against his forehead with a smack. "Oh, I almost forgot." He hurried indoors and came back with a letter in his hand. "A lad from South Carolina brought it three days gone."

When Anne saw the letter was from Alex she went off by herself to read it. In a little while she came back and handed it to Flora. "It's good news."

My dearest Wife:

Pray feel no anxiety on my account, for I am tolerably well off and safe enough here at Charleston. On first coming to this place, Lord Cornwallis was good enough to make use of me. This employment being completed and no other offering, he thinks it good that I go to General Clinton in New York. I shall write you from thence when a safe bearer can be had. I beg you inform Flora that her son Jamie and David made their way here in safety and have been commissioned lieutenants in Tarleton's Legion. They are in tolerable health and spirits. I have no fears for myself, but the welfare of you and the children, far from my side, is on my heart by day and night. Pray look after the servants as best you can. With all affection and love, I am

Your devoted Husband,

ALEXANDER

Charleston

Month followed month. Flora worked at household tasks, trying to forget, to ease the ache in her heart. The millhouse gradually took on the appearance of a home. They let a few trusted people know where they were living. They had alarms and more than once fled to the woods, but the danger passed.

No direct word came from Allan, but news reached them roundabout that he had been allowed to go to New York on parole to arrange his own exchange.

From Campbelltown they heard that Farquard Campbell had made his peace with the Provincial Congress, taken an oath of allegiance to the Whigs and so secured his release from imprisonment.

One morning about a year later one of Farquard Campbell's men rode out with news and a letter from Alex MacLeod. The arrangements the letter covered were not secret, and Farquard could afford to see it was delivered without compromising himself with the Whigs.

Efforts to secure a passport for Flora and Anne and the children had proved successful. Alex had arranged for a schooner to carry them from Wilmington to New York, where he would meet them. They were to go to Wilmington to take ship.

As Anne read the letter aloud she gave special emphasis to the last little paragraph: "Soon we will go to Nova Scotia, where Allan is, and we will all go home to Skye, my dearest. So lift up your hearts, for we shall soon be together again."

There was little sleep for either of them that night; their minds were too full. Toward morning, Anne came into her mother's room. "We'll need money, Mother. I don't know where we can get it. I've thought and thought, but I see no way."

"Don't worry, my child," Flora said. "I have a little, and then there is my silver which I saved, the teapot, jugs, bowls and tray. Surely I can sell them when we get to Wilmington."

Before they left, Flora took Robin, Anne's servant, and rode over to the MacDonald place. At the entrance she came on Moira's aunt and uncle sitting in a waggon. "We had to come up this way," Mr. MacQueen said. "Moira wanted a few minutes at Dougald's grave. If you go up the hill you'll find her there."

Flora left them there, and went through the pillaged farm and began to climb the hill, walking staunchly erect. There was a cairn at the grave now. Flora felt grateful to each of the unknown friends who had laid a stone there to Dougald's memory.

She had come quite close before Moira turned and saw her. The girl came running to her and buried her face in Flora's breast. "Oh, Flora! Flora!" she cried.

After a time they sat by the grave, where Moira had laid a bunch of wild flowers, and talked quietly of Dougald. "He is happy, Flora, I know that," Moira insisted earnestly. "In a way, I'm glad it turned out as it has. He would have been hurt in his heart by this cruel, cruel war. Instead, he died a hero's death." Tears came to her eyes, but she smiled a little. "David said the same thing in a letter to me. He wrote, 'It was always I who was going to be a great warrior, but it was Dougald who turned out the hero. All I could do was slip away and run."

Flora laid her hand on Moira's. "You must comfort David when he comes back, Moira. He will come, never fear. Only you and he knew the real Dougald and what went on in his heart."

The girl's cheek grew pinker. "Yes, Flora, I know. When he comes back from the fighting, he will need comforting."

Flora kissed Moira tenderly. "Keep Dougald in your heart, Moira, but do not let his death blight your life. He would not like that."

The girl's voice was low. "I know, Flora, I know."

Flora went back down the hill, then, for the last time. She was content to leave now. The visit had given her tranquillity. Moira would be all right now, and David. Dougald lay at peace here, under the great tree, in the keeping of earth and forest.

Tomorrow they would start for Wilmington, and then a ship to the north, toward Allan in far-away Nova Scotia.

Flora's destiny of sadness was moving onward. She could not know the fate of her two sons lost at sea, nor that, after a brief meeting in Nova Scotia, she and Allan must live their lives apart for many a year.

But she would go on, perhaps pulling out by night what she had woven by day in profitless expense of time, waiting for her Ulysses to come home, but return one day to her arms he must.

Her heart sang. Allan, her beloved Allan, and her dear Isle of Skye ... once more they would be hers, and hers forever.